COVEN

JENNIFER DUGAN

KIT SEATON

putnam

G. P. PUTNAM'S SONS

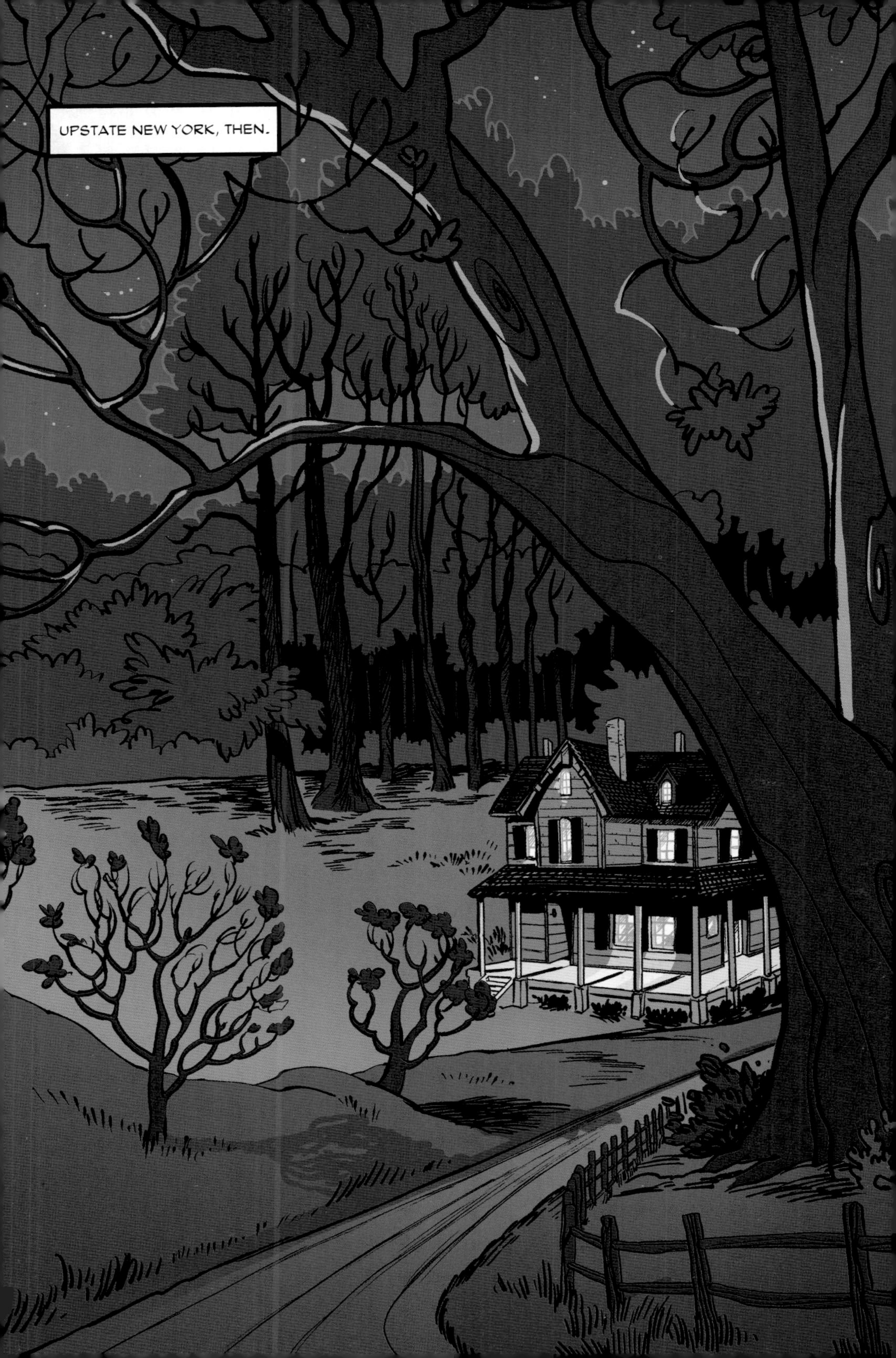
UPSTATE NEW YORK, THEN.

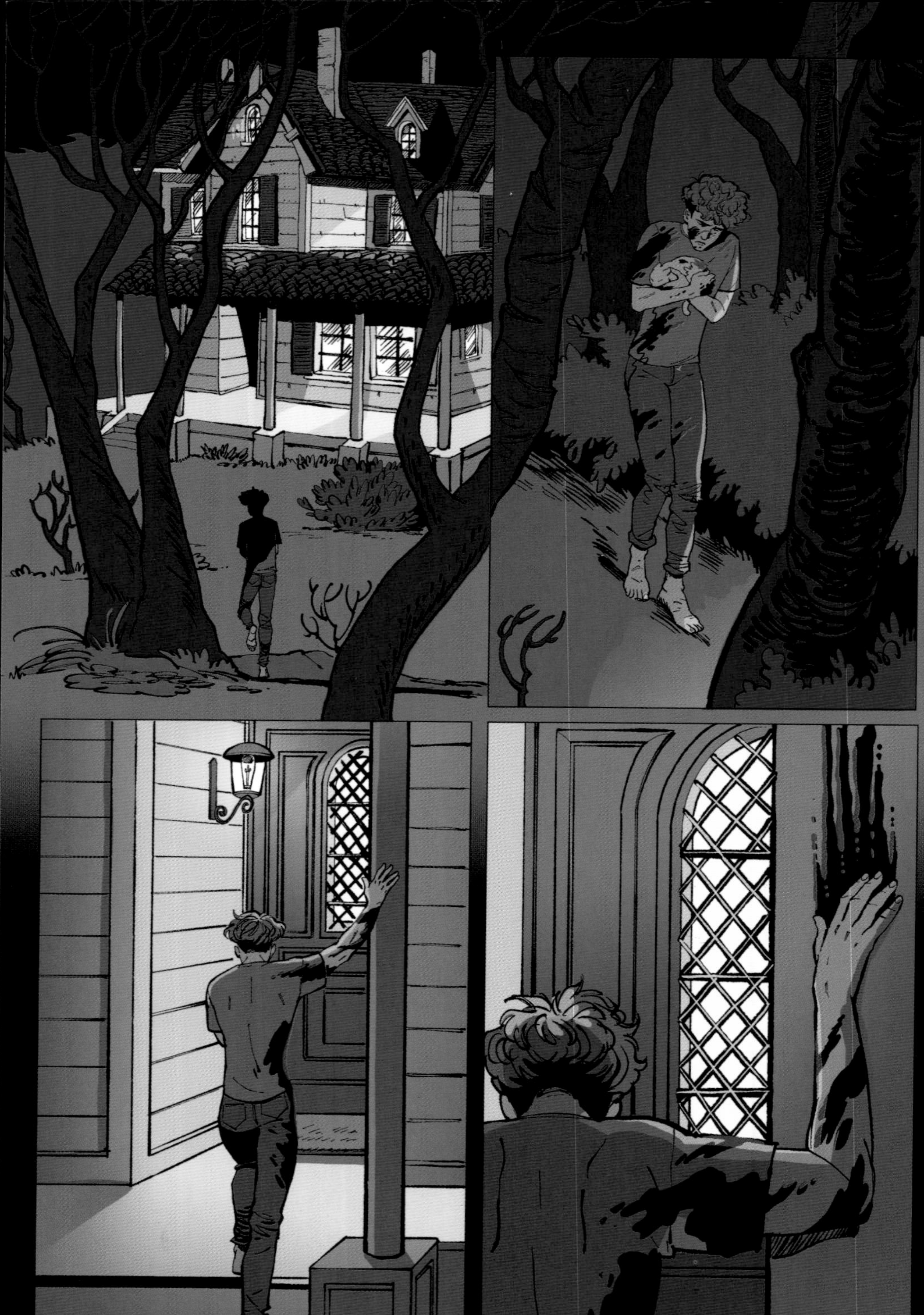

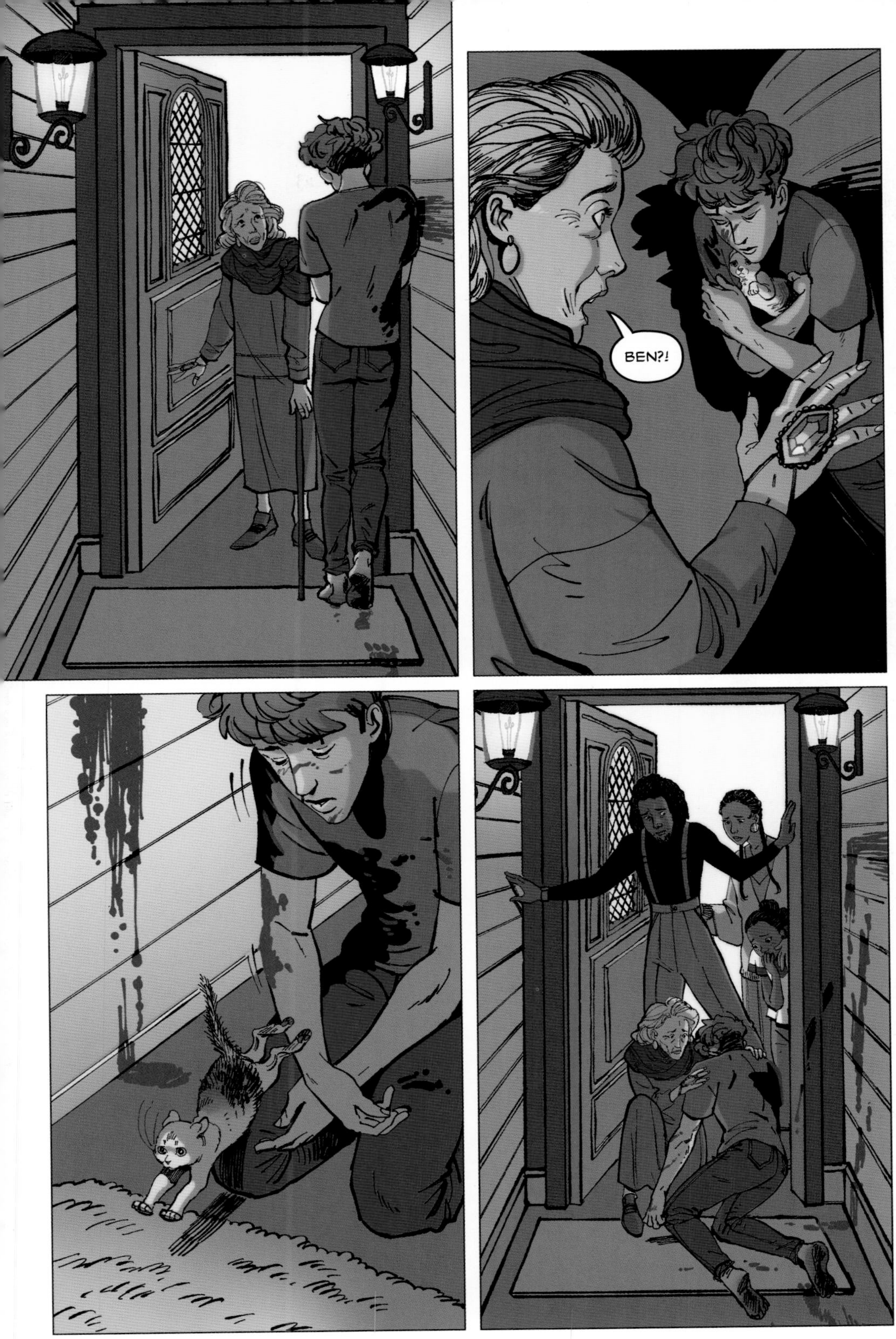
BEN?!

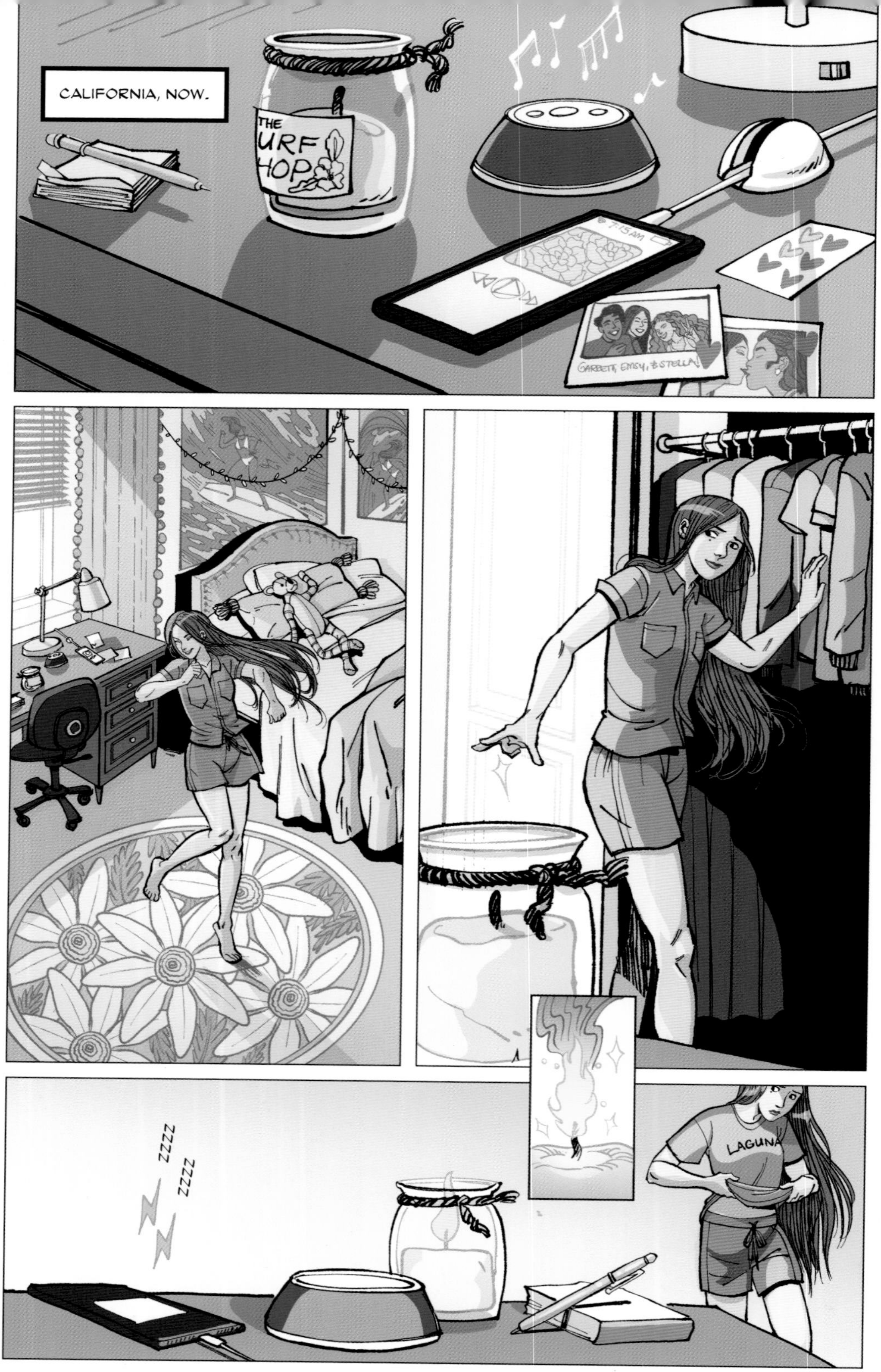
CALIFORNIA, NOW.
THE
URF
HOP
7:15AM
GARRETT, EMSY, & STELLA!
ZZZZ
ZZZZ
LAGUNA

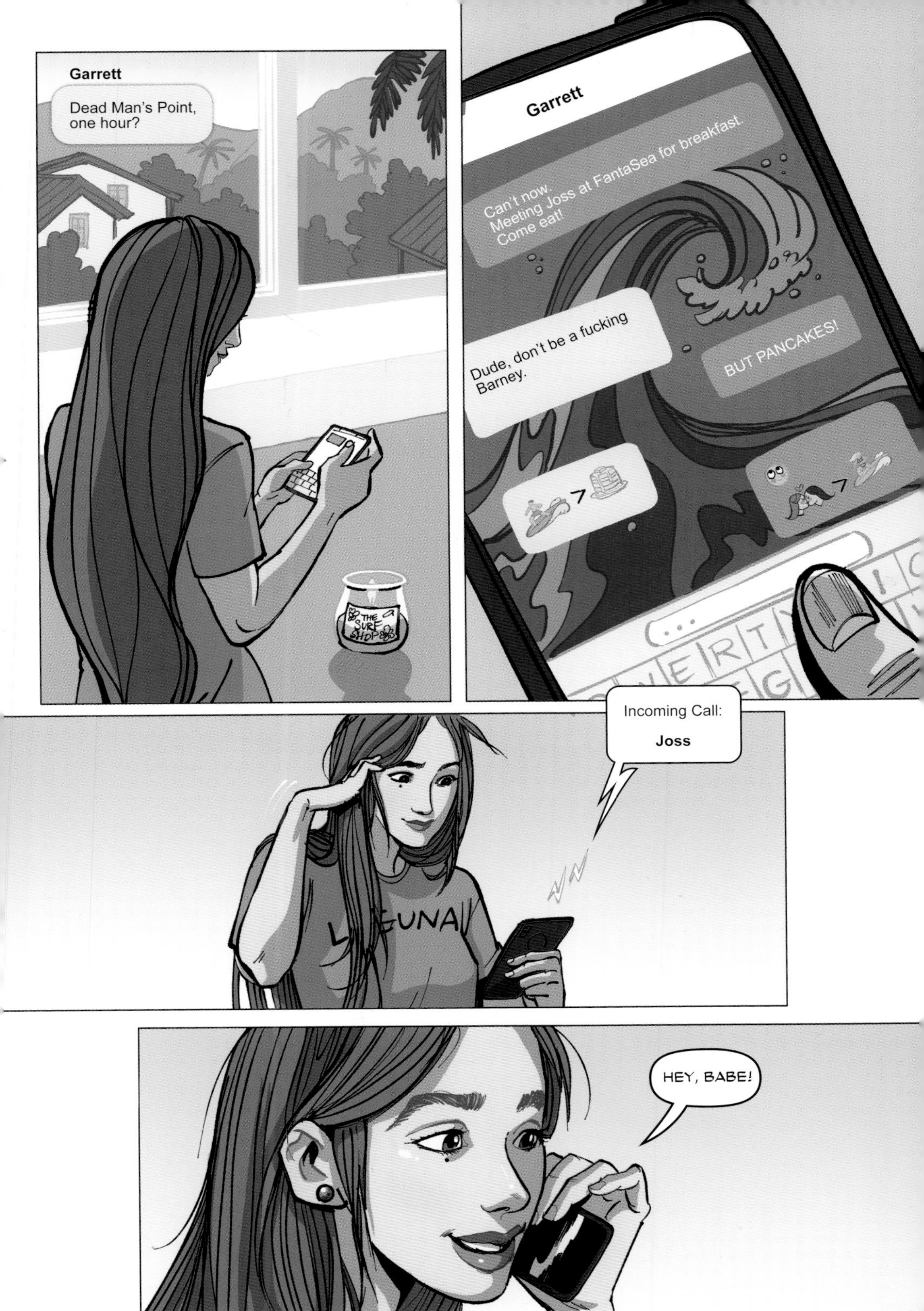
Garrett
Dead Man's Point, one hour?
Garrett
Can't now. Meeting Joss at FantaSea for breakfast. Come eat!
Dude, don't be a fucking Barney.
BUT PANCAKES!
Incoming Call:
Joss
HEY, BABE!

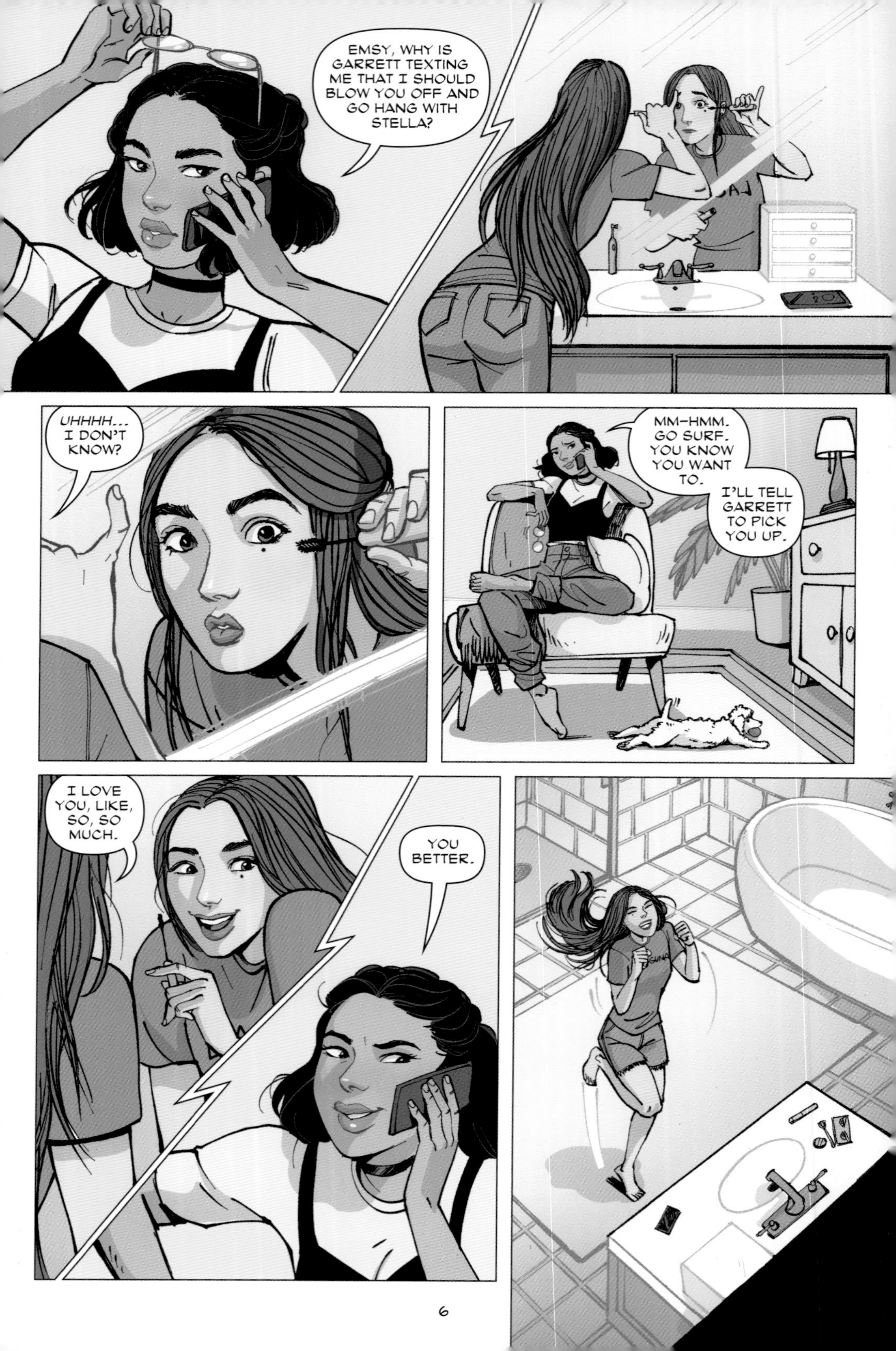
EMSY, WHY IS GARRETT TEXTING ME THAT I SHOULD BLOW YOU OFF AND GO HANG WITH STELLA?
UHHHH... I DON'T KNOW?
MM-HMM. GO SURF. YOU KNOW YOU WANT TO.
I'LL TELL GARRETT TO PICK YOU UP.
I LOVE YOU, LIKE, SO, SO MUCH.
YOU BETTER.

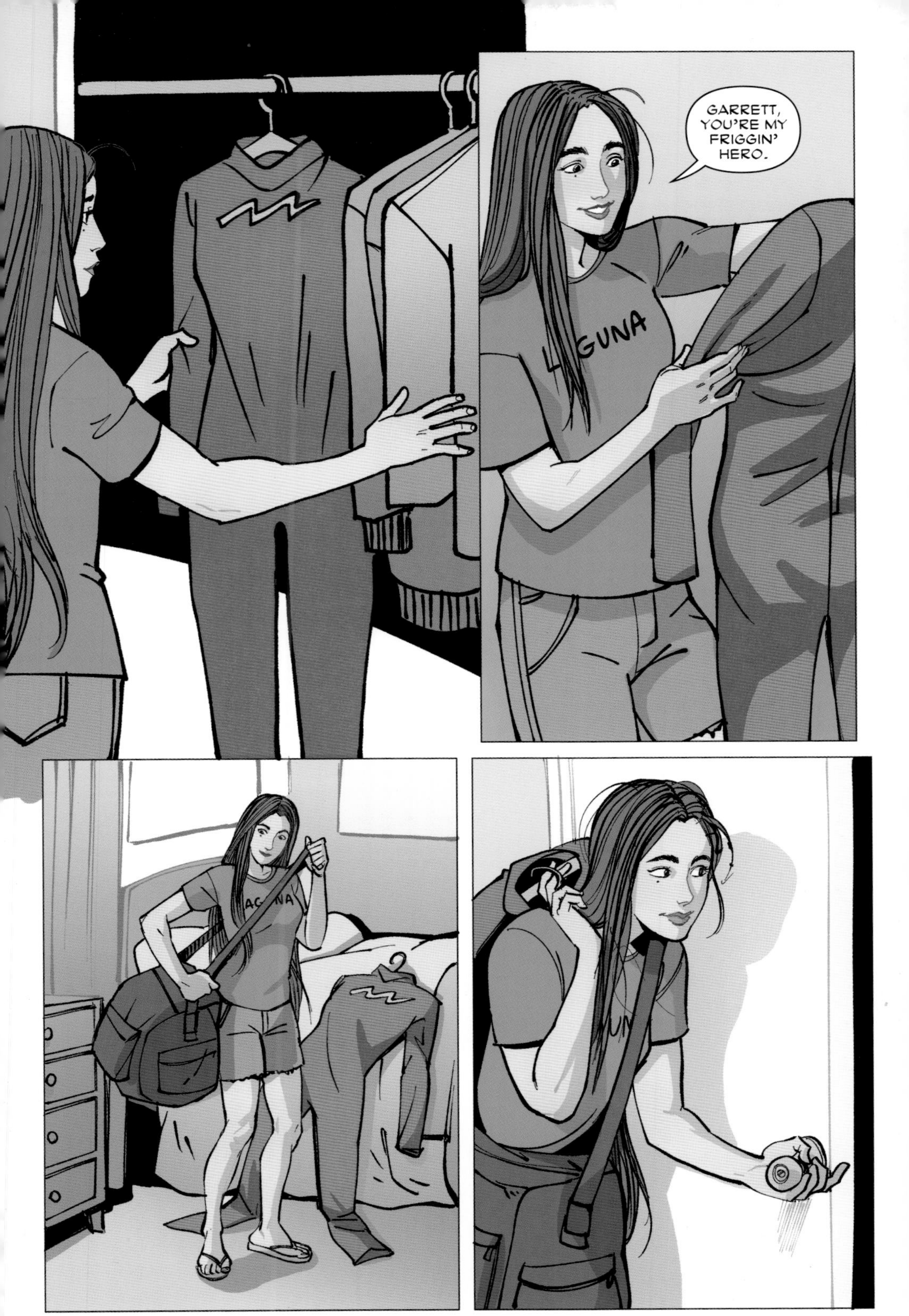
GARRETT, YOU'RE MY FRIGGIN' HERO.
LAGUNA

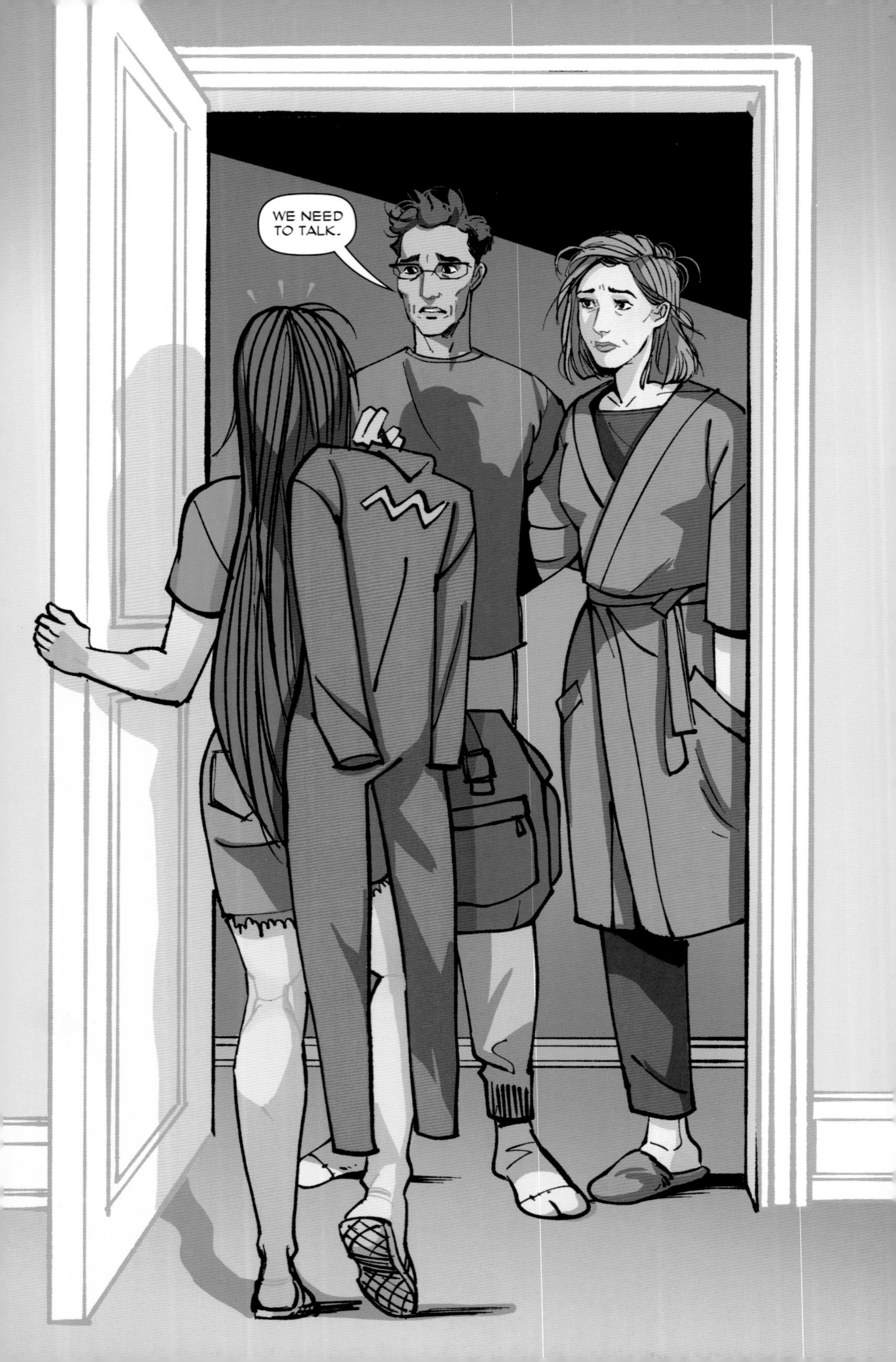
WE NEED TO TALK.

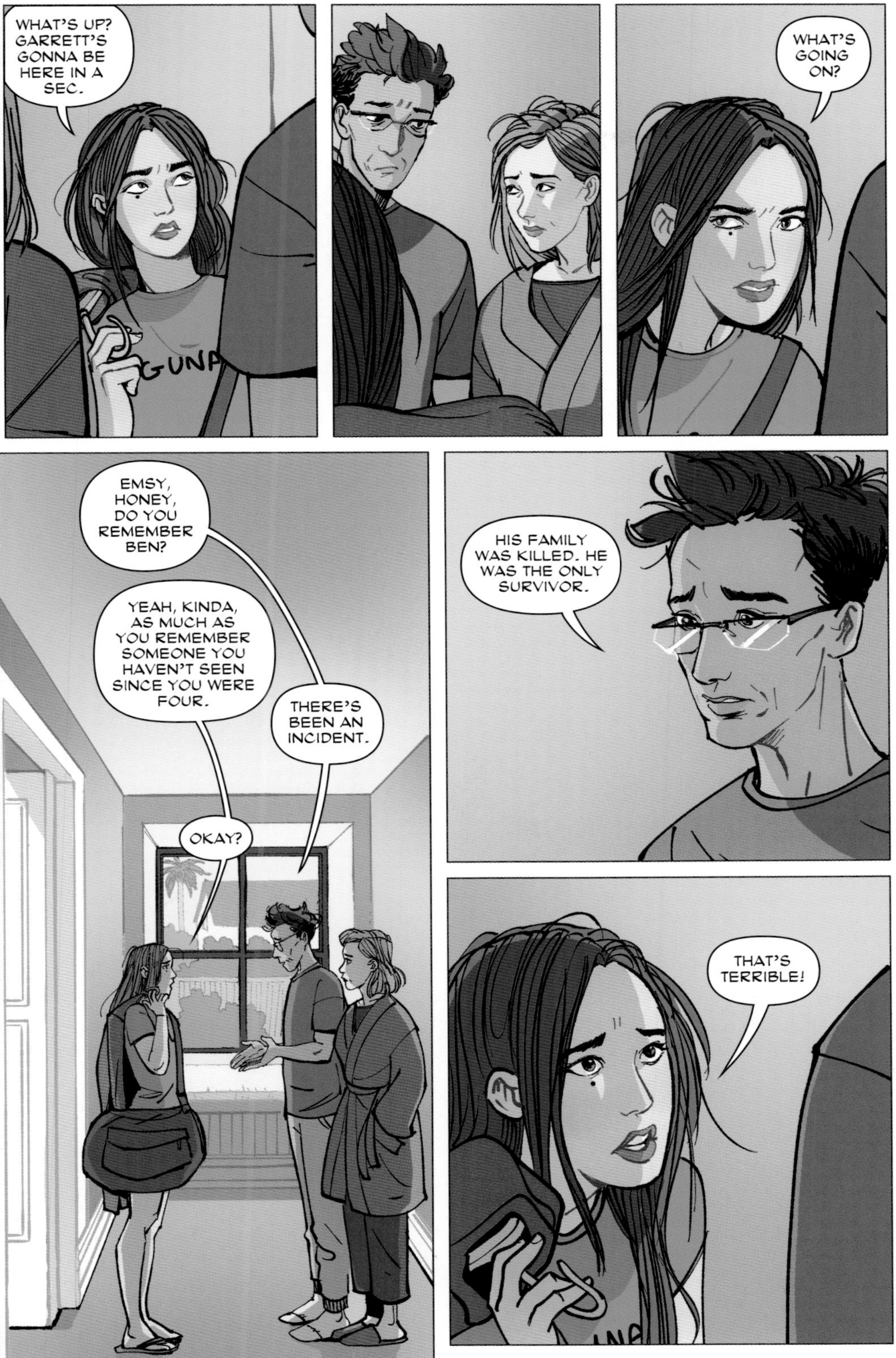
WHAT'S UP? GARRETT'S GONNA BE HERE IN A SEC.
WHAT'S GOING ON?
EMSY, HONEY, DO YOU REMEMBER BEN?
YEAH, KINDA, AS MUCH AS YOU REMEMBER SOMEONE YOU HAVEN'T SEEN SINCE YOU WERE FOUR.
THERE'S BEEN AN INCIDENT.
OKAY?
HIS FAMILY WAS KILLED. HE WAS THE ONLY SURVIVOR.
THAT'S TERRIBLE!

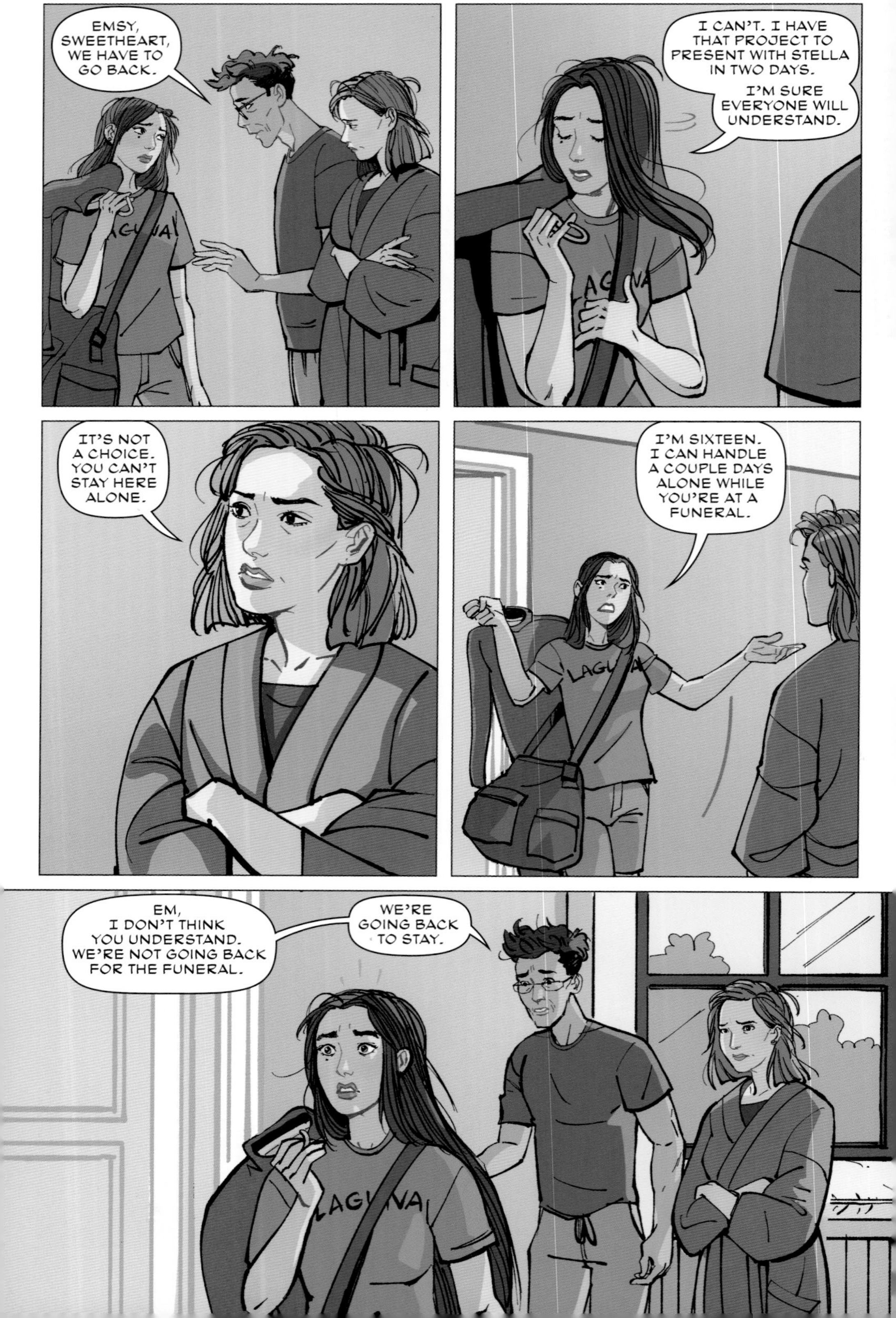
EMSY, SWEETHEART, WE HAVE TO GO BACK.
I CAN'T. I HAVE THAT PROJECT TO PRESENT WITH STELLA IN TWO DAYS.
I'M SURE EVERYONE WILL UNDERSTAND.
LAGUNA
IT'S NOT A CHOICE. YOU CAN'T STAY HERE ALONE.
I'M SIXTEEN. I CAN HANDLE A COUPLE DAYS ALONE WHILE YOU'RE AT A FUNERAL.
EM, I DON'T THINK YOU UNDERSTAND. WE'RE NOT GOING BACK FOR THE FUNERAL.
WE'RE GOING BACK TO STAY.

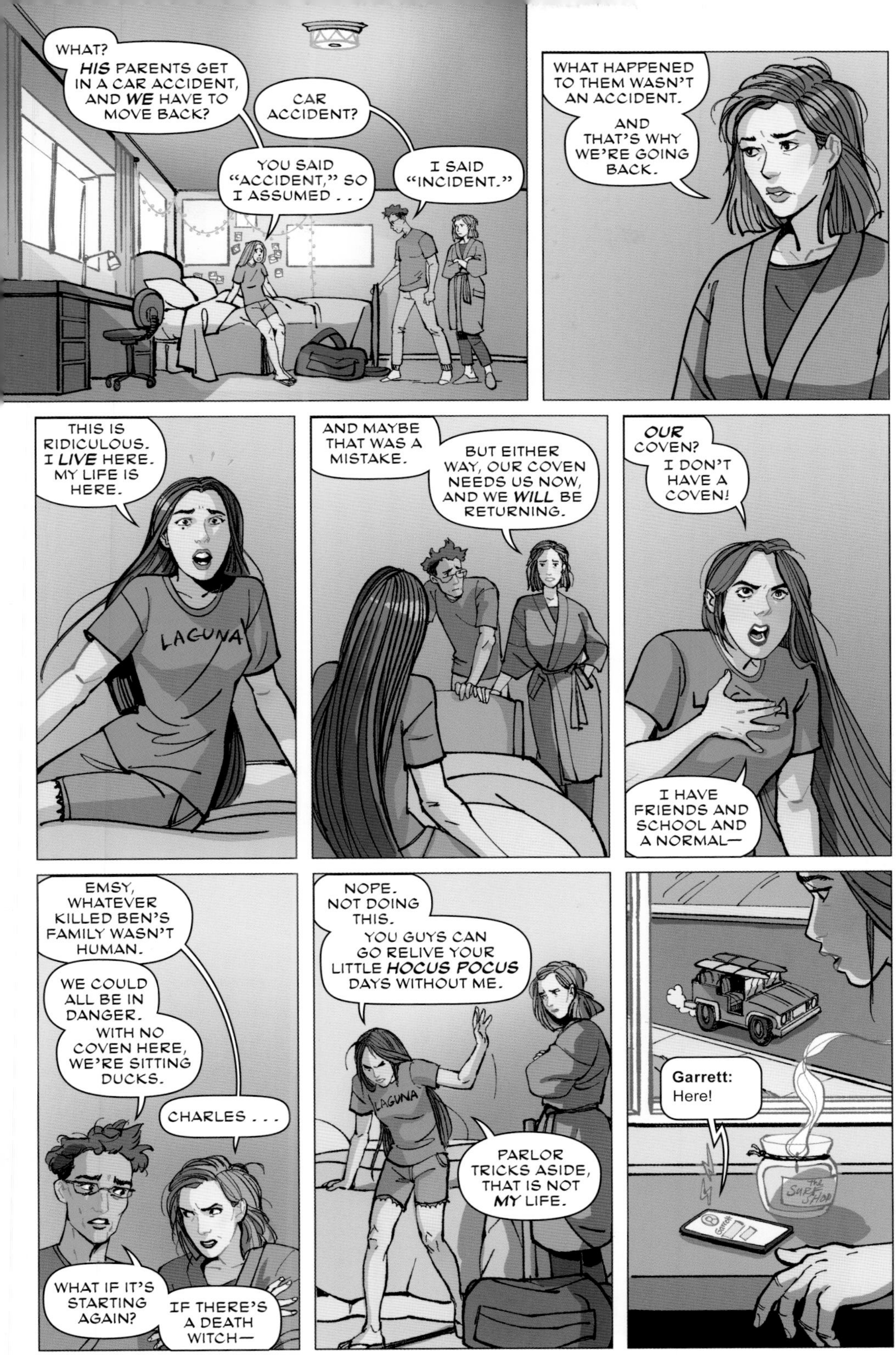

WHAT? *HIS* PARENTS GET IN A CAR ACCIDENT, AND *WE* HAVE TO MOVE BACK?
CAR ACCIDENT?
YOU SAID "ACCIDENT," SO I ASSUMED . . .
I SAID "INCIDENT."
WHAT HAPPENED TO THEM WASN'T AN ACCIDENT.
AND THAT'S WHY WE'RE GOING BACK.
THIS IS RIDICULOUS. I *LIVE* HERE. MY LIFE IS HERE.
LAGUNA
AND MAYBE THAT WAS A MISTAKE.
BUT EITHER WAY, OUR COVEN NEEDS US NOW, AND WE *WILL* BE RETURNING.
OUR COVEN?
I DON'T HAVE A COVEN!
I HAVE FRIENDS AND SCHOOL AND A NORMAL—
EMSY, WHATEVER KILLED BEN'S FAMILY WASN'T HUMAN.
WE COULD ALL BE IN DANGER.
WITH NO COVEN HERE, WE'RE SITTING DUCKS.
CHARLES . . .
WHAT IF IT'S STARTING AGAIN?
IF THERE'S A DEATH WITCH—
NOPE. NOT DOING THIS.
YOU GUYS CAN GO RELIVE YOUR LITTLE *HOCUS POCUS* DAYS WITHOUT ME.
LAGUNA
PARLOR TRICKS ASIDE, THAT IS NOT *MY* LIFE.
Garrett:
Here!
Garrett
the SURF SHOP

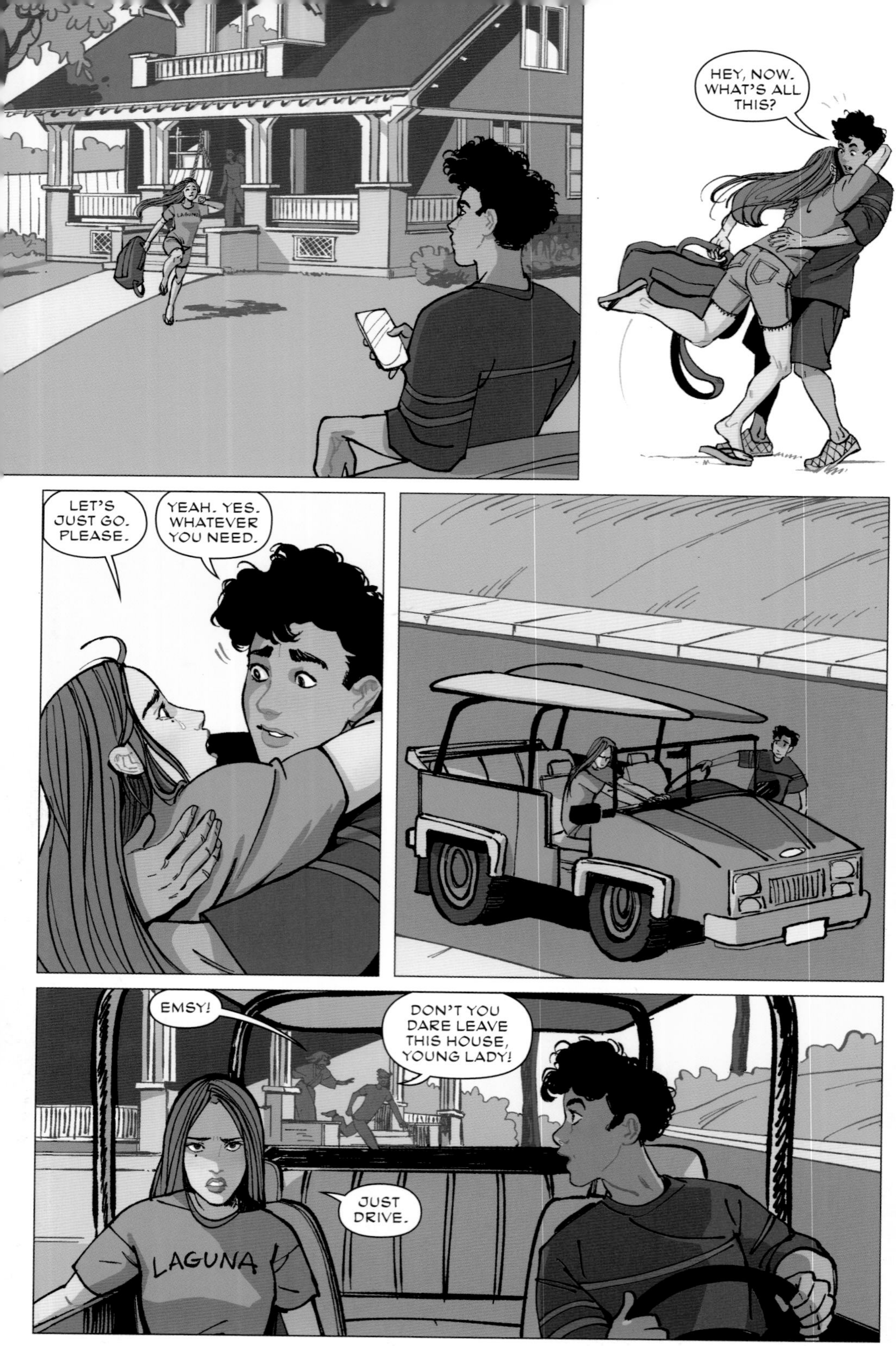
HEY, NOW. WHAT'S ALL THIS?
LET'S JUST GO. PLEASE.
YEAH. YES. WHATEVER YOU NEED.
LAGUNA
EMSY!
DON'T YOU DARE LEAVE THIS HOUSE, YOUNG LADY!
JUST DRIVE.

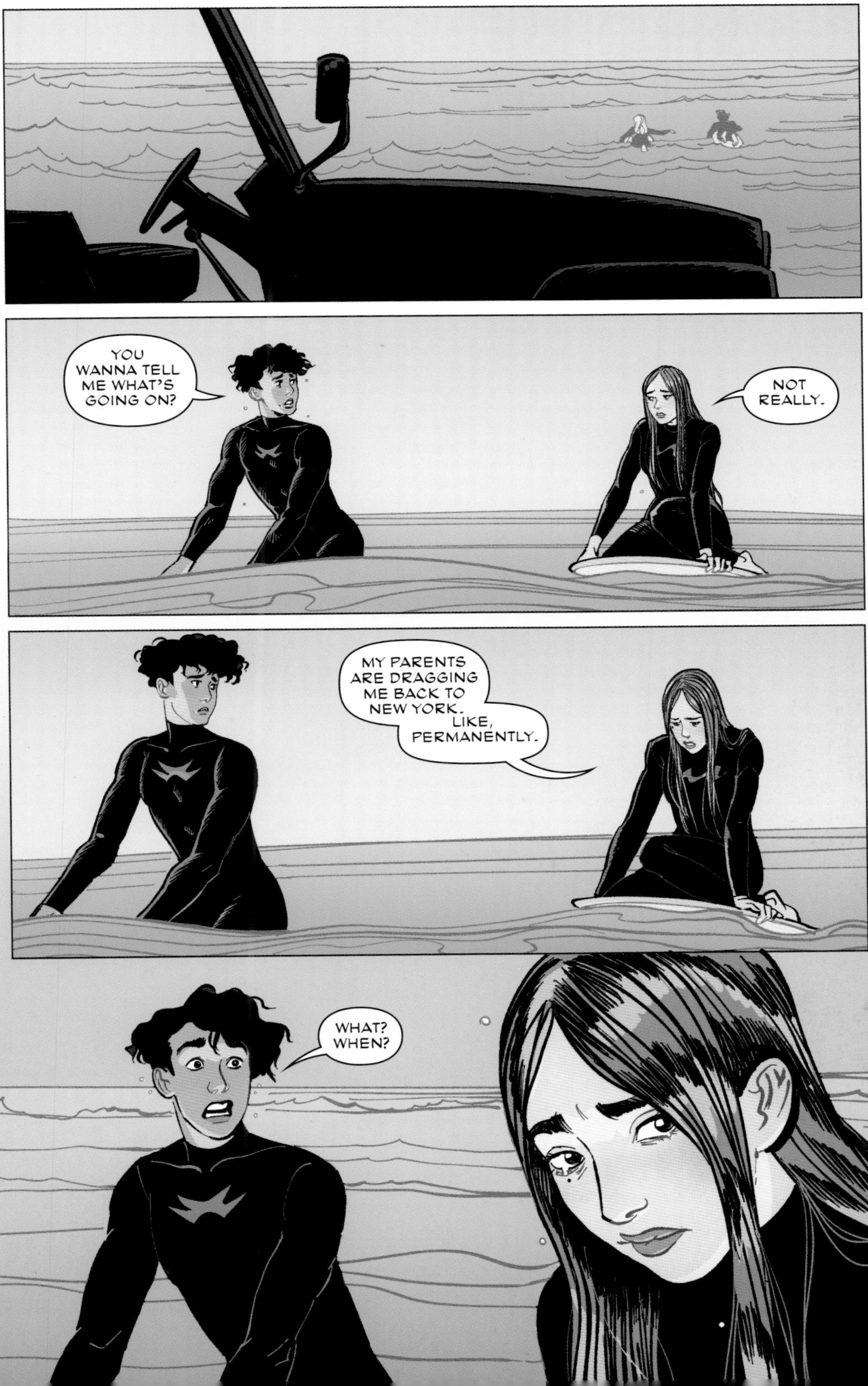
YOU WANNA TELL ME WHAT'S GOING ON?
NOT REALLY.
MY PARENTS ARE DRAGGING ME BACK TO NEW YORK.
LIKE, PERMANENTLY.
WHAT? WHEN?

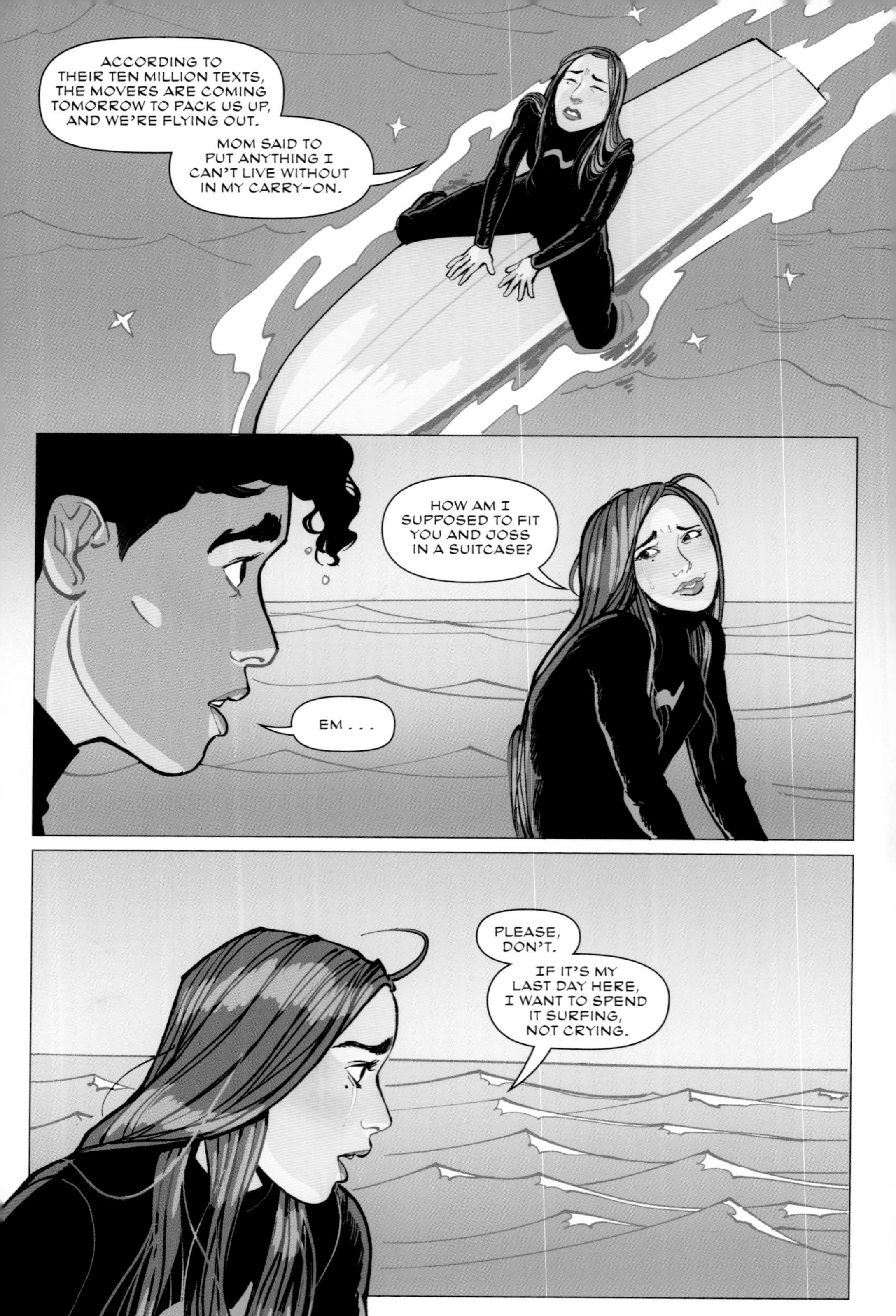
ACCORDING TO THEIR TEN MILLION TEXTS, THE MOVERS ARE COMING TOMORROW TO PACK US UP, AND WE'RE FLYING OUT.
MOM SAID TO PUT ANYTHING I CAN'T LIVE WITHOUT IN MY CARRY-ON.
HOW AM I SUPPOSED TO FIT YOU AND JOSS IN A SUITCASE?
EM . . .
PLEASE, DON'T.
IF IT'S MY LAST DAY HERE, I WANT TO SPEND IT SURFING, NOT CRYING.

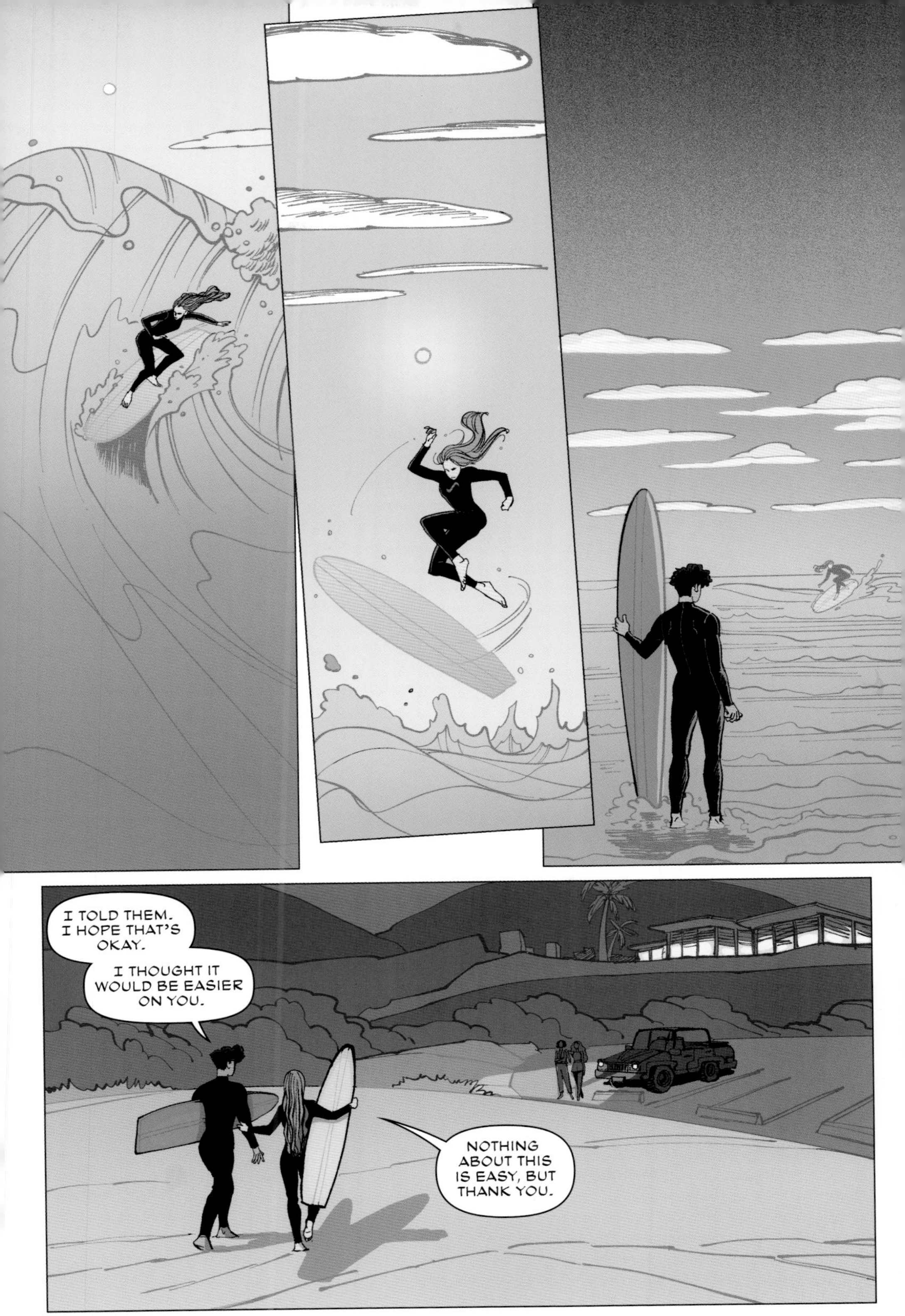
I TOLD THEM. I HOPE THAT'S OKAY.
I THOUGHT IT WOULD BE EASIER ON YOU.
NOTHING ABOUT THIS IS EASY, BUT THANK YOU.

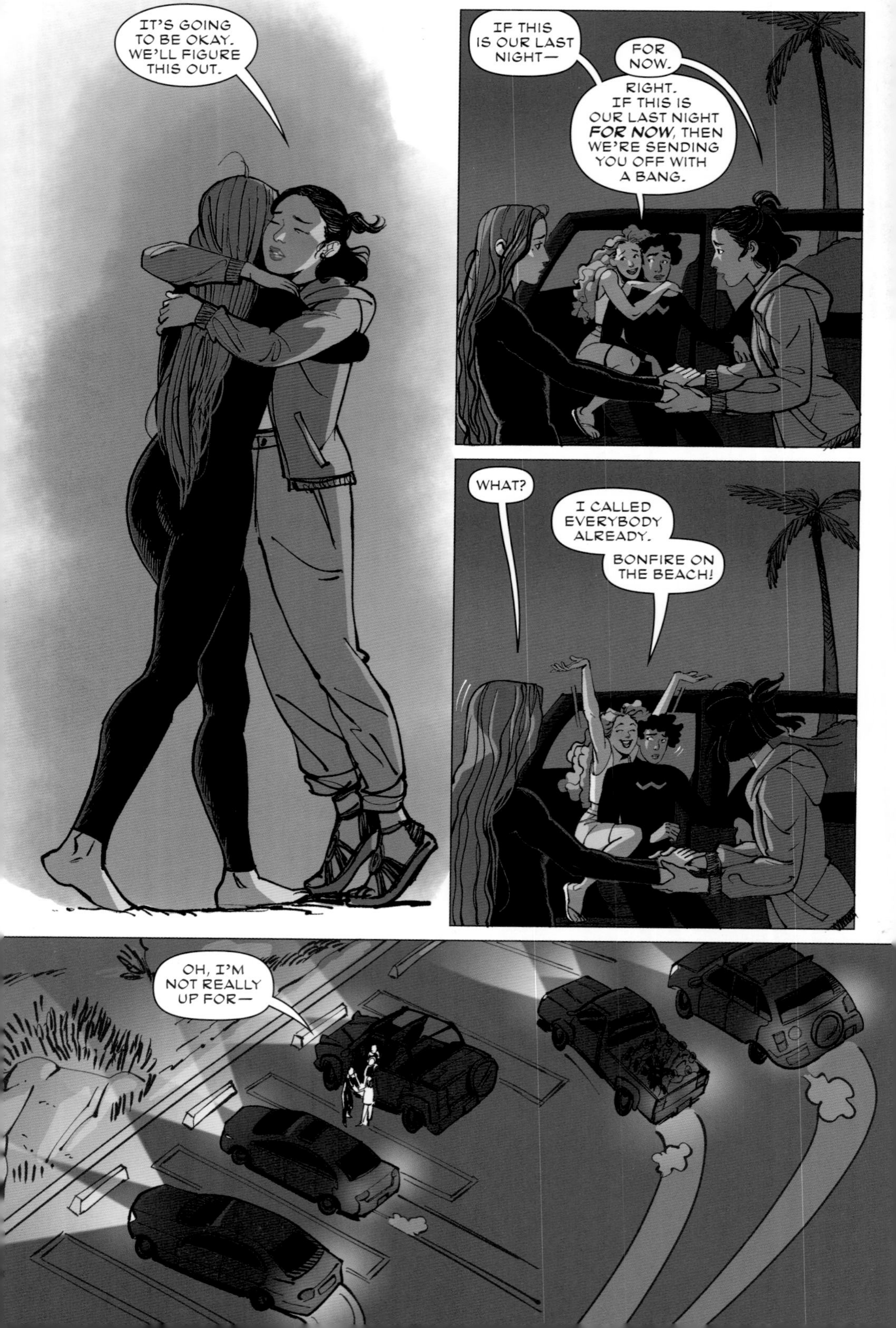
IT'S GOING TO BE OKAY. WE'LL FIGURE THIS OUT.
IF THIS IS OUR LAST NIGHT—
FOR NOW.
RIGHT. IF THIS IS OUR LAST NIGHT *FOR NOW*, THEN WE'RE SENDING YOU OFF WITH A BANG.
WHAT?
I CALLED EVERYBODY ALREADY.
BONFIRE ON THE BEACH!
OH, I'M NOT REALLY UP FOR—

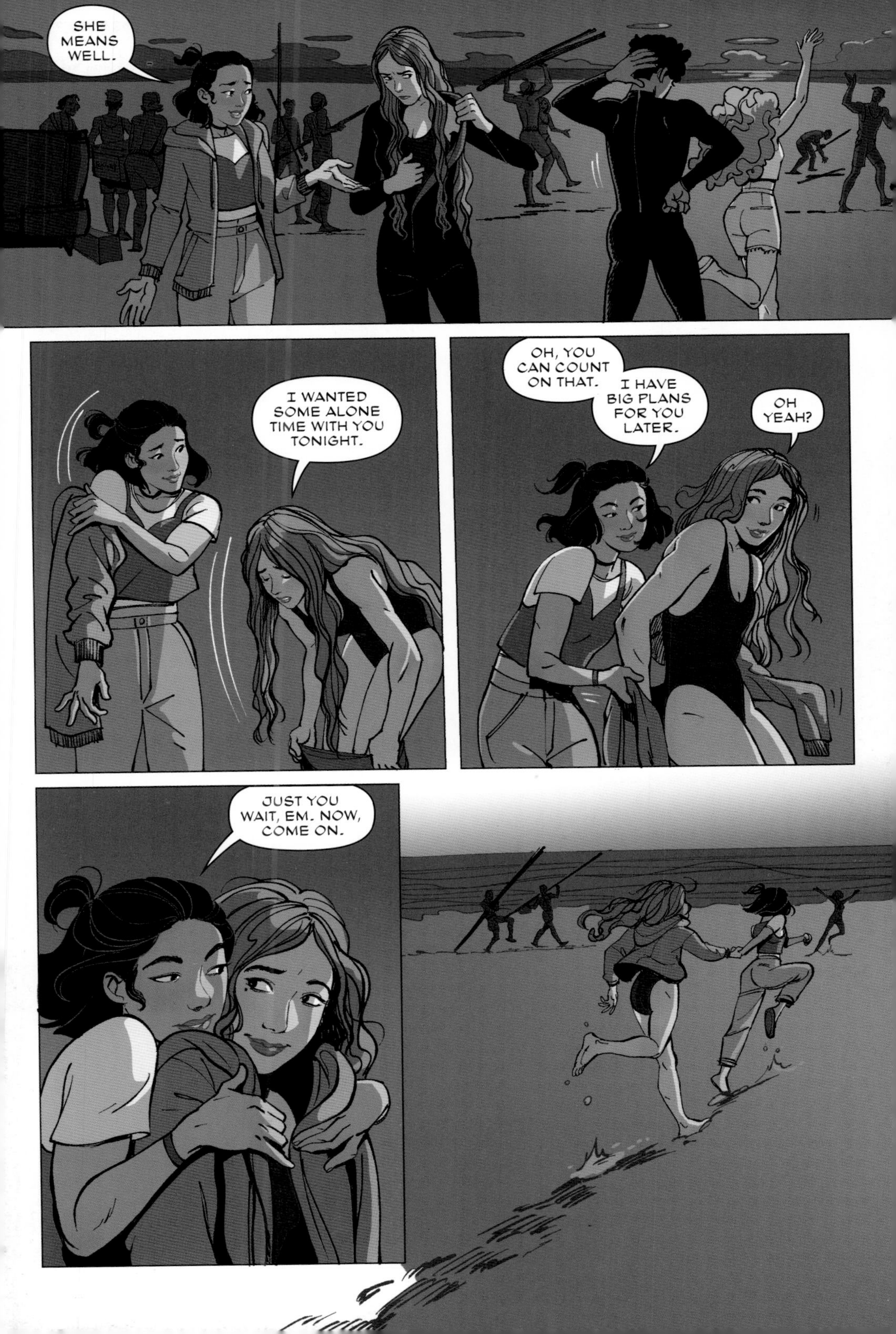
SHE MEANS WELL.
I WANTED SOME ALONE TIME WITH YOU TONIGHT.
OH, YOU CAN COUNT ON THAT.
I HAVE BIG PLANS FOR YOU LATER.
OH YEAH?
JUST YOU WAIT, EM. NOW, COME ON.

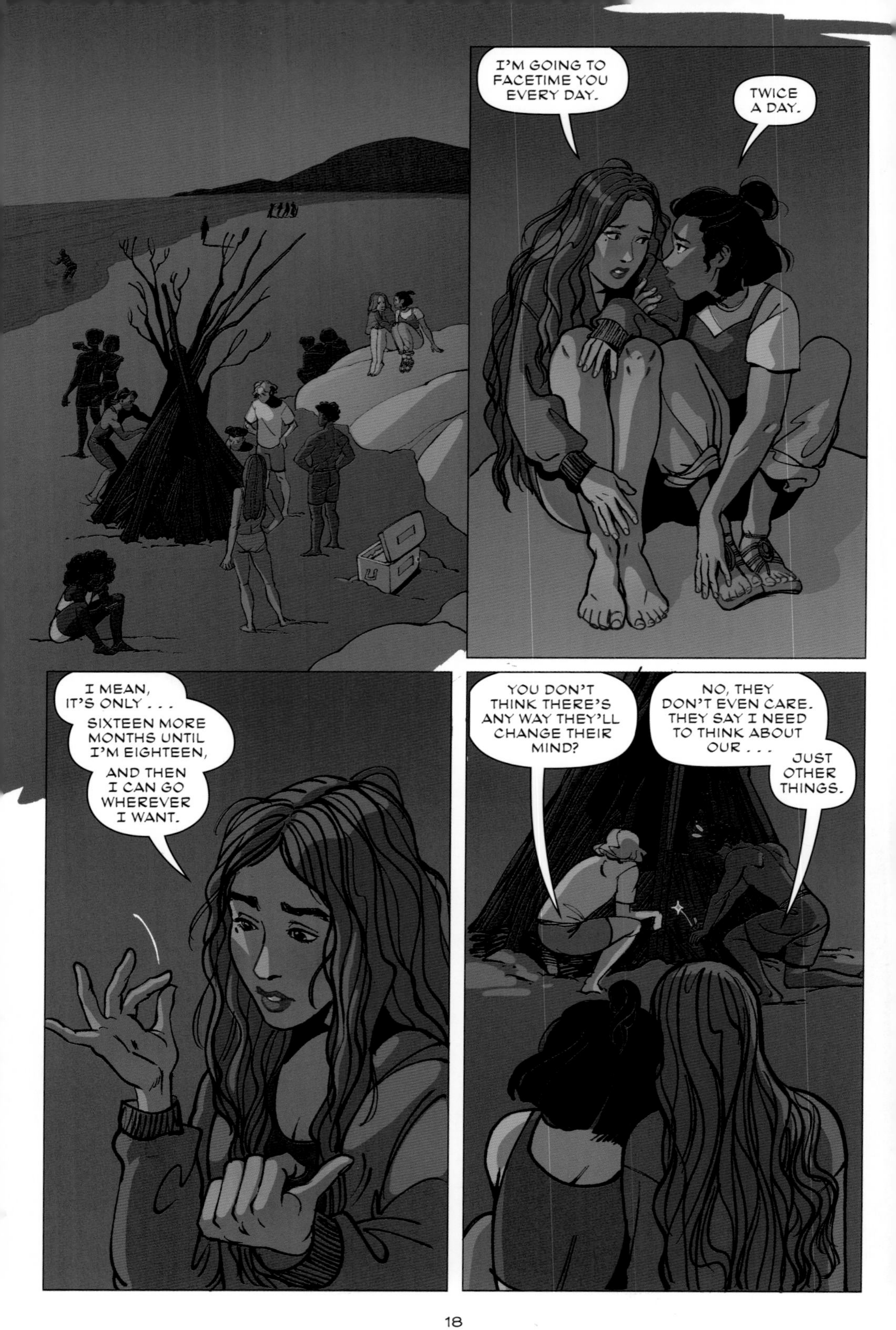

I'M GOING TO FACETIME YOU EVERY DAY.
TWICE A DAY.
I MEAN, IT'S ONLY . . .
SIXTEEN MORE MONTHS UNTIL I'M EIGHTEEN,
AND THEN I CAN GO WHEREVER I WANT.
YOU DON'T THINK THERE'S ANY WAY THEY'LL CHANGE THEIR MIND?
NO, THEY DON'T EVEN CARE. THEY SAY I NEED TO THINK ABOUT OUR . . .
JUST OTHER THINGS.

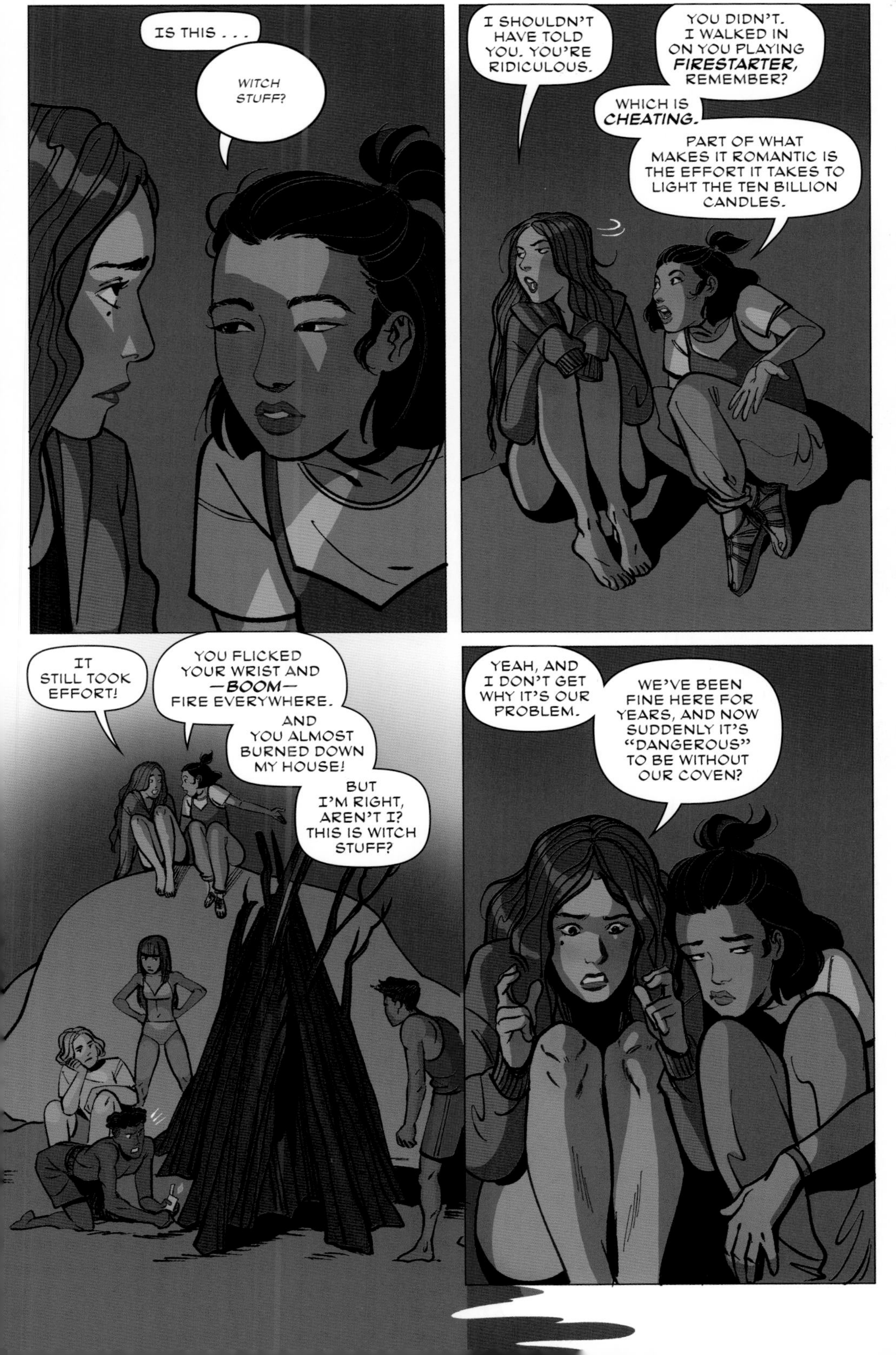
IS THIS . . .
WITCH STUFF?
I SHOULDN'T HAVE TOLD YOU. YOU'RE RIDICULOUS.
YOU DIDN'T. I WALKED IN ON YOU PLAYING *FIRESTARTER,* REMEMBER?
WHICH IS *CHEATING.*
PART OF WHAT MAKES IT ROMANTIC IS THE EFFORT IT TAKES TO LIGHT THE TEN BILLION CANDLES.
IT STILL TOOK EFFORT!
YOU FLICKED YOUR WRIST AND —*BOOM*— FIRE EVERYWHERE.
AND YOU ALMOST BURNED DOWN MY HOUSE!
BUT I'M RIGHT, AREN'T I? THIS IS WITCH STUFF?
YEAH, AND I DON'T GET WHY IT'S OUR PROBLEM.
WE'VE BEEN FINE HERE FOR YEARS, AND NOW SUDDENLY IT'S "DANGEROUS" TO BE WITHOUT OUR COVEN?

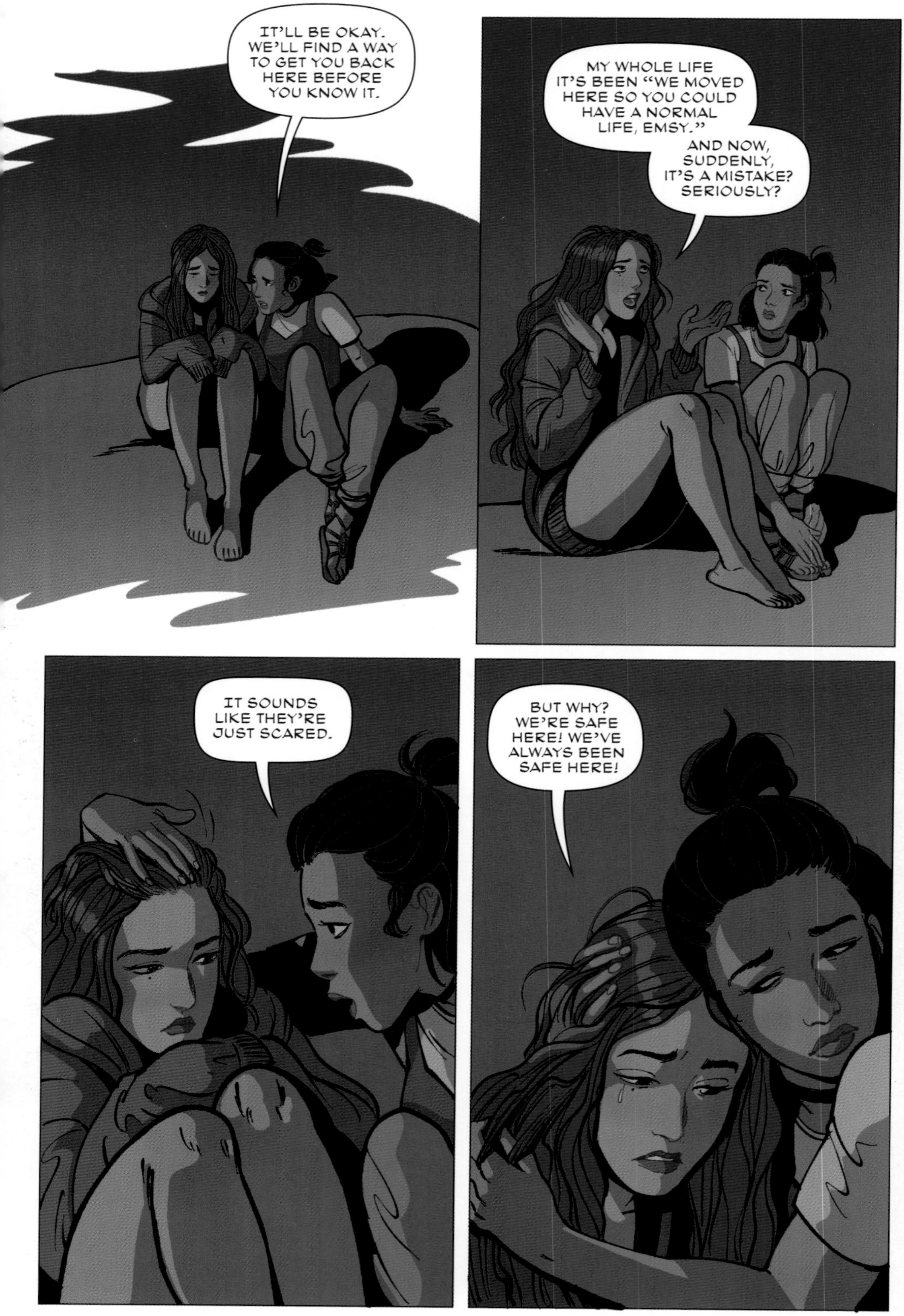
IT'LL BE OKAY. WE'LL FIND A WAY TO GET YOU BACK HERE BEFORE YOU KNOW IT.
MY WHOLE LIFE IT'S BEEN "WE MOVED HERE SO YOU COULD HAVE A NORMAL LIFE, EMSY."
AND NOW, SUDDENLY, IT'S A MISTAKE? SERIOUSLY?
IT SOUNDS LIKE THEY'RE JUST SCARED.
BUT WHY? WE'RE SAFE HERE! WE'VE ALWAYS BEEN SAFE HERE!

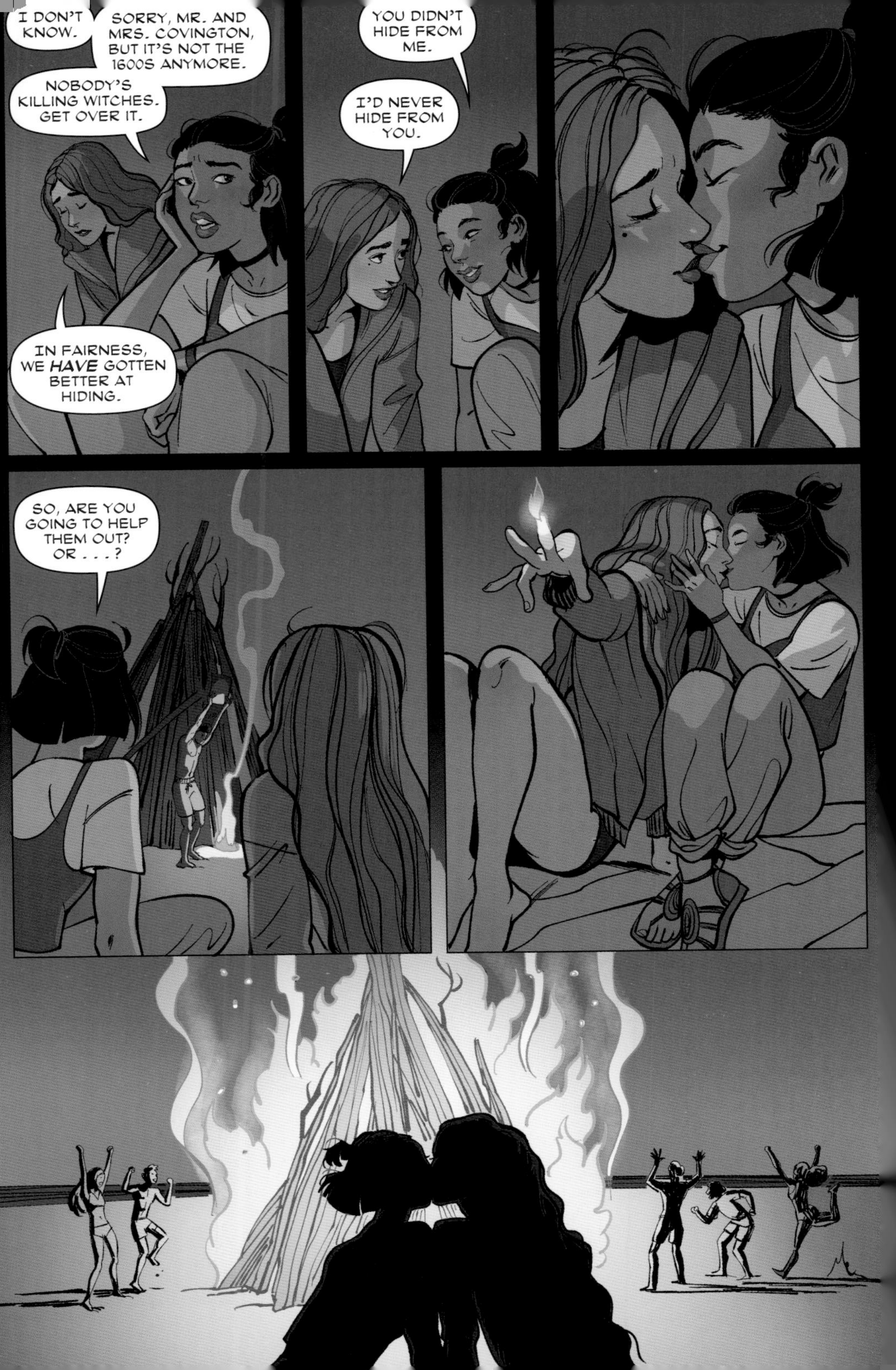

I DON'T KNOW.
SORRY, MR. AND MRS. COVINGTON, BUT IT'S NOT THE 1600S ANYMORE.
NOBODY'S KILLING WITCHES. GET OVER IT.
IN FAIRNESS, WE ***HAVE*** GOTTEN BETTER AT HIDING.
YOU DIDN'T HIDE FROM ME.
I'D NEVER HIDE FROM YOU.
SO, ARE YOU GOING TO HELP THEM OUT? OR . . . ?

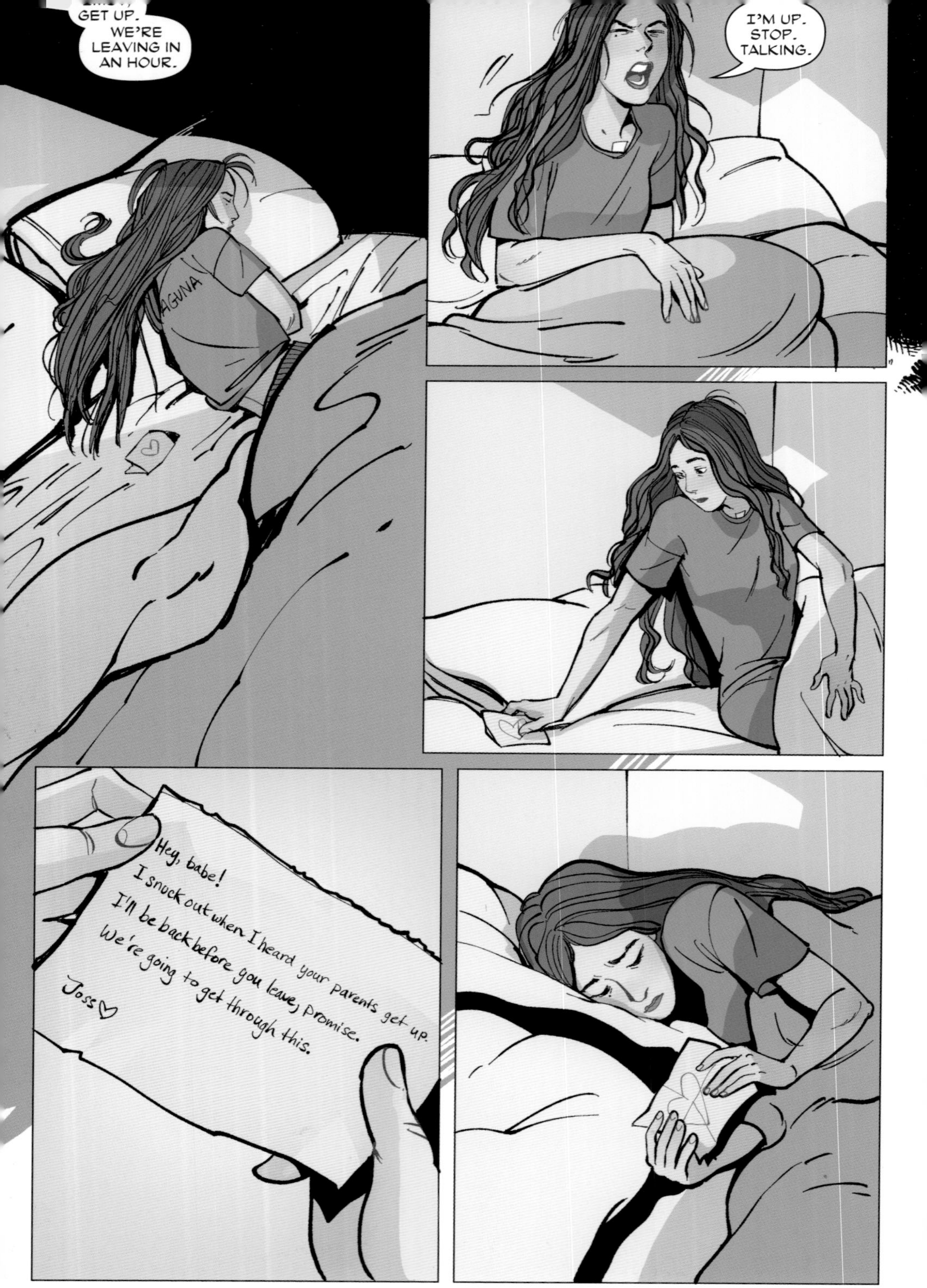

GET UP. WE'RE LEAVING IN AN HOUR.
I'M UP. STOP. TALKING.
Hey, babe!
I snuck out when I heard your parents get up.
I'll be back before you leave, promise.
We're going to get through this.
Joss♡

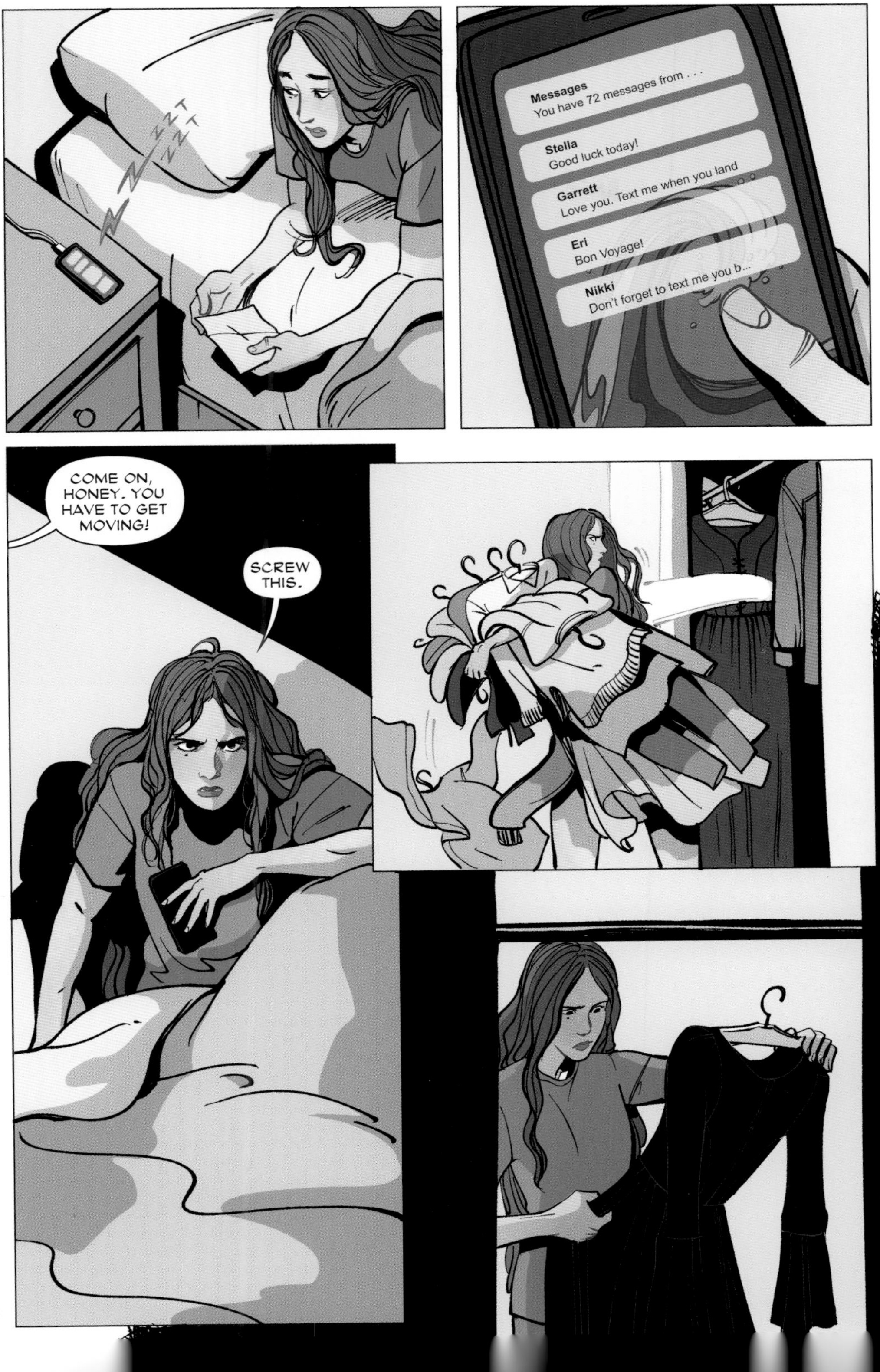
ZZZT
ZZZT
Messages
You have 72 messages from . . .
Stella
Good luck today!
Garrett
Love you. Text me when you land
Eri
Bon Voyage!
Nikki
Don't forget to text me you b...
COME ON, HONEY. YOU HAVE TO GET MOVING!
SCREW THIS.

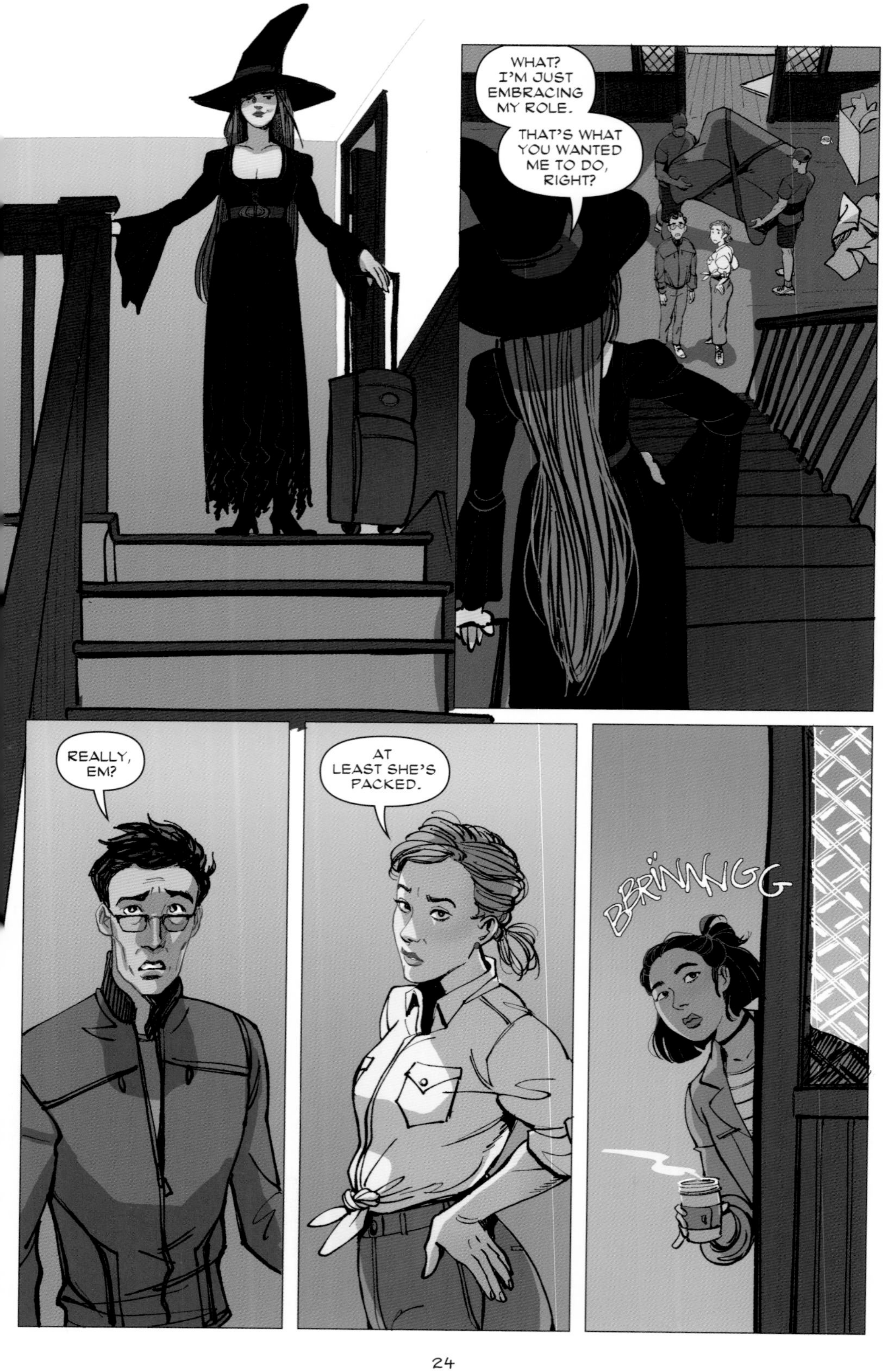
WHAT? I'M JUST EMBRACING MY ROLE.
THAT'S WHAT YOU WANTED ME TO DO, RIGHT?
REALLY, EM?
AT LEAST SHE'S PACKED.
BBRINNNGG

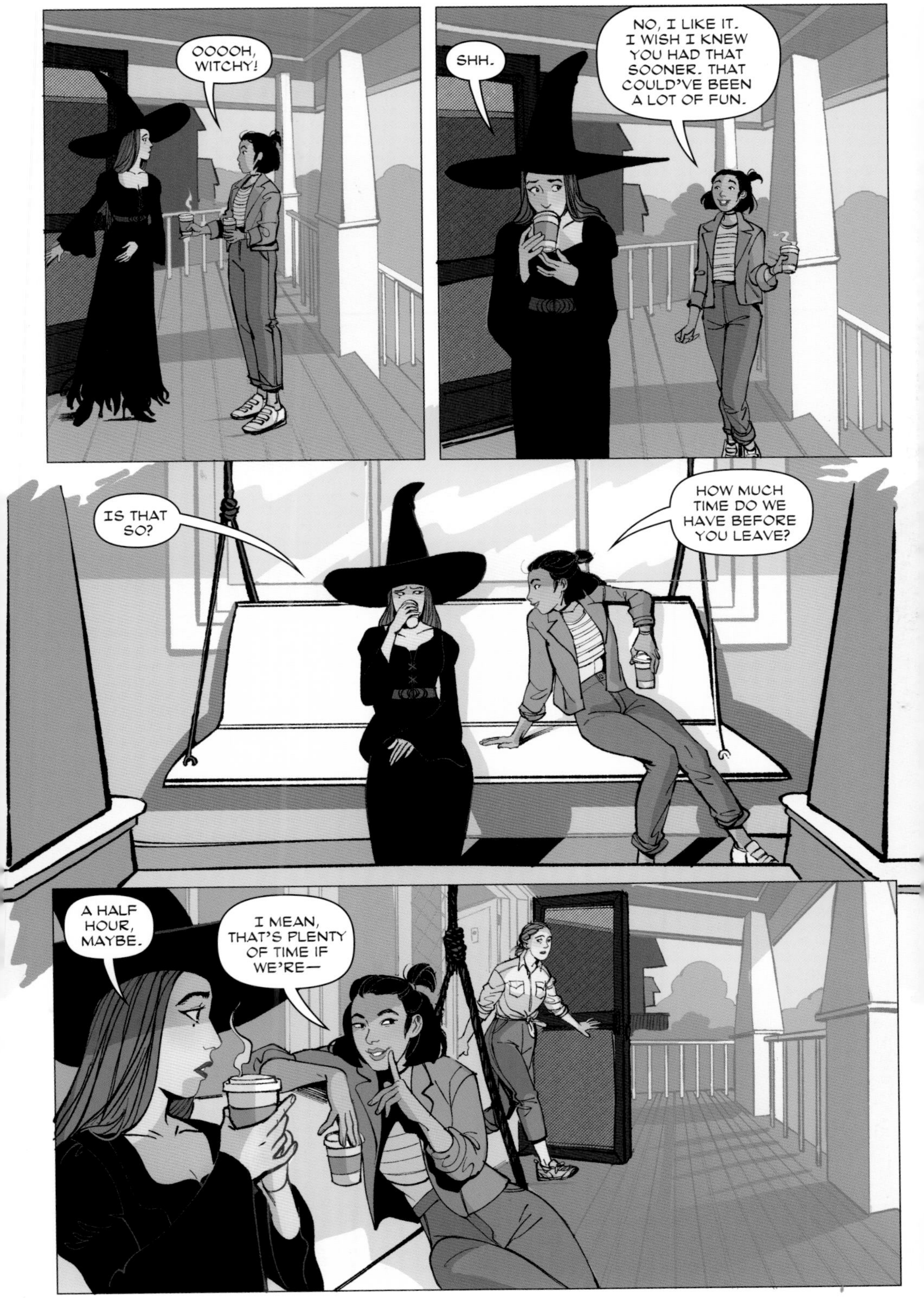
OOOOH, WITCHY!
SHH.
NO, I LIKE IT. I WISH I KNEW YOU HAD THAT SOONER. THAT COULD'VE BEEN A LOT OF FUN.
IS THAT SO?
HOW MUCH TIME DO WE HAVE BEFORE YOU LEAVE?
A HALF HOUR, MAYBE.
I MEAN, THAT'S PLENTY OF TIME IF WE'RE—

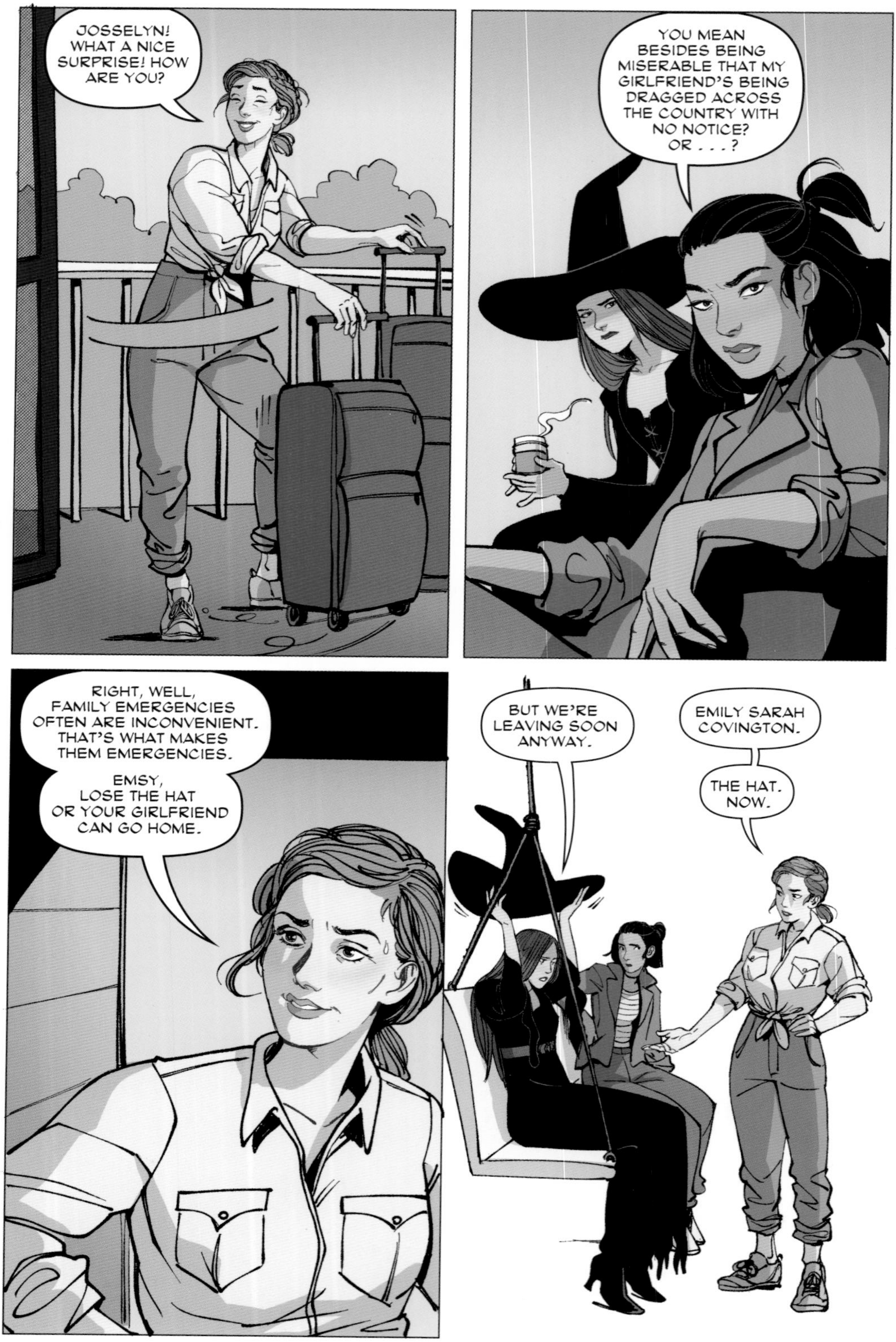
JOSSELYN! WHAT A NICE SURPRISE! HOW ARE YOU?
YOU MEAN BESIDES BEING MISERABLE THAT MY GIRLFRIEND'S BEING DRAGGED ACROSS THE COUNTRY WITH NO NOTICE? OR . . . ?
RIGHT, WELL, FAMILY EMERGENCIES OFTEN ARE INCONVENIENT. THAT'S WHAT MAKES THEM EMERGENCIES.
EMSY, LOSE THE HAT OR YOUR GIRLFRIEND CAN GO HOME.
BUT WE'RE LEAVING SOON ANYWAY.
EMILY SARAH COVINGTON.
THE HAT. NOW.

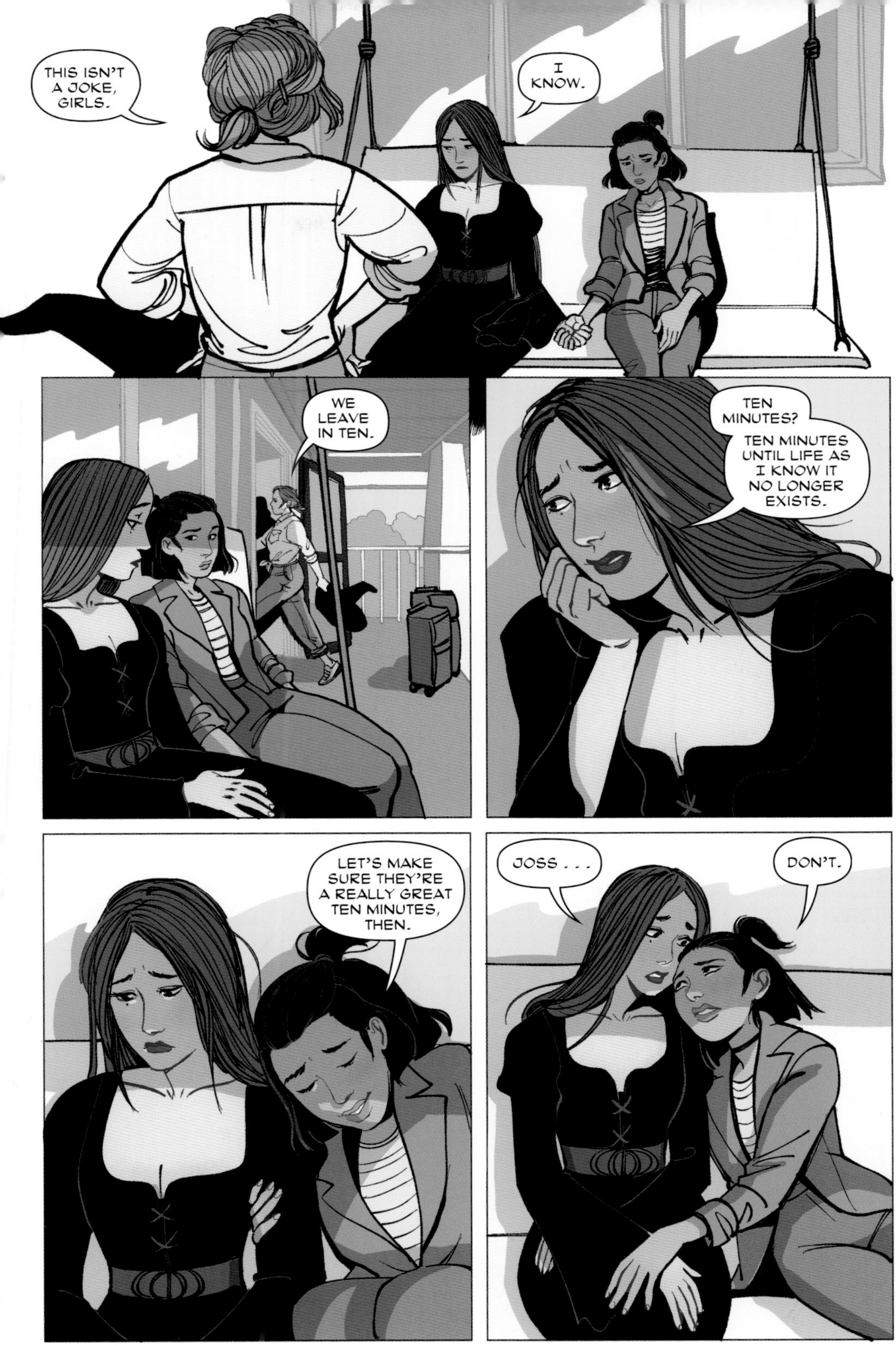
THIS ISN'T A JOKE, GIRLS.
I KNOW.
WE LEAVE IN TEN.
TEN MINUTES?
TEN MINUTES UNTIL LIFE AS I KNOW IT NO LONGER EXISTS.
LET'S MAKE SURE THEY'RE A REALLY GREAT TEN MINUTES, THEN.
JOSS . . .
DON'T.

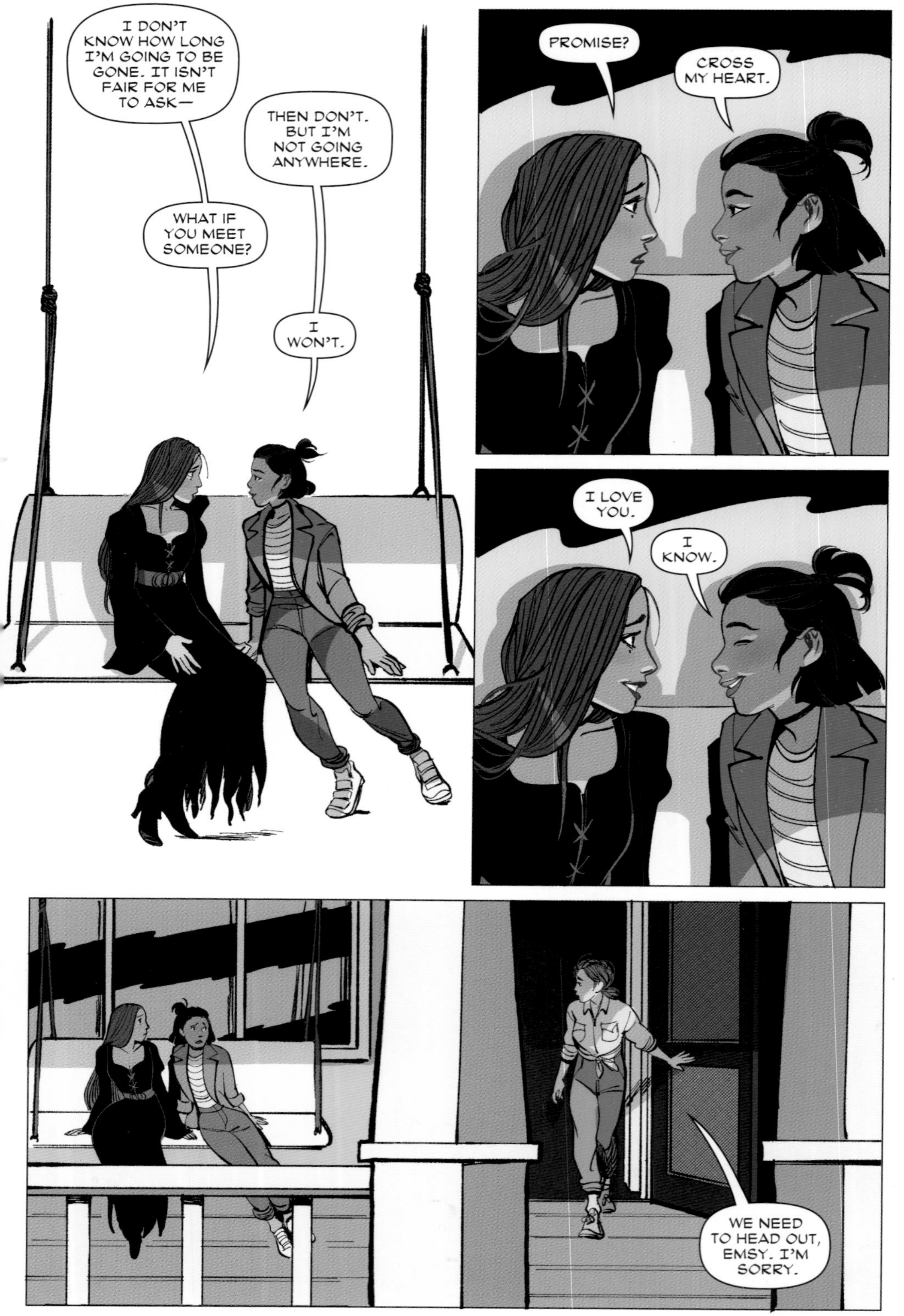
I DON'T KNOW HOW LONG I'M GOING TO BE GONE. IT ISN'T FAIR FOR ME TO ASK—
THEN DON'T. BUT I'M NOT GOING ANYWHERE.
WHAT IF YOU MEET SOMEONE?
I WON'T.
PROMISE?
CROSS MY HEART.
I LOVE YOU.
I KNOW.
WE NEED TO HEAD OUT, EMSY. I'M SORRY.

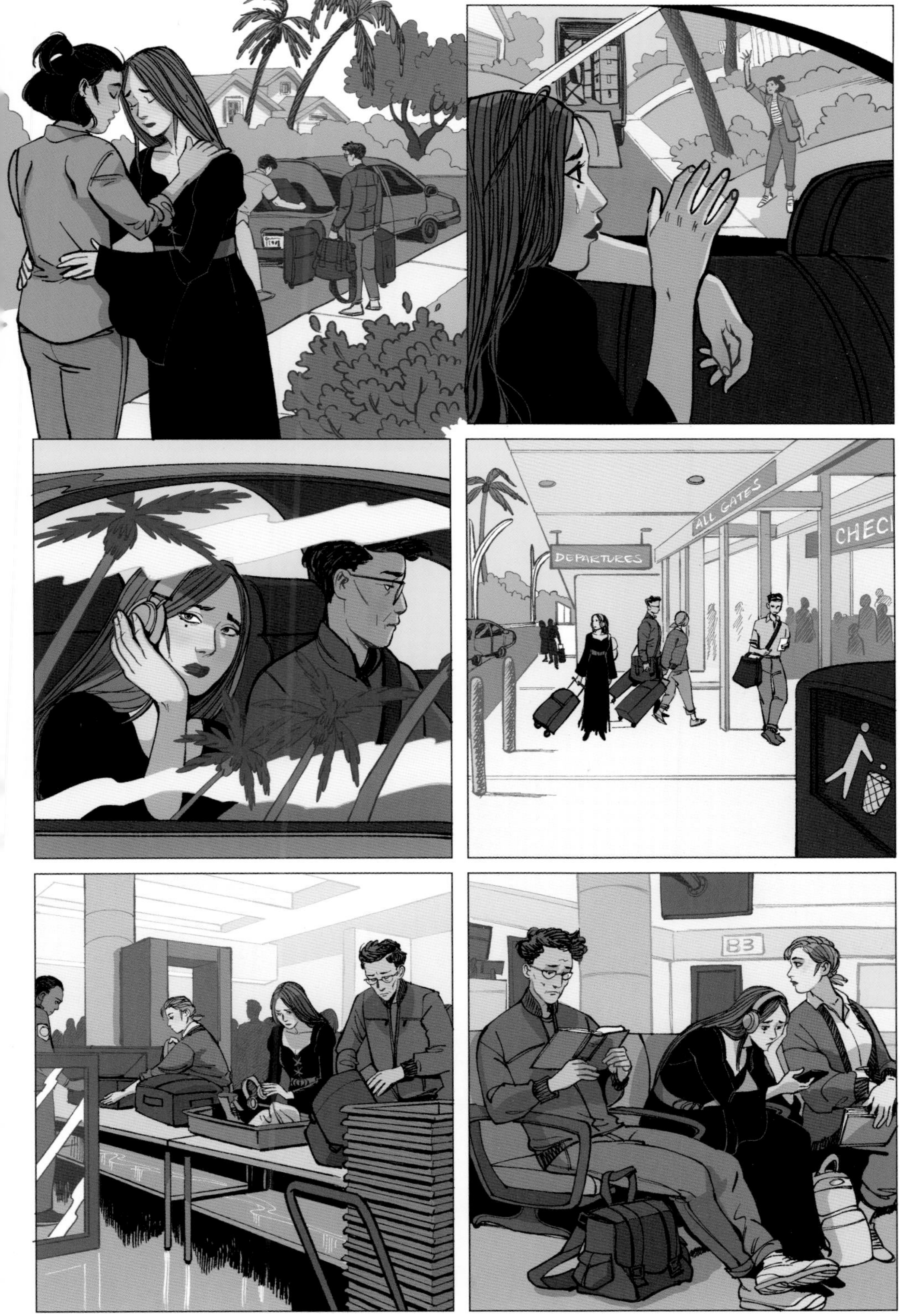
DEPARTURES
ALL GATES
CHECK
B3

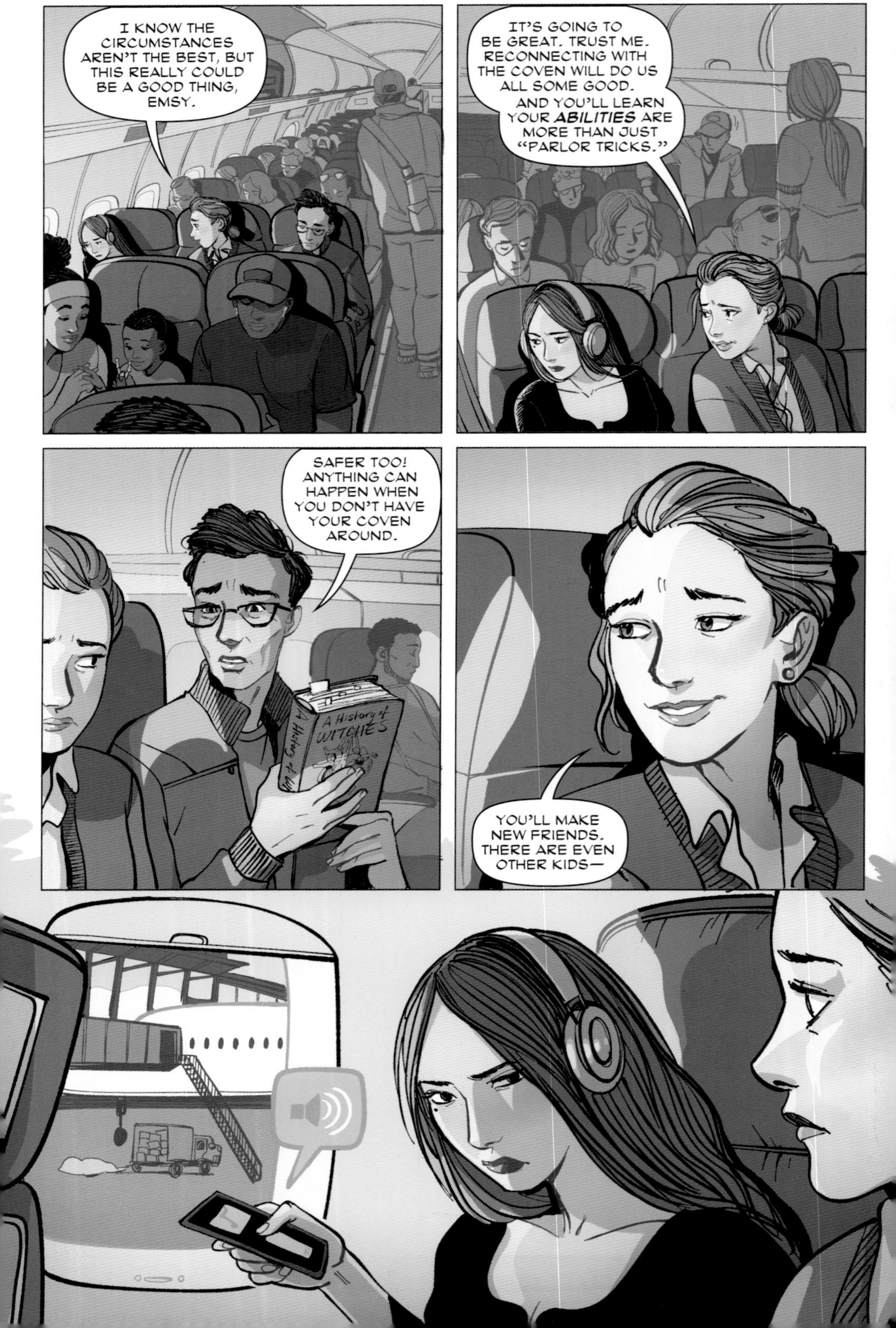

I KNOW THE CIRCUMSTANCES AREN'T THE BEST, BUT THIS REALLY COULD BE A GOOD THING, EMSY.
IT'S GOING TO BE GREAT. TRUST ME. RECONNECTING WITH THE COVEN WILL DO US ALL SOME GOOD.
AND YOU'LL LEARN YOUR ABILITIES ARE MORE THAN JUST "PARLOR TRICKS."
SAFER TOO! ANYTHING CAN HAPPEN WHEN YOU DON'T HAVE YOUR COVEN AROUND.
A History of WITCHES
YOU'LL MAKE NEW FRIENDS. THERE ARE EVEN OTHER KIDS—

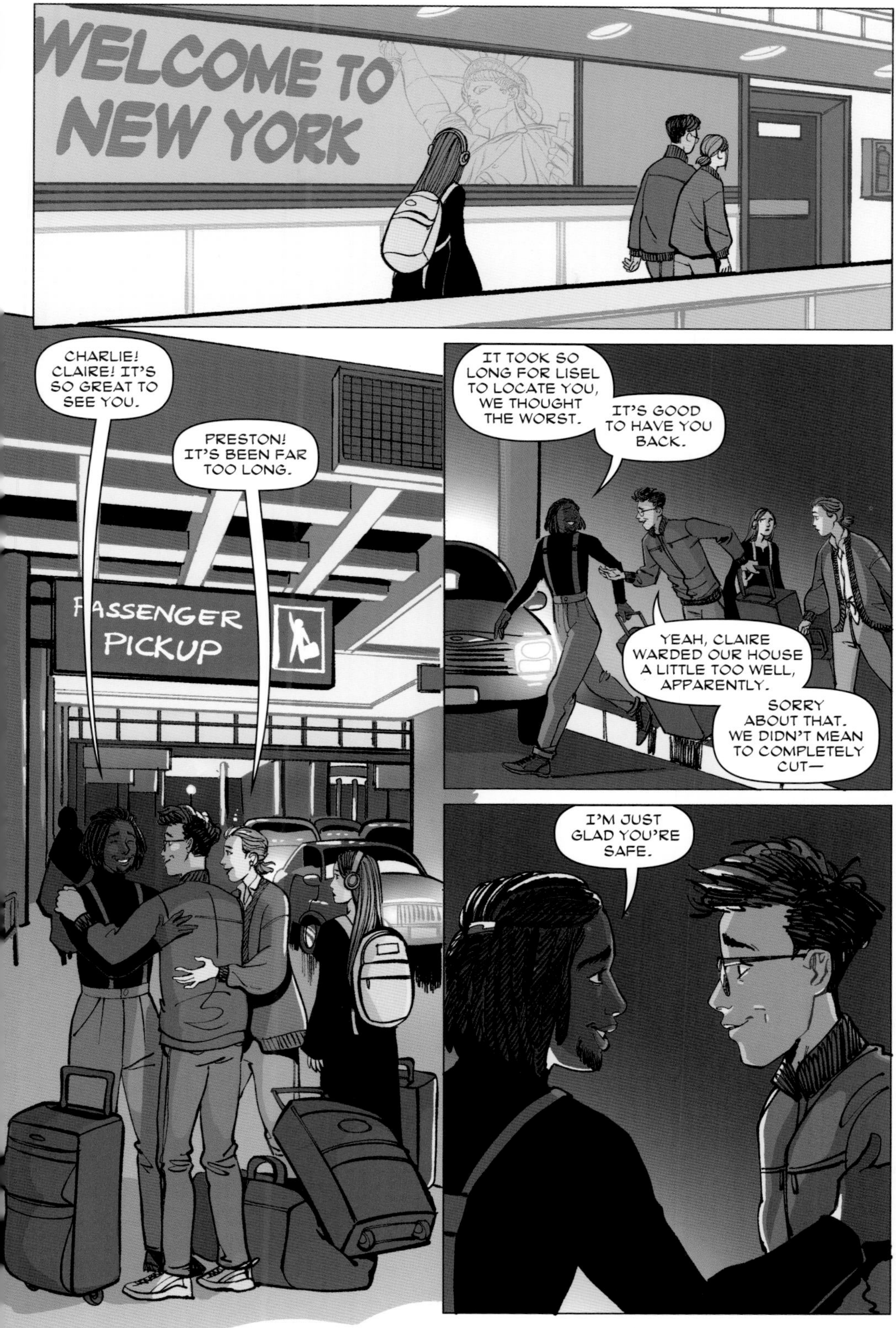

WELCOME TO NEW YORK
CHARLIE! CLAIRE! IT'S SO GREAT TO SEE YOU.
PRESTON! IT'S BEEN FAR TOO LONG.
PASSENGER PICKUP
IT TOOK SO LONG FOR LISEL TO LOCATE YOU, WE THOUGHT THE WORST.
IT'S GOOD TO HAVE YOU BACK.
YEAH, CLAIRE WARDED OUR HOUSE A LITTLE TOO WELL, APPARENTLY.
SORRY ABOUT THAT. WE DIDN'T MEAN TO COMPLETELY CUT—
I'M JUST GLAD YOU'RE SAFE.

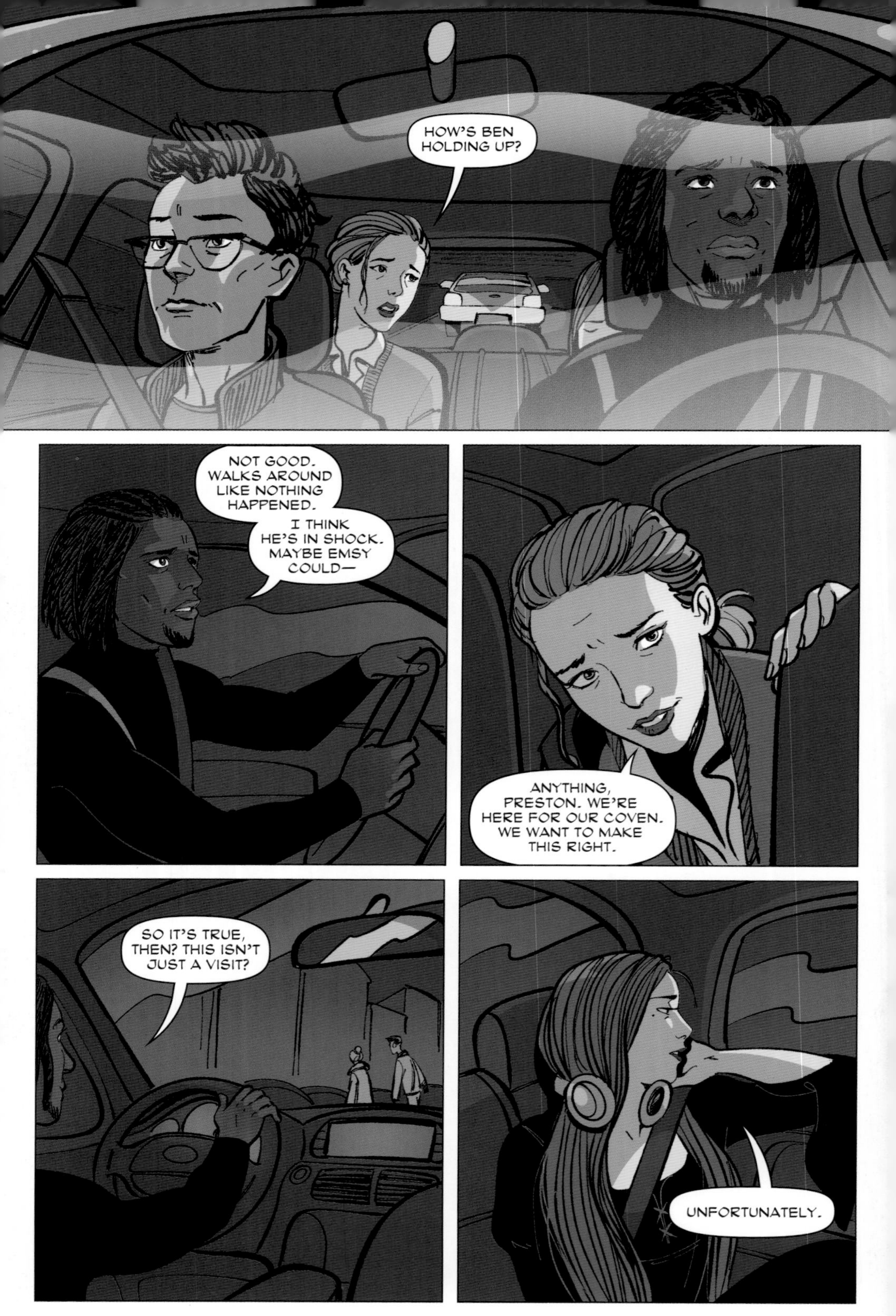
HOW'S BEN HOLDING UP?
NOT GOOD. WALKS AROUND LIKE NOTHING HAPPENED.
I THINK HE'S IN SHOCK. MAYBE EMSY COULD—
ANYTHING, PRESTON. WE'RE HERE FOR OUR COVEN. WE WANT TO MAKE THIS RIGHT.
SO IT'S TRUE, THEN? THIS ISN'T JUST A VISIT?
UNFORTUNATELY.

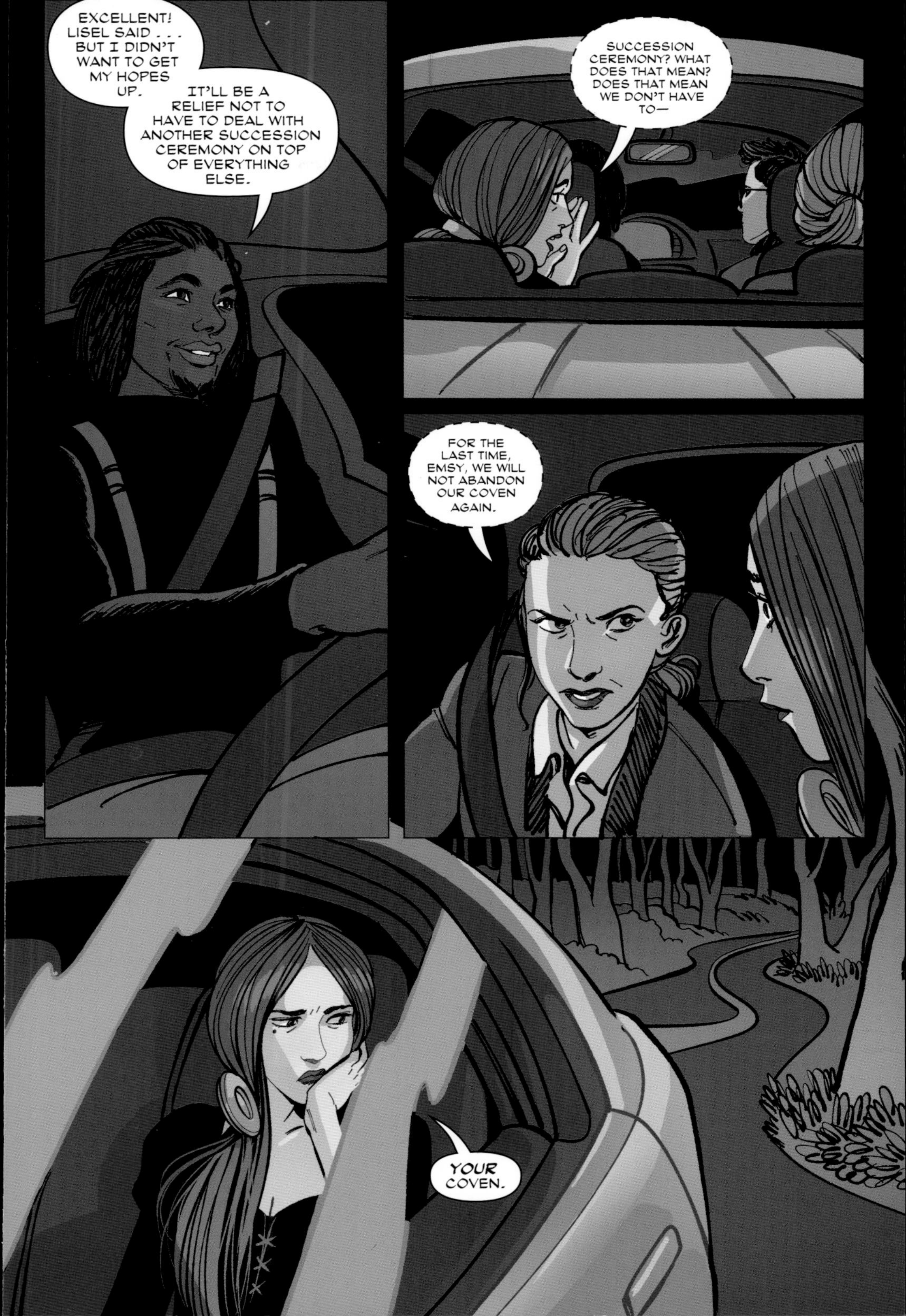
EXCELLENT! LISEL SAID . . . BUT I DIDN'T WANT TO GET MY HOPES UP.
IT'LL BE A RELIEF NOT TO HAVE TO DEAL WITH ANOTHER SUCCESSION CEREMONY ON TOP OF EVERYTHING ELSE.
SUCCESSION CEREMONY? WHAT DOES THAT MEAN? DOES THAT MEAN WE DON'T HAVE TO—
FOR THE LAST TIME, EMSY, WE WILL NOT ABANDON OUR COVEN AGAIN.
YOUR COVEN.

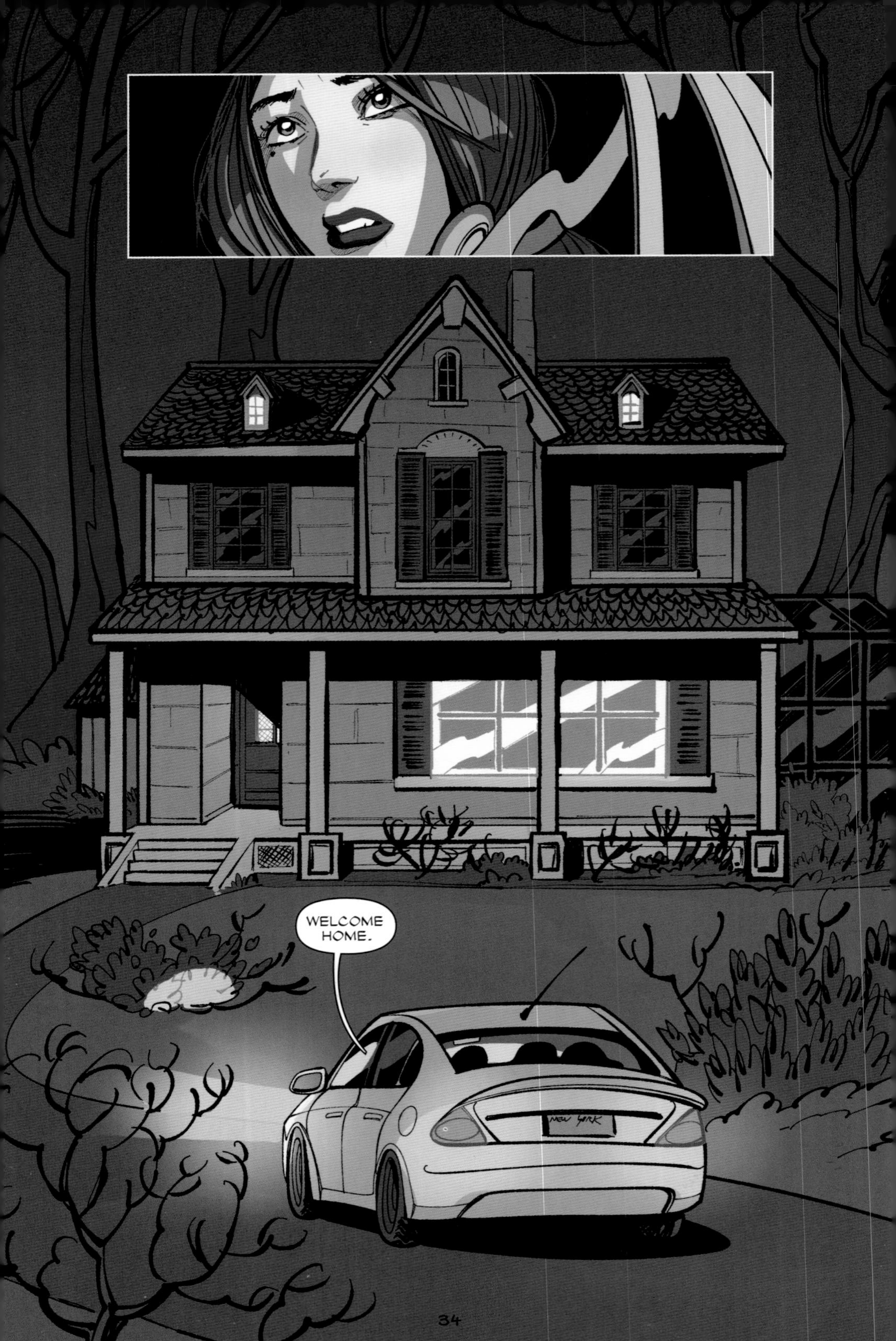
WELCOME HOME.
NEW YORK

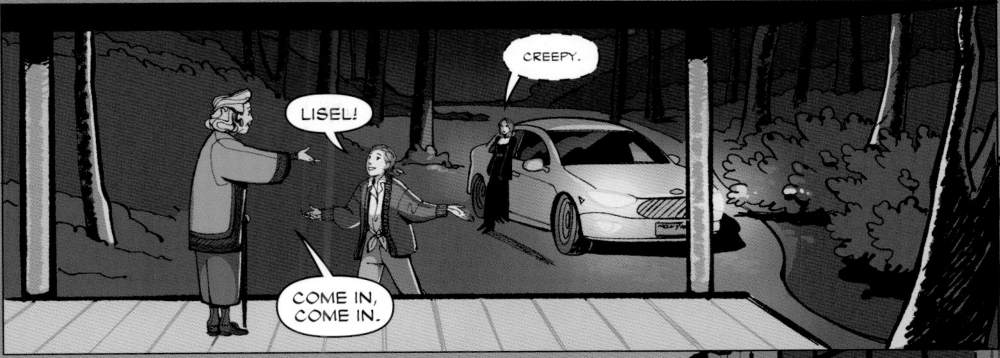
CREEPY.
LISEL!
COME IN, COME IN.

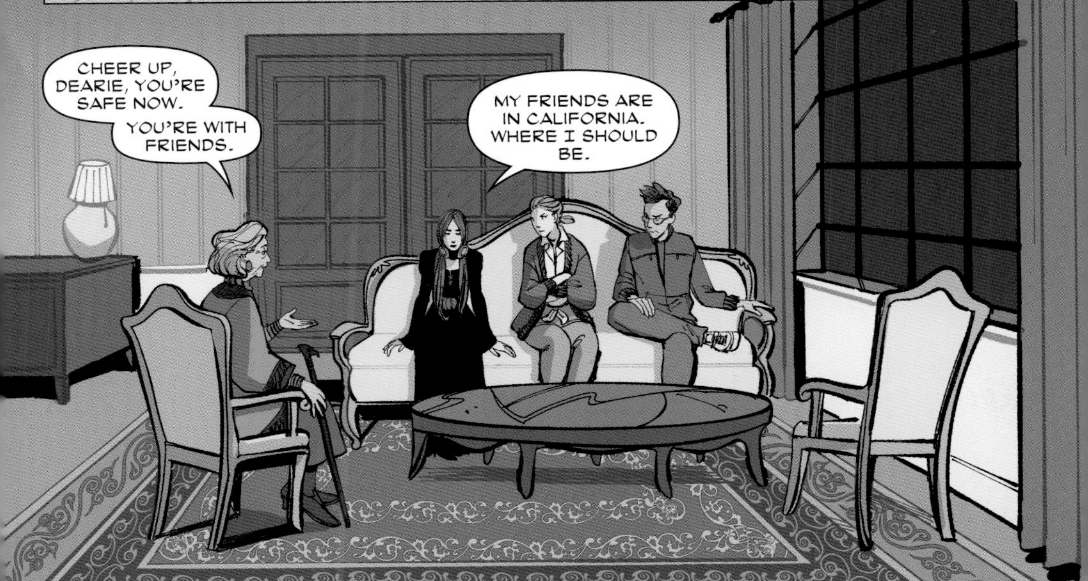
CHEER UP, DEARIE, YOU'RE SAFE NOW.
YOU'RE WITH FRIENDS.
MY FRIENDS ARE IN CALIFORNIA. WHERE I SHOULD BE.

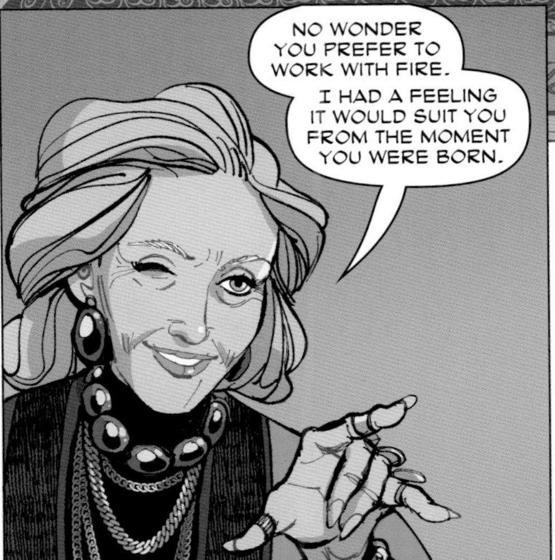
NO WONDER YOU PREFER TO WORK WITH FIRE.
I HAD A FEELING IT WOULD SUIT YOU FROM THE MOMENT YOU WERE BORN.

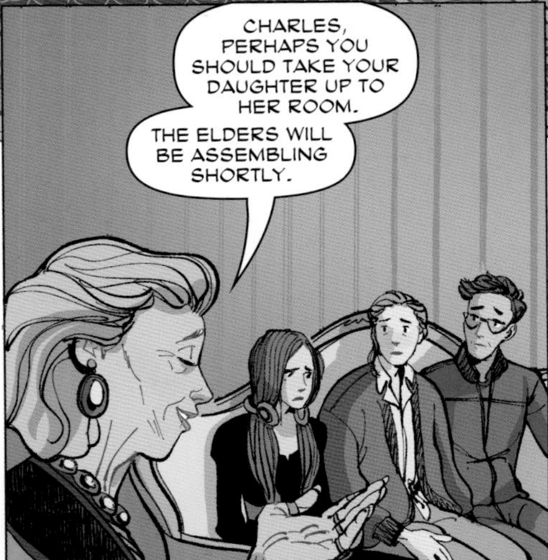
CHARLES, PERHAPS YOU SHOULD TAKE YOUR DAUGHTER UP TO HER ROOM.
THE ELDERS WILL BE ASSEMBLING SHORTLY.

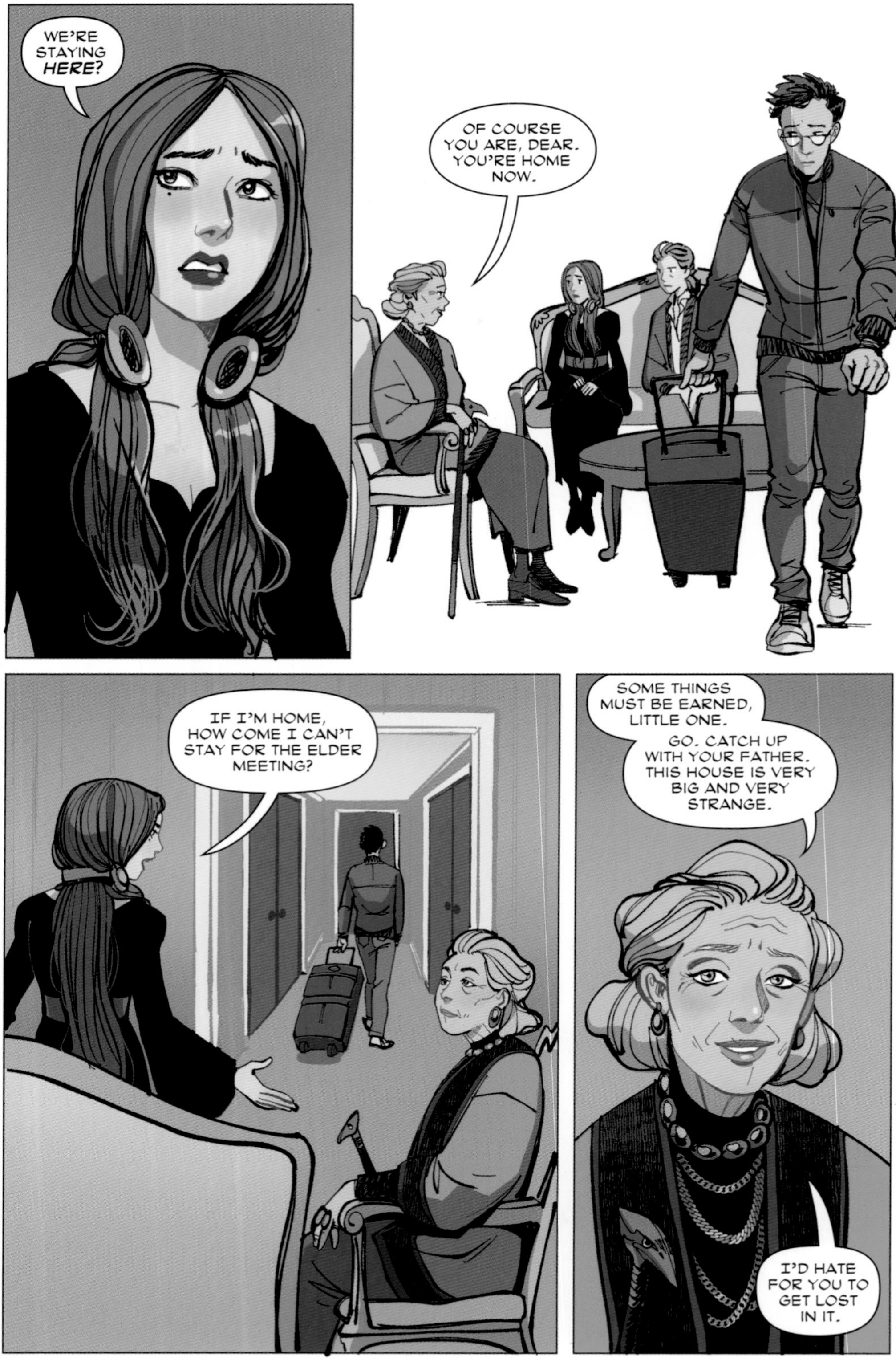
WE'RE STAYING *HERE*?
OF COURSE YOU ARE, DEAR. YOU'RE HOME NOW.
IF I'M HOME, HOW COME I CAN'T STAY FOR THE ELDER MEETING?
SOME THINGS MUST BE EARNED, LITTLE ONE.
GO. CATCH UP WITH YOUR FATHER. THIS HOUSE IS VERY BIG AND VERY STRANGE.
I'D HATE FOR YOU TO GET LOST IN IT.

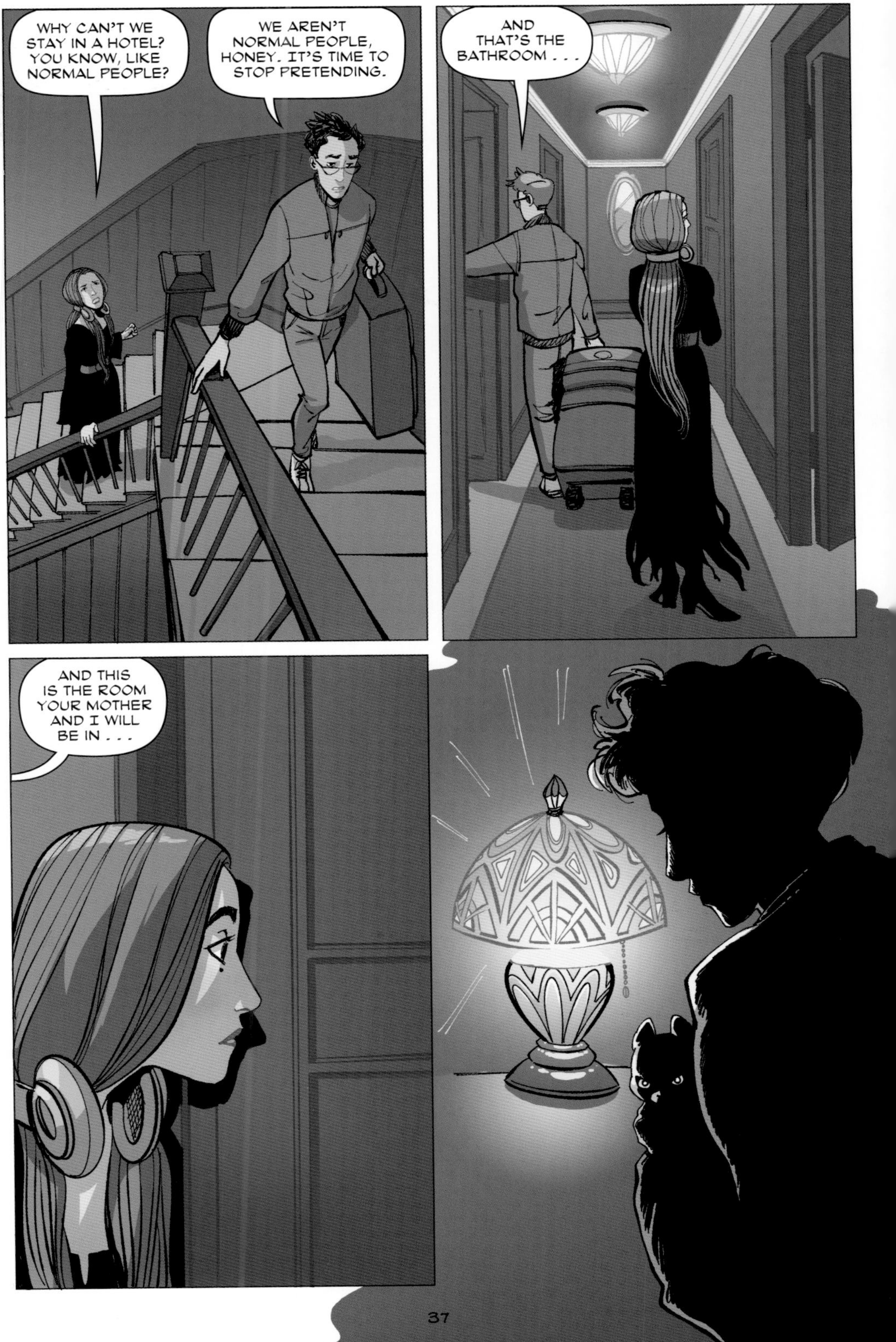
WHY CAN'T WE STAY IN A HOTEL? YOU KNOW, LIKE NORMAL PEOPLE?
WE AREN'T NORMAL PEOPLE, HONEY. IT'S TIME TO STOP PRETENDING.
AND THAT'S THE BATHROOM . . .
AND THIS IS THE ROOM YOUR MOTHER AND I WILL BE IN . . .

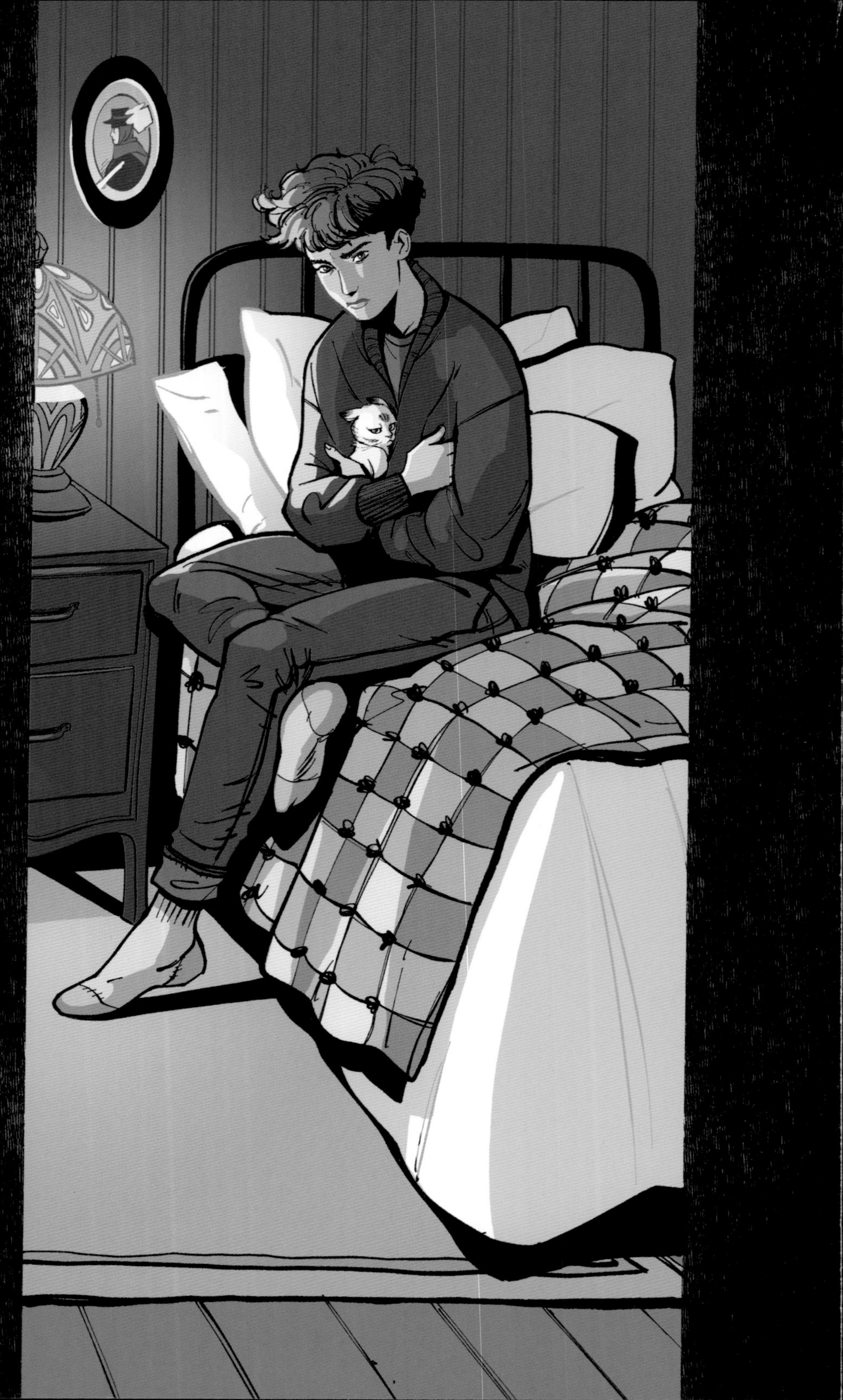

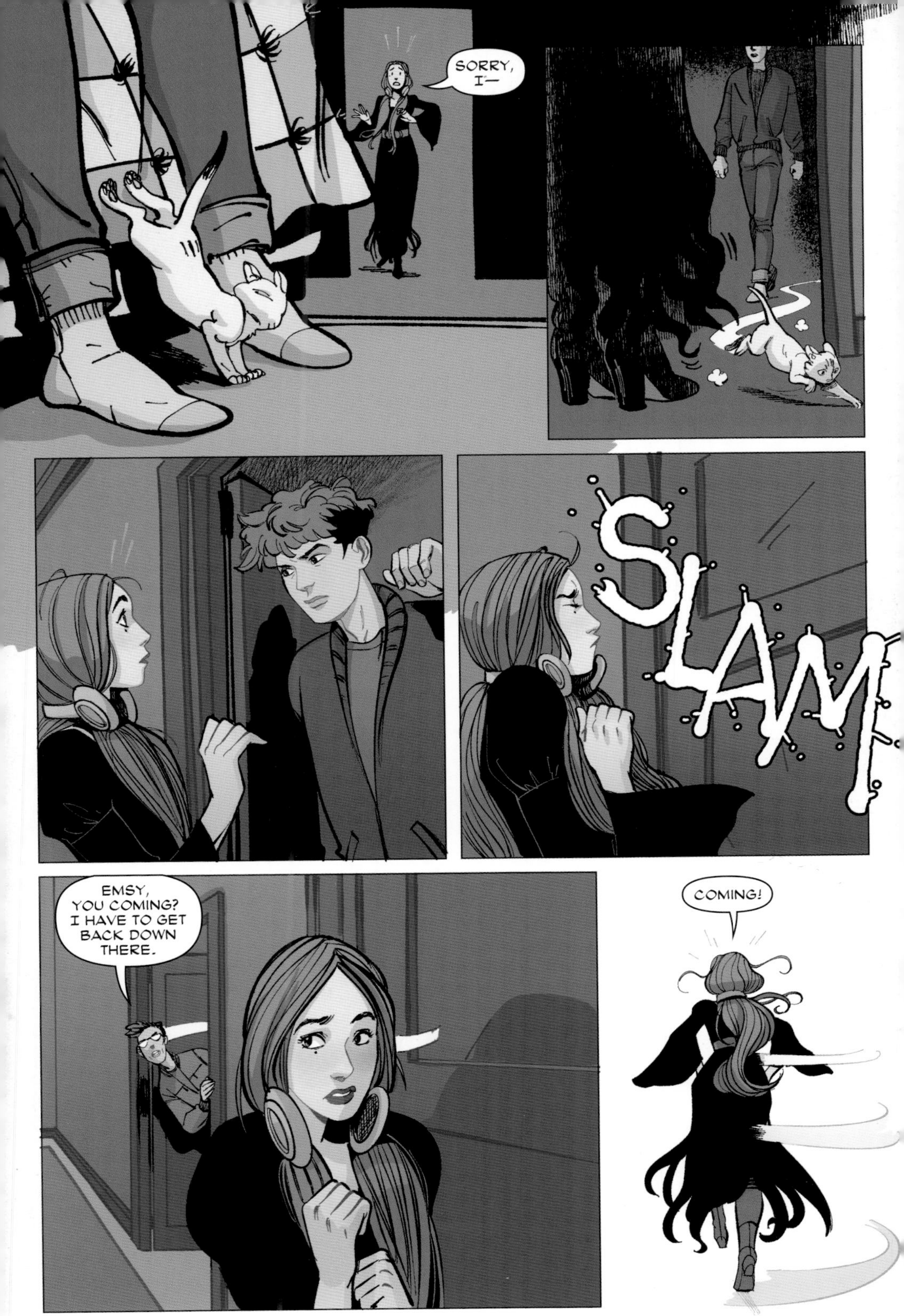
SORRY, I—
SLAM
EMSY, YOU COMING? I HAVE TO GET BACK DOWN THERE.
COMING!

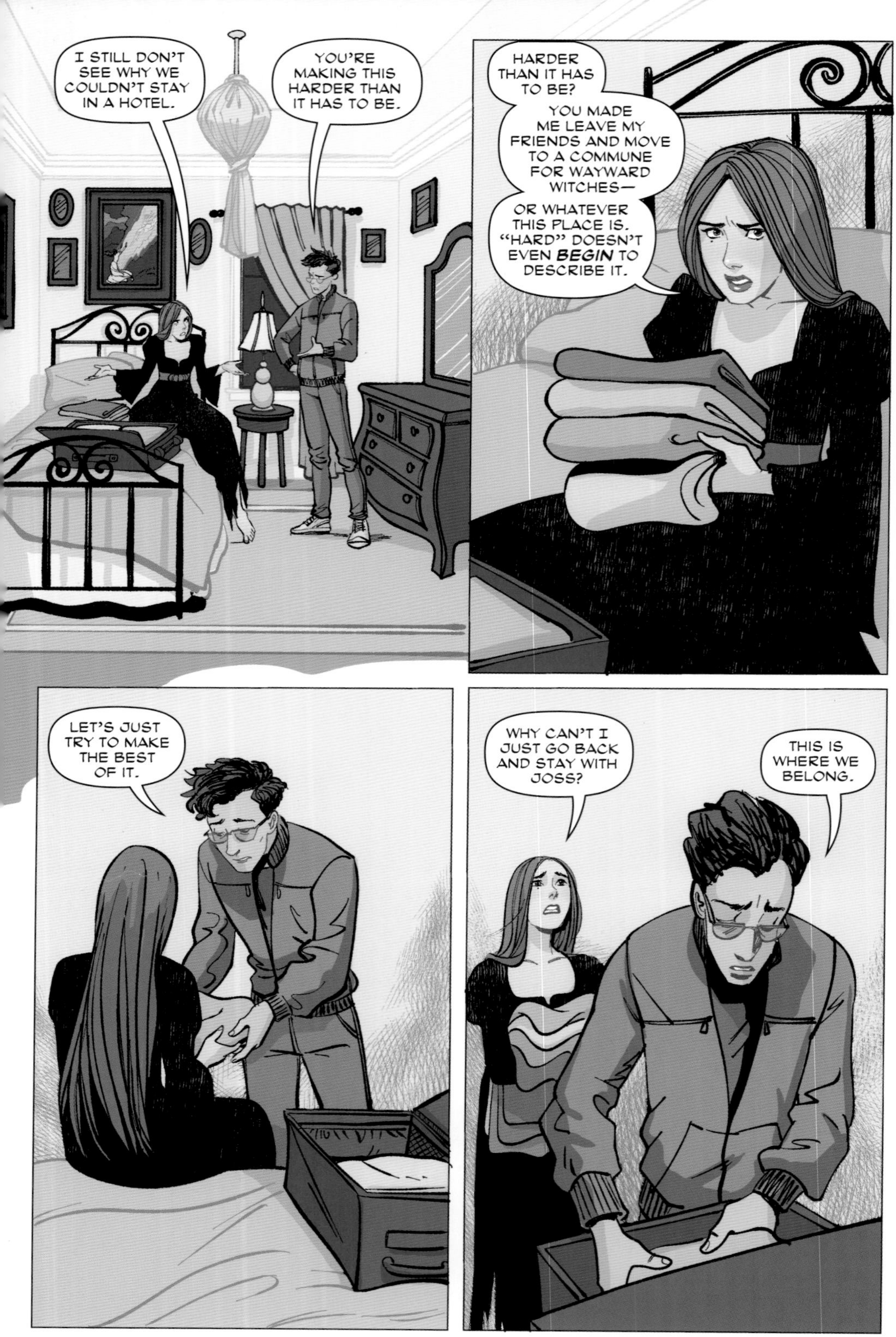
I STILL DON'T SEE WHY WE COULDN'T STAY IN A HOTEL.
YOU'RE MAKING THIS HARDER THAN IT HAS TO BE.
HARDER THAN IT HAS TO BE?
YOU MADE ME LEAVE MY FRIENDS AND MOVE TO A COMMUNE FOR WAYWARD WITCHES—
OR WHATEVER THIS PLACE IS. "HARD" DOESN'T EVEN BEGIN TO DESCRIBE IT.
LET'S JUST TRY TO MAKE THE BEST OF IT.
WHY CAN'T I JUST GO BACK AND STAY WITH JOSS?
THIS IS WHERE WE BELONG.

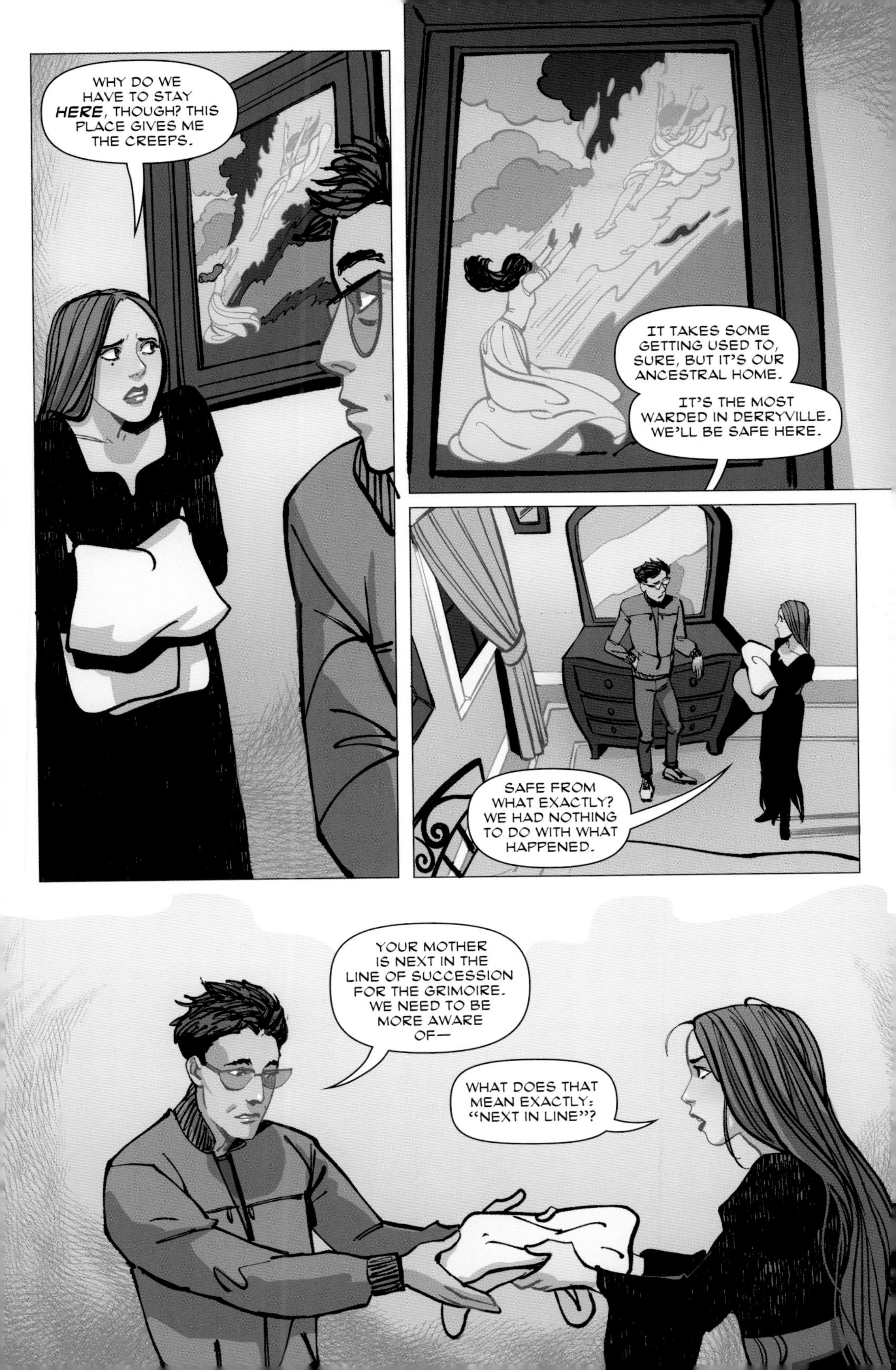
WHY DO WE HAVE TO STAY *HERE*, THOUGH? THIS PLACE GIVES ME THE CREEPS.
IT TAKES SOME GETTING USED TO, SURE, BUT IT'S OUR ANCESTRAL HOME.
IT'S THE MOST WARDED IN DERRYVILLE. WE'LL BE SAFE HERE.
SAFE FROM WHAT EXACTLY? WE HAD NOTHING TO DO WITH WHAT HAPPENED.
YOUR MOTHER IS NEXT IN THE LINE OF SUCCESSION FOR THE GRIMOIRE. WE NEED TO BE MORE AWARE OF—
WHAT DOES THAT MEAN EXACTLY: "NEXT IN LINE"?

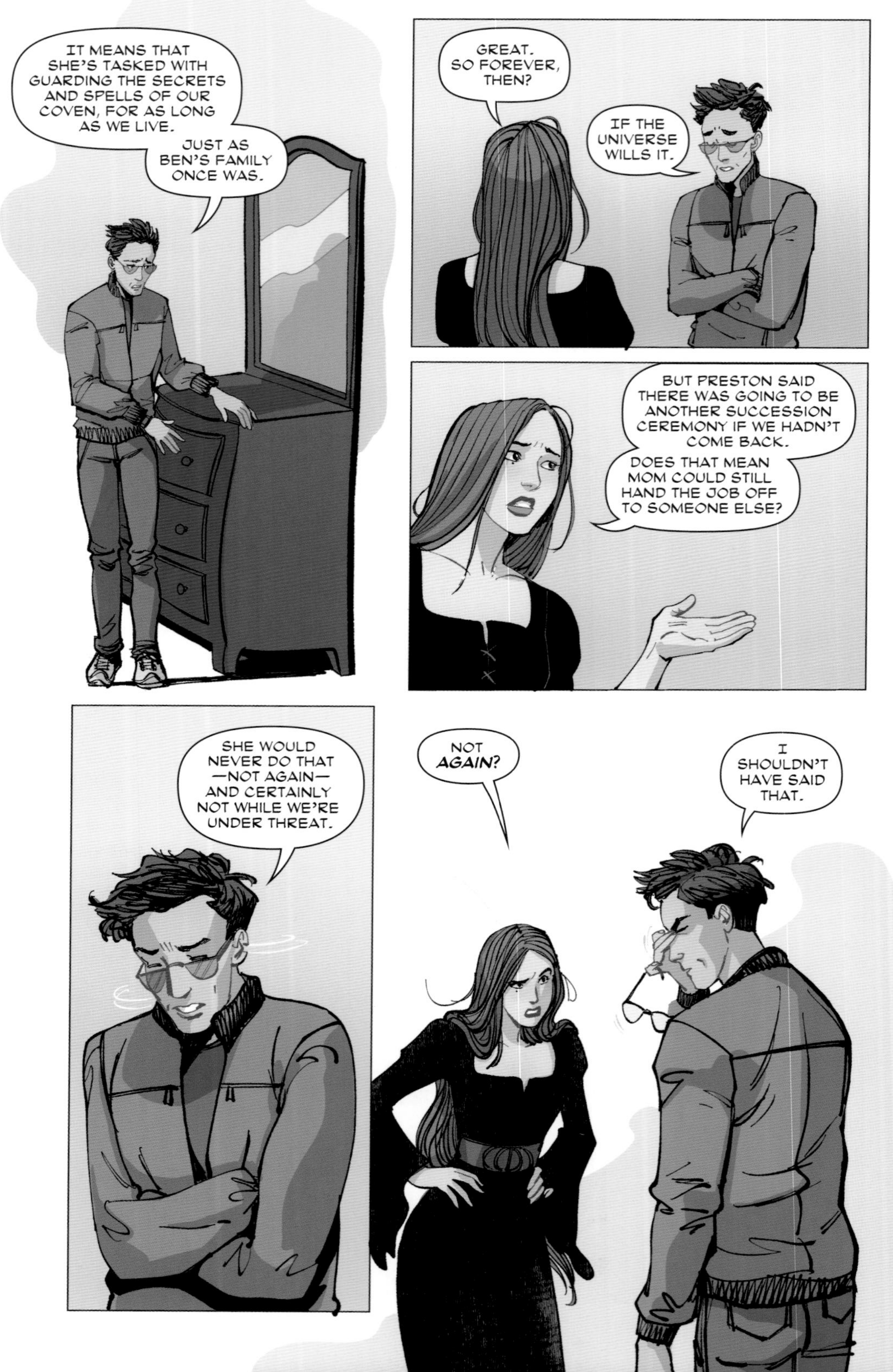
IT MEANS THAT SHE'S TASKED WITH GUARDING THE SECRETS AND SPELLS OF OUR COVEN, FOR AS LONG AS WE LIVE.
JUST AS BEN'S FAMILY ONCE WAS.
GREAT. SO FOREVER, THEN?
IF THE UNIVERSE WILLS IT.
BUT PRESTON SAID THERE WAS GOING TO BE ANOTHER SUCCESSION CEREMONY IF WE HADN'T COME BACK.
DOES THAT MEAN MOM COULD STILL HAND THE JOB OFF TO SOMEONE ELSE?
SHE WOULD NEVER DO THAT —NOT AGAIN— AND CERTAINLY NOT WHILE WE'RE UNDER THREAT.
NOT *AGAIN*?
I SHOULDN'T HAVE SAID THAT.

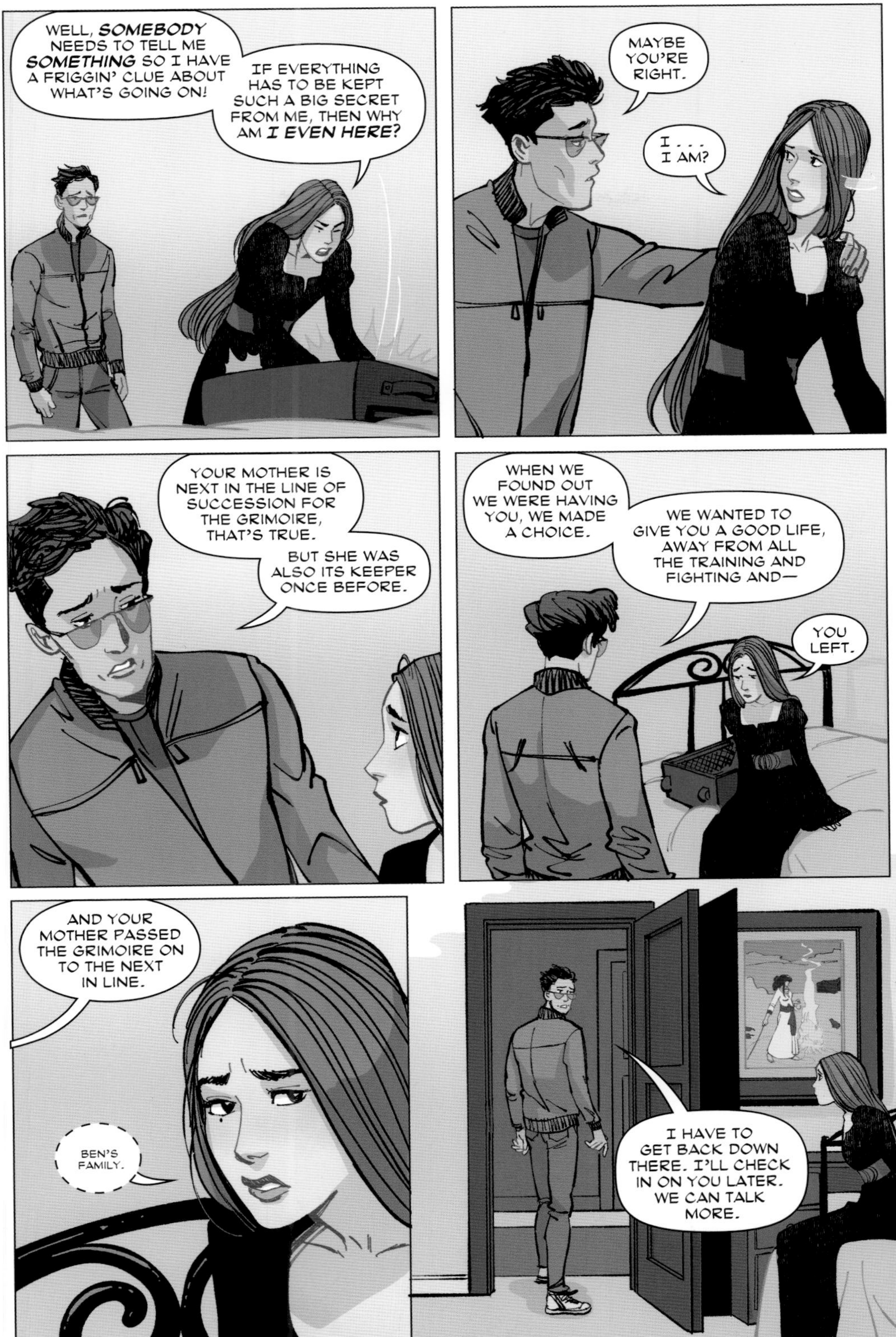
WELL, SOMEBODY NEEDS TO TELL ME SOMETHING SO I HAVE A FRIGGIN' CLUE ABOUT WHAT'S GOING ON!
IF EVERYTHING HAS TO BE KEPT SUCH A BIG SECRET FROM ME, THEN WHY AM I EVEN HERE?
MAYBE YOU'RE RIGHT.
I . . . I AM?
YOUR MOTHER IS NEXT IN THE LINE OF SUCCESSION FOR THE GRIMOIRE, THAT'S TRUE.
BUT SHE WAS ALSO ITS KEEPER ONCE BEFORE.
WHEN WE FOUND OUT WE WERE HAVING YOU, WE MADE A CHOICE.
WE WANTED TO GIVE YOU A GOOD LIFE, AWAY FROM ALL THE TRAINING AND FIGHTING AND—
YOU LEFT.
AND YOUR MOTHER PASSED THE GRIMOIRE ON TO THE NEXT IN LINE.
BEN'S FAMILY.
I HAVE TO GET BACK DOWN THERE. I'LL CHECK IN ON YOU LATER. WE CAN TALK MORE.

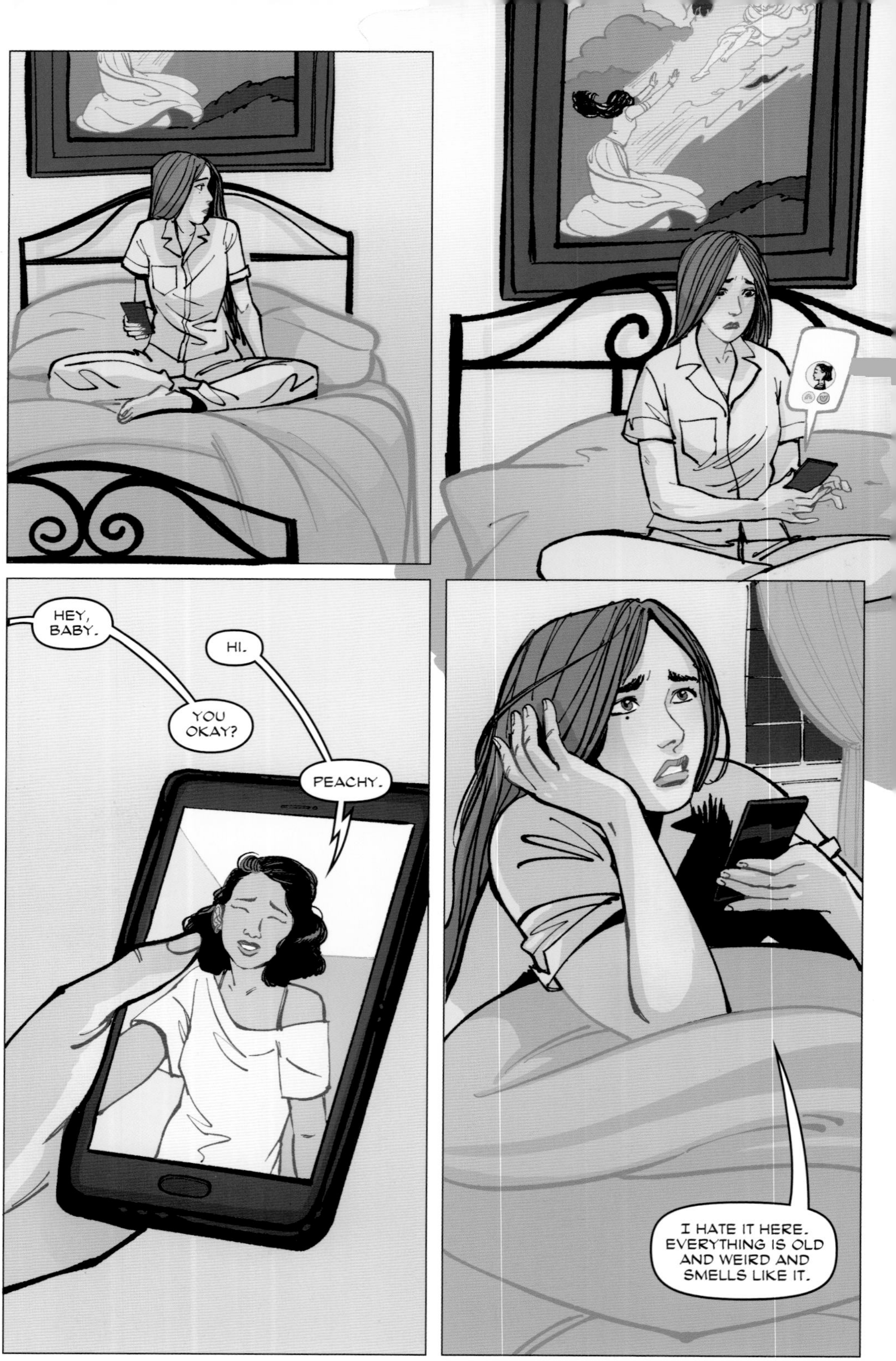
HEY, BABY.
HI.
YOU OKAY?
PEACHY.
I HATE IT HERE. EVERYTHING IS OLD AND WEIRD AND SMELLS LIKE IT.

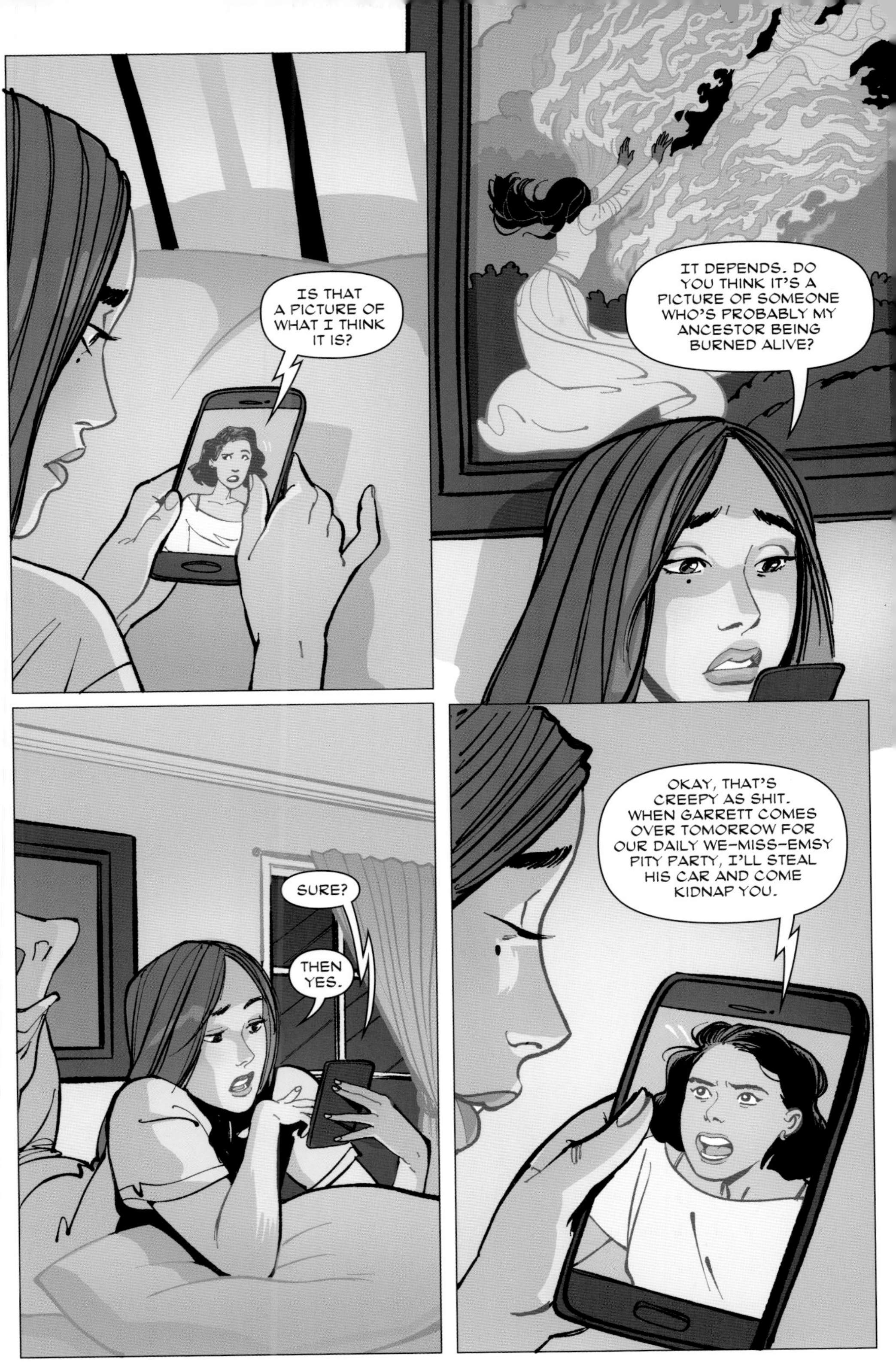
IS THAT A PICTURE OF WHAT I THINK IT IS?
IT DEPENDS. DO YOU THINK IT'S A PICTURE OF SOMEONE WHO'S PROBABLY MY ANCESTOR BEING BURNED ALIVE?
SURE?
THEN YES.
OKAY, THAT'S CREEPY AS SHIT. WHEN GARRETT COMES OVER TOMORROW FOR OUR DAILY WE-MISS-EMSY PITY PARTY, I'LL STEAL HIS CAR AND COME KIDNAP YOU.

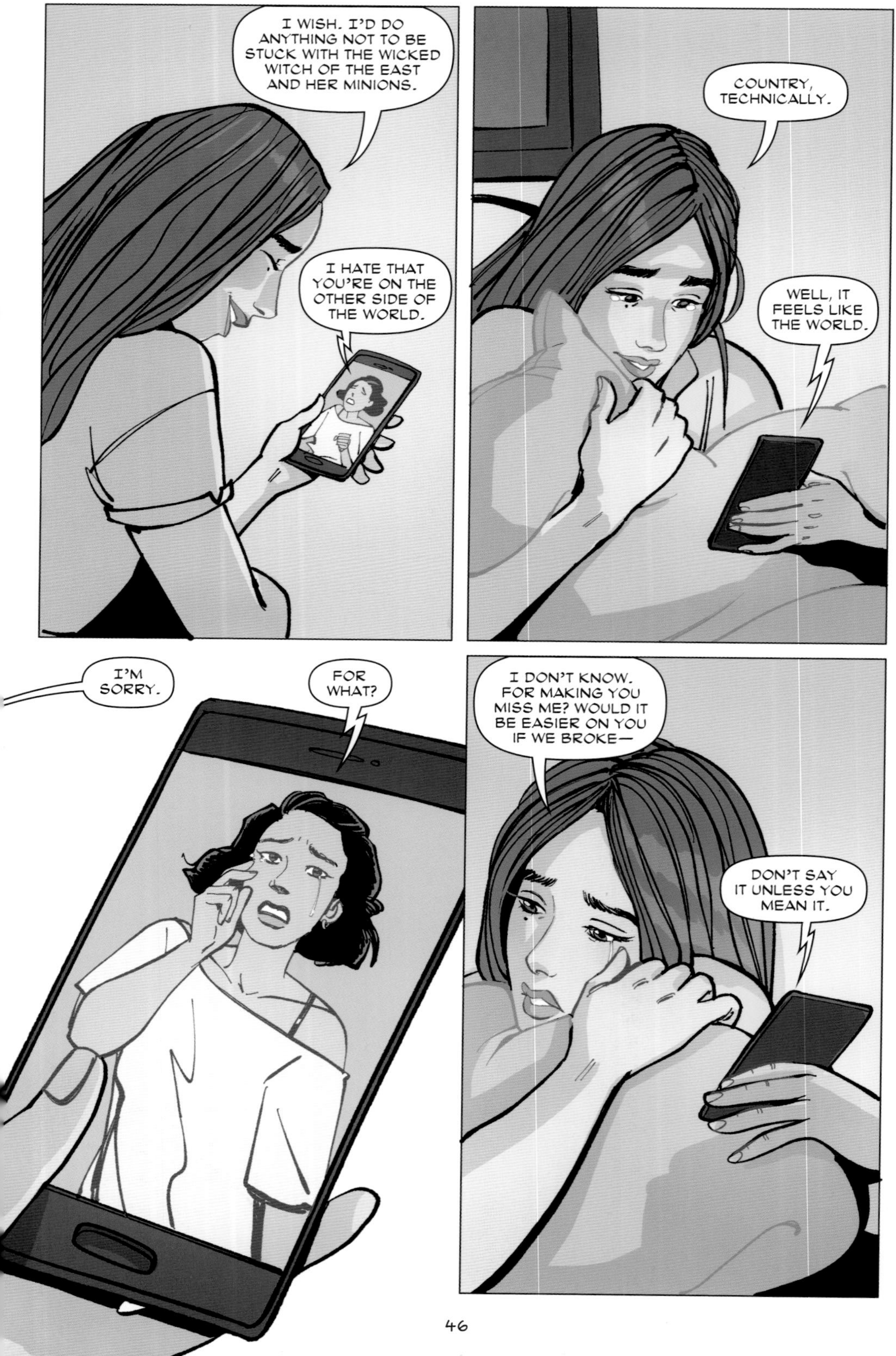
I WISH. I'D DO ANYTHING NOT TO BE STUCK WITH THE WICKED WITCH OF THE EAST AND HER MINIONS.
I HATE THAT YOU'RE ON THE OTHER SIDE OF THE WORLD.
COUNTRY, TECHNICALLY.
WELL, IT FEELS LIKE THE WORLD.
I'M SORRY.
FOR WHAT?
I DON'T KNOW. FOR MAKING YOU MISS ME? WOULD IT BE EASIER ON YOU IF WE BROKE—
DON'T SAY IT UNLESS YOU MEAN IT.

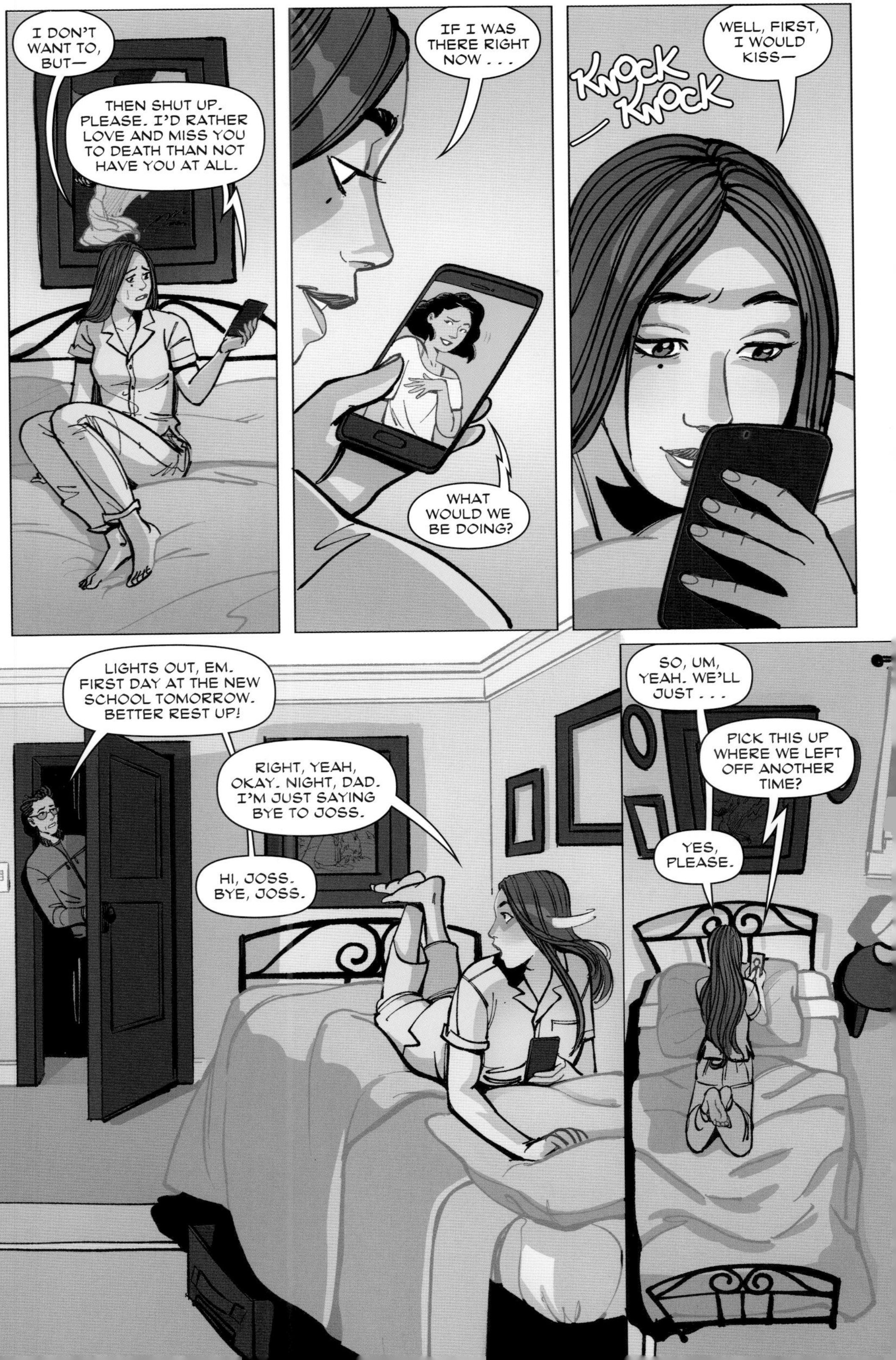

I DON'T WANT TO, BUT—
THEN SHUT UP. PLEASE. I'D RATHER LOVE AND MISS YOU TO DEATH THAN NOT HAVE YOU AT ALL.
IF I WAS THERE RIGHT NOW . . .
WHAT WOULD WE BE DOING?
WELL, FIRST, I WOULD KISS—
KNOCK KNOCK
LIGHTS OUT, EM. FIRST DAY AT THE NEW SCHOOL TOMORROW. BETTER REST UP!
RIGHT, YEAH, OKAY. NIGHT, DAD. I'M JUST SAYING BYE TO JOSS.
HI, JOSS. BYE, JOSS.
SO, UM, YEAH. WE'LL JUST . . .
PICK THIS UP WHERE WE LEFT OFF ANOTHER TIME?
YES, PLEASE.

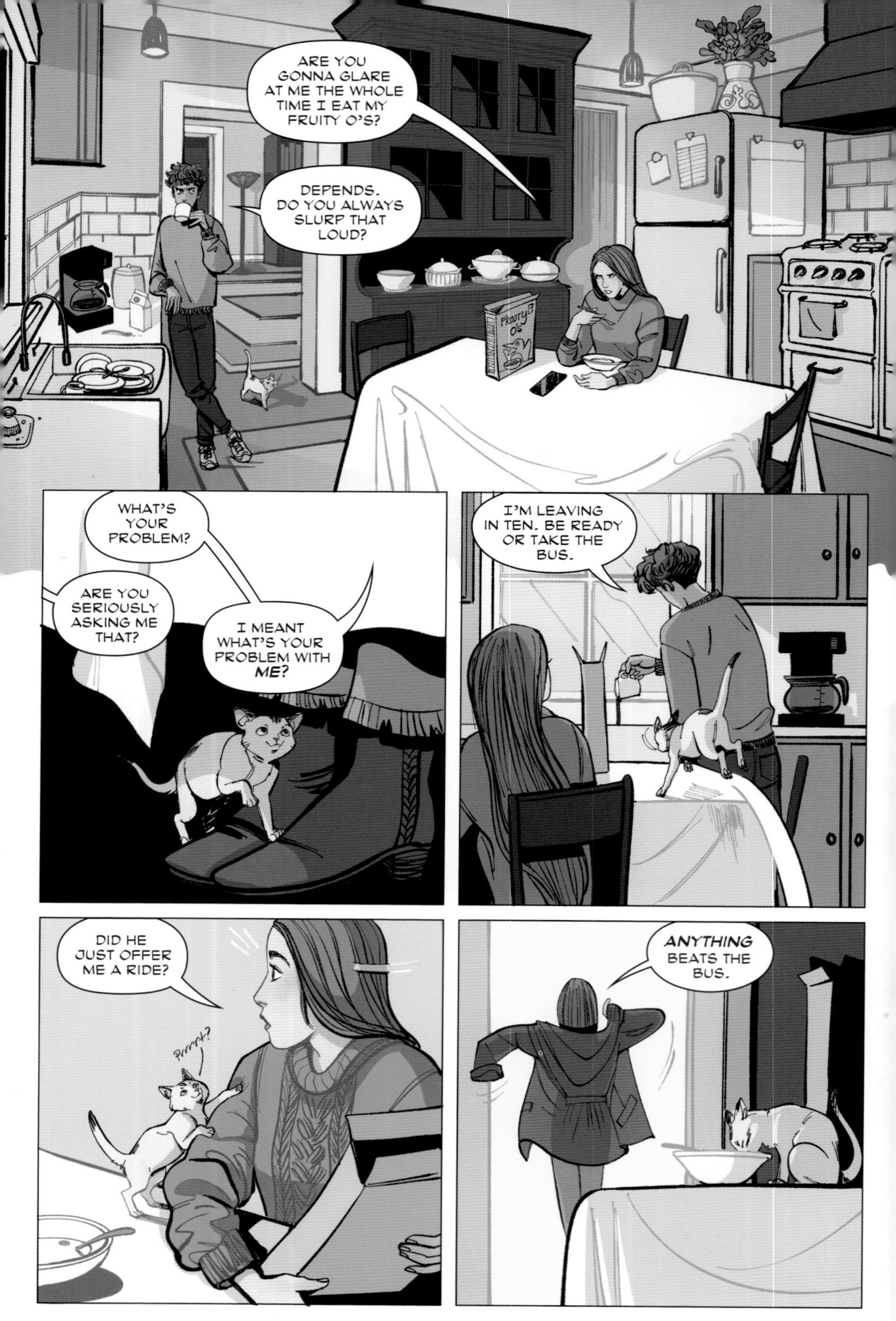
ARE YOU GONNA GLARE AT ME THE WHOLE TIME I EAT MY FRUITY O'S?
DEPENDS. DO YOU ALWAYS SLURP THAT LOUD?
Fruity O's
WHAT'S YOUR PROBLEM?
ARE YOU SERIOUSLY ASKING ME THAT?
I MEANT WHAT'S YOUR PROBLEM WITH *ME?*
I'M LEAVING IN TEN. BE READY OR TAKE THE BUS.
DID HE JUST OFFER ME A RIDE?
Prrrrt?
ANYTHING BEATS THE BUS.

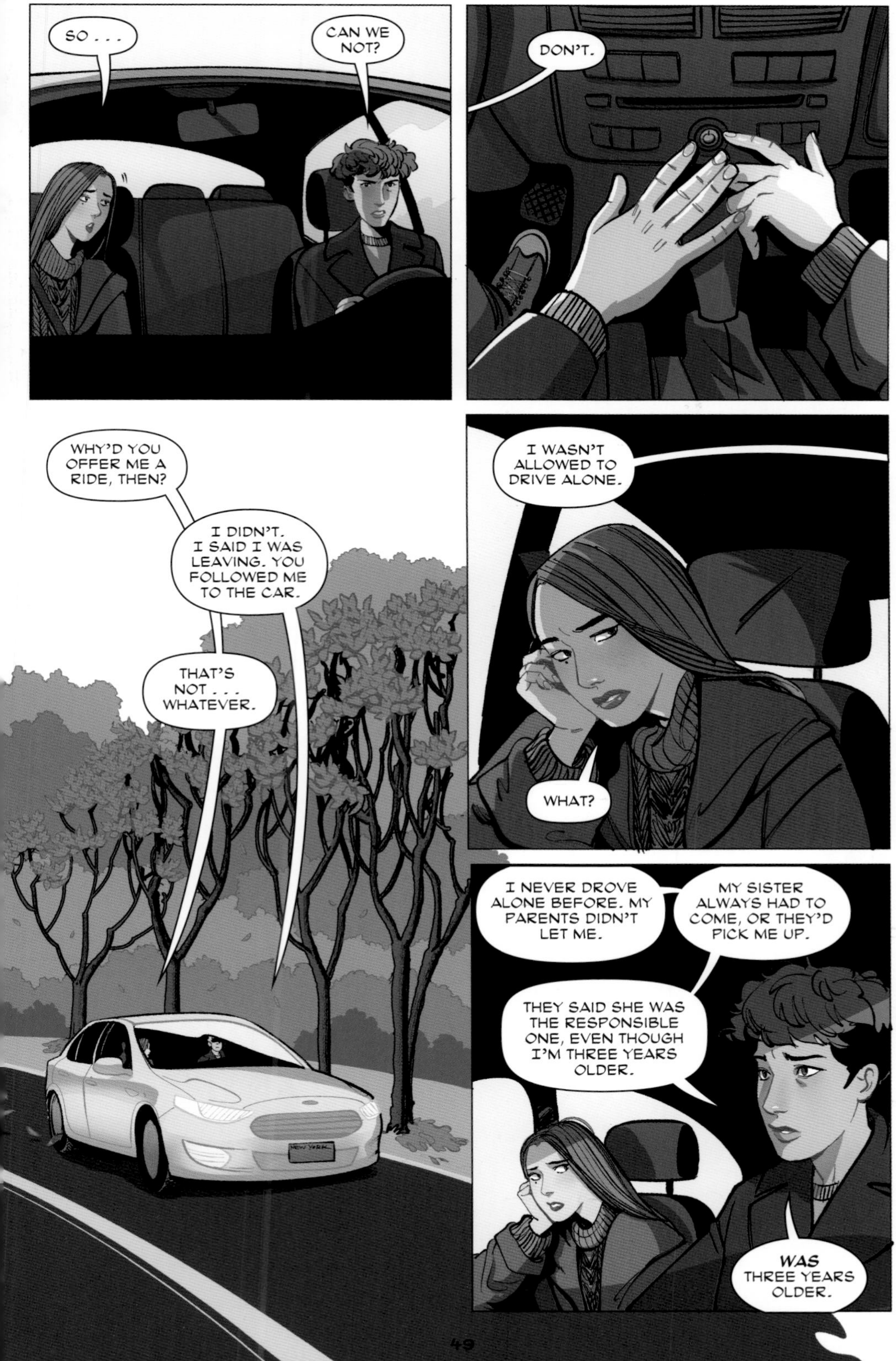
SO . . .
CAN WE NOT?
DON'T.
WHY'D YOU OFFER ME A RIDE, THEN?
I DIDN'T. I SAID I WAS LEAVING. YOU FOLLOWED ME TO THE CAR.
THAT'S NOT . . . WHATEVER.
NEW YORK
I WASN'T ALLOWED TO DRIVE ALONE.
WHAT?
I NEVER DROVE ALONE BEFORE. MY PARENTS DIDN'T LET ME.
MY SISTER ALWAYS HAD TO COME, OR THEY'D PICK ME UP.
THEY SAID SHE WAS THE RESPONSIBLE ONE, EVEN THOUGH I'M THREE YEARS OLDER.
WAS THREE YEARS OLDER.

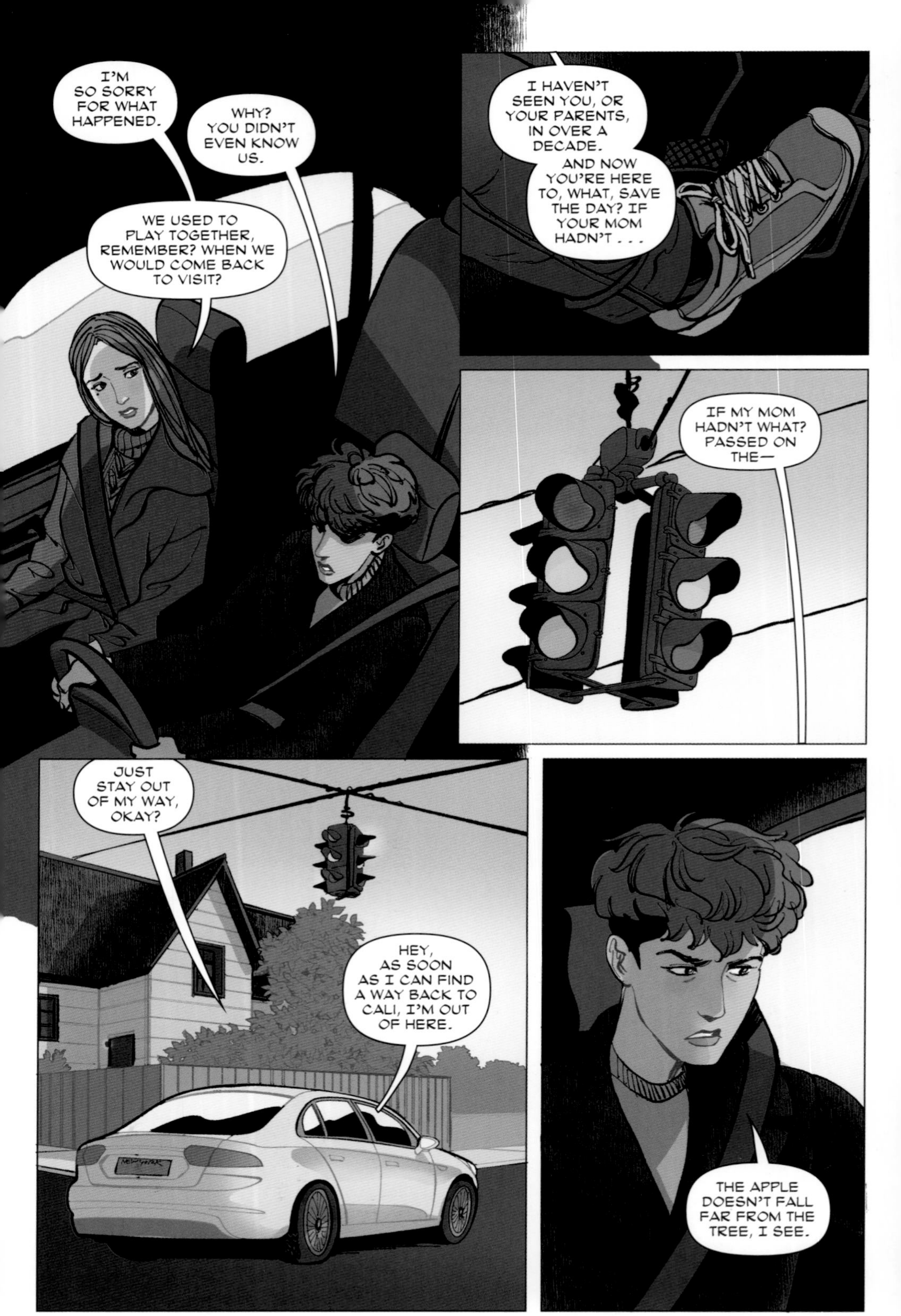
I'M SO SORRY FOR WHAT HAPPENED.
WHY? YOU DIDN'T EVEN KNOW US.
WE USED TO PLAY TOGETHER, REMEMBER? WHEN WE WOULD COME BACK TO VISIT?
I HAVEN'T SEEN YOU, OR YOUR PARENTS, IN OVER A DECADE.
AND NOW YOU'RE HERE TO, WHAT, SAVE THE DAY? IF YOUR MOM HADN'T . . .
IF MY MOM HADN'T WHAT? PASSED ON THE—
JUST STAY OUT OF MY WAY, OKAY?
HEY, AS SOON AS I CAN FIND A WAY BACK TO CALI, I'M OUT OF HERE.
THE APPLE DOESN'T FALL FAR FROM THE TREE, I SEE.

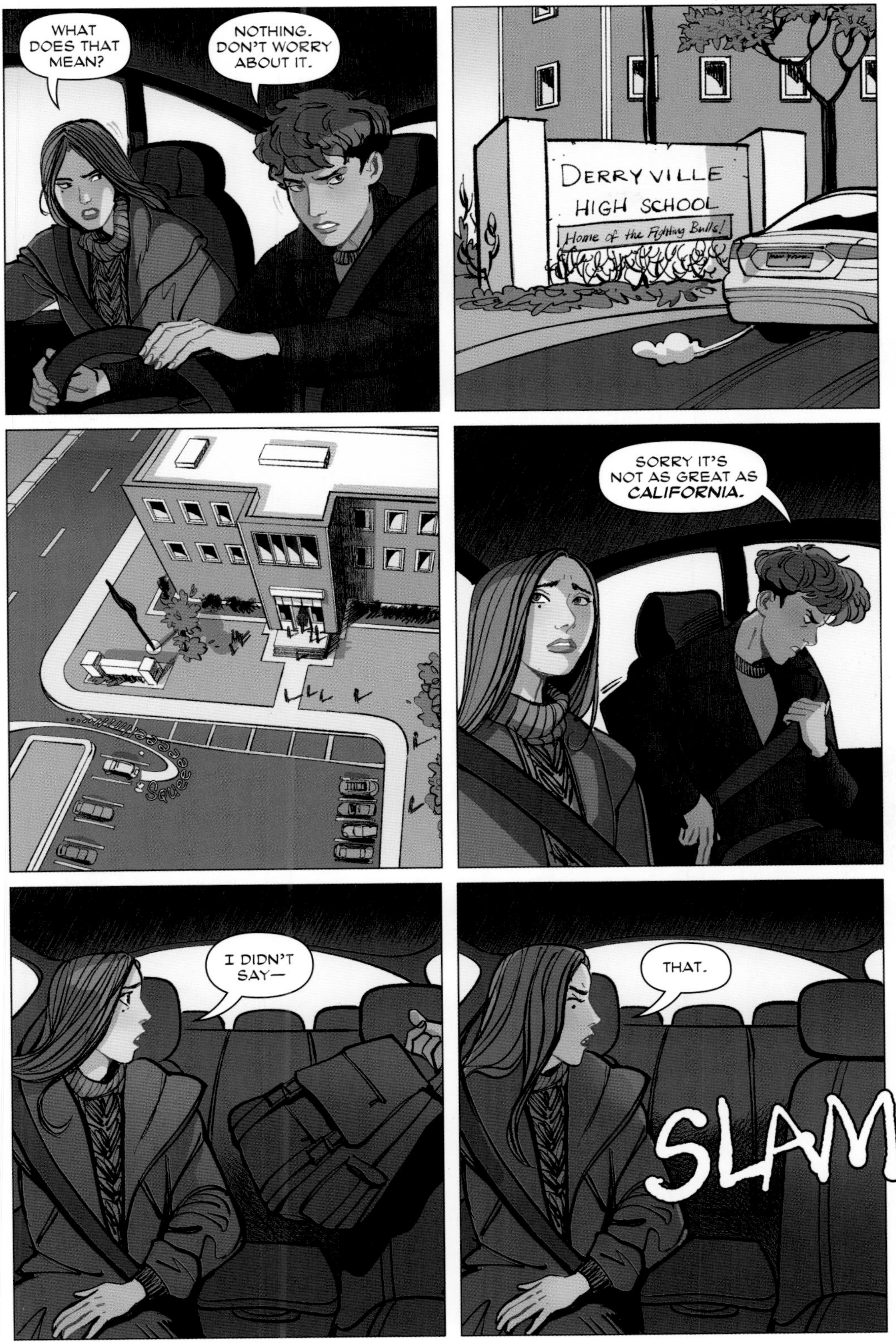
WHAT DOES THAT MEAN?
NOTHING. DON'T WORRY ABOUT IT.
DERRYVILLE HIGH SCHOOL
Home of the Fighting Bulls!
SORRY IT'S NOT AS GREAT AS **CALIFORNIA.**
I DIDN'T SAY—
THAT.
SLAM

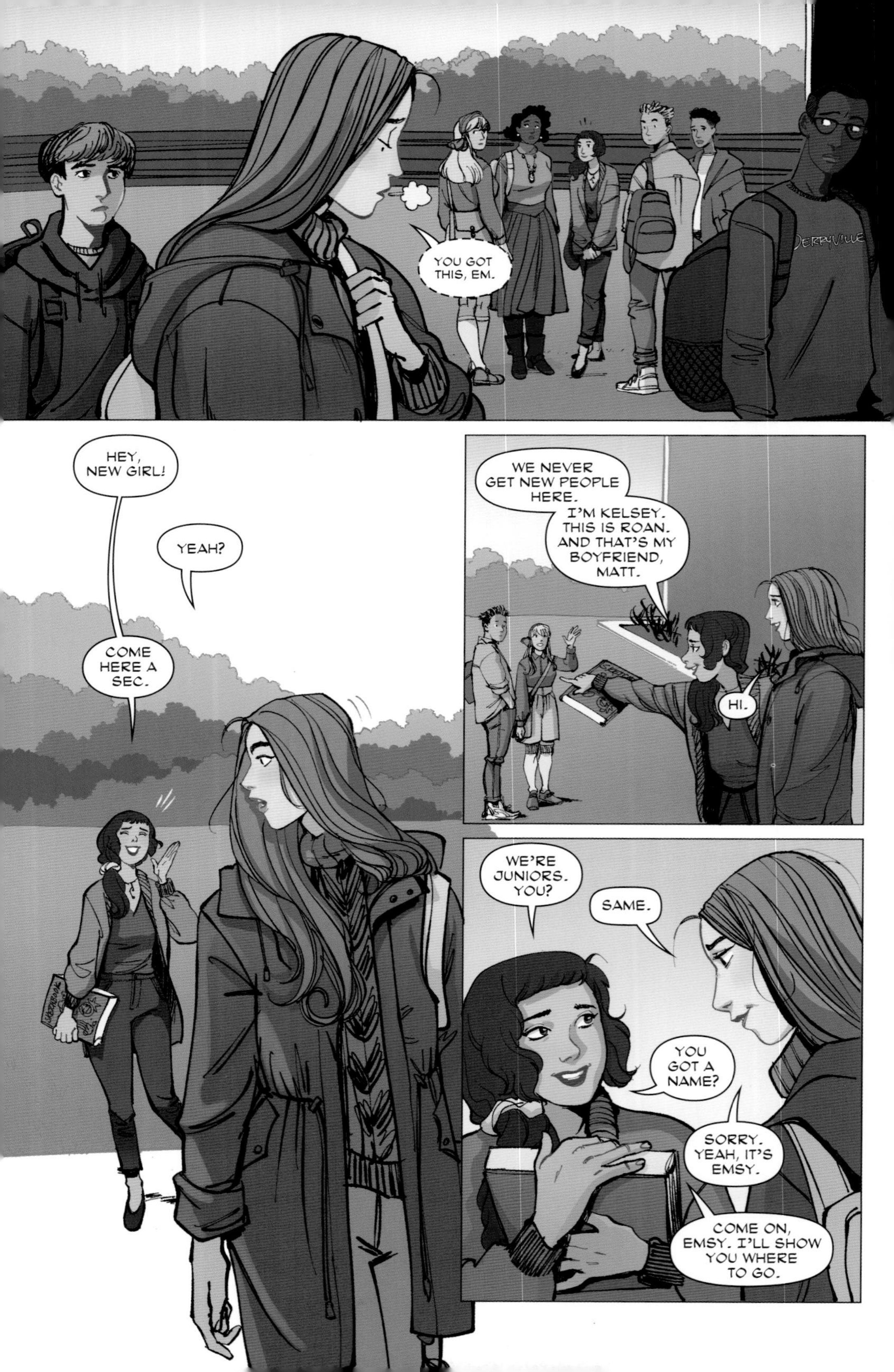
DERRYVILLE
YOU GOT THIS, EM.
HEY, NEW GIRL!
YEAH?
COME HERE A SEC.
WE NEVER GET NEW PEOPLE HERE.
I'M KELSEY. THIS IS ROAN. AND THAT'S MY BOYFRIEND, MATT.
HI.
WE'RE JUNIORS. YOU?
SAME.
YOU GOT A NAME?
SORRY. YEAH, IT'S EMSY.
COME ON, EMSY. I'LL SHOW YOU WHERE TO GO.

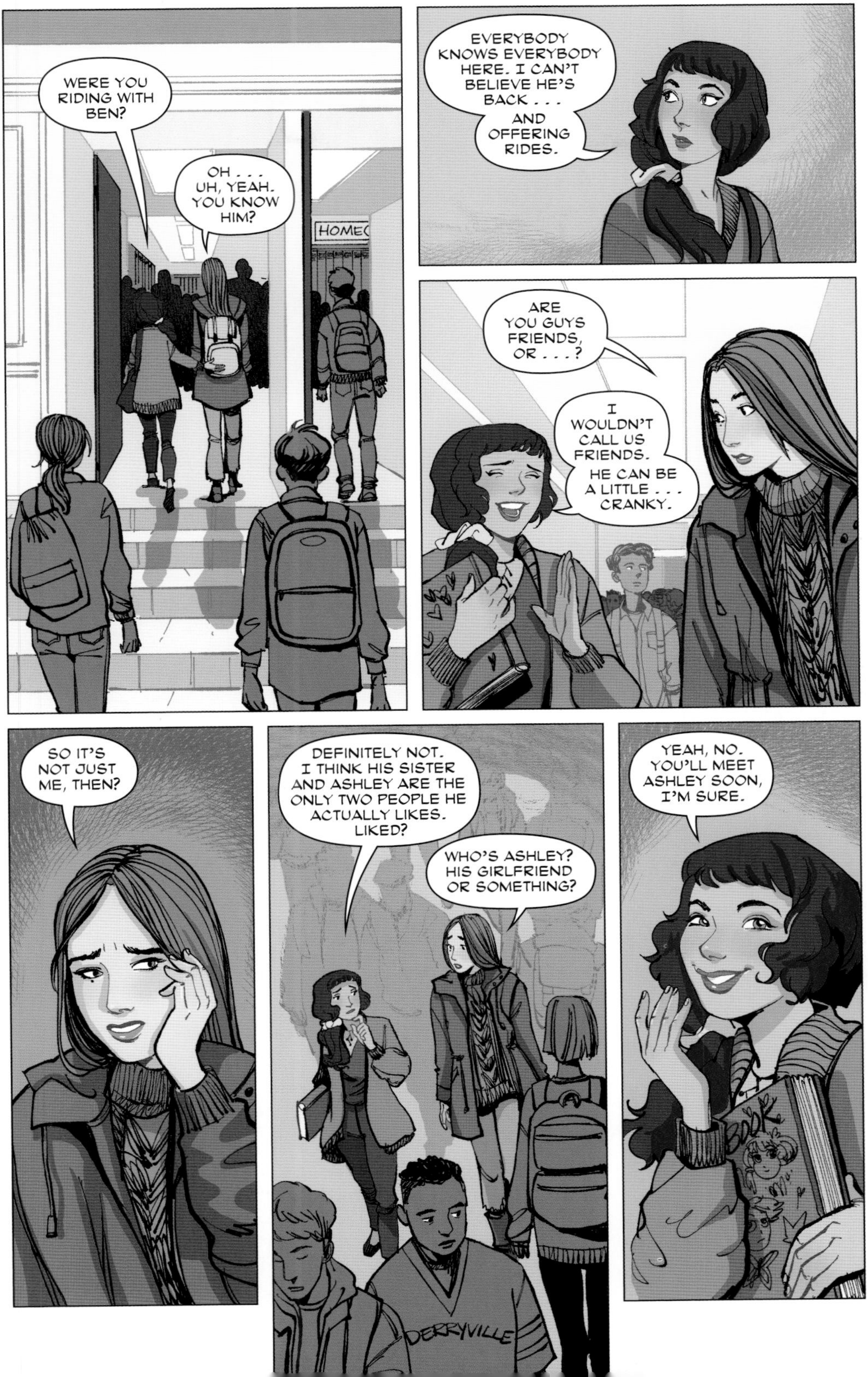
WERE YOU RIDING WITH BEN?
OH . . . UH, YEAH. YOU KNOW HIM?
HOMEC
EVERYBODY KNOWS EVERYBODY HERE. I CAN'T BELIEVE HE'S BACK . . .
AND OFFERING RIDES.
ARE YOU GUYS FRIENDS, OR . . . ?
I WOULDN'T CALL US FRIENDS.
HE CAN BE A LITTLE . . . CRANKY.
SO IT'S NOT JUST ME, THEN?
DEFINITELY NOT. I THINK HIS SISTER AND ASHLEY ARE THE ONLY TWO PEOPLE HE ACTUALLY LIKES. LIKED?
WHO'S ASHLEY? HIS GIRLFRIEND OR SOMETHING?
DERRYVILLE
YEAH, NO. YOU'LL MEET ASHLEY SOON, I'M SURE.
BOOK

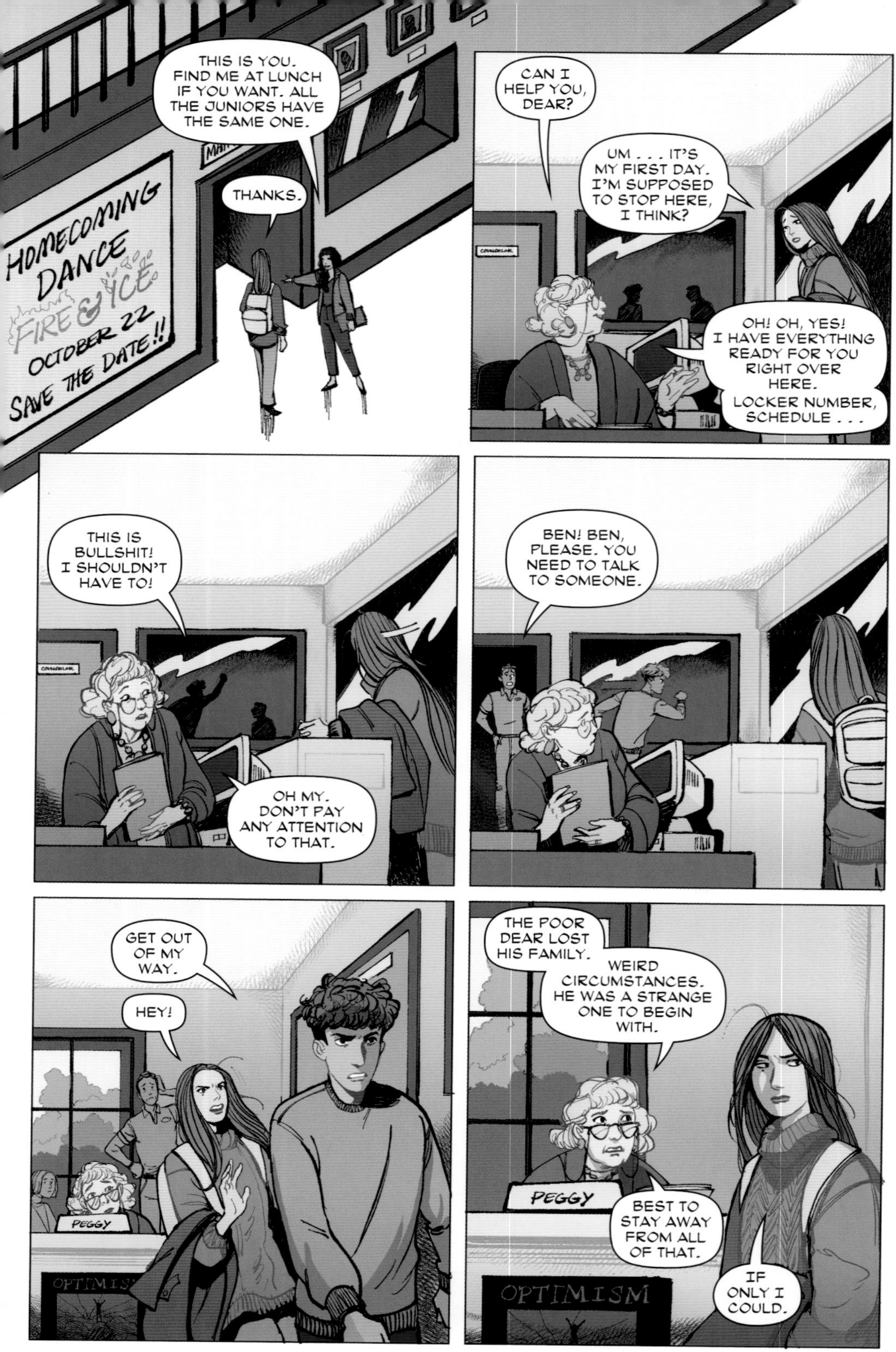
THIS IS YOU. FIND ME AT LUNCH IF YOU WANT. ALL THE JUNIORS HAVE THE SAME ONE.
THANKS.
HOMECOMING DANCE FIRE & ICE OCTOBER 22 SAVE THE DATE!!
CAN I HELP YOU, DEAR?
UM . . . IT'S MY FIRST DAY. I'M SUPPOSED TO STOP HERE, I THINK?
OH! OH, YES! I HAVE EVERYTHING READY FOR YOU RIGHT OVER HERE.
LOCKER NUMBER, SCHEDULE . . .
THIS IS BULLSHIT! I SHOULDN'T HAVE TO!
OH MY. DON'T PAY ANY ATTENTION TO THAT.
BEN! BEN, PLEASE. YOU NEED TO TALK TO SOMEONE.
GET OUT OF MY WAY.
HEY!
PEGGY
OPTIMISM
THE POOR DEAR LOST HIS FAMILY.
WEIRD CIRCUMSTANCES. HE WAS A STRANGE ONE TO BEGIN WITH.
PEGGY
BEST TO STAY AWAY FROM ALL OF THAT.
IF ONLY I COULD.
OPTIMISM

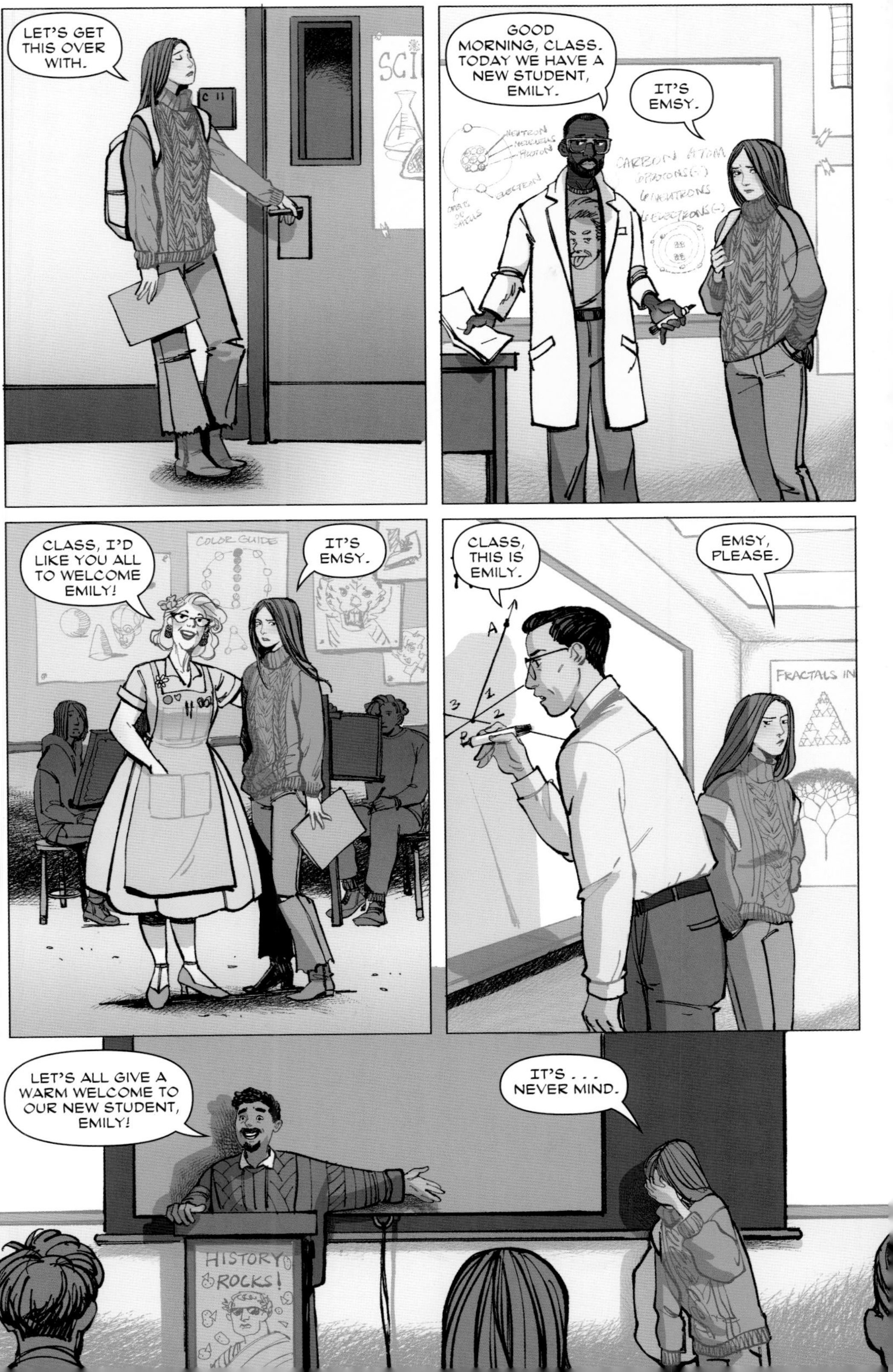
LET'S GET THIS OVER WITH.
SCI
GOOD MORNING, CLASS. TODAY WE HAVE A NEW STUDENT, EMILY.
IT'S EMSY.
CARBON ATOM
CLASS, I'D LIKE YOU ALL TO WELCOME EMILY!
IT'S EMSY.
COLOR GUIDE
CLASS, THIS IS EMILY.
EMSY, PLEASE.
FRACTALS IN
LET'S ALL GIVE A WARM WELCOME TO OUR NEW STUDENT, EMILY!
IT'S . . . NEVER MIND.
HISTORY ROCKS!

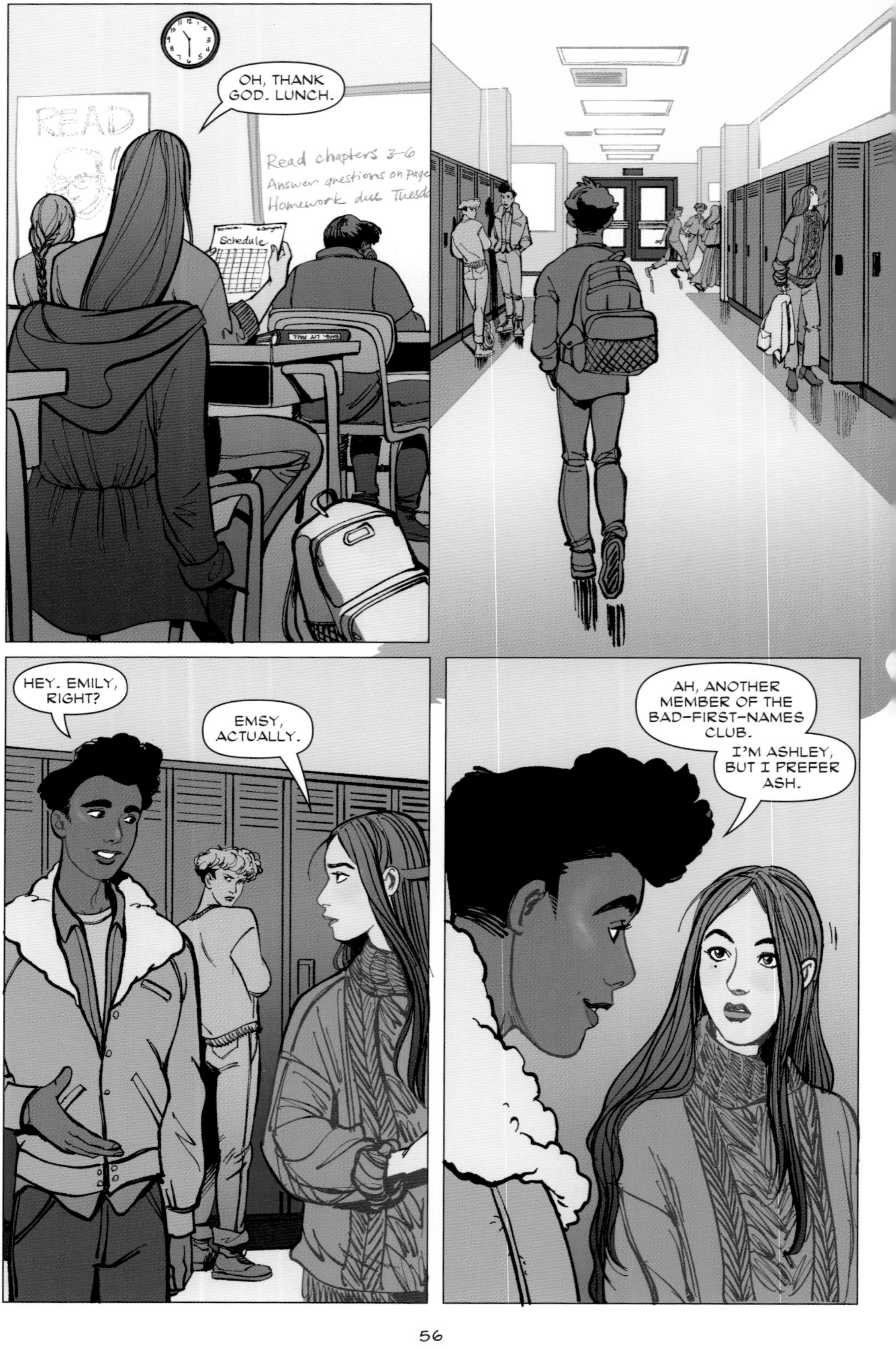
READ
Read chapters 3-6
Schedule
OH, THANK GOD. LUNCH.
HEY. EMILY, RIGHT?
EMSY, ACTUALLY.
AH, ANOTHER MEMBER OF THE BAD-FIRST-NAMES CLUB.
I'M ASHLEY, BUT I PREFER ASH.

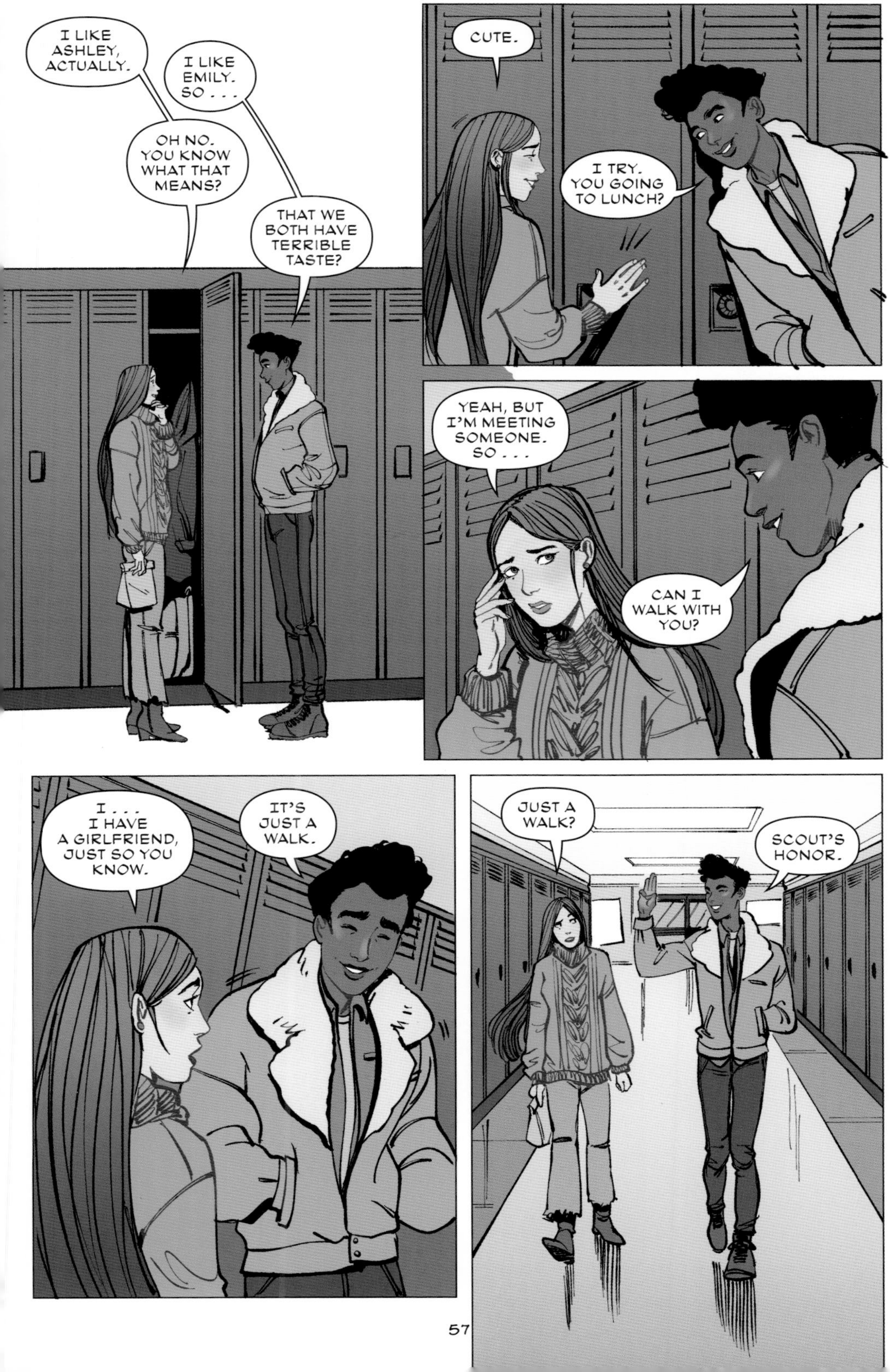
I LIKE ASHLEY, ACTUALLY.
I LIKE EMILY. SO . . .
OH NO. YOU KNOW WHAT THAT MEANS?
THAT WE BOTH HAVE TERRIBLE TASTE?
CUTE.
I TRY. YOU GOING TO LUNCH?
YEAH, BUT I'M MEETING SOMEONE. SO . . .
CAN I WALK WITH YOU?
I . . . I HAVE A GIRLFRIEND, JUST SO YOU KNOW.
IT'S JUST A WALK.
JUST A WALK?
SCOUT'S HONOR.

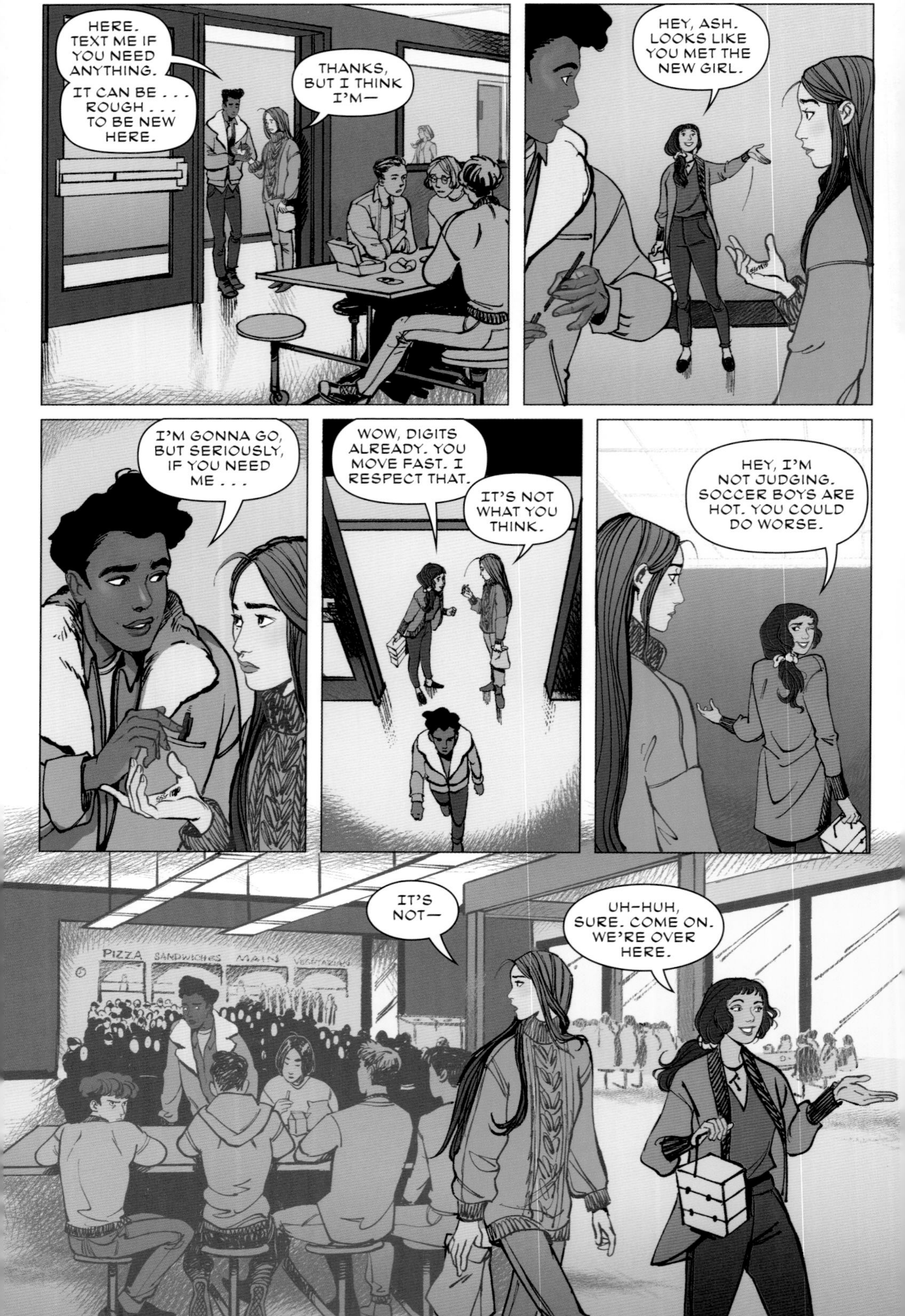
HERE. TEXT ME IF YOU NEED ANYTHING.
IT CAN BE . . . ROUGH . . . TO BE NEW HERE.
THANKS, BUT I THINK I'M—
HEY, ASH. LOOKS LIKE YOU MET THE NEW GIRL.
I'M GONNA GO, BUT SERIOUSLY, IF YOU NEED ME . . .
WOW, DIGITS ALREADY. YOU MOVE FAST. I RESPECT THAT.
IT'S NOT WHAT YOU THINK.
HEY, I'M NOT JUDGING. SOCCER BOYS ARE HOT. YOU COULD DO WORSE.
IT'S NOT—
UH-HUH, SURE. COME ON. WE'RE OVER HERE.
PIZZA
SANDWICHES
MAIN
VEGETARIAN

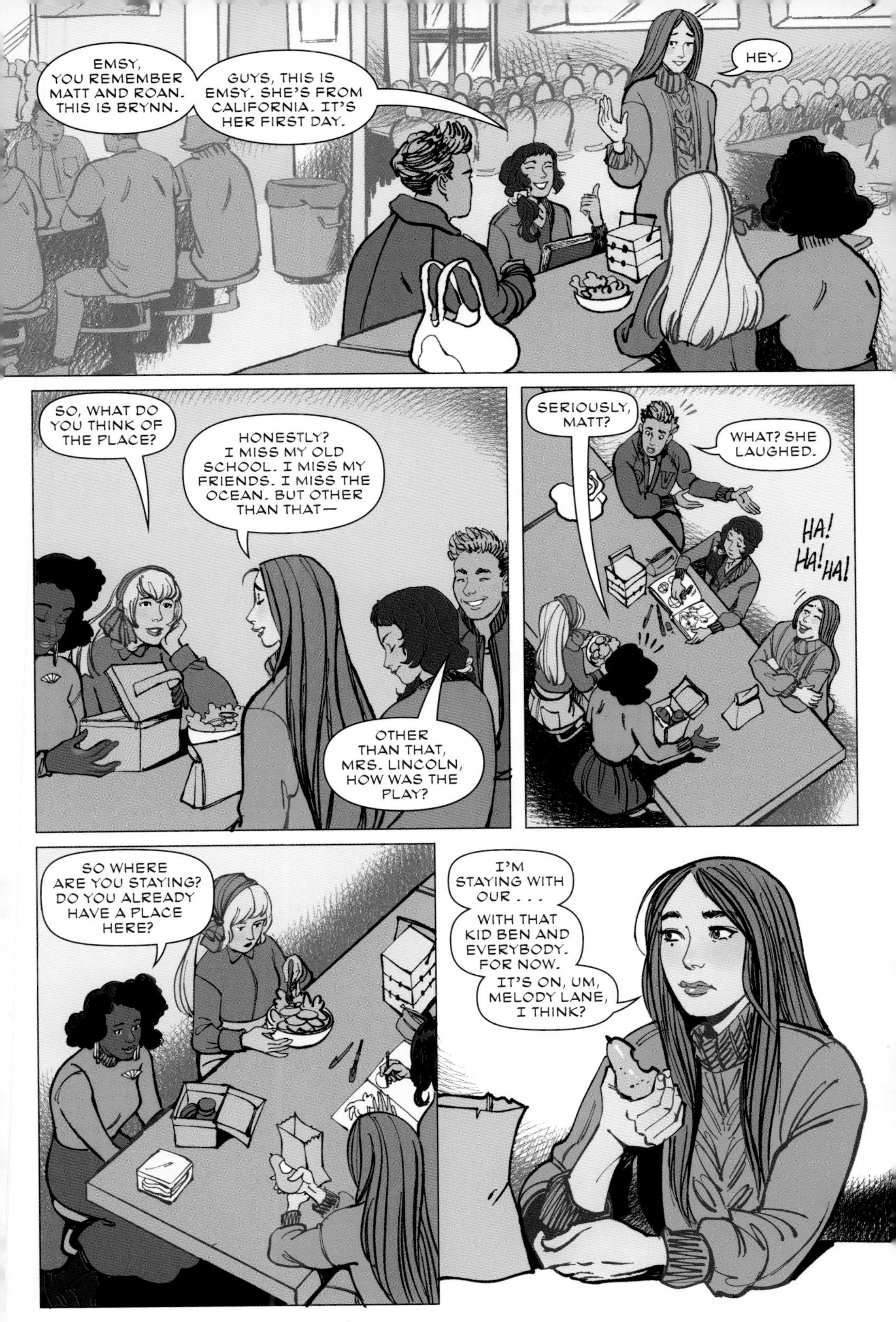
EMSY, YOU REMEMBER MATT AND ROAN. THIS IS BRYNN.
GUYS, THIS IS EMSY. SHE'S FROM CALIFORNIA. IT'S HER FIRST DAY.
HEY.
SO, WHAT DO YOU THINK OF THE PLACE?
HONESTLY? I MISS MY OLD SCHOOL. I MISS MY FRIENDS. I MISS THE OCEAN. BUT OTHER THAN THAT—
OTHER THAN THAT, MRS. LINCOLN, HOW WAS THE PLAY?
SERIOUSLY, MATT?
WHAT? SHE LAUGHED.
HA! HA! HA!
SO WHERE ARE YOU STAYING? DO YOU ALREADY HAVE A PLACE HERE?
I'M STAYING WITH OUR . . .
WITH THAT KID BEN AND EVERYBODY. FOR NOW.
IT'S ON, UM, MELODY LANE, I THINK?

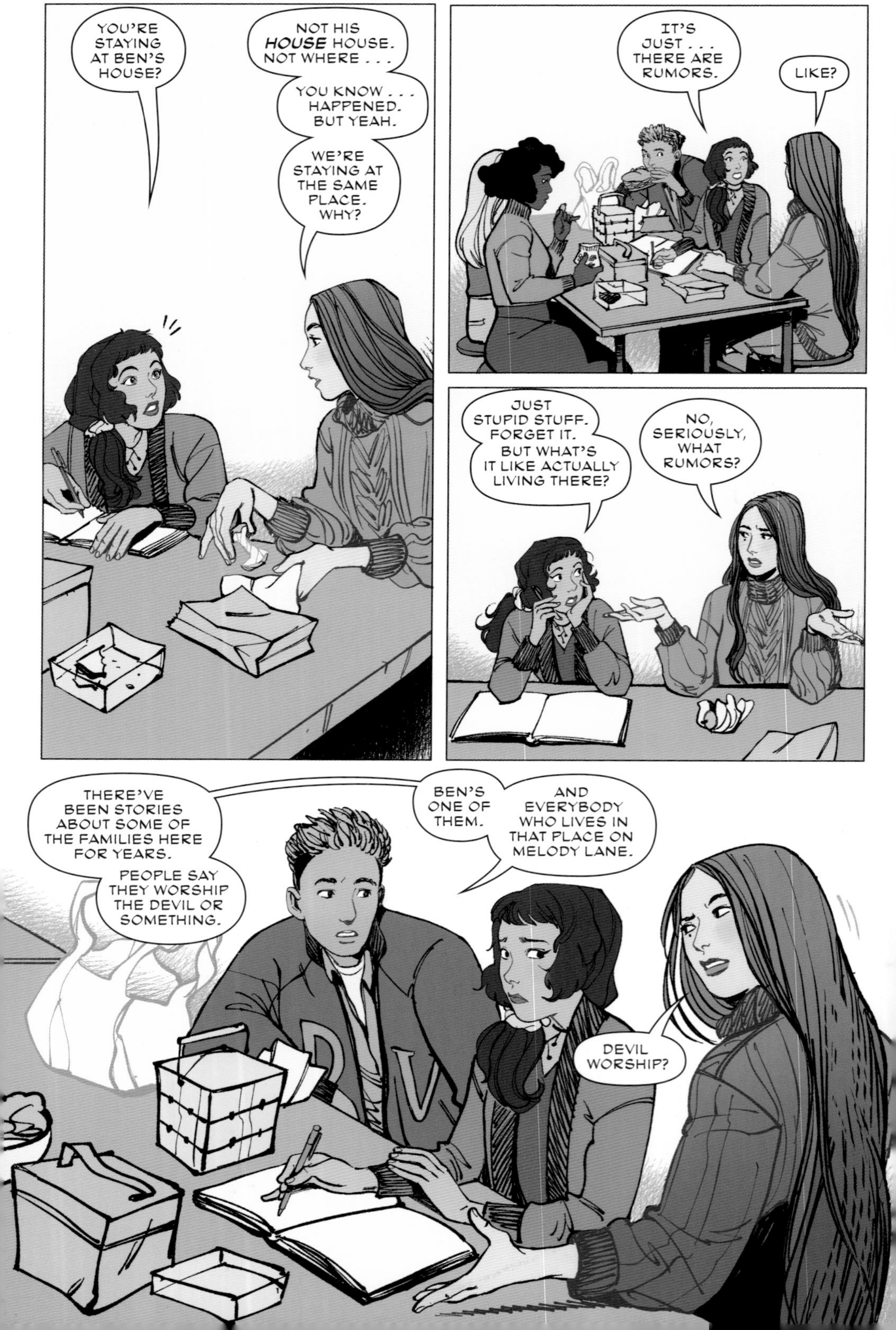
YOU'RE STAYING AT BEN'S HOUSE?
NOT HIS *HOUSE* HOUSE. NOT WHERE . . .
YOU KNOW . . . HAPPENED. BUT YEAH.
WE'RE STAYING AT THE SAME PLACE. WHY?
IT'S JUST . . . THERE ARE RUMORS.
LIKE?
JUST STUPID STUFF. FORGET IT.
BUT WHAT'S IT LIKE ACTUALLY LIVING THERE?
NO, SERIOUSLY, WHAT RUMORS?
THERE'VE BEEN STORIES ABOUT SOME OF THE FAMILIES HERE FOR YEARS.
PEOPLE SAY THEY WORSHIP THE DEVIL OR SOMETHING.
BEN'S ONE OF THEM.
AND EVERYBODY WHO LIVES IN THAT PLACE ON MELODY LANE.
DEVIL WORSHIP?

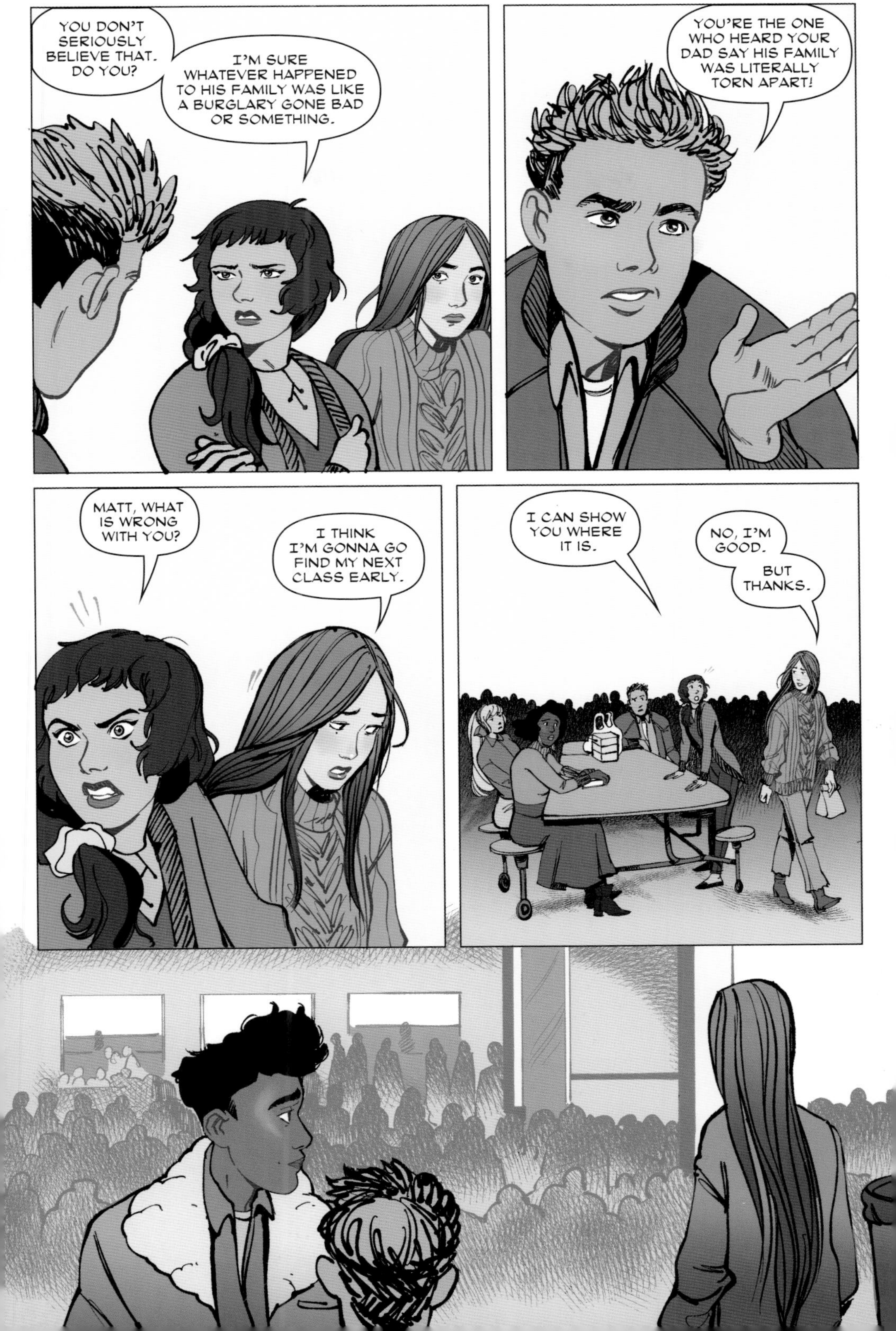

YOU DON'T SERIOUSLY BELIEVE THAT. DO YOU?
I'M SURE WHATEVER HAPPENED TO HIS FAMILY WAS LIKE A BURGLARY GONE BAD OR SOMETHING.
YOU'RE THE ONE WHO HEARD YOUR DAD SAY HIS FAMILY WAS LITERALLY TORN APART!
MATT, WHAT IS WRONG WITH YOU?
I THINK I'M GONNA GO FIND MY NEXT CLASS EARLY.
I CAN SHOW YOU WHERE IT IS.
NO, I'M GOOD.
BUT THANKS.

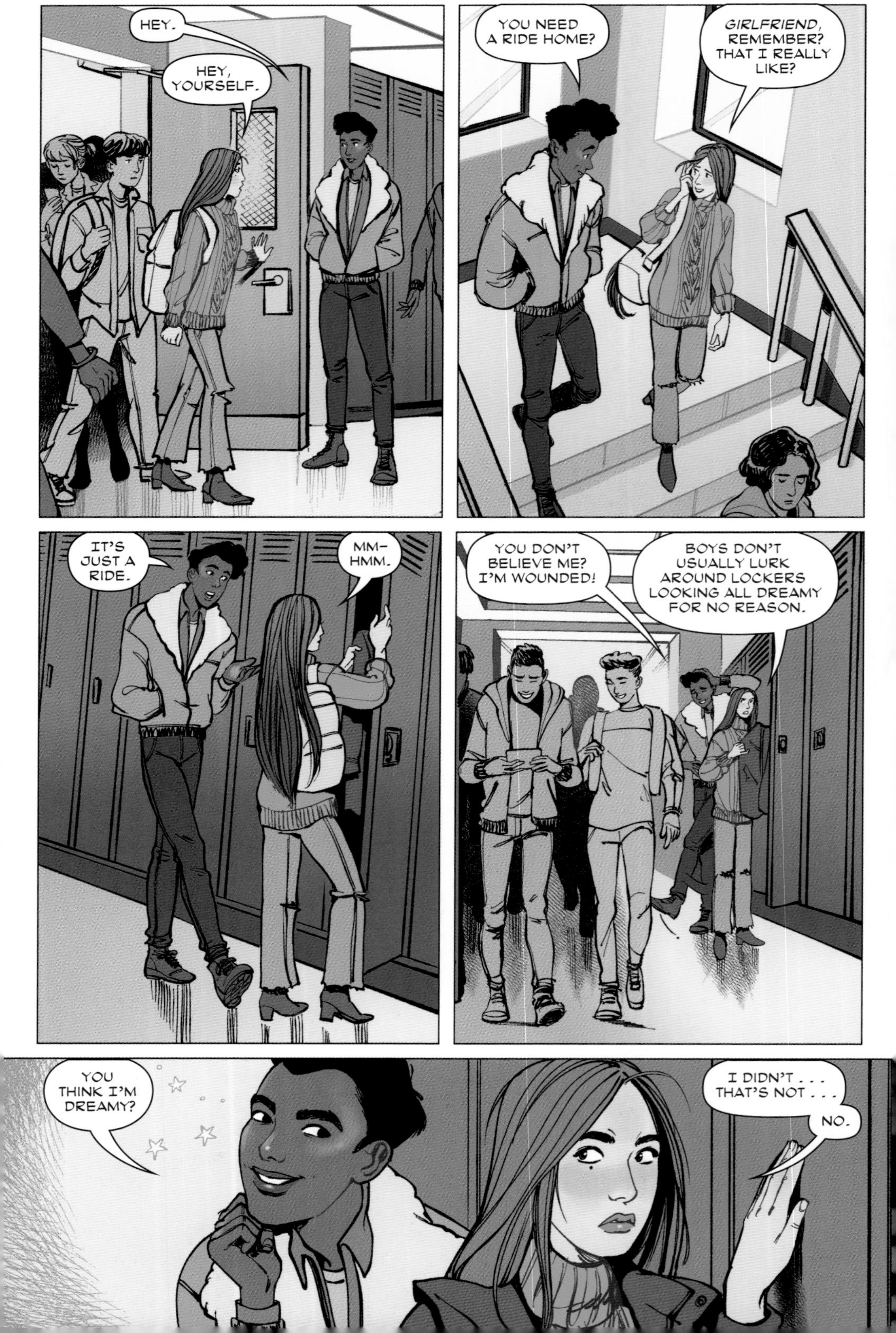
HEY.
HEY, YOURSELF.
YOU NEED A RIDE HOME?
GIRLFRIEND, REMEMBER? THAT I REALLY LIKE?
IT'S JUST A RIDE.
MM-HMM.
YOU DON'T BELIEVE ME? I'M WOUNDED!
BOYS DON'T USUALLY LURK AROUND LOCKERS LOOKING ALL DREAMY FOR NO REASON.
YOU THINK I'M DREAMY?
I DIDN'T . . . THAT'S NOT . . .
NO.

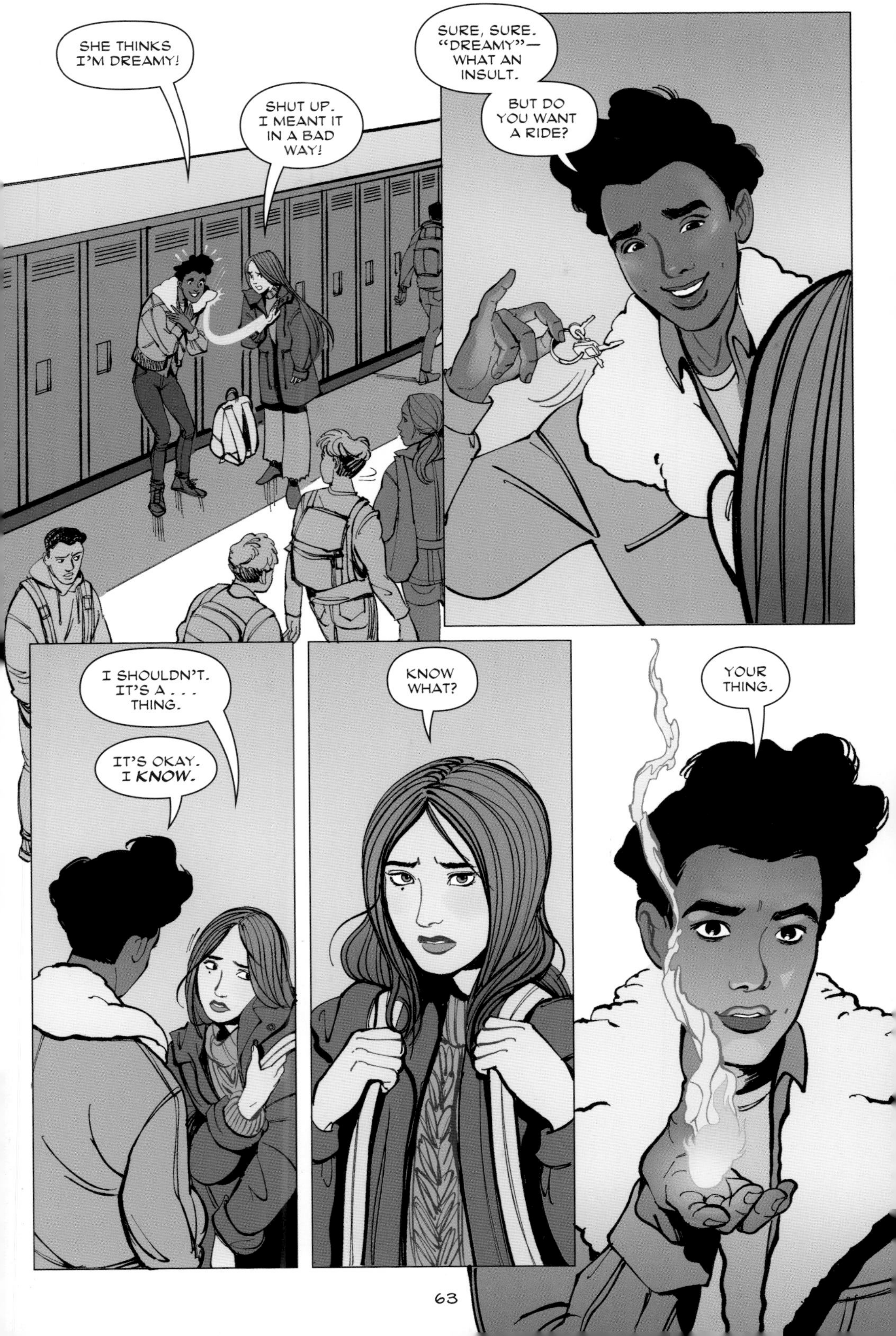
SHE THINKS I'M DREAMY!
SHUT UP. I MEANT IT IN A BAD WAY!
SURE, SURE. "DREAMY"— WHAT AN INSULT.
BUT DO YOU WANT A RIDE?
I SHOULDN'T. IT'S A . . . THING.
IT'S OKAY. I **KNOW**.
KNOW WHAT?
YOUR THING.

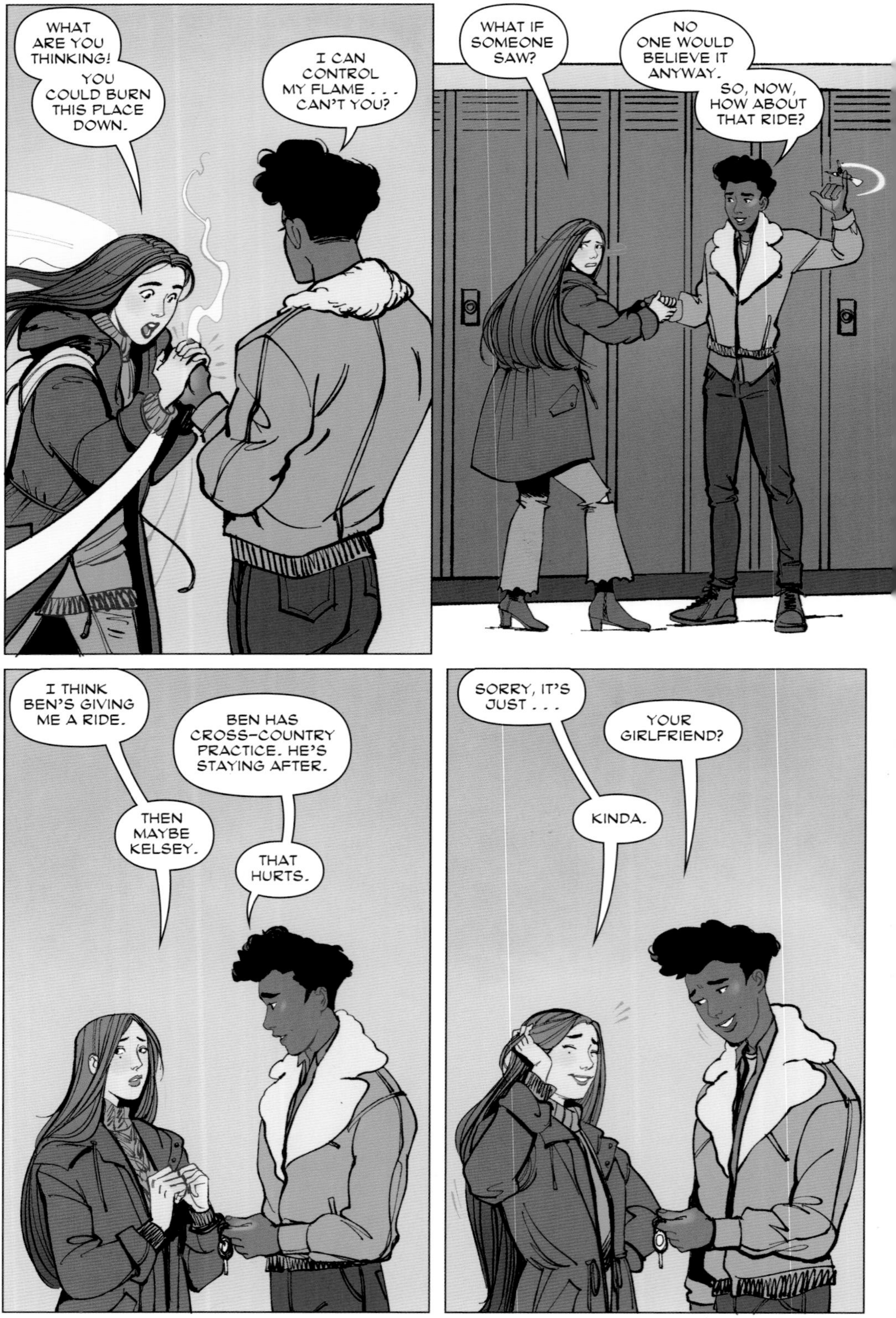
WHAT ARE YOU THINKING!
YOU COULD BURN THIS PLACE DOWN.
I CAN CONTROL MY FLAME . . . CAN'T YOU?
WHAT IF SOMEONE SAW?
NO ONE WOULD BELIEVE IT ANYWAY.
SO, NOW, HOW ABOUT THAT RIDE?
I THINK BEN'S GIVING ME A RIDE.
BEN HAS CROSS-COUNTRY PRACTICE. HE'S STAYING AFTER.
THEN MAYBE KELSEY.
THAT HURTS.
SORRY, IT'S JUST . . .
YOUR GIRLFRIEND?
KINDA.

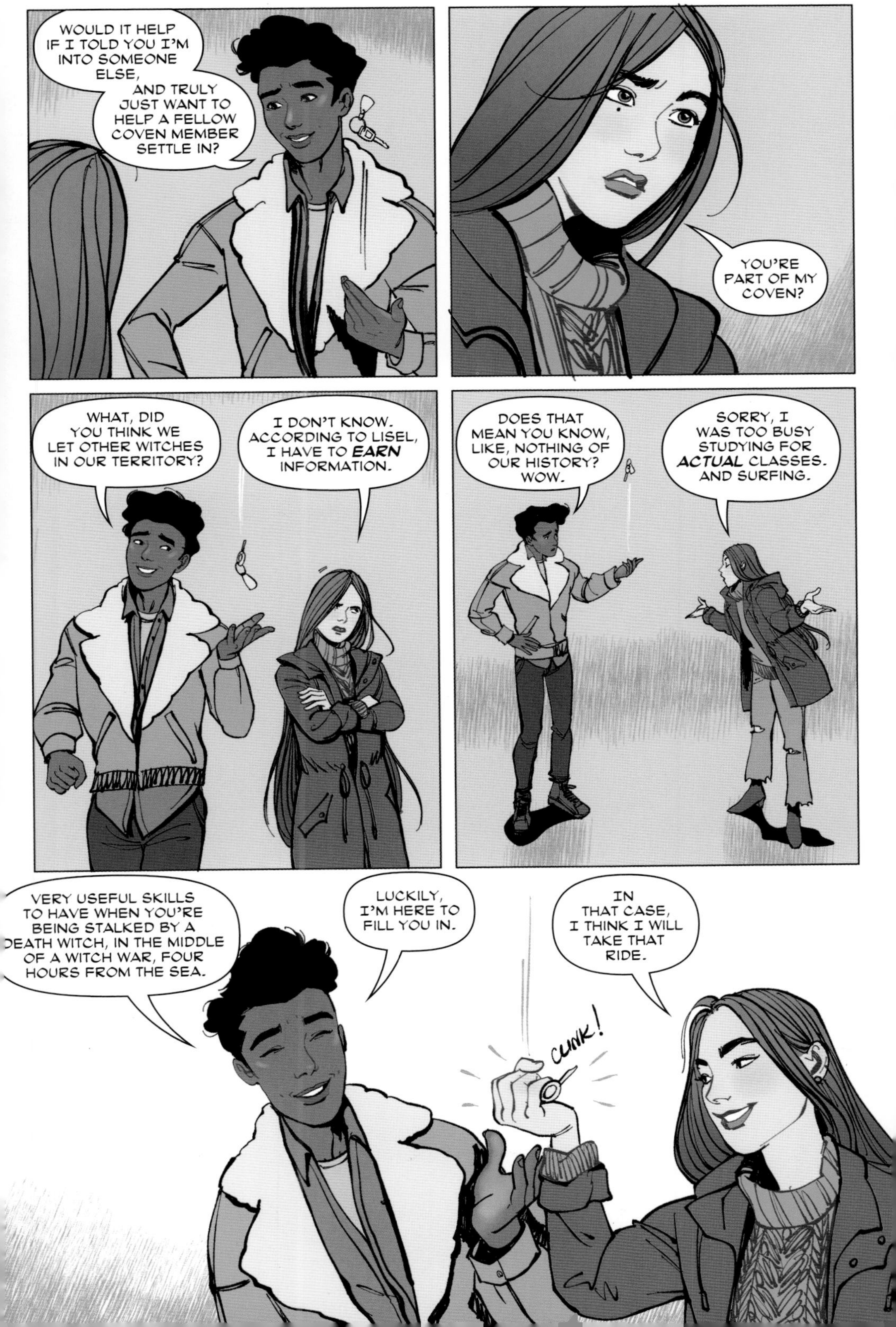
WOULD IT HELP IF I TOLD YOU I'M INTO SOMEONE ELSE,
AND TRULY JUST WANT TO HELP A FELLOW COVEN MEMBER SETTLE IN?
YOU'RE PART OF MY COVEN?
WHAT, DID YOU THINK WE LET OTHER WITCHES IN OUR TERRITORY?
I DON'T KNOW. ACCORDING TO LISEL, I HAVE TO EARN INFORMATION.
DOES THAT MEAN YOU KNOW, LIKE, NOTHING OF OUR HISTORY? WOW.
SORRY, I WAS TOO BUSY STUDYING FOR ACTUAL CLASSES. AND SURFING.
VERY USEFUL SKILLS TO HAVE WHEN YOU'RE BEING STALKED BY A DEATH WITCH, IN THE MIDDLE OF A WITCH WAR, FOUR HOURS FROM THE SEA.
LUCKILY, I'M HERE TO FILL YOU IN.
IN THAT CASE, I THINK I WILL TAKE THAT RIDE.
CLINK!

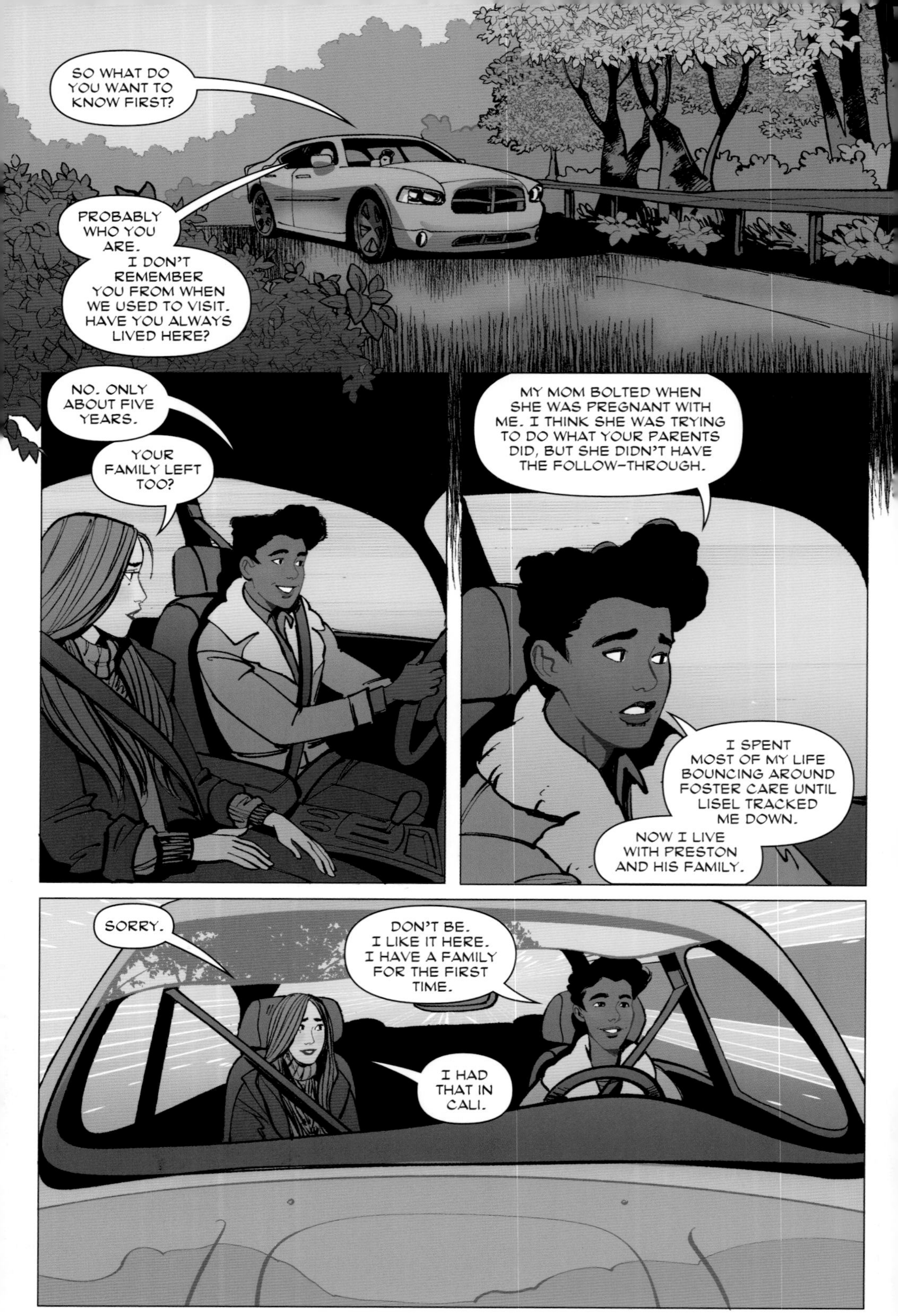
SO WHAT DO YOU WANT TO KNOW FIRST?
PROBABLY WHO YOU ARE. I DON'T REMEMBER YOU FROM WHEN WE USED TO VISIT. HAVE YOU ALWAYS LIVED HERE?
NO. ONLY ABOUT FIVE YEARS.
YOUR FAMILY LEFT TOO?
MY MOM BOLTED WHEN SHE WAS PREGNANT WITH ME. I THINK SHE WAS TRYING TO DO WHAT YOUR PARENTS DID, BUT SHE DIDN'T HAVE THE FOLLOW-THROUGH.
I SPENT MOST OF MY LIFE BOUNCING AROUND FOSTER CARE UNTIL LISEL TRACKED ME DOWN.
NOW I LIVE WITH PRESTON AND HIS FAMILY.
SORRY.
DON'T BE. I LIKE IT HERE. I HAVE A FAMILY FOR THE FIRST TIME.
I HAD THAT IN CALI.

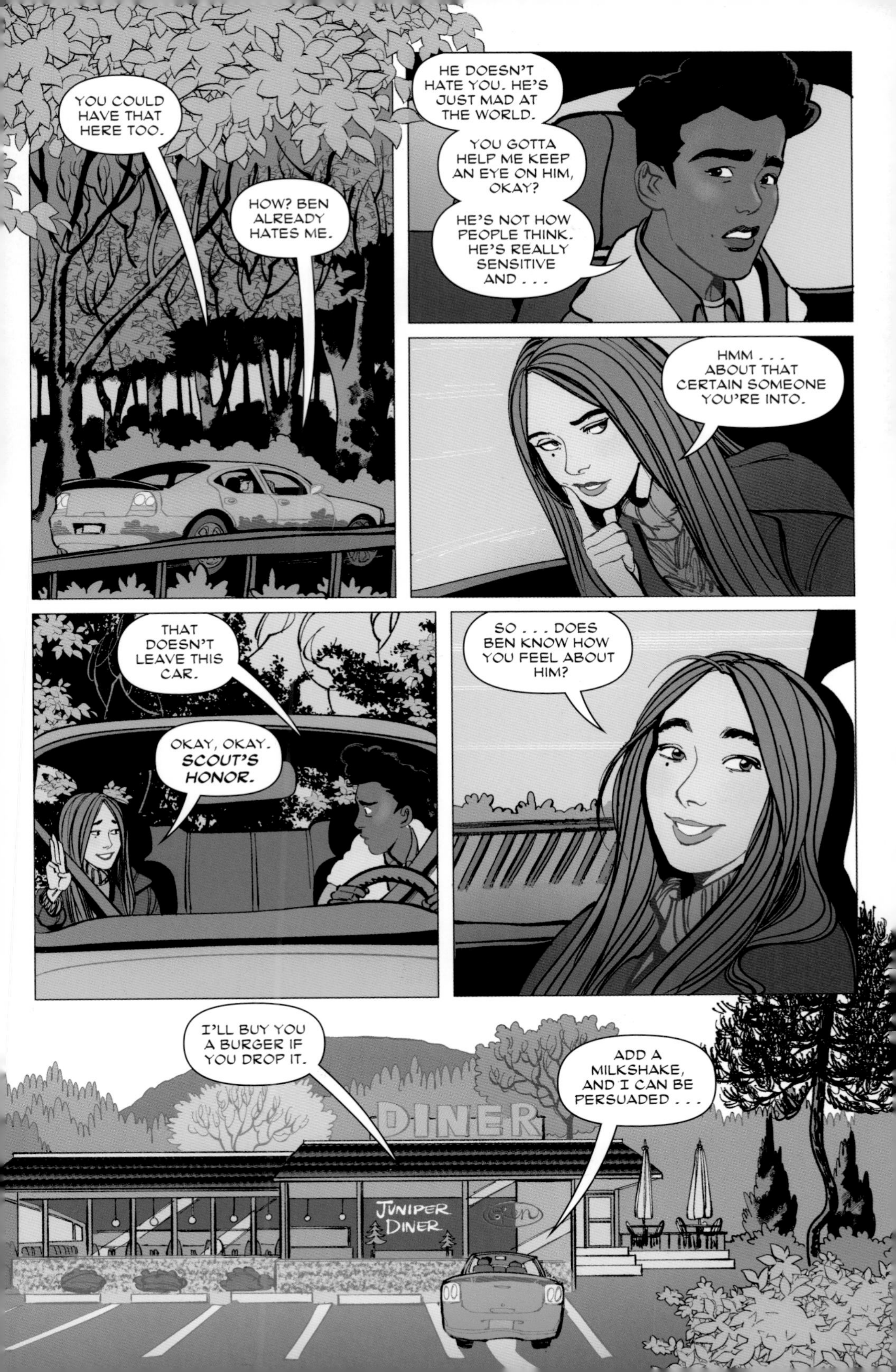
YOU COULD HAVE THAT HERE TOO.
HOW? BEN ALREADY HATES ME.
HE DOESN'T HATE YOU. HE'S JUST MAD AT THE WORLD.
YOU GOTTA HELP ME KEEP AN EYE ON HIM, OKAY?
HE'S NOT HOW PEOPLE THINK. HE'S REALLY SENSITIVE AND . . .
HMM . . . ABOUT THAT CERTAIN SOMEONE YOU'RE INTO.
THAT DOESN'T LEAVE THIS CAR.
OKAY, OKAY. SCOUT'S HONOR.
SO . . . DOES BEN KNOW HOW YOU FEEL ABOUT HIM?
I'LL BUY YOU A BURGER IF YOU DROP IT.
DINER
JUNIPER DINER
ADD A MILKSHAKE, AND I CAN BE PERSUADED . . .

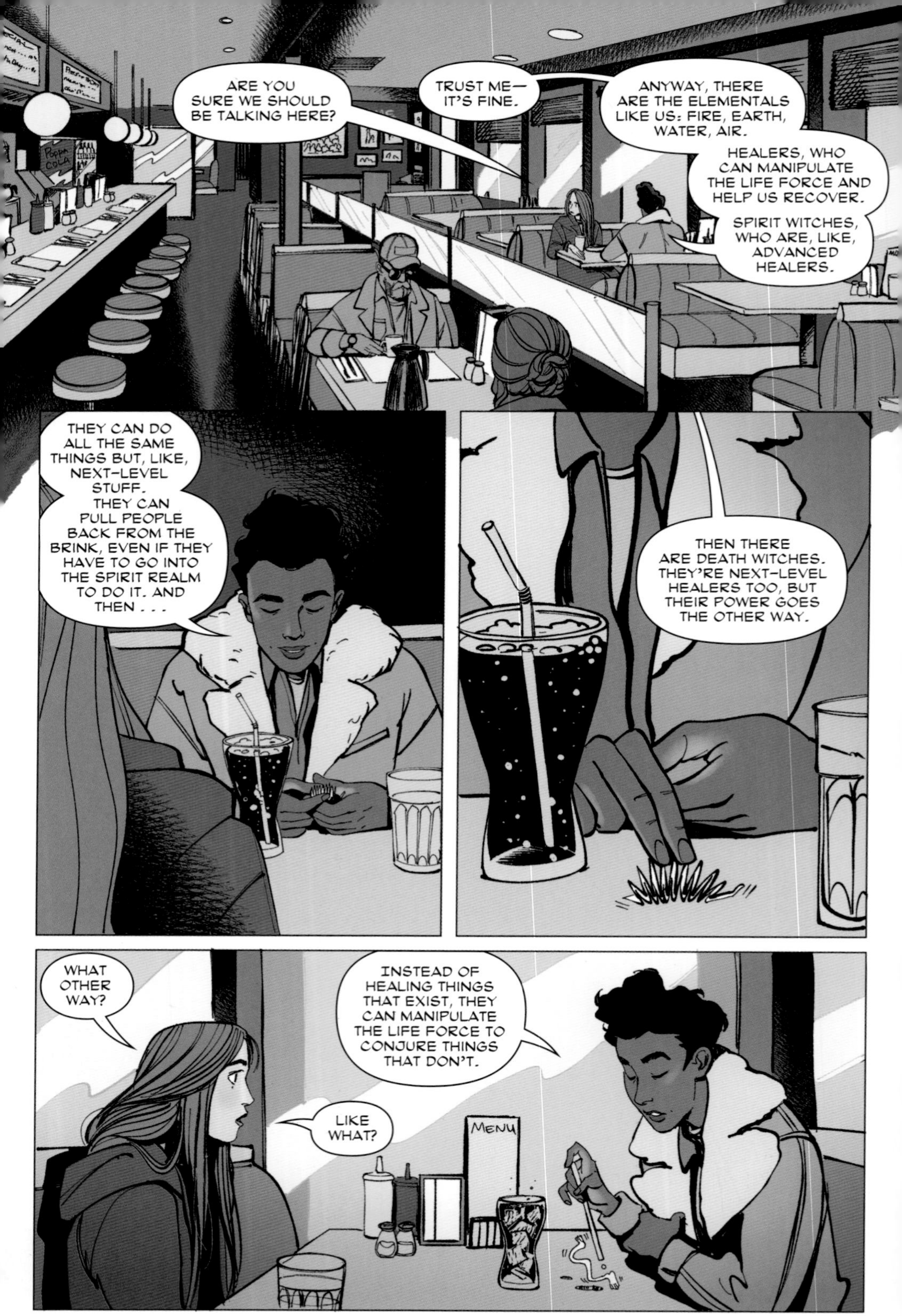
ARE YOU SURE WE SHOULD BE TALKING HERE?
TRUST ME— IT'S FINE.
ANYWAY, THERE ARE THE ELEMENTALS LIKE US: FIRE, EARTH, WATER, AIR.
HEALERS, WHO CAN MANIPULATE THE LIFE FORCE AND HELP US RECOVER.
SPIRIT WITCHES, WHO ARE, LIKE, ADVANCED HEALERS.
POPPA COLA
THEY CAN DO ALL THE SAME THINGS BUT, LIKE, NEXT-LEVEL STUFF.
THEY CAN PULL PEOPLE BACK FROM THE BRINK, EVEN IF THEY HAVE TO GO INTO THE SPIRIT REALM TO DO IT. AND THEN . . .
THEN THERE ARE DEATH WITCHES. THEY'RE NEXT-LEVEL HEALERS TOO, BUT THEIR POWER GOES THE OTHER WAY.
WHAT OTHER WAY?
INSTEAD OF HEALING THINGS THAT EXIST, THEY CAN MANIPULATE THE LIFE FORCE TO CONJURE THINGS THAT DON'T.
LIKE WHAT?
MENU

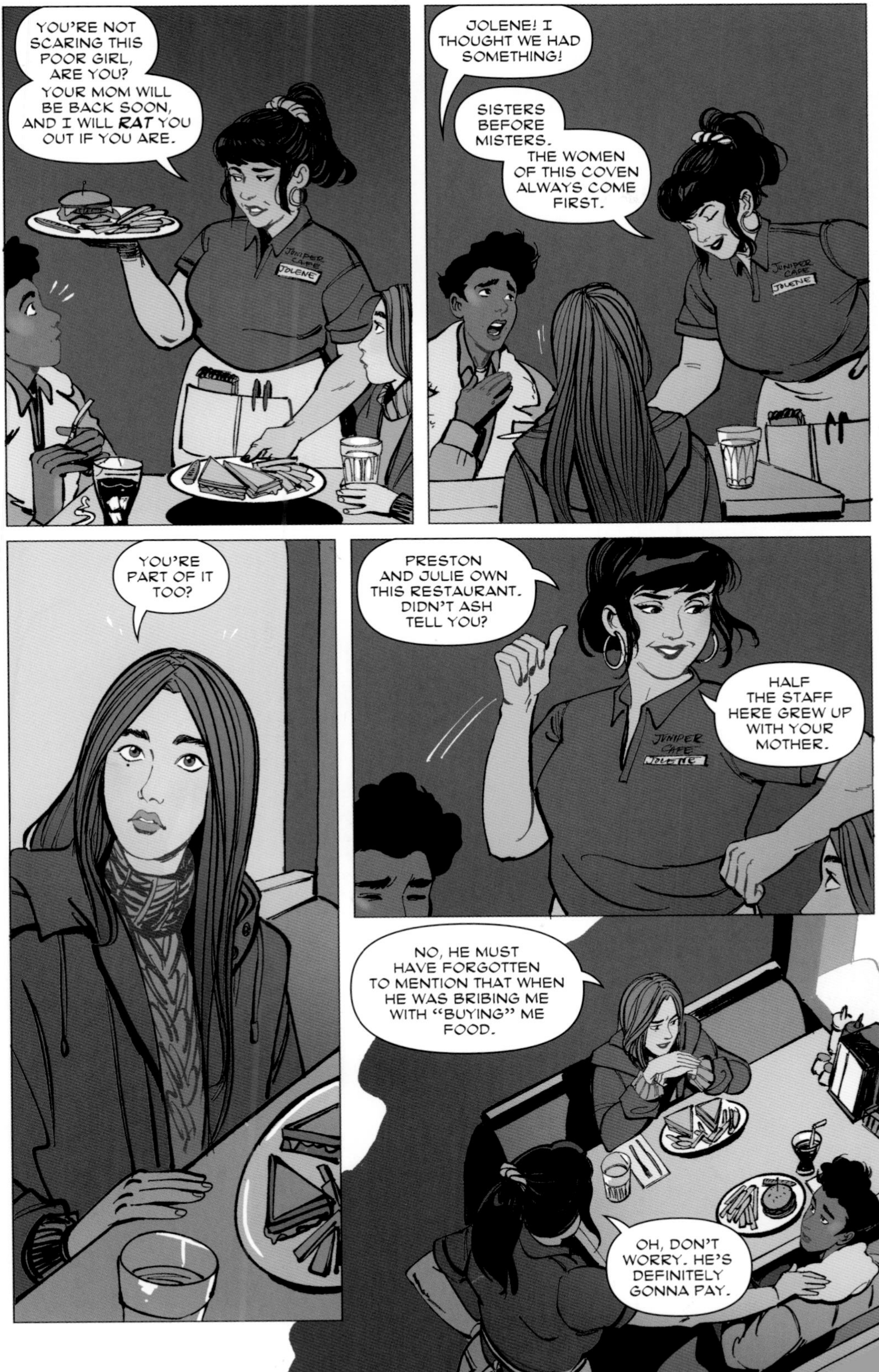
YOU'RE NOT SCARING THIS POOR GIRL, ARE YOU?
YOUR MOM WILL BE BACK SOON, AND I WILL **RAT** YOU OUT IF YOU ARE.
JUNIPER CAFE
JOLENE
JOLENE! I THOUGHT WE HAD SOMETHING!
SISTERS BEFORE MISTERS.
THE WOMEN OF THIS COVEN ALWAYS COME FIRST.
JUNIPER CAFE
JOLENE
YOU'RE PART OF IT TOO?
PRESTON AND JULIE OWN THIS RESTAURANT. DIDN'T ASH TELL YOU?
HALF THE STAFF HERE GREW UP WITH YOUR MOTHER.
JUNIPER CAFE
NO, HE MUST HAVE FORGOTTEN TO MENTION THAT WHEN HE WAS BRIBING ME WITH "BUYING" ME FOOD.
OH, DON'T WORRY. HE'S DEFINITELY GONNA PAY.

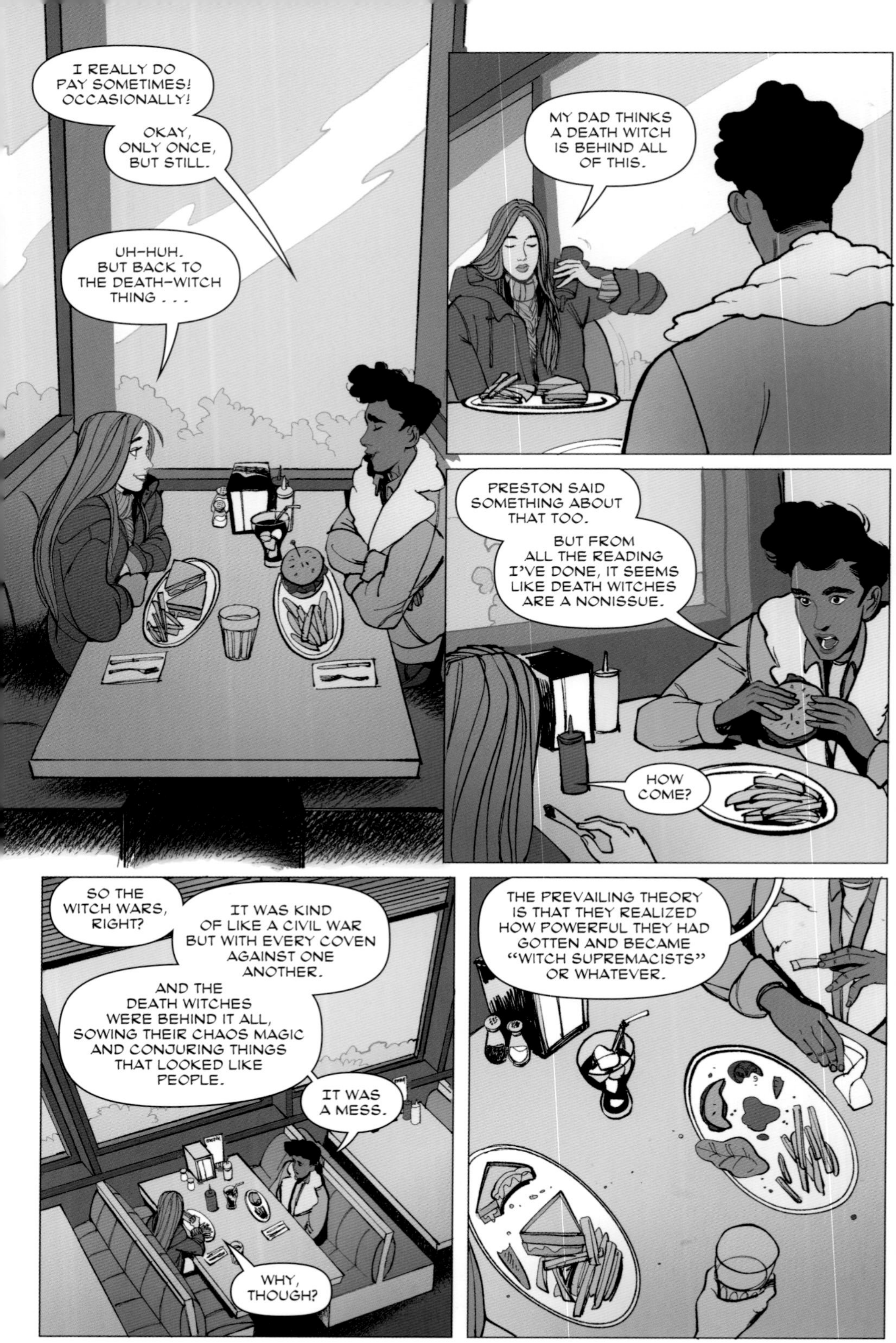

I REALLY DO PAY SOMETIMES! OCCASIONALLY!
OKAY, ONLY ONCE, BUT STILL.
UH-HUH. BUT BACK TO THE DEATH-WITCH THING . . .
MY DAD THINKS A DEATH WITCH IS BEHIND ALL OF THIS.
PRESTON SAID SOMETHING ABOUT THAT TOO.
BUT FROM ALL THE READING I'VE DONE, IT SEEMS LIKE DEATH WITCHES ARE A NONISSUE.
HOW COME?
SO THE WITCH WARS, RIGHT?
IT WAS KIND OF LIKE A CIVIL WAR BUT WITH EVERY COVEN AGAINST ONE ANOTHER.
AND THE DEATH WITCHES WERE BEHIND IT ALL, SOWING THEIR CHAOS MAGIC AND CONJURING THINGS THAT LOOKED LIKE PEOPLE.
IT WAS A MESS.
WHY, THOUGH?
THE PREVAILING THEORY IS THAT THEY REALIZED HOW POWERFUL THEY HAD GOTTEN AND BECAME "WITCH SUPREMACISTS" OR WHATEVER.

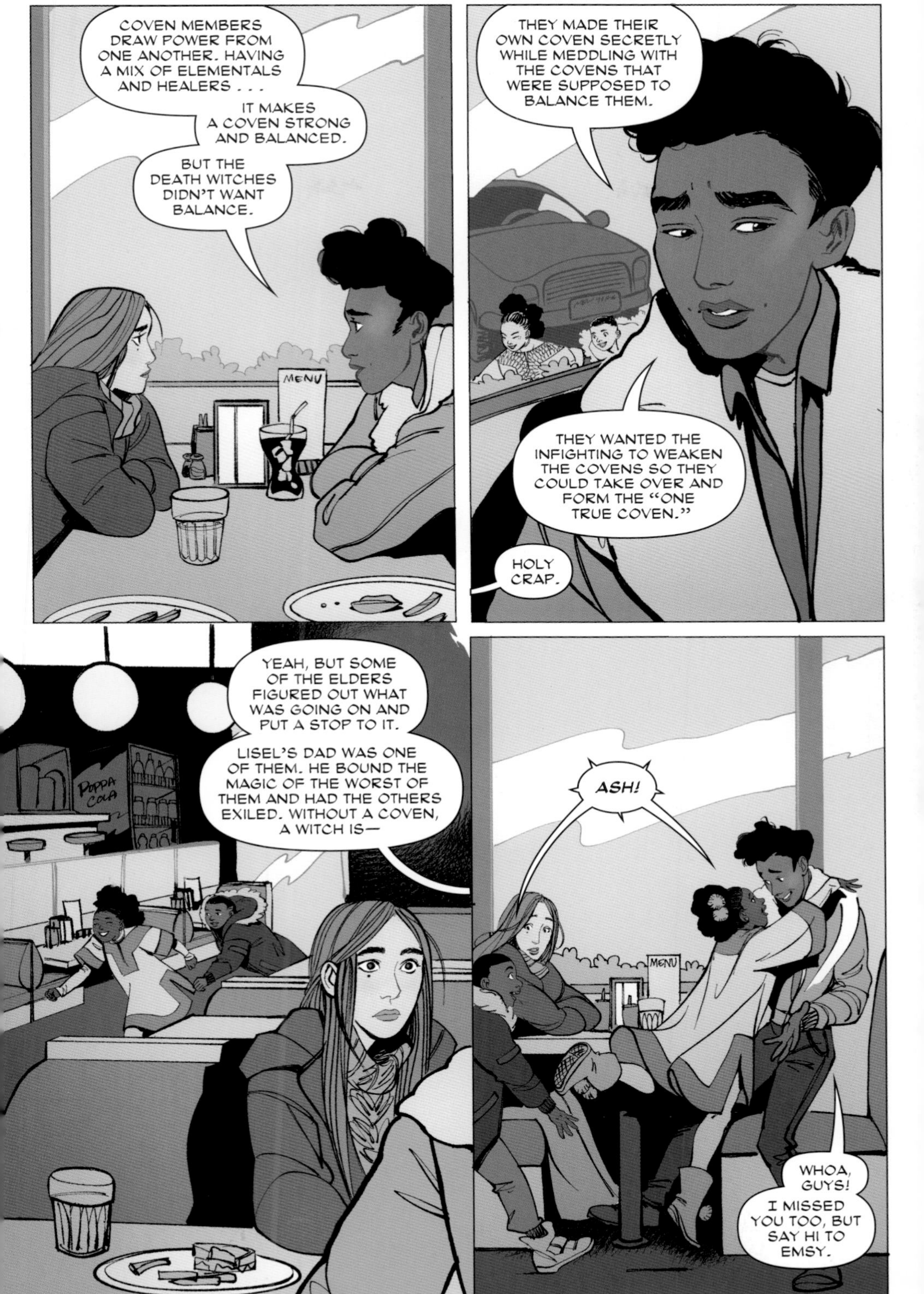
COVEN MEMBERS DRAW POWER FROM ONE ANOTHER. HAVING A MIX OF ELEMENTALS AND HEALERS . . .
IT MAKES A COVEN STRONG AND BALANCED.
BUT THE DEATH WITCHES DIDN'T WANT BALANCE.
MENU
THEY MADE THEIR OWN COVEN SECRETLY WHILE MEDDLING WITH THE COVENS THAT WERE SUPPOSED TO BALANCE THEM.
THEY WANTED THE INFIGHTING TO WEAKEN THE COVENS SO THEY COULD TAKE OVER AND FORM THE "ONE TRUE COVEN."
HOLY CRAP.
YEAH, BUT SOME OF THE ELDERS FIGURED OUT WHAT WAS GOING ON AND PUT A STOP TO IT.
LISEL'S DAD WAS ONE OF THEM. HE BOUND THE MAGIC OF THE WORST OF THEM AND HAD THE OTHERS EXILED. WITHOUT A COVEN, A WITCH IS—
POPPA COLA
ASH!
MENU
WHOA, GUYS!
I MISSED YOU TOO, BUT SAY HI TO EMSY.

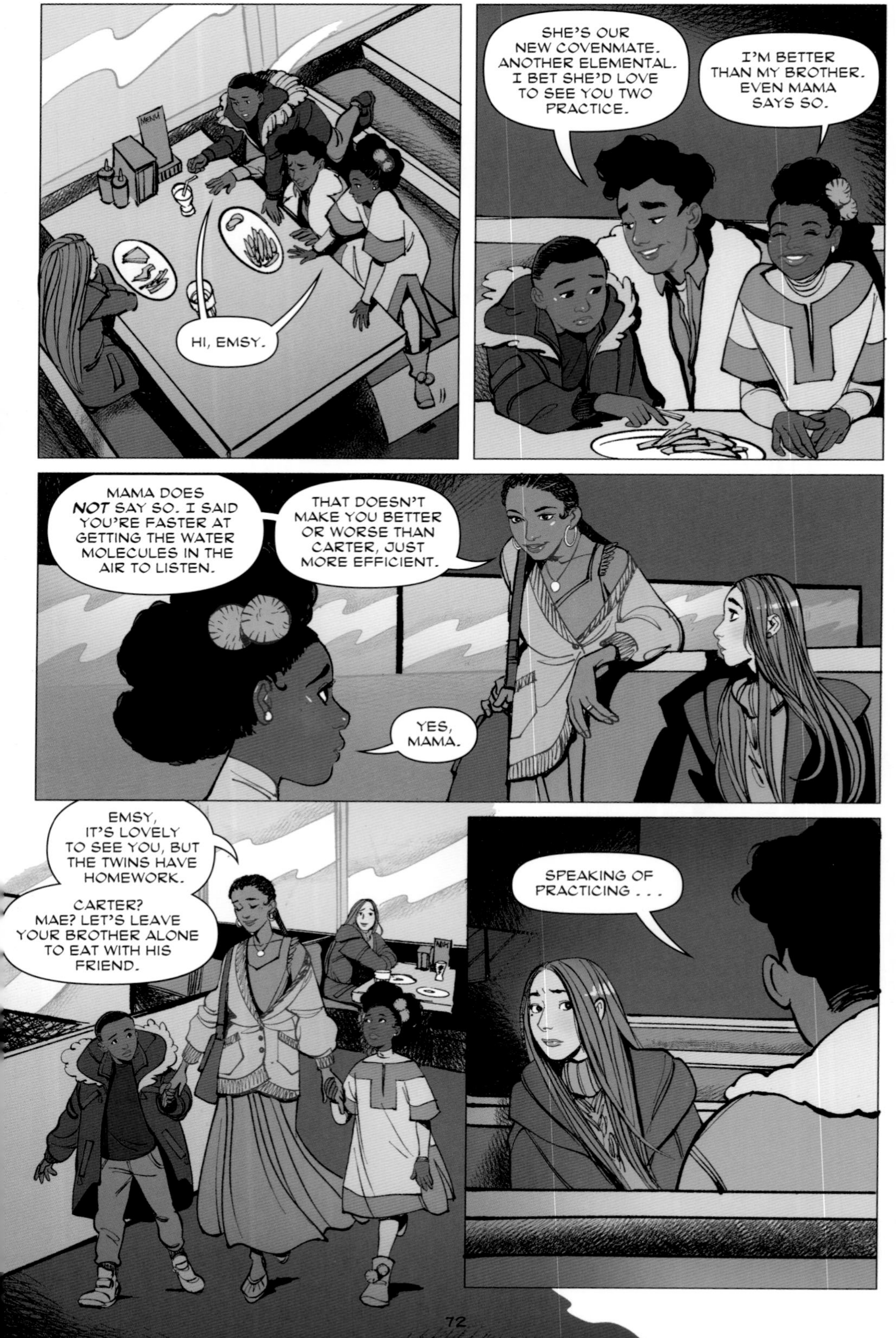
HI, EMSY.
SHE'S OUR NEW COVENMATE. ANOTHER ELEMENTAL. I BET SHE'D LOVE TO SEE YOU TWO PRACTICE.
I'M BETTER THAN MY BROTHER. EVEN MAMA SAYS SO.
MAMA DOES *NOT* SAY SO. I SAID YOU'RE FASTER AT GETTING THE WATER MOLECULES IN THE AIR TO LISTEN.
THAT DOESN'T MAKE YOU BETTER OR WORSE THAN CARTER, JUST MORE EFFICIENT.
YES, MAMA.
EMSY, IT'S LOVELY TO SEE YOU, BUT THE TWINS HAVE HOMEWORK.
CARTER? MAE? LET'S LEAVE YOUR BROTHER ALONE TO EAT WITH HIS FRIEND.
SPEAKING OF PRACTICING . . .

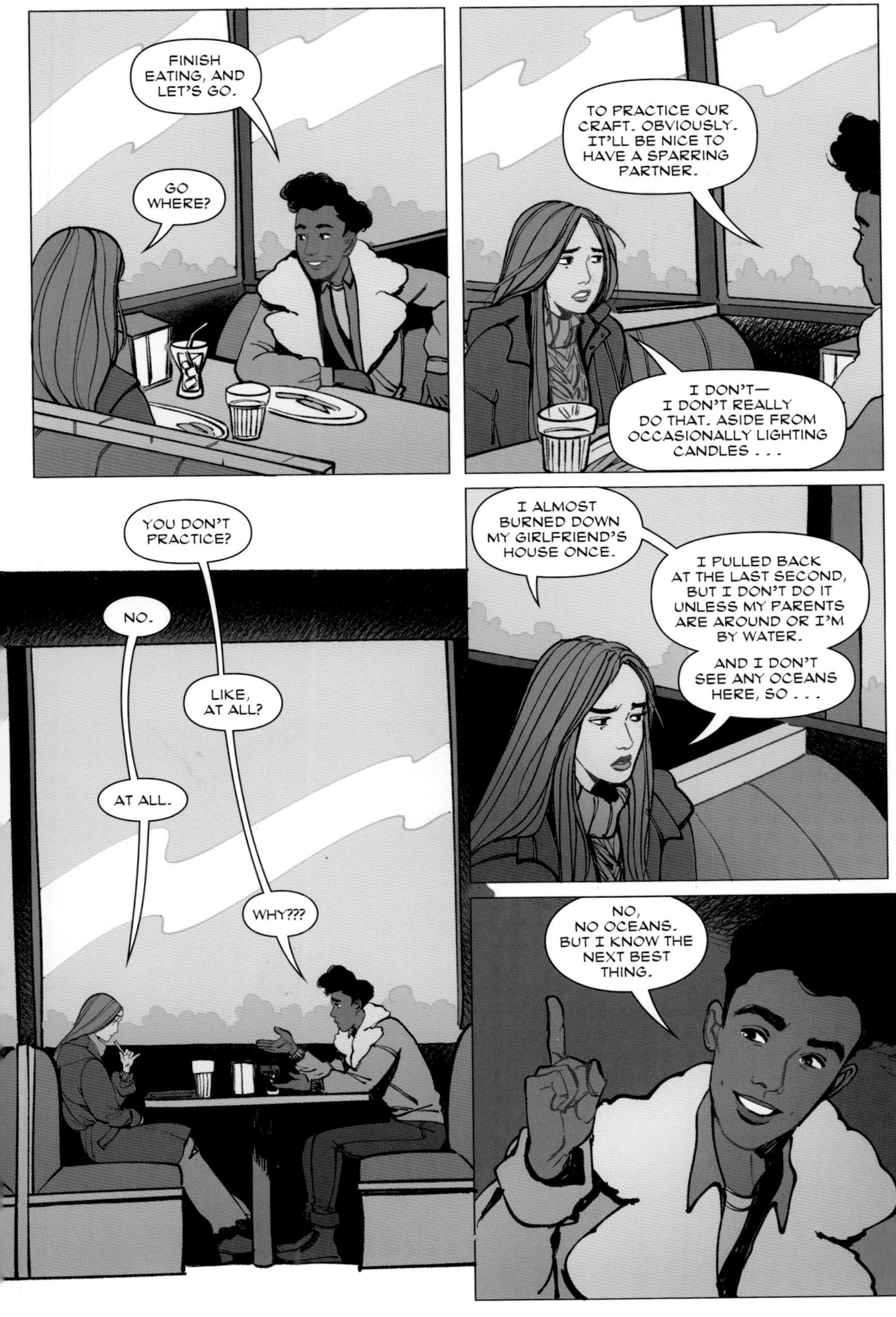
FINISH EATING, AND LET'S GO.
GO WHERE?
TO PRACTICE OUR CRAFT. OBVIOUSLY. IT'LL BE NICE TO HAVE A SPARRING PARTNER.
I DON'T— I DON'T REALLY DO THAT. ASIDE FROM OCCASIONALLY LIGHTING CANDLES . . .
YOU DON'T PRACTICE?
NO.
LIKE, AT ALL?
AT ALL.
WHY???
I ALMOST BURNED DOWN MY GIRLFRIEND'S HOUSE ONCE.
I PULLED BACK AT THE LAST SECOND, BUT I DON'T DO IT UNLESS MY PARENTS ARE AROUND OR I'M BY WATER.
AND I DON'T SEE ANY OCEANS HERE, SO . . .
NO, NO OCEANS. BUT I KNOW THE NEXT BEST THING.

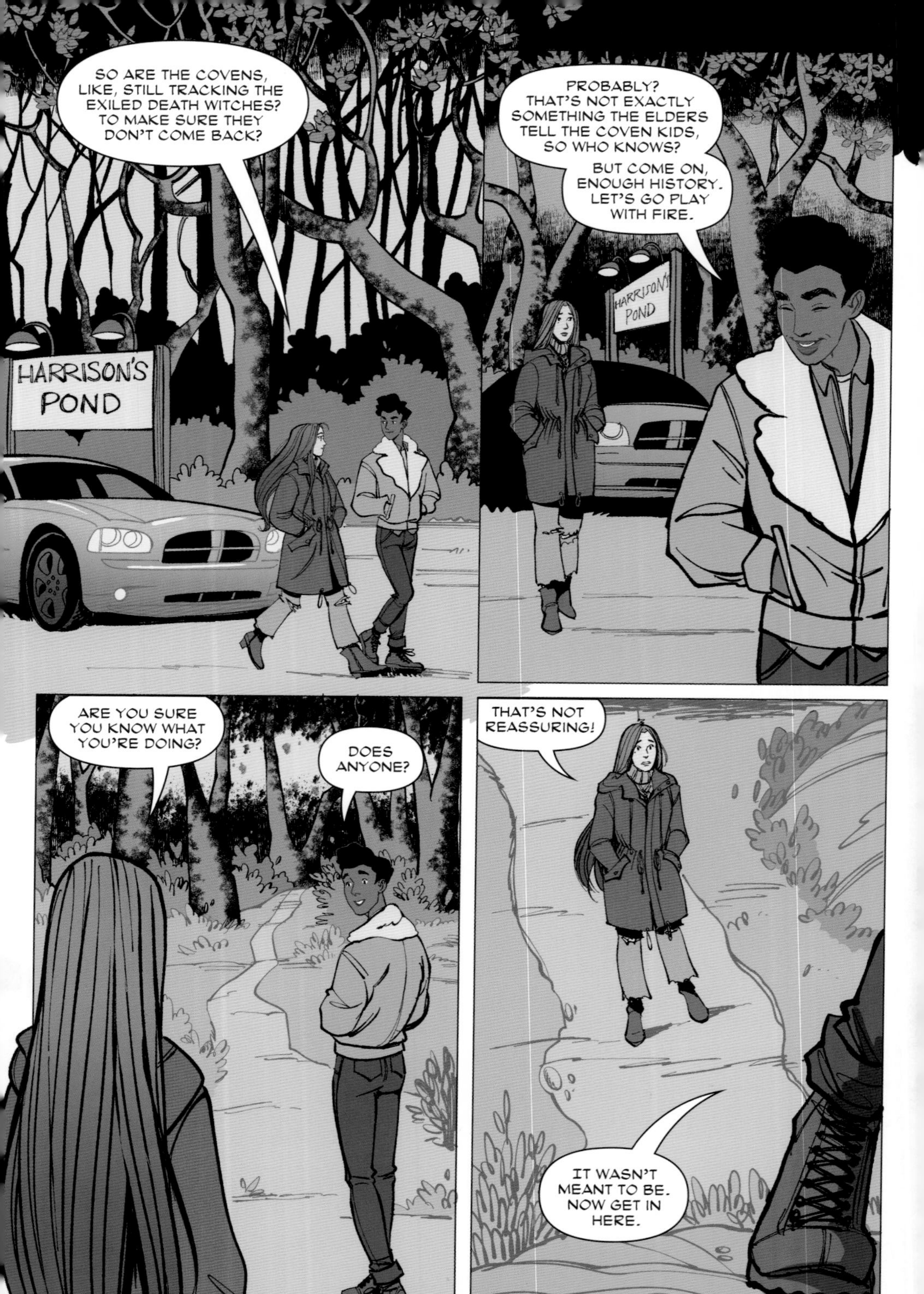
SO ARE THE COVENS, LIKE, STILL TRACKING THE EXILED DEATH WITCHES? TO MAKE SURE THEY DON'T COME BACK?
HARRISON'S POND
PROBABLY? THAT'S NOT EXACTLY SOMETHING THE ELDERS TELL THE COVEN KIDS, SO WHO KNOWS?
BUT COME ON, ENOUGH HISTORY. LET'S GO PLAY WITH FIRE.
HARRISON'S POND
ARE YOU SURE YOU KNOW WHAT YOU'RE DOING?
DOES ANYONE?
THAT'S NOT REASSURING!
IT WASN'T MEANT TO BE. NOW GET IN HERE.

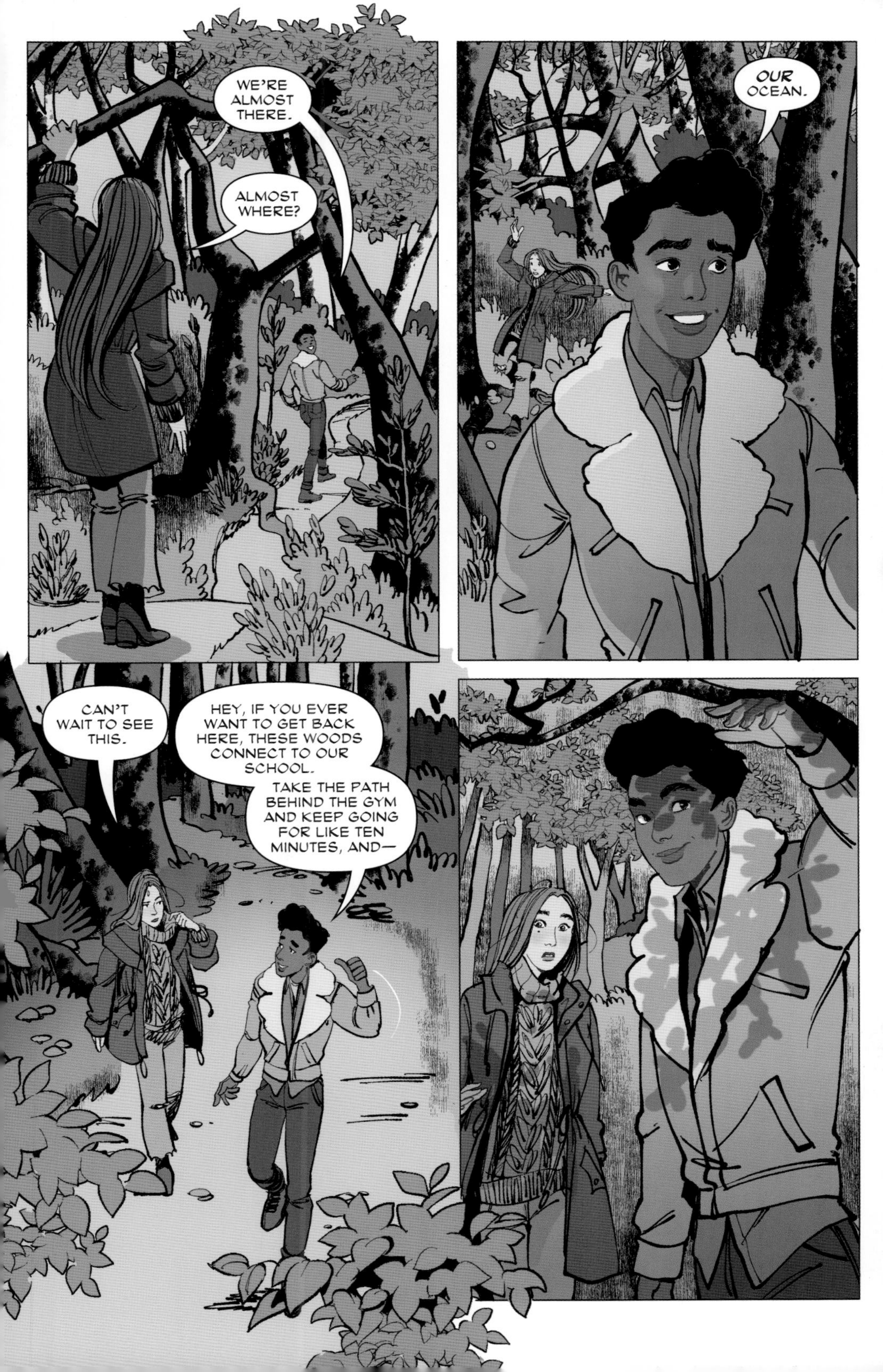
WE'RE ALMOST THERE.
ALMOST WHERE?
OUR OCEAN.
CAN'T WAIT TO SEE THIS.
HEY, IF YOU EVER WANT TO GET BACK HERE, THESE WOODS CONNECT TO OUR SCHOOL.
TAKE THE PATH BEHIND THE GYM AND KEEP GOING FOR LIKE TEN MINUTES, AND—

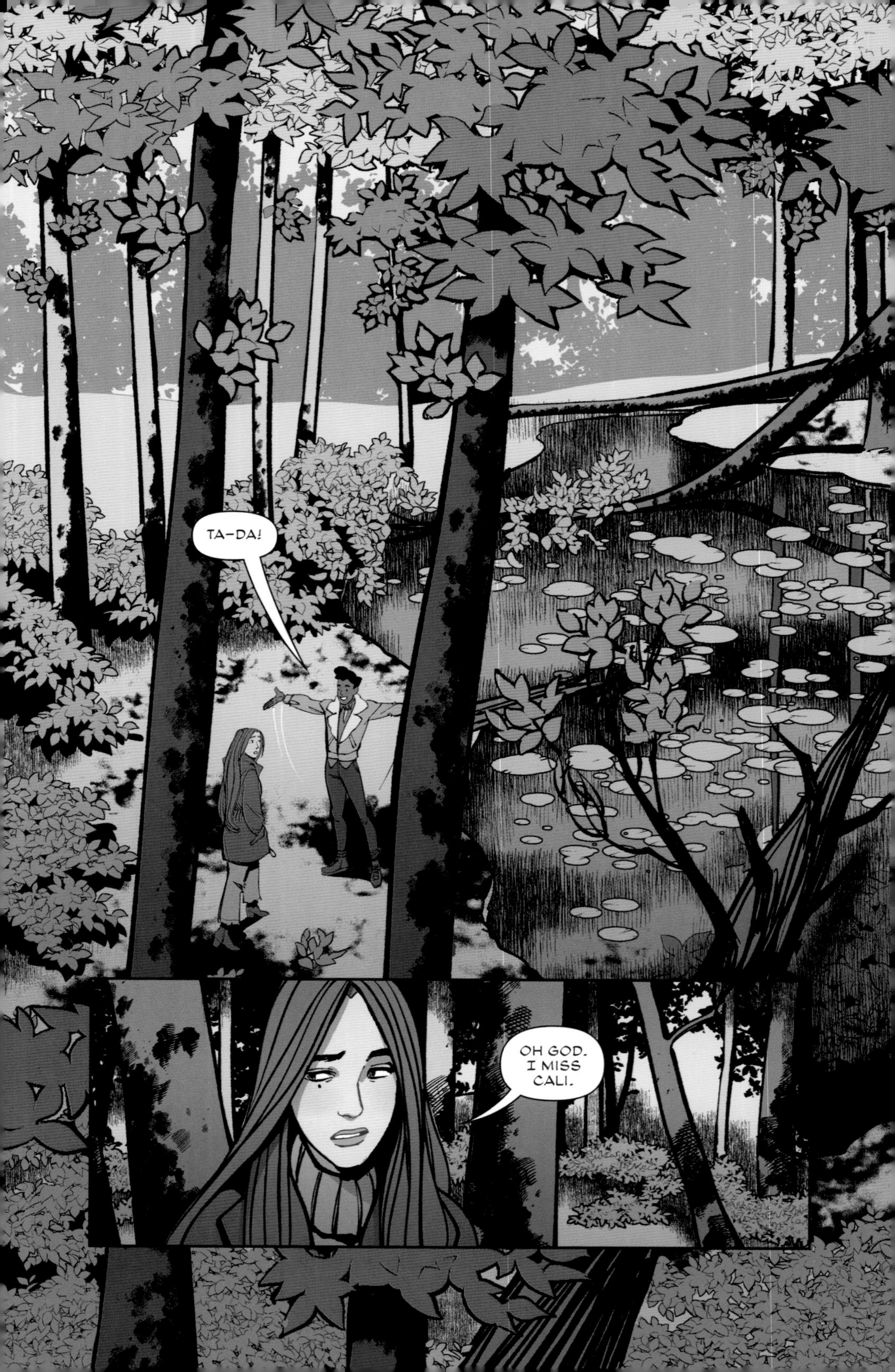
TA-DA!
OH GOD. I MISS CALI.

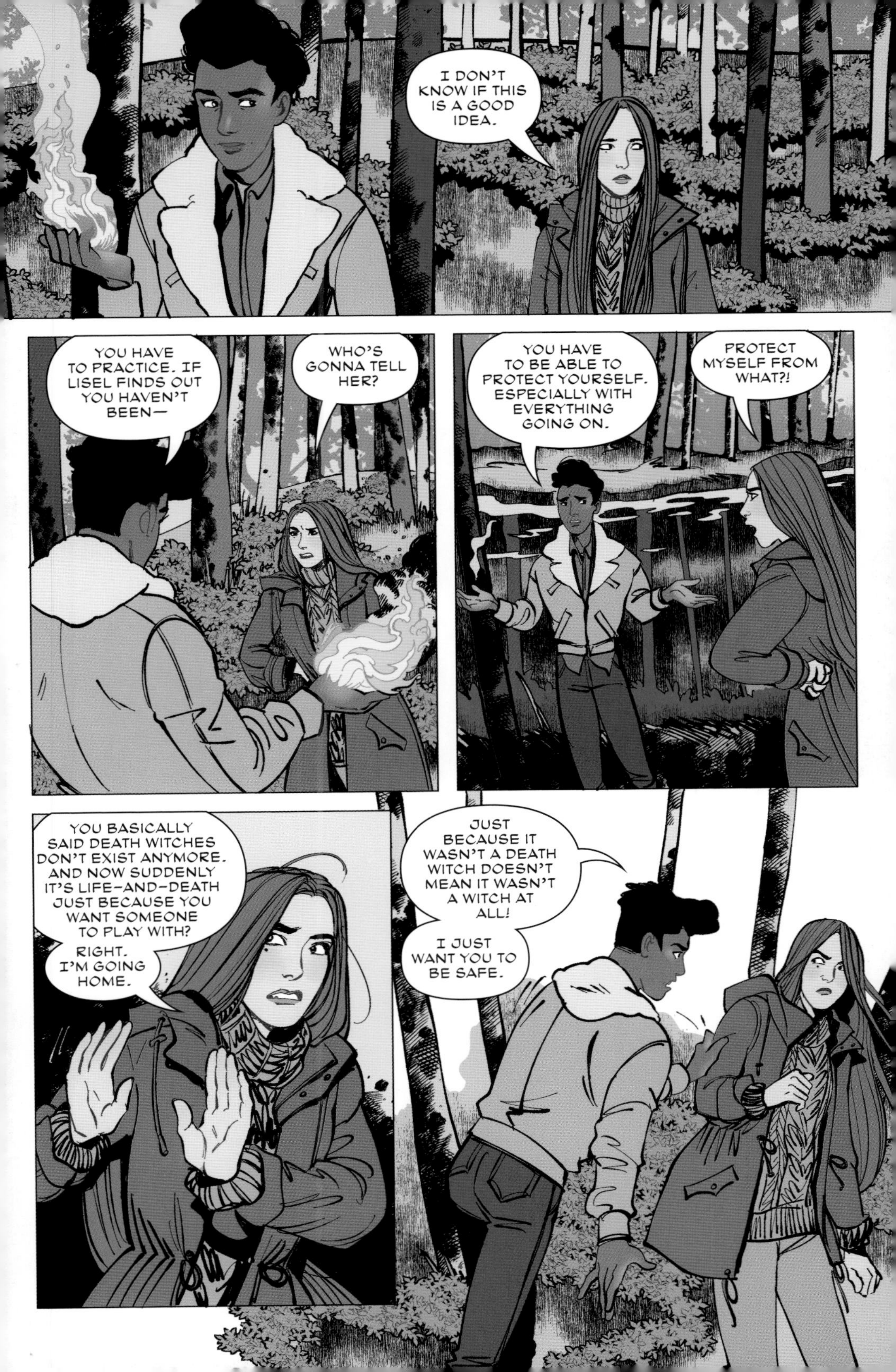
I DON'T KNOW IF THIS IS A GOOD IDEA.
YOU HAVE TO PRACTICE. IF LISEL FINDS OUT YOU HAVEN'T BEEN—
WHO'S GONNA TELL HER?
YOU HAVE TO BE ABLE TO PROTECT YOURSELF. ESPECIALLY WITH EVERYTHING GOING ON.
PROTECT MYSELF FROM WHAT?!
YOU BASICALLY SAID DEATH WITCHES DON'T EXIST ANYMORE. AND NOW SUDDENLY IT'S LIFE-AND-DEATH JUST BECAUSE YOU WANT SOMEONE TO PLAY WITH?
RIGHT. I'M GOING HOME.
JUST BECAUSE IT WASN'T A DEATH WITCH DOESN'T MEAN IT WASN'T A WITCH AT ALL!
I JUST WANT YOU TO BE SAFE.

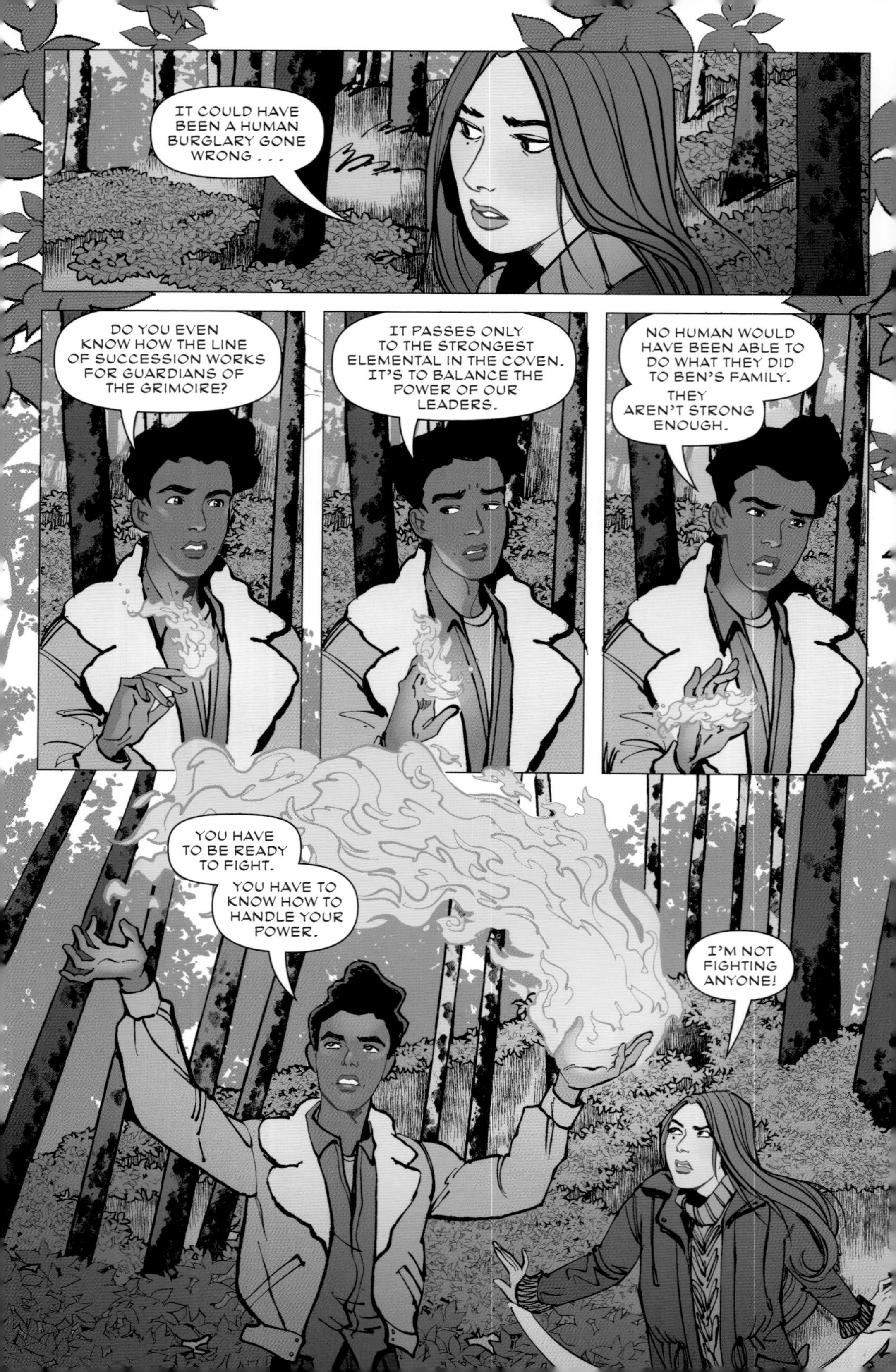

IT COULD HAVE BEEN A HUMAN BURGLARY GONE WRONG . . .
DO YOU EVEN KNOW HOW THE LINE OF SUCCESSION WORKS FOR GUARDIANS OF THE GRIMOIRE?
IT PASSES ONLY TO THE STRONGEST ELEMENTAL IN THE COVEN. IT'S TO BALANCE THE POWER OF OUR LEADERS.
NO HUMAN WOULD HAVE BEEN ABLE TO DO WHAT THEY DID TO BEN'S FAMILY.
THEY AREN'T STRONG ENOUGH.
YOU HAVE TO BE READY TO FIGHT.
YOU HAVE TO KNOW HOW TO HANDLE YOUR POWER.
I'M NOT FIGHTING ANYONE!

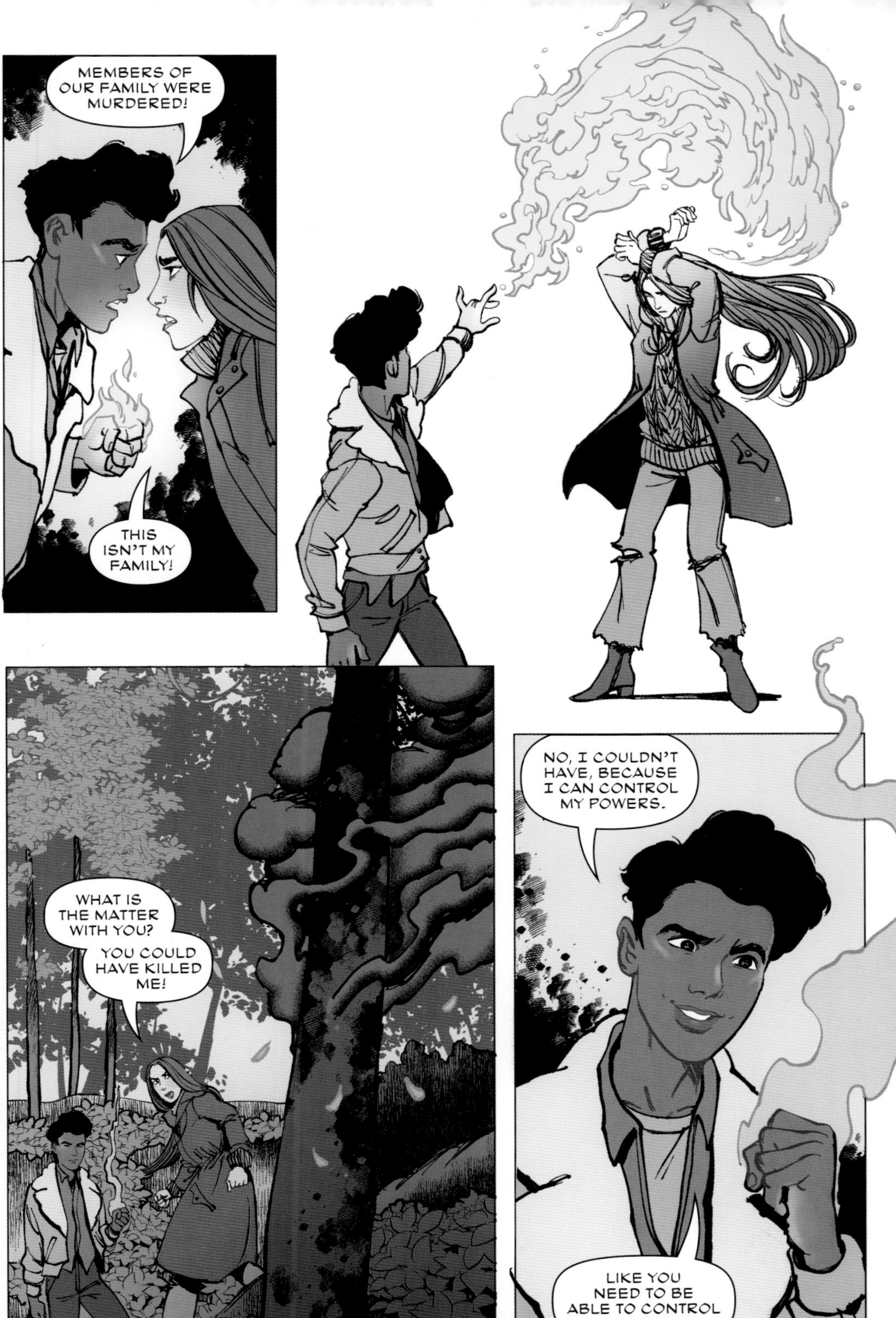
MEMBERS OF OUR FAMILY WERE MURDERED!
THIS ISN'T MY FAMILY!
WHAT IS THE MATTER WITH YOU?
YOU COULD HAVE KILLED ME!
NO, I COULDN'T HAVE, BECAUSE I CAN CONTROL MY POWERS.
LIKE YOU NEED TO BE ABLE TO CONTROL YOURS.

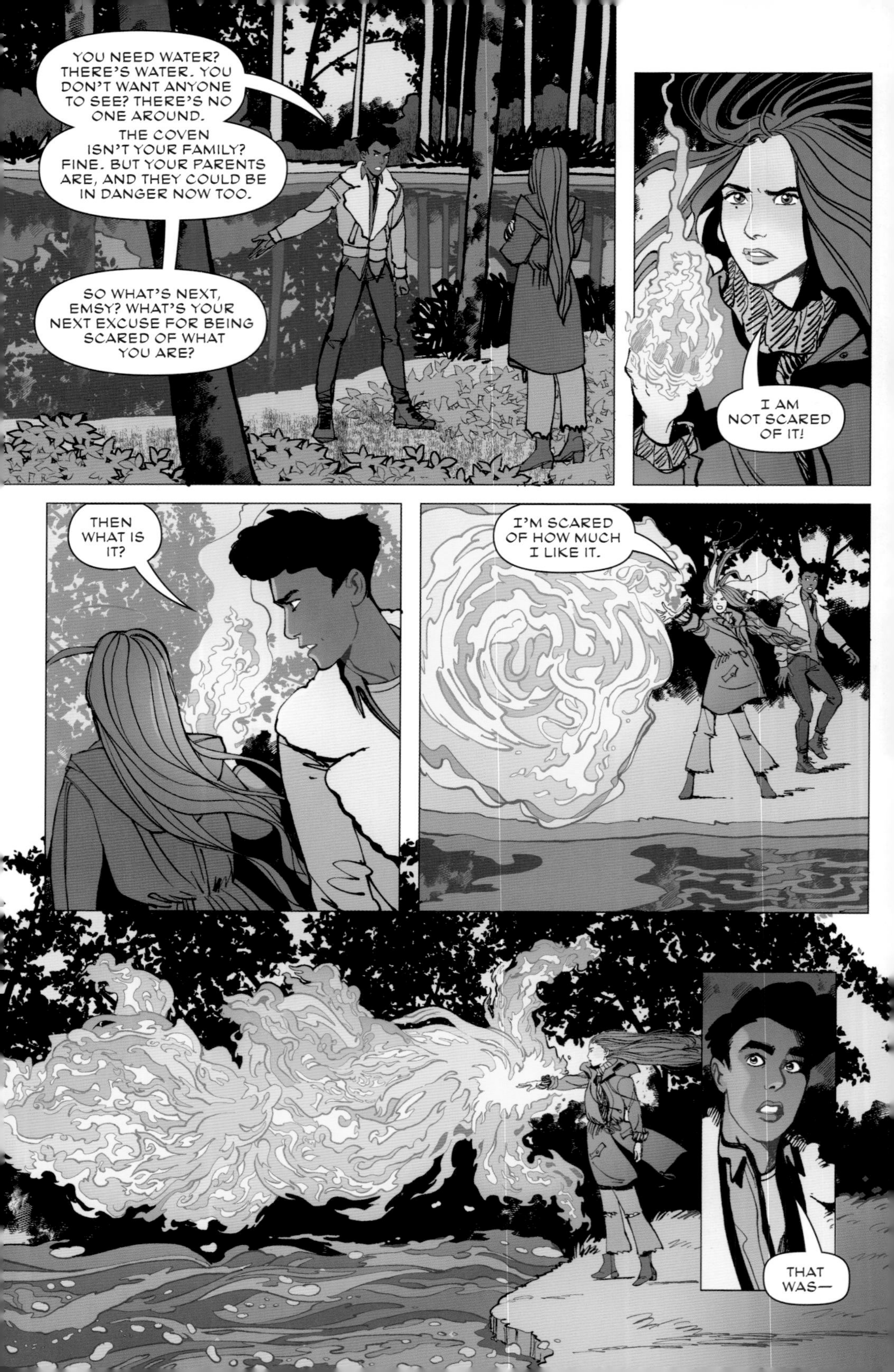
YOU NEED WATER? THERE'S WATER. YOU DON'T WANT ANYONE TO SEE? THERE'S NO ONE AROUND.
THE COVEN ISN'T YOUR FAMILY? FINE. BUT YOUR PARENTS ARE, AND THEY COULD BE IN DANGER NOW TOO.
SO WHAT'S NEXT, EMSY? WHAT'S YOUR NEXT EXCUSE FOR BEING SCARED OF WHAT YOU ARE?
I AM NOT SCARED OF IT!
THEN WHAT IS IT?
I'M SCARED OF HOW MUCH I LIKE IT.
THAT WAS—

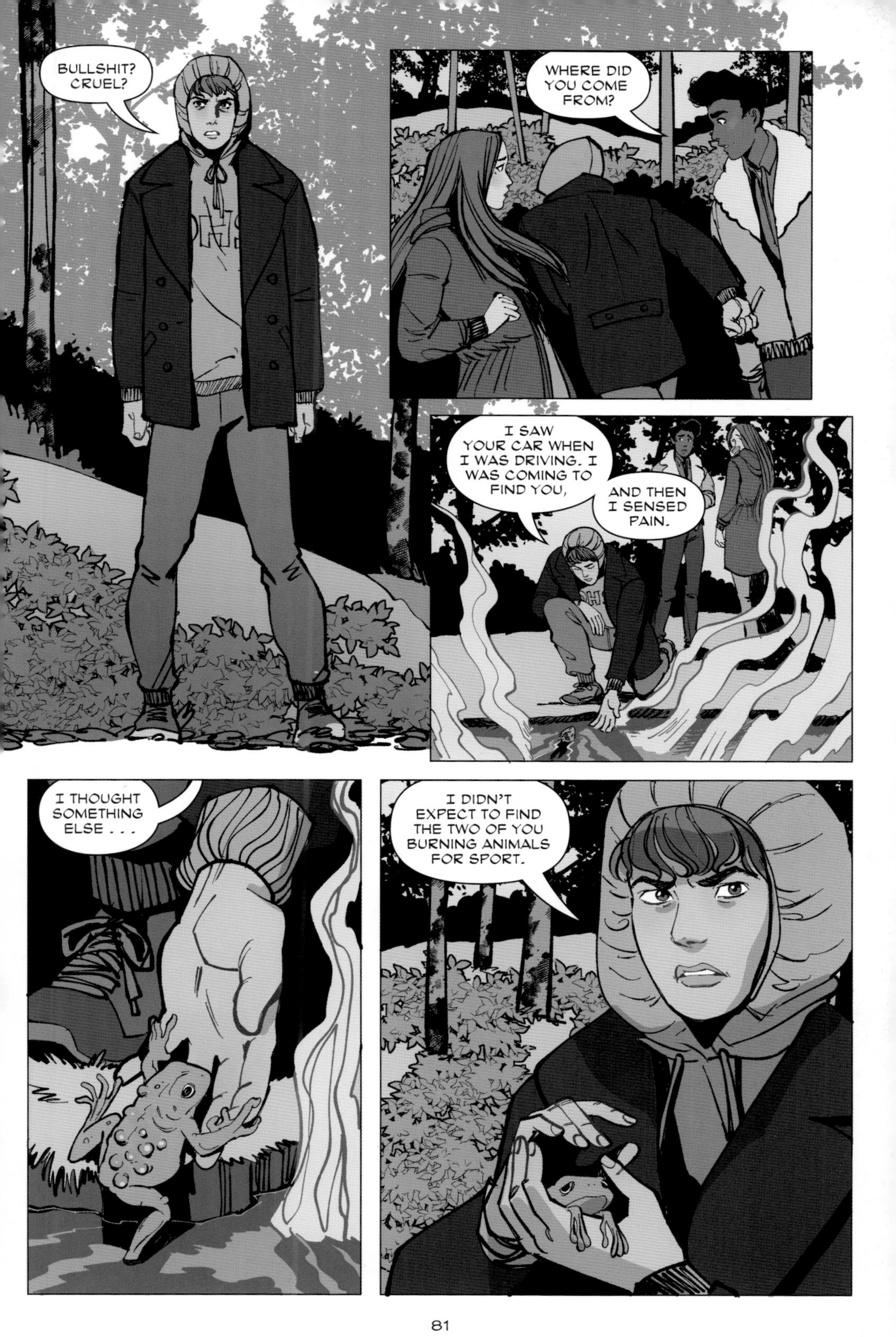

BULLSHIT? CRUEL?
WHERE DID YOU COME FROM?
I SAW YOUR CAR WHEN I WAS DRIVING. I WAS COMING TO FIND YOU,
AND THEN I SENSED PAIN.
I THOUGHT SOMETHING ELSE . . .
I DIDN'T EXPECT TO FIND THE TWO OF YOU BURNING ANIMALS FOR SPORT.

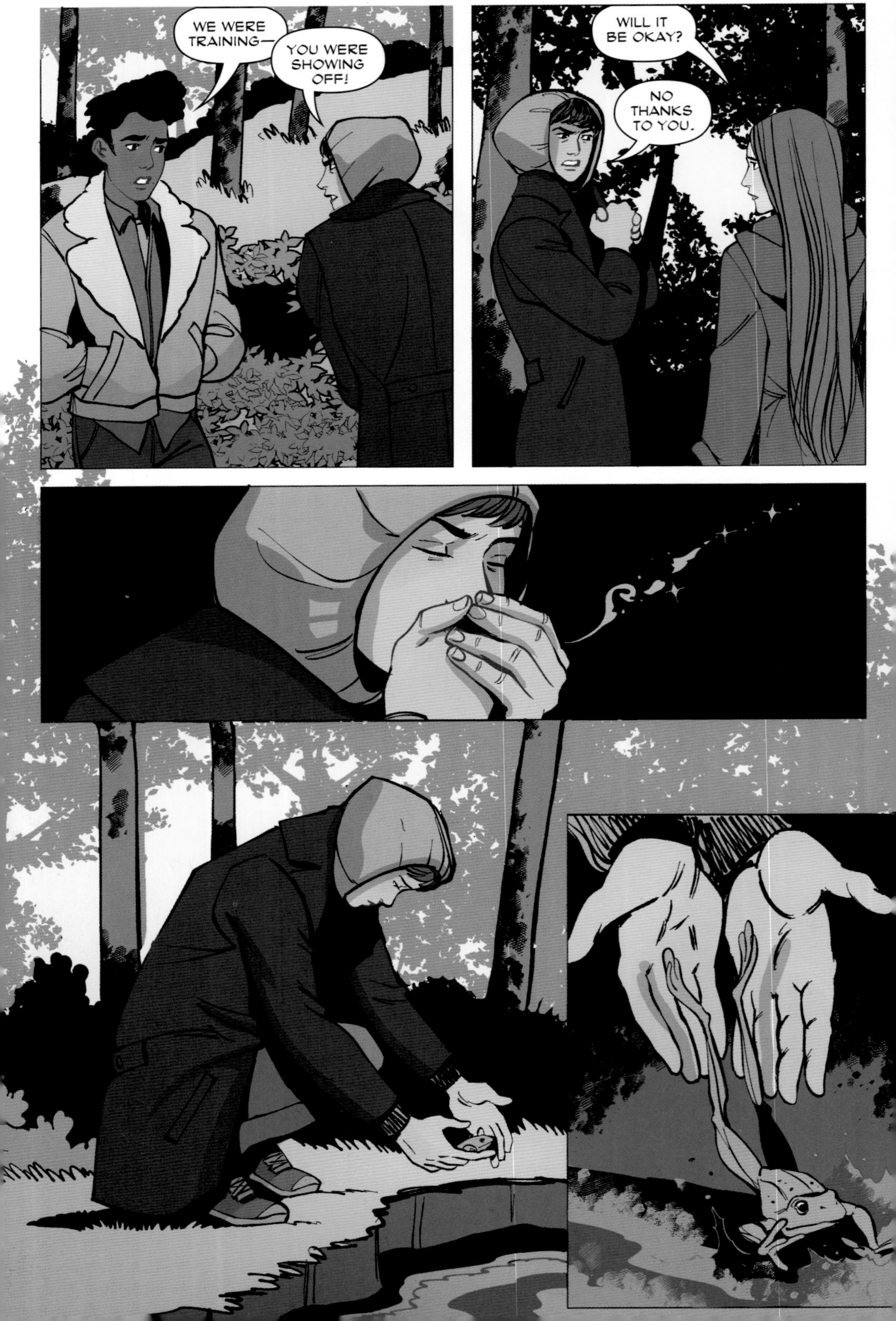
WE WERE TRAINING—
YOU WERE SHOWING OFF!
WILL IT BE OKAY?
NO THANKS TO YOU.

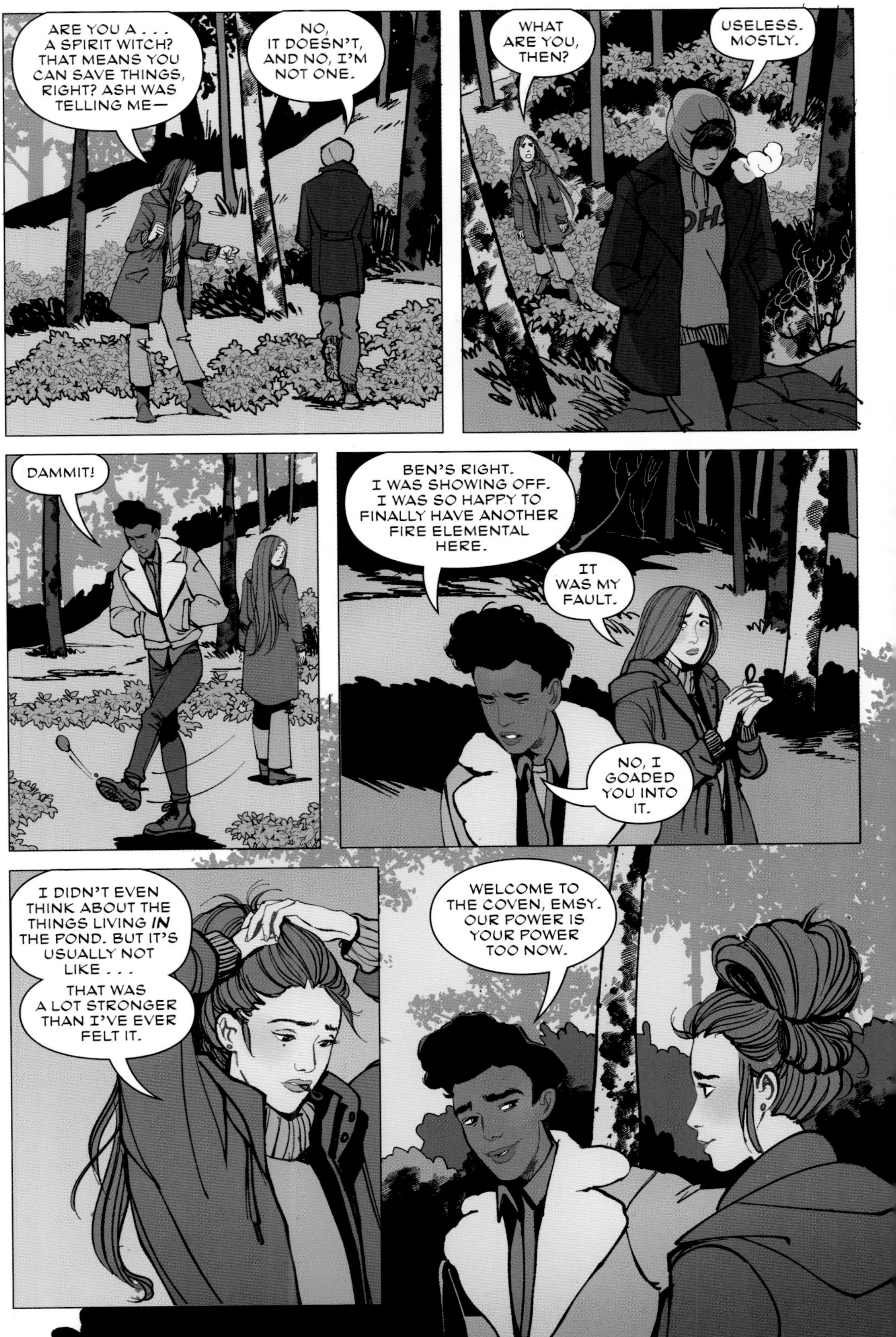
ARE YOU A . . . A SPIRIT WITCH? THAT MEANS YOU CAN SAVE THINGS, RIGHT? ASH WAS TELLING ME—
NO, IT DOESN'T, AND NO, I'M NOT ONE.
WHAT ARE YOU, THEN?
USELESS. MOSTLY.
DAMMIT!
BEN'S RIGHT. I WAS SHOWING OFF. I WAS SO HAPPY TO FINALLY HAVE ANOTHER FIRE ELEMENTAL HERE.
IT WAS MY FAULT.
NO, I GOADED YOU INTO IT.
I DIDN'T EVEN THINK ABOUT THE THINGS LIVING *IN* THE POND. BUT IT'S USUALLY NOT LIKE . . .
THAT WAS A LOT STRONGER THAN I'VE EVER FELT IT.
WELCOME TO THE COVEN, EMSY. OUR POWER IS YOUR POWER TOO NOW.

DAY ONE IN A NEW PLACE WITH NEW FRIENDS AND YOU SET A FROG ON FIRE?

NOT ON PURPOSE!

ALSO, LIKE TODAY COULDN'T GET ANY SHITTIER, I SOMEHOW HAVE A TON OF HOMEWORK EVEN THOUGH IT'S MY FIRST DAY.

I'M SORRY, BABY. I WOULD HELP IF I COULD.

DID YOU AT LEAST FIND OUT ANYTHING THAT MIGHT HELP GET YOU BACK HOME?

YOU DON'T WANT TO KNOW.

TRY ME.

LET'S JUST SAY TODAY WAS A CRASH COURSE IN WITCH HISTORY.

AND IT'S MORE BLOOD AND BACKSTABBING THAN FUN AND GAMES.

YIKES.

YEAH.

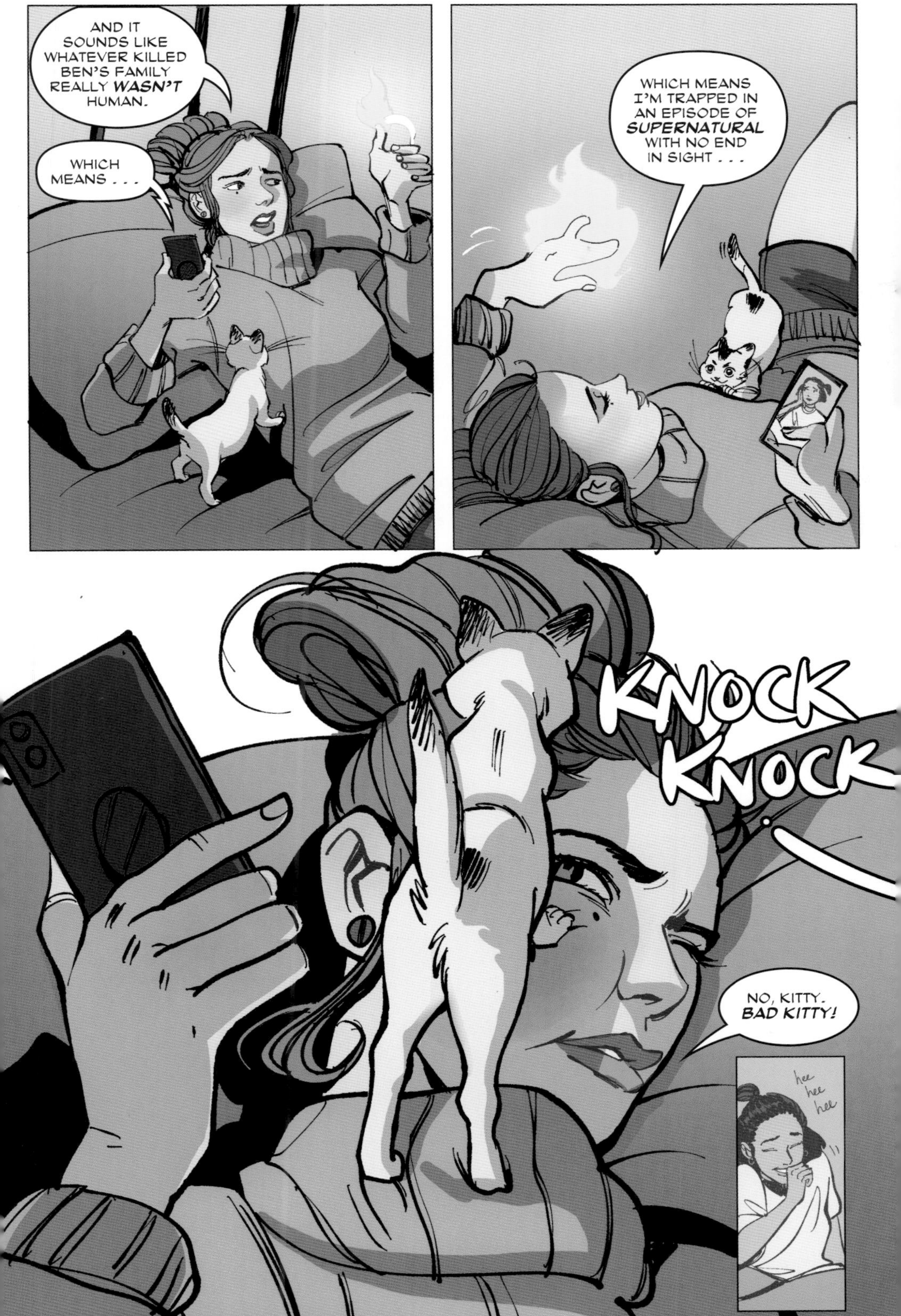
AND IT SOUNDS LIKE WHATEVER KILLED BEN'S FAMILY REALLY ***WASN'T*** HUMAN.
WHICH MEANS . . .
WHICH MEANS I'M TRAPPED IN AN EPISODE OF ***SUPERNATURAL*** WITH NO END IN SIGHT . . .
KNOCK KNOCK
NO, KITTY. ***BAD KITTY!***
hee hee hee

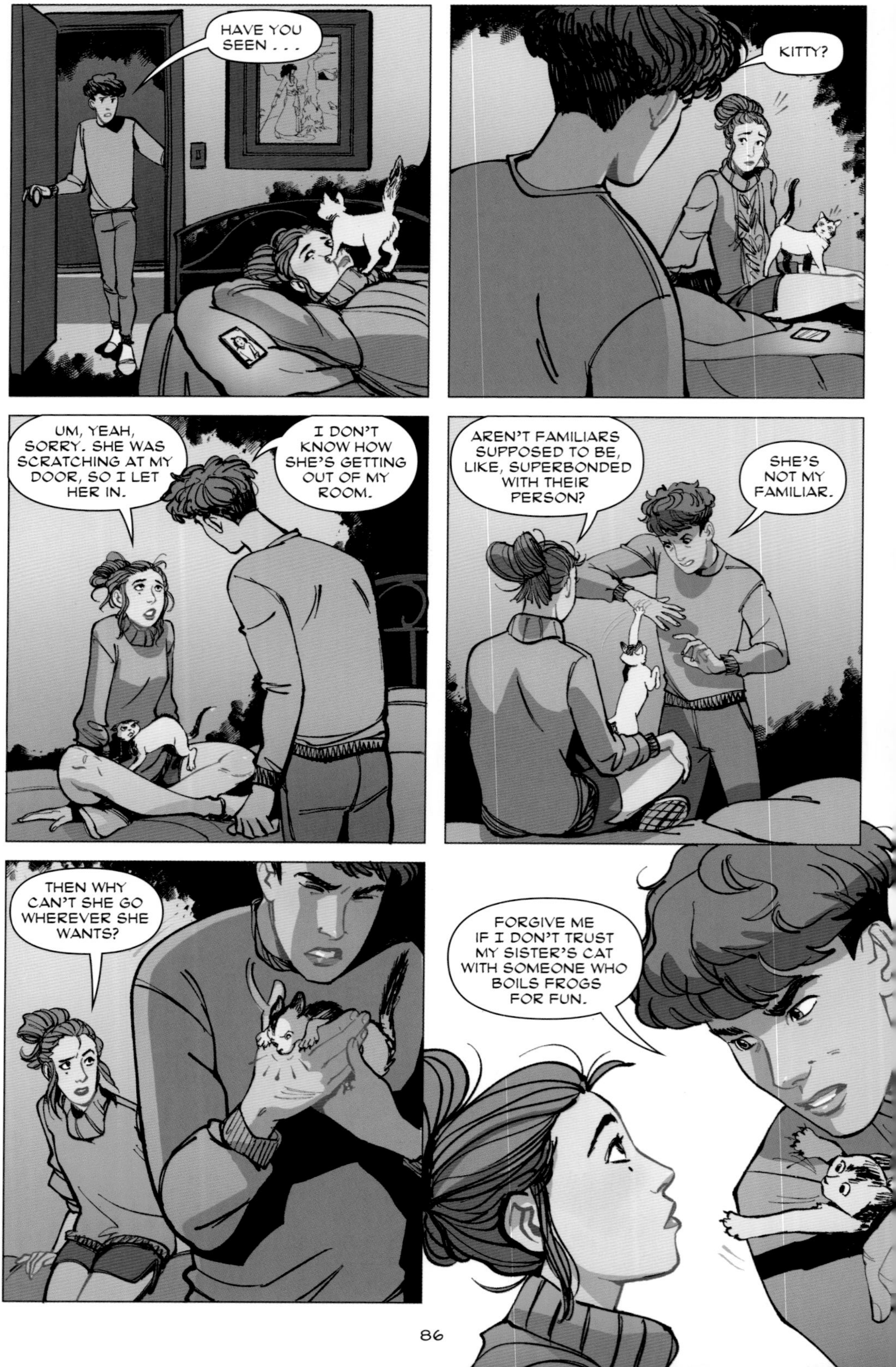
HAVE YOU SEEN . . .
KITTY?
UM, YEAH, SORRY. SHE WAS SCRATCHING AT MY DOOR, SO I LET HER IN.
I DON'T KNOW HOW SHE'S GETTING OUT OF MY ROOM.
AREN'T FAMILIARS SUPPOSED TO BE, LIKE, SUPERBONDED WITH THEIR PERSON?
SHE'S NOT MY FAMILIAR.
THEN WHY CAN'T SHE GO WHEREVER SHE WANTS?
FORGIVE ME IF I DON'T TRUST MY SISTER'S CAT WITH SOMEONE WHO BOILS FROGS FOR FUN.

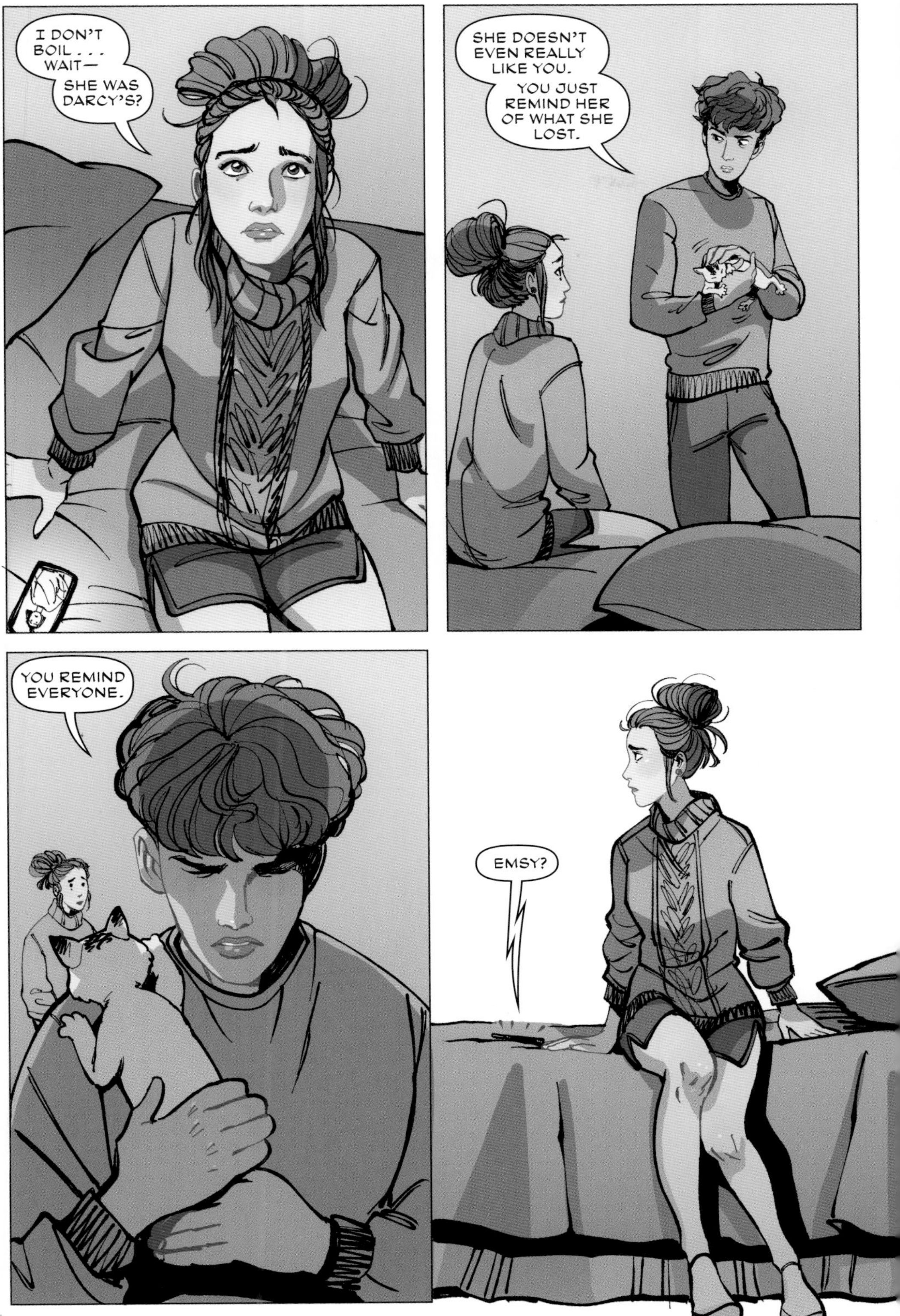

I DON'T BOIL . . . WAIT—
SHE WAS DARCY'S?
SHE DOESN'T EVEN REALLY LIKE YOU.
YOU JUST REMIND HER OF WHAT SHE LOST.
YOU REMIND EVERYONE.
EMSY?

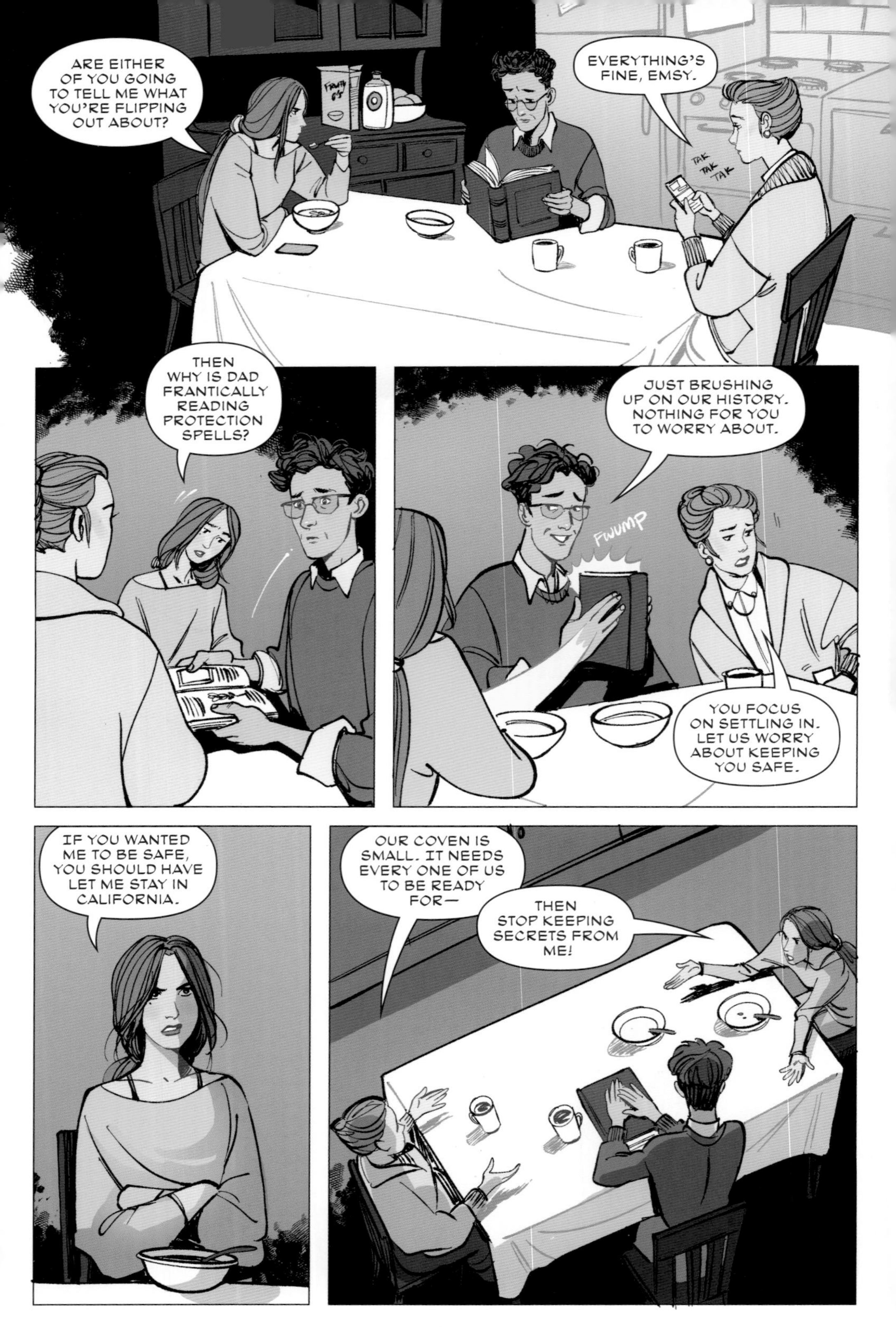
ARE EITHER OF YOU GOING TO TELL ME WHAT YOU'RE FLIPPING OUT ABOUT?
EVERYTHING'S FINE, EMSY.
TAK TAK TAK
THEN WHY IS DAD FRANTICALLY READING PROTECTION SPELLS?
JUST BRUSHING UP ON OUR HISTORY. NOTHING FOR YOU TO WORRY ABOUT.
FWUMP
YOU FOCUS ON SETTLING IN. LET US WORRY ABOUT KEEPING YOU SAFE.
IF YOU WANTED ME TO BE SAFE, YOU SHOULD HAVE LET ME STAY IN CALIFORNIA.
OUR COVEN IS SMALL. IT NEEDS EVERY ONE OF US TO BE READY FOR—
THEN STOP KEEPING SECRETS FROM ME!

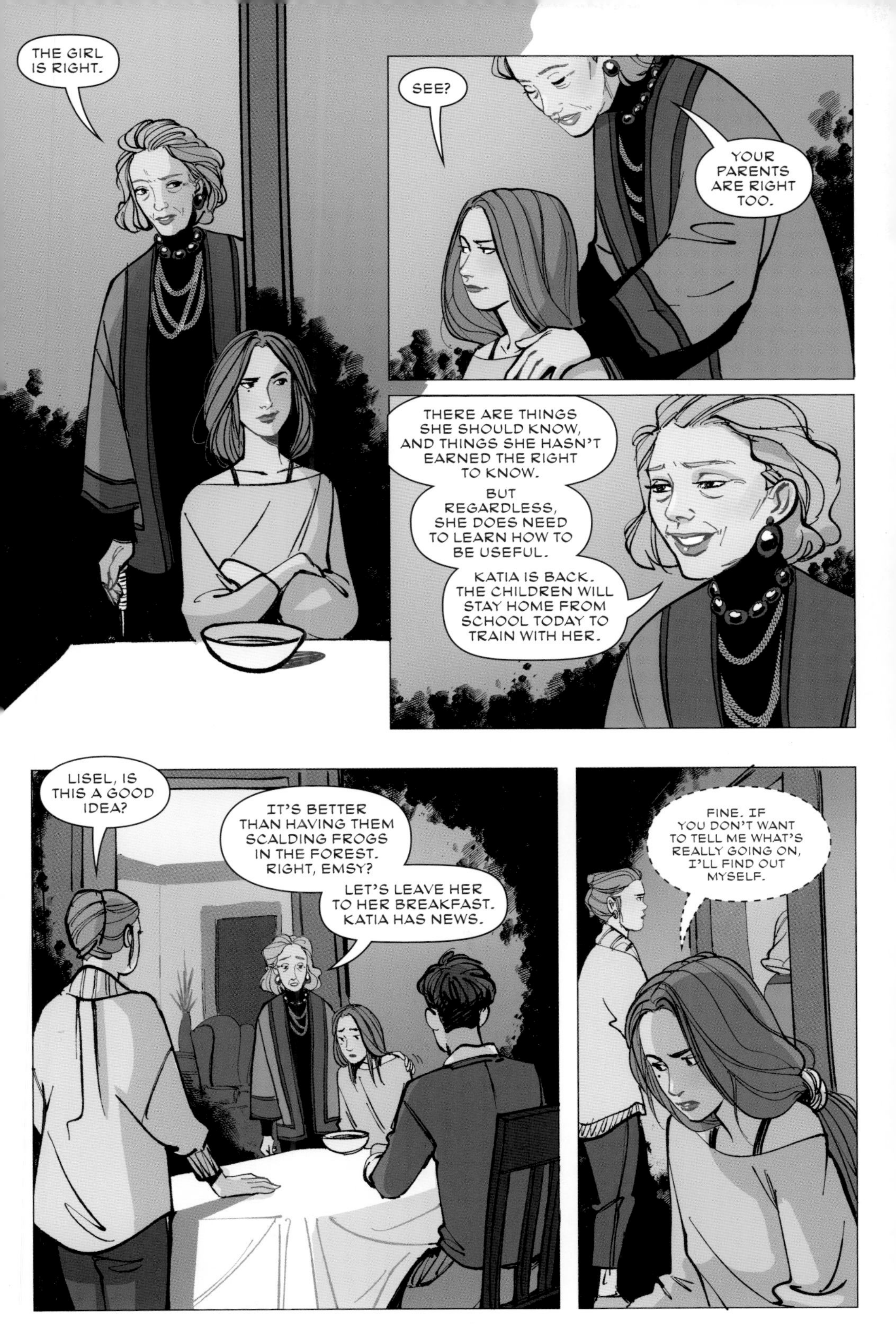

THE GIRL IS RIGHT.
SEE?
YOUR PARENTS ARE RIGHT TOO.
THERE ARE THINGS SHE SHOULD KNOW, AND THINGS SHE HASN'T EARNED THE RIGHT TO KNOW.
BUT REGARDLESS, SHE DOES NEED TO LEARN HOW TO BE USEFUL.
KATIA IS BACK. THE CHILDREN WILL STAY HOME FROM SCHOOL TODAY TO TRAIN WITH HER.
LISEL, IS THIS A GOOD IDEA?
IT'S BETTER THAN HAVING THEM SCALDING FROGS IN THE FOREST. RIGHT, EMSY?
LET'S LEAVE HER TO HER BREAKFAST. KATIA HAS NEWS.
FINE. IF YOU DON'T WANT TO TELL ME WHAT'S REALLY GOING ON, I'LL FIND OUT MYSELF.

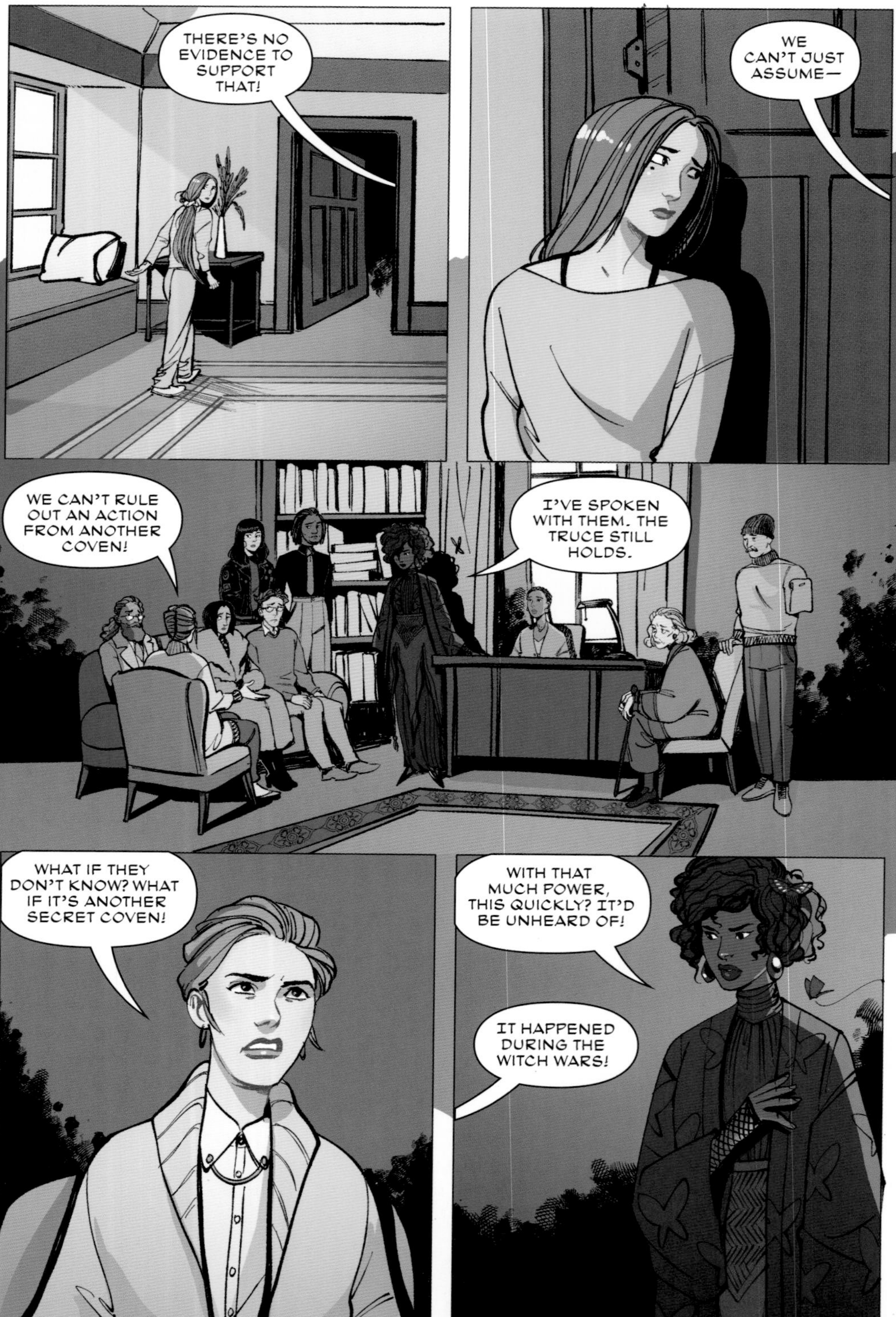
THERE'S NO EVIDENCE TO SUPPORT THAT!
WE CAN'T JUST ASSUME—
WE CAN'T RULE OUT AN ACTION FROM ANOTHER COVEN!
I'VE SPOKEN WITH THEM. THE TRUCE STILL HOLDS.
WHAT IF THEY DON'T KNOW? WHAT IF IT'S ANOTHER SECRET COVEN!
WITH THAT MUCH POWER, THIS QUICKLY? IT'D BE UNHEARD OF!
IT HAPPENED DURING THE WITCH WARS!

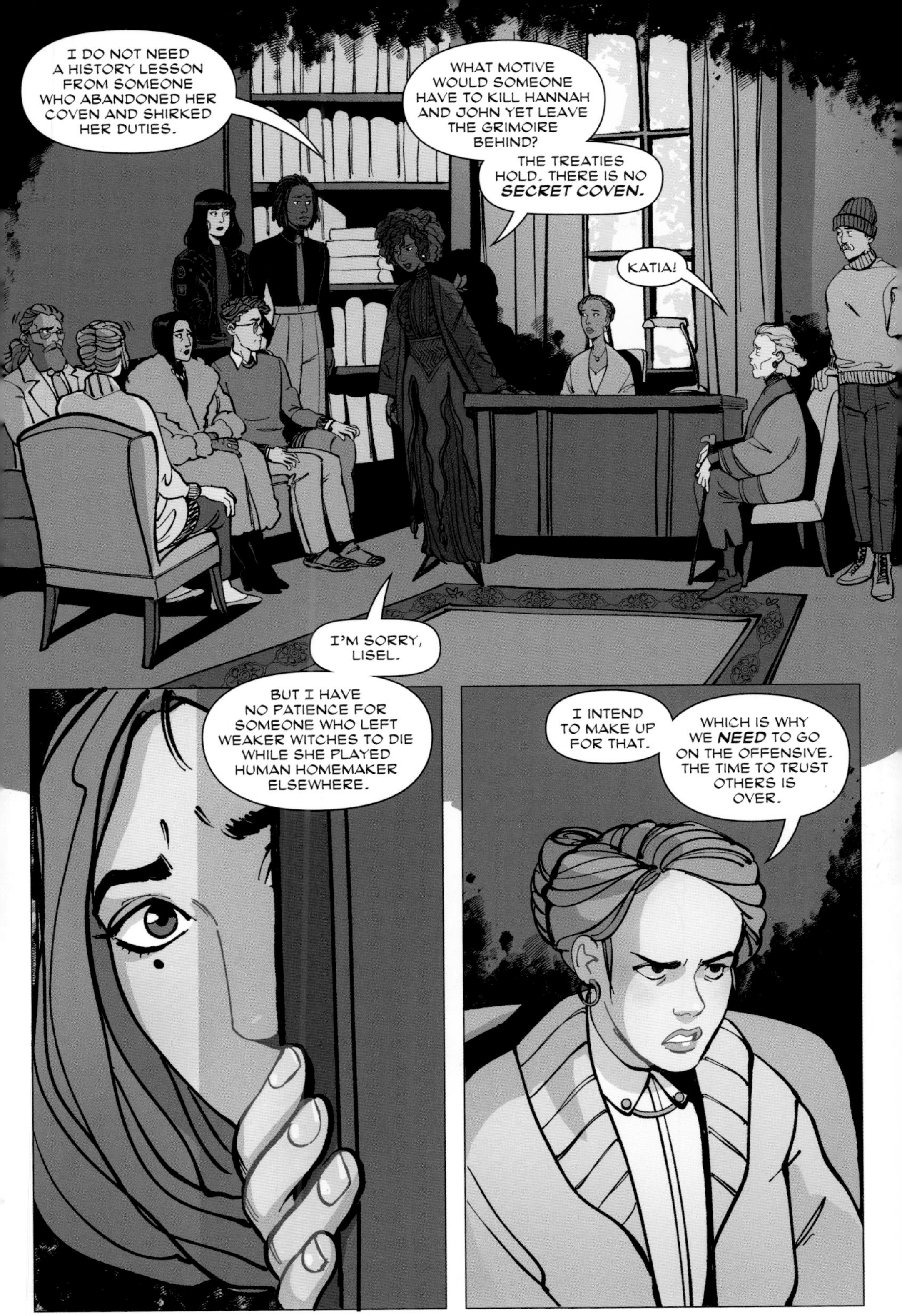

I DO NOT NEED A HISTORY LESSON FROM SOMEONE WHO ABANDONED HER COVEN AND SHIRKED HER DUTIES.
WHAT MOTIVE WOULD SOMEONE HAVE TO KILL HANNAH AND JOHN YET LEAVE THE GRIMOIRE BEHIND?
THE TREATIES HOLD. THERE IS NO *SECRET COVEN.*
KATIA!
I'M SORRY, LISEL.
BUT I HAVE NO PATIENCE FOR SOMEONE WHO LEFT WEAKER WITCHES TO DIE WHILE SHE PLAYED HUMAN HOMEMAKER ELSEWHERE.
I INTEND TO MAKE UP FOR THAT.
WHICH IS WHY WE ***NEED*** TO GO ON THE OFFENSIVE. THE TIME TO TRUST OTHERS IS OVER.

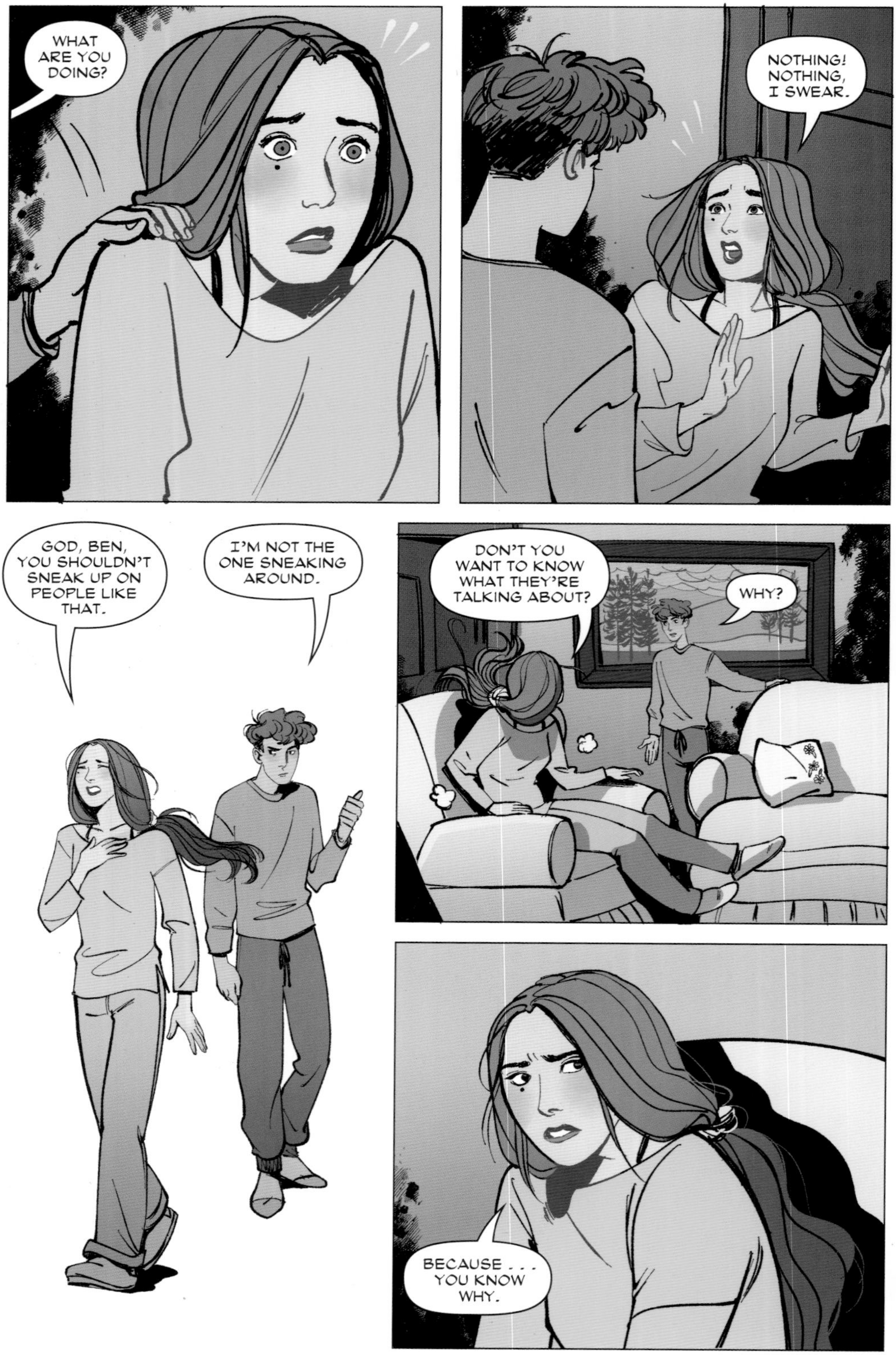
WHAT ARE YOU DOING?
NOTHING! NOTHING, I SWEAR.
GOD, BEN, YOU SHOULDN'T SNEAK UP ON PEOPLE LIKE THAT.
I'M NOT THE ONE SNEAKING AROUND.
DON'T YOU WANT TO KNOW WHAT THEY'RE TALKING ABOUT?
WHY?
BECAUSE . . . YOU KNOW WHY.

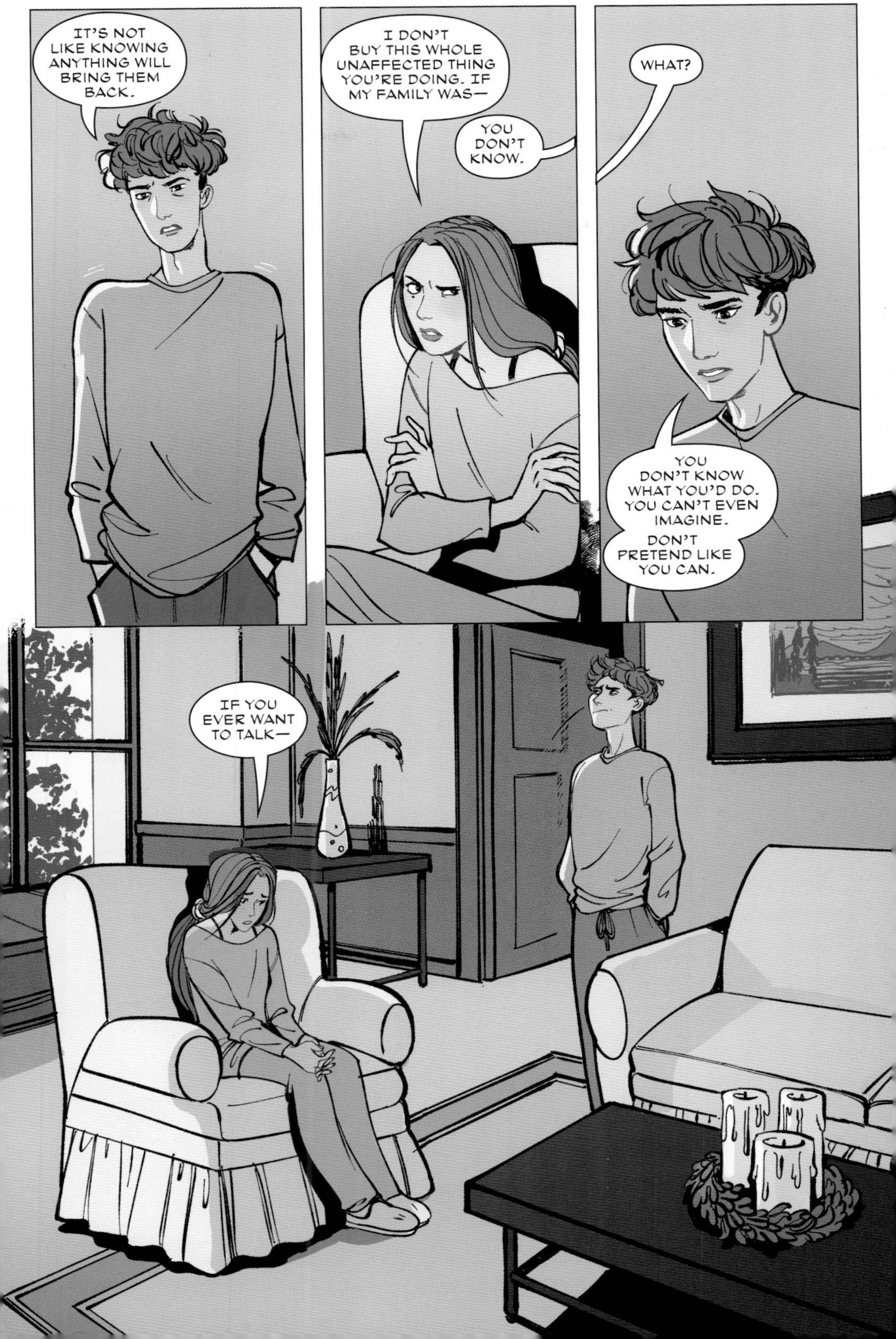
IT'S NOT LIKE KNOWING ANYTHING WILL BRING THEM BACK.
I DON'T BUY THIS WHOLE UNAFFECTED THING YOU'RE DOING. IF MY FAMILY WAS—
YOU DON'T KNOW.
WHAT?
YOU DON'T KNOW WHAT YOU'D DO. YOU CAN'T EVEN IMAGINE.
DON'T PRETEND LIKE YOU CAN.
IF YOU EVER WANT TO TALK—

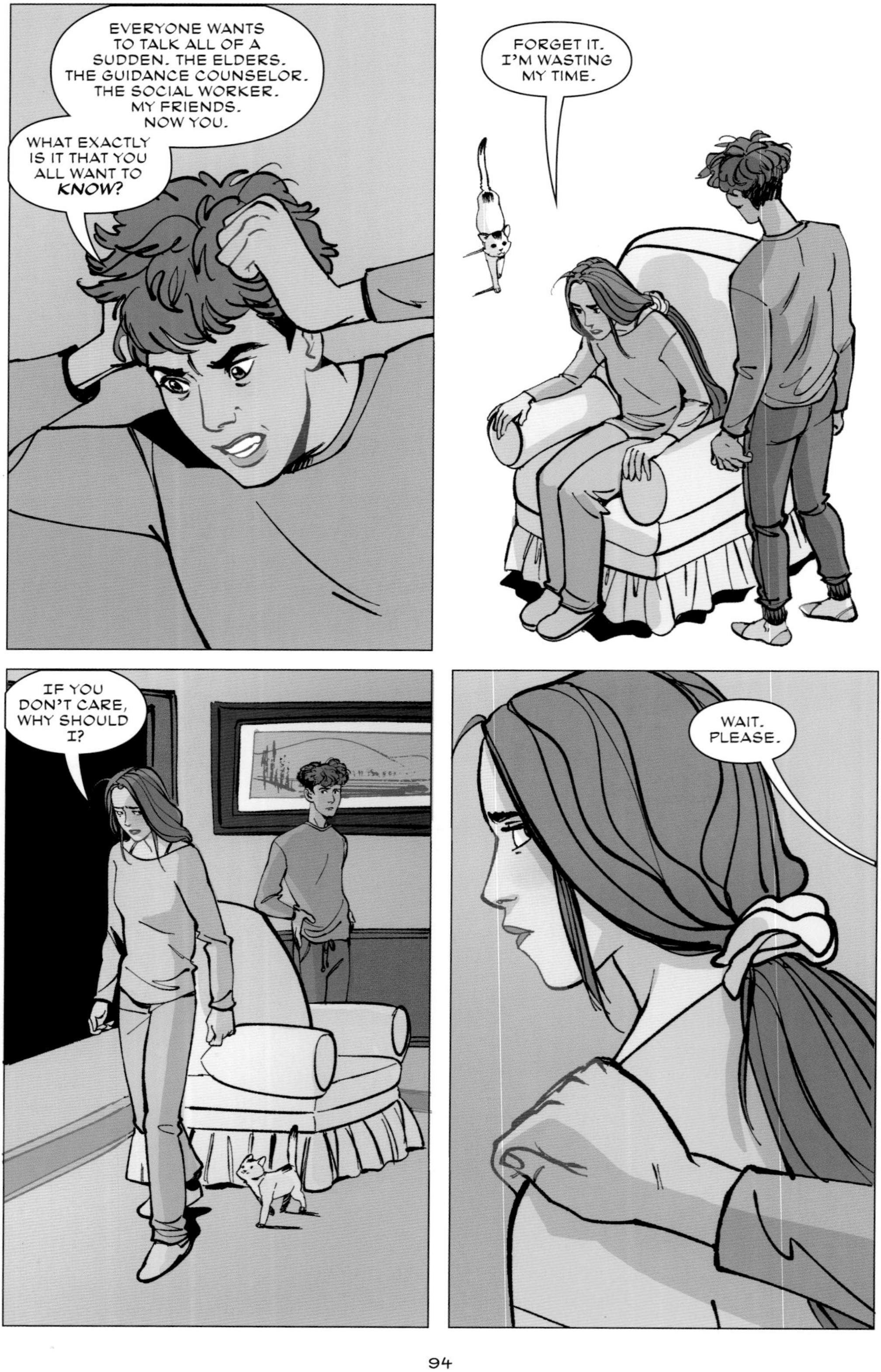
EVERYONE WANTS TO TALK ALL OF A SUDDEN. THE ELDERS. THE GUIDANCE COUNSELOR. THE SOCIAL WORKER. MY FRIENDS. NOW YOU.
WHAT EXACTLY IS IT THAT YOU ALL WANT TO KNOW?
FORGET IT. I'M WASTING MY TIME.
IF YOU DON'T CARE, WHY SHOULD I?
WAIT. PLEASE.

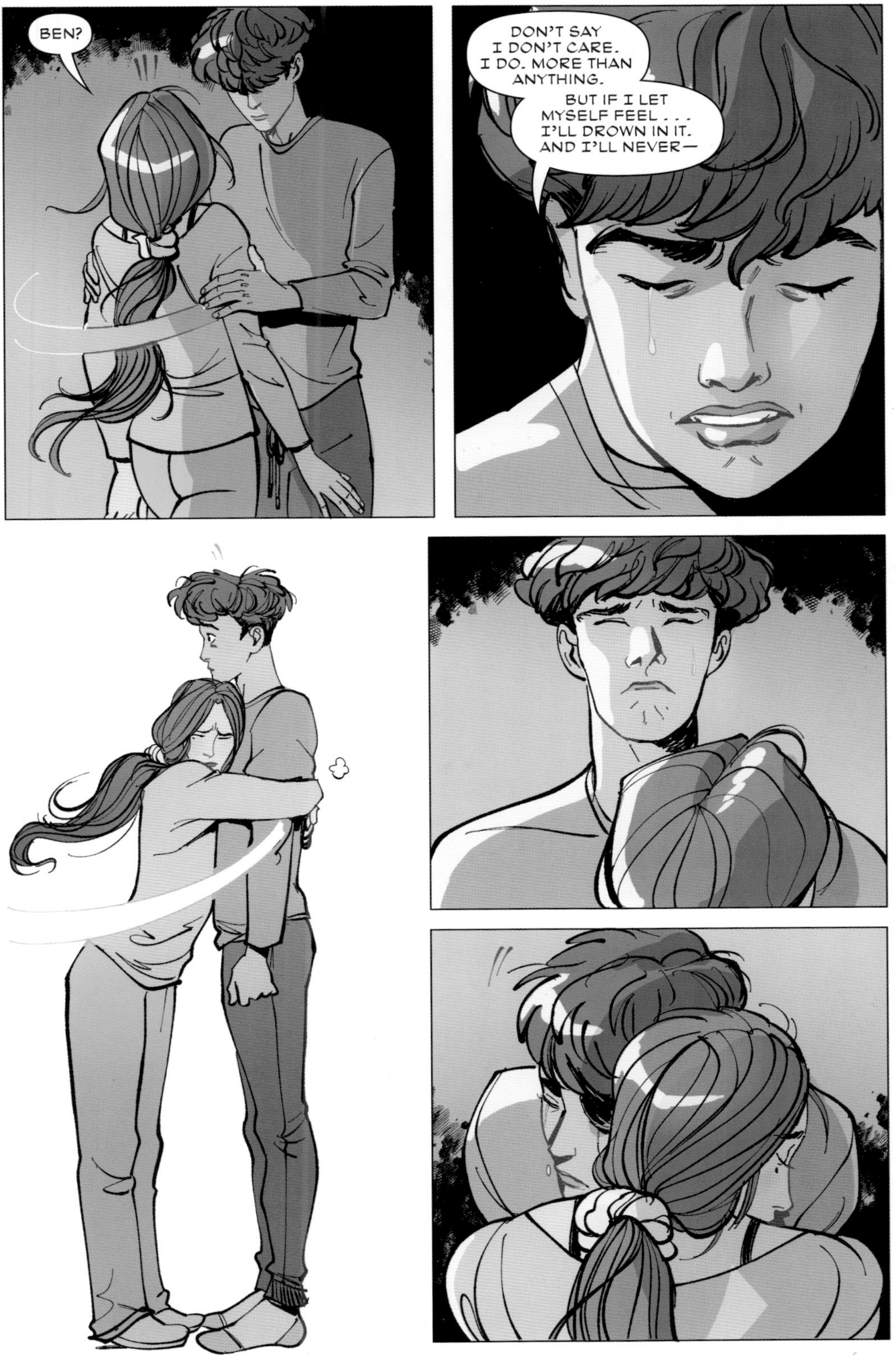
BEN?
DON'T SAY I DON'T CARE. I DO. MORE THAN ANYTHING.
BUT IF I LET MYSELF FEEL . . . I'LL DROWN IN IT. AND I'LL NEVER—

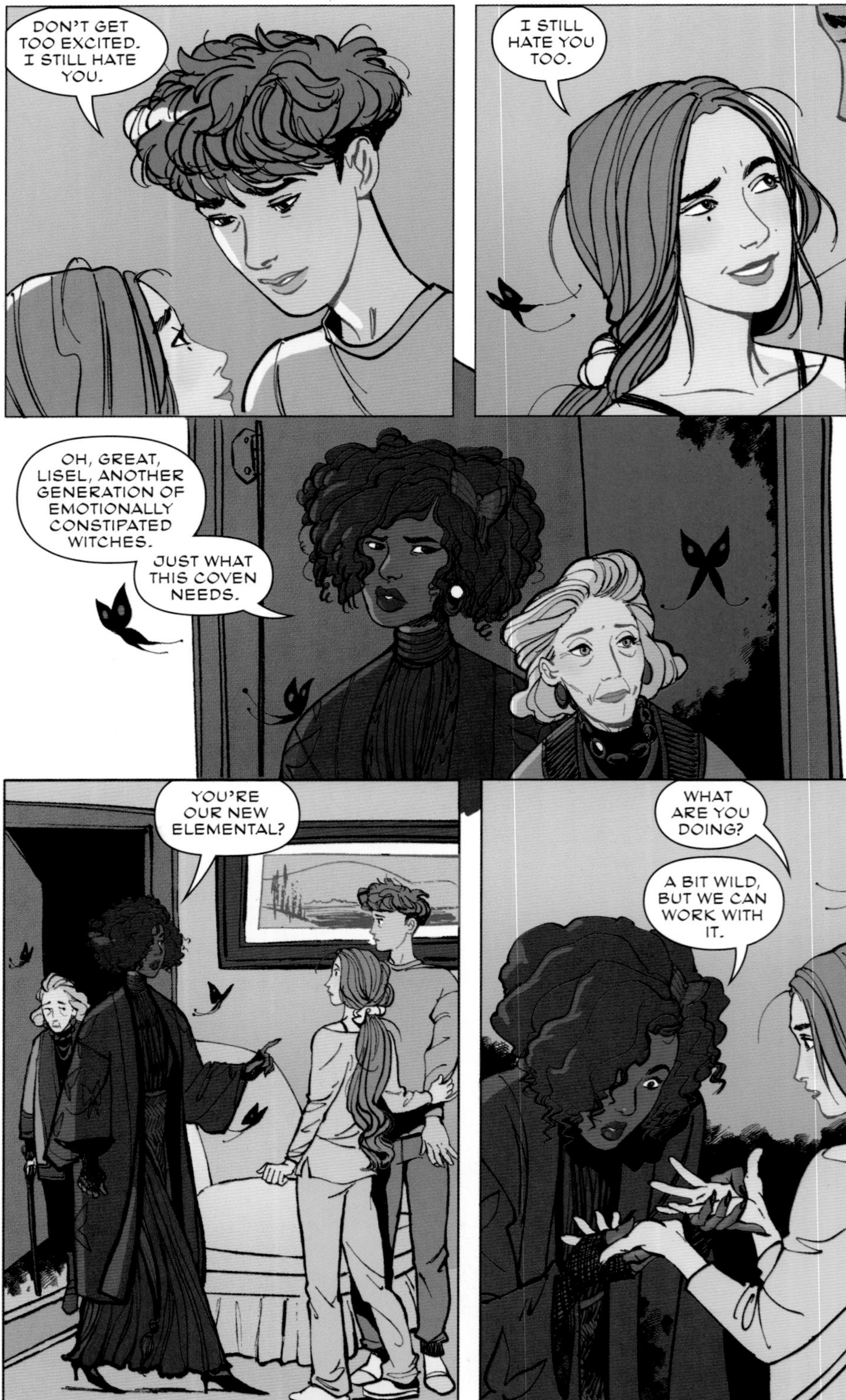
DON'T GET TOO EXCITED. I STILL HATE YOU.
I STILL HATE YOU TOO.
OH, GREAT, LISEL, ANOTHER GENERATION OF EMOTIONALLY CONSTIPATED WITCHES.
JUST WHAT THIS COVEN NEEDS.
YOU'RE OUR NEW ELEMENTAL?
WHAT ARE YOU DOING?
A BIT WILD, BUT WE CAN WORK WITH IT.

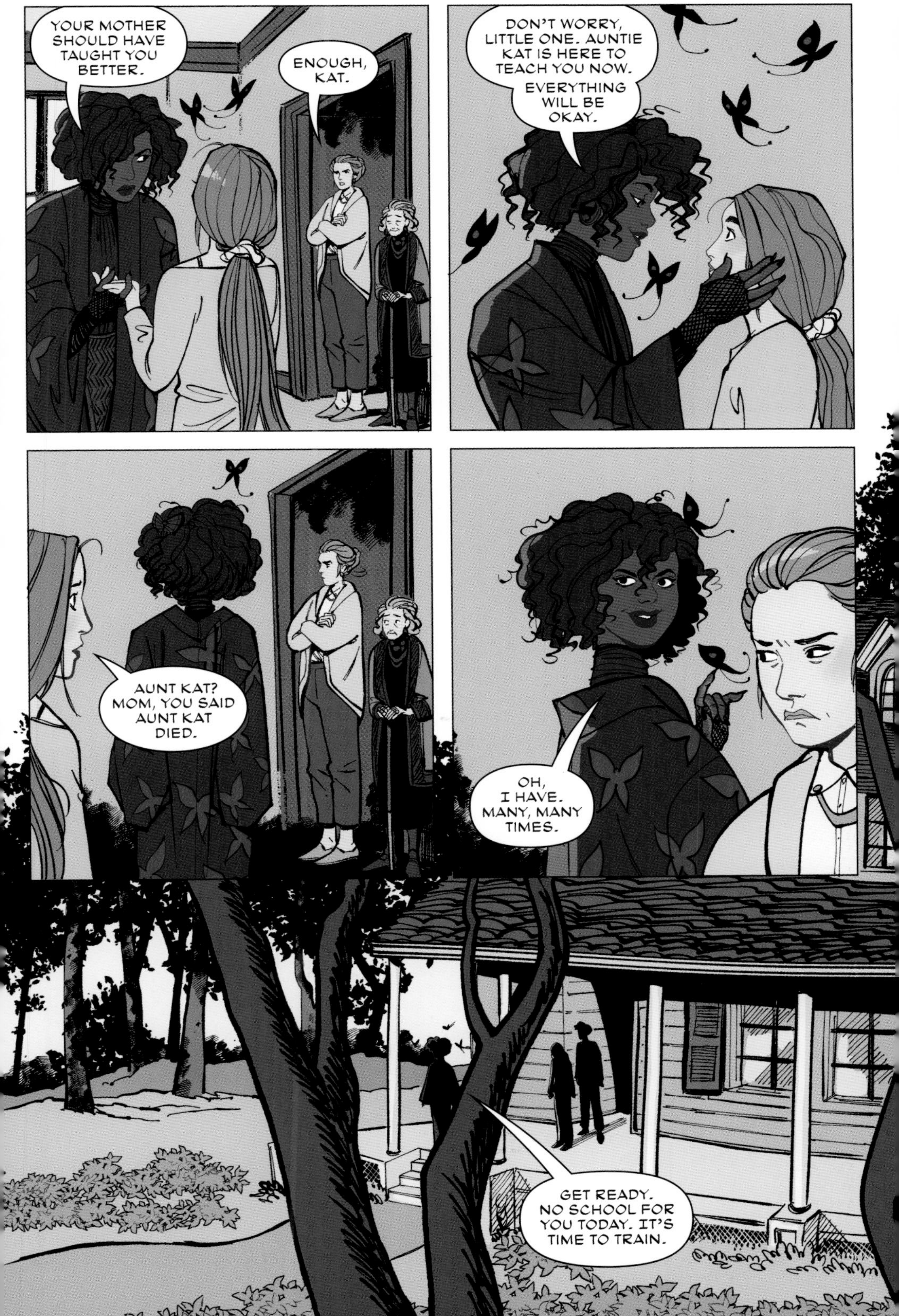
YOUR MOTHER SHOULD HAVE TAUGHT YOU BETTER.
ENOUGH, KAT.
DON'T WORRY, LITTLE ONE. AUNTIE KAT IS HERE TO TEACH YOU NOW.
EVERYTHING WILL BE OKAY.
AUNT KAT? MOM, YOU SAID AUNT KAT DIED.
OH, I HAVE. MANY, MANY TIMES.
GET READY. NO SCHOOL FOR YOU TODAY. IT'S TIME TO TRAIN.

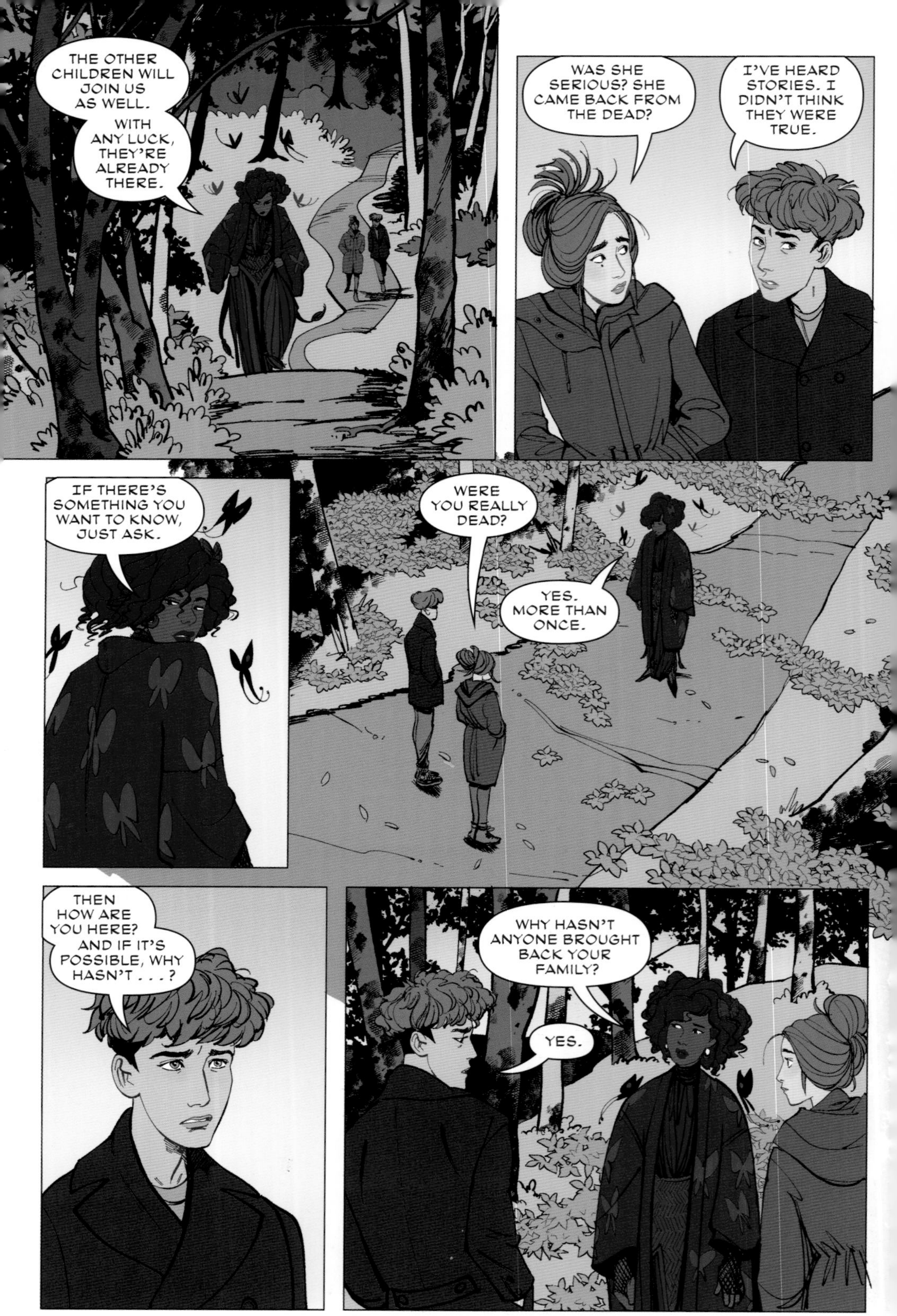
THE OTHER CHILDREN WILL JOIN US AS WELL.
WITH ANY LUCK, THEY'RE ALREADY THERE.
WAS SHE SERIOUS? SHE CAME BACK FROM THE DEAD?
I'VE HEARD STORIES. I DIDN'T THINK THEY WERE TRUE.
IF THERE'S SOMETHING YOU WANT TO KNOW, JUST ASK.
WERE YOU REALLY DEAD?
YES. MORE THAN ONCE.
THEN HOW ARE YOU HERE? AND IF IT'S POSSIBLE, WHY HASN'T . . . ?
WHY HASN'T ANYONE BROUGHT BACK YOUR FAMILY?
YES.

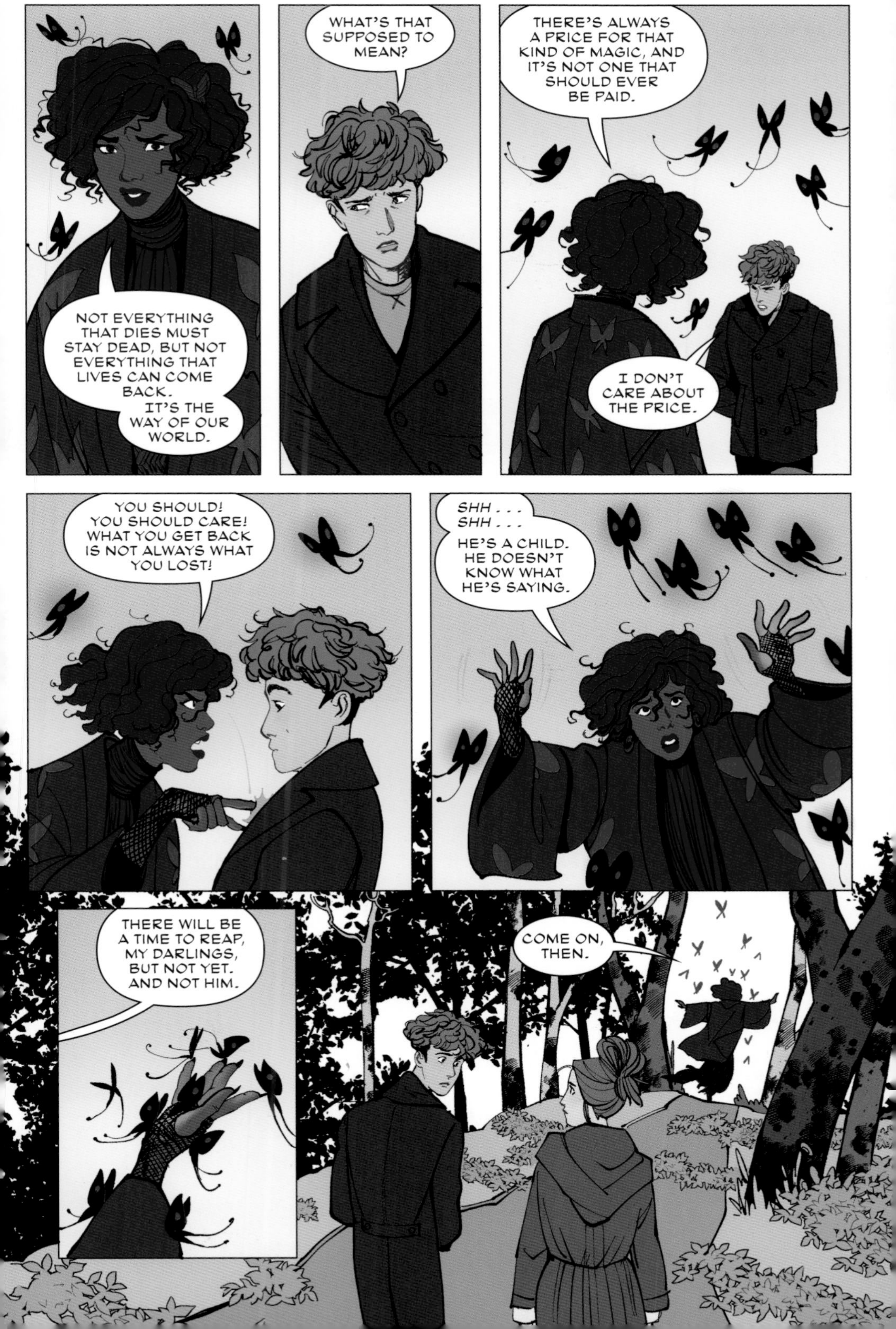
NOT EVERYTHING THAT DIES MUST STAY DEAD, BUT NOT EVERYTHING THAT LIVES CAN COME BACK.
IT'S THE WAY OF OUR WORLD.
WHAT'S THAT SUPPOSED TO MEAN?
THERE'S ALWAYS A PRICE FOR THAT KIND OF MAGIC, AND IT'S NOT ONE THAT SHOULD EVER BE PAID.
I DON'T CARE ABOUT THE PRICE.
YOU SHOULD! YOU SHOULD CARE! WHAT YOU GET BACK IS NOT ALWAYS WHAT YOU LOST!
SHH . . . SHH . . .
HE'S A CHILD. HE DOESN'T KNOW WHAT HE'S SAYING.
THERE WILL BE A TIME TO REAP, MY DARLINGS, BUT NOT YET. AND NOT HIM.
COME ON, THEN.

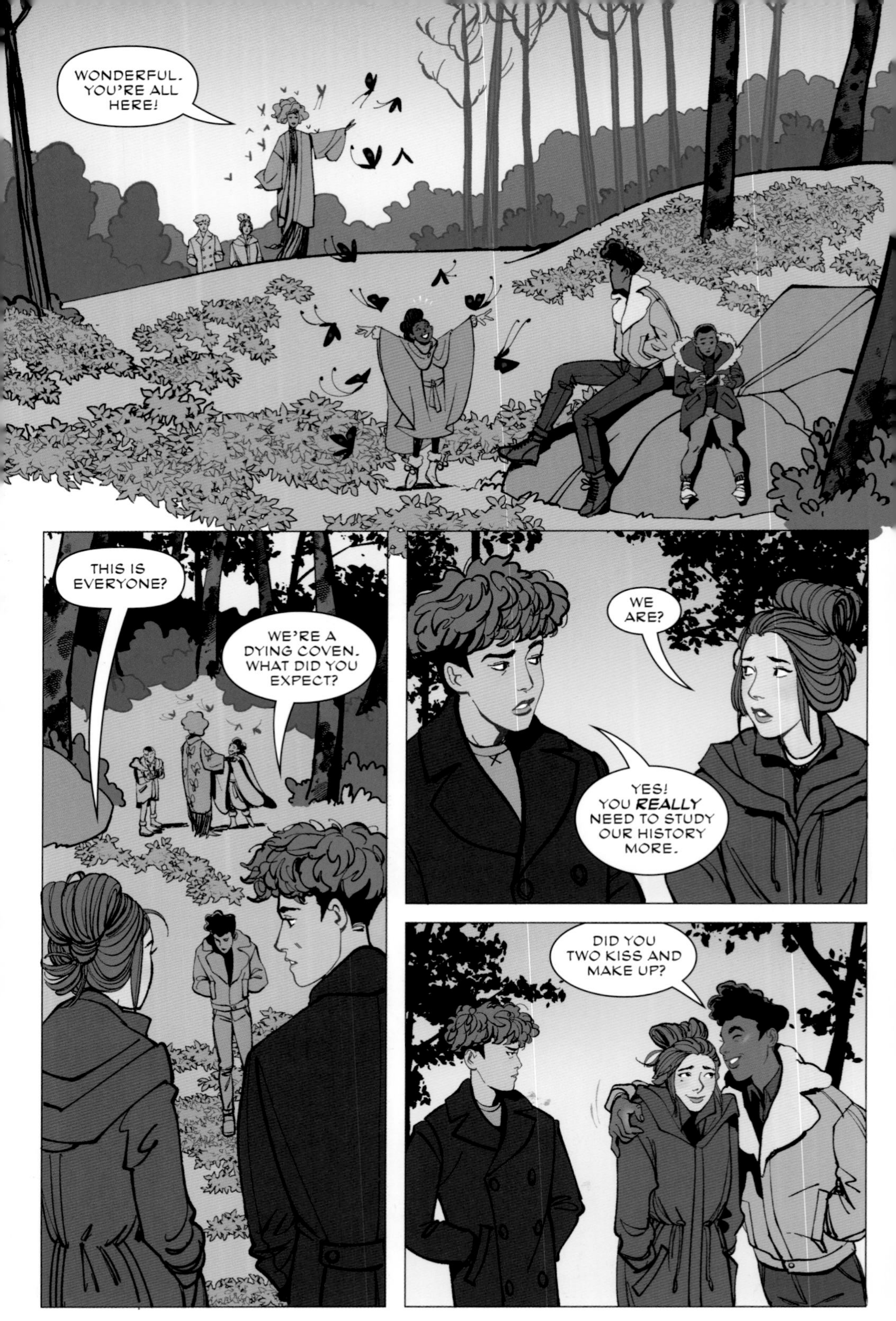
WONDERFUL. YOU'RE ALL HERE!
THIS IS EVERYONE?
WE'RE A DYING COVEN. WHAT DID YOU EXPECT?
WE ARE?
YES! YOU **REALLY** NEED TO STUDY OUR HISTORY MORE.
DID YOU TWO KISS AND MAKE UP?

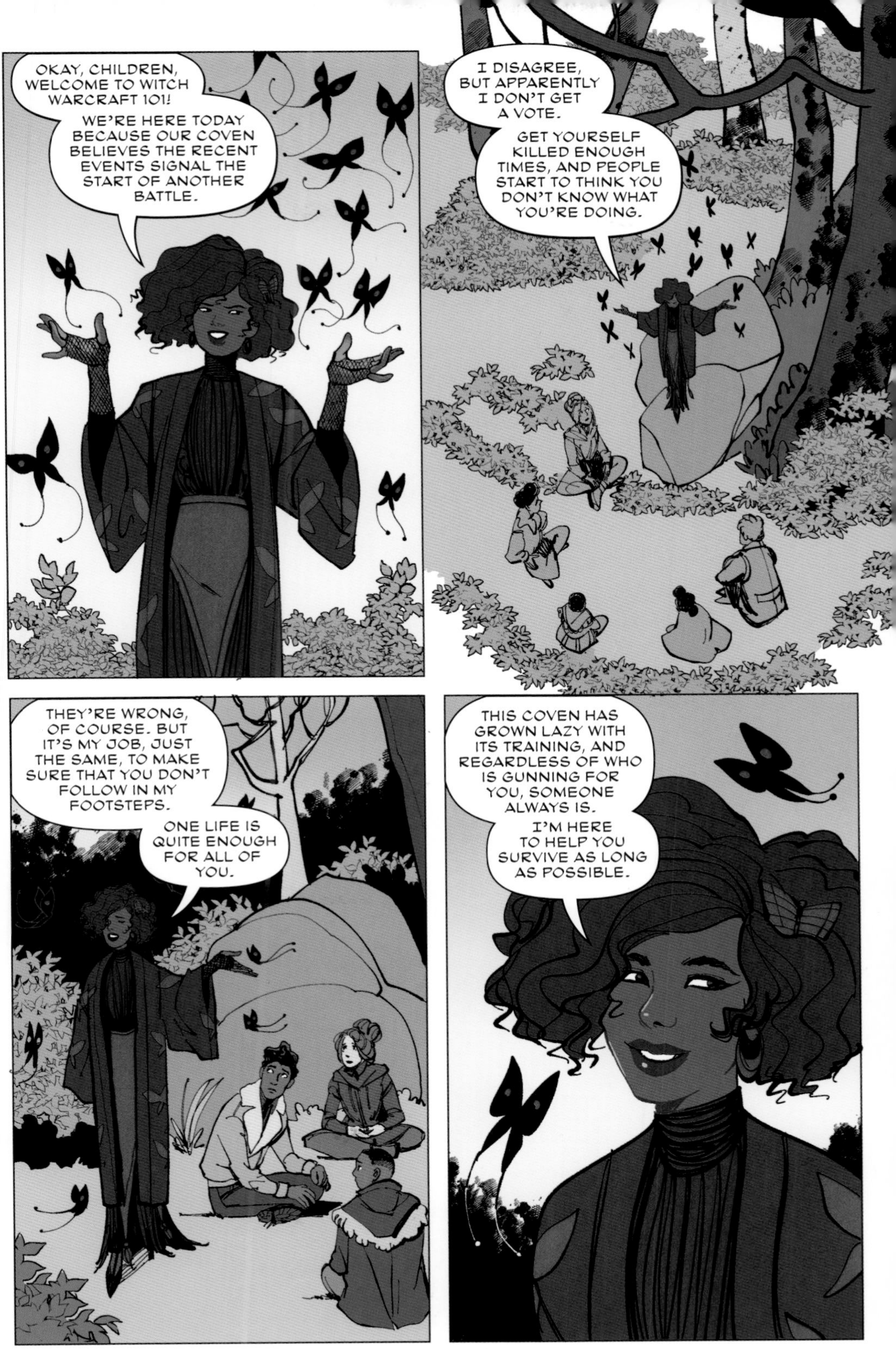

OKAY, CHILDREN, WELCOME TO WITCH WARCRAFT 101!
WE'RE HERE TODAY BECAUSE OUR COVEN BELIEVES THE RECENT EVENTS SIGNAL THE START OF ANOTHER BATTLE.
I DISAGREE, BUT APPARENTLY I DON'T GET A VOTE.
GET YOURSELF KILLED ENOUGH TIMES, AND PEOPLE START TO THINK YOU DON'T KNOW WHAT YOU'RE DOING.
THEY'RE WRONG, OF COURSE. BUT IT'S MY JOB, JUST THE SAME, TO MAKE SURE THAT YOU DON'T FOLLOW IN MY FOOTSTEPS.
ONE LIFE IS QUITE ENOUGH FOR ALL OF YOU.
THIS COVEN HAS GROWN LAZY WITH ITS TRAINING, AND REGARDLESS OF WHO IS GUNNING FOR YOU, SOMEONE ALWAYS IS.
I'M HERE TO HELP YOU SURVIVE AS LONG AS POSSIBLE.

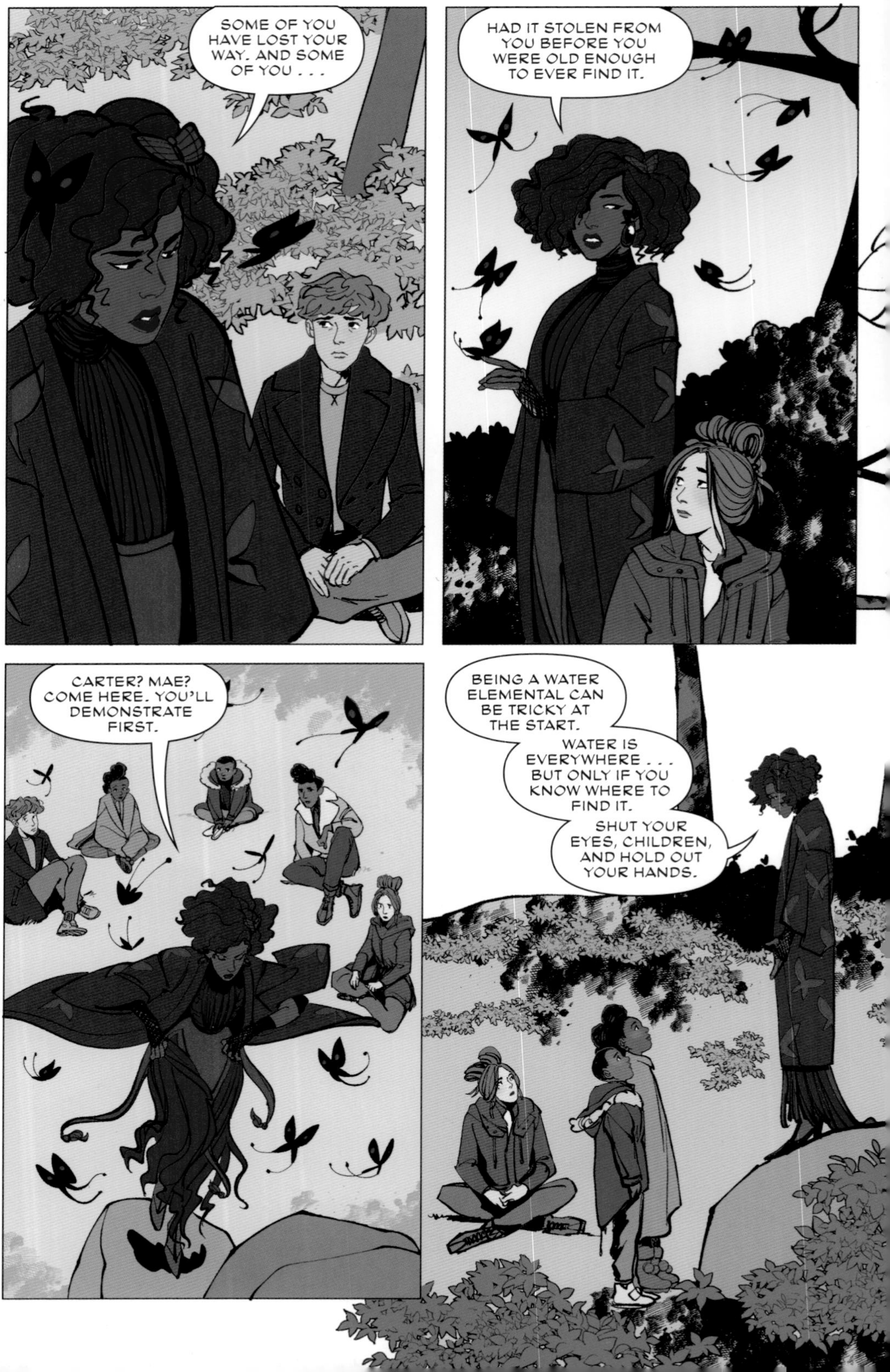
SOME OF YOU HAVE LOST YOUR WAY. AND SOME OF YOU . . .
HAD IT STOLEN FROM YOU BEFORE YOU WERE OLD ENOUGH TO EVER FIND IT.
CARTER? MAE? COME HERE. YOU'LL DEMONSTRATE FIRST.
BEING A WATER ELEMENTAL CAN BE TRICKY AT THE START.
WATER IS EVERYWHERE . . . BUT ONLY IF YOU KNOW WHERE TO FIND IT.
SHUT YOUR EYES, CHILDREN, AND HOLD OUT YOUR HANDS.

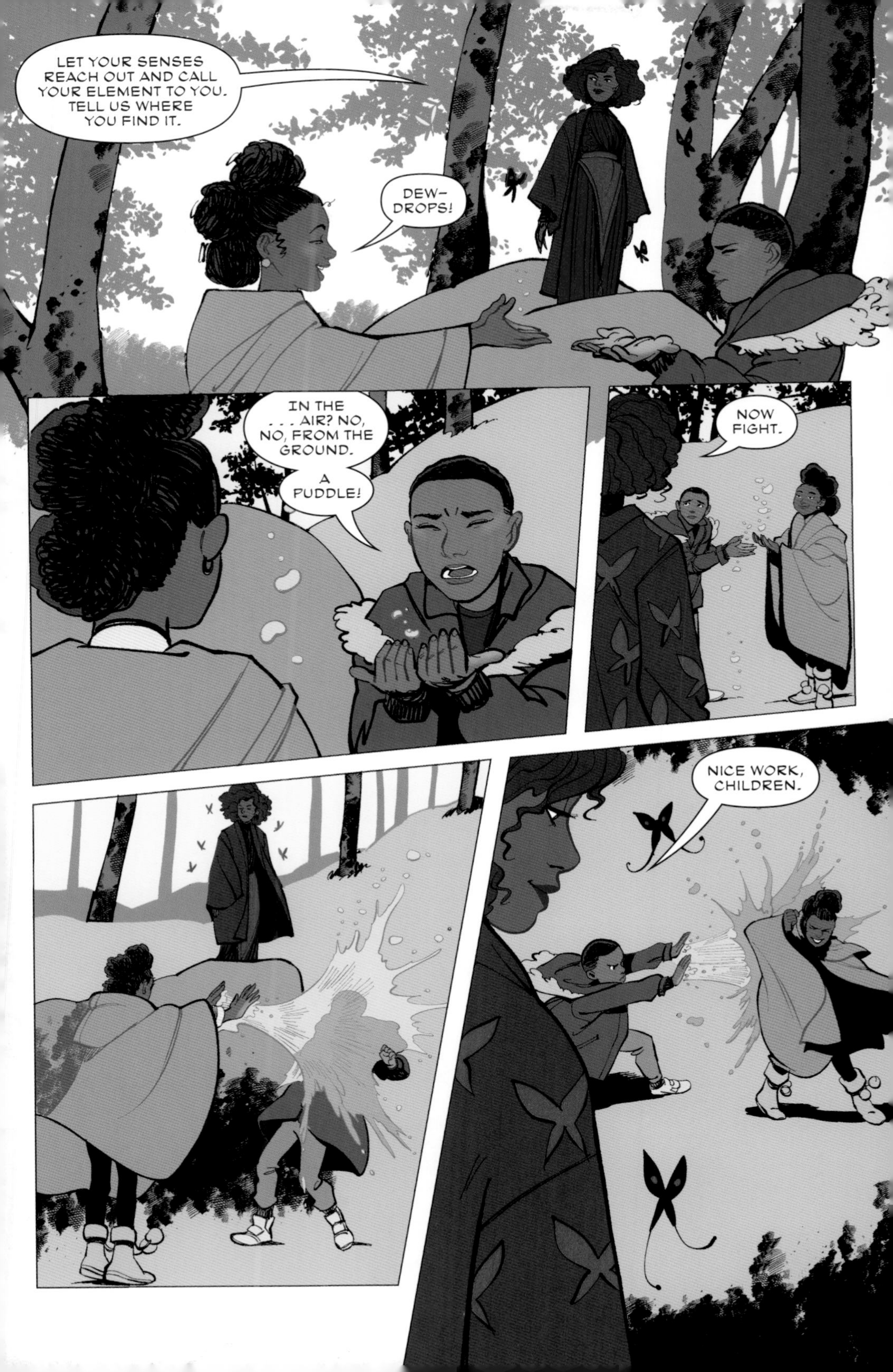
LET YOUR SENSES REACH OUT AND CALL YOUR ELEMENT TO YOU. TELL US WHERE YOU FIND IT.
DEW-DROPS!
IN THE . . . AIR? NO, NO, FROM THE GROUND.
A PUDDLE!
NOW FIGHT.
NICE WORK, CHILDREN.

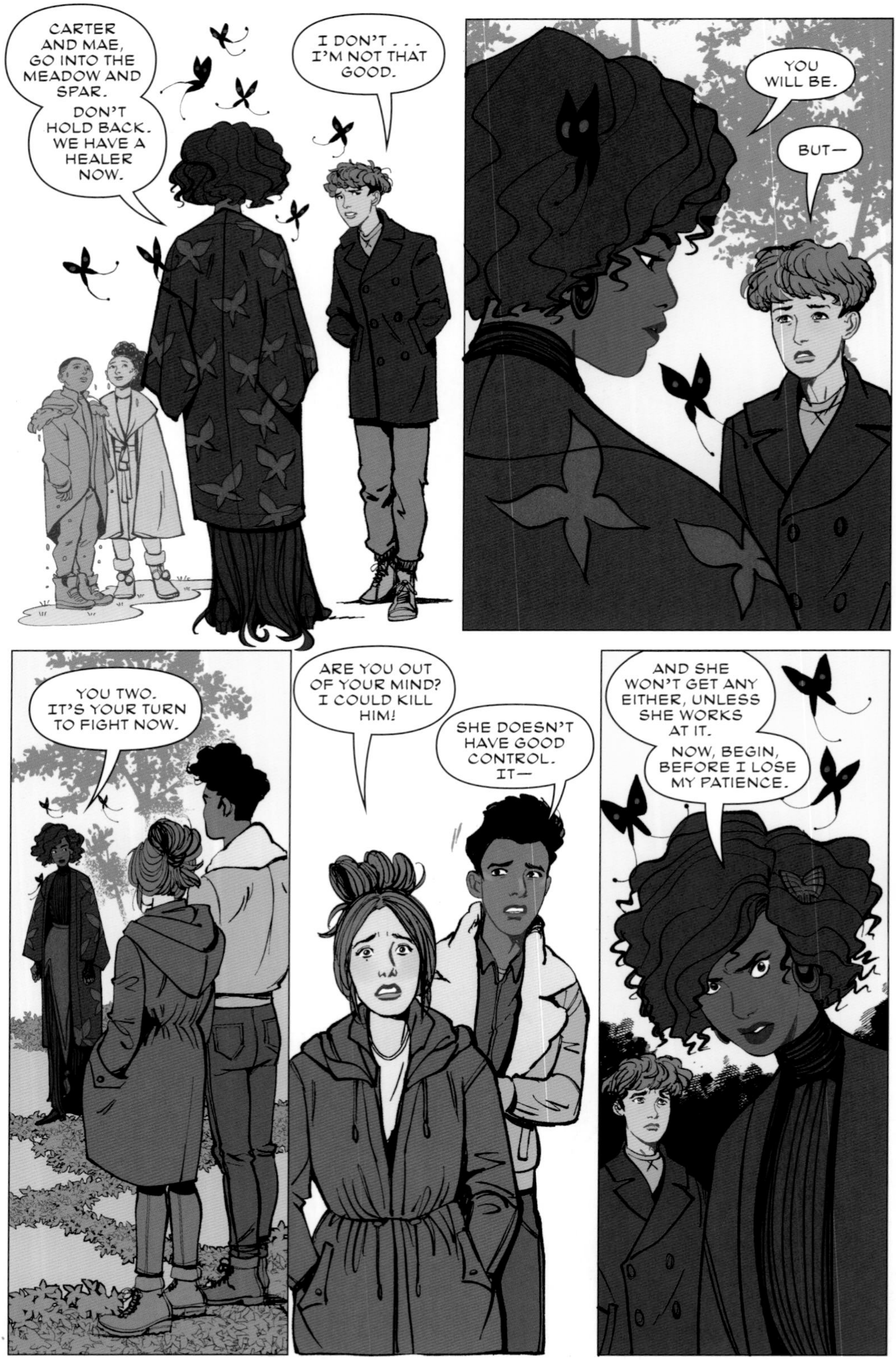
CARTER AND MAE, GO INTO THE MEADOW AND SPAR.
DON'T HOLD BACK. WE HAVE A HEALER NOW.
I DON'T . . . I'M NOT THAT GOOD.
YOU WILL BE.
BUT—
YOU TWO. IT'S YOUR TURN TO FIGHT NOW.
ARE YOU OUT OF YOUR MIND? I COULD KILL HIM!
SHE DOESN'T HAVE GOOD CONTROL. IT—
AND SHE WON'T GET ANY EITHER, UNLESS SHE WORKS AT IT.
NOW, BEGIN, BEFORE I LOSE MY PATIENCE.

I DON'T WANT TO HURT YOU.

I CAN TAKE IT. BESIDES, YOU THINK I'M NOT BLOCKING YOU?

I'M NOT THE ONE OUT OF PRACTICE HERE.

OKAY.

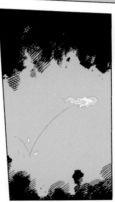

I'M SORRY. I CAN'T DO THIS. I WON'T HURT MY FRIEND!

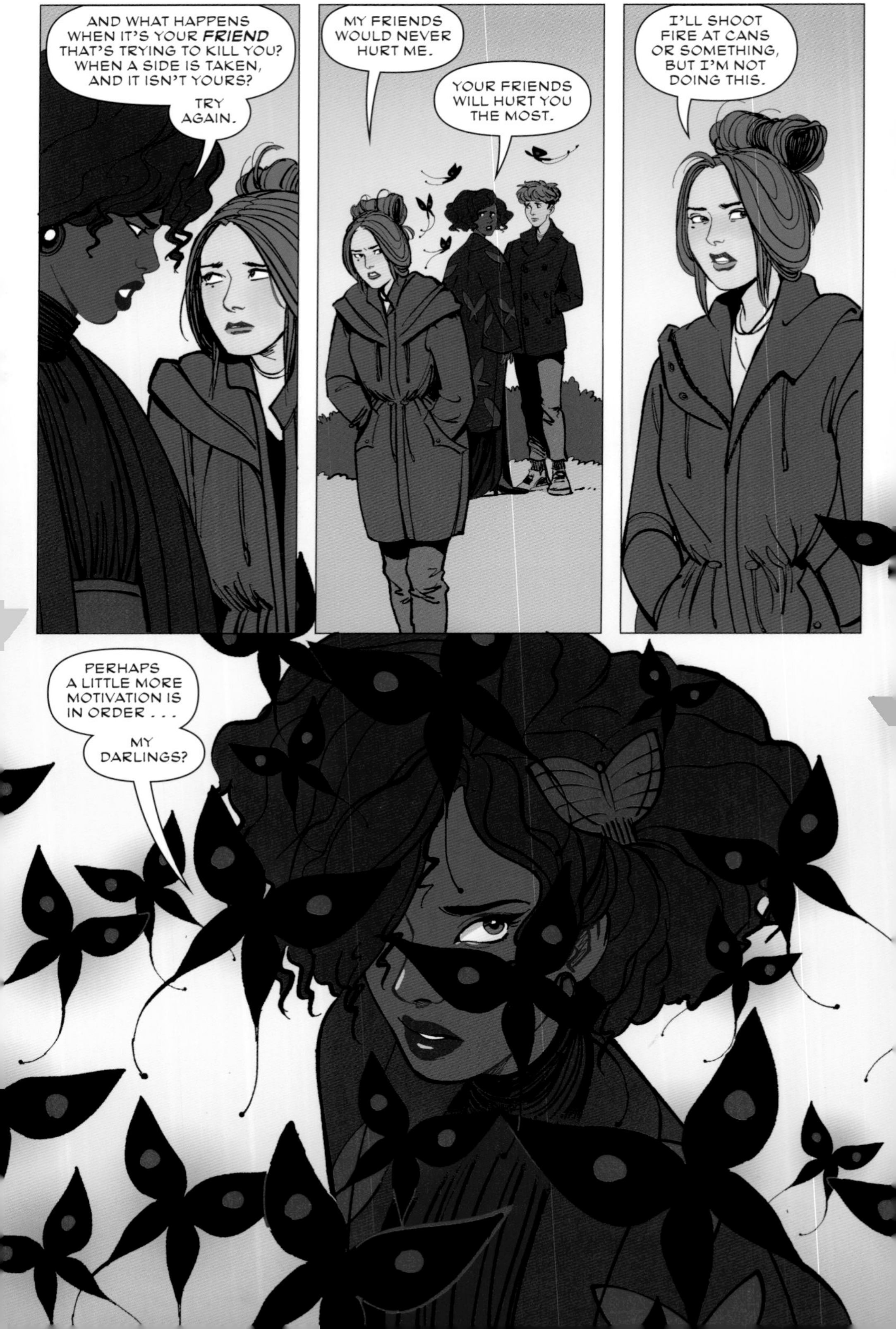
AND WHAT HAPPENS WHEN IT'S YOUR *FRIEND* THAT'S TRYING TO KILL YOU? WHEN A SIDE IS TAKEN, AND IT ISN'T YOURS?
TRY AGAIN.
MY FRIENDS WOULD NEVER HURT ME.
YOUR FRIENDS WILL HURT YOU THE MOST.
I'LL SHOOT FIRE AT CANS OR SOMETHING, BUT I'M NOT DOING THIS.
PERHAPS A LITTLE MORE MOTIVATION IS IN ORDER . . .
MY DARLINGS?

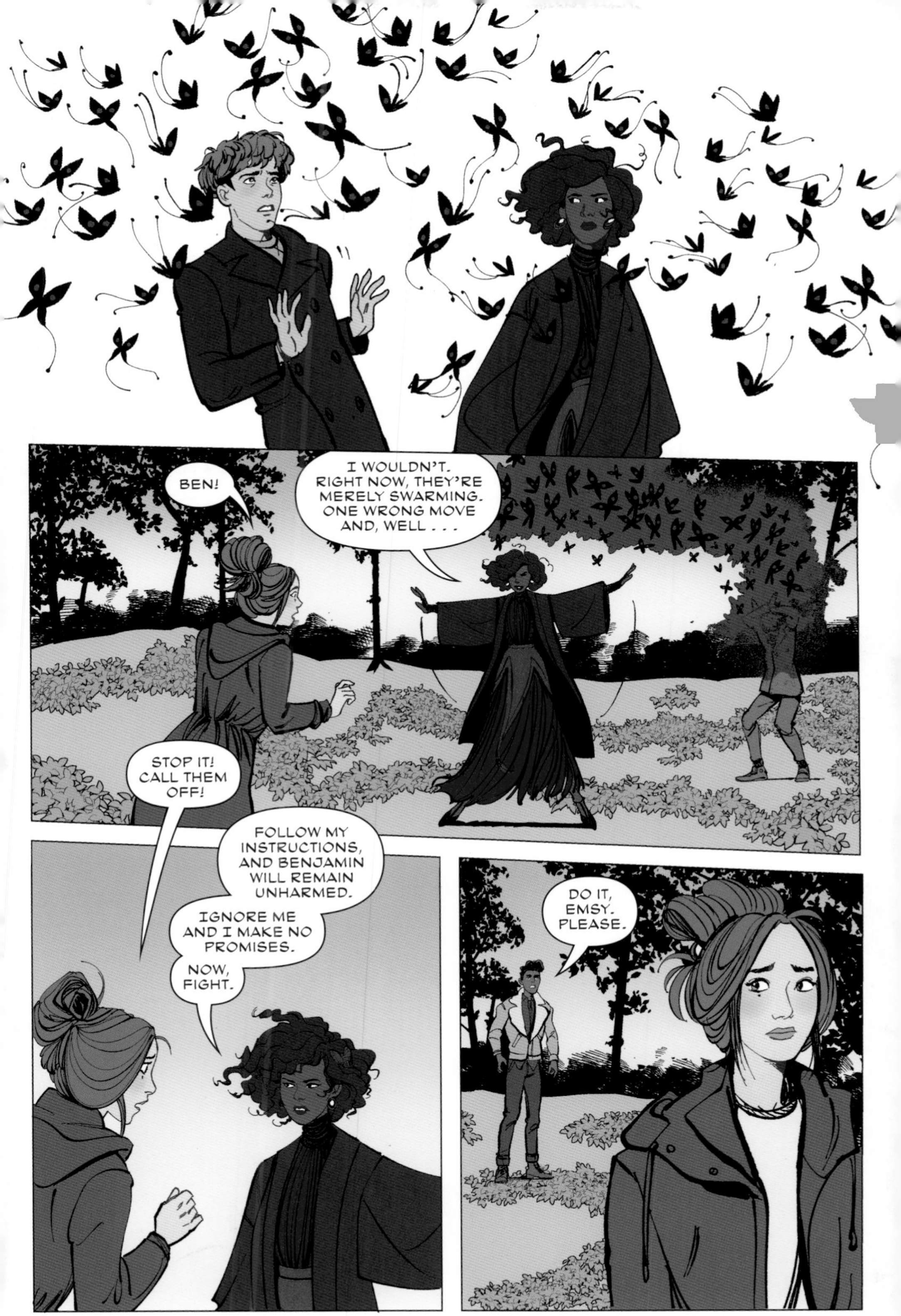
BEN!
I WOULDN'T. RIGHT NOW, THEY'RE MERELY SWARMING. ONE WRONG MOVE AND, WELL . . .
STOP IT! CALL THEM OFF!
FOLLOW MY INSTRUCTIONS, AND BENJAMIN WILL REMAIN UNHARMED.
IGNORE ME AND I MAKE NO PROMISES.
NOW, FIGHT.
DO IT, EMSY. PLEASE.

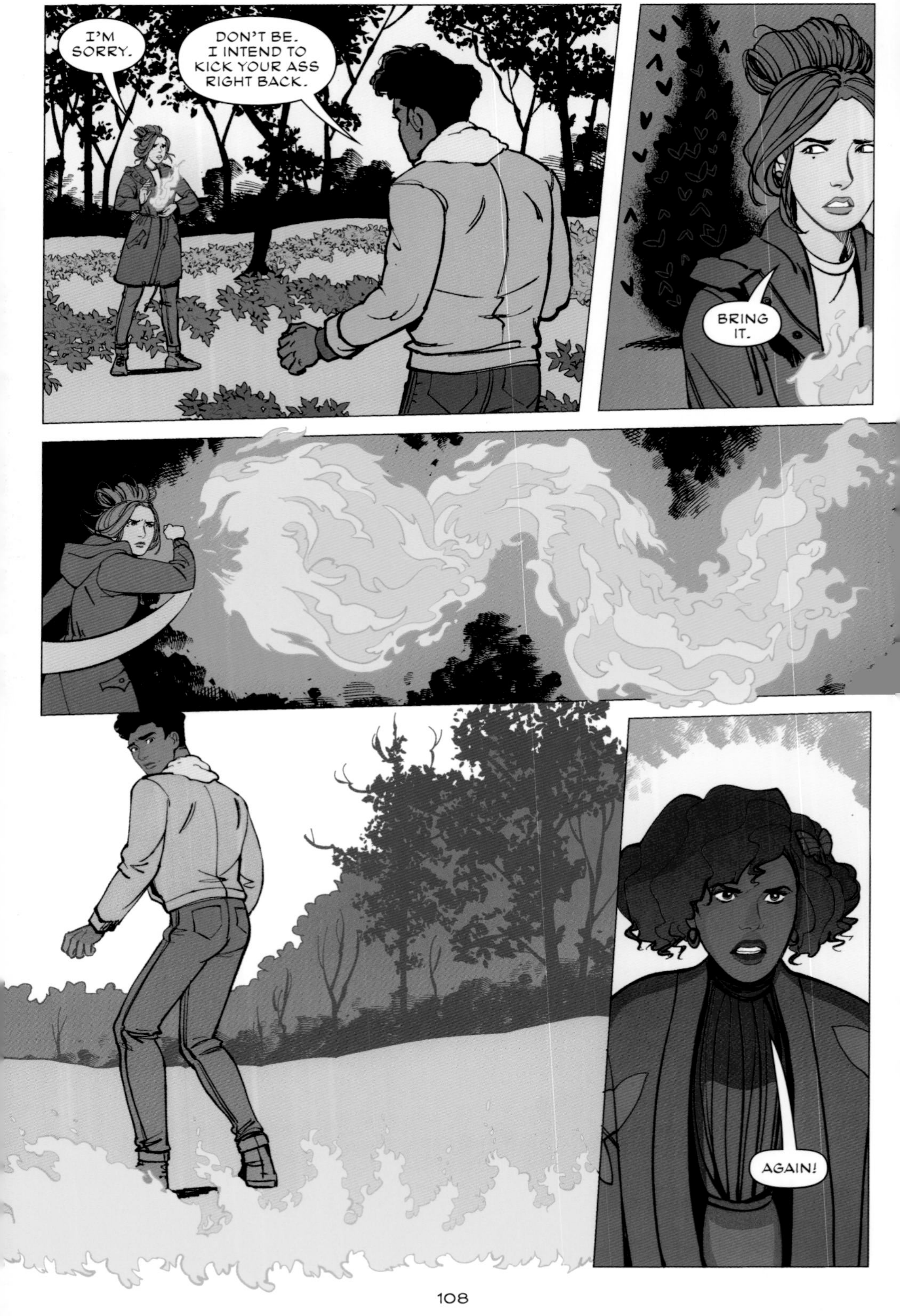
I'M SORRY.
DON'T BE. I INTEND TO KICK YOUR ASS RIGHT BACK.
BRING IT.
AGAIN!

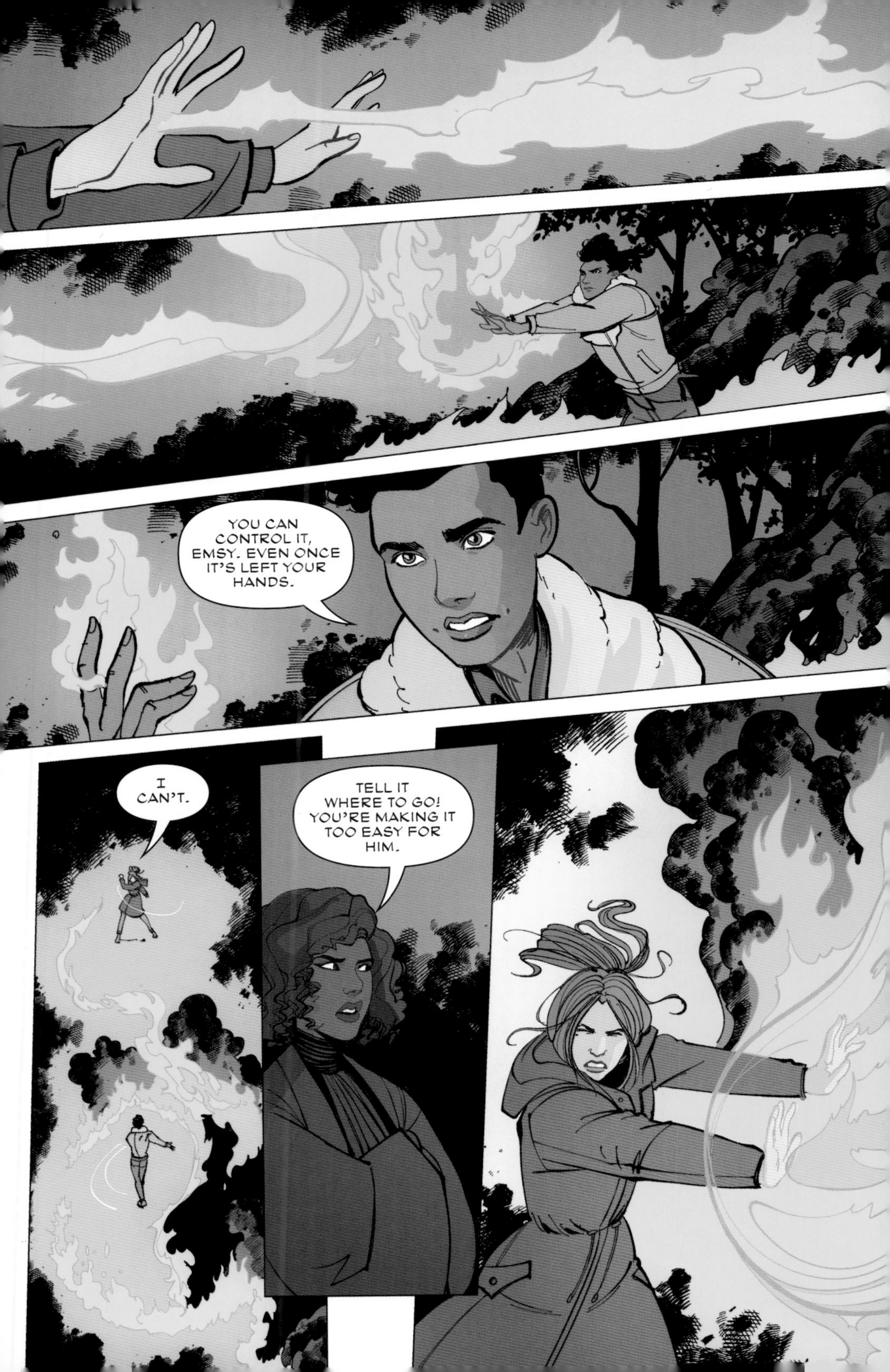
YOU CAN CONTROL IT, EMSY. EVEN ONCE IT'S LEFT YOUR HANDS.
I CAN'T.
TELL IT WHERE TO GO! YOU'RE MAKING IT TOO EASY FOR HIM.

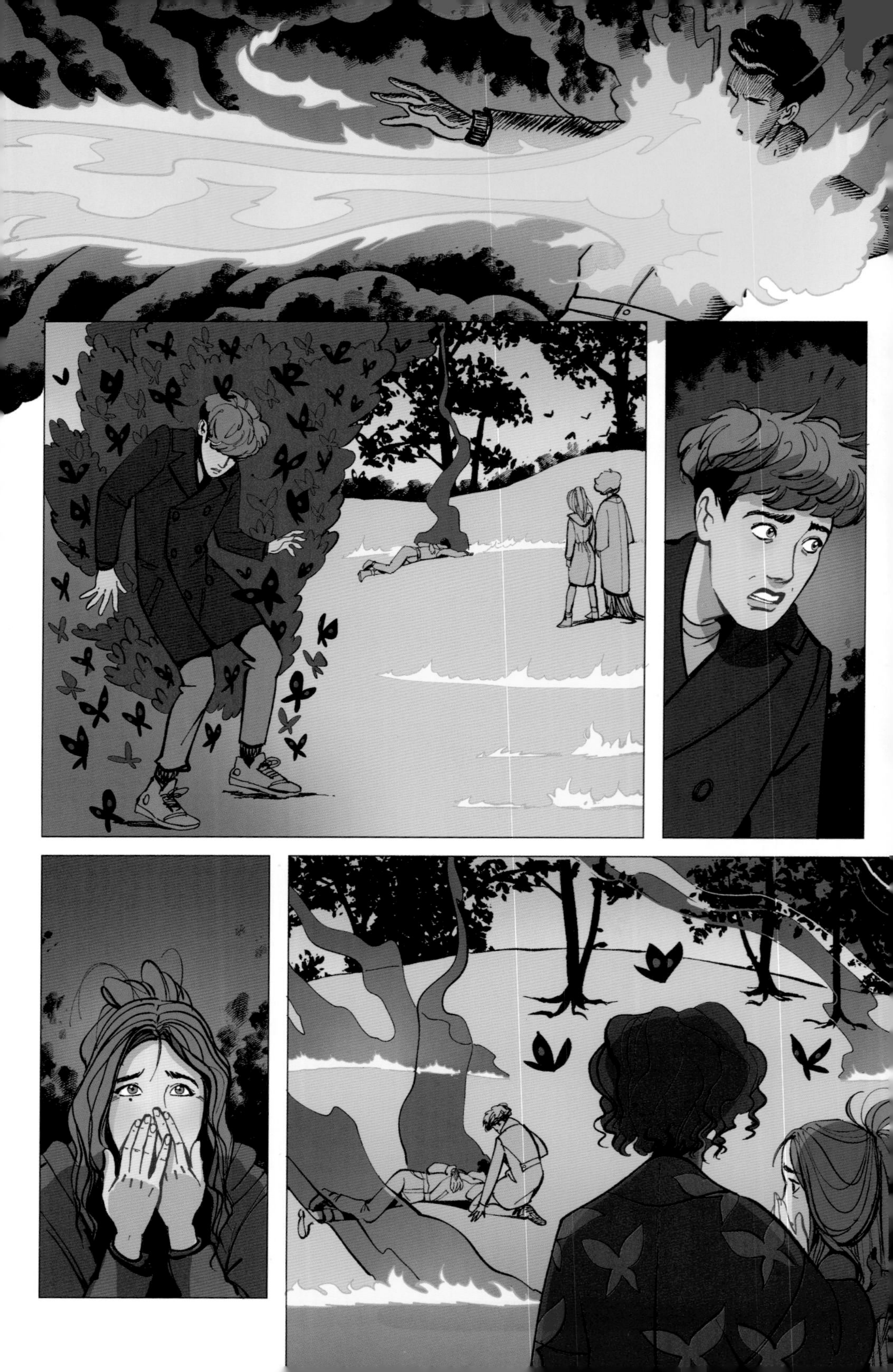

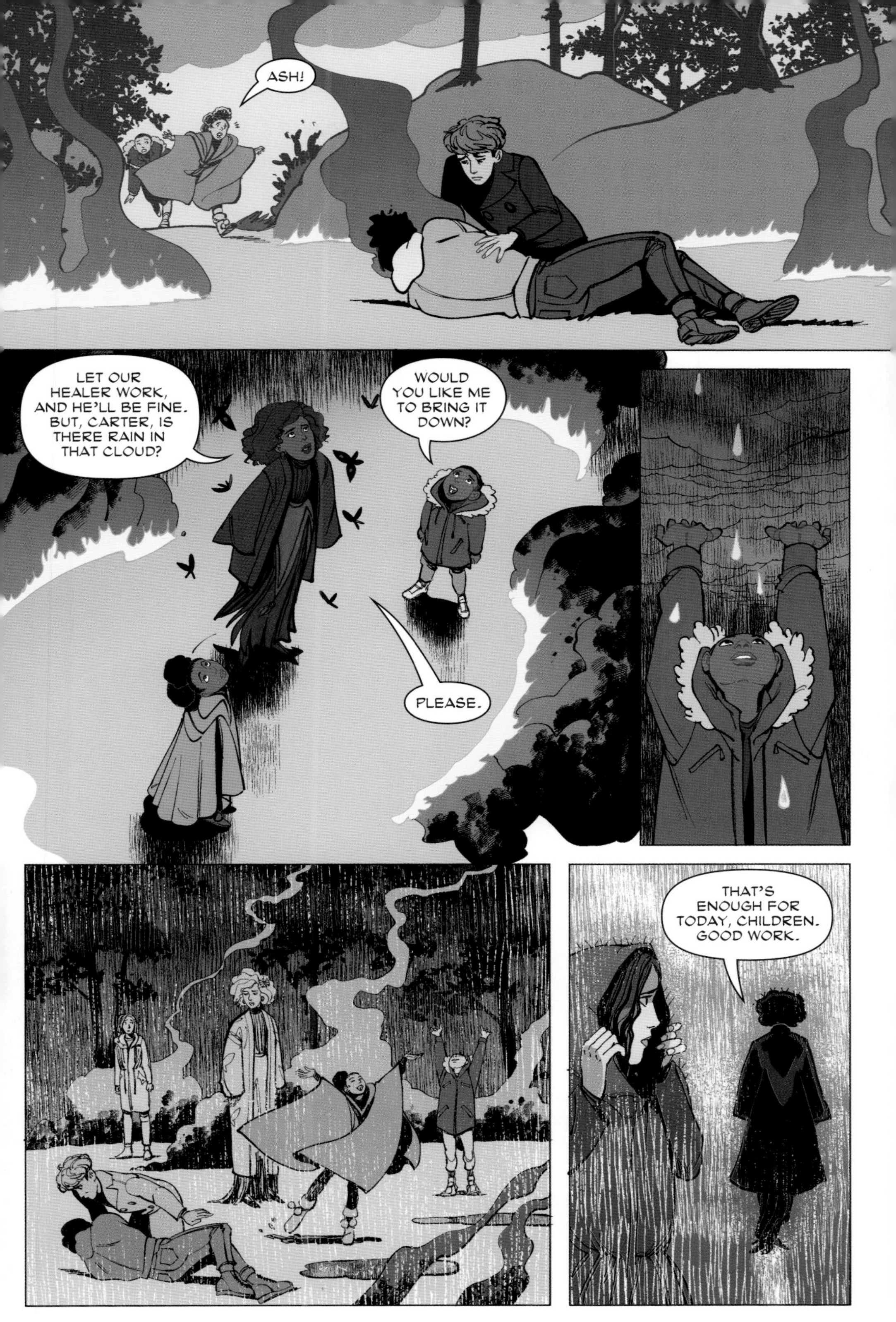
ASH!
LET OUR HEALER WORK, AND HE'LL BE FINE. BUT, CARTER, IS THERE RAIN IN THAT CLOUD?
WOULD YOU LIKE ME TO BRING IT DOWN?
PLEASE.
THAT'S ENOUGH FOR TODAY, CHILDREN. GOOD WORK.

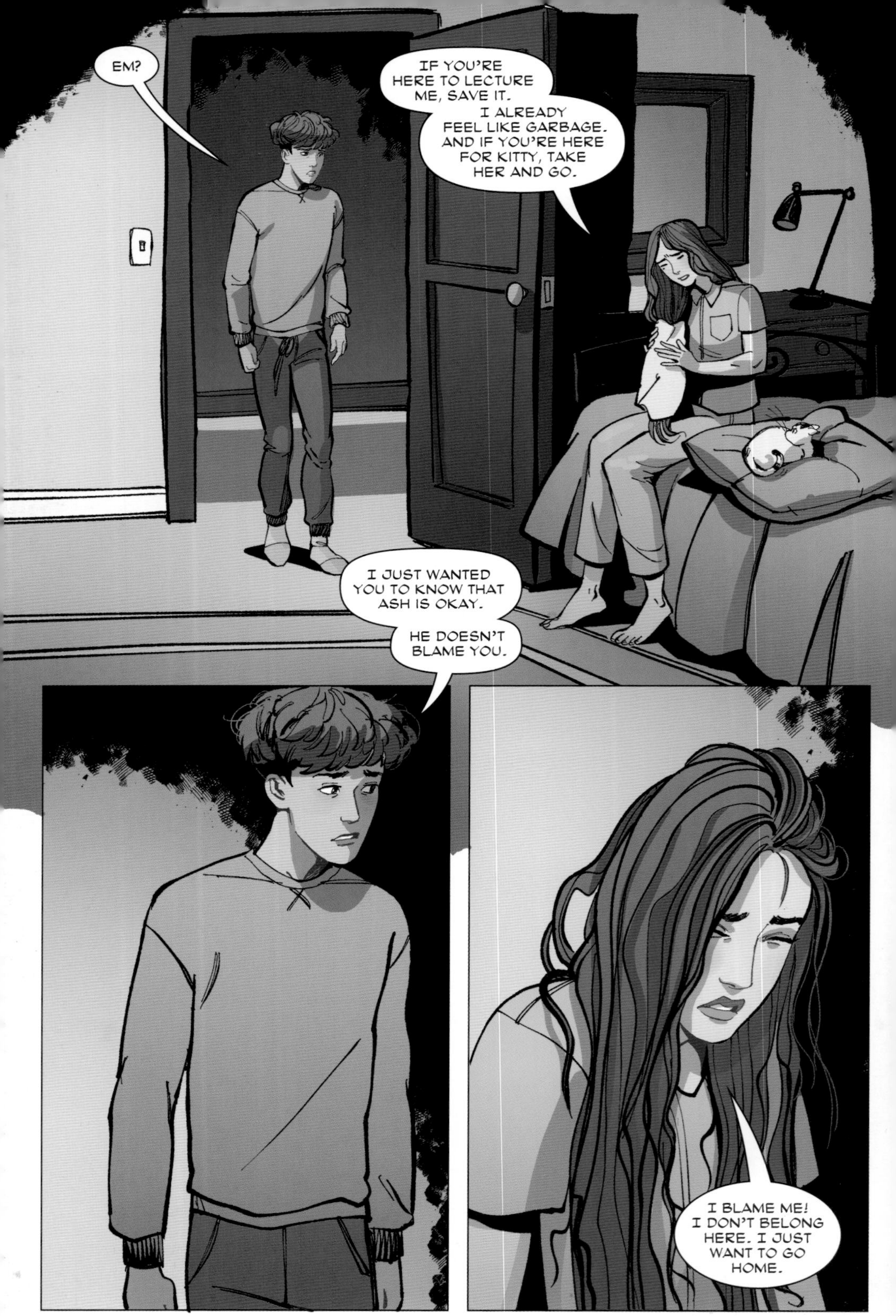
EM?
IF YOU'RE HERE TO LECTURE ME, SAVE IT.
I ALREADY FEEL LIKE GARBAGE. AND IF YOU'RE HERE FOR KITTY, TAKE HER AND GO.
I JUST WANTED YOU TO KNOW THAT ASH IS OKAY.
HE DOESN'T BLAME YOU.
I BLAME ME! I DON'T BELONG HERE. I JUST WANT TO GO HOME.

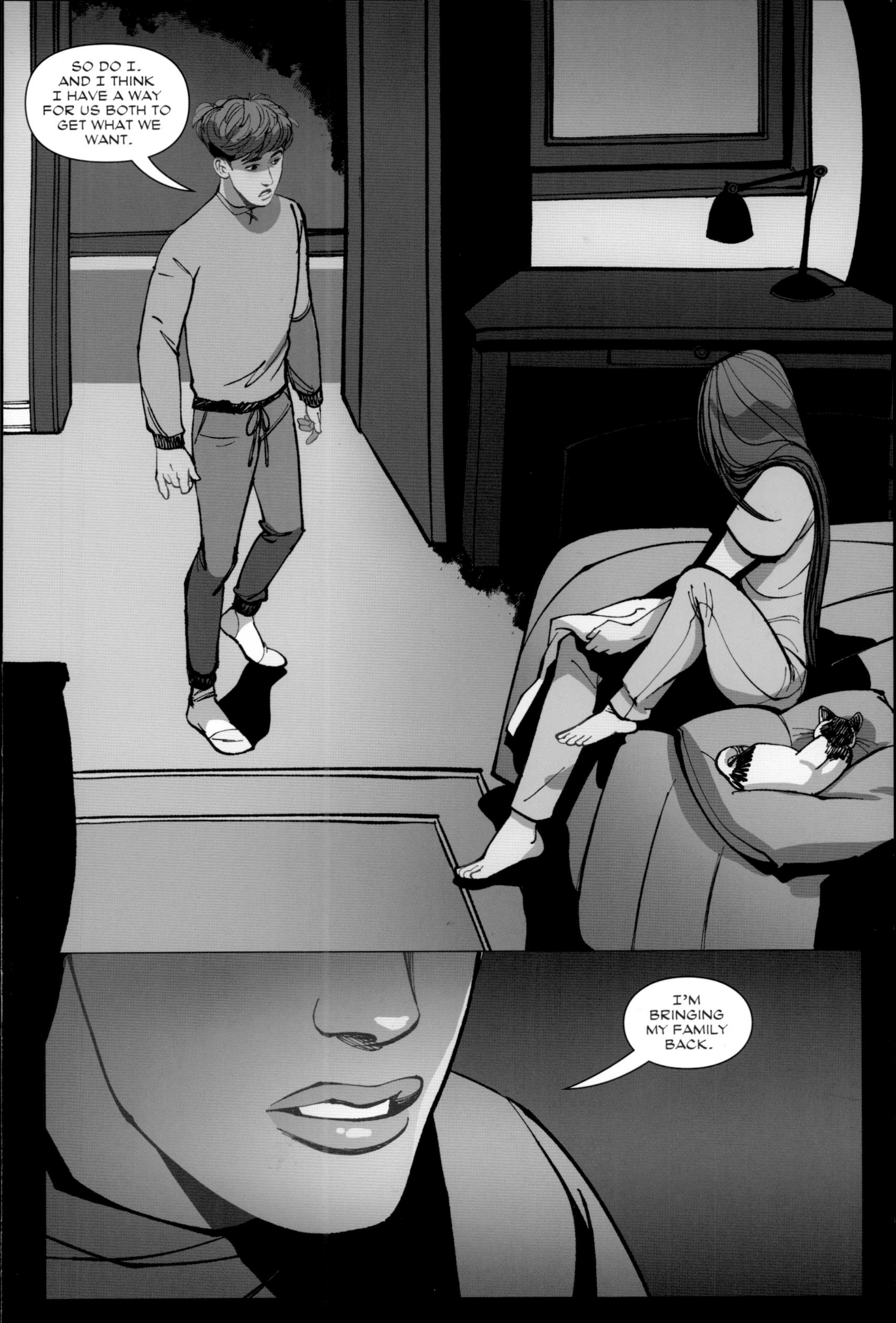
SO DO I. AND I THINK I HAVE A WAY FOR US BOTH TO GET WHAT WE WANT.
I'M BRINGING MY FAMILY BACK.

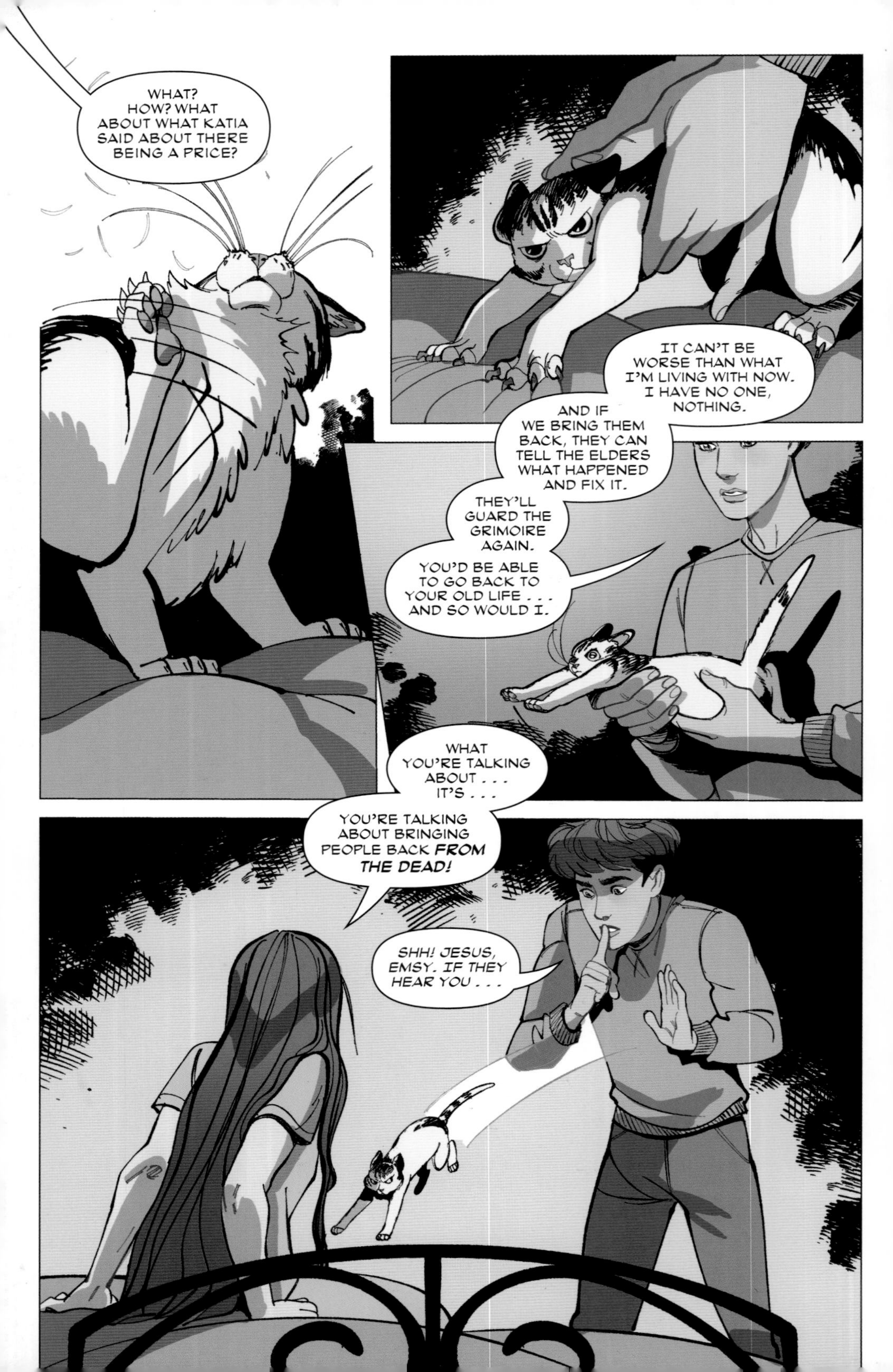
WHAT? HOW? WHAT ABOUT WHAT KATIA SAID ABOUT THERE BEING A PRICE?
IT CAN'T BE WORSE THAN WHAT I'M LIVING WITH NOW. I HAVE NO ONE, NOTHING.
AND IF WE BRING THEM BACK, THEY CAN TELL THE ELDERS WHAT HAPPENED AND FIX IT.
THEY'LL GUARD THE GRIMOIRE AGAIN.
YOU'D BE ABLE TO GO BACK TO YOUR OLD LIFE . . . AND SO WOULD I.
WHAT YOU'RE TALKING ABOUT . . . IT'S . . .
YOU'RE TALKING ABOUT BRINGING PEOPLE BACK *FROM THE DEAD!*
SHH! JESUS, EMSY. IF THEY HEAR YOU . . .

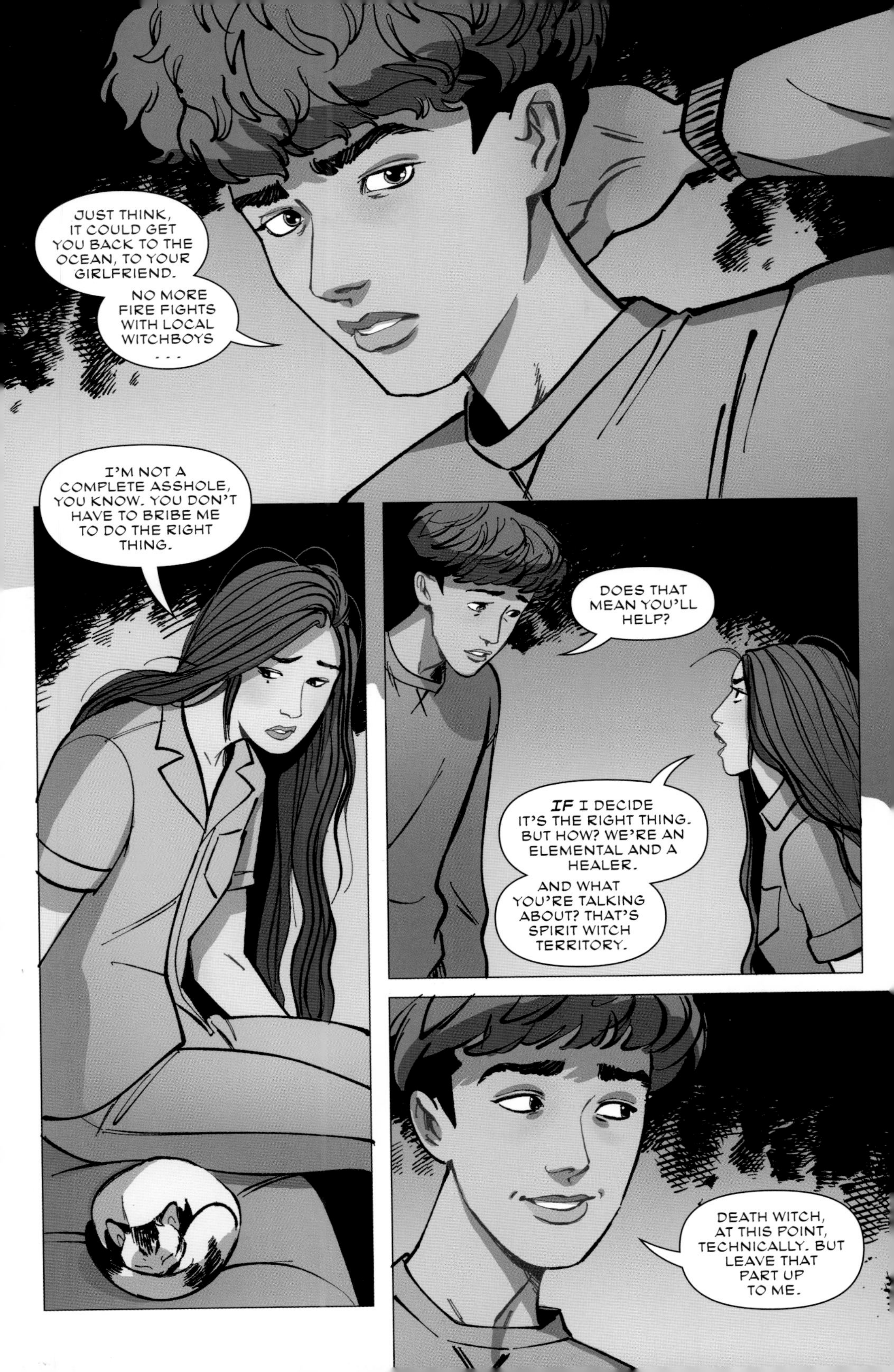
JUST THINK, IT COULD GET YOU BACK TO THE OCEAN, TO YOUR GIRLFRIEND.
NO MORE FIRE FIGHTS WITH LOCAL WITCHBOYS . . .
I'M NOT A COMPLETE ASSHOLE, YOU KNOW. YOU DON'T HAVE TO BRIBE ME TO DO THE RIGHT THING.
DOES THAT MEAN YOU'LL HELP?
IF I DECIDE IT'S THE RIGHT THING. BUT HOW? WE'RE AN ELEMENTAL AND A HEALER.
AND WHAT YOU'RE TALKING ABOUT? THAT'S SPIRIT WITCH TERRITORY.
DEATH WITCH, AT THIS POINT, TECHNICALLY. BUT LEAVE THAT PART UP TO ME.

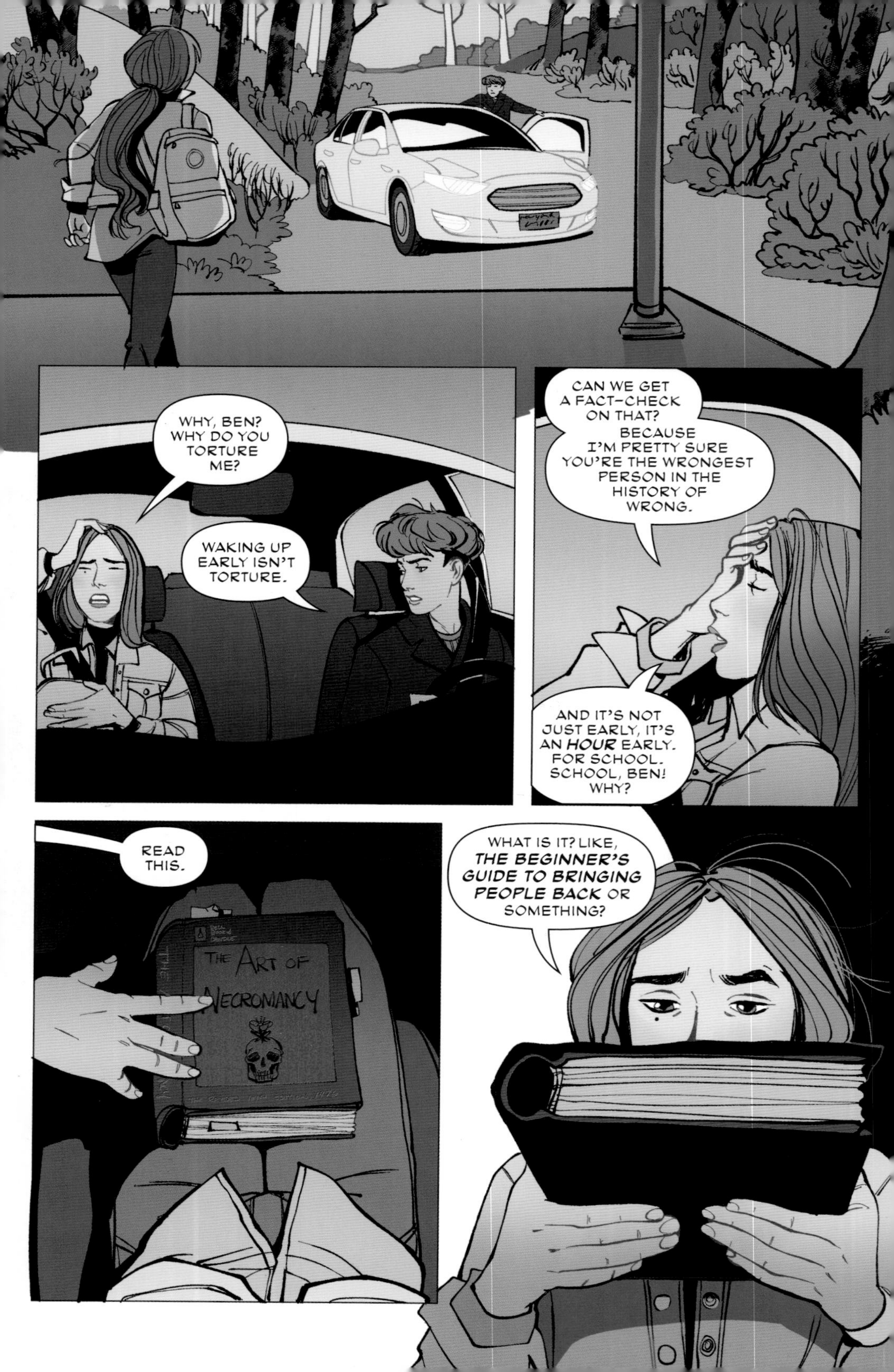
WHY, BEN? WHY DO YOU TORTURE ME?
WAKING UP EARLY ISN'T TORTURE.
CAN WE GET A FACT-CHECK ON THAT?
BECAUSE I'M PRETTY SURE YOU'RE THE WRONGEST PERSON IN THE HISTORY OF WRONG.
AND IT'S NOT JUST EARLY, IT'S AN *HOUR* EARLY. FOR SCHOOL. SCHOOL, BEN! WHY?
READ THIS.
THE ART OF NECROMANCY
WHAT IS IT? LIKE, ***THE BEGINNER'S GUIDE TO BRINGING PEOPLE BACK*** OR SOMETHING?

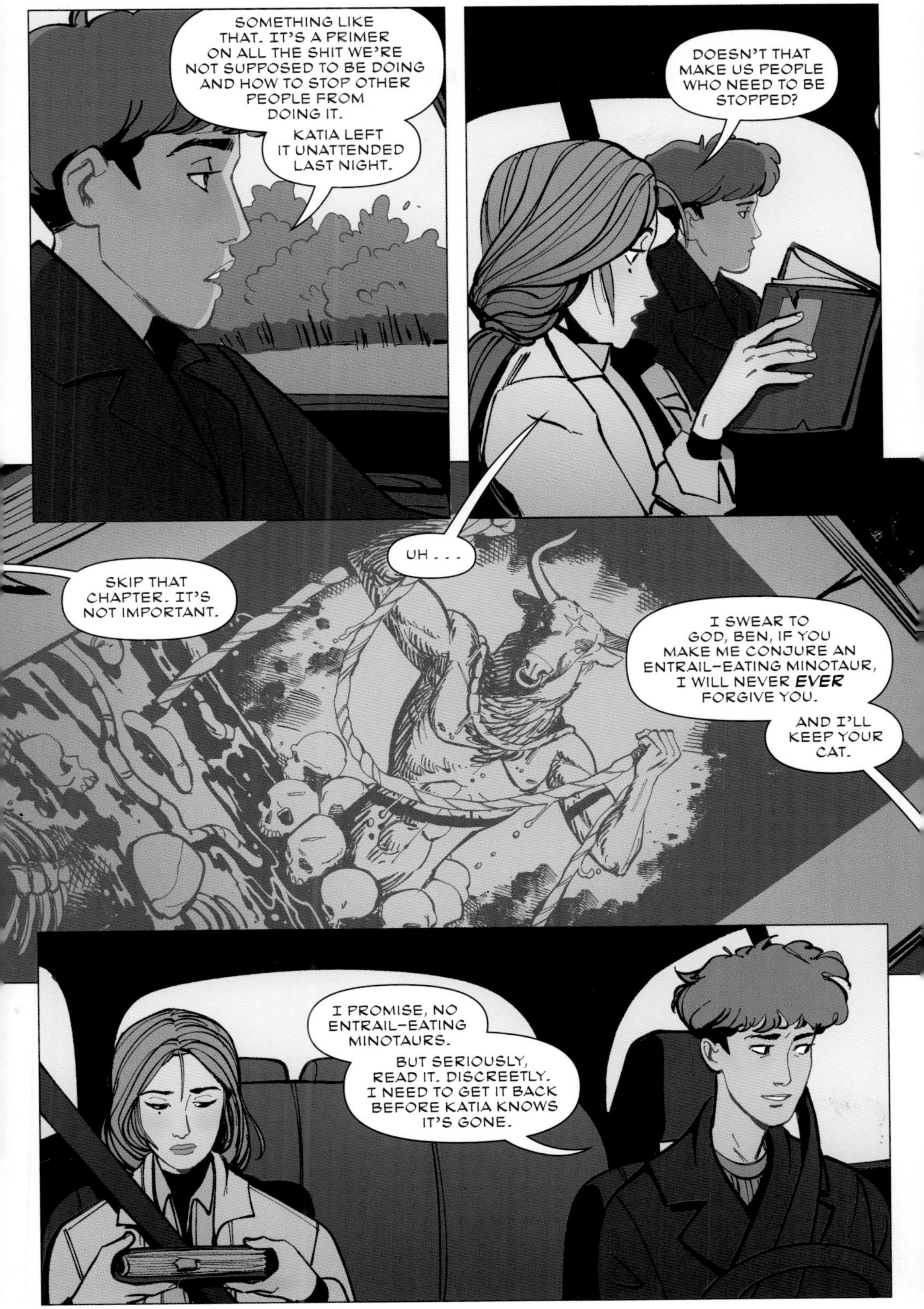
SOMETHING LIKE THAT. IT'S A PRIMER ON ALL THE SHIT WE'RE NOT SUPPOSED TO BE DOING AND HOW TO STOP OTHER PEOPLE FROM DOING IT.
KATIA LEFT IT UNATTENDED LAST NIGHT.
DOESN'T THAT MAKE US PEOPLE WHO NEED TO BE STOPPED?
UH . . .
SKIP THAT CHAPTER. IT'S NOT IMPORTANT.
I SWEAR TO GOD, BEN, IF YOU MAKE ME CONJURE AN ENTRAIL-EATING MINOTAUR, I WILL NEVER ***EVER*** FORGIVE YOU.
AND I'LL KEEP YOUR CAT.
I PROMISE, NO ENTRAIL-EATING MINOTAURS.
BUT SERIOUSLY, READ IT. DISCREETLY. I NEED TO GET IT BACK BEFORE KATIA KNOWS IT'S GONE.

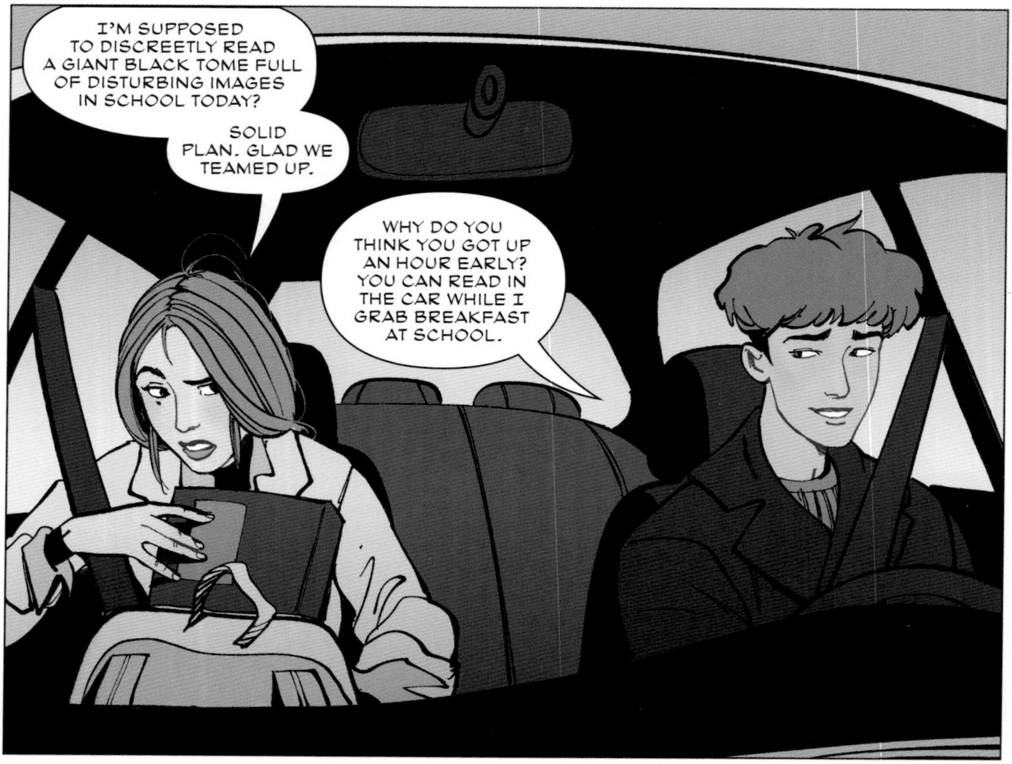
I'M SUPPOSED TO DISCREETLY READ A GIANT BLACK TOME FULL OF DISTURBING IMAGES IN SCHOOL TODAY?
SOLID PLAN. GLAD WE TEAMED UP.
WHY DO YOU THINK YOU GOT UP AN HOUR EARLY? YOU CAN READ IN THE CAR WHILE I GRAB BREAKFAST AT SCHOOL.

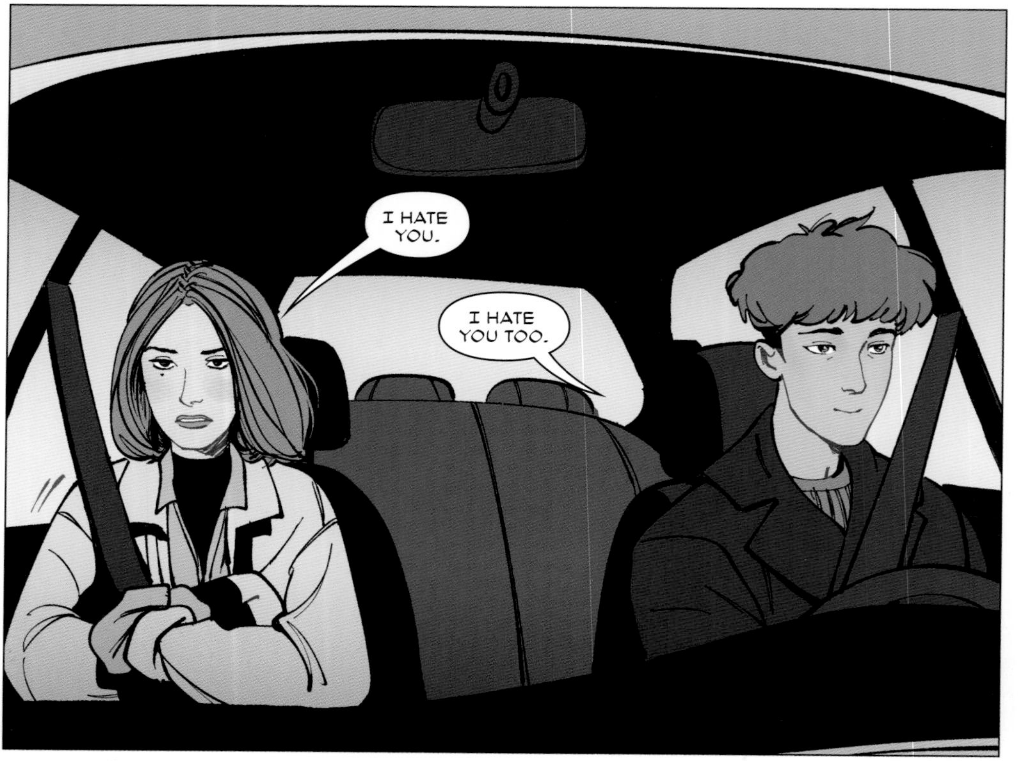
I HATE YOU.
I HATE YOU TOO.

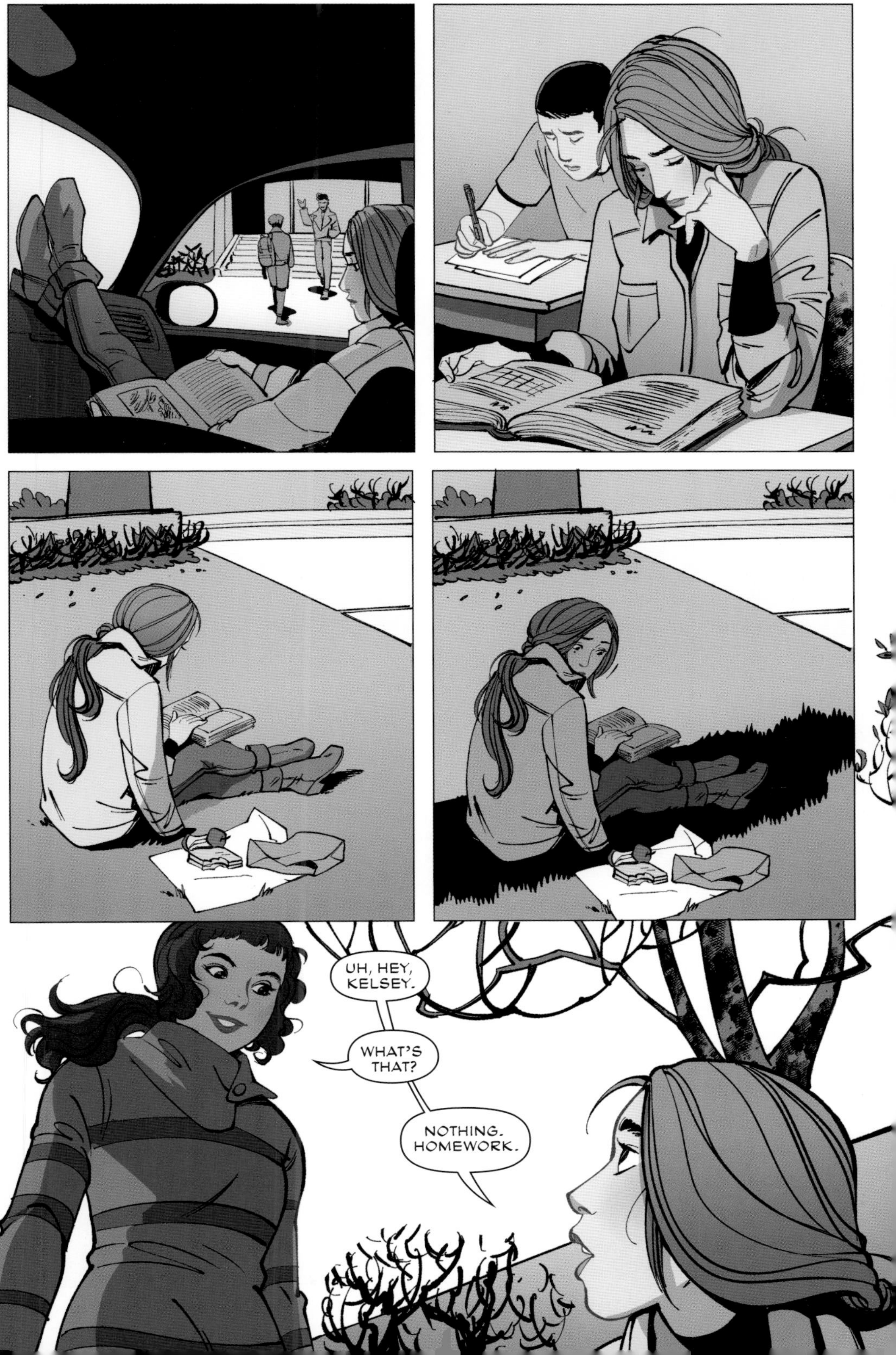
UH, HEY, KELSEY.
WHAT'S THAT?
NOTHING. HOMEWORK.

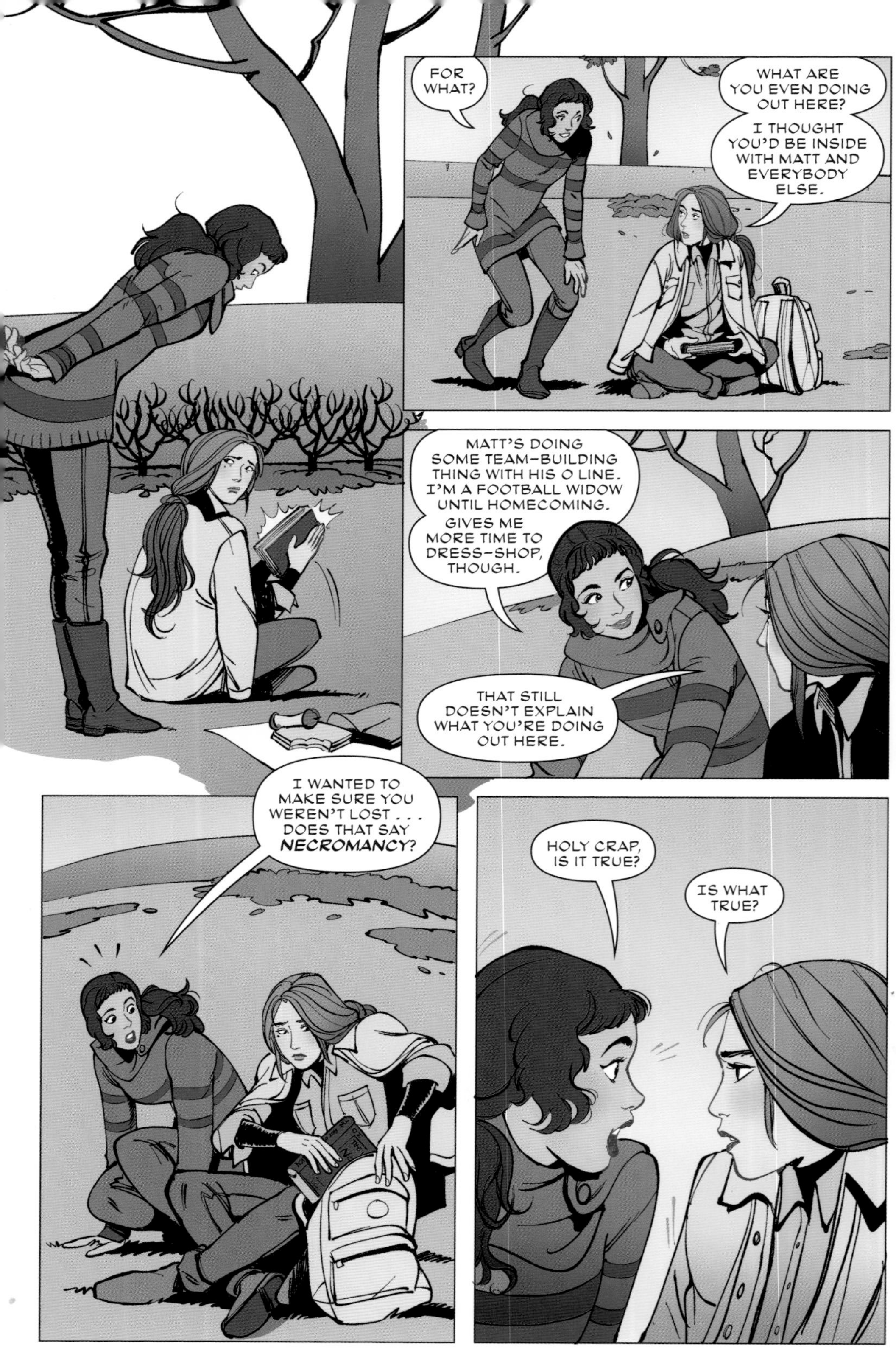
FOR WHAT?
WHAT ARE YOU EVEN DOING OUT HERE?
I THOUGHT YOU'D BE INSIDE WITH MATT AND EVERYBODY ELSE.
MATT'S DOING SOME TEAM-BUILDING THING WITH HIS O LINE. I'M A FOOTBALL WIDOW UNTIL HOMECOMING.
GIVES ME MORE TIME TO DRESS-SHOP, THOUGH.
THAT STILL DOESN'T EXPLAIN WHAT YOU'RE DOING OUT HERE.
I WANTED TO MAKE SURE YOU WEREN'T LOST . . . DOES THAT SAY ***NECROMANCY***?
HOLY CRAP, IS IT TRUE?
IS WHAT TRUE?

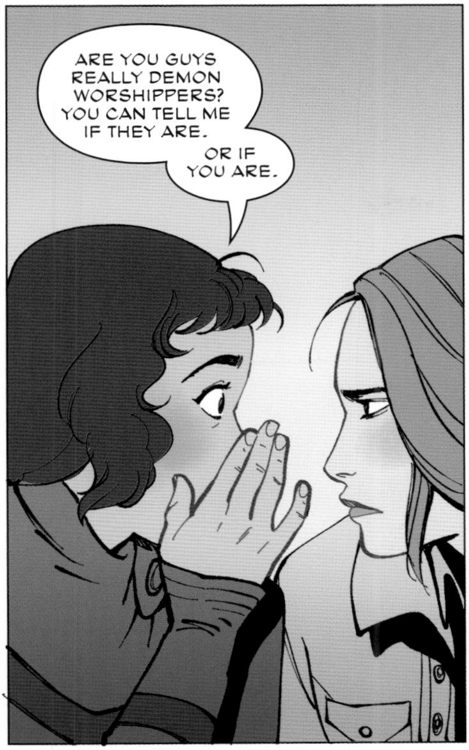
ARE YOU GUYS REALLY DEMON WORSHIPPERS? YOU CAN TELL ME IF THEY ARE.
OR IF YOU ARE.

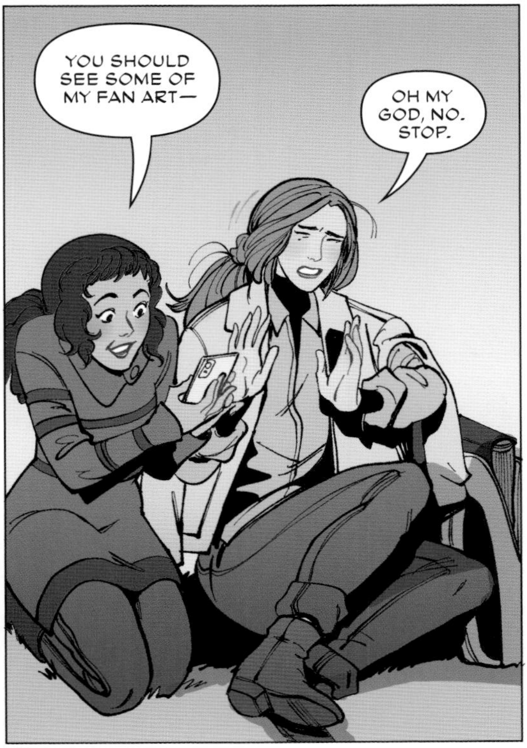
YOU SHOULD SEE SOME OF MY FAN ART—
OH MY GOD, NO. STOP.

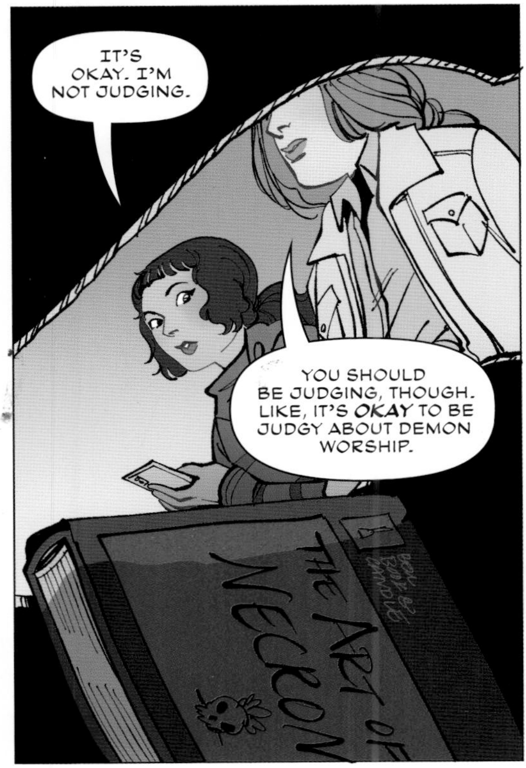
IT'S OKAY. I'M NOT JUDGING.
YOU SHOULD BE JUDGING, THOUGH. LIKE, IT'S *OKAY* TO BE JUDGY ABOUT DEMON WORSHIP.

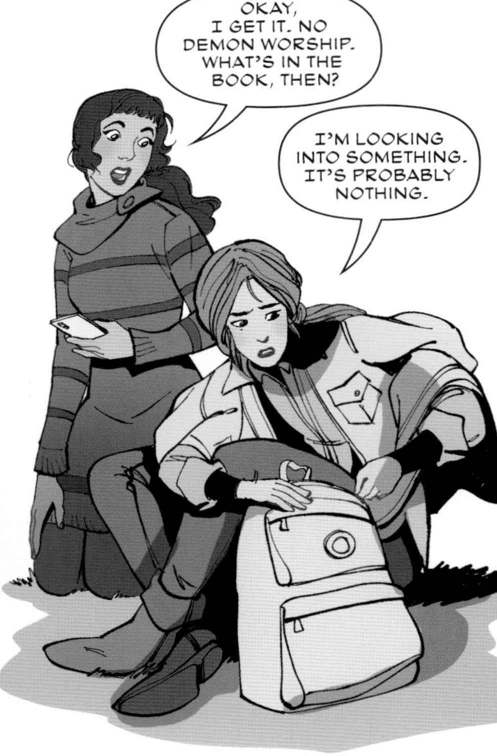
OKAY, I GET IT. NO DEMON WORSHIP. WHAT'S IN THE BOOK, THEN?
I'M LOOKING INTO SOMETHING. IT'S PROBABLY NOTHING.

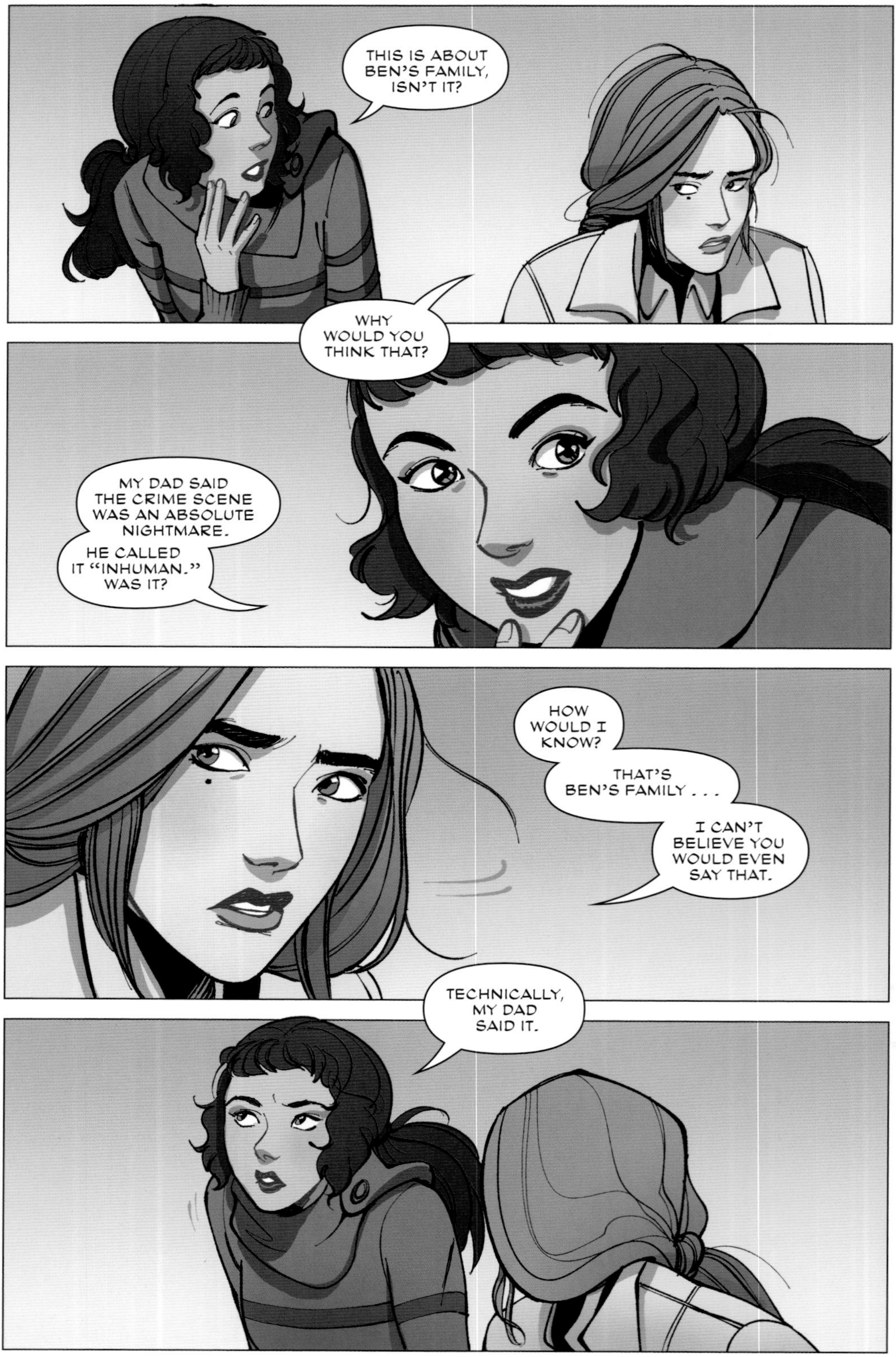
THIS IS ABOUT BEN'S FAMILY, ISN'T IT?
WHY WOULD YOU THINK THAT?
MY DAD SAID THE CRIME SCENE WAS AN ABSOLUTE NIGHTMARE.
HE CALLED IT "INHUMAN." WAS IT?
HOW WOULD I KNOW?
THAT'S BEN'S FAMILY . . .
I CAN'T BELIEVE YOU WOULD EVEN SAY THAT.
TECHNICALLY, MY DAD SAID IT.

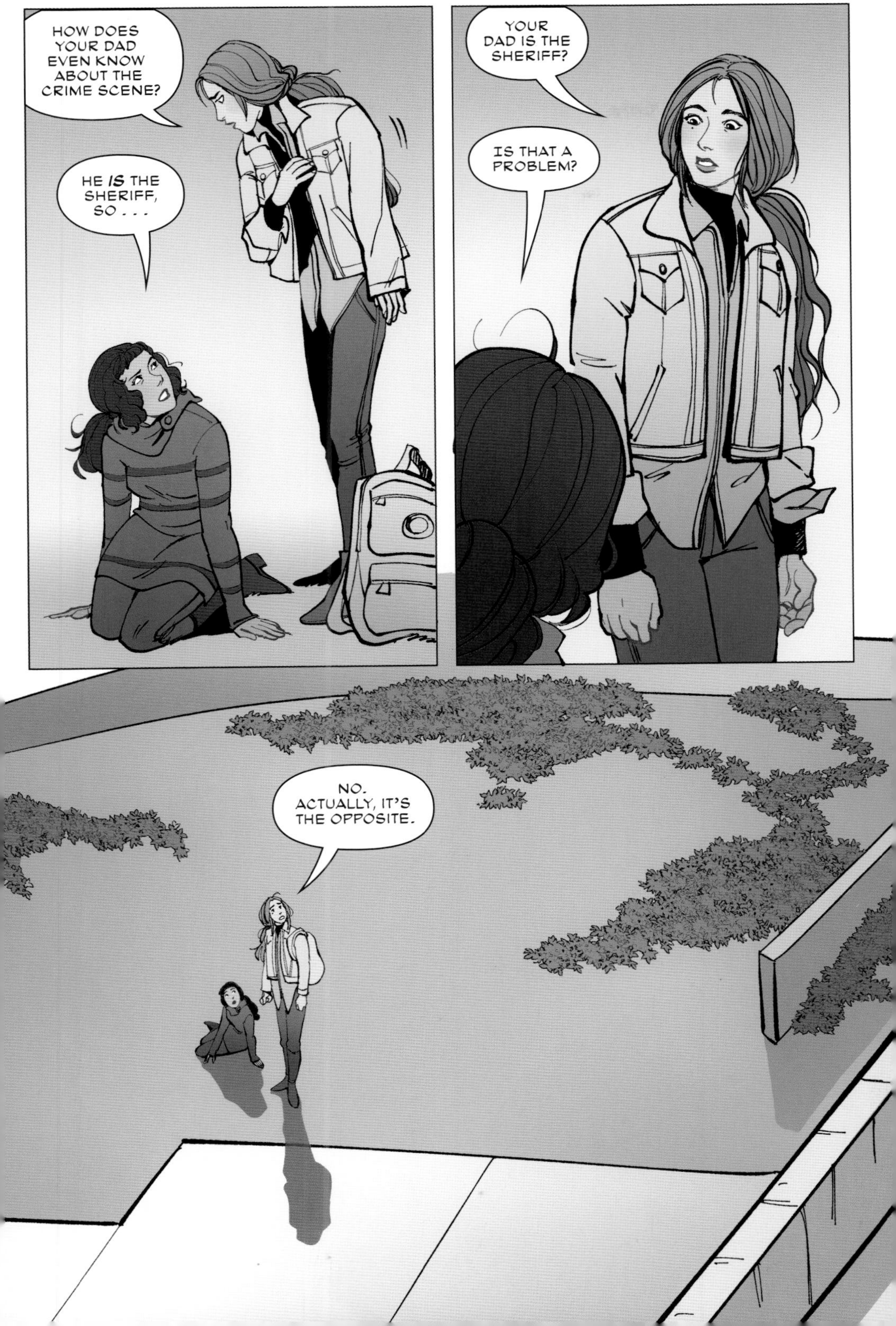
HOW DOES YOUR DAD EVEN KNOW ABOUT THE CRIME SCENE?
HE *IS* THE SHERIFF, SO . . .
YOUR DAD IS THE SHERIFF?
IS THAT A PROBLEM?
NO. ACTUALLY, IT'S THE OPPOSITE.

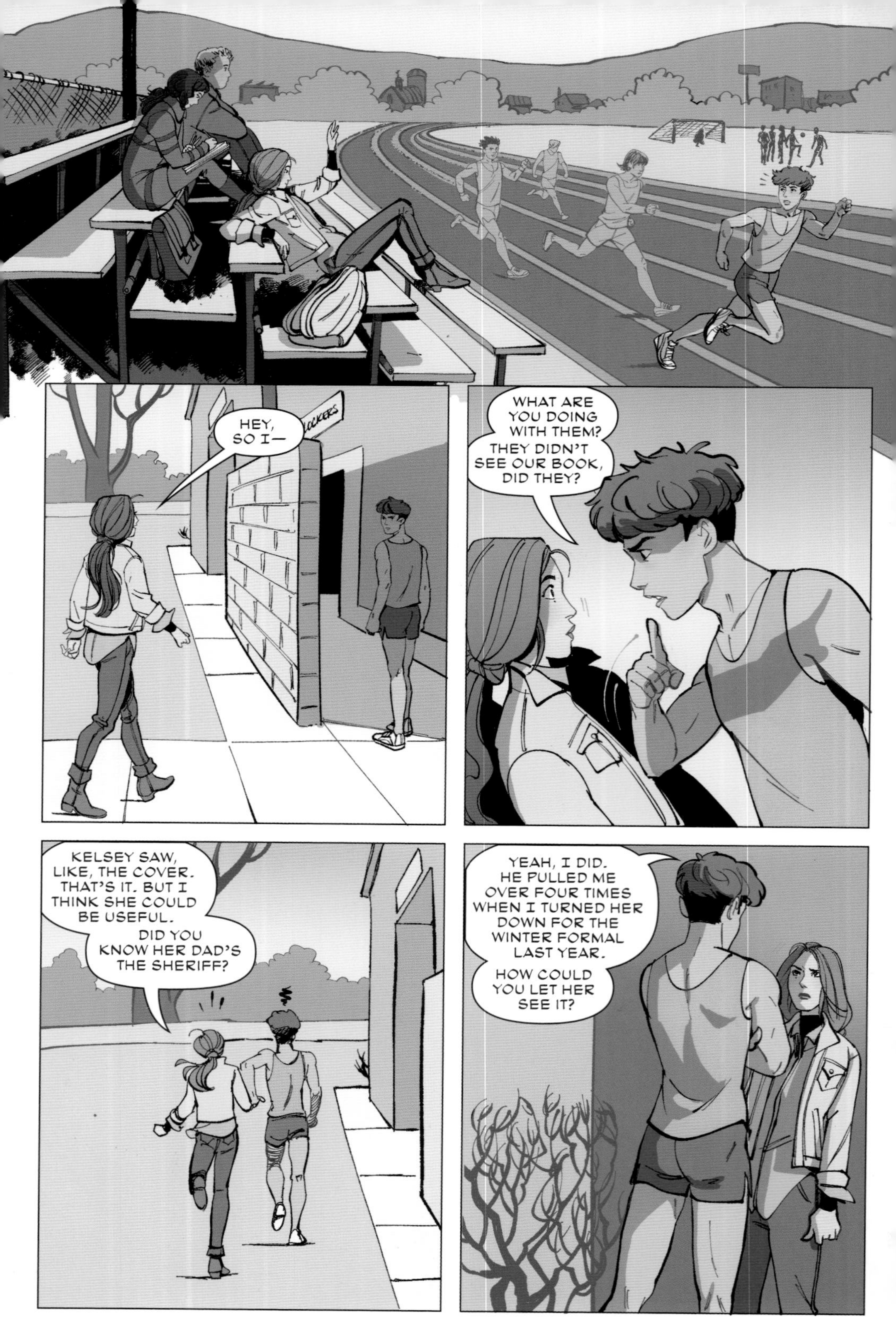
LOCKERS
HEY, SO I—
WHAT ARE YOU DOING WITH THEM?
THEY DIDN'T SEE OUR BOOK, DID THEY?
KELSEY SAW, LIKE, THE COVER. THAT'S IT. BUT I THINK SHE COULD BE USEFUL.
DID YOU KNOW HER DAD'S THE SHERIFF?
YEAH, I DID. HE PULLED ME OVER FOUR TIMES WHEN I TURNED HER DOWN FOR THE WINTER FORMAL LAST YEAR.
HOW COULD YOU LET HER SEE IT?

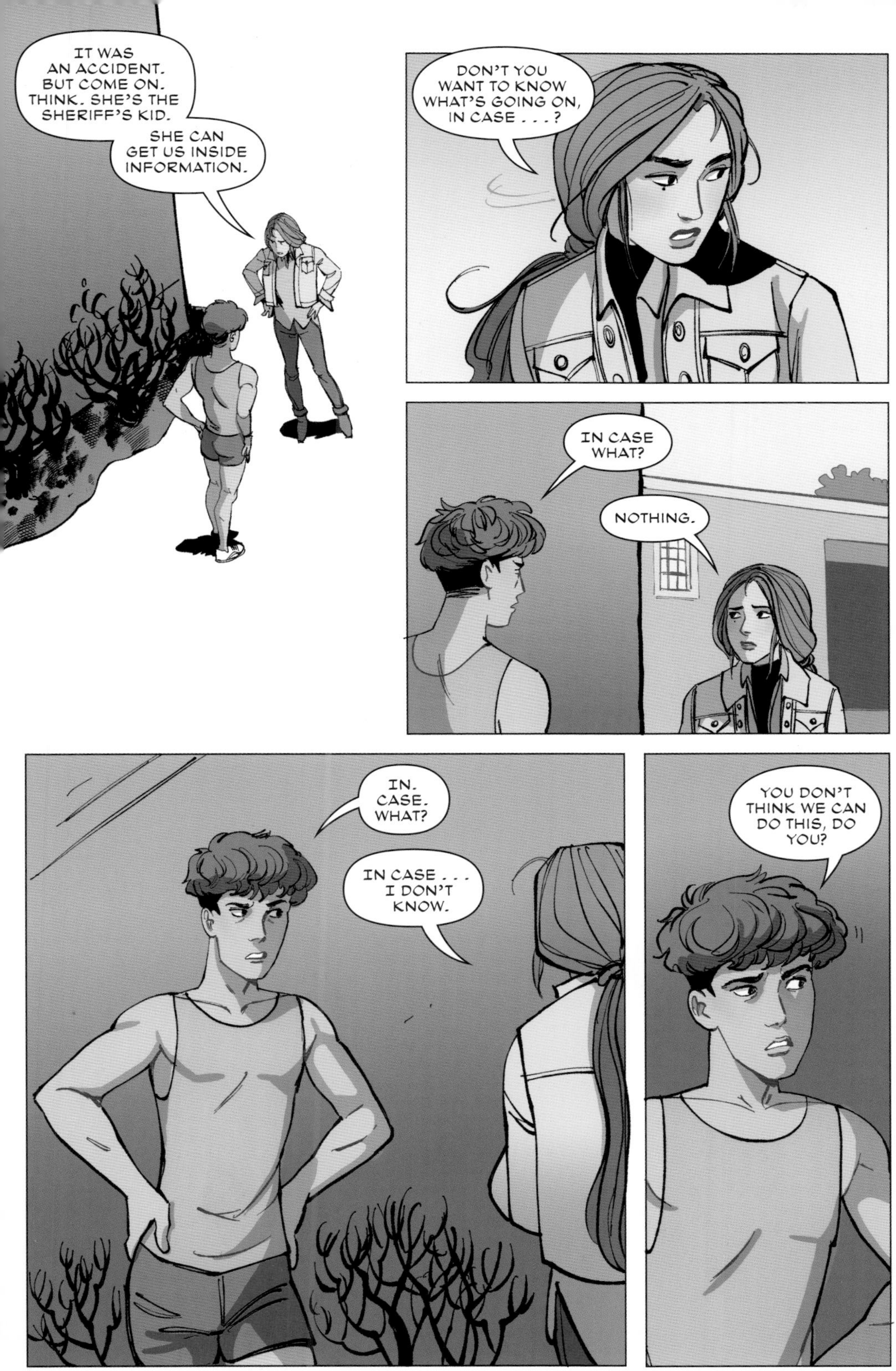
IT WAS AN ACCIDENT. BUT COME ON. THINK. SHE'S THE SHERIFF'S KID.
SHE CAN GET US INSIDE INFORMATION.
DON'T YOU WANT TO KNOW WHAT'S GOING ON, IN CASE . . . ?
IN CASE WHAT?
NOTHING.
IN. CASE. WHAT?
IN CASE . . . I DON'T KNOW.
YOU DON'T THINK WE CAN DO THIS, DO YOU?

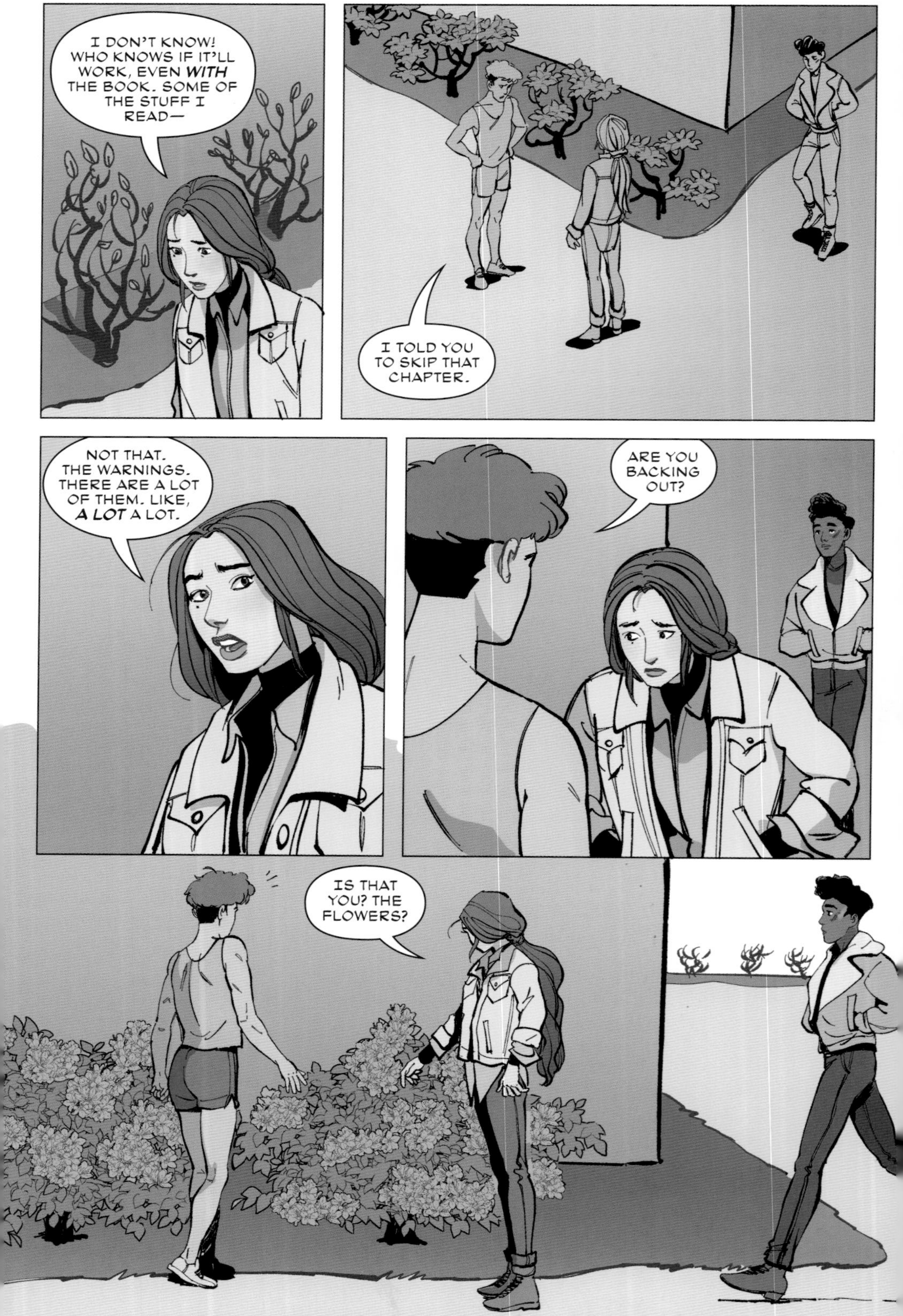

I DON'T KNOW! WHO KNOWS IF IT'LL WORK, EVEN *WITH* THE BOOK. SOME OF THE STUFF I READ—
I TOLD YOU TO SKIP THAT CHAPTER.
NOT THAT. THE WARNINGS. THERE ARE A LOT OF THEM. LIKE, ***A LOT*** A LOT.
ARE YOU BACKING OUT?
IS THAT YOU? THE FLOWERS?

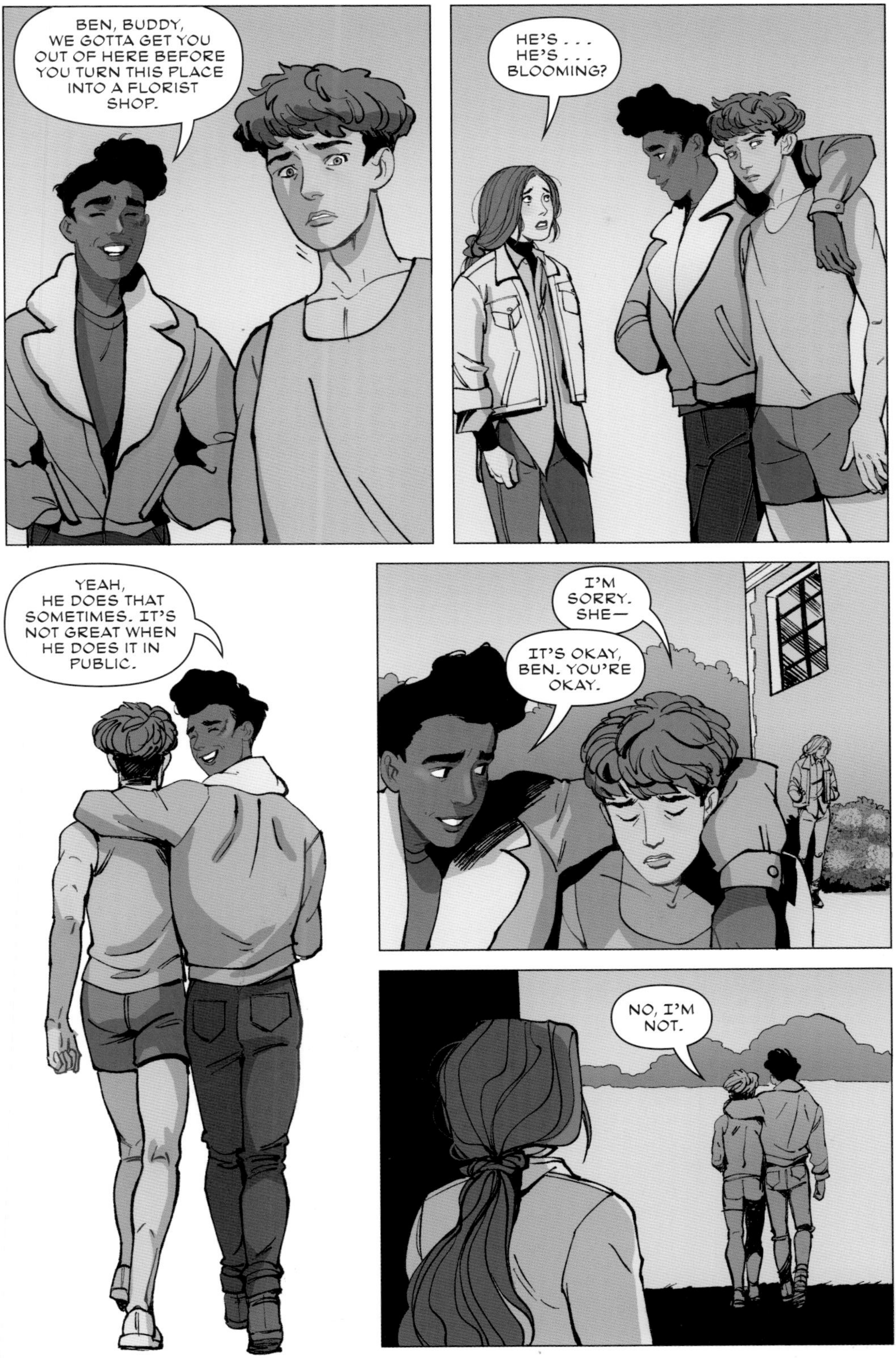
BEN, BUDDY, WE GOTTA GET YOU OUT OF HERE BEFORE YOU TURN THIS PLACE INTO A FLORIST SHOP.
HE'S . . . HE'S . . . BLOOMING?
YEAH, HE DOES THAT SOMETIMES. IT'S NOT GREAT WHEN HE DOES IT IN PUBLIC.
I'M SORRY. SHE—
IT'S OKAY, BEN. YOU'RE OKAY.
NO, I'M NOT.

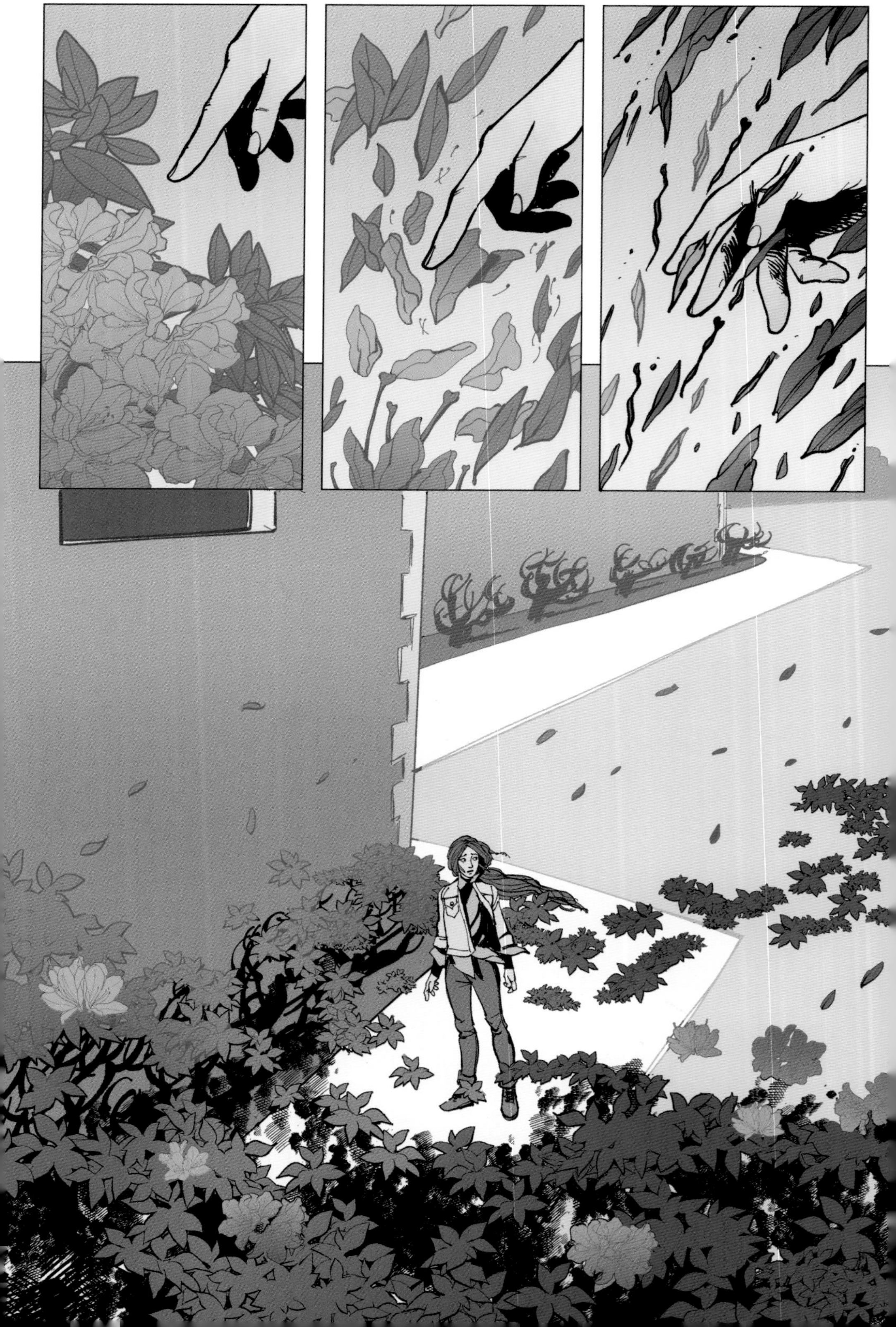

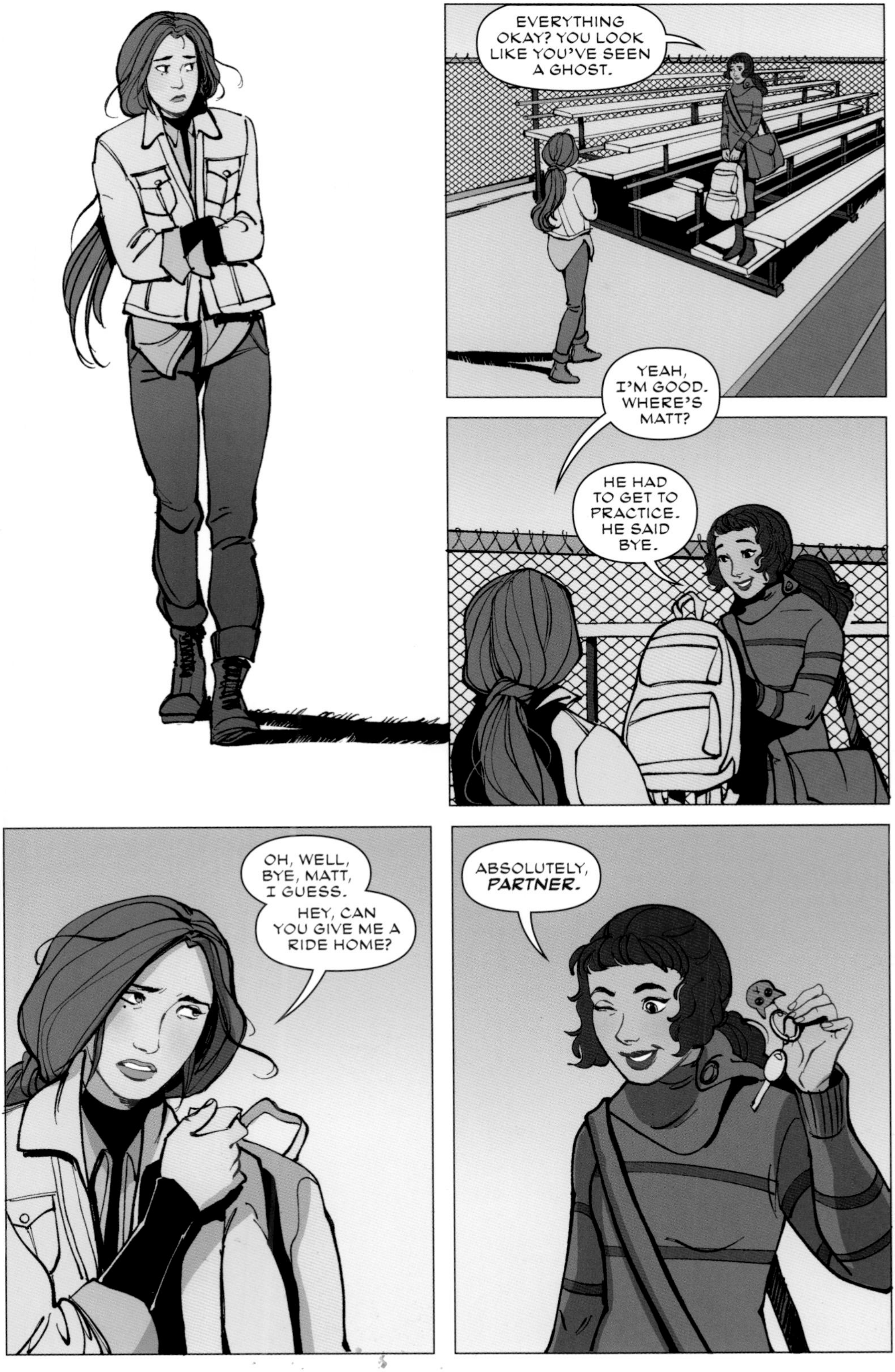
EVERYTHING OKAY? YOU LOOK LIKE YOU'VE SEEN A GHOST.
YEAH, I'M GOOD. WHERE'S MATT?
HE HAD TO GET TO PRACTICE. HE SAID BYE.
OH, WELL, BYE, MATT, I GUESS.
HEY, CAN YOU GIVE ME A RIDE HOME?
ABSOLUTELY, *PARTNER.*

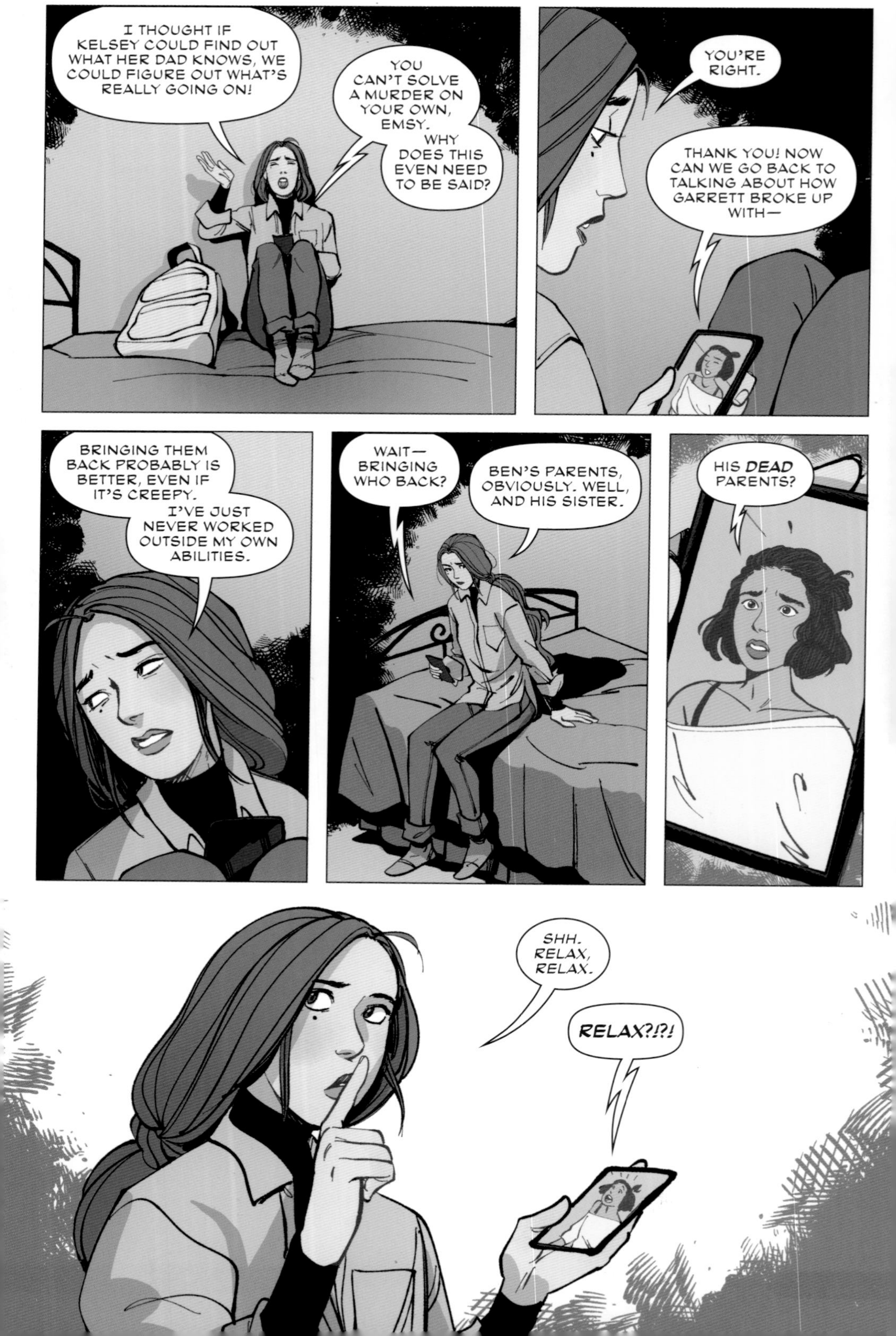
I THOUGHT IF KELSEY COULD FIND OUT WHAT HER DAD KNOWS, WE COULD FIGURE OUT WHAT'S REALLY GOING ON!
YOU CAN'T SOLVE A MURDER ON YOUR OWN, EMSY.
WHY DOES THIS EVEN NEED TO BE SAID?
YOU'RE RIGHT.
THANK YOU! NOW CAN WE GO BACK TO TALKING ABOUT HOW GARRETT BROKE UP WITH—
BRINGING THEM BACK PROBABLY IS BETTER, EVEN IF IT'S CREEPY.
I'VE JUST NEVER WORKED OUTSIDE MY OWN ABILITIES.
WAIT— BRINGING WHO BACK?
BEN'S PARENTS, OBVIOUSLY. WELL, AND HIS SISTER.
HIS ***DEAD*** PARENTS?
SHH. RELAX, RELAX.
RELAX?!?!

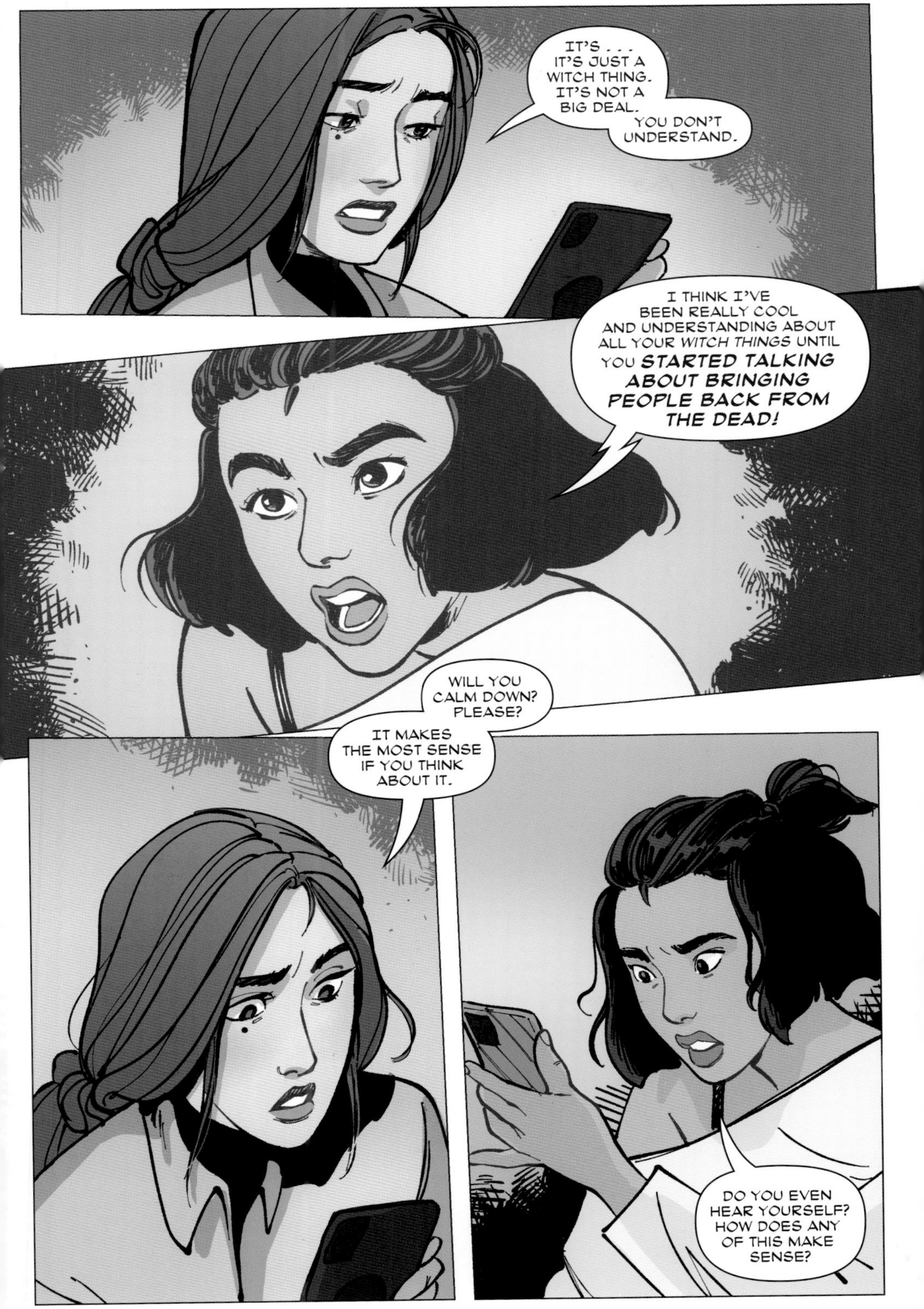
IT'S . . . IT'S JUST A WITCH THING. IT'S NOT A BIG DEAL.
YOU DON'T UNDERSTAND.
I THINK I'VE BEEN REALLY COOL AND UNDERSTANDING ABOUT ALL YOUR *WITCH THINGS* UNTIL YOU **STARTED TALKING ABOUT BRINGING PEOPLE BACK FROM THE DEAD!**
WILL YOU CALM DOWN? PLEASE?
IT MAKES THE MOST SENSE IF YOU THINK ABOUT IT.
DO YOU EVEN HEAR YOURSELF? HOW DOES ANY OF THIS MAKE SENSE?

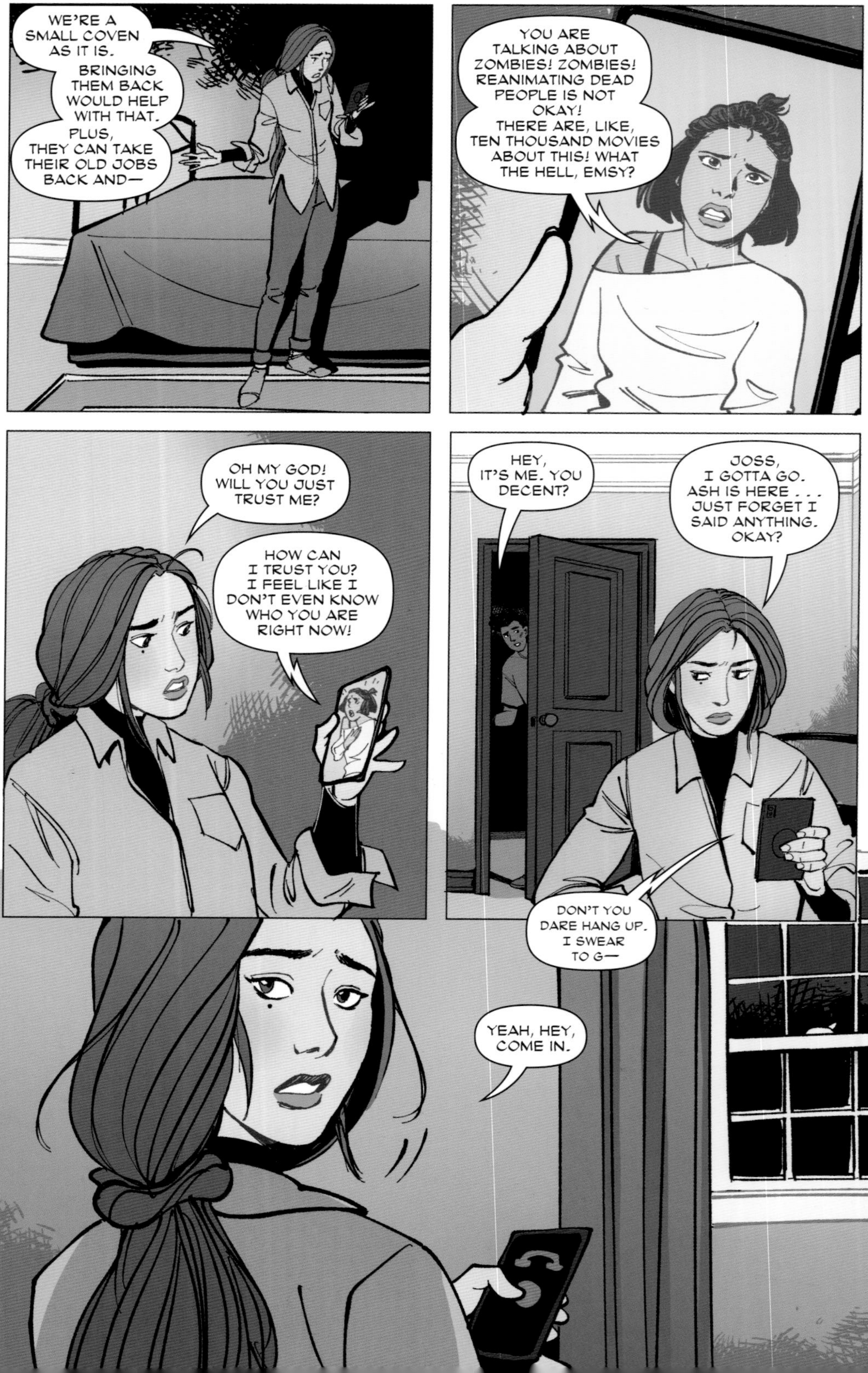
WE'RE A SMALL COVEN AS IT IS.
BRINGING THEM BACK WOULD HELP WITH THAT.
PLUS, THEY CAN TAKE THEIR OLD JOBS BACK AND—
YOU ARE TALKING ABOUT ZOMBIES! ZOMBIES! REANIMATING DEAD PEOPLE IS NOT OKAY!
THERE ARE, LIKE, TEN THOUSAND MOVIES ABOUT THIS! WHAT THE HELL, EMSY?
OH MY GOD! WILL YOU JUST TRUST ME?
HOW CAN I TRUST YOU? I FEEL LIKE I DON'T EVEN KNOW WHO YOU ARE RIGHT NOW!
HEY, IT'S ME. YOU DECENT?
JOSS, I GOTTA GO. ASH IS HERE . . . JUST FORGET I SAID ANYTHING. OKAY?
DON'T YOU DARE HANG UP. I SWEAR TO G—
YEAH, HEY, COME IN.

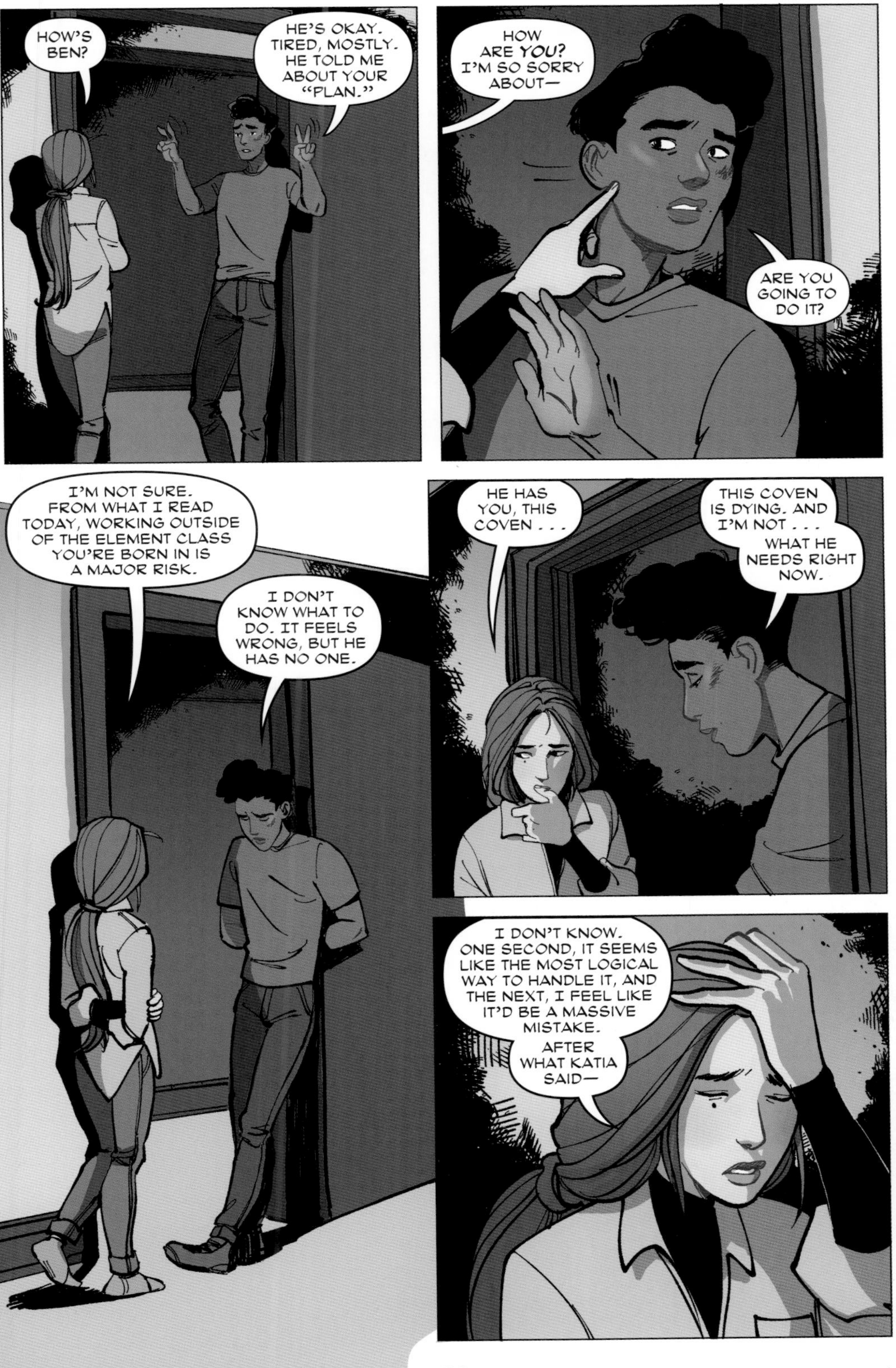
HOW'S BEN?
HE'S OKAY. TIRED, MOSTLY. HE TOLD ME ABOUT YOUR "PLAN."
HOW ARE *YOU*? I'M SO SORRY ABOUT—
ARE YOU GOING TO DO IT?
I'M NOT SURE. FROM WHAT I READ TODAY, WORKING OUTSIDE OF THE ELEMENT CLASS YOU'RE BORN IN IS A MAJOR RISK.
I DON'T KNOW WHAT TO DO. IT FEELS WRONG, BUT HE HAS NO ONE.
HE HAS YOU, THIS COVEN . . .
THIS COVEN IS DYING. AND I'M NOT . . .
WHAT HE NEEDS RIGHT NOW.
I DON'T KNOW. ONE SECOND, IT SEEMS LIKE THE MOST LOGICAL WAY TO HANDLE IT, AND THE NEXT, I FEEL LIKE IT'D BE A MASSIVE MISTAKE.
AFTER WHAT KATIA SAID—

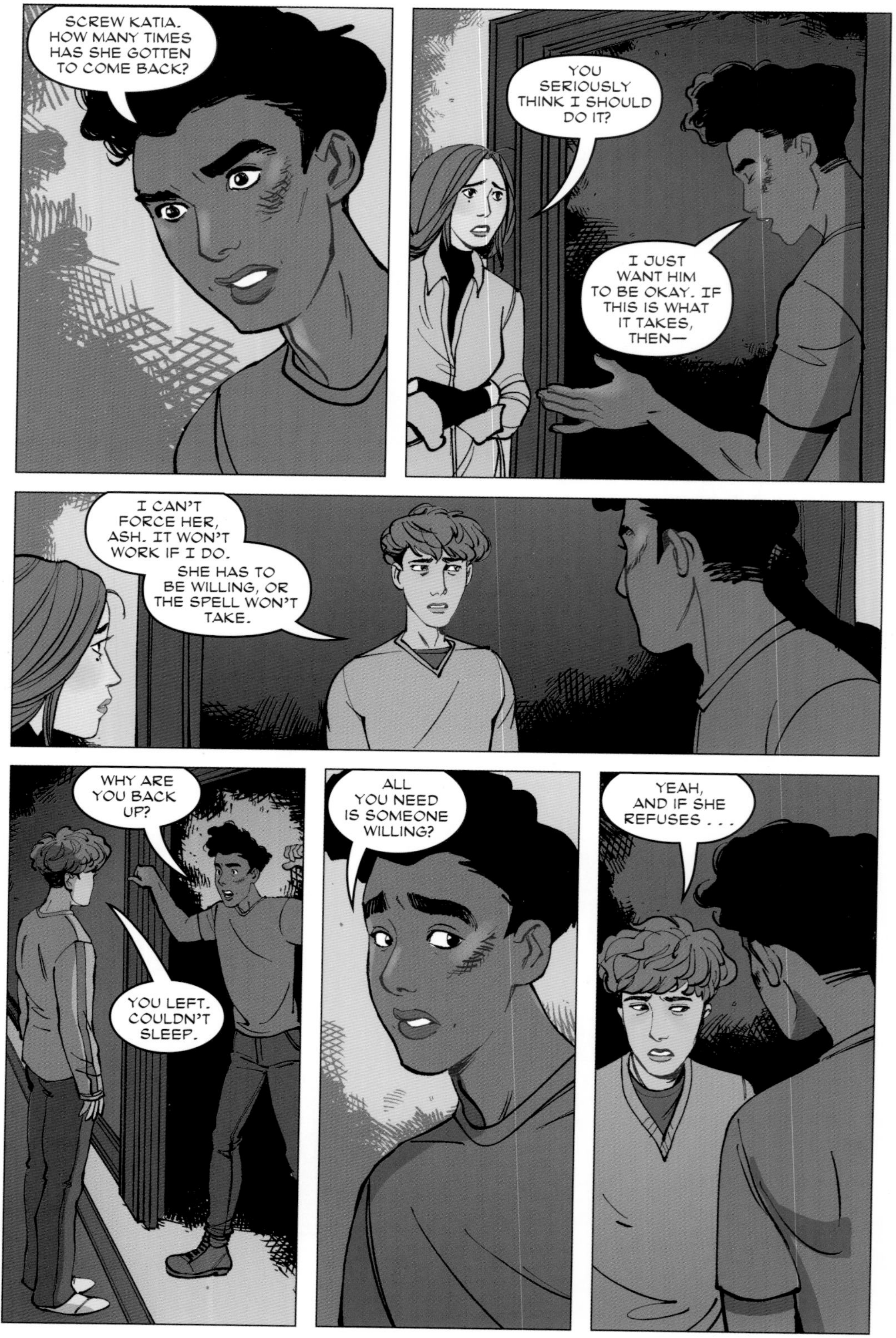
SCREW KATIA. HOW MANY TIMES HAS SHE GOTTEN TO COME BACK?
YOU SERIOUSLY THINK I SHOULD DO IT?
I JUST WANT HIM TO BE OKAY. IF THIS IS WHAT IT TAKES, THEN—
I CAN'T FORCE HER, ASH. IT WON'T WORK IF I DO.
SHE HAS TO BE WILLING, OR THE SPELL WON'T TAKE.
WHY ARE YOU BACK UP?
YOU LEFT. COULDN'T SLEEP.
ALL YOU NEED IS SOMEONE WILLING?
YEAH, AND IF SHE REFUSES . . .

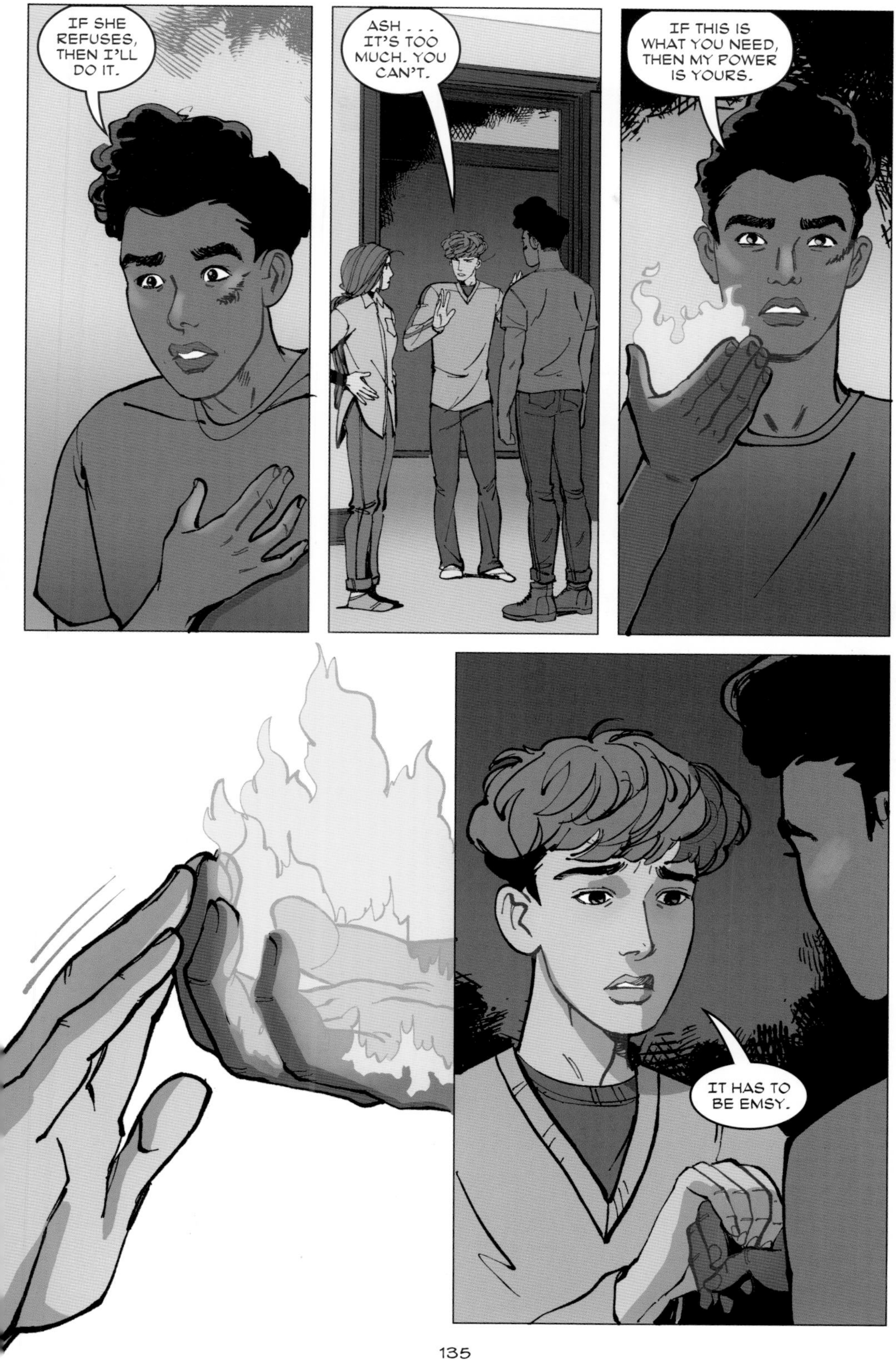
IF SHE REFUSES, THEN I'LL DO IT.
ASH . . . IT'S TOO MUCH. YOU CAN'T.
IF THIS IS WHAT YOU NEED, THEN MY POWER IS YOURS.
IT HAS TO BE EMSY.

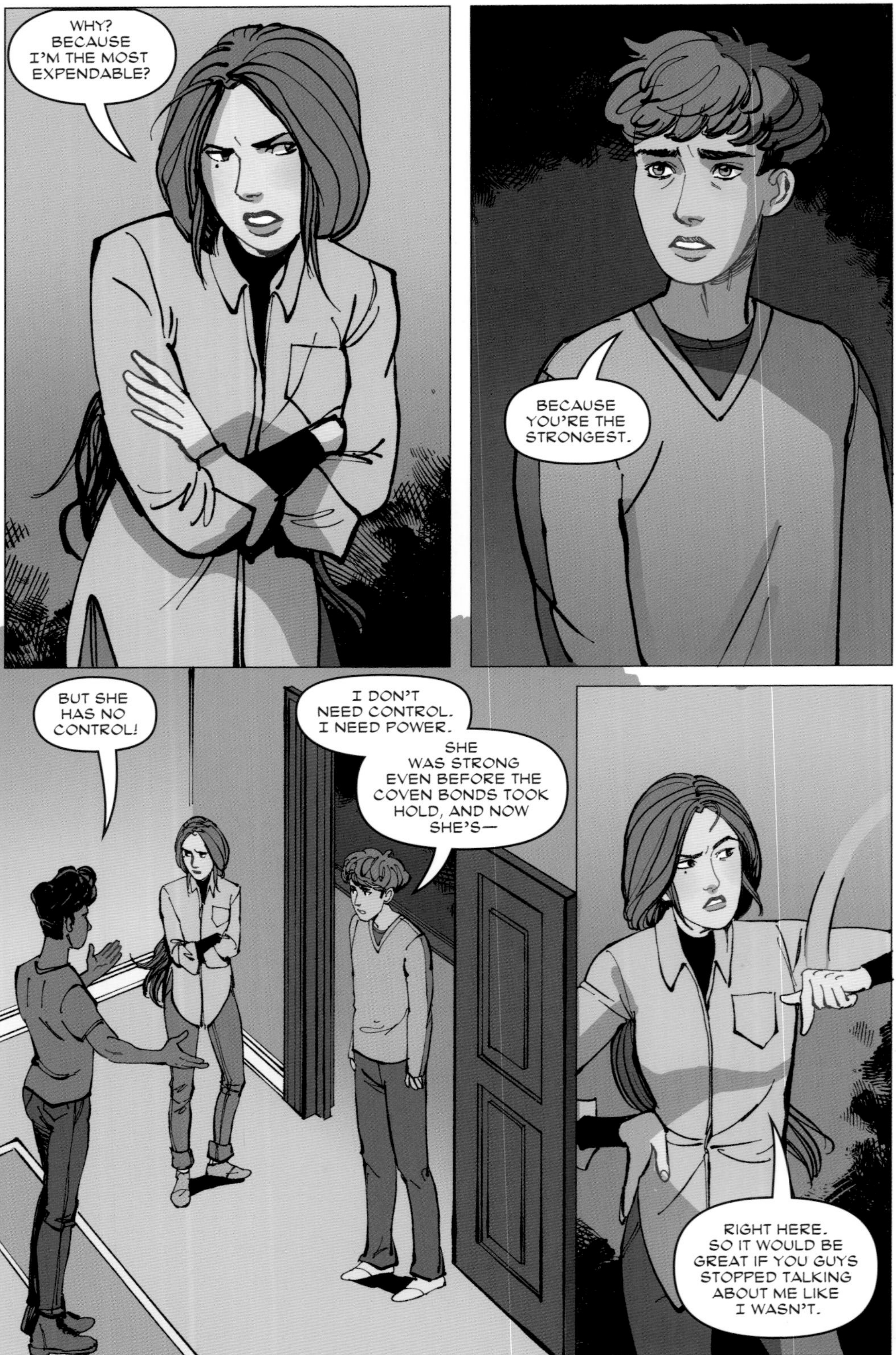
WHY? BECAUSE I'M THE MOST EXPENDABLE?
BECAUSE YOU'RE THE STRONGEST.
BUT SHE HAS NO CONTROL!
I DON'T NEED CONTROL. I NEED POWER.
SHE WAS STRONG EVEN BEFORE THE COVEN BONDS TOOK HOLD, AND NOW SHE'S—
RIGHT HERE. SO IT WOULD BE GREAT IF YOU GUYS STOPPED TALKING ABOUT ME LIKE I WASN'T.

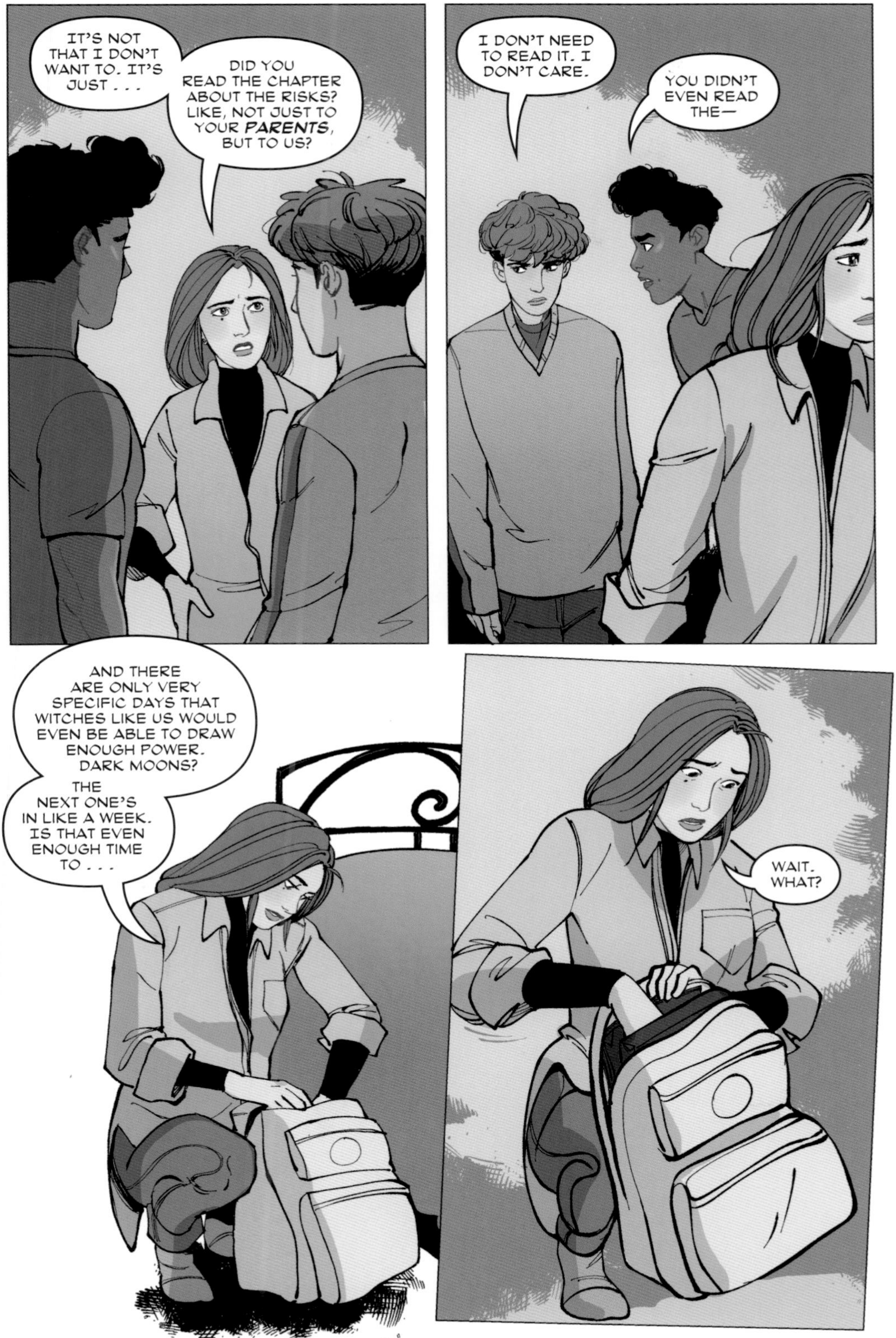
IT'S NOT THAT I DON'T WANT TO. IT'S JUST . . .
DID YOU READ THE CHAPTER ABOUT THE RISKS? LIKE, NOT JUST TO YOUR **PARENTS**, BUT TO US?
I DON'T NEED TO READ IT. I DON'T CARE.
YOU DIDN'T EVEN READ THE—
AND THERE ARE ONLY VERY SPECIFIC DAYS THAT WITCHES LIKE US WOULD EVEN BE ABLE TO DRAW ENOUGH POWER. DARK MOONS?
THE NEXT ONE'S IN LIKE A WEEK. IS THAT EVEN ENOUGH TIME TO . . .
WAIT. WHAT?

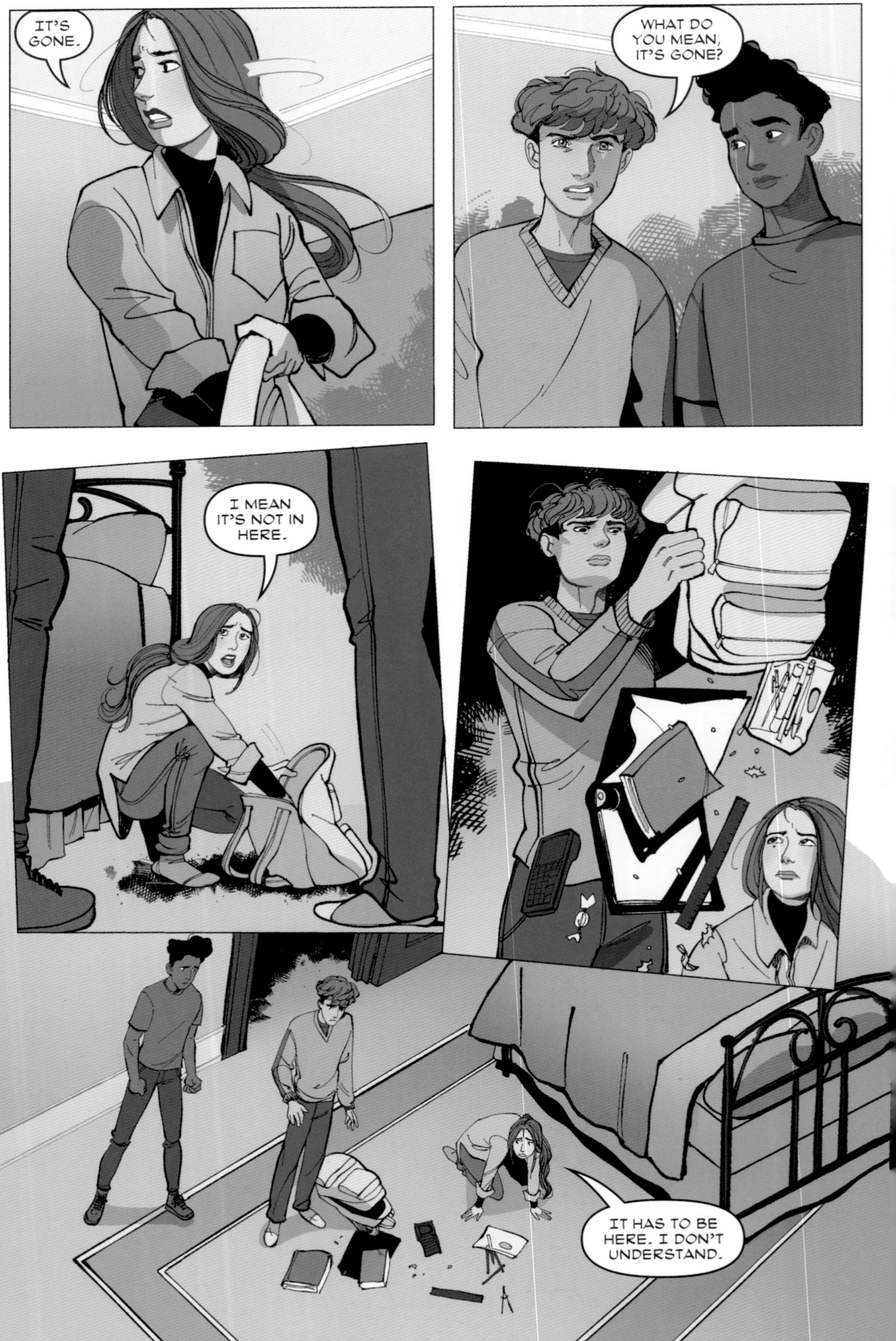

IT'S GONE.
WHAT DO YOU MEAN, IT'S GONE?
I MEAN IT'S NOT IN HERE.
IT HAS TO BE HERE. I DON'T UNDERSTAND.

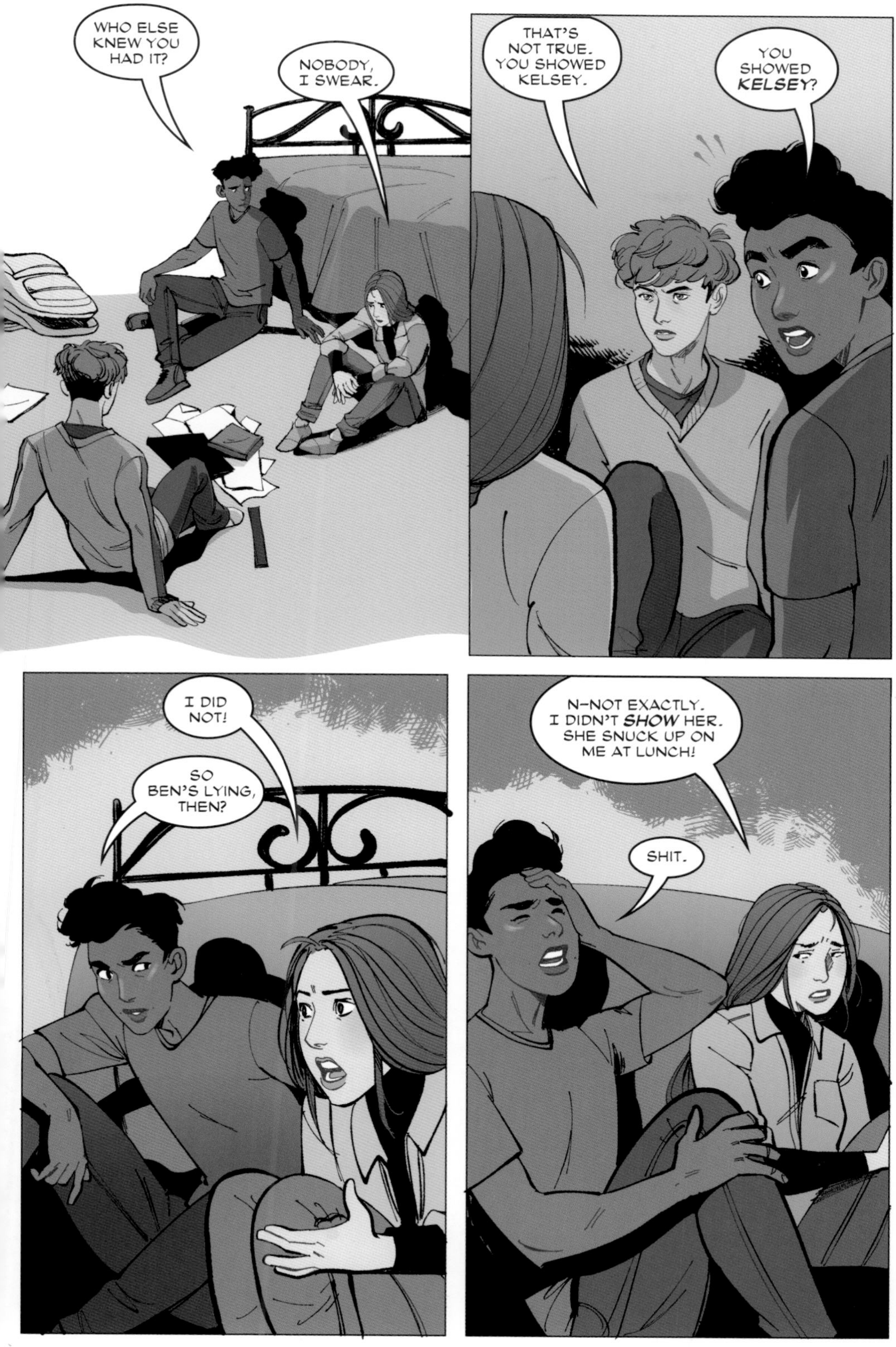
WHO ELSE KNEW YOU HAD IT?
NOBODY, I SWEAR.
THAT'S NOT TRUE. YOU SHOWED KELSEY.
YOU SHOWED KELSEY?
I DID NOT!
SO BEN'S LYING, THEN?
N-NOT EXACTLY. I DIDN'T SHOW HER. SHE SNUCK UP ON ME AT LUNCH!
SHIT.

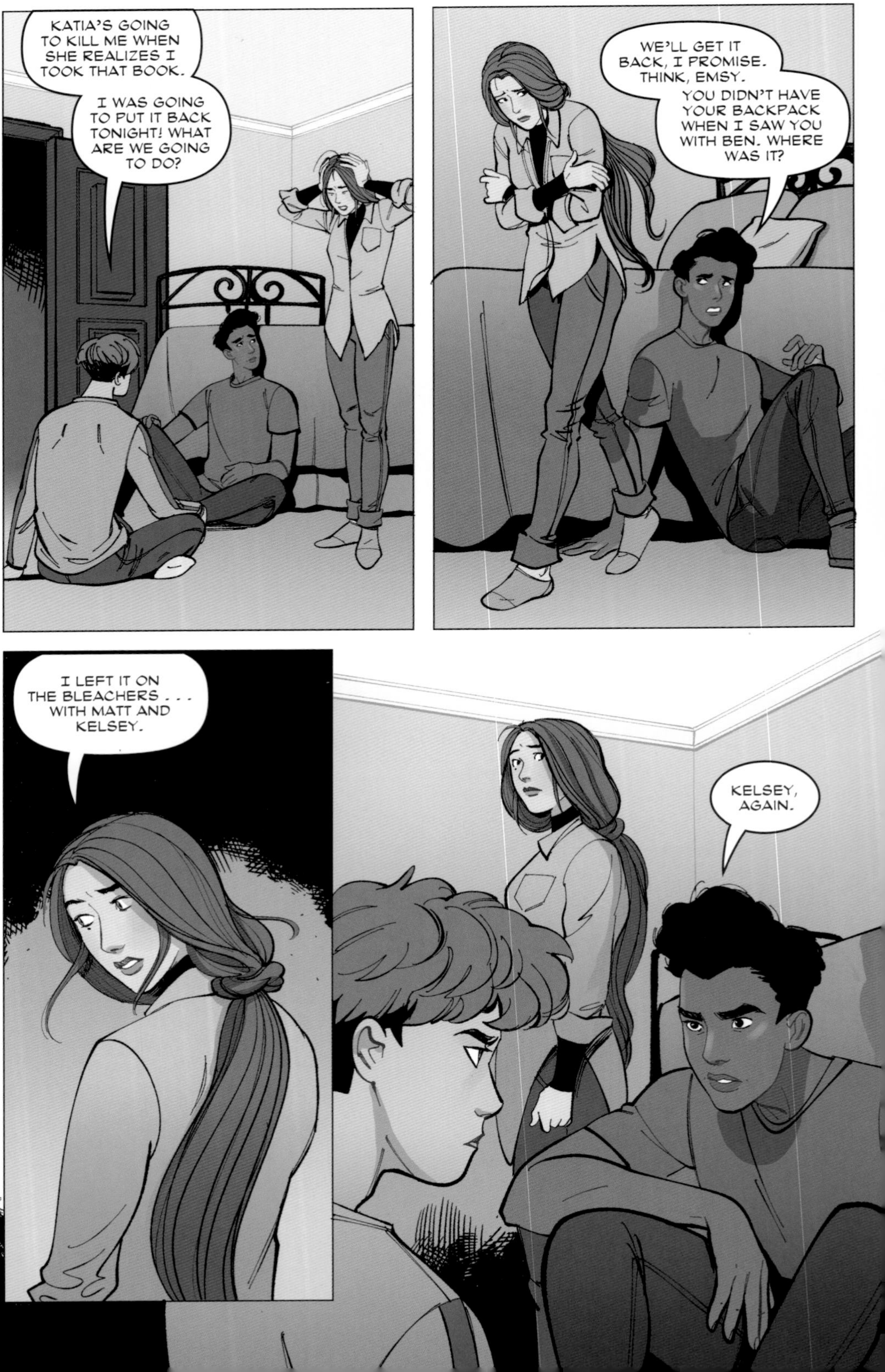
KATIA'S GOING TO KILL ME WHEN SHE REALIZES I TOOK THAT BOOK.
I WAS GOING TO PUT IT BACK TONIGHT! WHAT ARE WE GOING TO DO?
WE'LL GET IT BACK, I PROMISE. THINK, EMSY.
YOU DIDN'T HAVE YOUR BACKPACK WHEN I SAW YOU WITH BEN. WHERE WAS IT?
I LEFT IT ON THE BLEACHERS . . . WITH MATT AND KELSEY.
KELSEY, AGAIN.

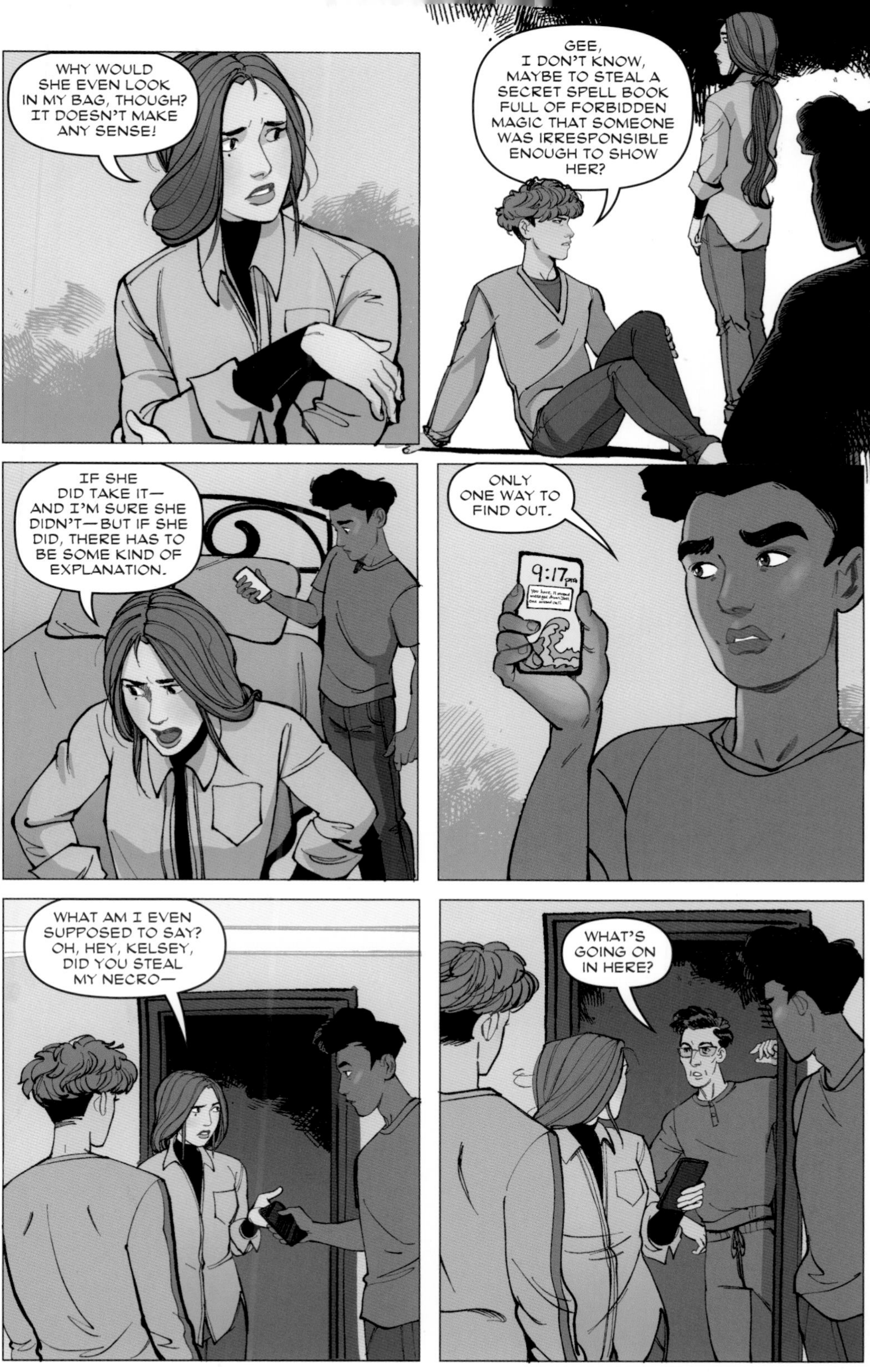
WHY WOULD SHE EVEN LOOK IN MY BAG, THOUGH? IT DOESN'T MAKE ANY SENSE!
GEE, I DON'T KNOW, MAYBE TO STEAL A SECRET SPELL BOOK FULL OF FORBIDDEN MAGIC THAT SOMEONE WAS IRRESPONSIBLE ENOUGH TO SHOW HER?
IF SHE DID TAKE IT— AND I'M SURE SHE DIDN'T— BUT IF SHE DID, THERE HAS TO BE SOME KIND OF EXPLANATION.
ONLY ONE WAY TO FIND OUT.
WHAT AM I EVEN SUPPOSED TO SAY? OH, HEY, KELSEY, DID YOU STEAL MY NECRO—
WHAT'S GOING ON IN HERE?

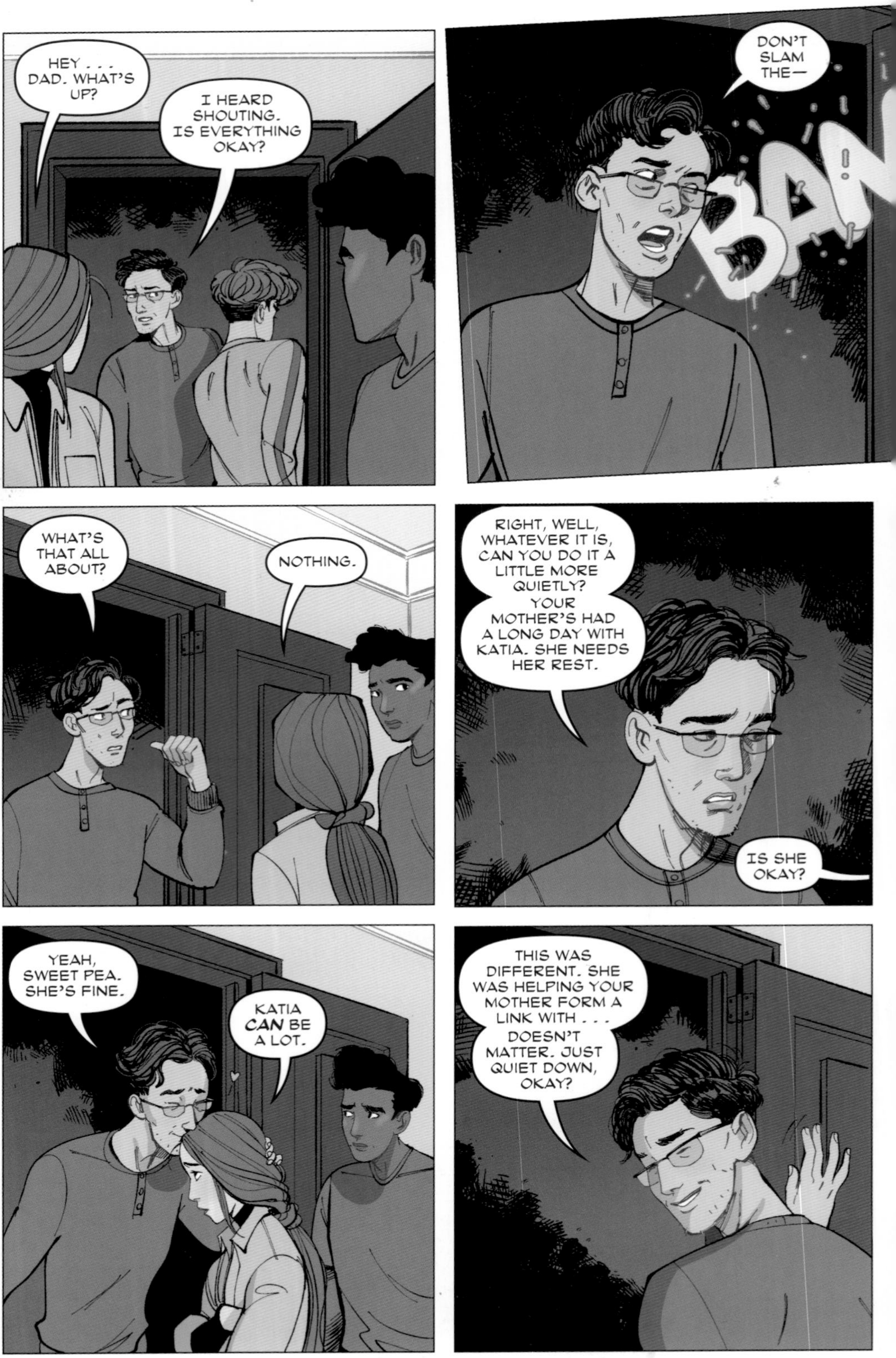
HEY . . . DAD. WHAT'S UP?
I HEARD SHOUTING. IS EVERYTHING OKAY?
DON'T SLAM THE—
BAM
WHAT'S THAT ALL ABOUT?
NOTHING.
RIGHT, WELL, WHATEVER IT IS, CAN YOU DO IT A LITTLE MORE QUIETLY?
YOUR MOTHER'S HAD A LONG DAY WITH KATIA. SHE NEEDS HER REST.
IS SHE OKAY?
YEAH, SWEET PEA. SHE'S FINE.
KATIA ***CAN*** BE A LOT.
THIS WAS DIFFERENT. SHE WAS HELPING YOUR MOTHER FORM A LINK WITH . . .
DOESN'T MATTER. JUST QUIET DOWN, OKAY?

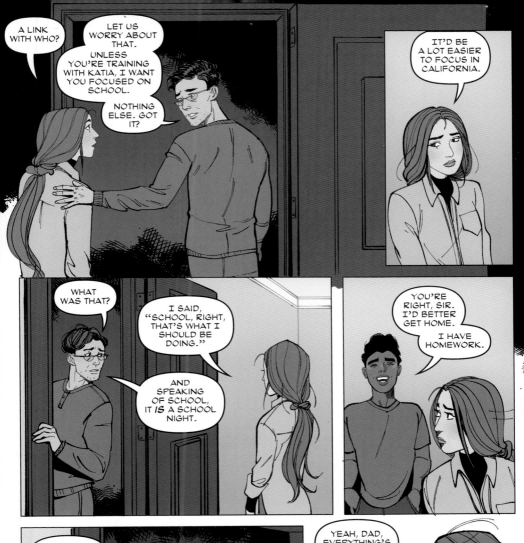

A LINK WITH WHO?

LET US WORRY ABOUT THAT. UNLESS YOU'RE TRAINING WITH KATIA, I WANT YOU FOCUSED ON SCHOOL.

NOTHING ELSE. GOT IT?

IT'D BE A LOT EASIER TO FOCUS IN CALIFORNIA.

WHAT WAS THAT?

I SAID, "SCHOOL, RIGHT, THAT'S WHAT I SHOULD BE DOING."

AND SPEAKING OF SCHOOL, IT *IS* A SCHOOL NIGHT.

YOU'RE RIGHT, SIR. I'D BETTER GET HOME.

I HAVE HOMEWORK.

ARE YOU SURE EVERYTHING'S OKAY?

YEAH, DAD, EVERYTHING'S JUST *PEACHY*.

You have 4 missed FaceTime calls, 6 missed calls, and 15 texts from Joss.

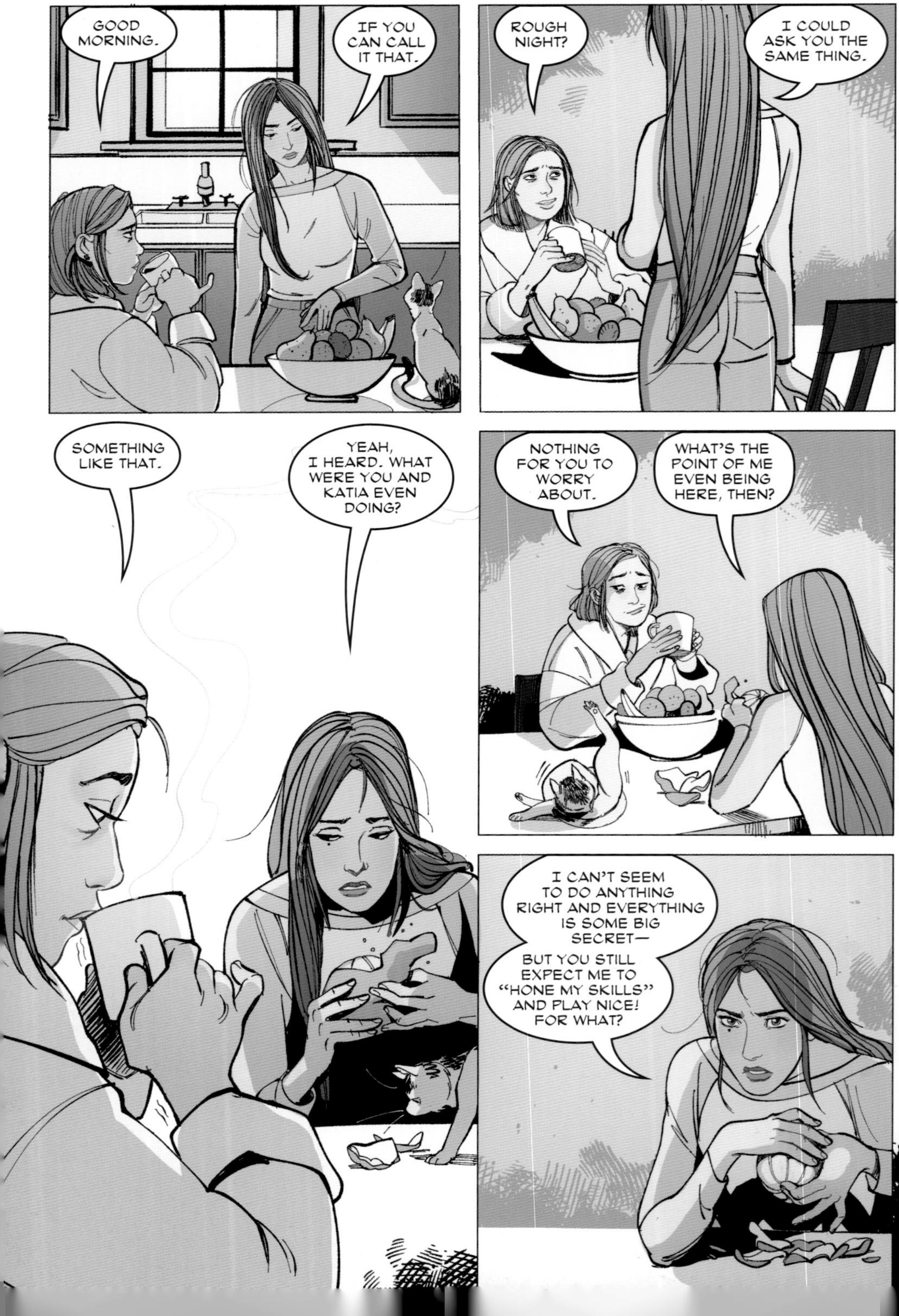
GOOD MORNING.
IF YOU CAN CALL IT THAT.
ROUGH NIGHT?
I COULD ASK YOU THE SAME THING.
SOMETHING LIKE THAT.
YEAH, I HEARD. WHAT WERE YOU AND KATIA EVEN DOING?
NOTHING FOR YOU TO WORRY ABOUT.
WHAT'S THE POINT OF ME EVEN BEING HERE, THEN?
I CAN'T SEEM TO DO ANYTHING RIGHT AND EVERYTHING IS SOME BIG SECRET—
BUT YOU STILL EXPECT ME TO "HONE MY SKILLS" AND PLAY NICE! FOR WHAT?

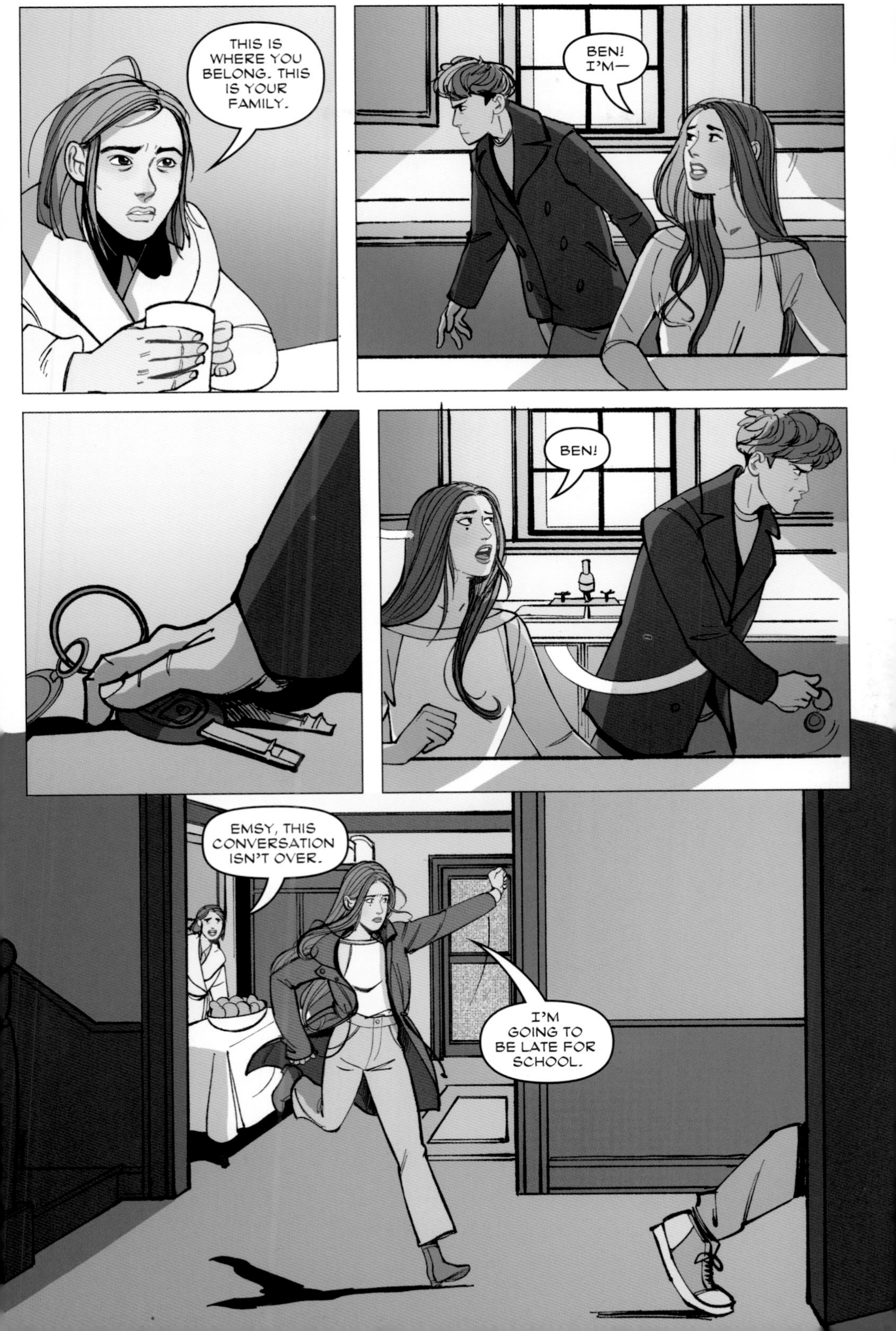

THIS IS WHERE YOU BELONG. THIS IS YOUR FAMILY.
BEN! I'M—
BEN!
EMSY, THIS CONVERSATION ISN'T OVER.
I'M GOING TO BE LATE FOR SCHOOL.

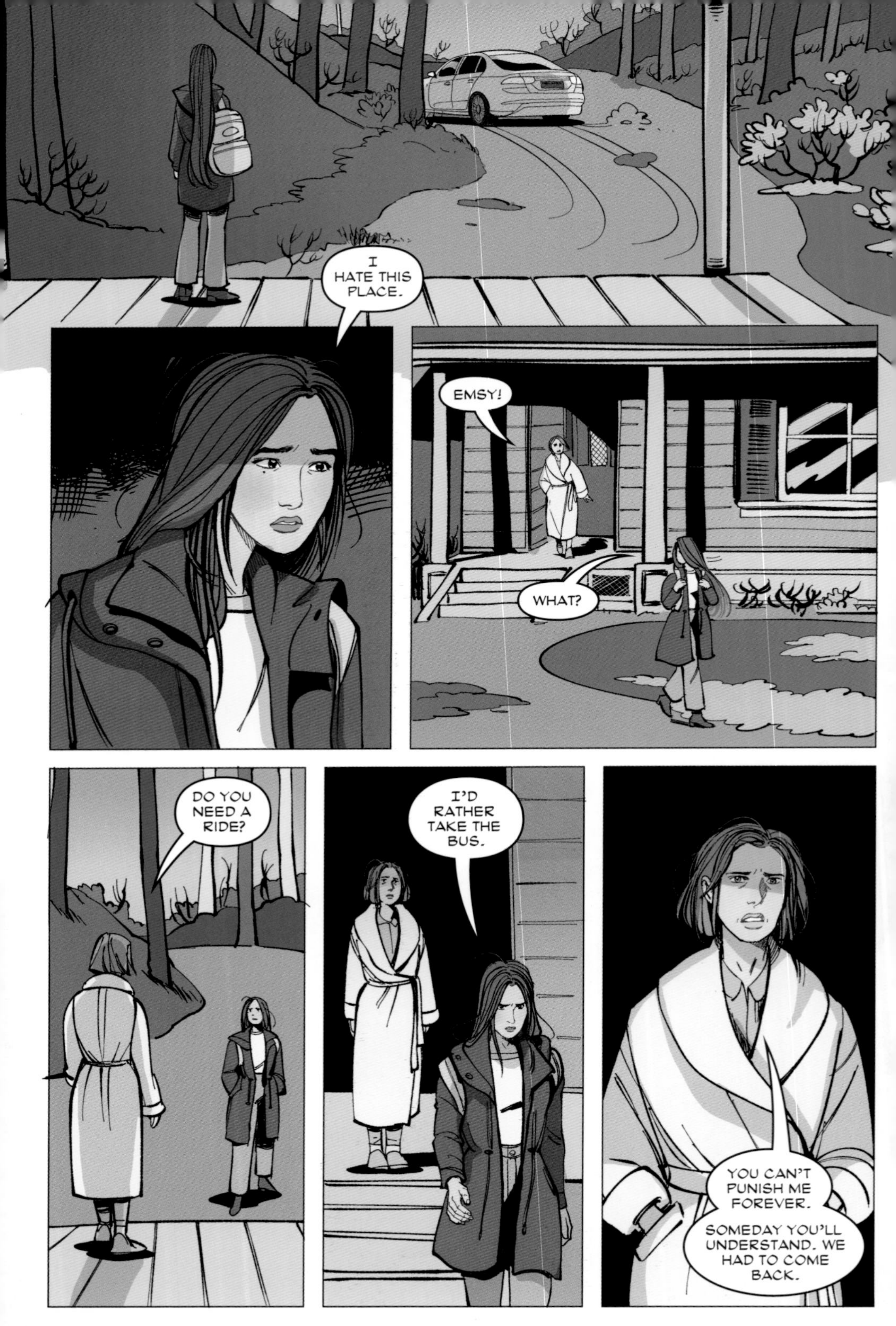
I HATE THIS PLACE.
EMSY!
WHAT?
DO YOU NEED A RIDE?
I'D RATHER TAKE THE BUS.
YOU CAN'T PUNISH ME FOREVER.
SOMEDAY YOU'LL UNDERSTAND. WE HAD TO COME BACK.

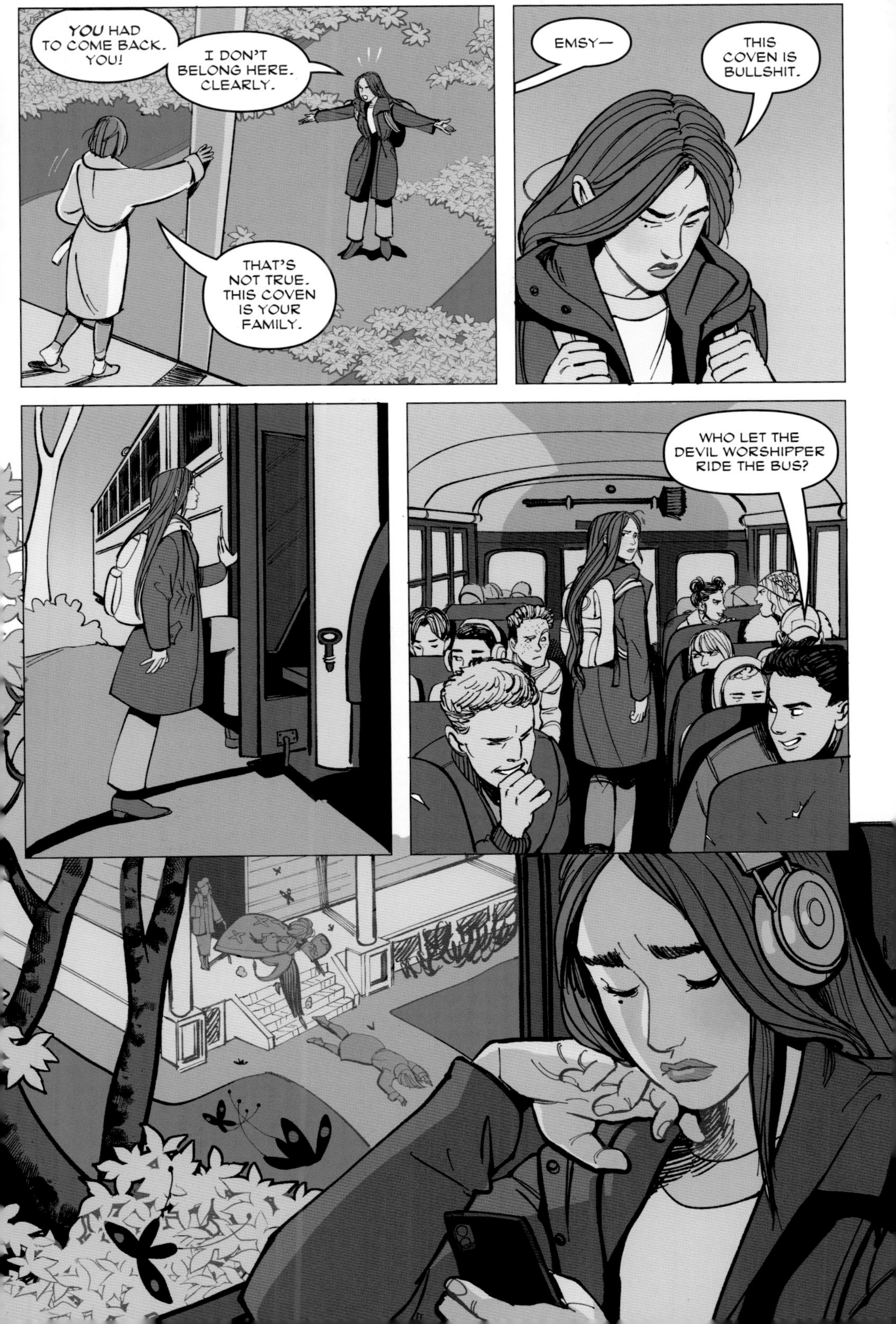
YOU HAD TO COME BACK. YOU!
I DON'T BELONG HERE. CLEARLY.
THAT'S NOT TRUE. THIS COVEN IS YOUR FAMILY.
EMSY—
THIS COVEN IS BULLSHIT.
WHO LET THE DEVIL WORSHIPPER RIDE THE BUS?

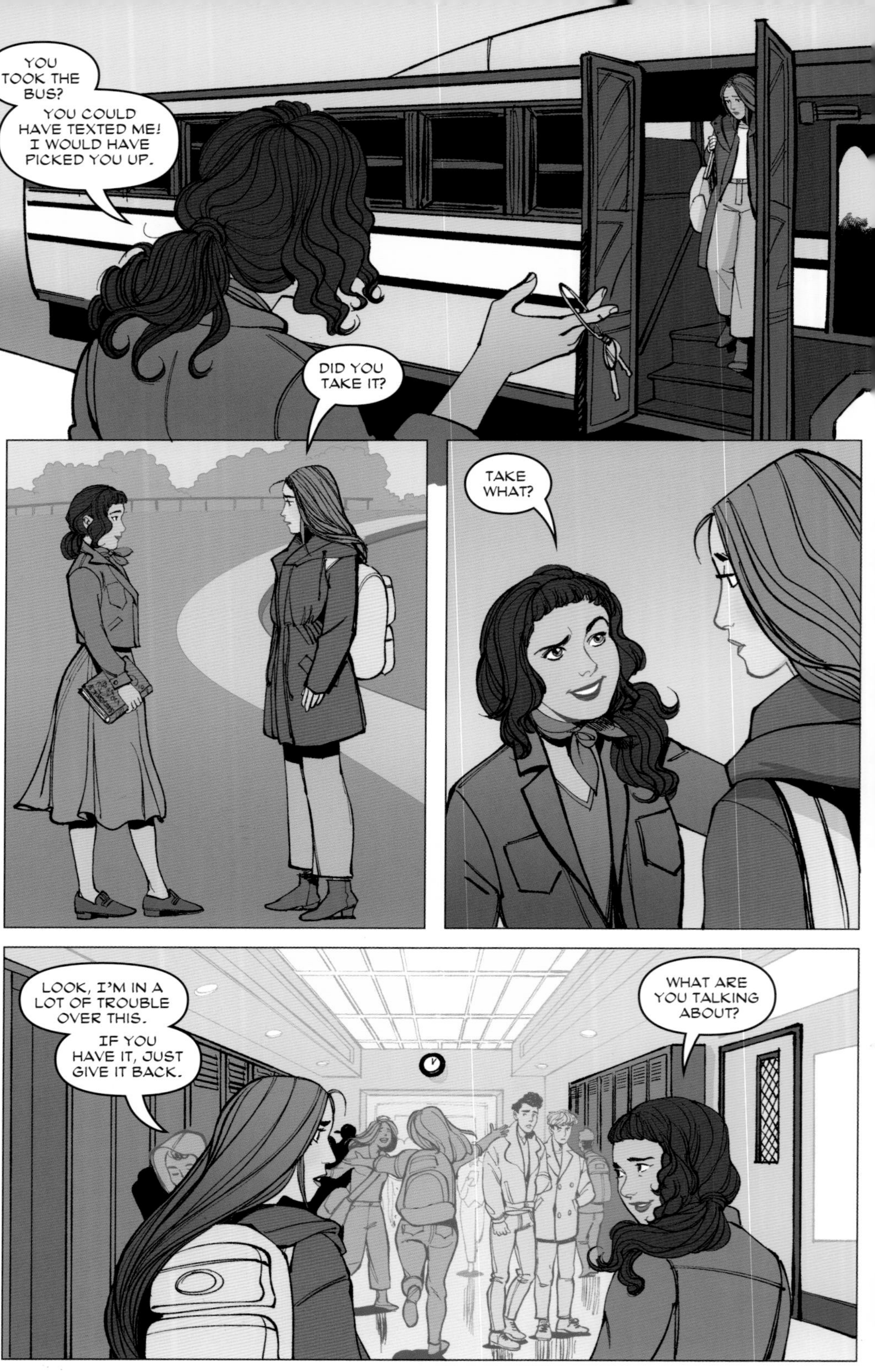
YOU TOOK THE BUS?
YOU COULD HAVE TEXTED ME! I WOULD HAVE PICKED YOU UP.
DID YOU TAKE IT?
TAKE WHAT?
LOOK, I'M IN A LOT OF TROUBLE OVER THIS.
IF YOU HAVE IT, JUST GIVE IT BACK.
WHAT ARE YOU TALKING ABOUT?

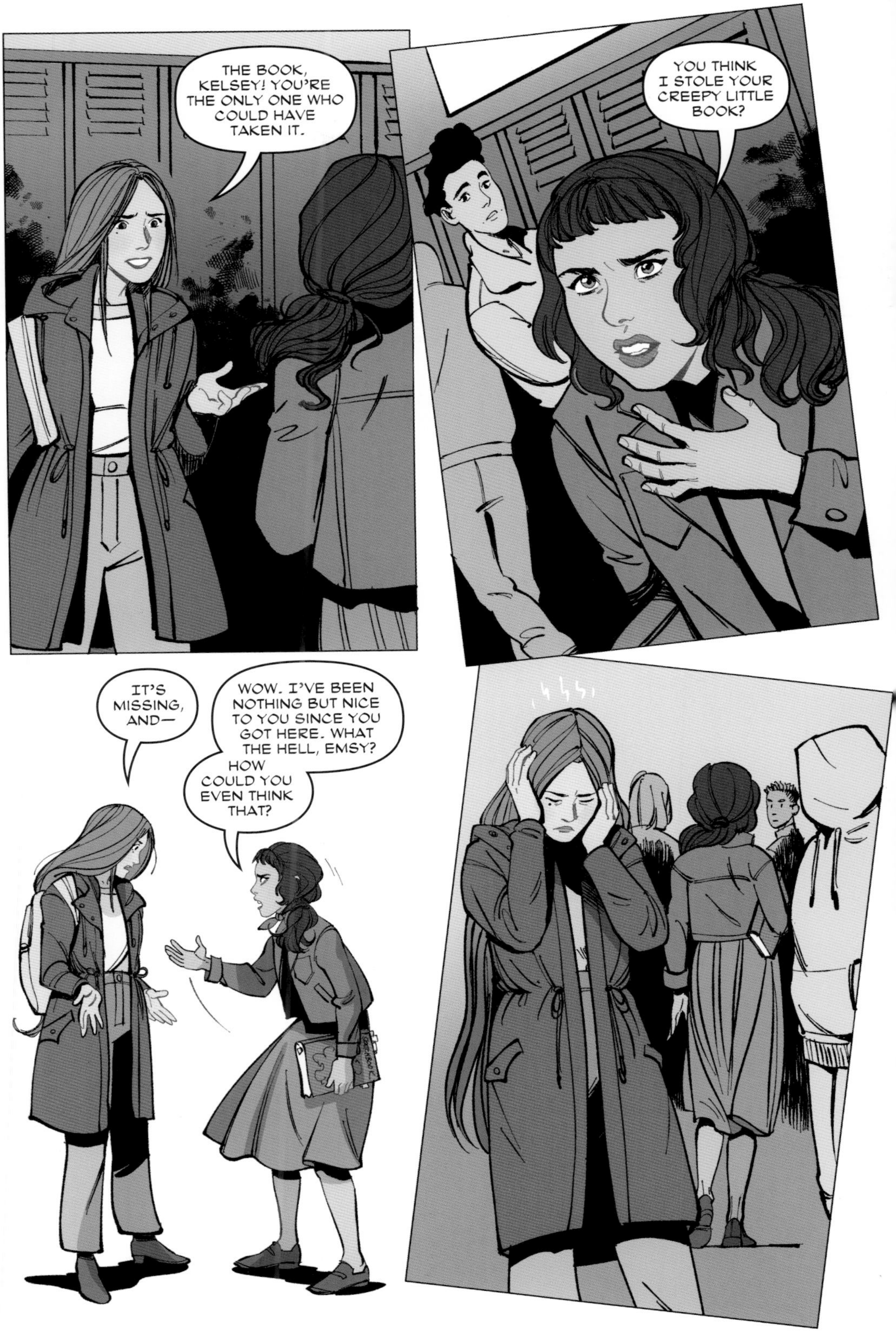

THE BOOK, KELSEY! YOU'RE THE ONLY ONE WHO COULD HAVE TAKEN IT.
YOU THINK I STOLE YOUR CREEPY LITTLE BOOK?
IT'S MISSING, AND—
WOW. I'VE BEEN NOTHING BUT NICE TO YOU SINCE YOU GOT HERE. WHAT THE HELL, EMSY?
HOW COULD YOU EVEN THINK THAT?

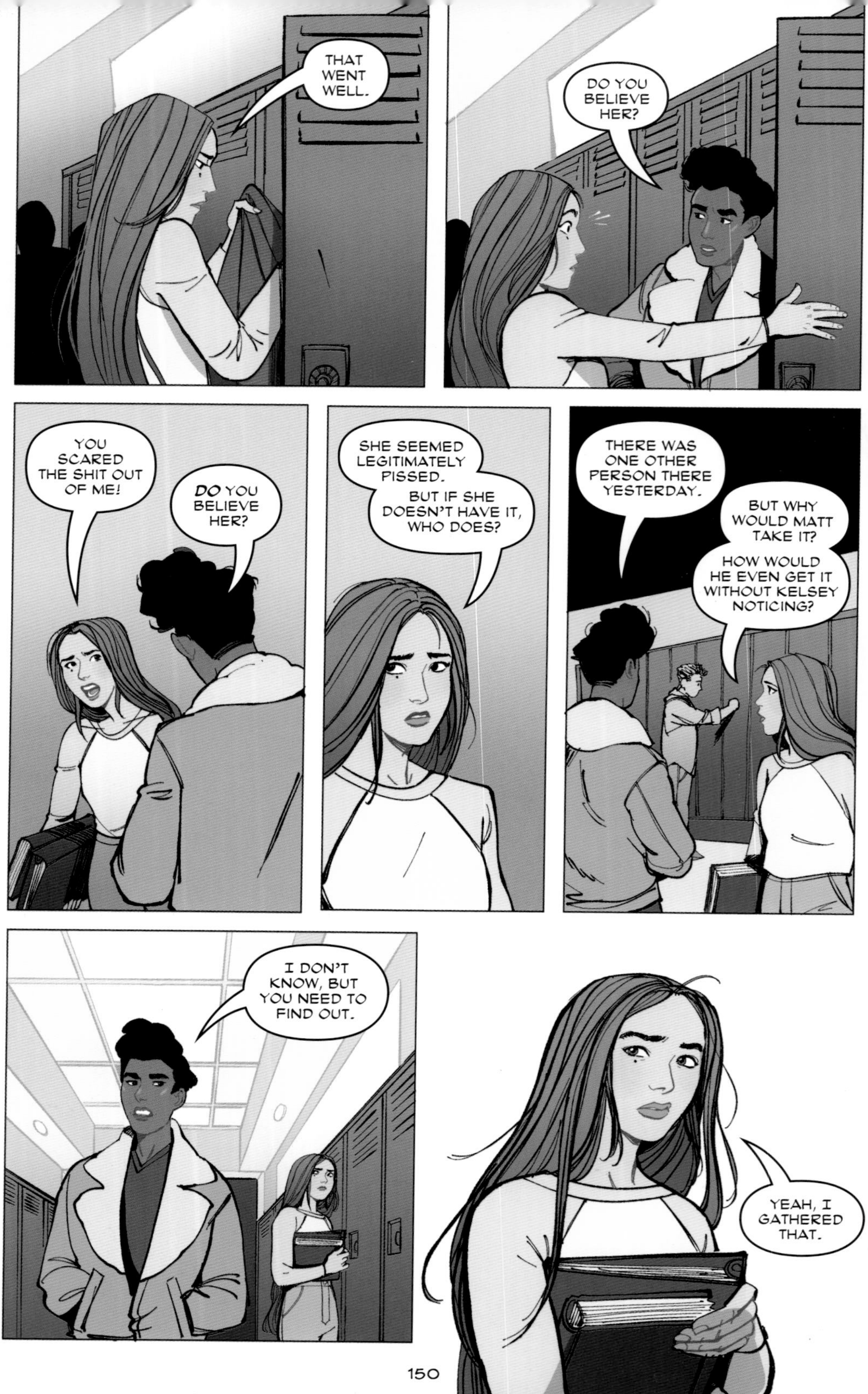

THAT WENT WELL.
DO YOU BELIEVE HER?
YOU SCARED THE SHIT OUT OF ME!
DO YOU BELIEVE HER?
SHE SEEMED LEGITIMATELY PISSED.
BUT IF SHE DOESN'T HAVE IT, WHO DOES?
THERE WAS ONE OTHER PERSON THERE YESTERDAY.
BUT WHY WOULD MATT TAKE IT?
HOW WOULD HE EVEN GET IT WITHOUT KELSEY NOTICING?
I DON'T KNOW, BUT YOU NEED TO FIND OUT.
YEAH, I GATHERED THAT.

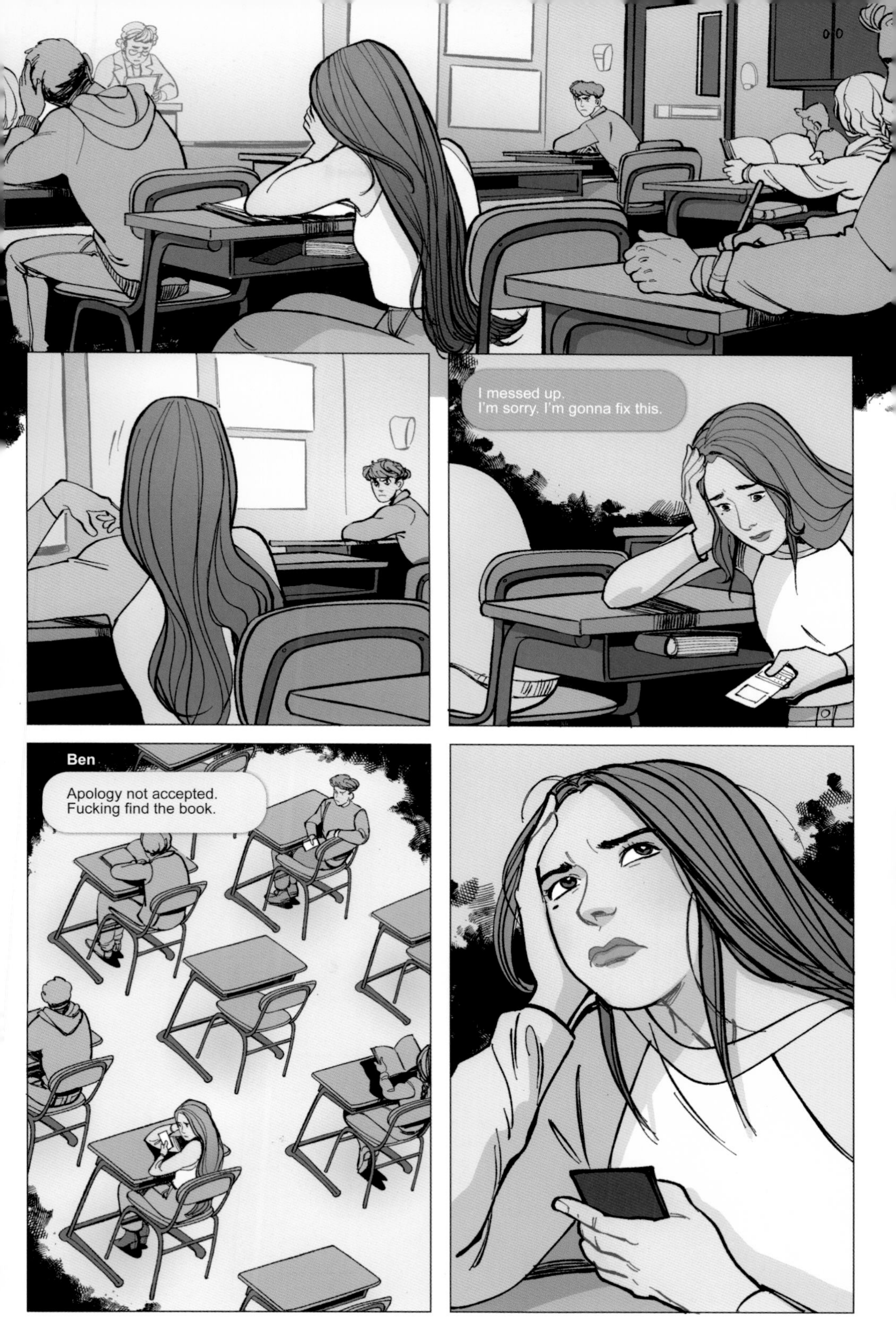
I messed up.
I'm sorry. I'm gonna fix this.
Ben
Apology not accepted.
Fucking find the book.

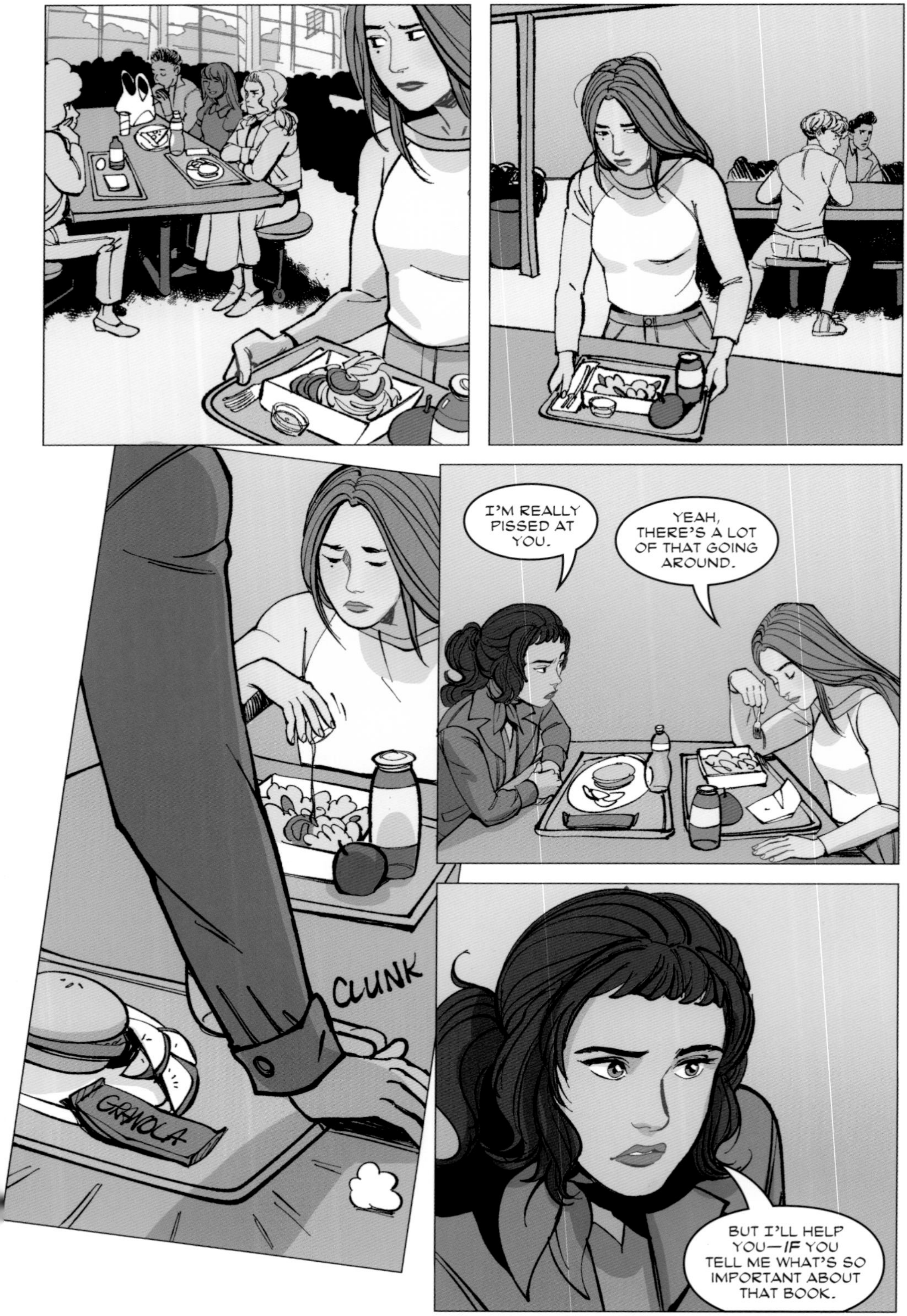
CLUNK
GRANOLA
I'M REALLY PISSED AT YOU.
YEAH, THERE'S A LOT OF THAT GOING AROUND.
BUT I'LL HELP YOU—*IF* YOU TELL ME WHAT'S SO IMPORTANT ABOUT THAT BOOK.

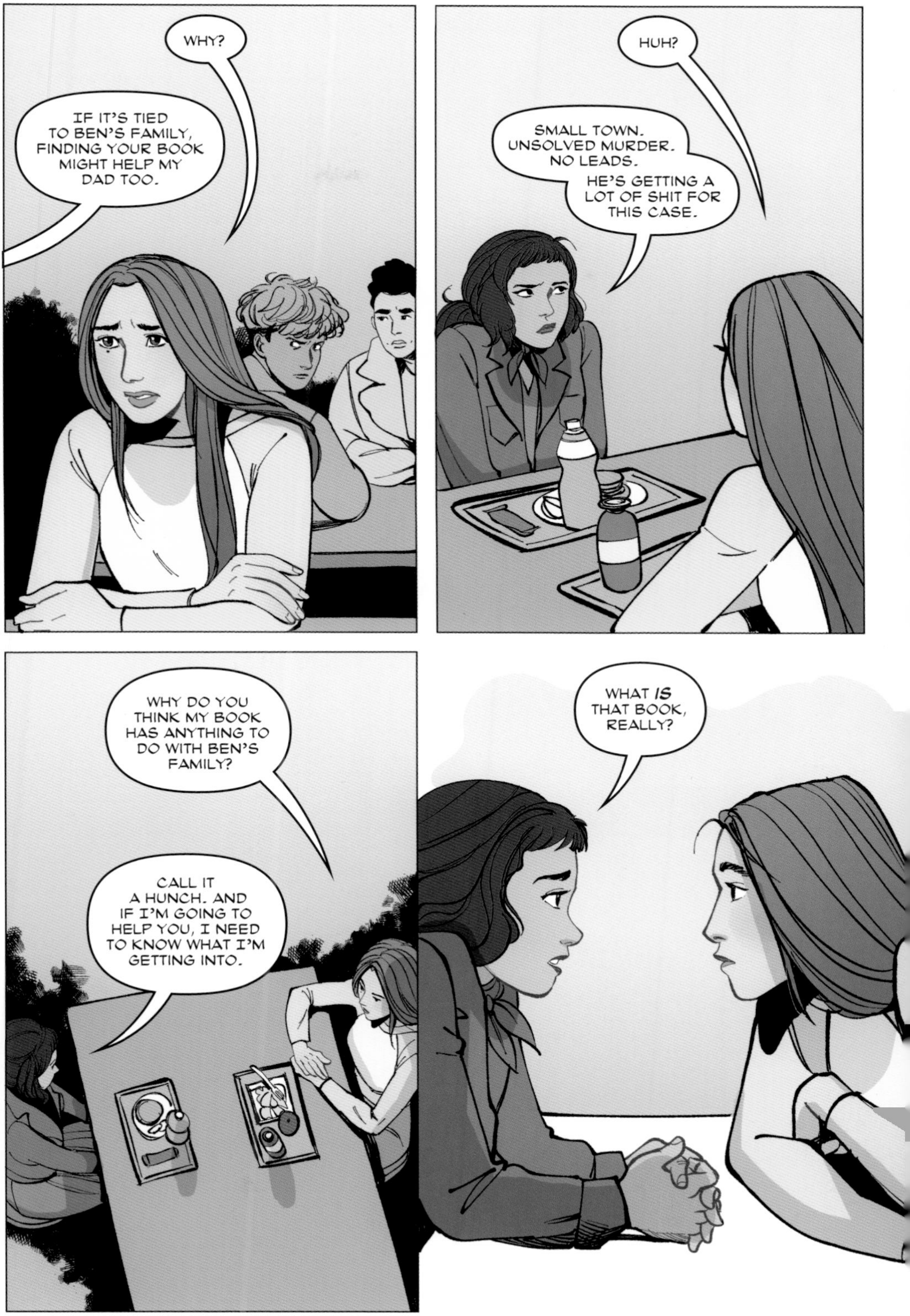
WHY?
IF IT'S TIED TO BEN'S FAMILY, FINDING YOUR BOOK MIGHT HELP MY DAD TOO.
HUH?
SMALL TOWN. UNSOLVED MURDER. NO LEADS.
HE'S GETTING A LOT OF SHIT FOR THIS CASE.
WHY DO YOU THINK MY BOOK HAS ANYTHING TO DO WITH BEN'S FAMILY?
CALL IT A HUNCH. AND IF I'M GOING TO HELP YOU, I NEED TO KNOW WHAT I'M GETTING INTO.
WHAT *IS* THAT BOOK, REALLY?

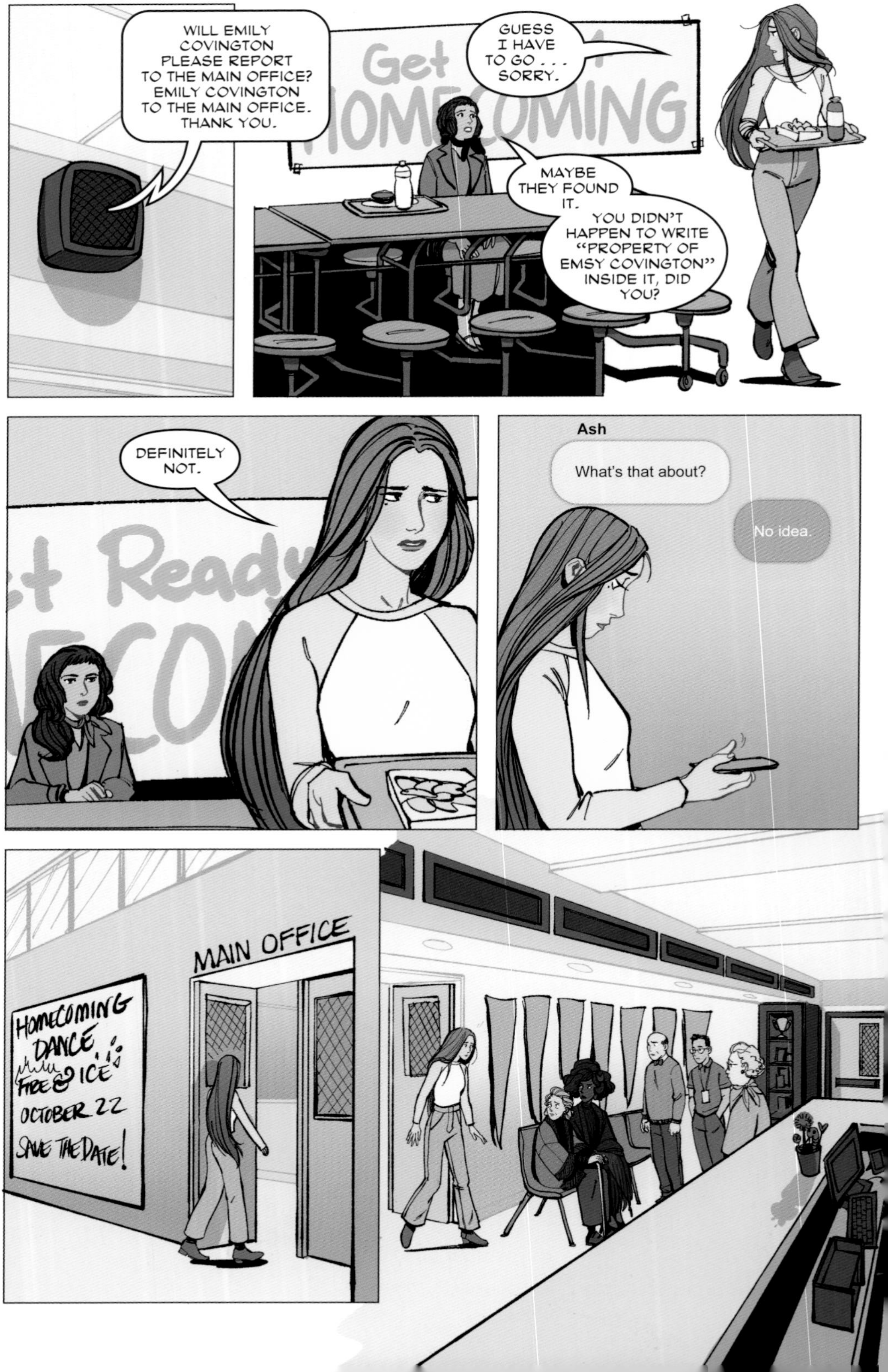
WILL EMILY COVINGTON PLEASE REPORT TO THE MAIN OFFICE? EMILY COVINGTON TO THE MAIN OFFICE. THANK YOU.
Get Ready HOMECOMING
GUESS I HAVE TO GO . . . SORRY.
MAYBE THEY FOUND IT.
YOU DIDN'T HAPPEN TO WRITE "PROPERTY OF EMSY COVINGTON" INSIDE IT, DID YOU?
DEFINITELY NOT.
Ash
What's that about?
No idea.
MAIN OFFICE
HOMECOMING DANCE FIRE & ICE OCTOBER 22 SAVE THE DATE!

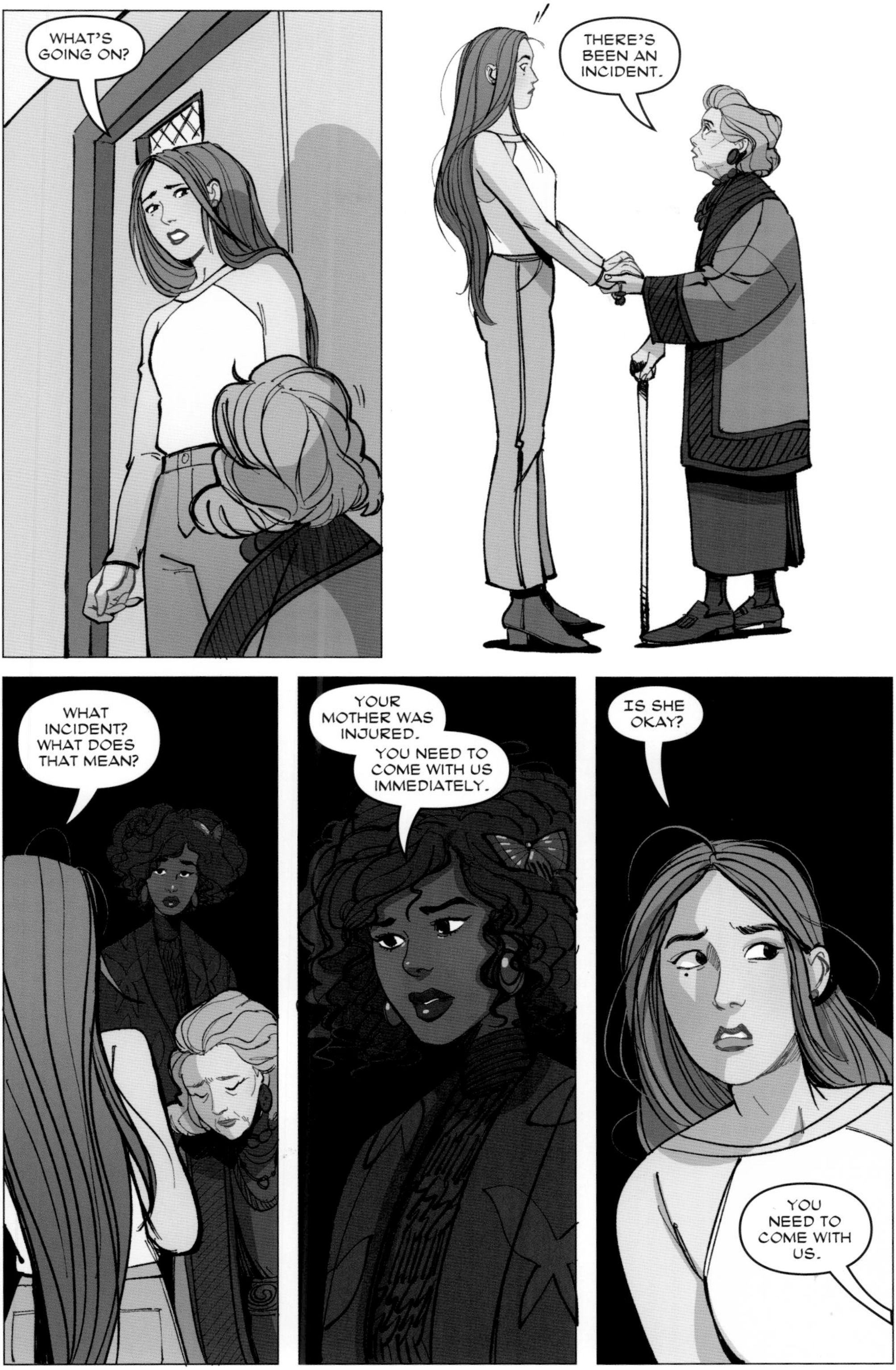
WHAT'S GOING ON?
THERE'S BEEN AN INCIDENT.
WHAT INCIDENT? WHAT DOES THAT MEAN?
YOUR MOTHER WAS INJURED.
YOU NEED TO COME WITH US IMMEDIATELY.
IS SHE OKAY?
YOU NEED TO COME WITH US.

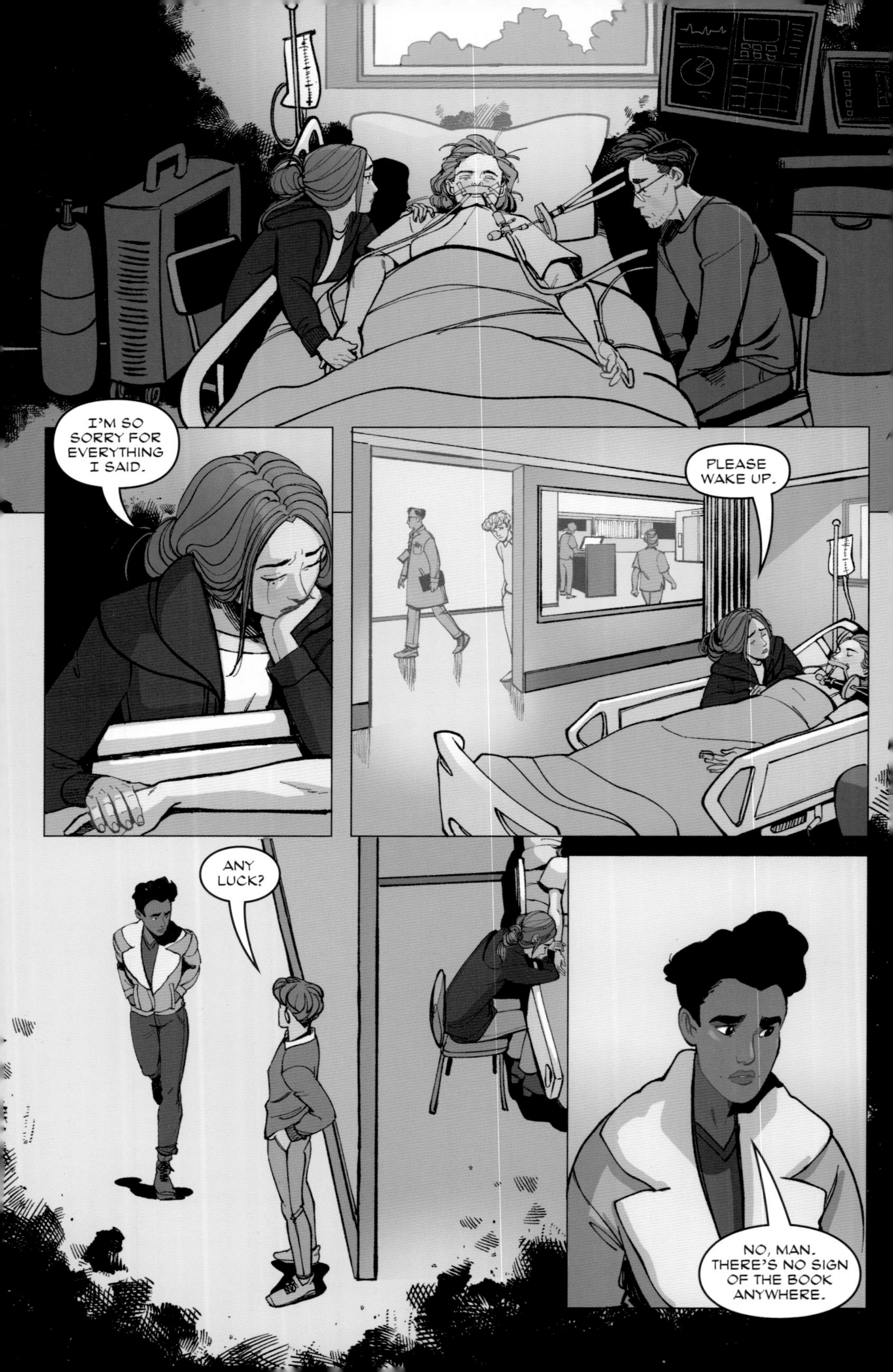
I'M SO SORRY FOR EVERYTHING I SAID.
PLEASE WAKE UP.
ANY LUCK?
NO, MAN. THERE'S NO SIGN OF THE BOOK ANYWHERE.

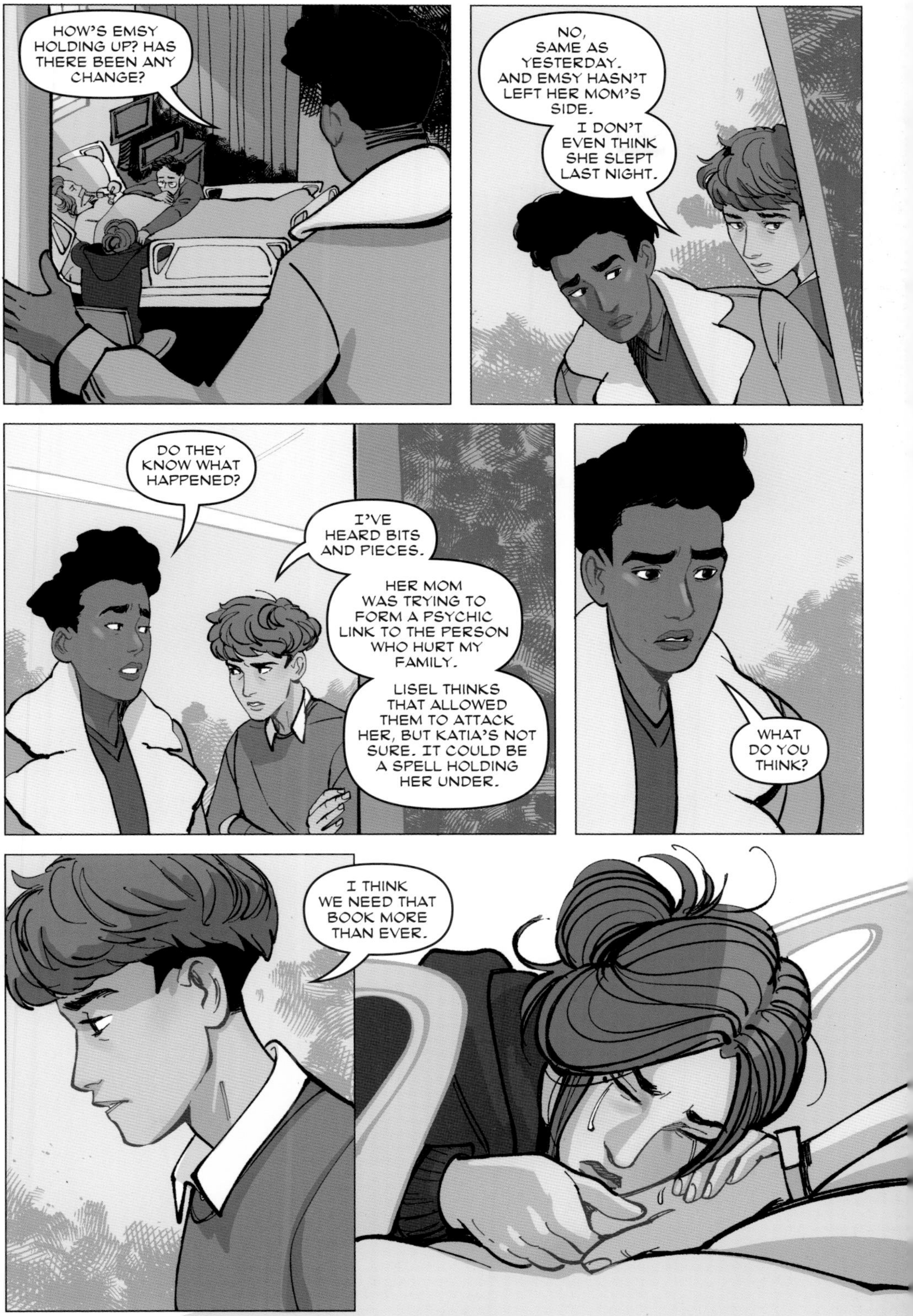
HOW'S EMSY HOLDING UP? HAS THERE BEEN ANY CHANGE?
NO, SAME AS YESTERDAY. AND EMSY HASN'T LEFT HER MOM'S SIDE.
I DON'T EVEN THINK SHE SLEPT LAST NIGHT.
DO THEY KNOW WHAT HAPPENED?
I'VE HEARD BITS AND PIECES.
HER MOM WAS TRYING TO FORM A PSYCHIC LINK TO THE PERSON WHO HURT MY FAMILY.
LISEL THINKS THAT ALLOWED THEM TO ATTACK HER, BUT KATIA'S NOT SURE. IT COULD BE A SPELL HOLDING HER UNDER.
WHAT DO YOU THINK?
I THINK WE NEED THAT BOOK MORE THAN EVER.

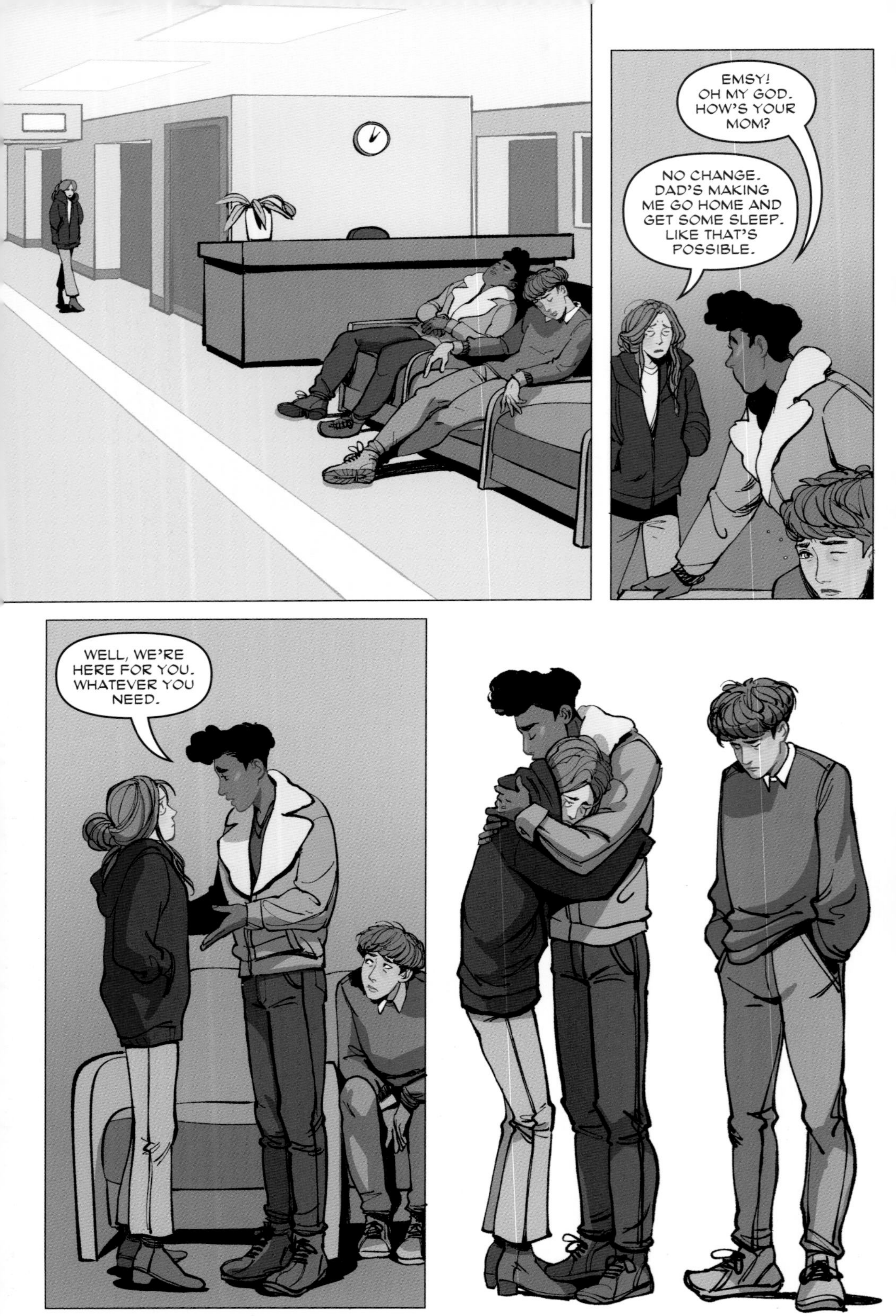
EMSY! OH MY GOD. HOW'S YOUR MOM?
NO CHANGE. DAD'S MAKING ME GO HOME AND GET SOME SLEEP. LIKE THAT'S POSSIBLE.
WELL, WE'RE HERE FOR YOU. WHATEVER YOU NEED.

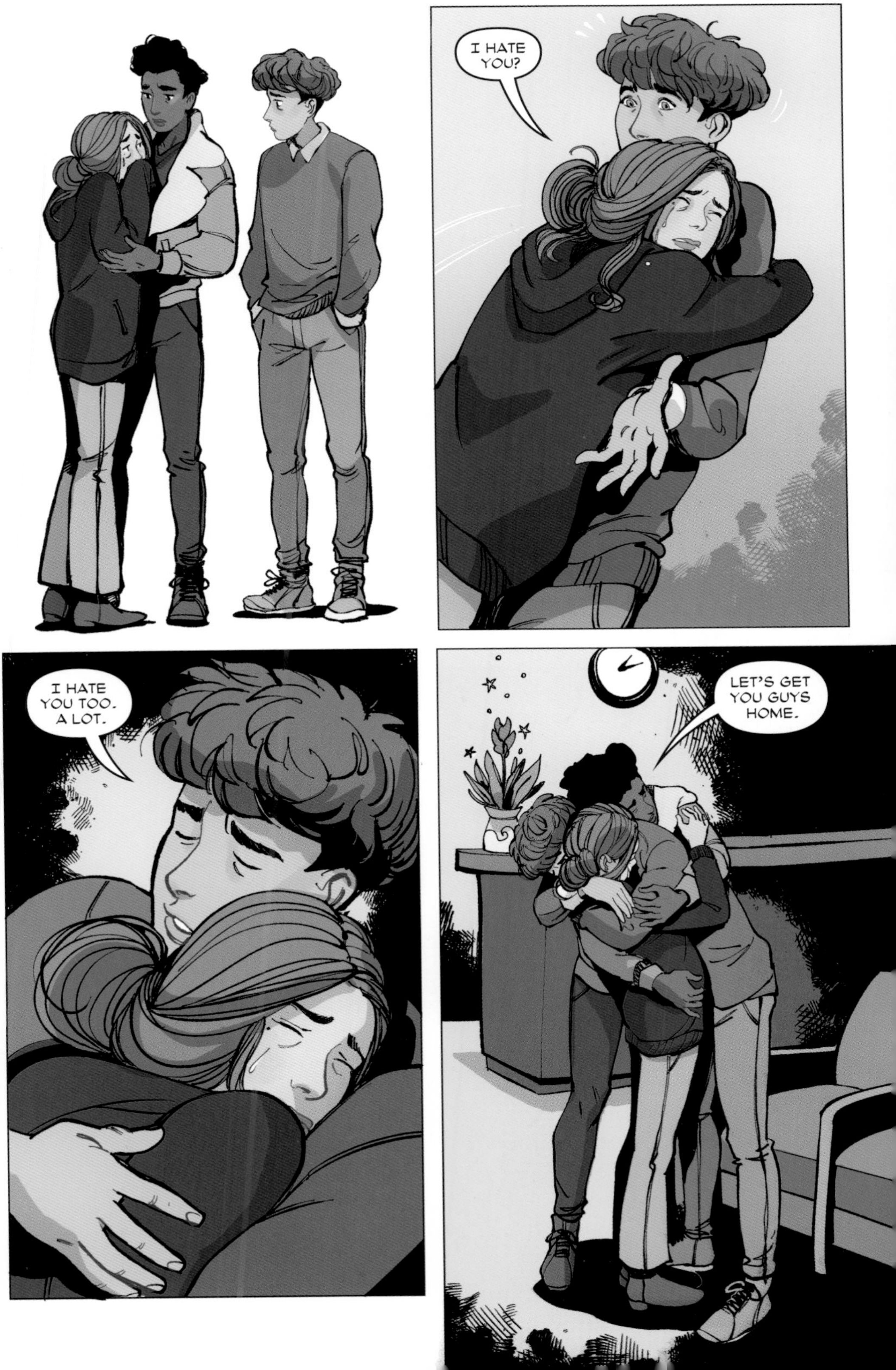
I HATE YOU?
I HATE YOU TOO. A LOT.
LET'S GET YOU GUYS HOME.

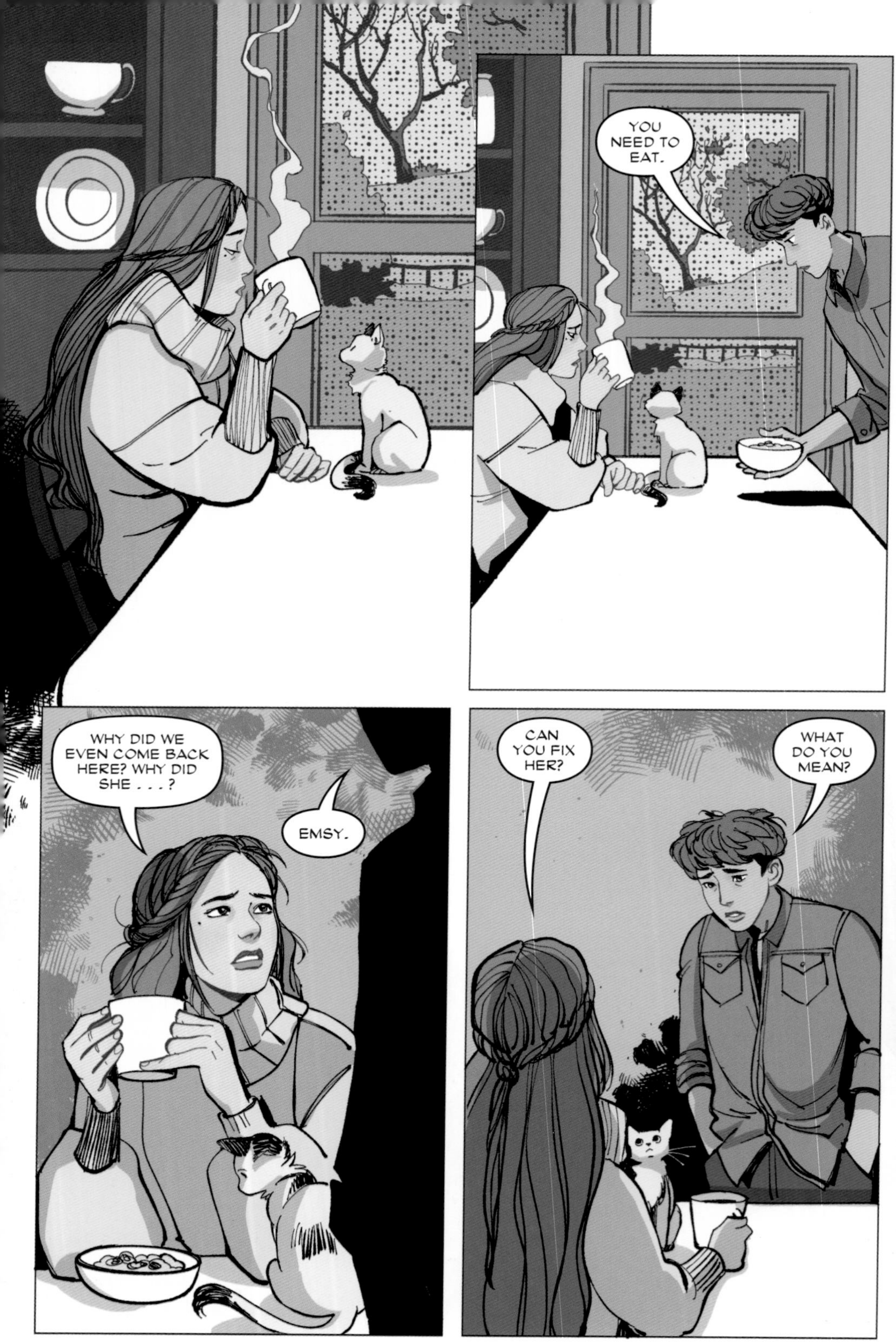
YOU NEED TO EAT.
WHY DID WE EVEN COME BACK HERE? WHY DID SHE . . . ?
EMSY.
CAN YOU FIX HER?
WHAT DO YOU MEAN?

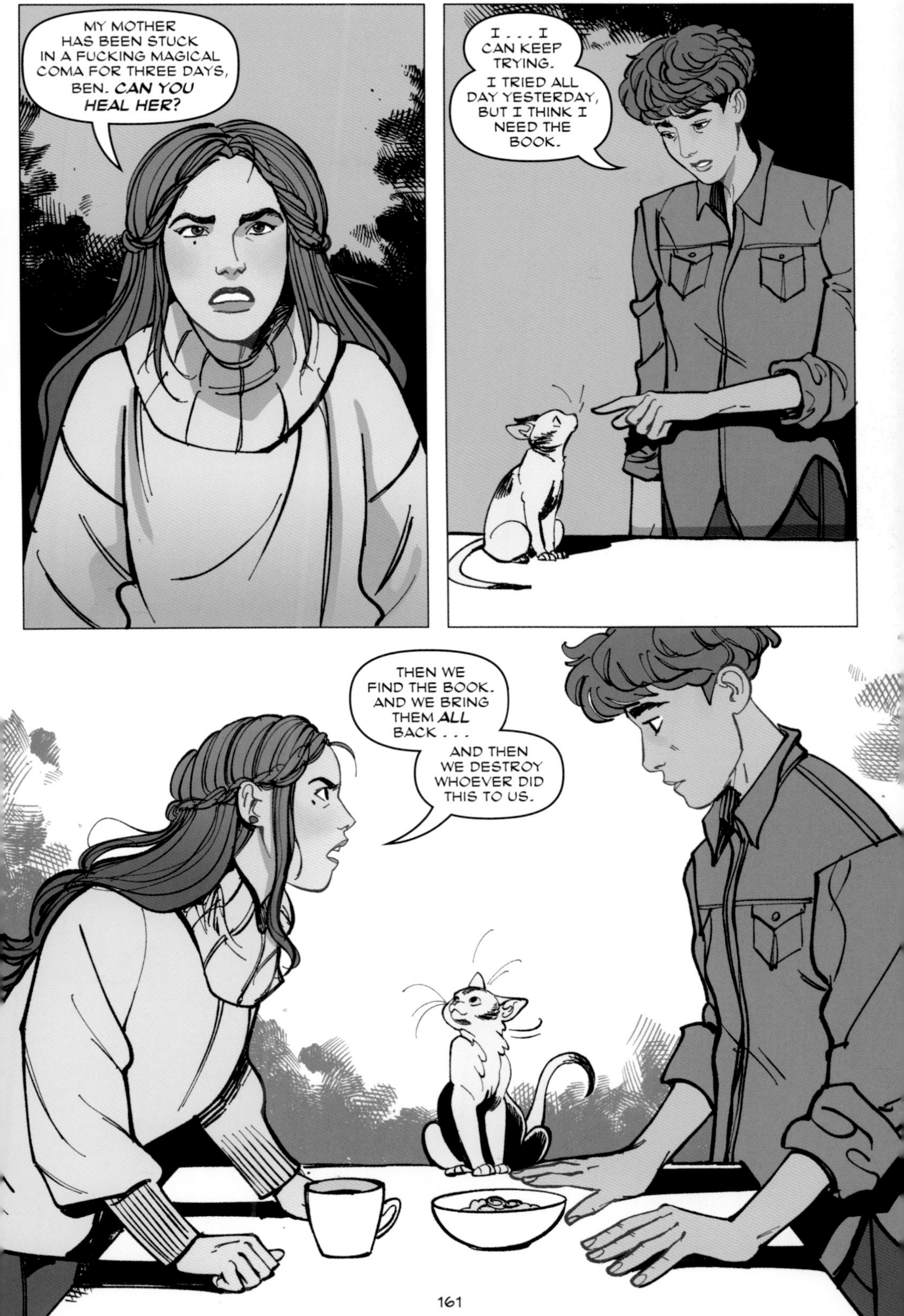
MY MOTHER HAS BEEN STUCK IN A FUCKING MAGICAL COMA FOR THREE DAYS, BEN. *CAN YOU HEAL HER?*
I . . . I CAN KEEP TRYING.
I TRIED ALL DAY YESTERDAY, BUT I THINK I NEED THE BOOK.
THEN WE FIND THE BOOK. AND WE BRING THEM *ALL* BACK . . .
AND THEN WE DESTROY WHOEVER DID THIS TO US.

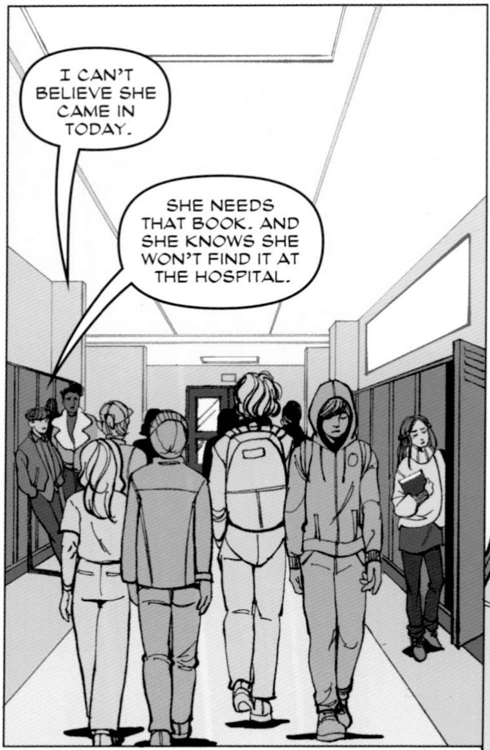
I CAN'T BELIEVE SHE CAME IN TODAY.
SHE NEEDS THAT BOOK. AND SHE KNOWS SHE WON'T FIND IT AT THE HOSPITAL.

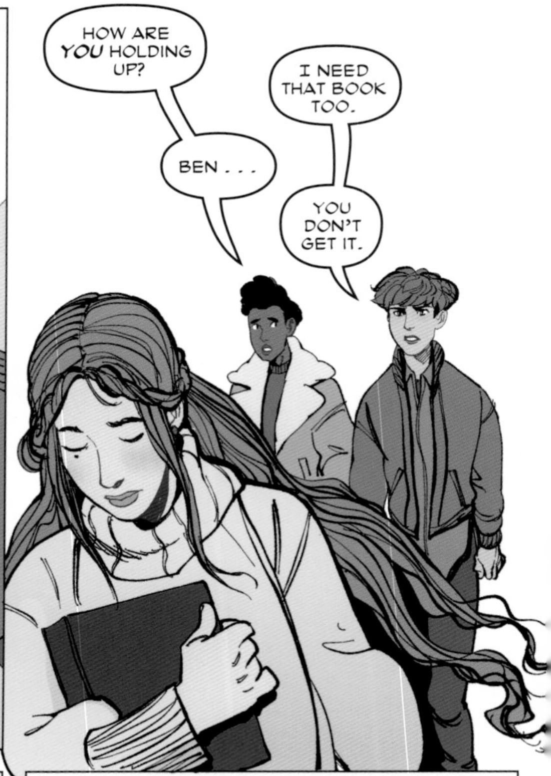
HOW ARE *YOU* HOLDING UP?
BEN . . .
I NEED THAT BOOK TOO.
YOU DON'T GET IT.

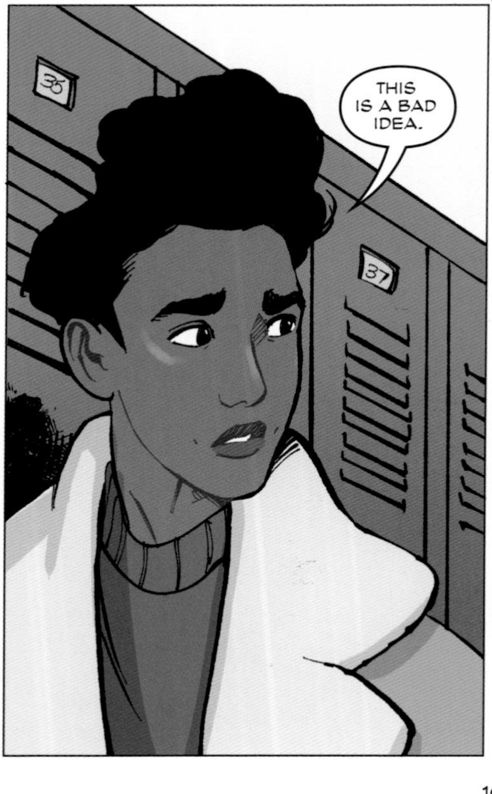
THIS IS A BAD IDEA.

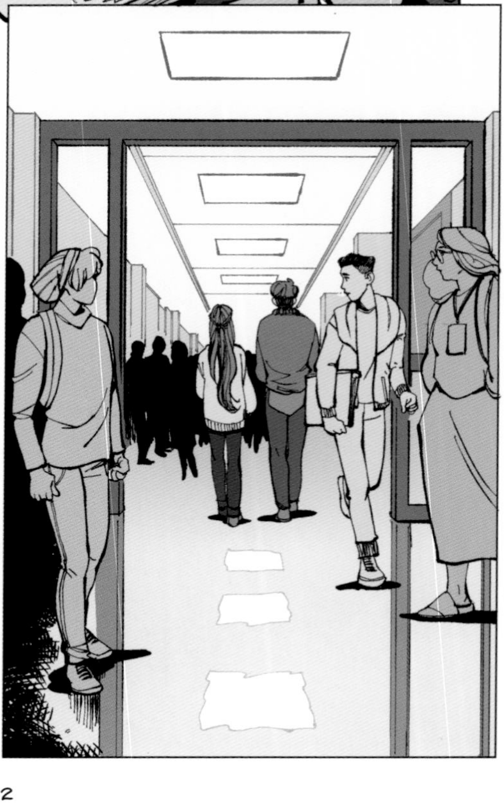

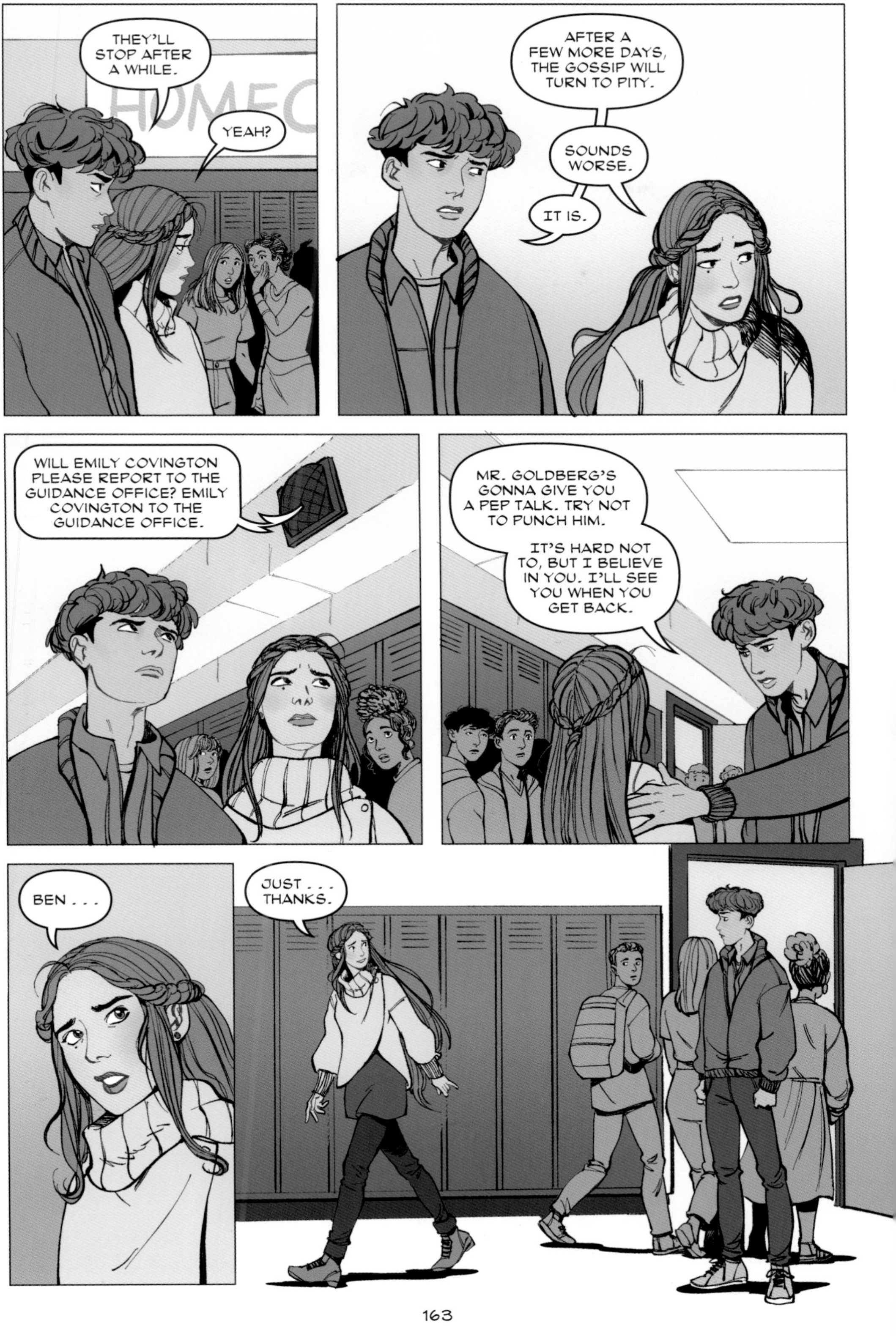
THEY'LL STOP AFTER A WHILE.
YEAH?
AFTER A FEW MORE DAYS, THE GOSSIP WILL TURN TO PITY.
SOUNDS WORSE.
IT IS.
WILL EMILY COVINGTON PLEASE REPORT TO THE GUIDANCE OFFICE? EMILY COVINGTON TO THE GUIDANCE OFFICE.
MR. GOLDBERG'S GONNA GIVE YOU A PEP TALK. TRY NOT TO PUNCH HIM.
IT'S HARD NOT TO, BUT I BELIEVE IN YOU. I'LL SEE YOU WHEN YOU GET BACK.
BEN . . .
JUST . . . THANKS.

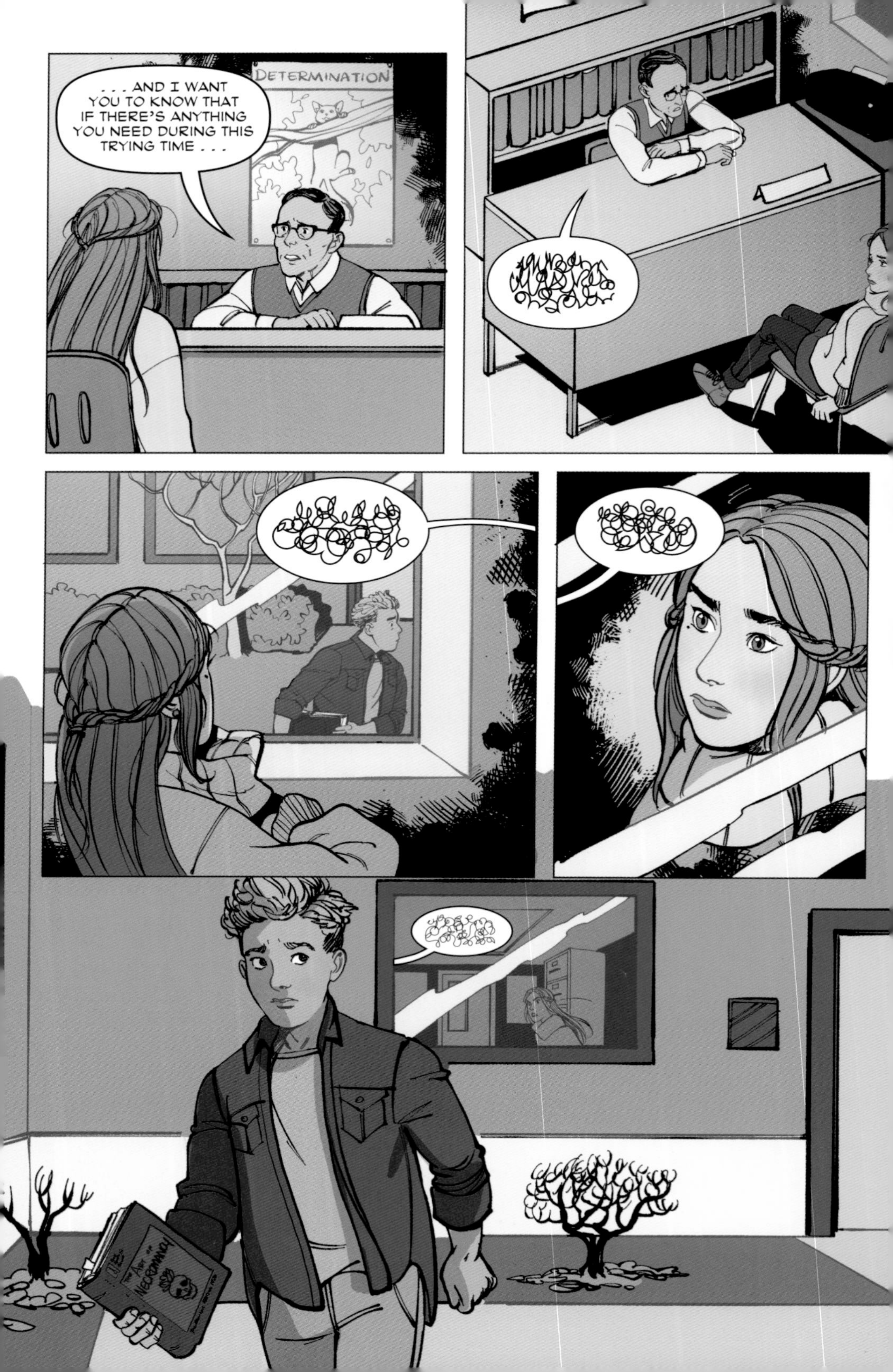
. . . AND I WANT YOU TO KNOW THAT IF THERE'S ANYTHING YOU NEED DURING THIS TRYING TIME . . .
DETERMINATION

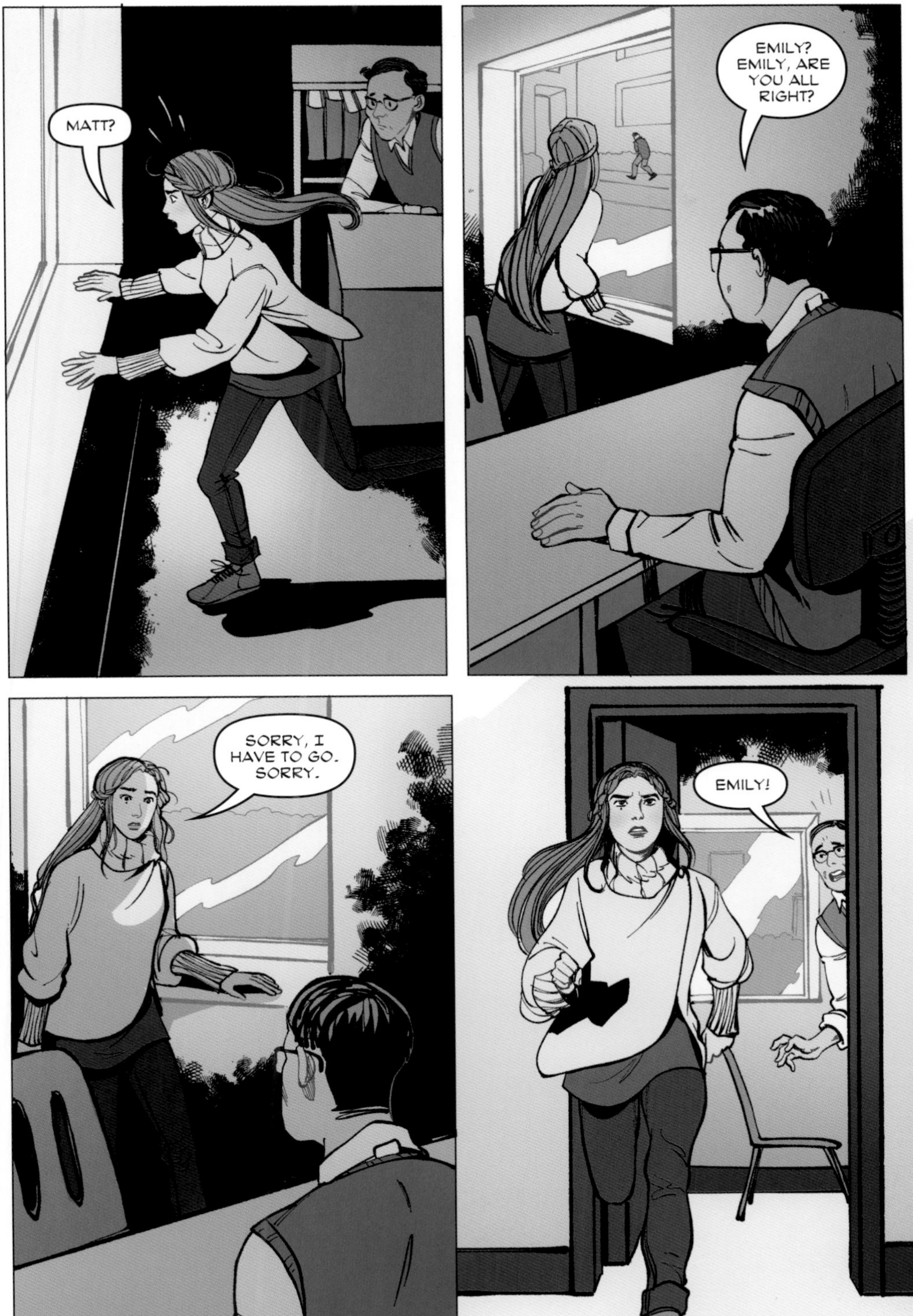
MATT?
EMILY? EMILY, ARE YOU ALL RIGHT?
SORRY, I HAVE TO GO. SORRY.
EMILY!

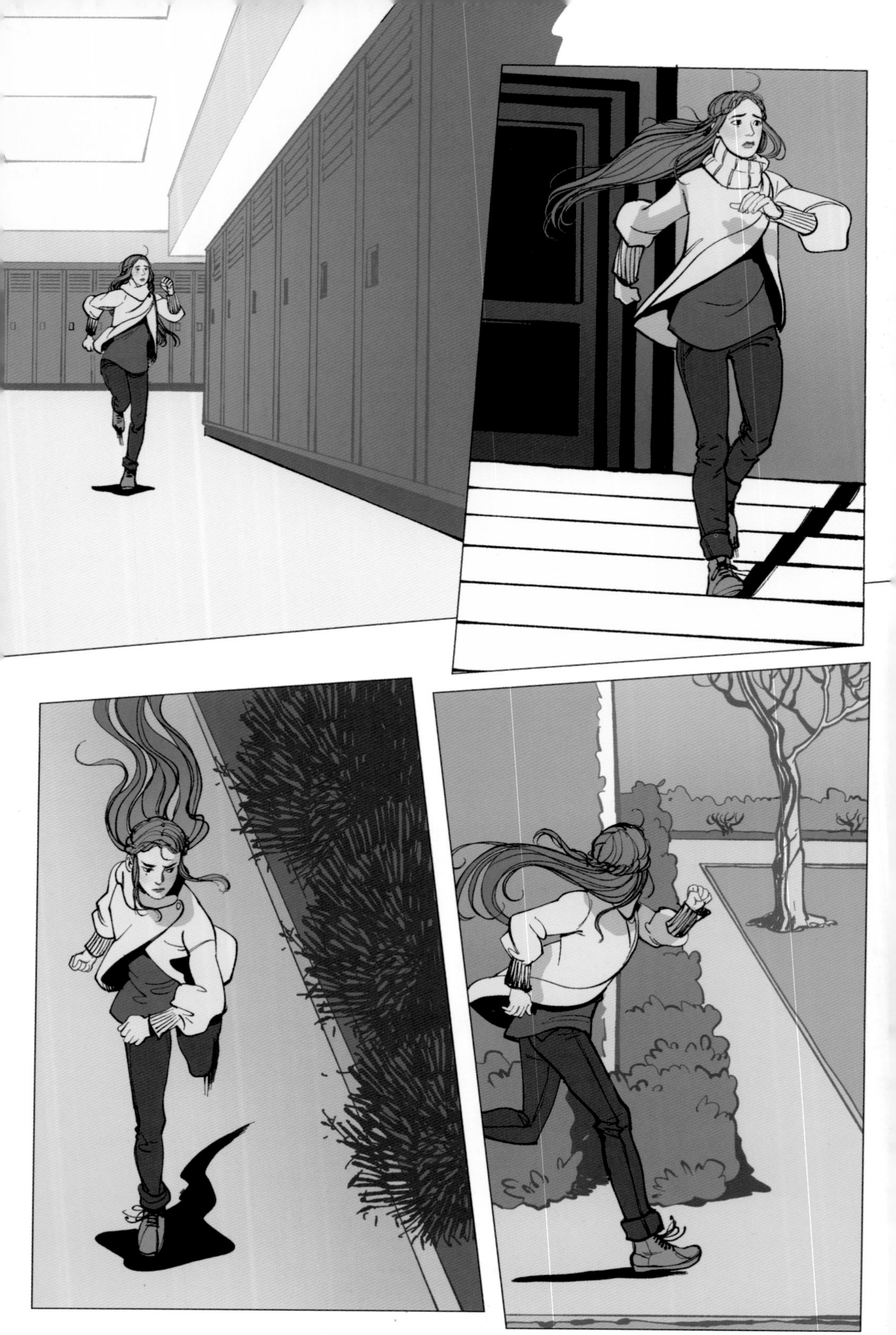

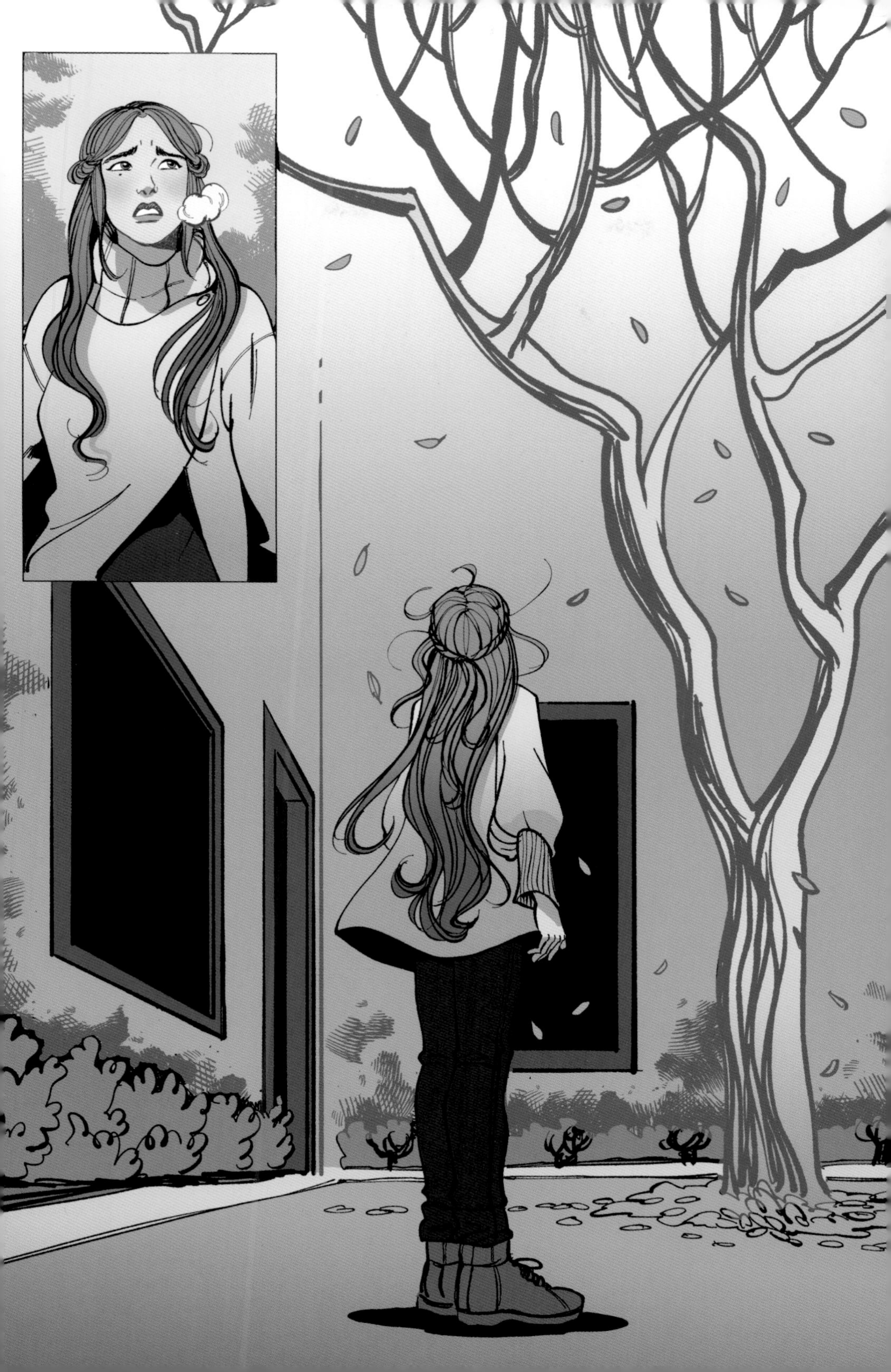

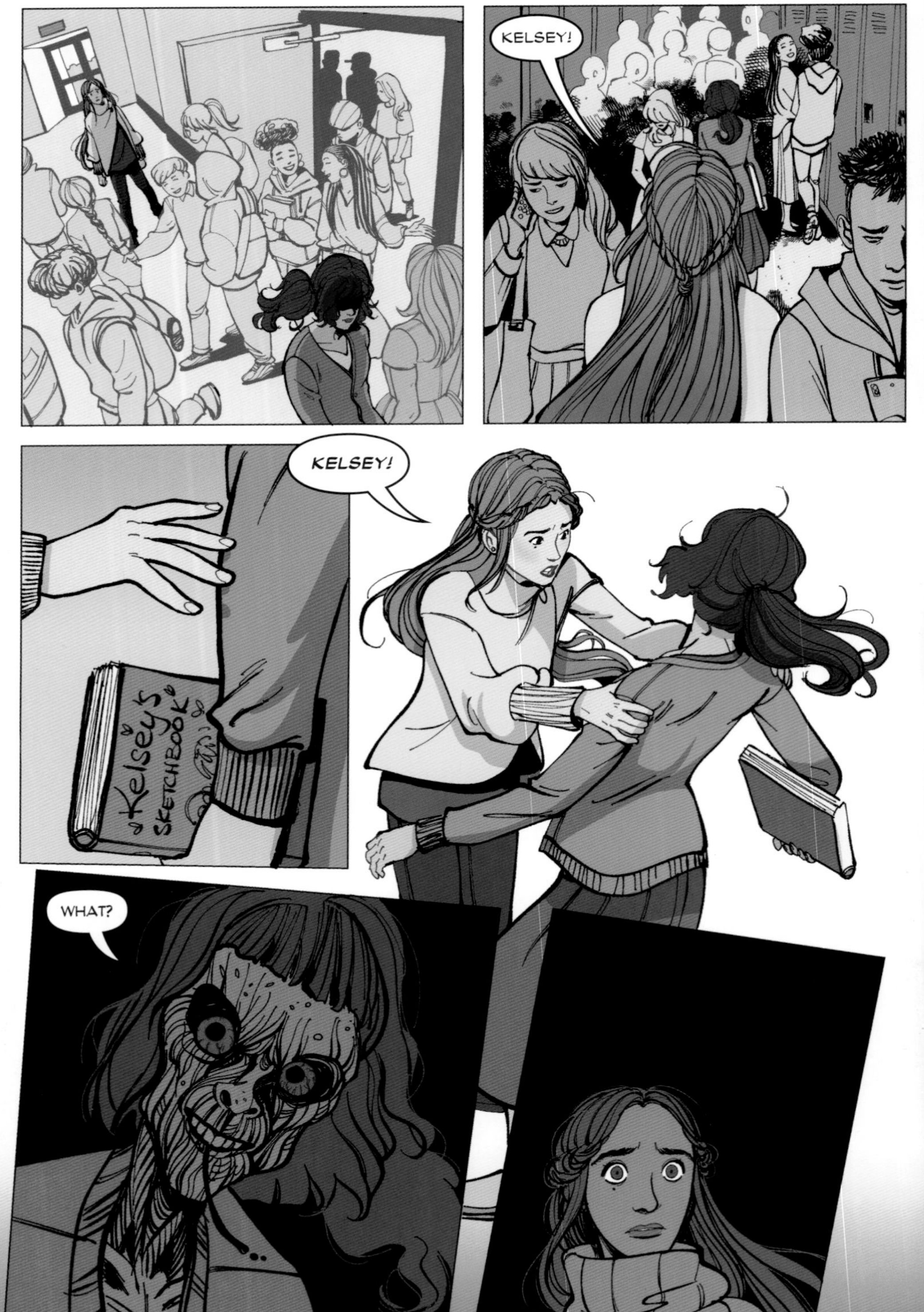
KELSEY!
KELSEY!
Kelsey's SKETCHBOOK
WHAT?

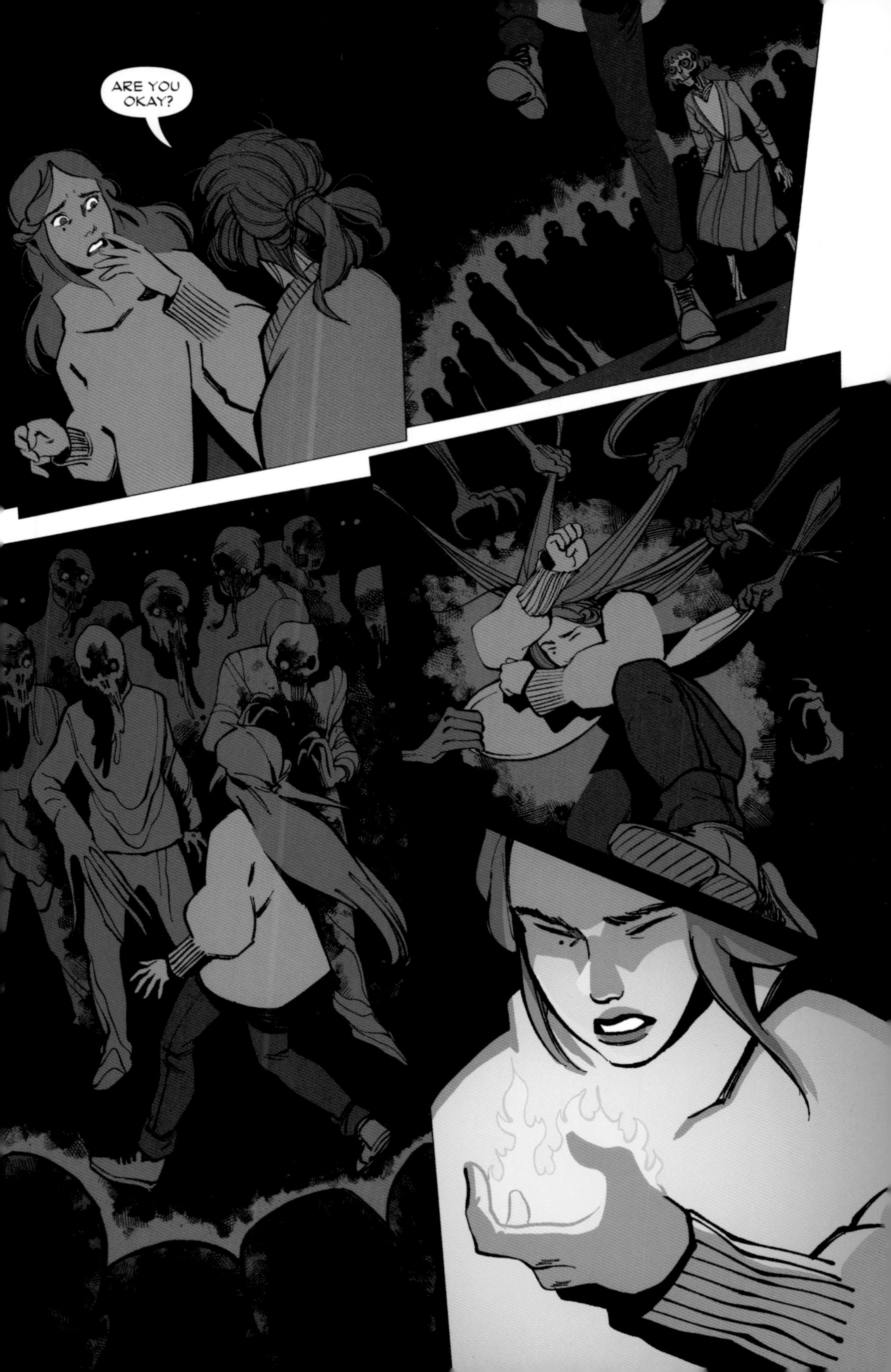
ARE YOU OKAY?

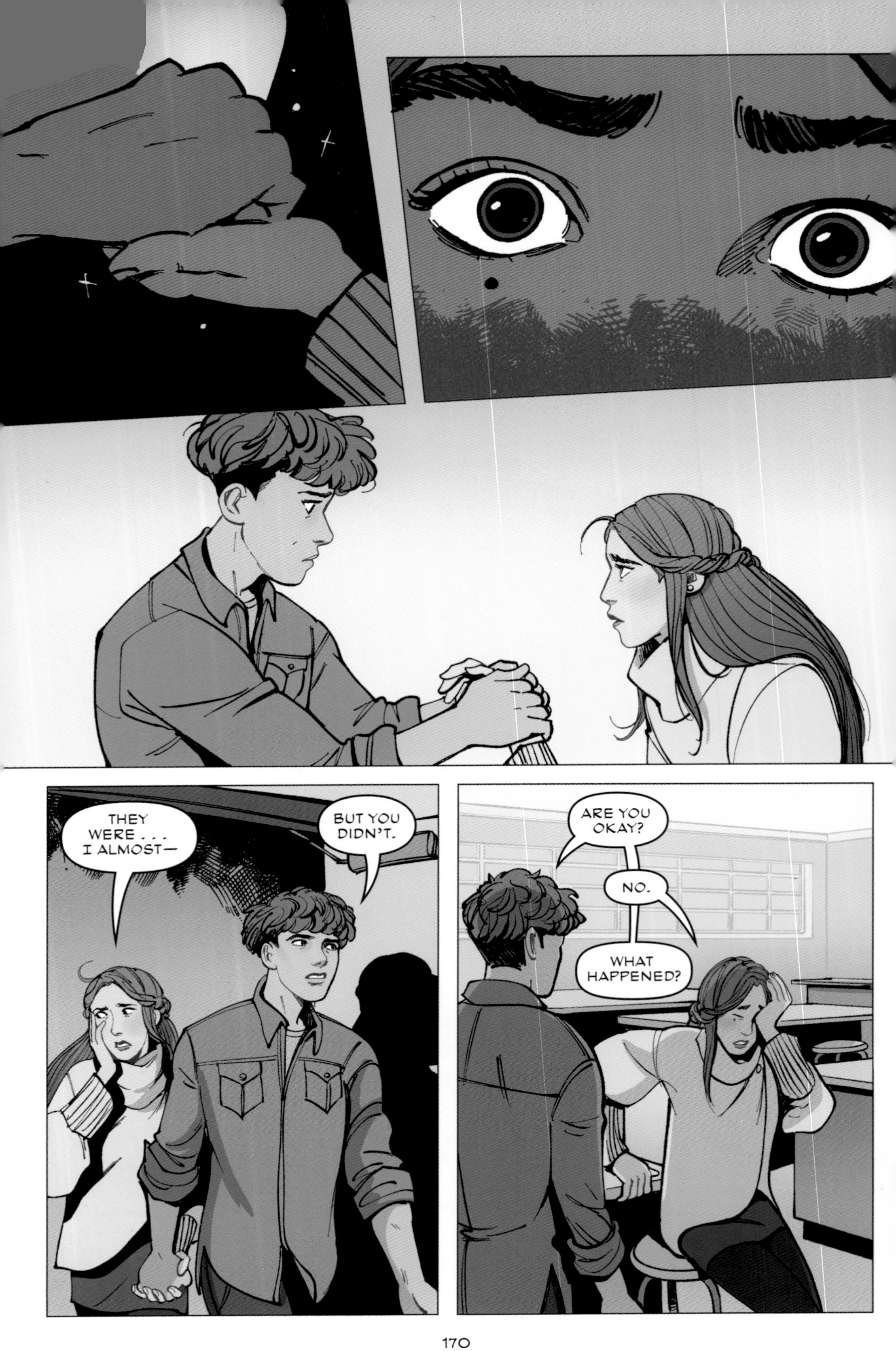
THEY WERE . . . I ALMOST—
BUT YOU DIDN'T.
ARE YOU OKAY?
NO.
WHAT HAPPENED?

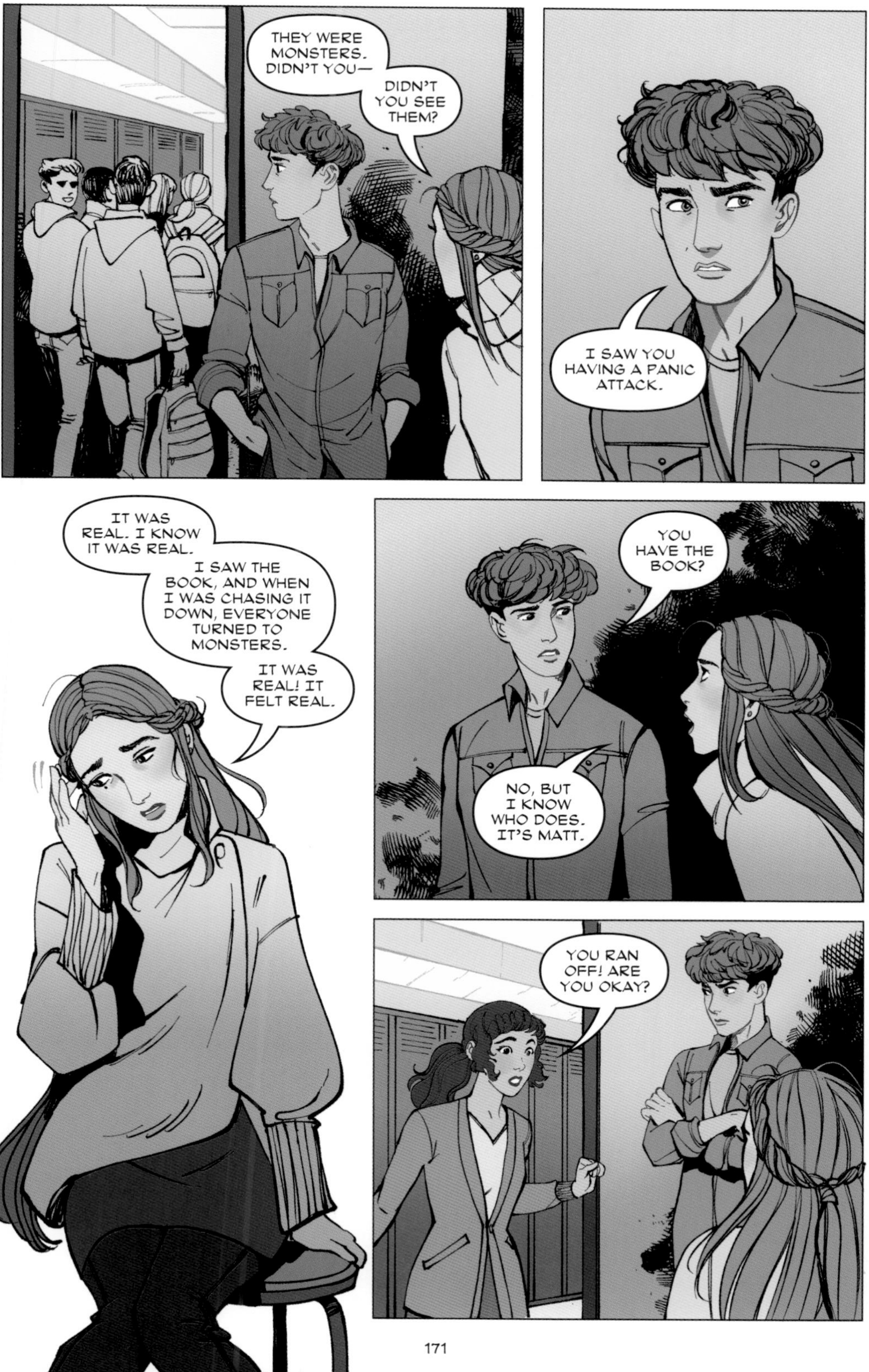
THEY WERE MONSTERS. DIDN'T YOU—
DIDN'T YOU SEE THEM?
I SAW YOU HAVING A PANIC ATTACK.
IT WAS REAL. I KNOW IT WAS REAL.
I SAW THE BOOK, AND WHEN I WAS CHASING IT DOWN, EVERYONE TURNED TO MONSTERS.
IT WAS REAL! IT FELT REAL.
YOU HAVE THE BOOK?
NO, BUT I KNOW WHO DOES. IT'S MATT.
YOU RAN OFF! ARE YOU OKAY?

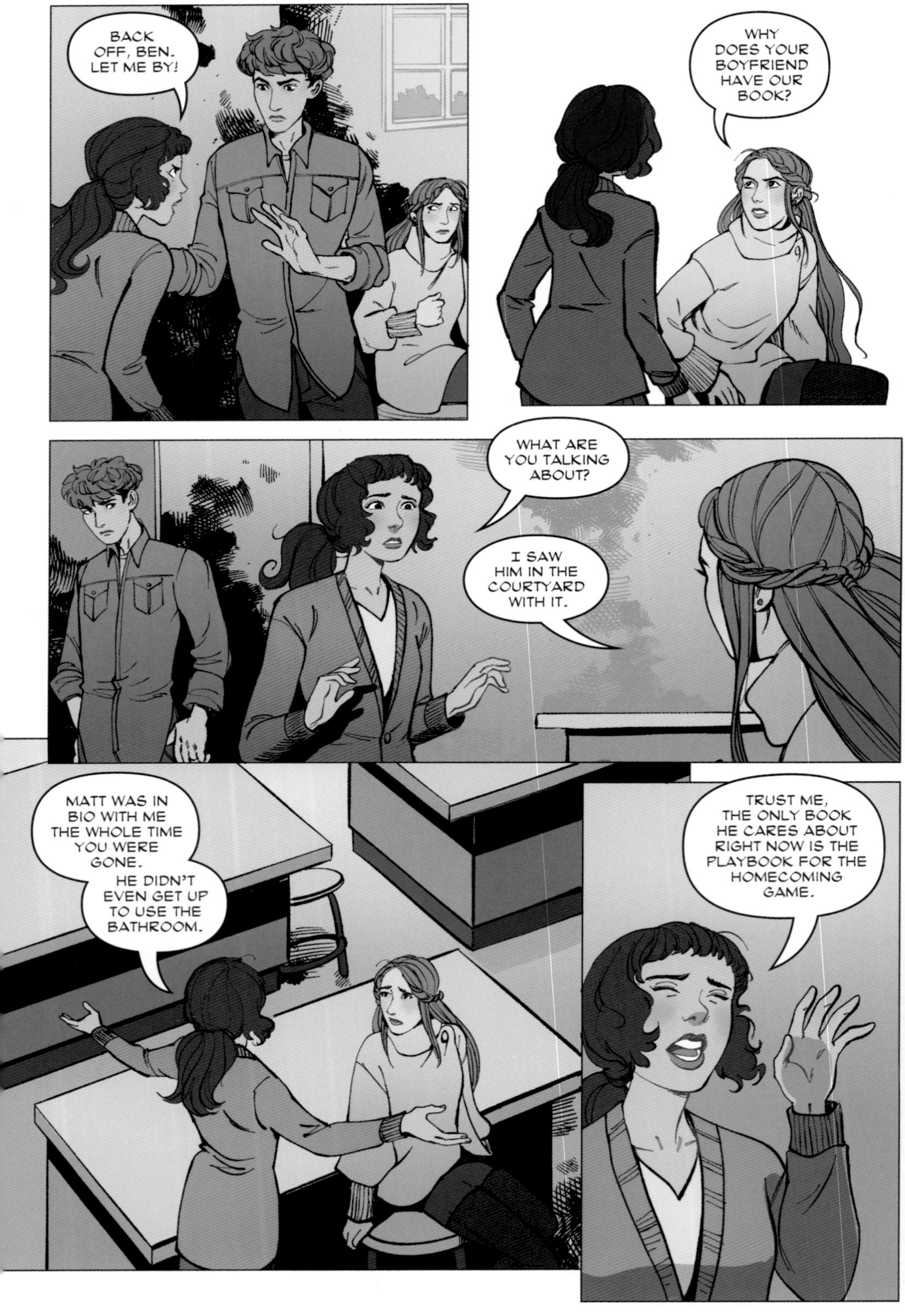
BACK OFF, BEN. LET ME BY!
WHY DOES YOUR BOYFRIEND HAVE OUR BOOK?
WHAT ARE YOU TALKING ABOUT?
I SAW HIM IN THE COURTYARD WITH IT.
MATT WAS IN BIO WITH ME THE WHOLE TIME YOU WERE GONE.
HE DIDN'T EVEN GET UP TO USE THE BATHROOM.
TRUST ME, THE ONLY BOOK HE CARES ABOUT RIGHT NOW IS THE PLAYBOOK FOR THE HOMECOMING GAME.

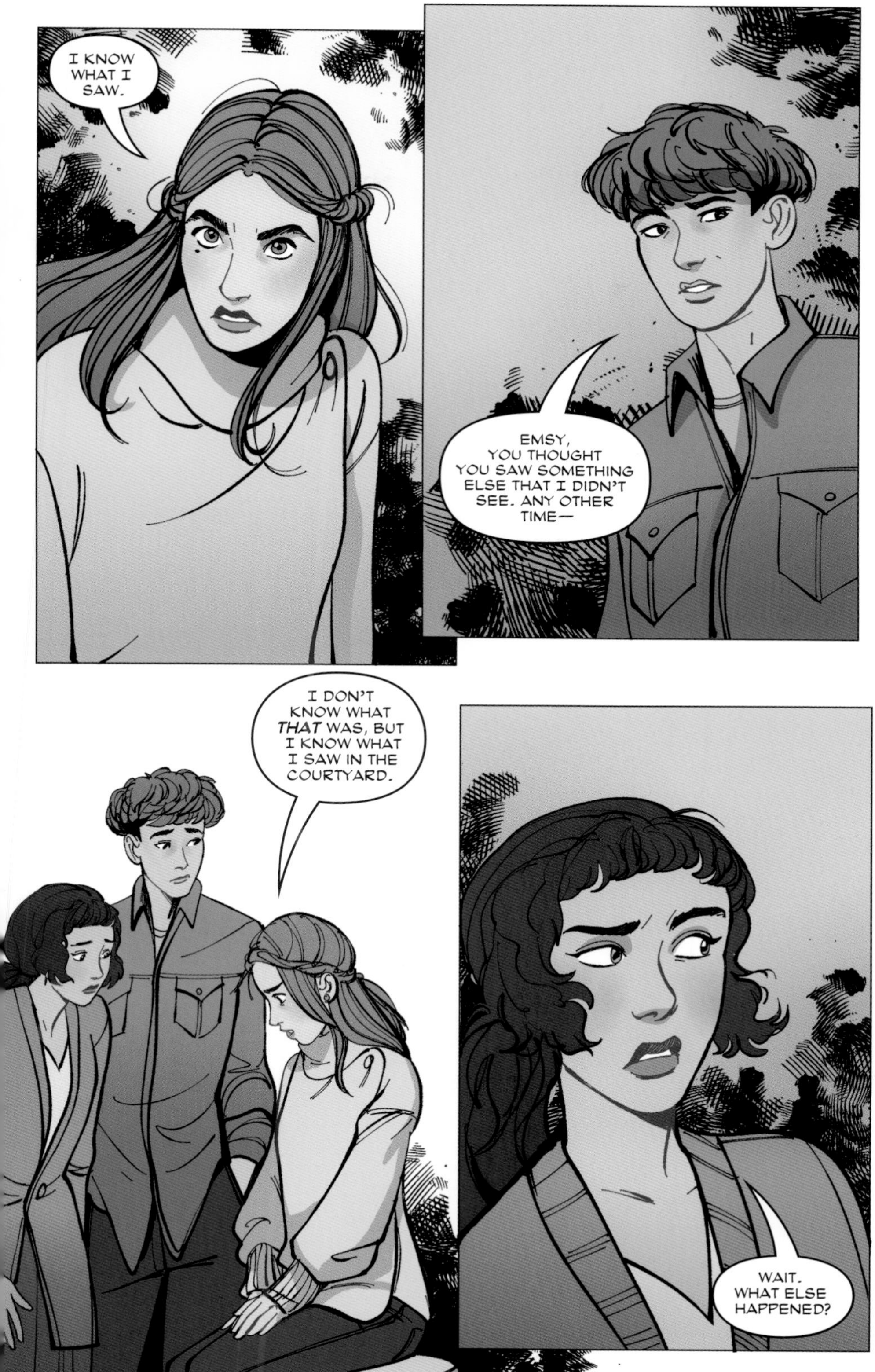
I KNOW WHAT I SAW.
EMSY, YOU THOUGHT YOU SAW SOMETHING ELSE THAT I DIDN'T SEE. ANY OTHER TIME—
I DON'T KNOW WHAT *THAT* WAS, BUT I KNOW WHAT I SAW IN THE COURTYARD.
WAIT. WHAT ELSE HAPPENED?

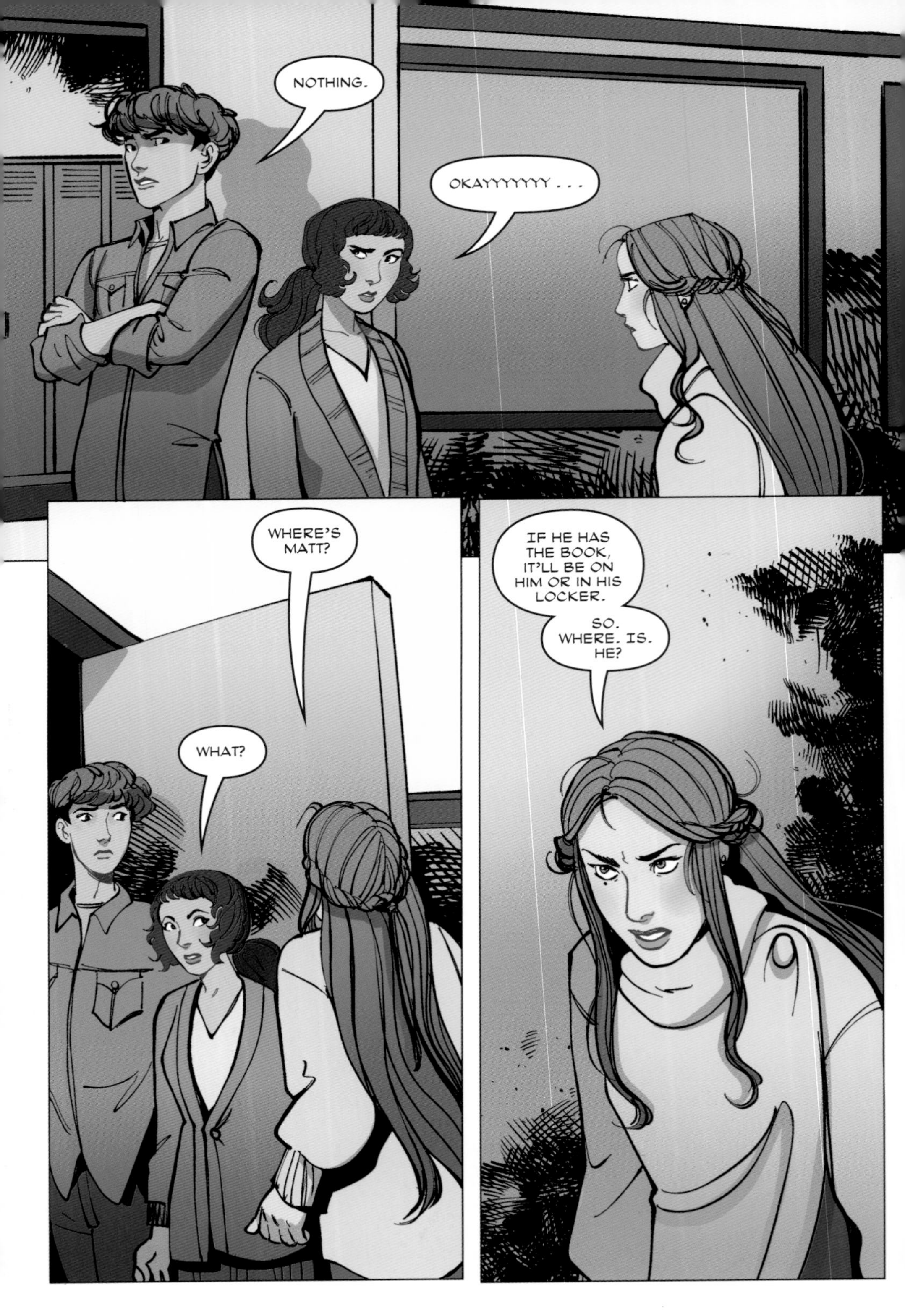
NOTHING.
OKAYYYYYYY . . .
WHERE'S MATT?
WHAT?
IF HE HAS THE BOOK, IT'LL BE ON HIM OR IN HIS LOCKER.
SO. WHERE. IS. HE?

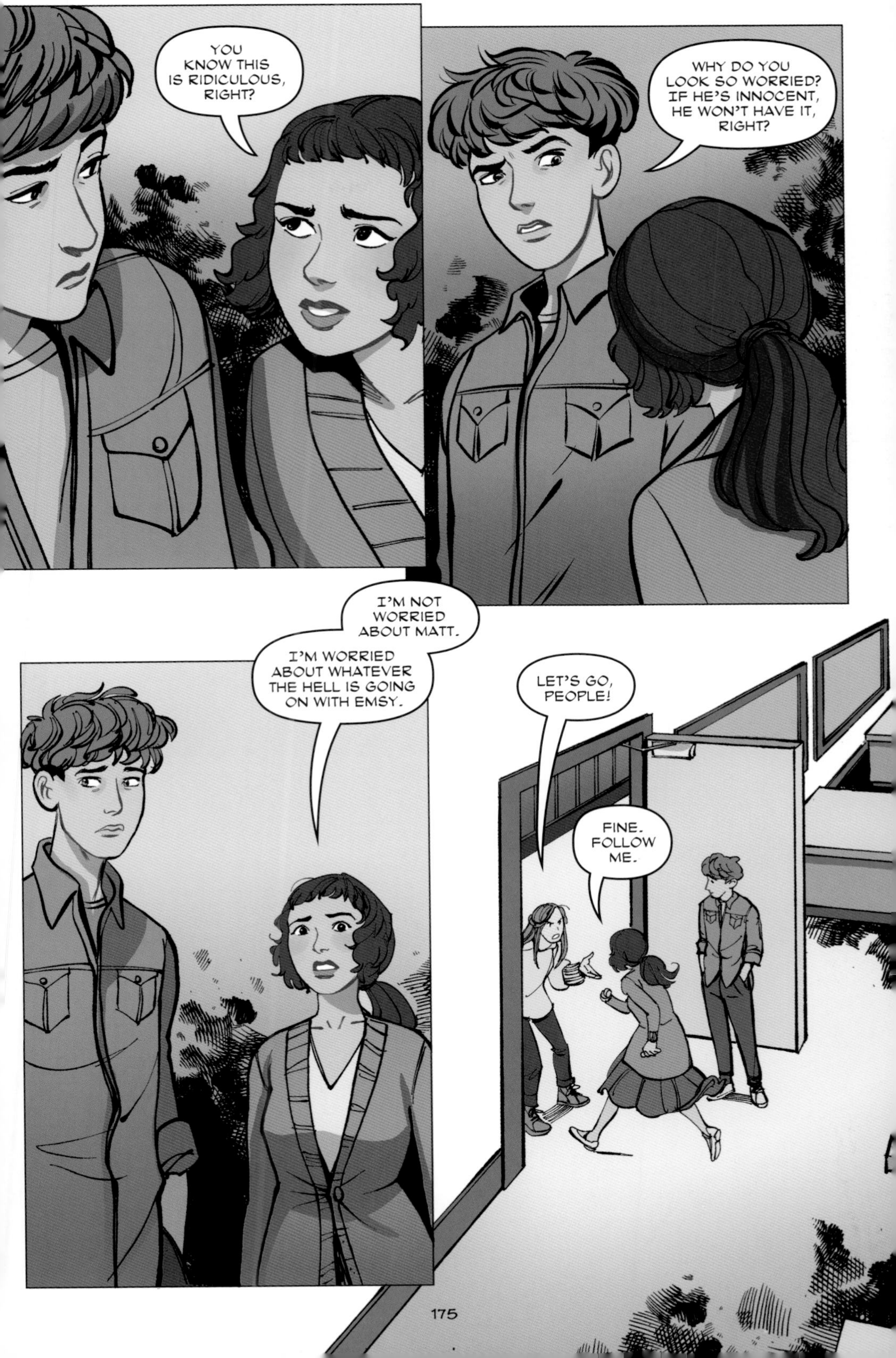
YOU KNOW THIS IS RIDICULOUS, RIGHT?
WHY DO YOU LOOK SO WORRIED? IF HE'S INNOCENT, HE WON'T HAVE IT, RIGHT?
I'M NOT WORRIED ABOUT MATT.
I'M WORRIED ABOUT WHATEVER THE HELL IS GOING ON WITH EMSY.
LET'S GO, PEOPLE!
FINE. FOLLOW ME.

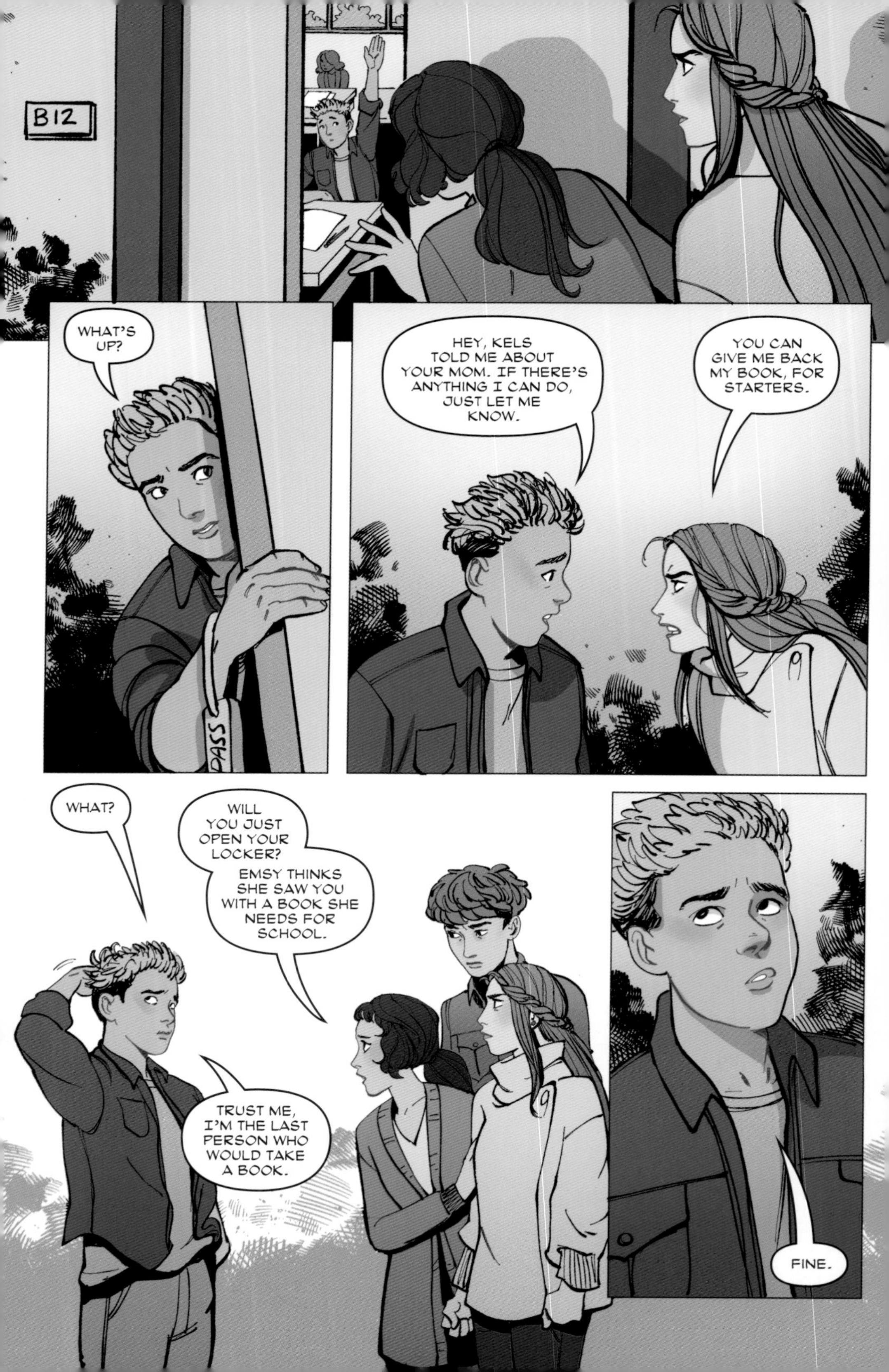
B12
WHAT'S UP?
HEY, KELS TOLD ME ABOUT YOUR MOM. IF THERE'S ANYTHING I CAN DO, JUST LET ME KNOW.
YOU CAN GIVE ME BACK MY BOOK, FOR STARTERS.
PASS
WHAT?
WILL YOU JUST OPEN YOUR LOCKER?
EMSY THINKS SHE SAW YOU WITH A BOOK SHE NEEDS FOR SCHOOL.
TRUST ME, I'M THE LAST PERSON WHO WOULD TAKE A BOOK.
FINE.

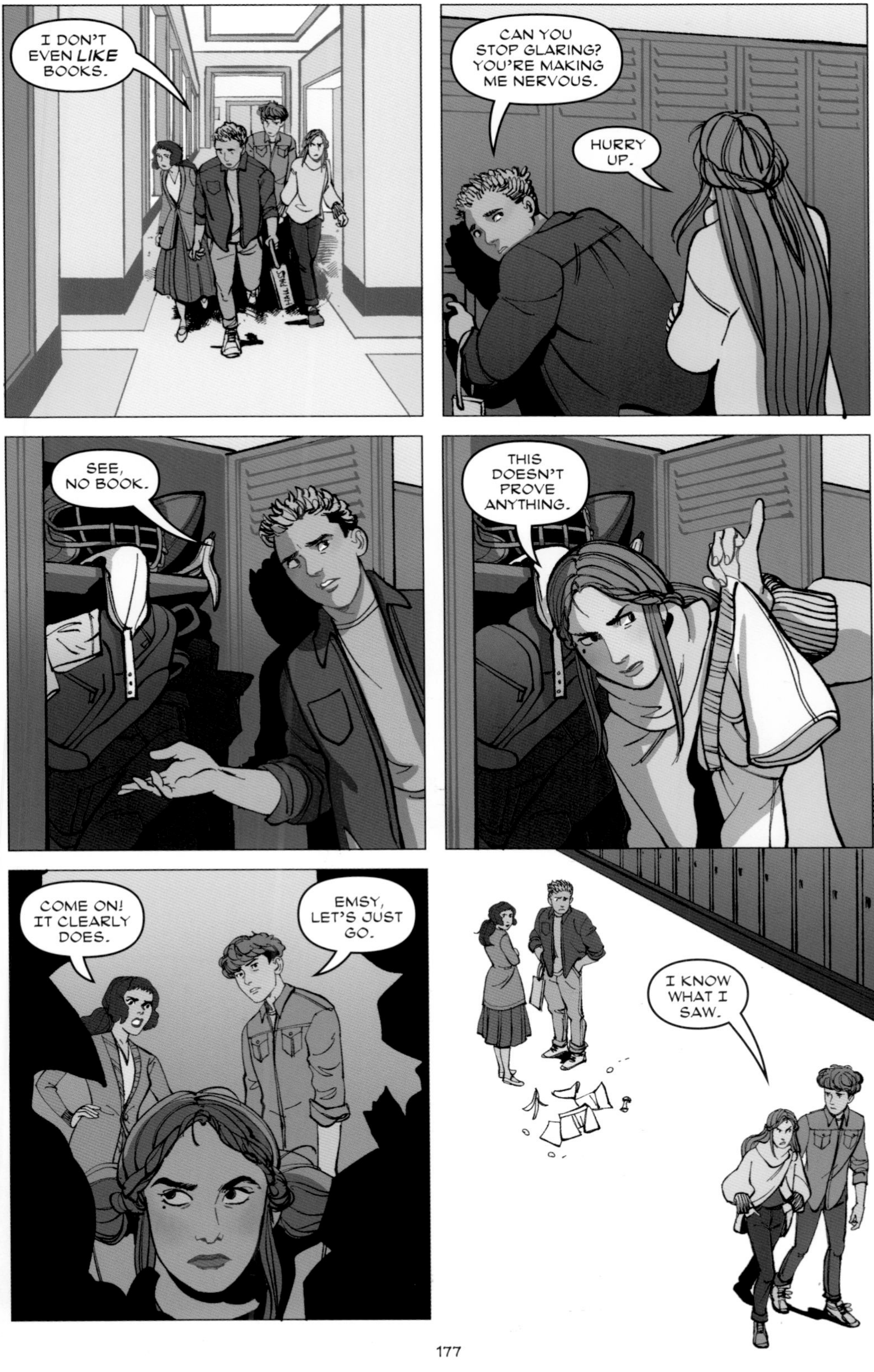
I DON'T EVEN LIKE BOOKS.
CAN YOU STOP GLARING? YOU'RE MAKING ME NERVOUS.
HURRY UP.
SEE, NO BOOK.
THIS DOESN'T PROVE ANYTHING.
COME ON! IT CLEARLY DOES.
EMSY, LET'S JUST GO.
I KNOW WHAT I SAW.

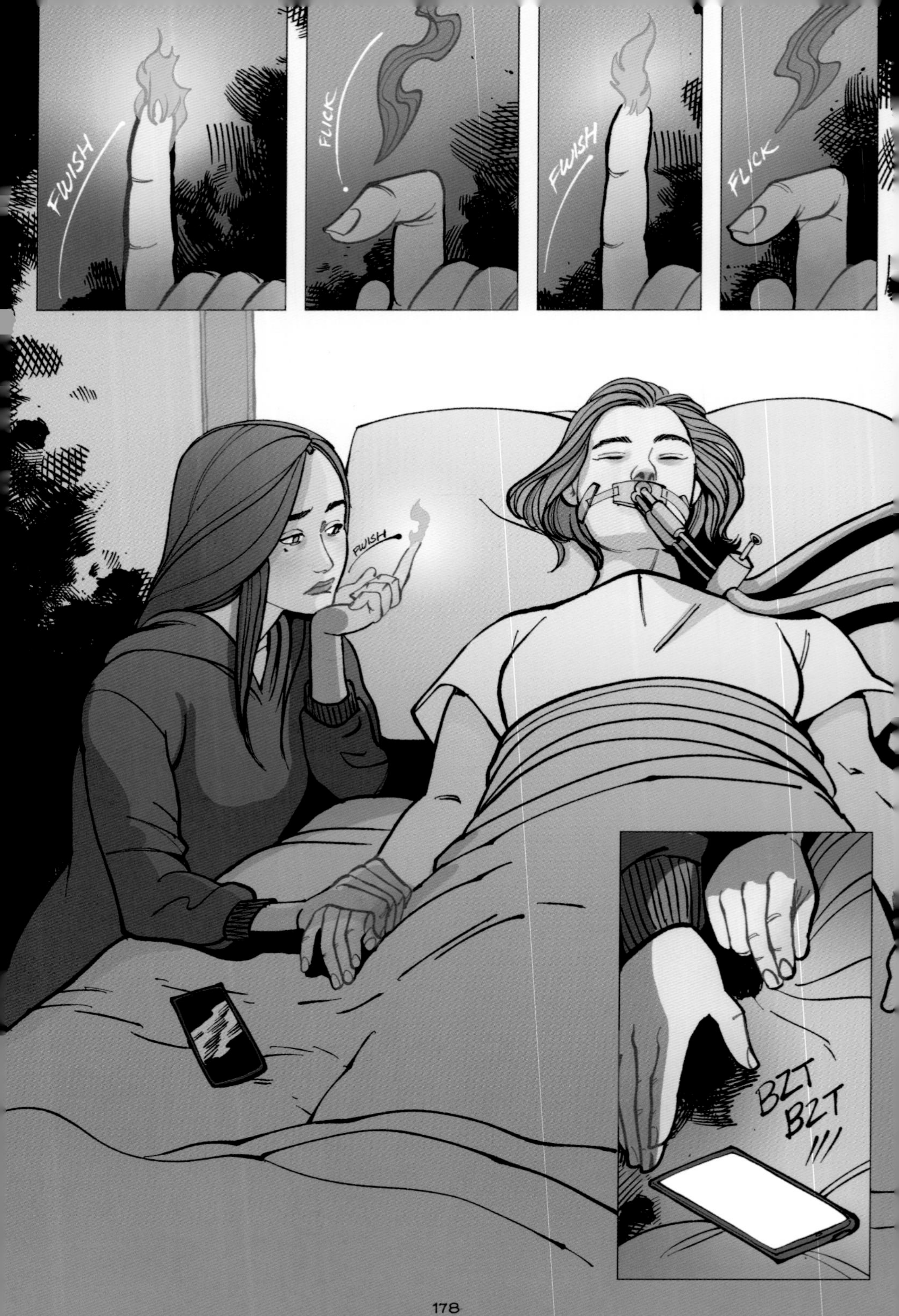
FWISH
FLICK
FWISH
FLICK
FWISH
BZT BZT

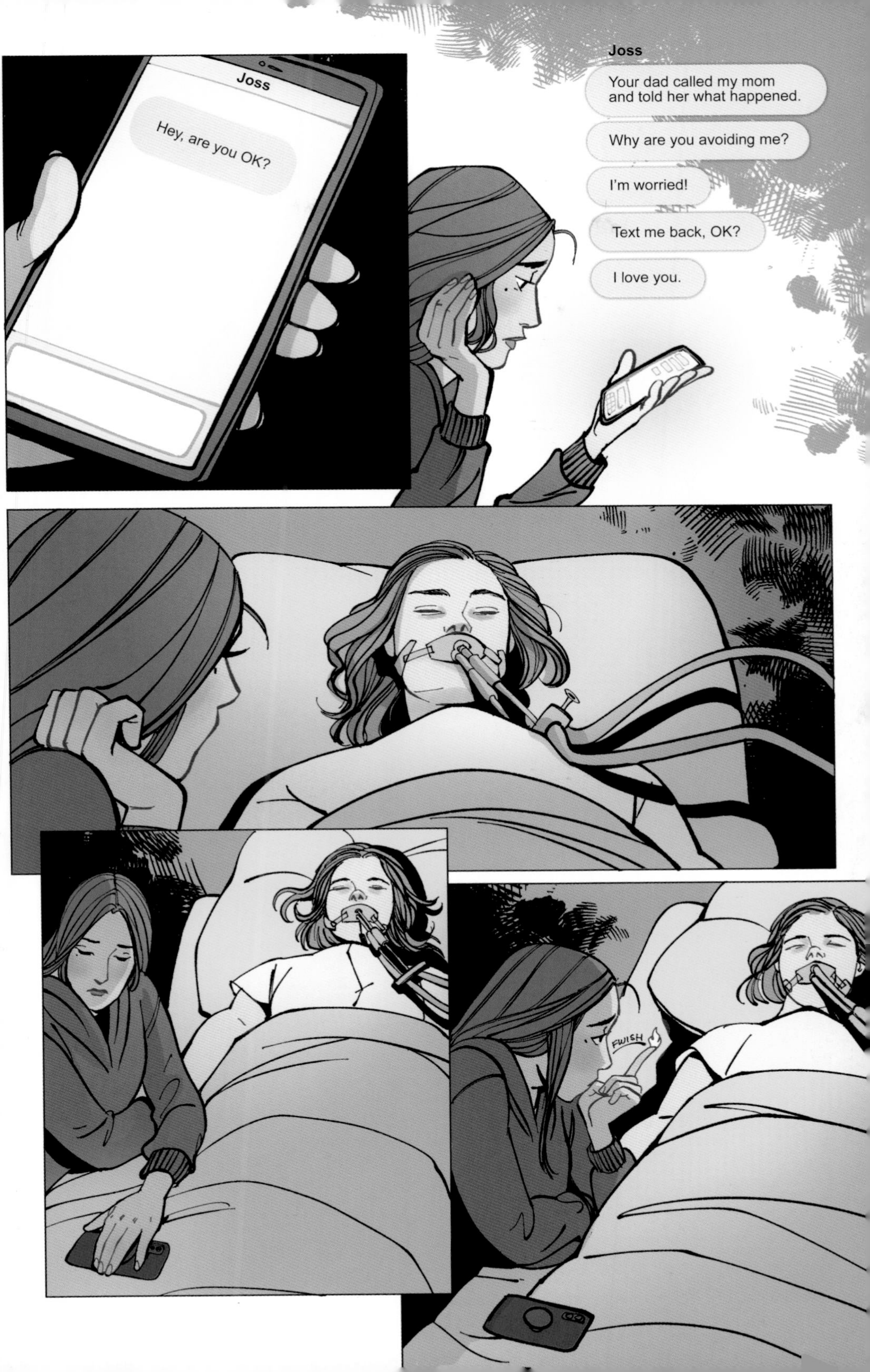
Joss
Hey, are you OK?
Joss
Your dad called my mom and told her what happened.
Why are you avoiding me?
I'm worried!
Text me back, OK?
I love you.
FWISH

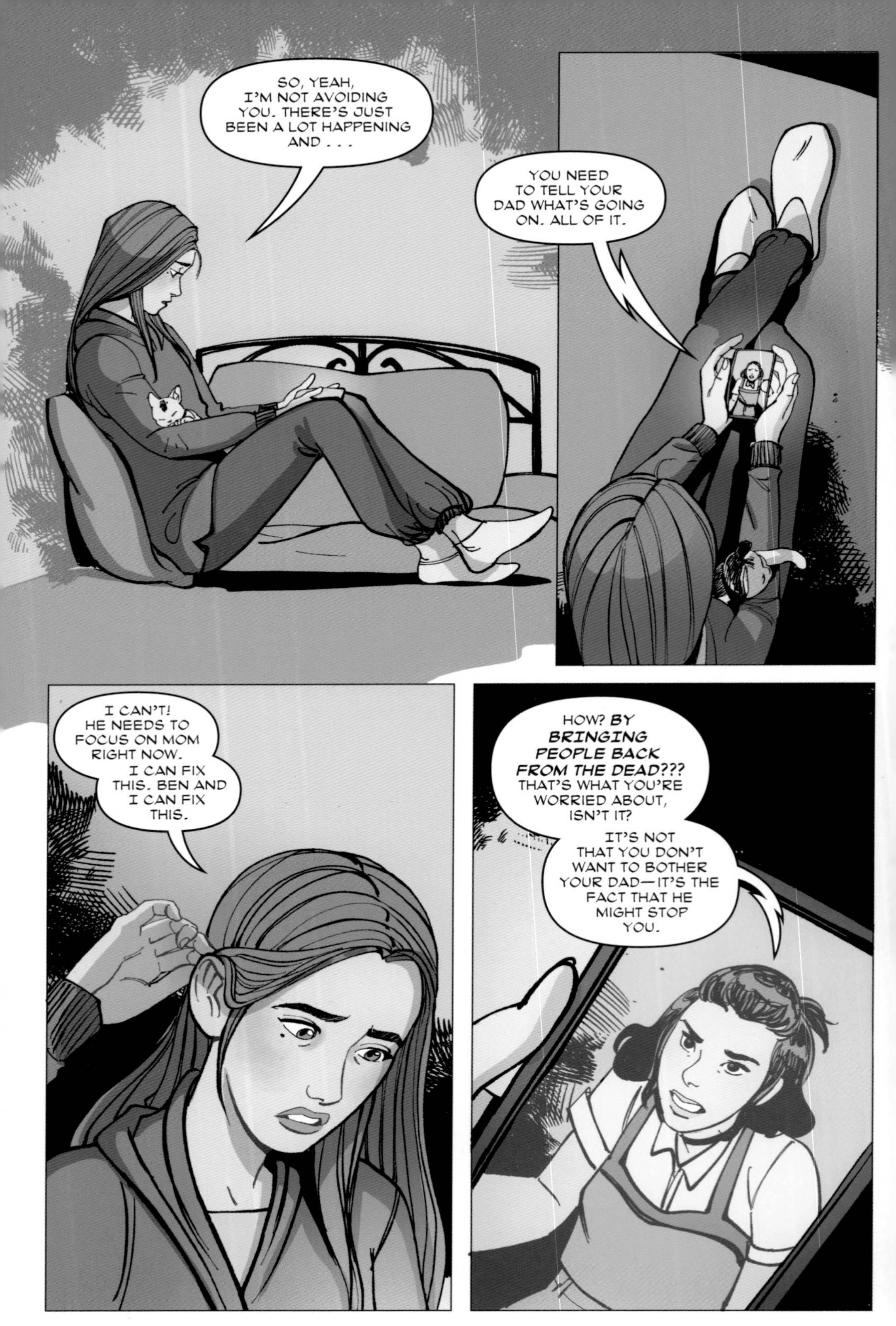
SO, YEAH, I'M NOT AVOIDING YOU. THERE'S JUST BEEN A LOT HAPPENING AND . . .
YOU NEED TO TELL YOUR DAD WHAT'S GOING ON. ALL OF IT.
I CAN'T! HE NEEDS TO FOCUS ON MOM RIGHT NOW.
I CAN FIX THIS. BEN AND I CAN FIX THIS.
HOW? **BY BRINGING PEOPLE BACK FROM THE DEAD???** THAT'S WHAT YOU'RE WORRIED ABOUT, ISN'T IT?
IT'S NOT THAT YOU DON'T WANT TO BOTHER YOUR DAD—IT'S THE FACT THAT HE MIGHT STOP YOU.

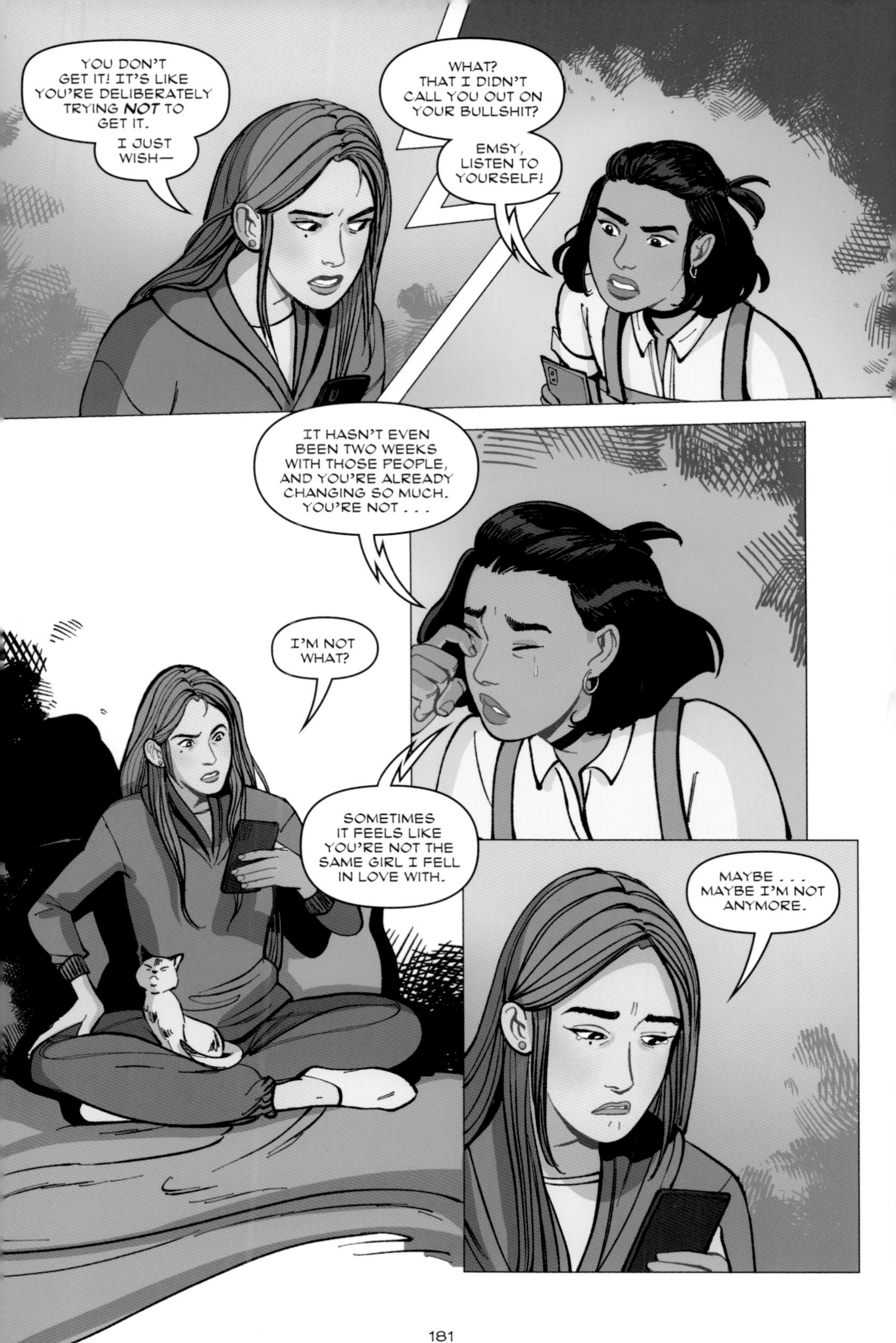
YOU DON'T GET IT! IT'S LIKE YOU'RE DELIBERATELY TRYING **NOT** TO GET IT.
I JUST WISH—
WHAT? THAT I DIDN'T CALL YOU OUT ON YOUR BULLSHIT?
EMSY, LISTEN TO YOURSELF!
IT HASN'T EVEN BEEN TWO WEEKS WITH THOSE PEOPLE, AND YOU'RE ALREADY CHANGING SO MUCH. YOU'RE NOT . . .
I'M NOT WHAT?
SOMETIMES IT FEELS LIKE YOU'RE NOT THE SAME GIRL I FELL IN LOVE WITH.
MAYBE . . . MAYBE I'M NOT ANYMORE.

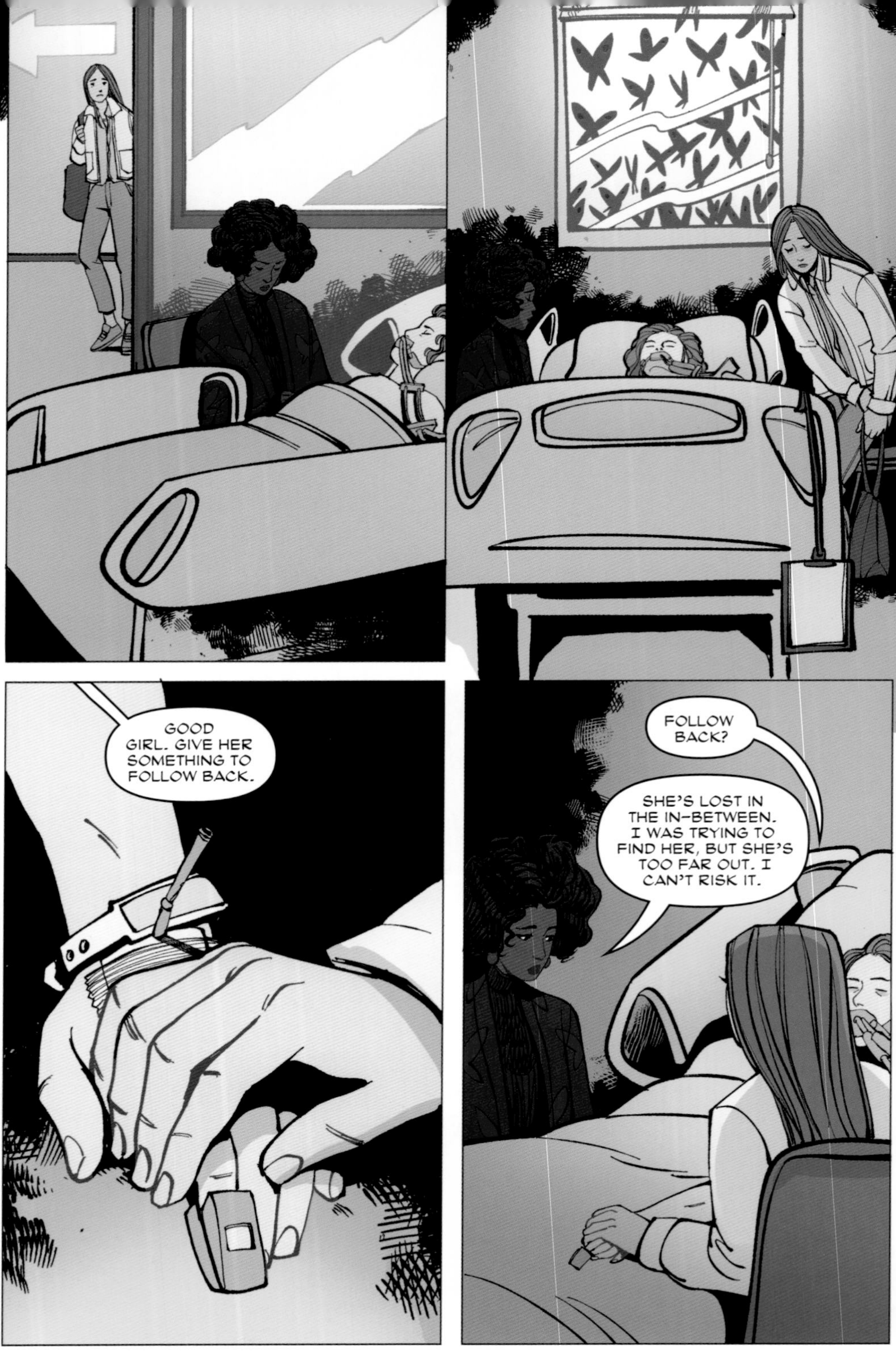
GOOD GIRL. GIVE HER SOMETHING TO FOLLOW BACK.
FOLLOW BACK?
SHE'S LOST IN THE IN-BETWEEN. I WAS TRYING TO FIND HER, BUT SHE'S TOO FAR OUT. I CAN'T RISK IT.

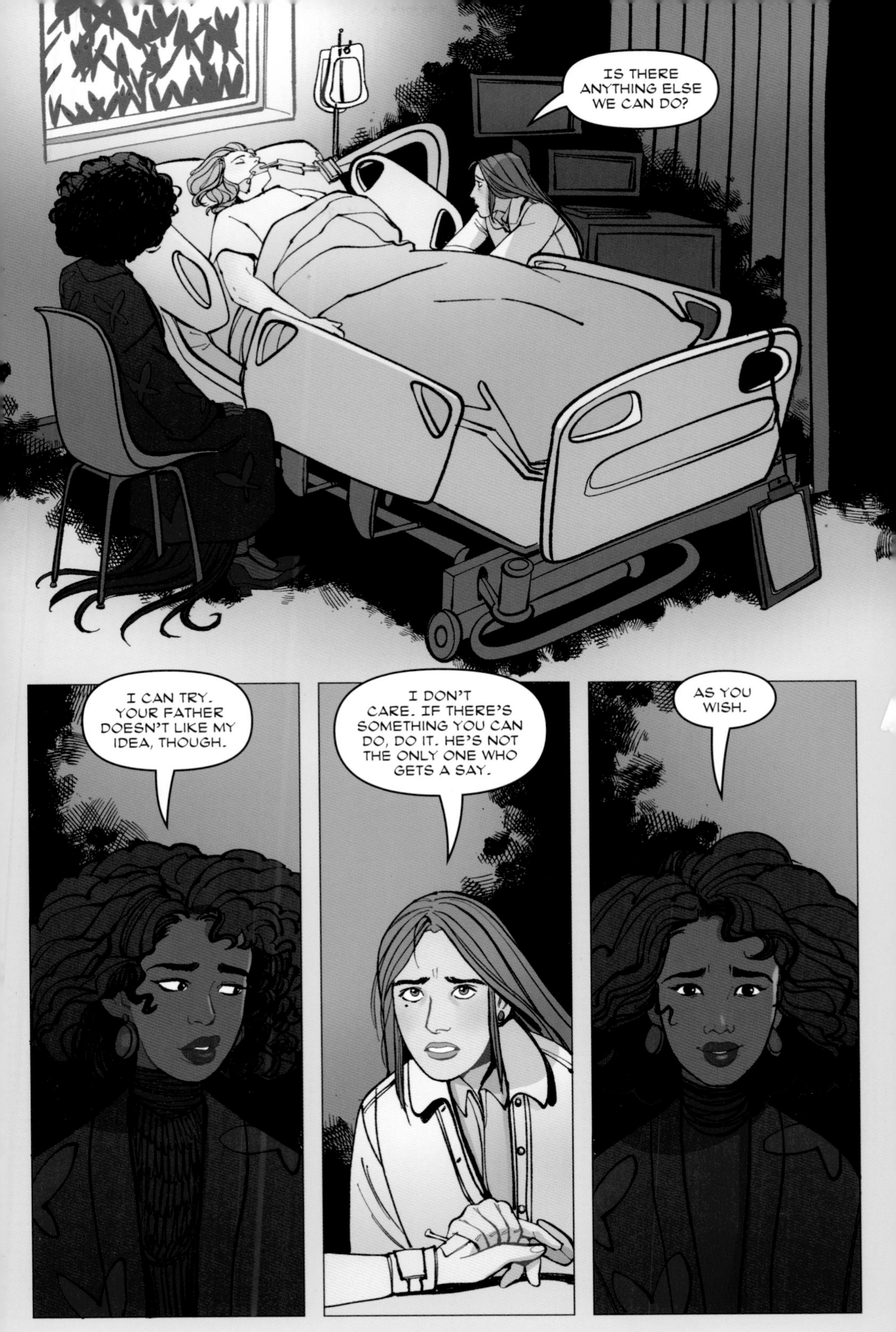
IS THERE ANYTHING ELSE WE CAN DO?
I CAN TRY. YOUR FATHER DOESN'T LIKE MY IDEA, THOUGH.
I DON'T CARE. IF THERE'S SOMETHING YOU CAN DO, DO IT. HE'S NOT THE ONLY ONE WHO GETS A SAY.
AS YOU WISH.

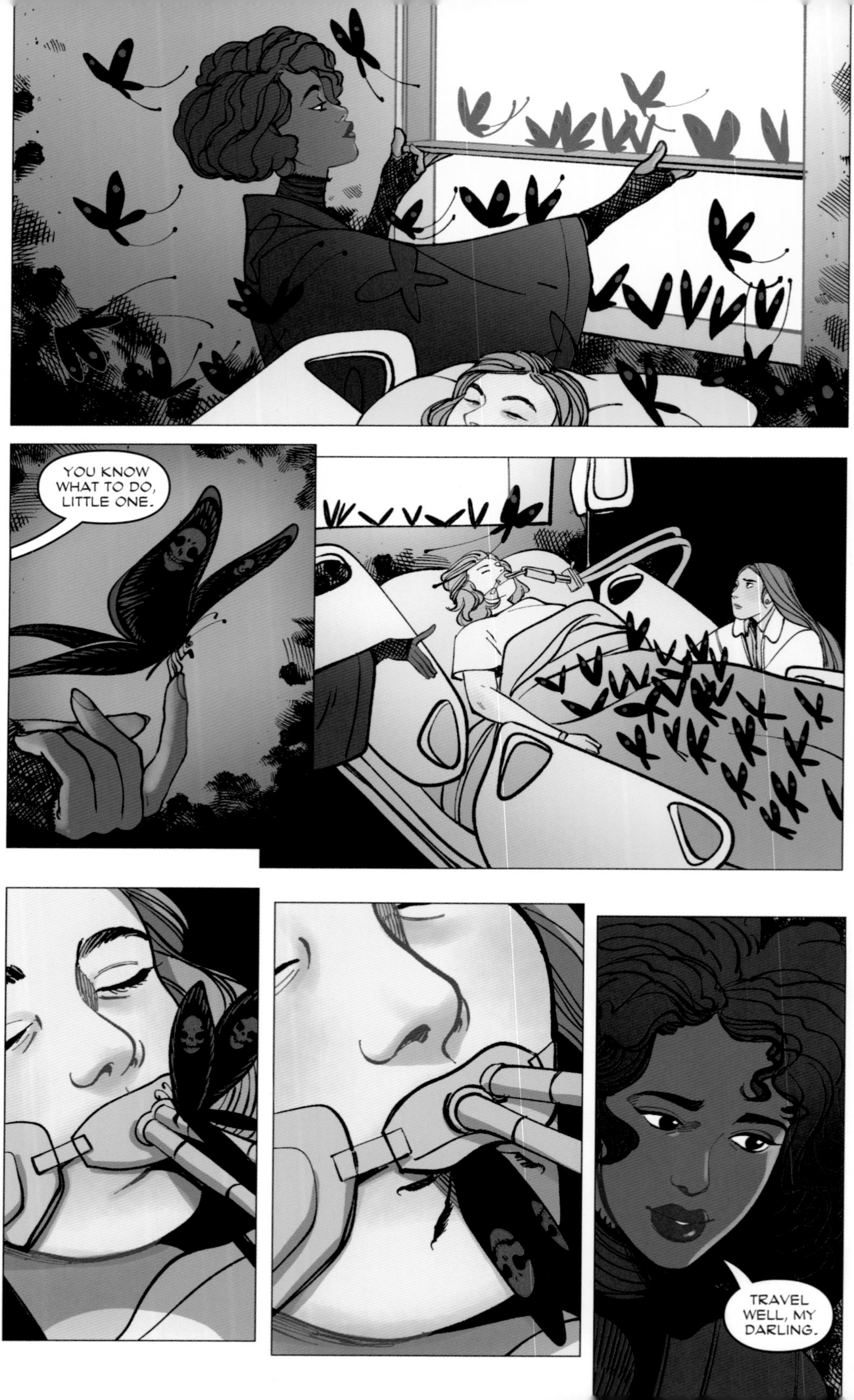
YOU KNOW WHAT TO DO, LITTLE ONE.
TRAVEL WELL, MY DARLING.

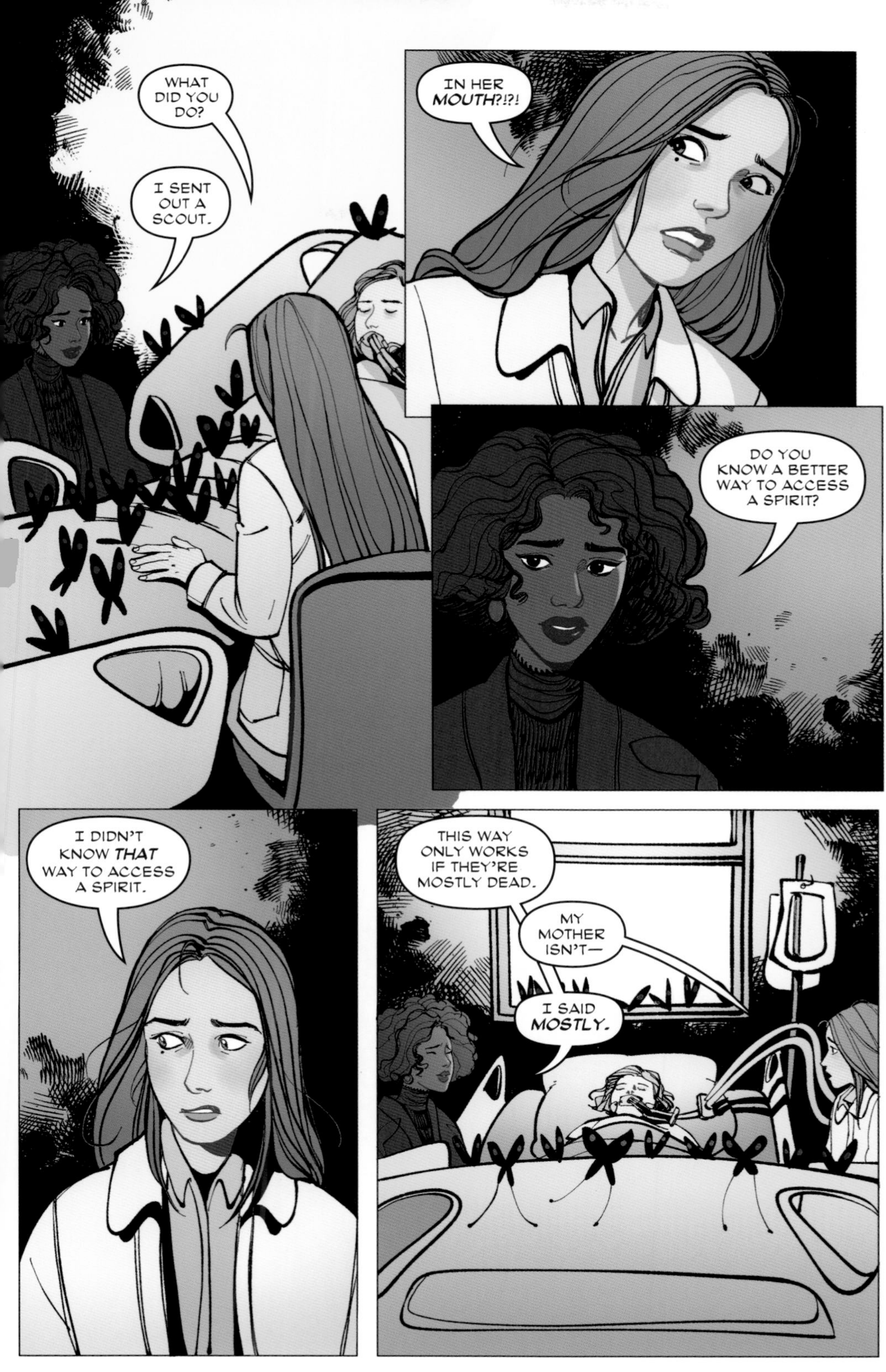
WHAT DID YOU DO?
I SENT OUT A SCOUT.
IN HER *MOUTH*?!?!
DO YOU KNOW A BETTER WAY TO ACCESS A SPIRIT?
I DIDN'T KNOW *THAT* WAY TO ACCESS A SPIRIT.
THIS WAY ONLY WORKS IF THEY'RE MOSTLY DEAD.
MY MOTHER ISN'T—
I SAID *MOSTLY*.

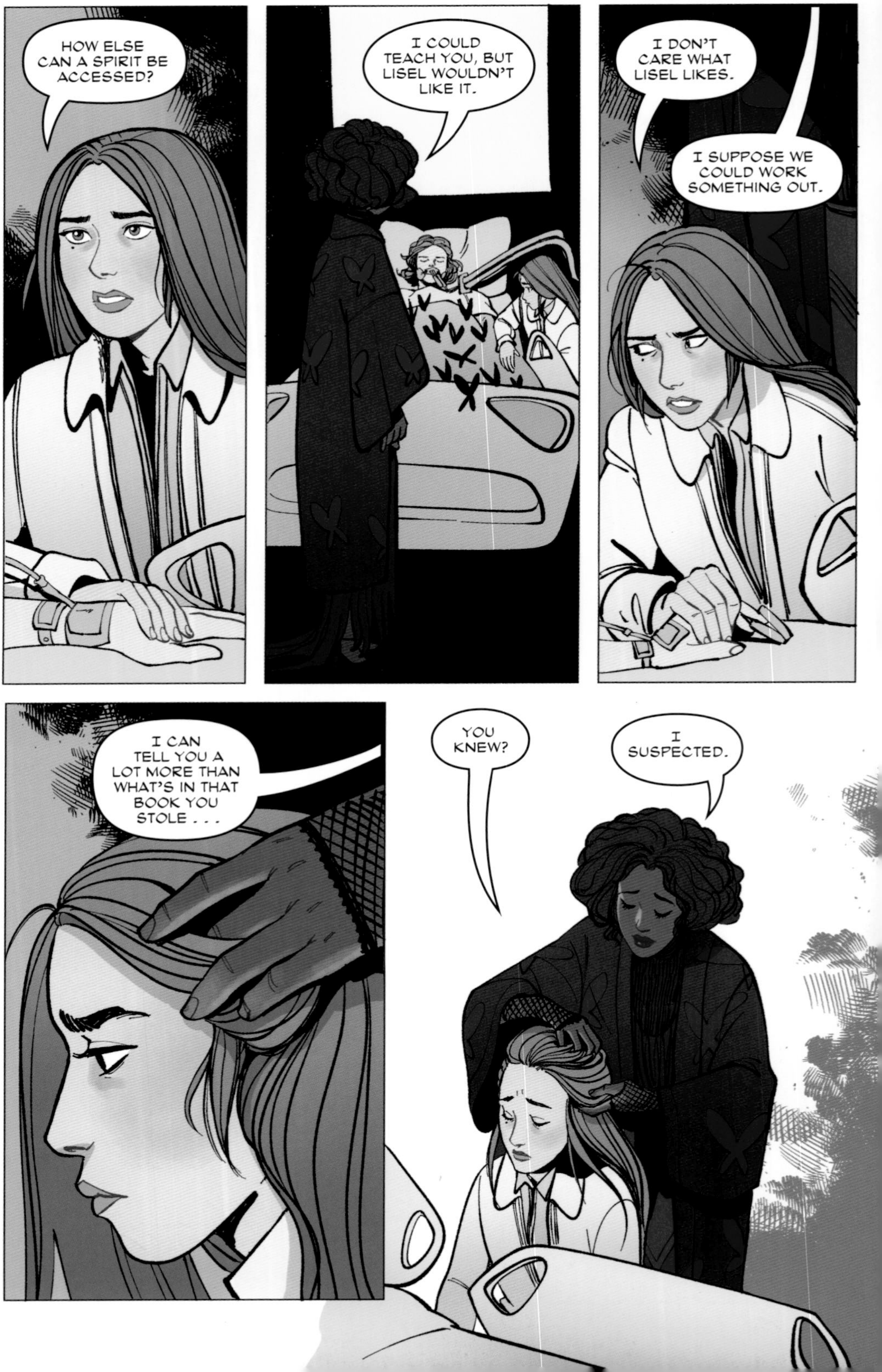
HOW ELSE CAN A SPIRIT BE ACCESSED?
I COULD TEACH YOU, BUT LISEL WOULDN'T LIKE IT.
I DON'T CARE WHAT LISEL LIKES.
I SUPPOSE WE COULD WORK SOMETHING OUT.
I CAN TELL YOU A LOT MORE THAN WHAT'S IN THAT BOOK YOU STOLE . . .
YOU KNEW?
I SUSPECTED.

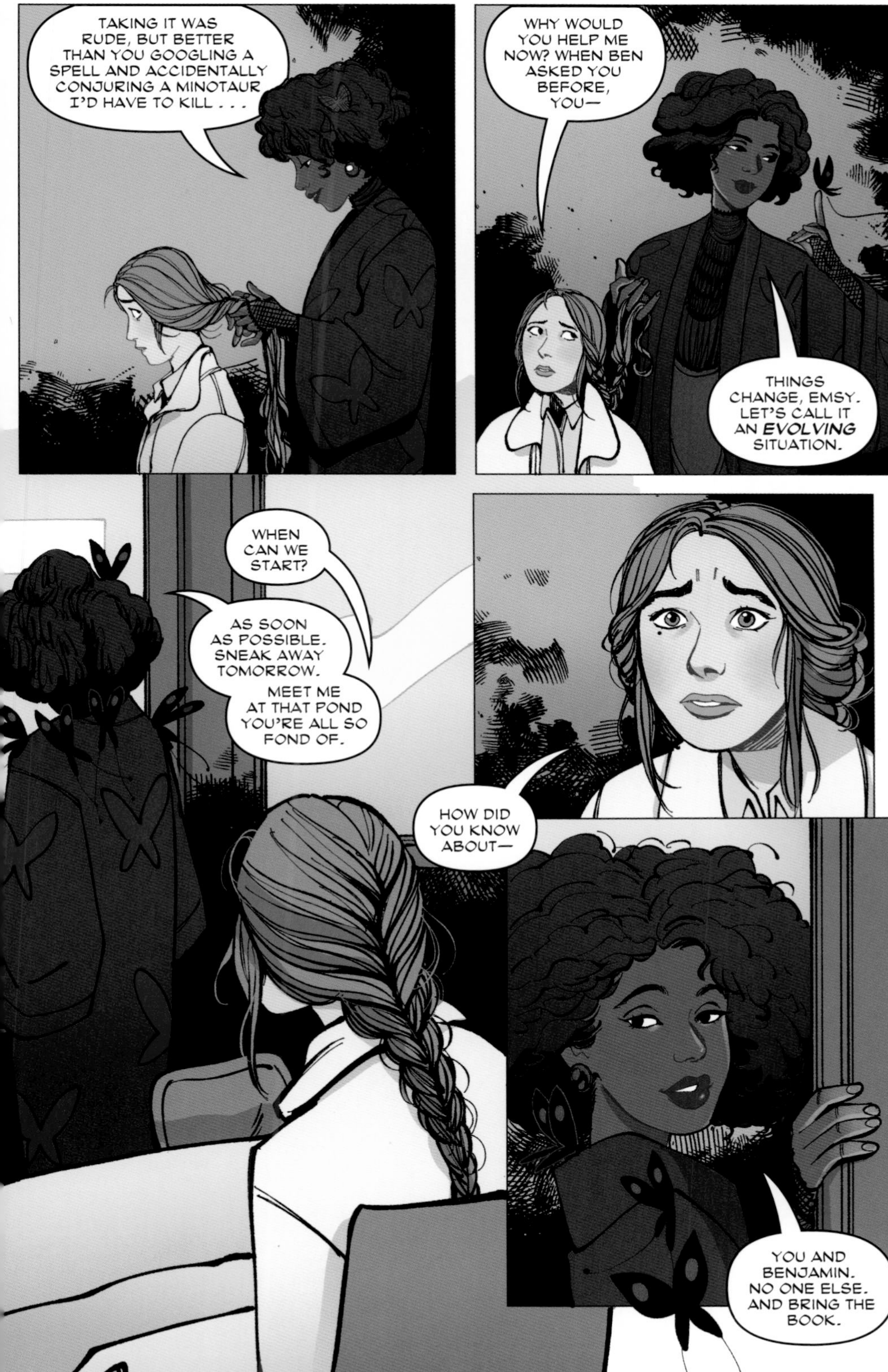
TAKING IT WAS RUDE, BUT BETTER THAN YOU GOOGLING A SPELL AND ACCIDENTALLY CONJURING A MINOTAUR I'D HAVE TO KILL . . .
WHY WOULD YOU HELP ME NOW? WHEN BEN ASKED YOU BEFORE, YOU—
THINGS CHANGE, EMSY. LET'S CALL IT AN *EVOLVING* SITUATION.
WHEN CAN WE START?
AS SOON AS POSSIBLE. SNEAK AWAY TOMORROW.
MEET ME AT THAT POND YOU'RE ALL SO FOND OF.
HOW DID YOU KNOW ABOUT—
YOU AND BENJAMIN. NO ONE ELSE. AND BRING THE BOOK.

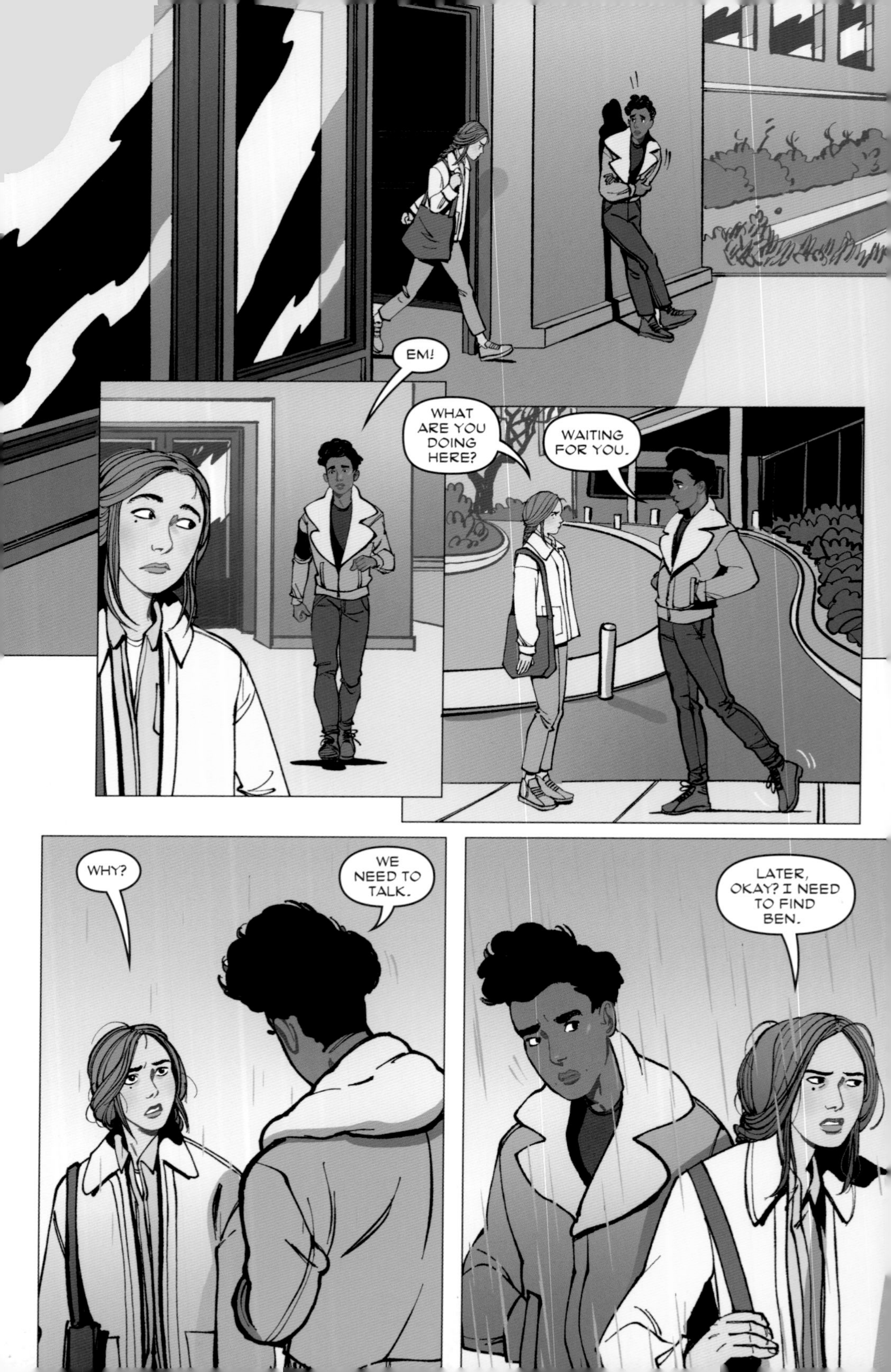
EM!
WHAT ARE YOU DOING HERE?
WAITING FOR YOU.
WHY?
WE NEED TO TALK.
LATER, OKAY? I NEED TO FIND BEN.

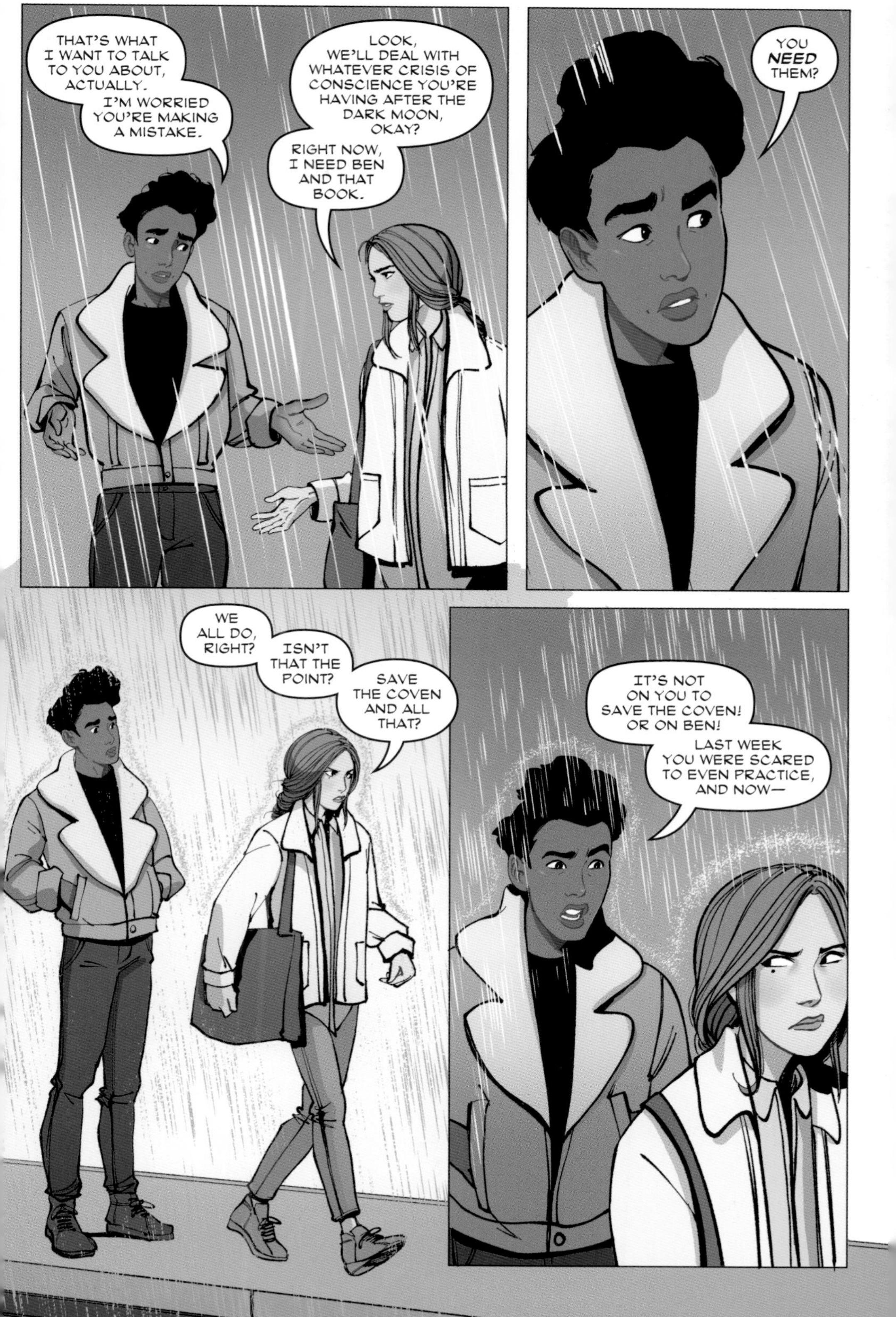
THAT'S WHAT I WANT TO TALK TO YOU ABOUT, ACTUALLY.
I'M WORRIED YOU'RE MAKING A MISTAKE.
LOOK, WE'LL DEAL WITH WHATEVER CRISIS OF CONSCIENCE YOU'RE HAVING AFTER THE DARK MOON, OKAY?
RIGHT NOW, I NEED BEN AND THAT BOOK.
YOU **NEED** THEM?
WE ALL DO, RIGHT?
ISN'T THAT THE POINT?
SAVE THE COVEN AND ALL THAT?
IT'S NOT ON YOU TO SAVE THE COVEN! OR ON BEN!
LAST WEEK YOU WERE SCARED TO EVEN PRACTICE, AND NOW—

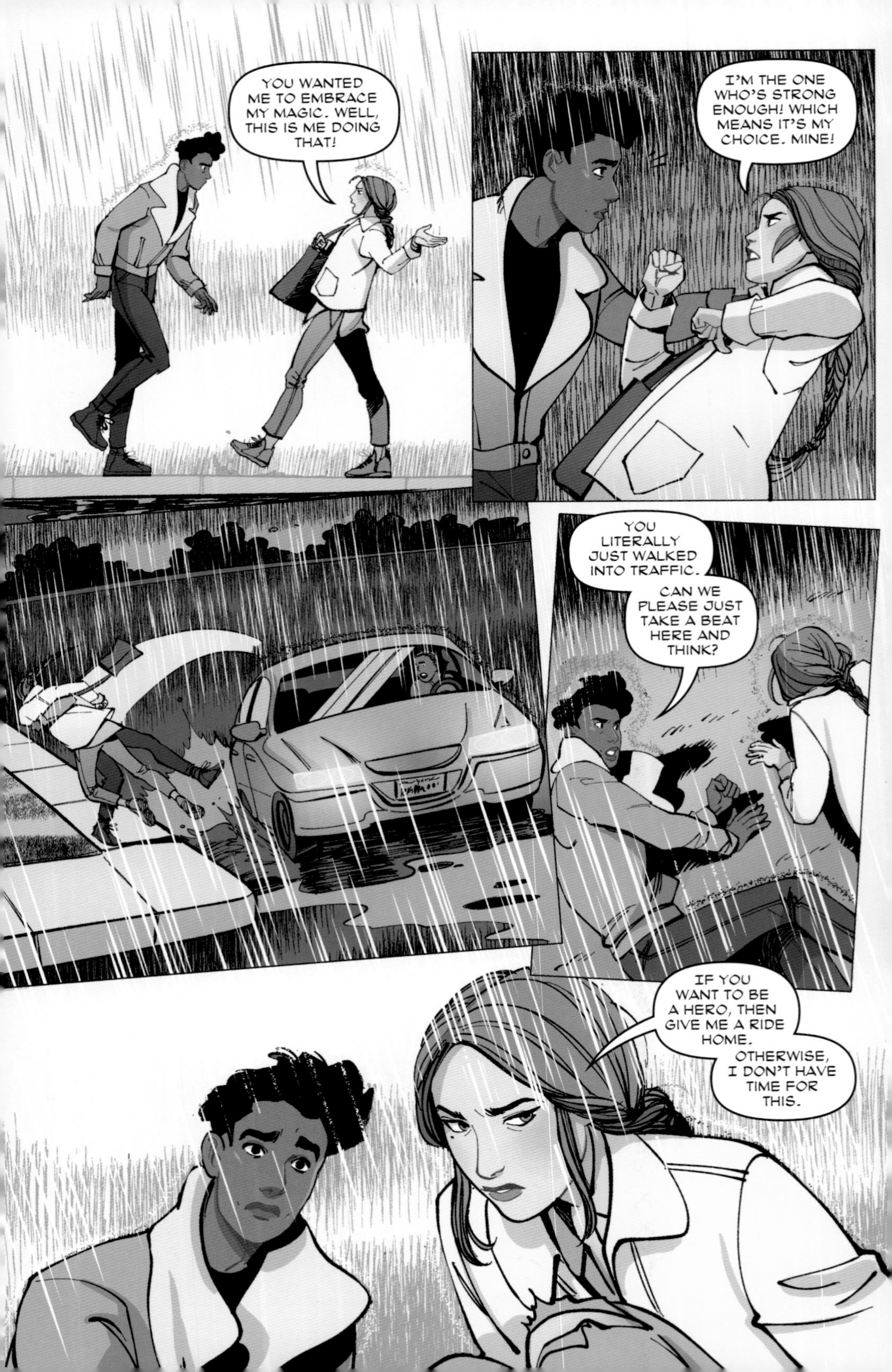
YOU WANTED ME TO EMBRACE MY MAGIC. WELL, THIS IS ME DOING THAT!
I'M THE ONE WHO'S STRONG ENOUGH! WHICH MEANS IT'S MY CHOICE. MINE!
YOU LITERALLY JUST WALKED INTO TRAFFIC.
CAN WE PLEASE JUST TAKE A BEAT HERE AND THINK?
IF YOU WANT TO BE A HERO, THEN GIVE ME A RIDE HOME.
OTHERWISE, I DON'T HAVE TIME FOR THIS.

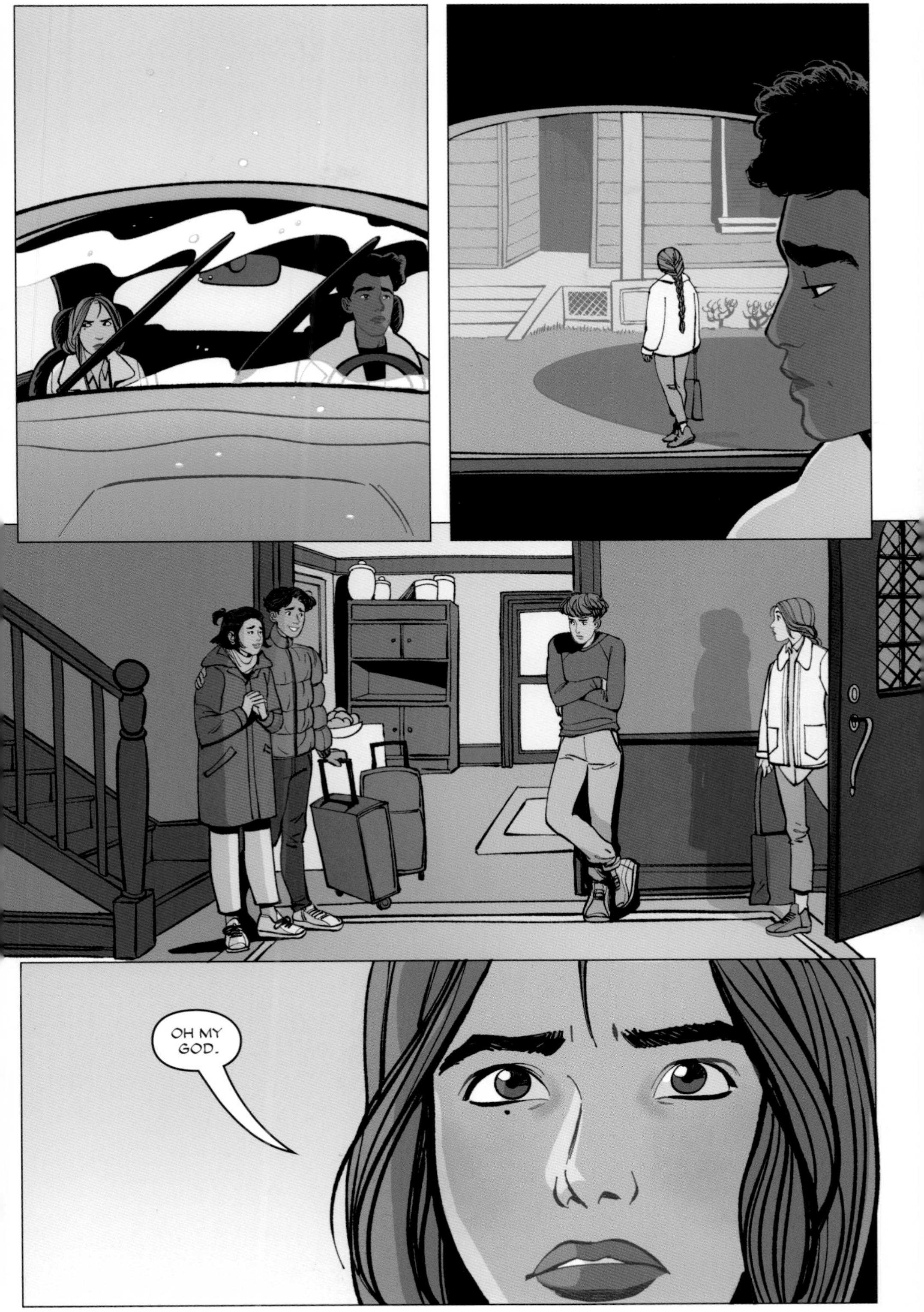
OH MY GOD.

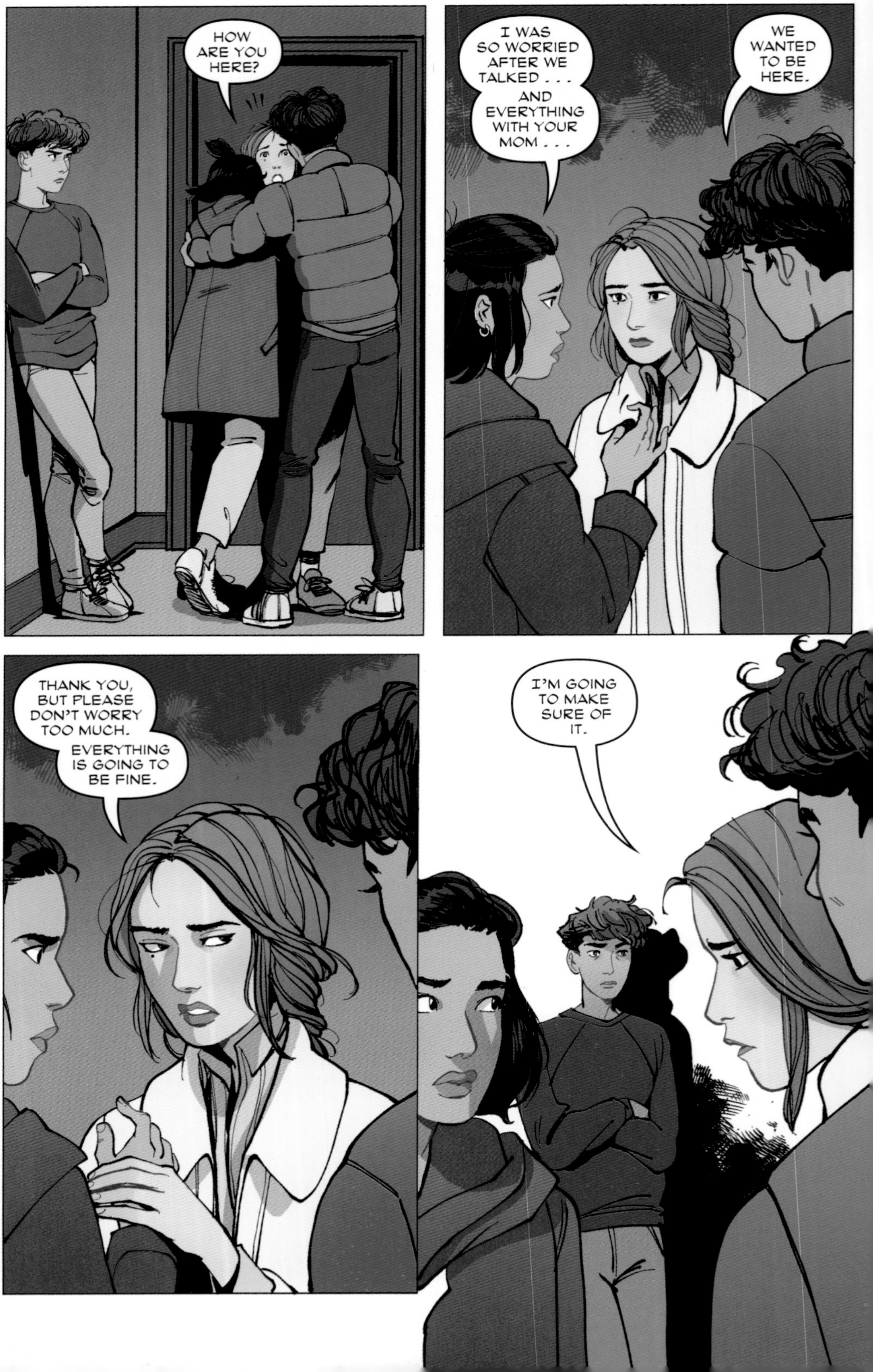
HOW ARE YOU HERE?
I WAS SO WORRIED AFTER WE TALKED . . .
AND EVERYTHING WITH YOUR MOM . . .
WE WANTED TO BE HERE.
THANK YOU, BUT PLEASE DON'T WORRY TOO MUCH.
EVERYTHING IS GOING TO BE FINE.
I'M GOING TO MAKE SURE OF IT.

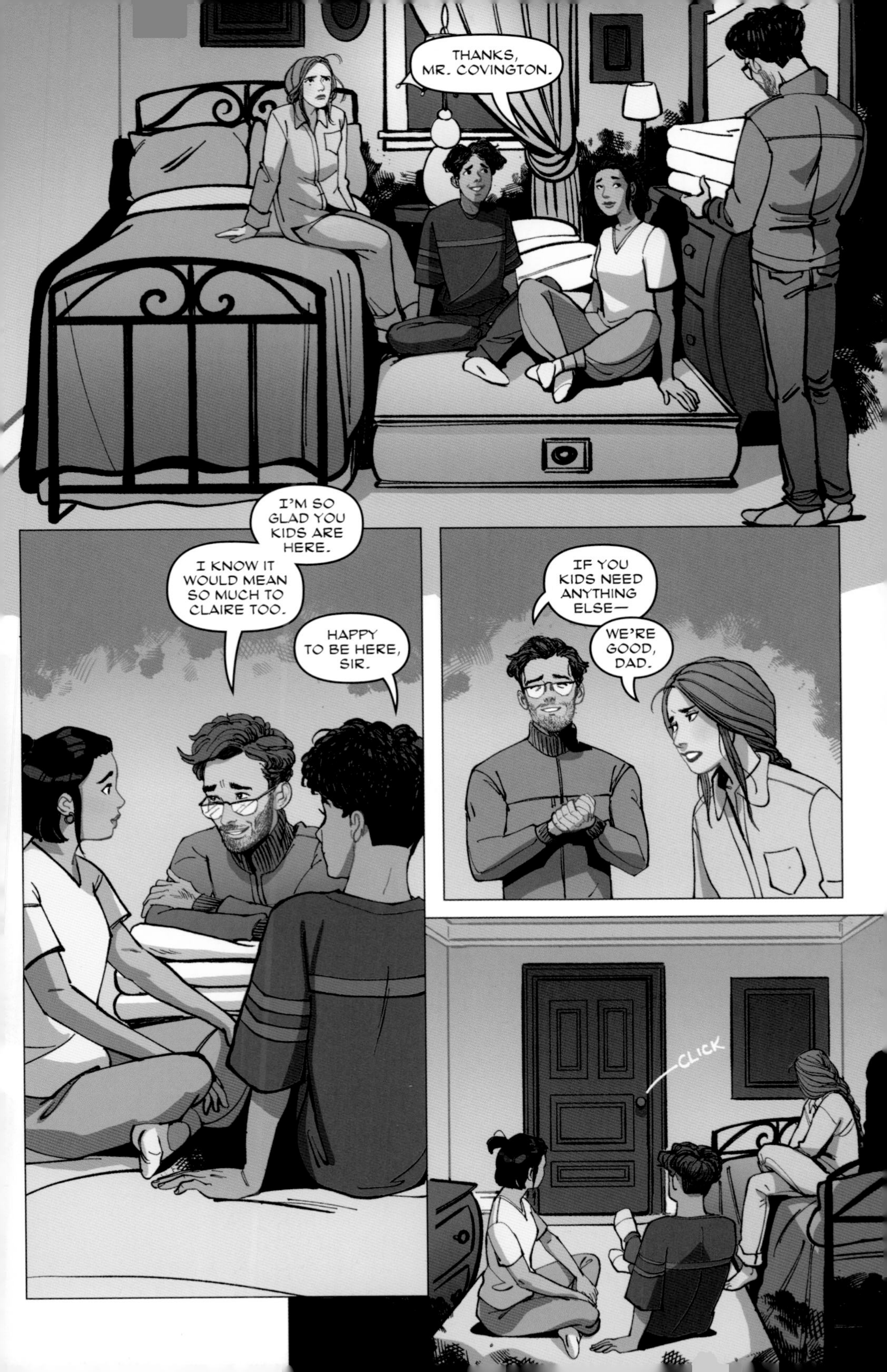
THANKS, MR. COVINGTON.
I'M SO GLAD YOU KIDS ARE HERE.
I KNOW IT WOULD MEAN SO MUCH TO CLAIRE TOO.
HAPPY TO BE HERE, SIR.
IF YOU KIDS NEED ANYTHING ELSE—
WE'RE GOOD, DAD.
CLICK

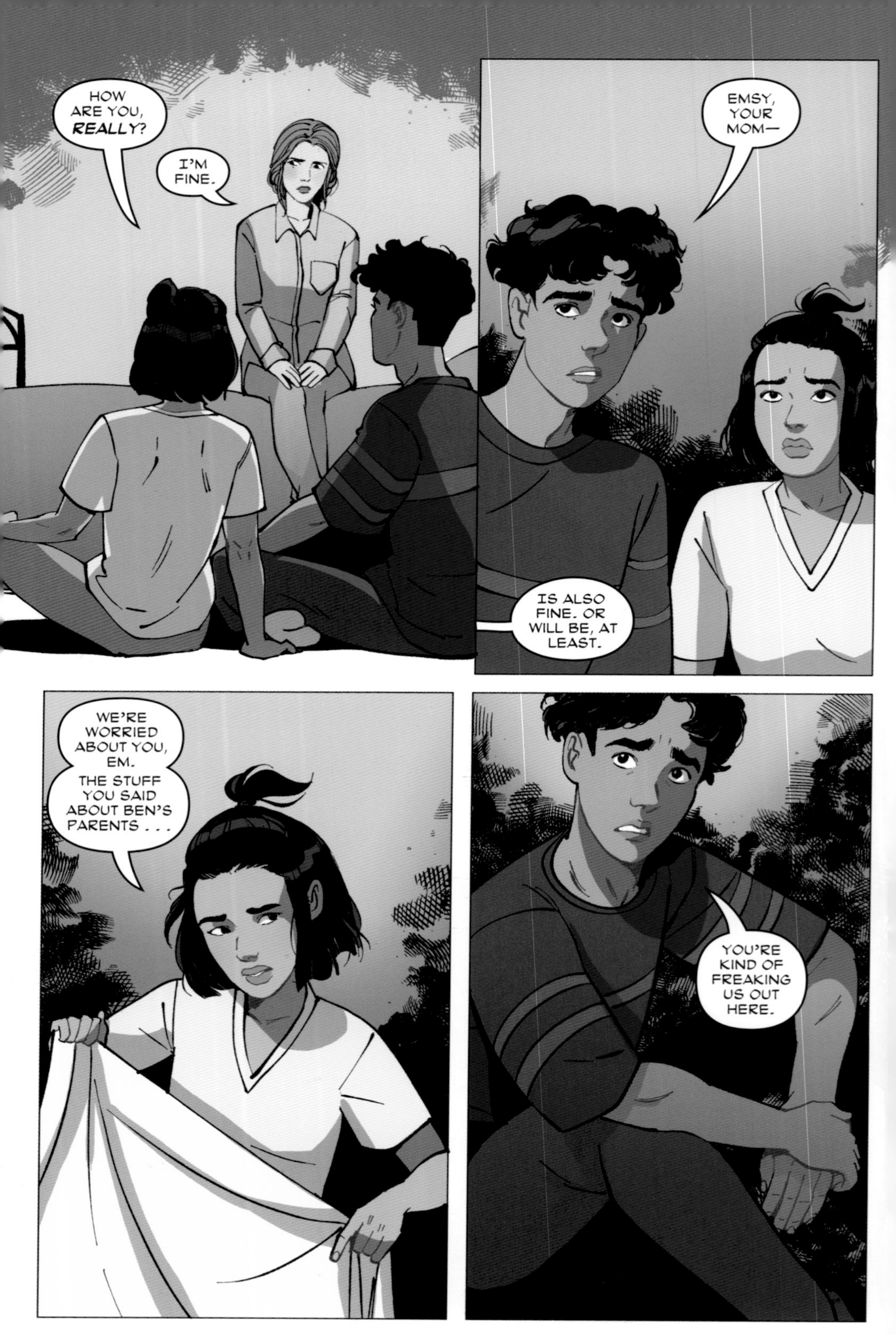
HOW ARE YOU, REALLY?
I'M FINE.
EMSY, YOUR MOM—
IS ALSO FINE. OR WILL BE, AT LEAST.
WE'RE WORRIED ABOUT YOU, EM.
THE STUFF YOU SAID ABOUT BEN'S PARENTS . . .
YOU'RE KIND OF FREAKING US OUT HERE.

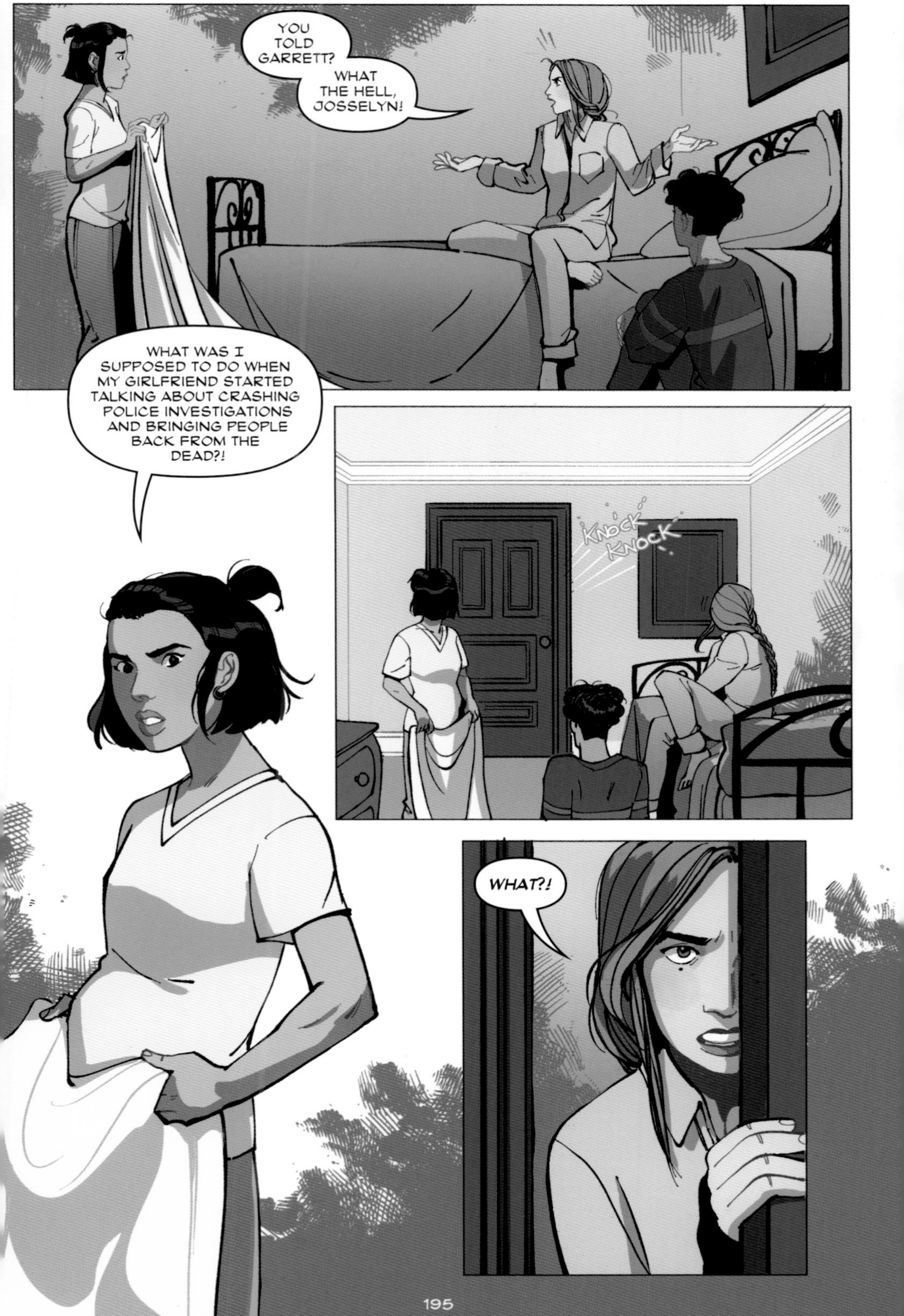
YOU TOLD GARRETT?
WHAT THE HELL, JOSSELYN!
WHAT WAS I SUPPOSED TO DO WHEN MY GIRLFRIEND STARTED TALKING ABOUT CRASHING POLICE INVESTIGATIONS AND BRINGING PEOPLE BACK FROM THE DEAD?!
KNOCK KNOCK
WHAT?!

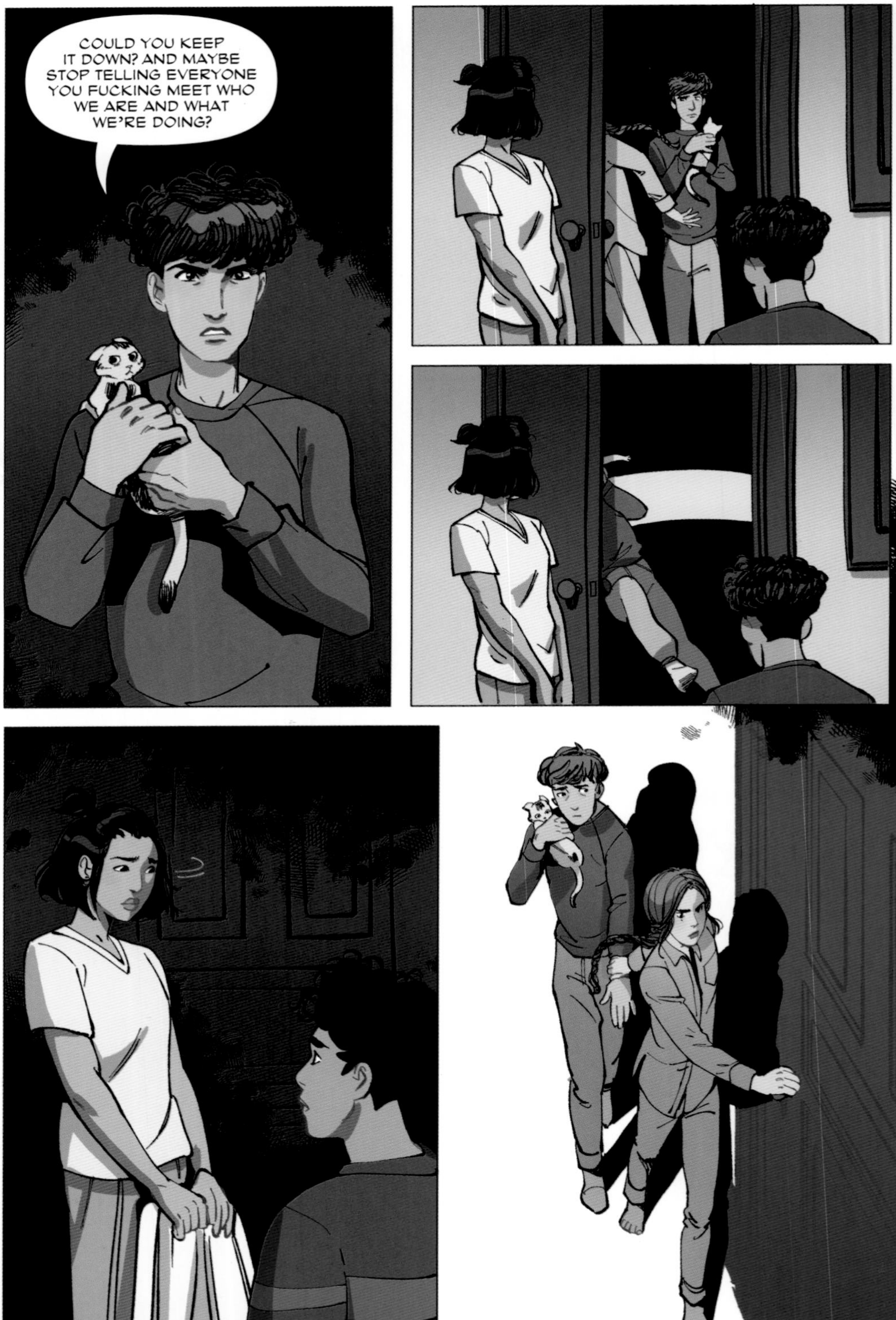
COULD YOU KEEP IT DOWN? AND MAYBE STOP TELLING EVERYONE YOU FUCKING MEET WHO WE ARE AND WHAT WE'RE DOING?

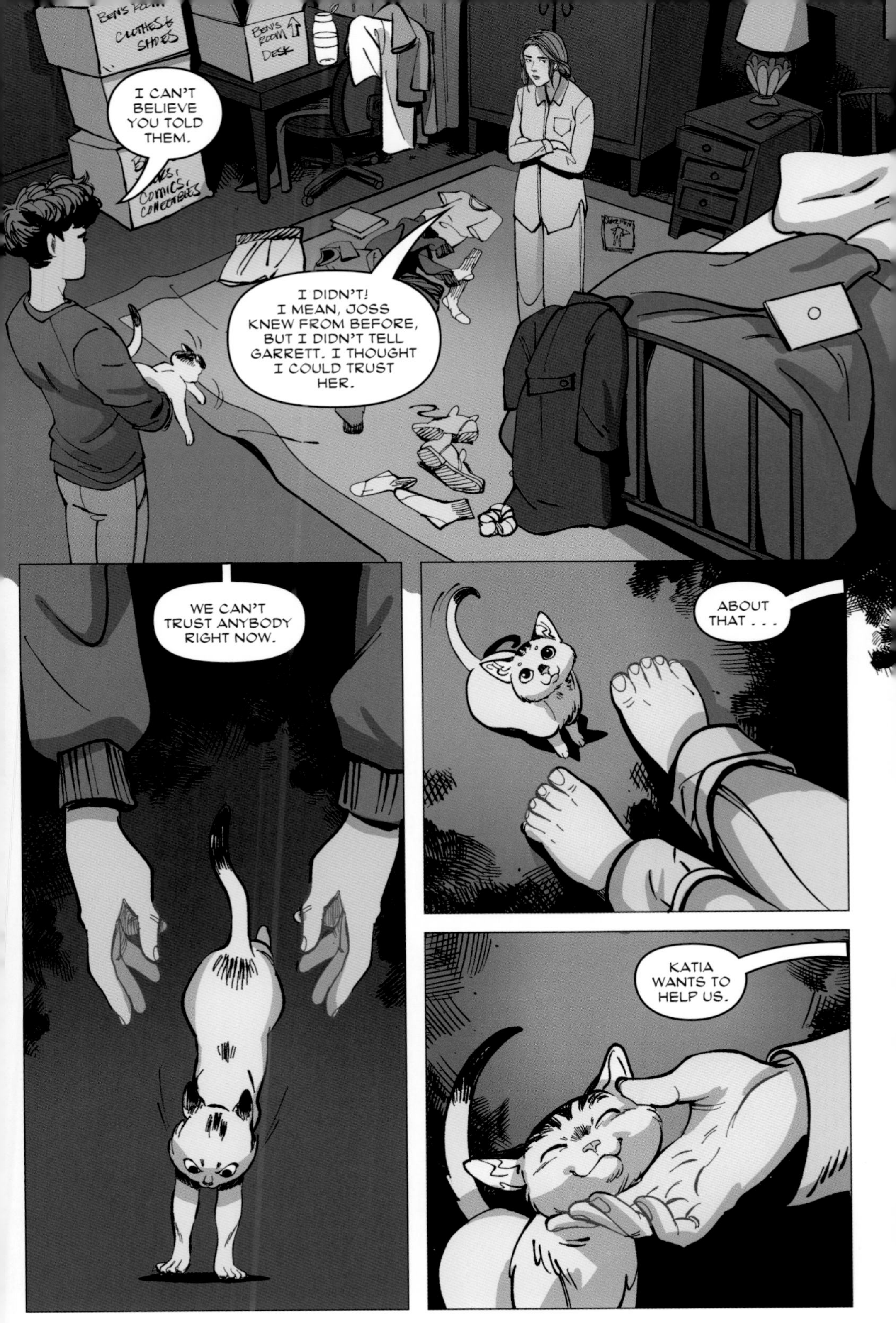
I CAN'T BELIEVE YOU TOLD THEM.
I DIDN'T! I MEAN, JOSS KNEW FROM BEFORE, BUT I DIDN'T TELL GARRETT. I THOUGHT I COULD TRUST HER.
WE CAN'T TRUST ANYBODY RIGHT NOW.
ABOUT THAT . . .
KATIA WANTS TO HELP US.

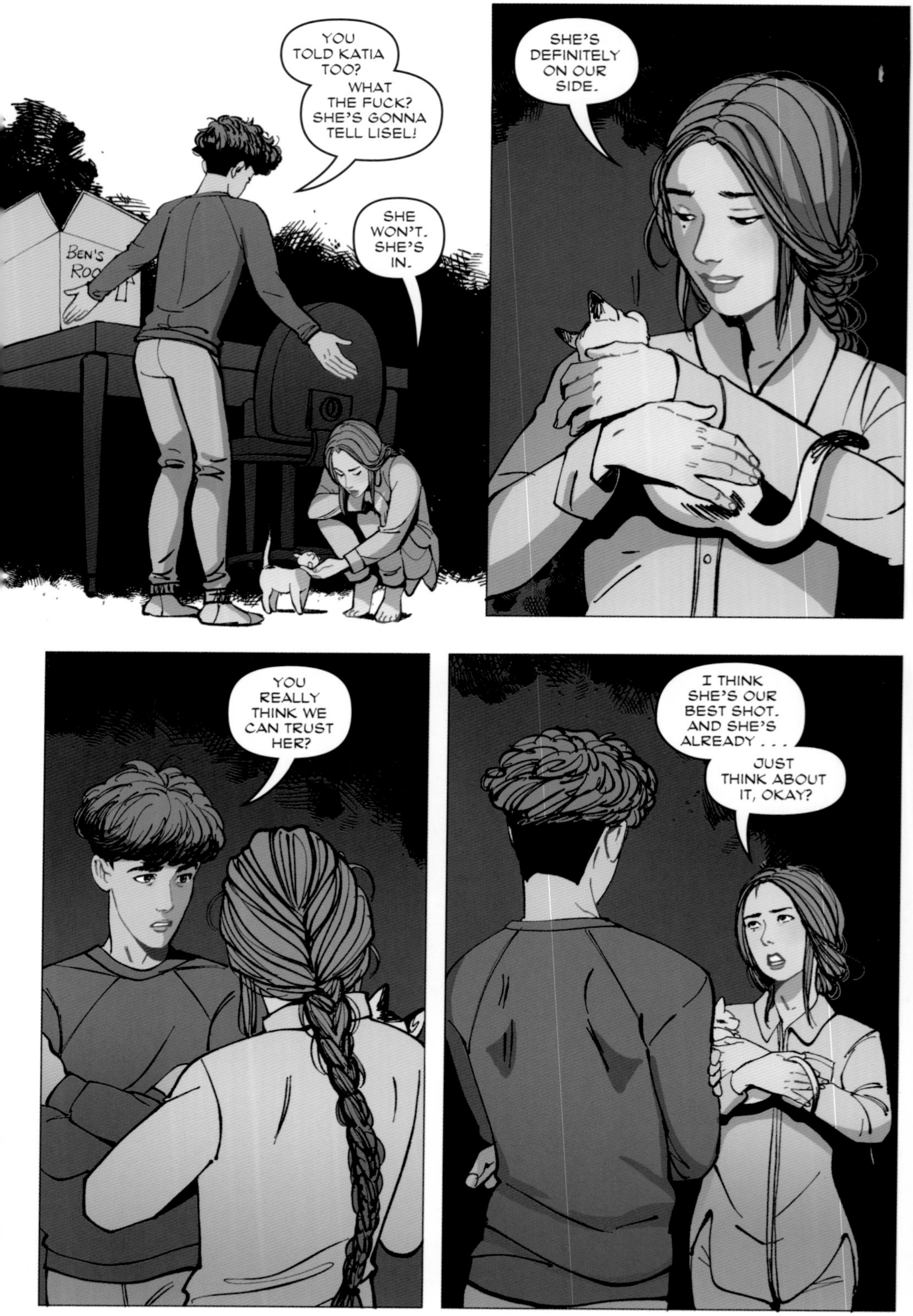
YOU TOLD KATIA TOO?
WHAT THE FUCK? SHE'S GONNA TELL LISEL!
BEN'S ROO
SHE WON'T. SHE'S IN.
SHE'S DEFINITELY ON OUR SIDE.
YOU REALLY THINK WE CAN TRUST HER?
I THINK SHE'S OUR BEST SHOT. AND SHE'S ALREADY . . .
JUST THINK ABOUT IT, OKAY?

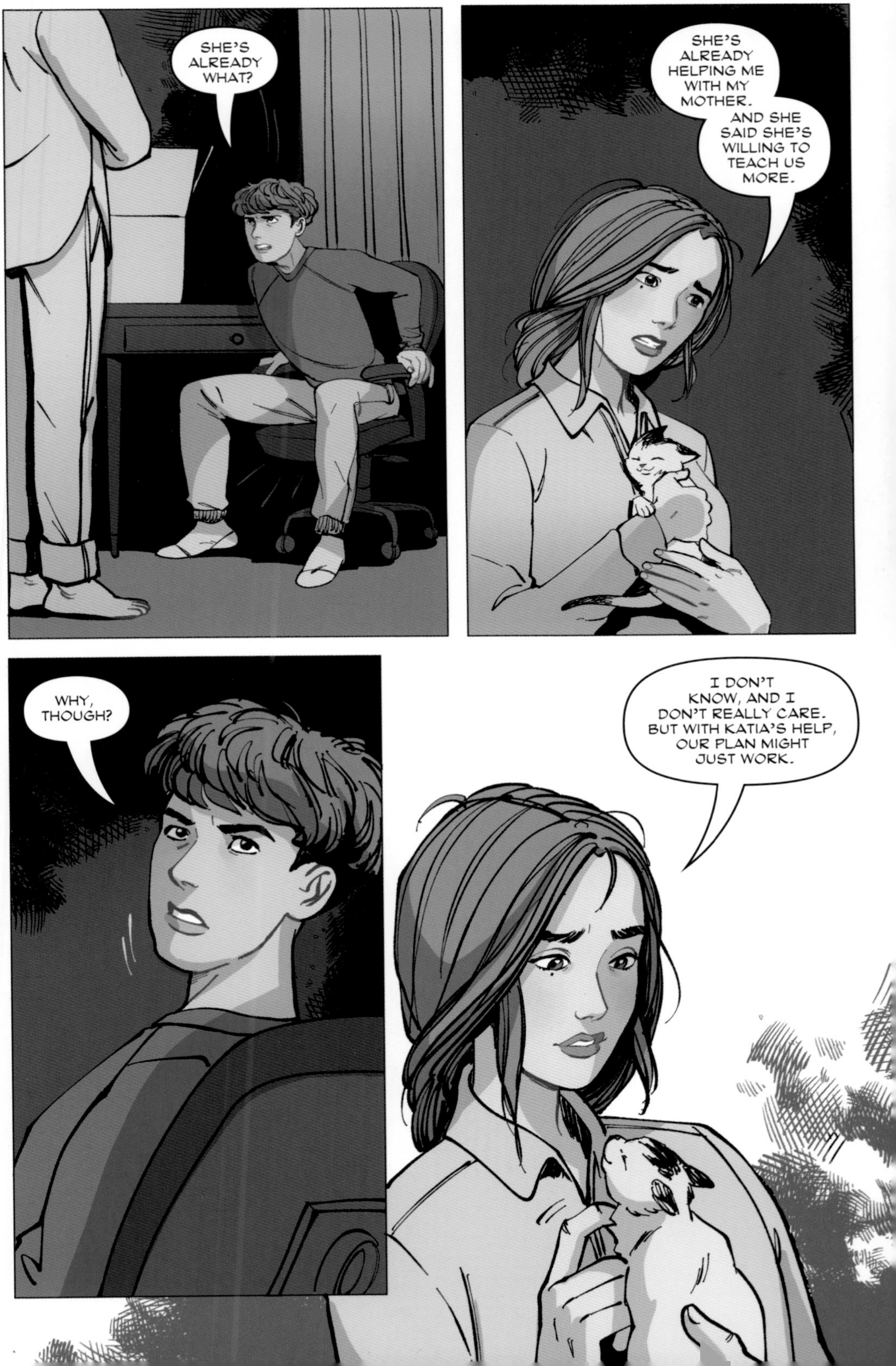
SHE'S ALREADY WHAT?
SHE'S ALREADY HELPING ME WITH MY MOTHER.
AND SHE SAID SHE'S WILLING TO TEACH US MORE.
WHY, THOUGH?
I DON'T KNOW, AND I DON'T REALLY CARE. BUT WITH KATIA'S HELP, OUR PLAN MIGHT JUST WORK.

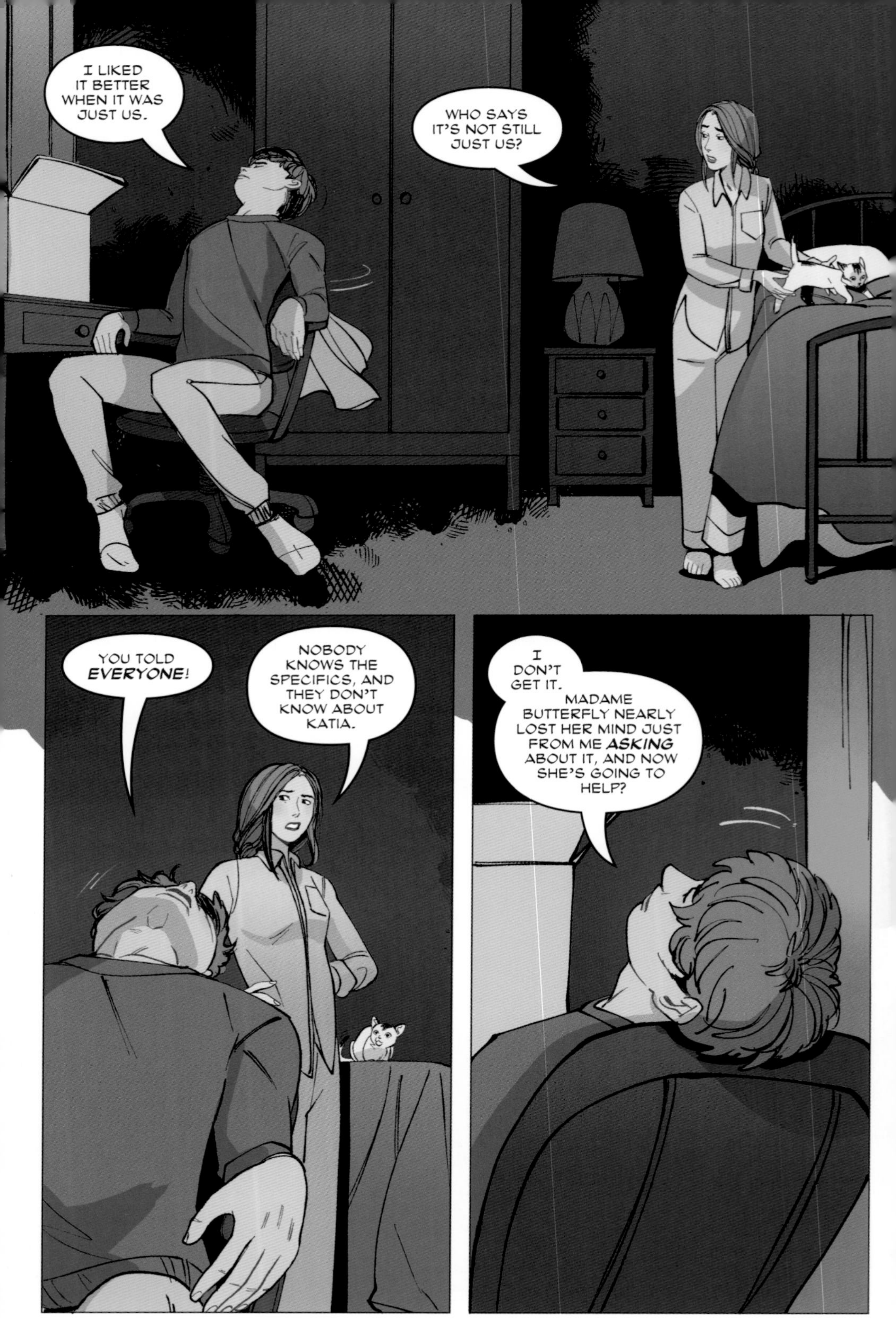
I LIKED IT BETTER WHEN IT WAS JUST US.
WHO SAYS IT'S NOT STILL JUST US?
YOU TOLD *EVERYONE*!
NOBODY KNOWS THE SPECIFICS, AND THEY DON'T KNOW ABOUT KATIA.
I DON'T GET IT.
MADAME BUTTERFLY NEARLY LOST HER MIND JUST FROM ME *ASKING* ABOUT IT, AND NOW SHE'S GOING TO HELP?

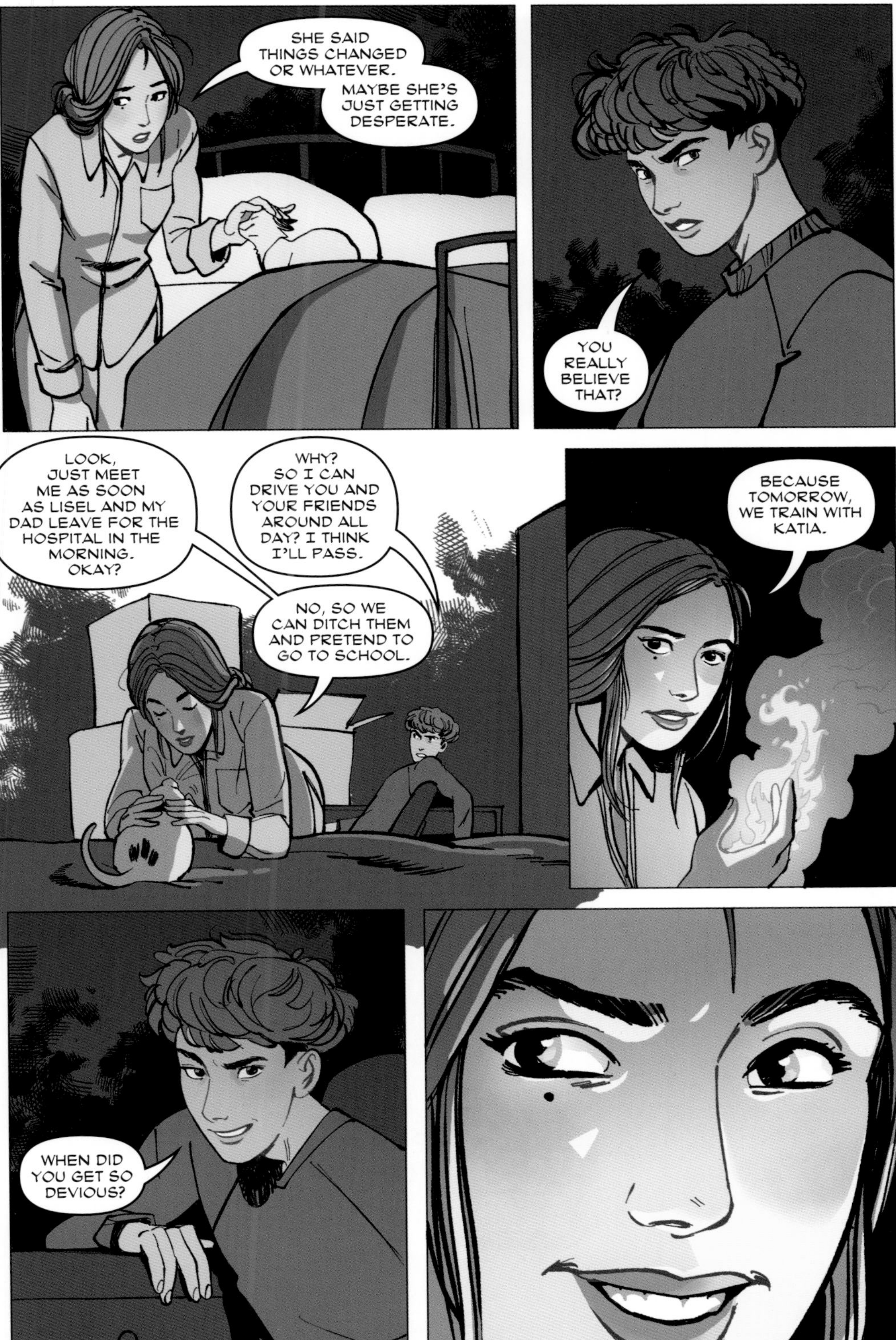
SHE SAID THINGS CHANGED OR WHATEVER.
MAYBE SHE'S JUST GETTING DESPERATE.
YOU REALLY BELIEVE THAT?
LOOK, JUST MEET ME AS SOON AS LISEL AND MY DAD LEAVE FOR THE HOSPITAL IN THE MORNING. OKAY?
WHY? SO I CAN DRIVE YOU AND YOUR FRIENDS AROUND ALL DAY? I THINK I'LL PASS.
NO, SO WE CAN DITCH THEM AND PRETEND TO GO TO SCHOOL.
BECAUSE TOMORROW, WE TRAIN WITH KATIA.
WHEN DID YOU GET SO DEVIOUS?

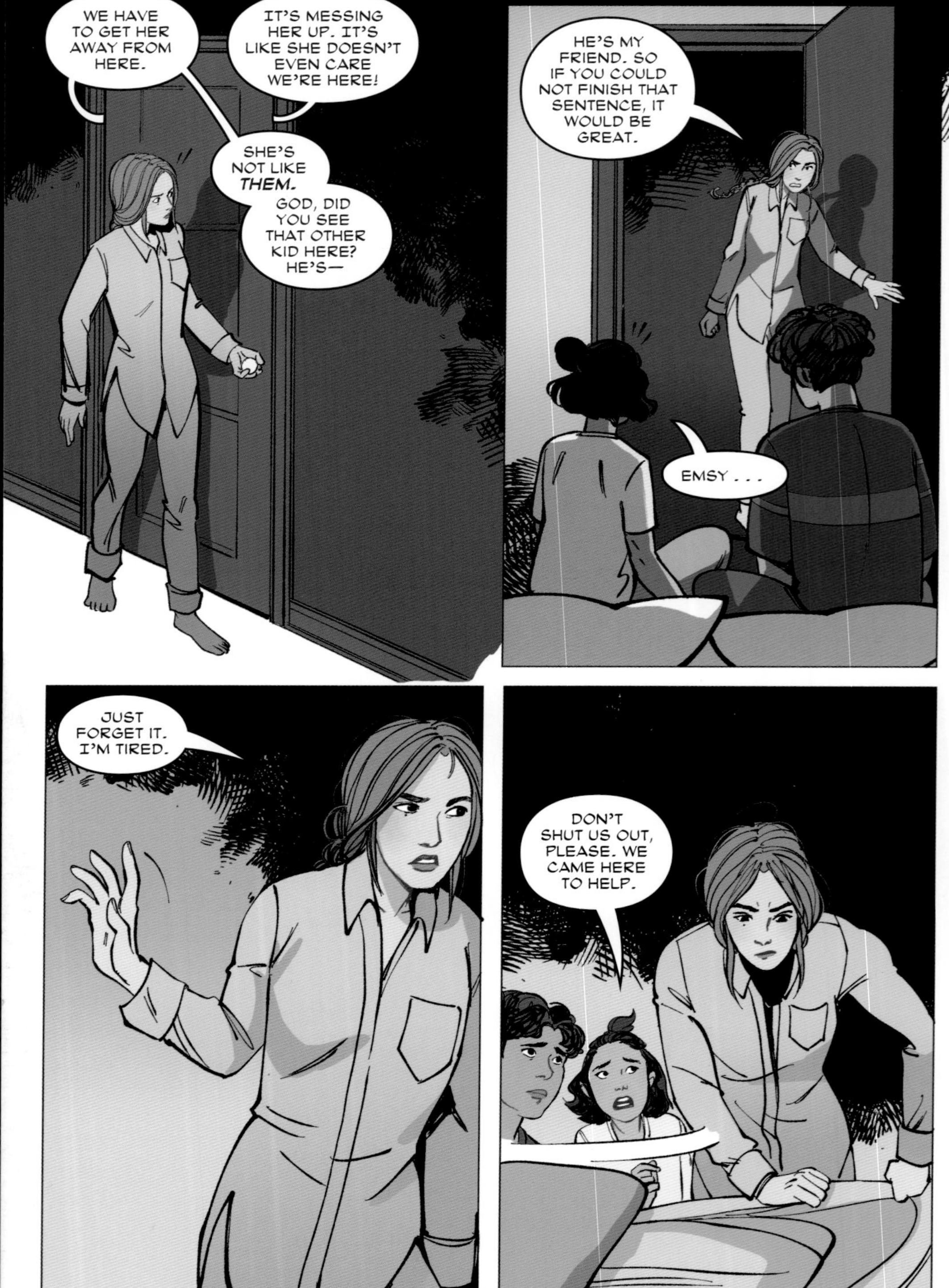
WE HAVE TO GET HER AWAY FROM HERE.
IT'S MESSING HER UP. IT'S LIKE SHE DOESN'T EVEN CARE WE'RE HERE!
SHE'S NOT LIKE *THEM.*
GOD, DID YOU SEE THAT OTHER KID HERE? HE'S—
HE'S MY FRIEND. SO IF YOU COULD NOT FINISH THAT SENTENCE, IT WOULD BE GREAT.
EMSY . . .
JUST FORGET IT. I'M TIRED.
DON'T SHUT US OUT, PLEASE. WE CAME HERE TO HELP.

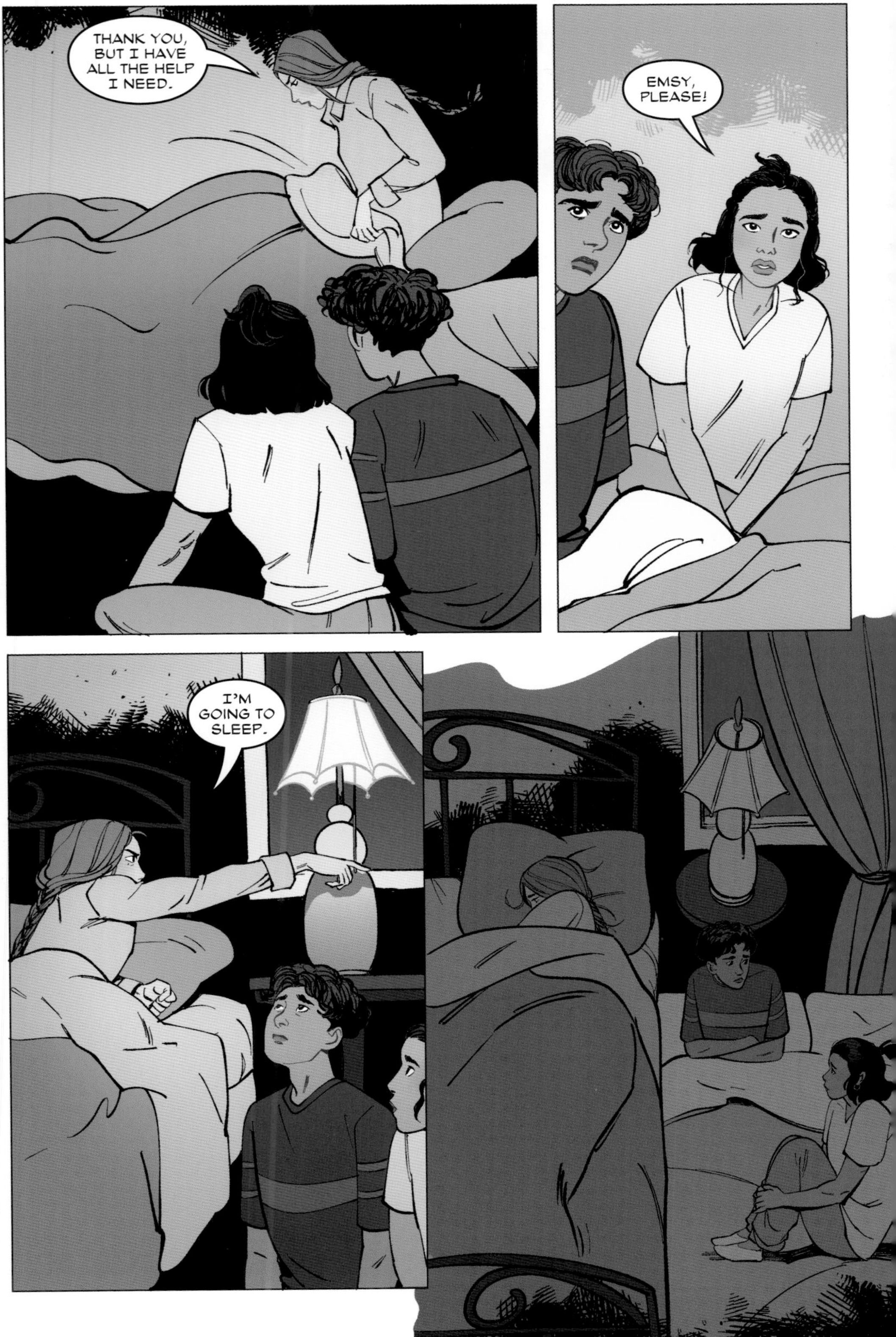
THANK YOU, BUT I HAVE ALL THE HELP I NEED.
EMSY, PLEASE!
I'M GOING TO SLEEP.

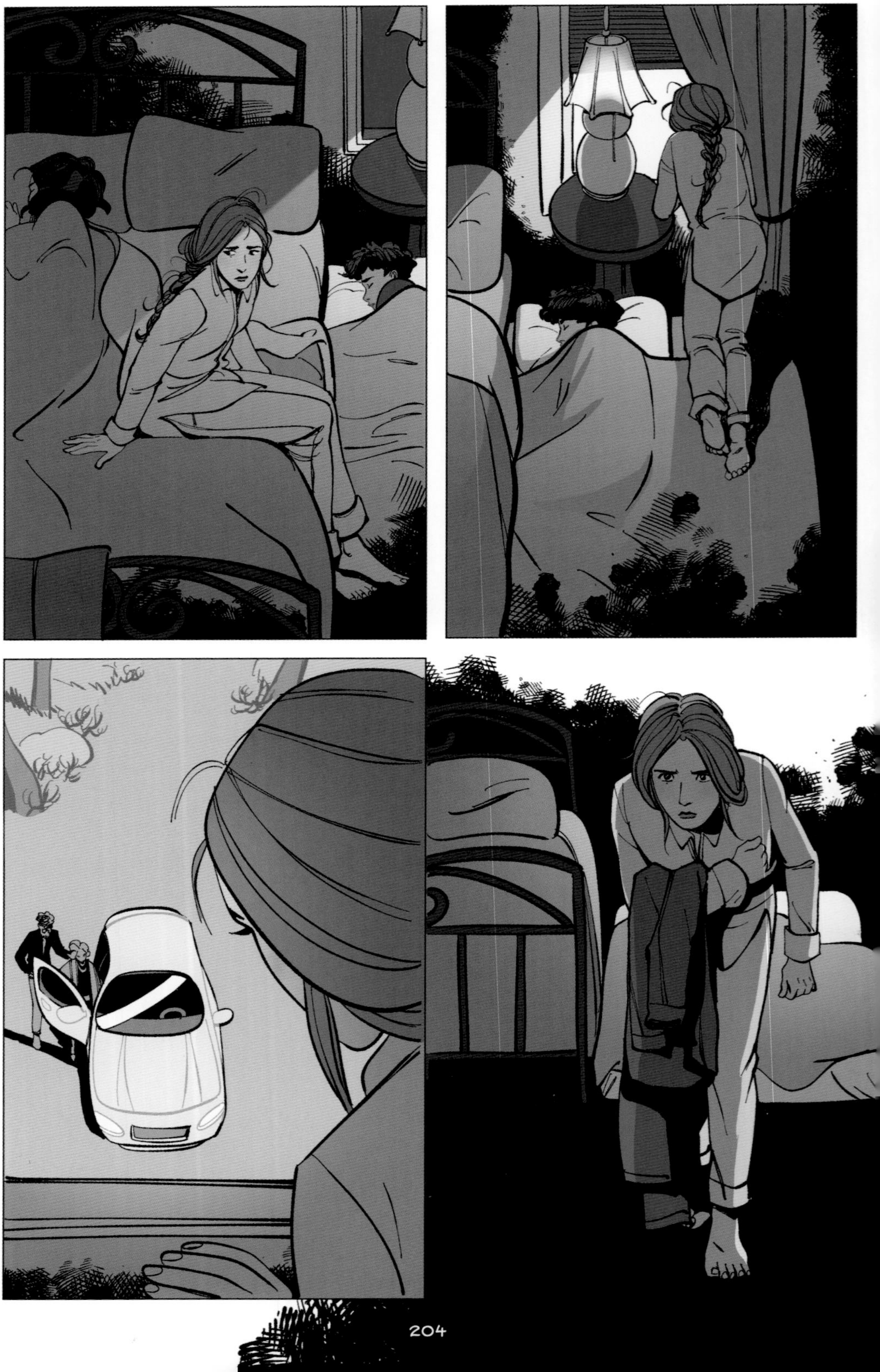

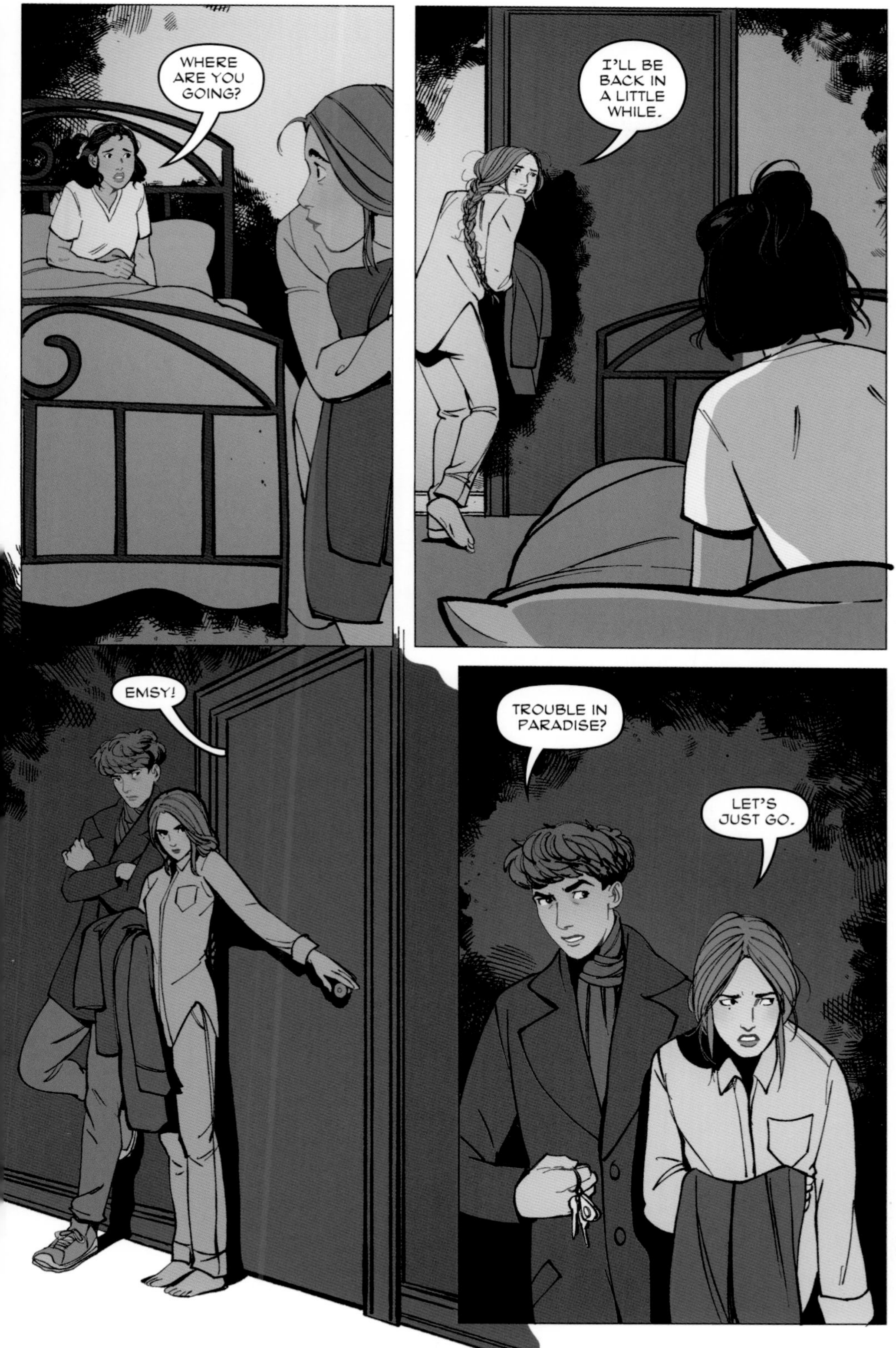
WHERE ARE YOU GOING?
I'LL BE BACK IN A LITTLE WHILE.
EMSY!
TROUBLE IN PARADISE?
LET'S JUST GO.

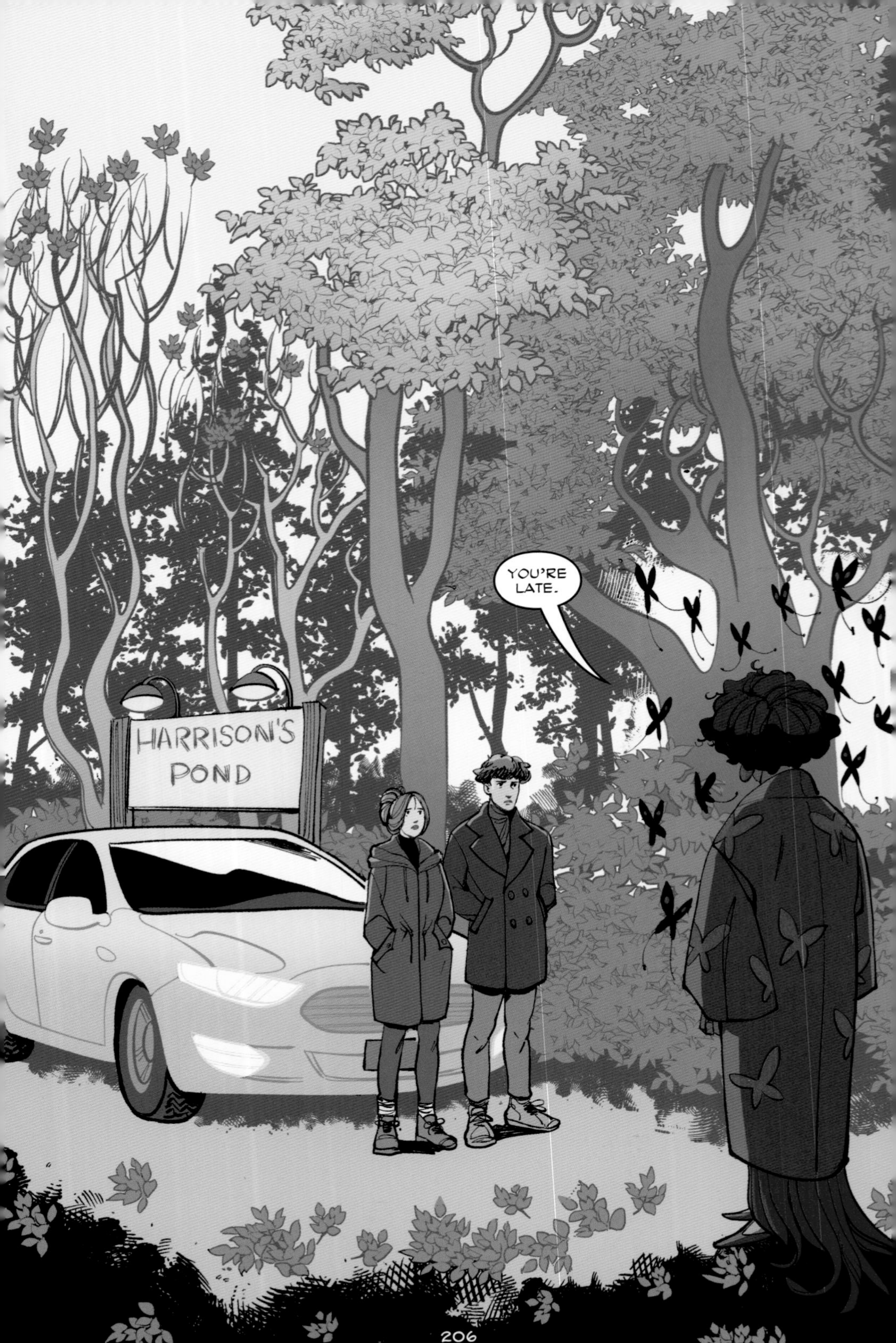
HARRISON'S
POND
YOU'RE
LATE.

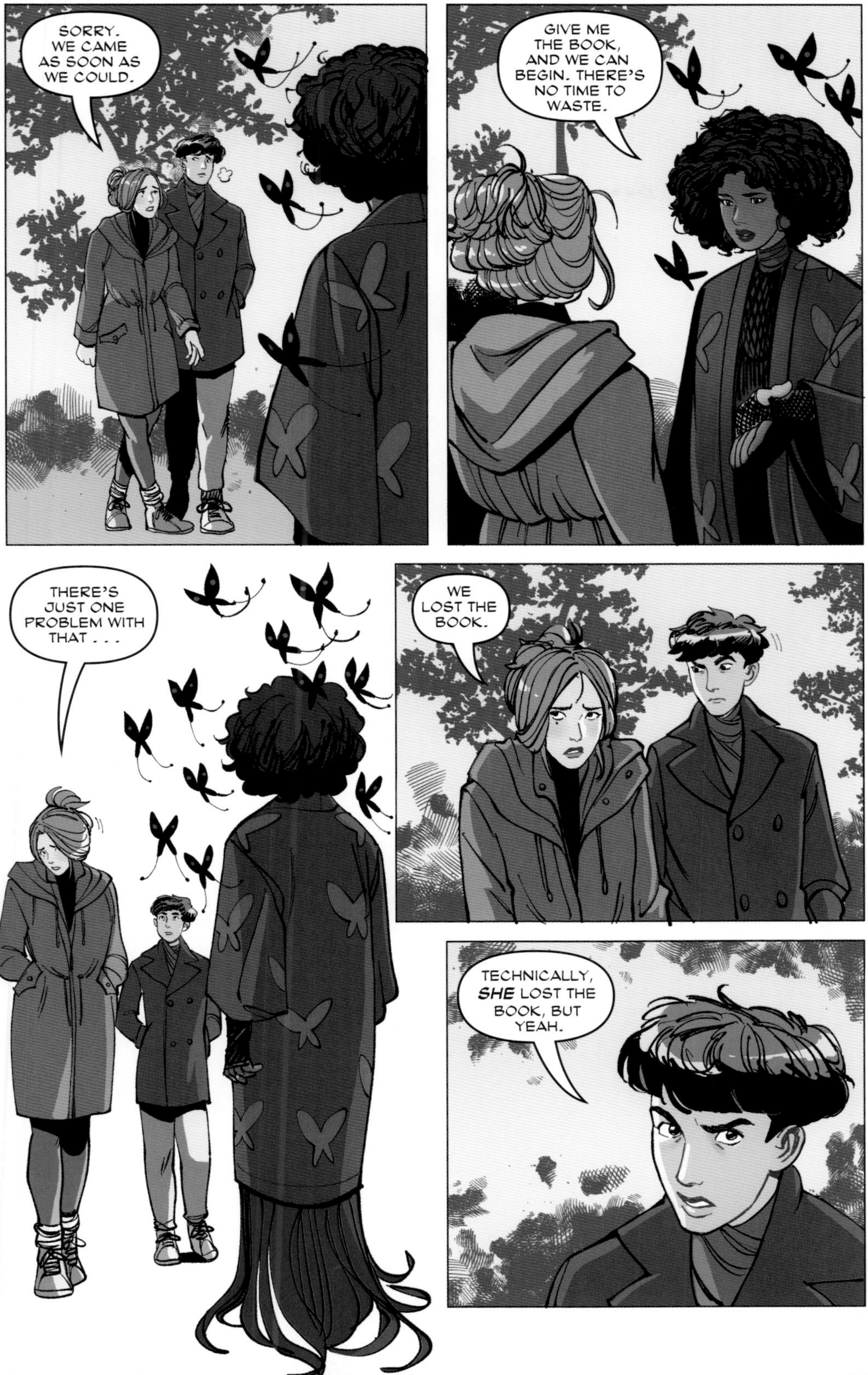
SORRY. WE CAME AS SOON AS WE COULD.
GIVE ME THE BOOK, AND WE CAN BEGIN. THERE'S NO TIME TO WASTE.
THERE'S JUST ONE PROBLEM WITH THAT . . .
WE LOST THE BOOK.
TECHNICALLY, **SHE** LOST THE BOOK, BUT YEAH.

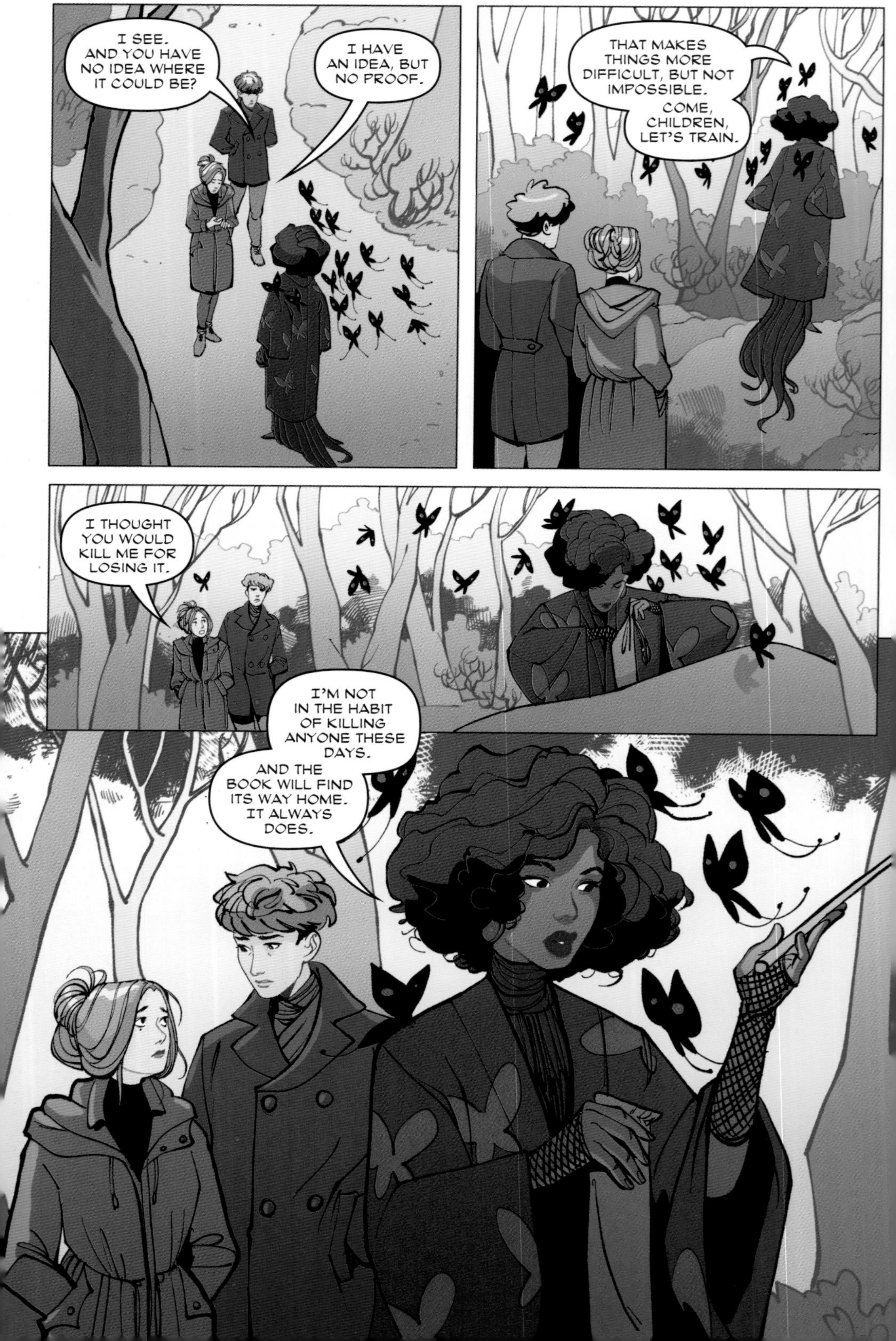
I SEE. AND YOU HAVE NO IDEA WHERE IT COULD BE?
I HAVE AN IDEA, BUT NO PROOF.
THAT MAKES THINGS MORE DIFFICULT, BUT NOT IMPOSSIBLE.
COME, CHILDREN, LET'S TRAIN.
I THOUGHT YOU WOULD KILL ME FOR LOSING IT.
I'M NOT IN THE HABIT OF KILLING ANYONE THESE DAYS.
AND THE BOOK WILL FIND ITS WAY HOME. IT ALWAYS DOES.

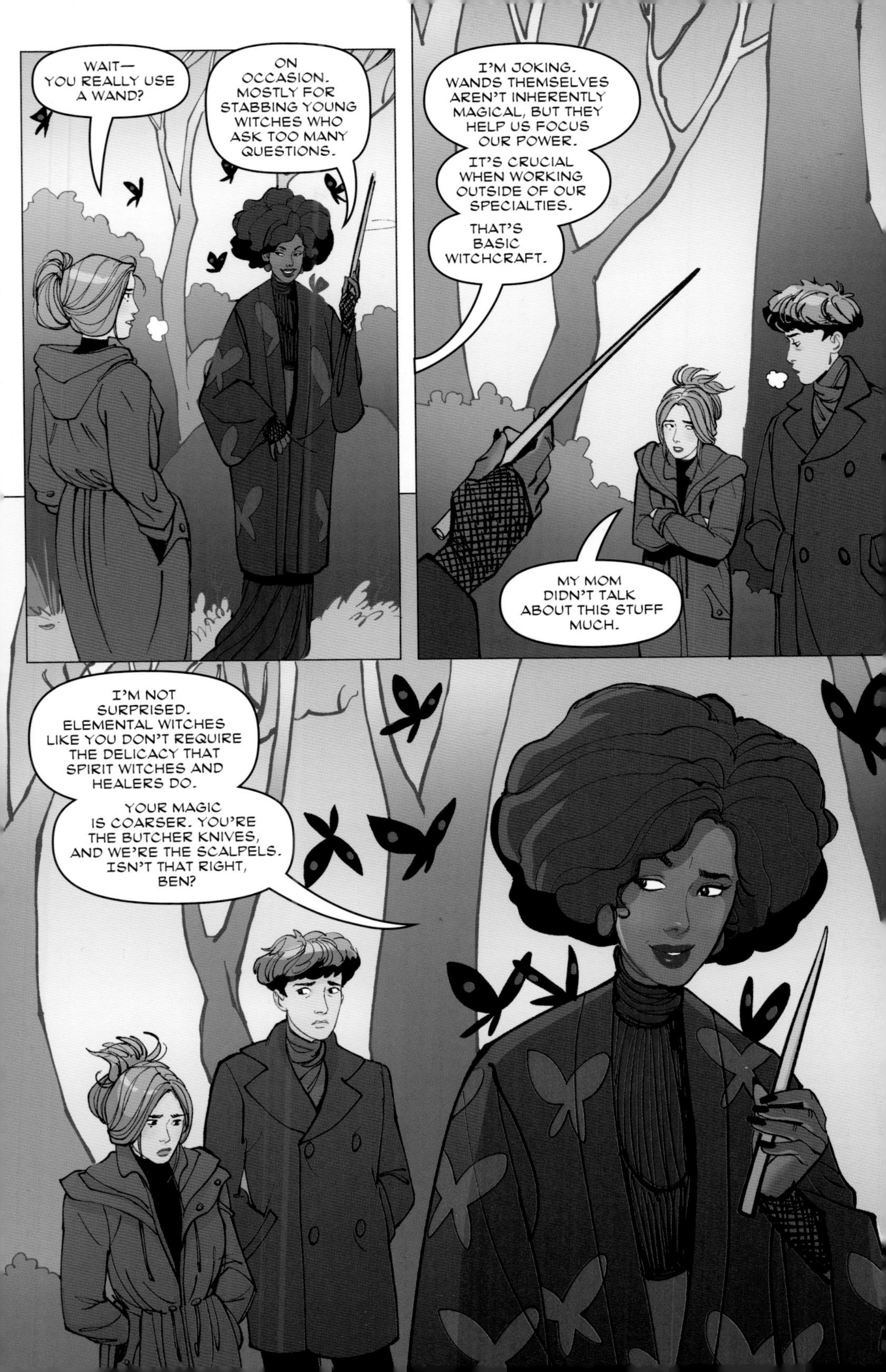
WAIT— YOU REALLY USE A WAND?
ON OCCASION. MOSTLY FOR STABBING YOUNG WITCHES WHO ASK TOO MANY QUESTIONS.
I'M JOKING. WANDS THEMSELVES AREN'T INHERENTLY MAGICAL, BUT THEY HELP US FOCUS OUR POWER.
IT'S CRUCIAL WHEN WORKING OUTSIDE OF OUR SPECIALTIES.
THAT'S BASIC WITCHCRAFT.
MY MOM DIDN'T TALK ABOUT THIS STUFF MUCH.
I'M NOT SURPRISED. ELEMENTAL WITCHES LIKE YOU DON'T REQUIRE THE DELICACY THAT SPIRIT WITCHES AND HEALERS DO.
YOUR MAGIC IS COARSER. YOU'RE THE BUTCHER KNIVES, AND WE'RE THE SCALPELS. ISN'T THAT RIGHT, BEN?

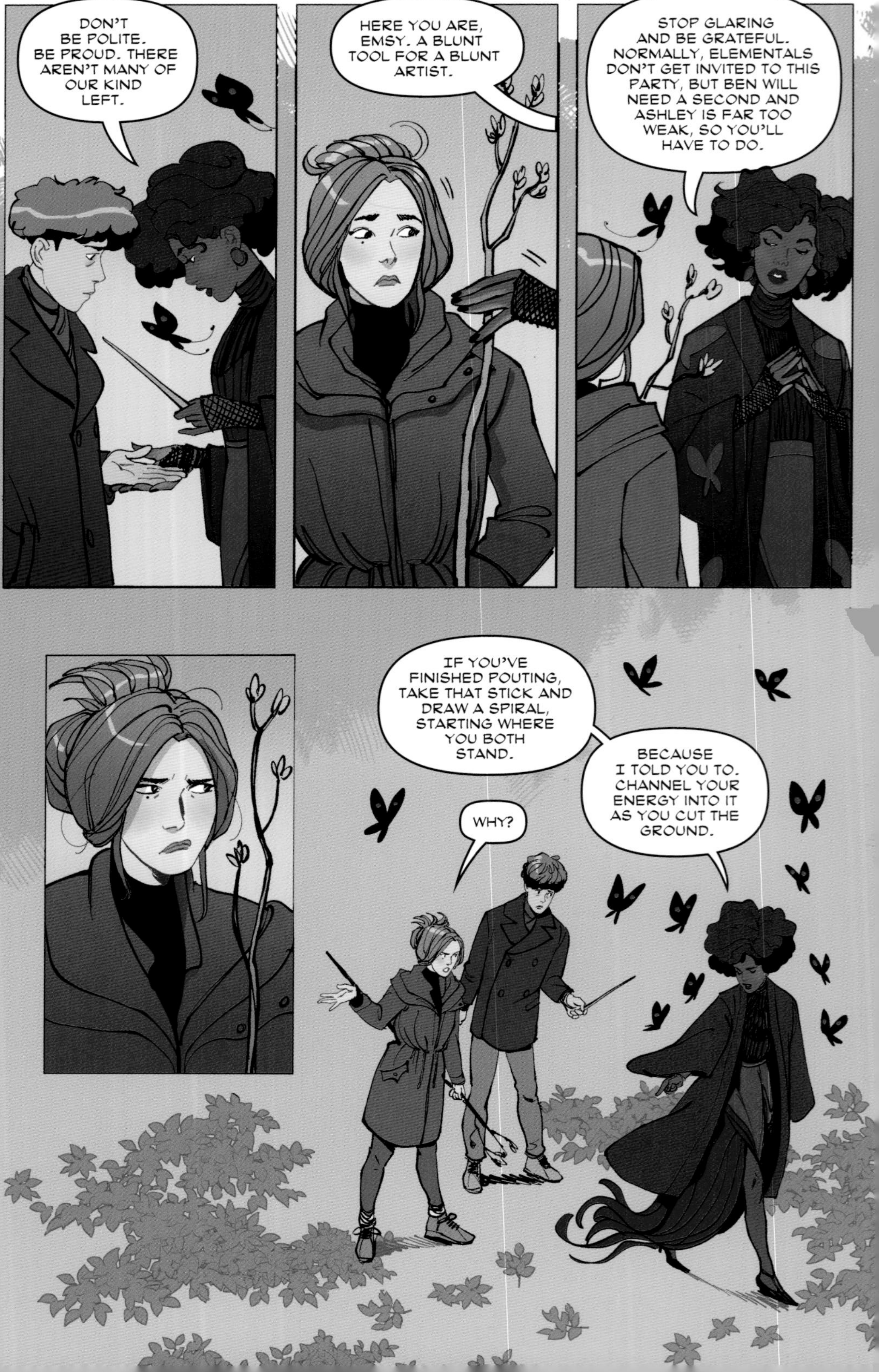
DON'T BE POLITE. BE PROUD. THERE AREN'T MANY OF OUR KIND LEFT.
HERE YOU ARE, EMSY. A BLUNT TOOL FOR A BLUNT ARTIST.
STOP GLARING AND BE GRATEFUL. NORMALLY, ELEMENTALS DON'T GET INVITED TO THIS PARTY, BUT BEN WILL NEED A SECOND AND ASHLEY IS FAR TOO WEAK, SO YOU'LL HAVE TO DO.
IF YOU'VE FINISHED POUTING, TAKE THAT STICK AND DRAW A SPIRAL, STARTING WHERE YOU BOTH STAND.
WHY?
BECAUSE I TOLD YOU TO. CHANNEL YOUR ENERGY INTO IT AS YOU CUT THE GROUND.

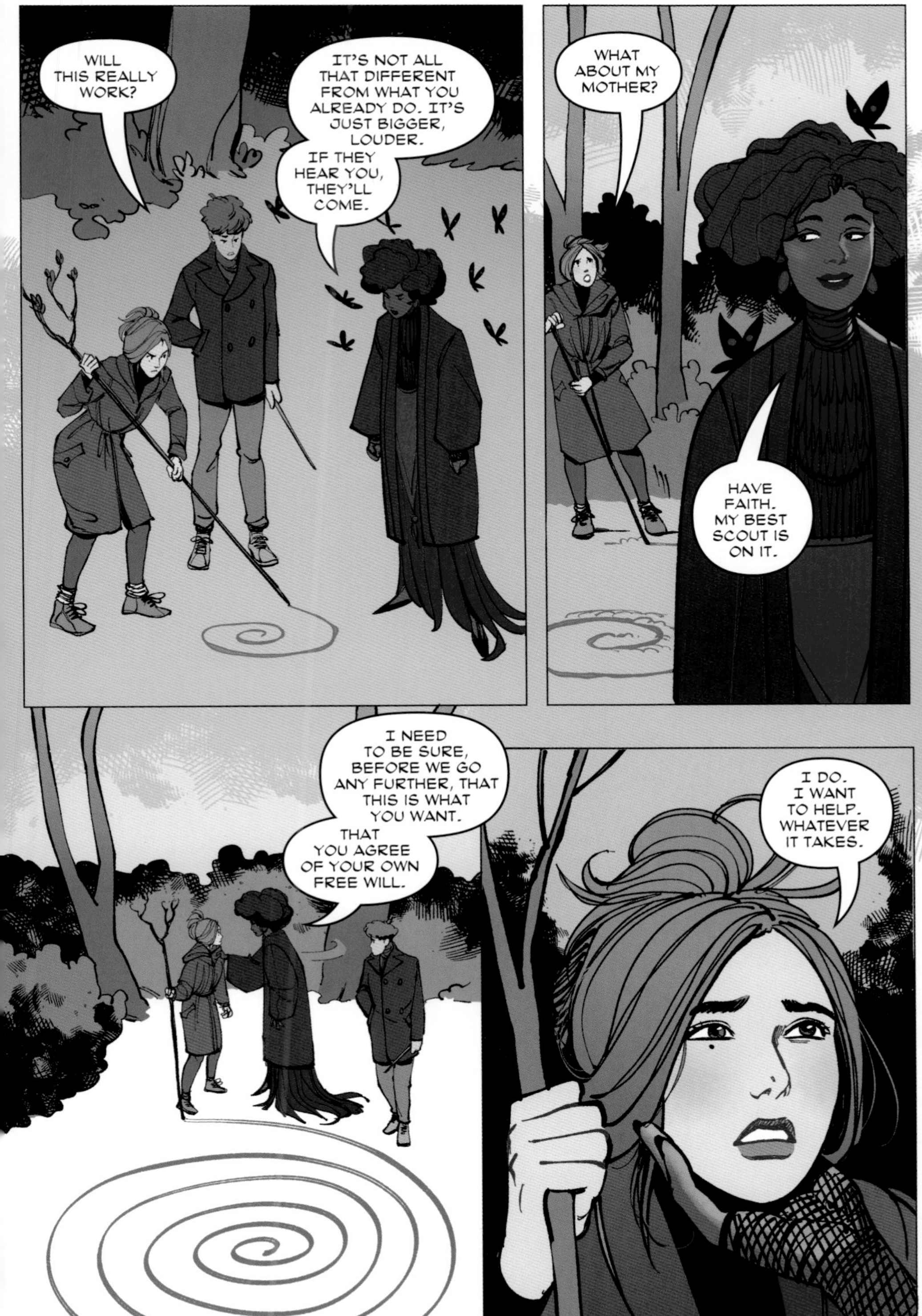
WILL THIS REALLY WORK?
IT'S NOT ALL THAT DIFFERENT FROM WHAT YOU ALREADY DO. IT'S JUST BIGGER, LOUDER.
IF THEY HEAR YOU, THEY'LL COME.
WHAT ABOUT MY MOTHER?
HAVE FAITH. MY BEST SCOUT IS ON IT.
I NEED TO BE SURE, BEFORE WE GO ANY FURTHER, THAT THIS IS WHAT YOU WANT.
THAT YOU AGREE OF YOUR OWN FREE WILL.
I DO. I WANT TO HELP. WHATEVER IT TAKES.

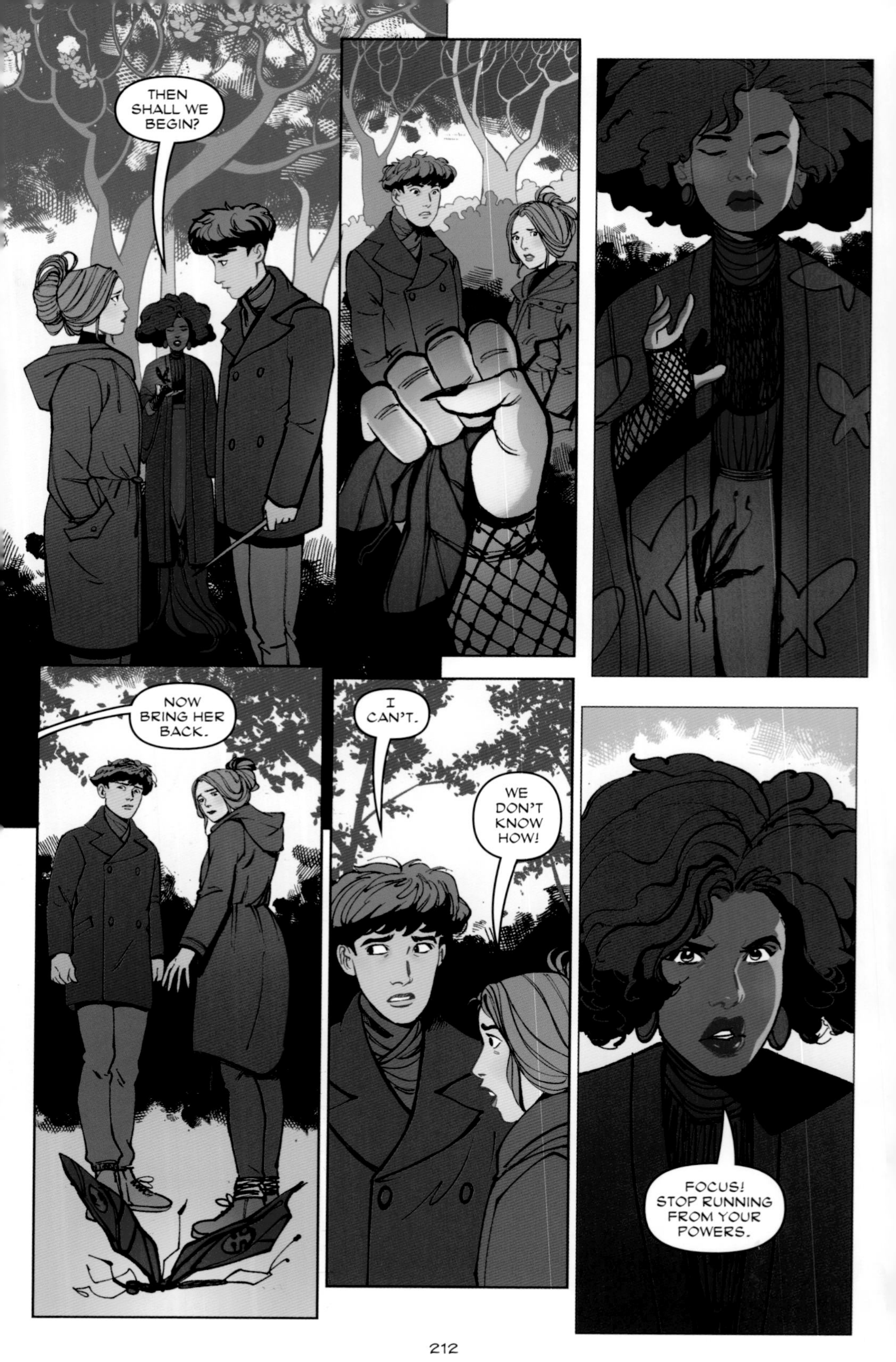
THEN SHALL WE BEGIN?
NOW BRING HER BACK.
I CAN'T.
WE DON'T KNOW HOW!
FOCUS! STOP RUNNING FROM YOUR POWERS.

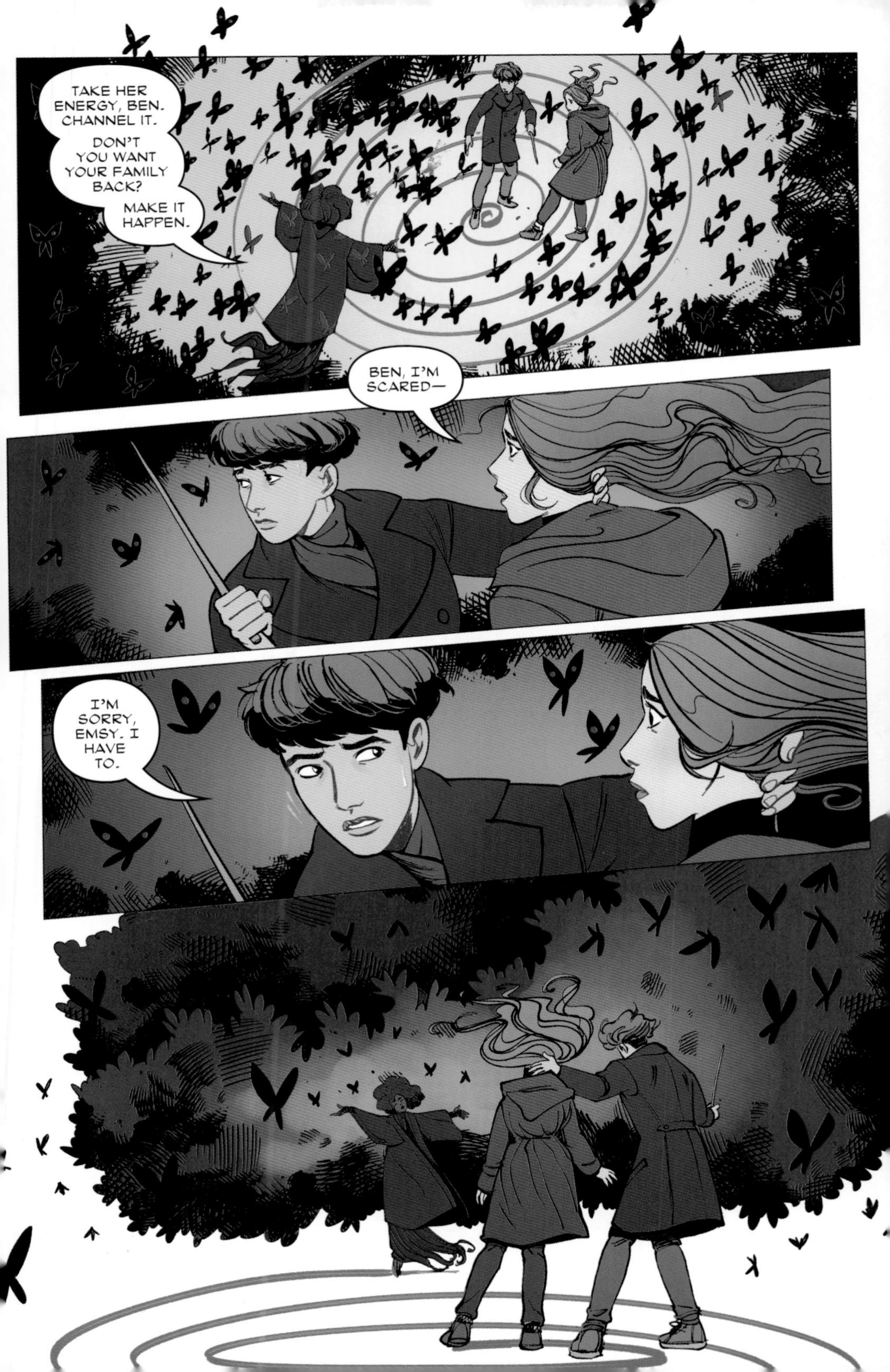
TAKE HER ENERGY, BEN. CHANNEL IT.
DON'T YOU WANT YOUR FAMILY BACK?
MAKE IT HAPPEN.
BEN, I'M SCARED—
I'M SORRY, EMSY. I HAVE TO.

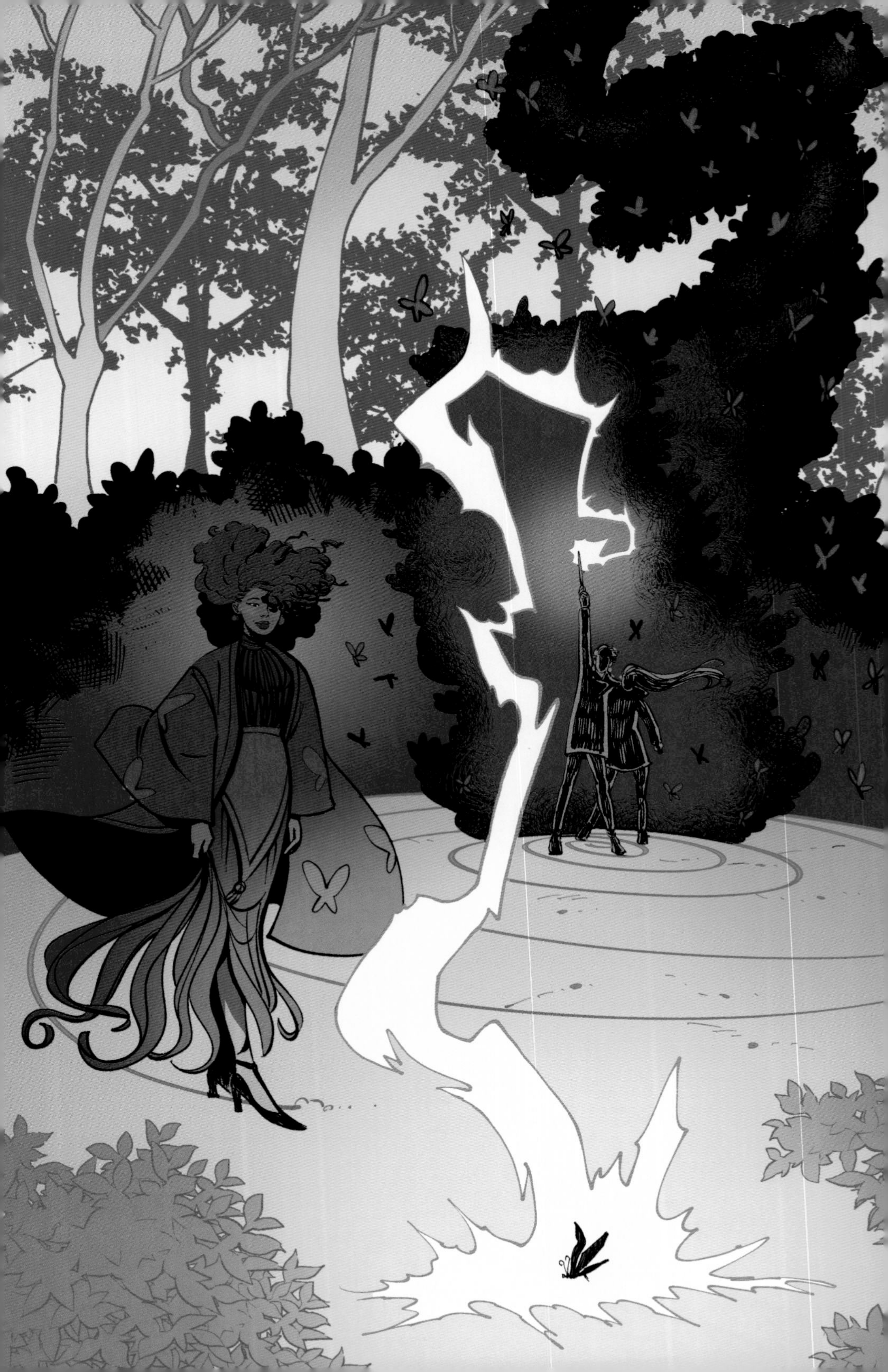

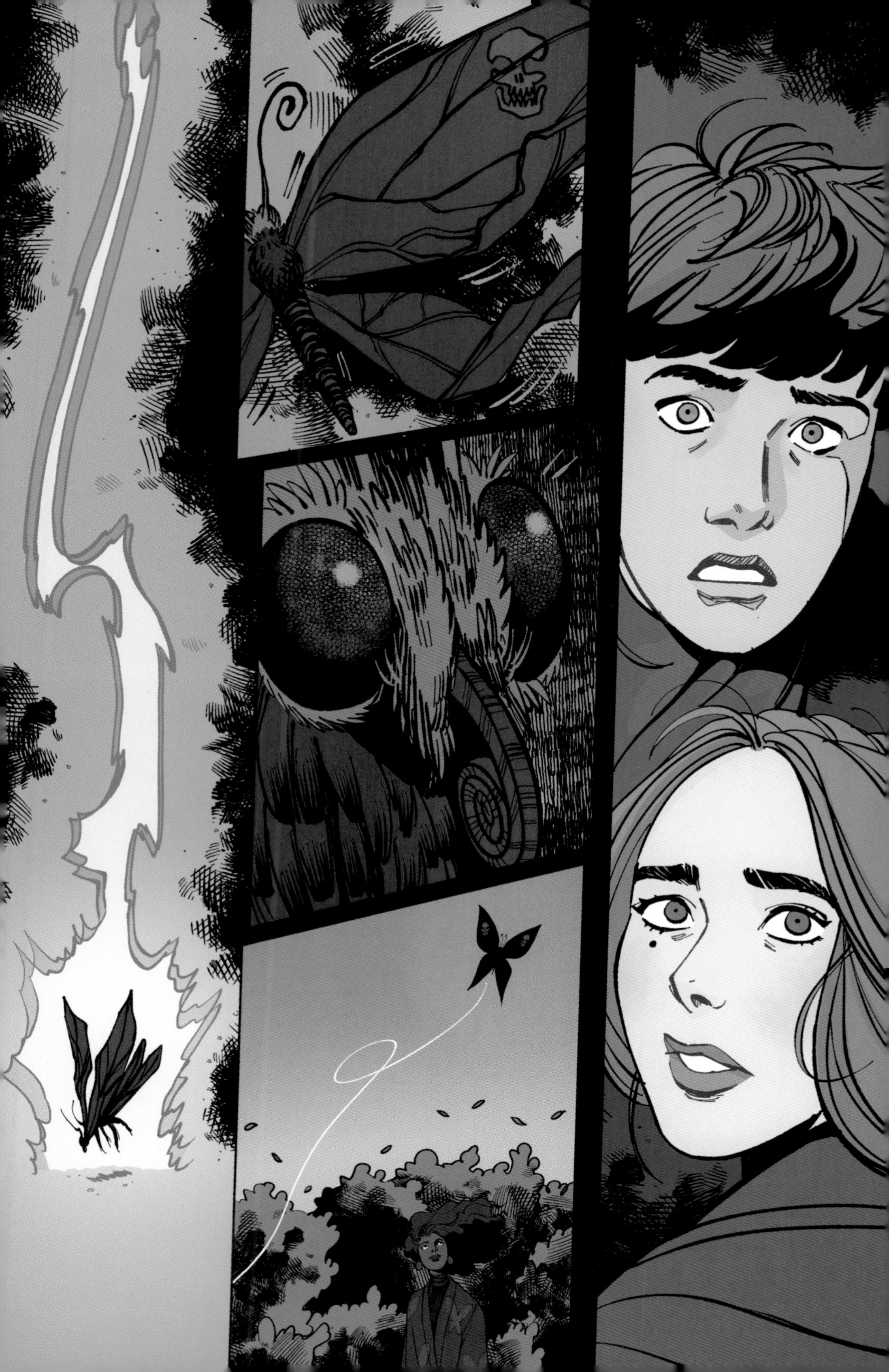

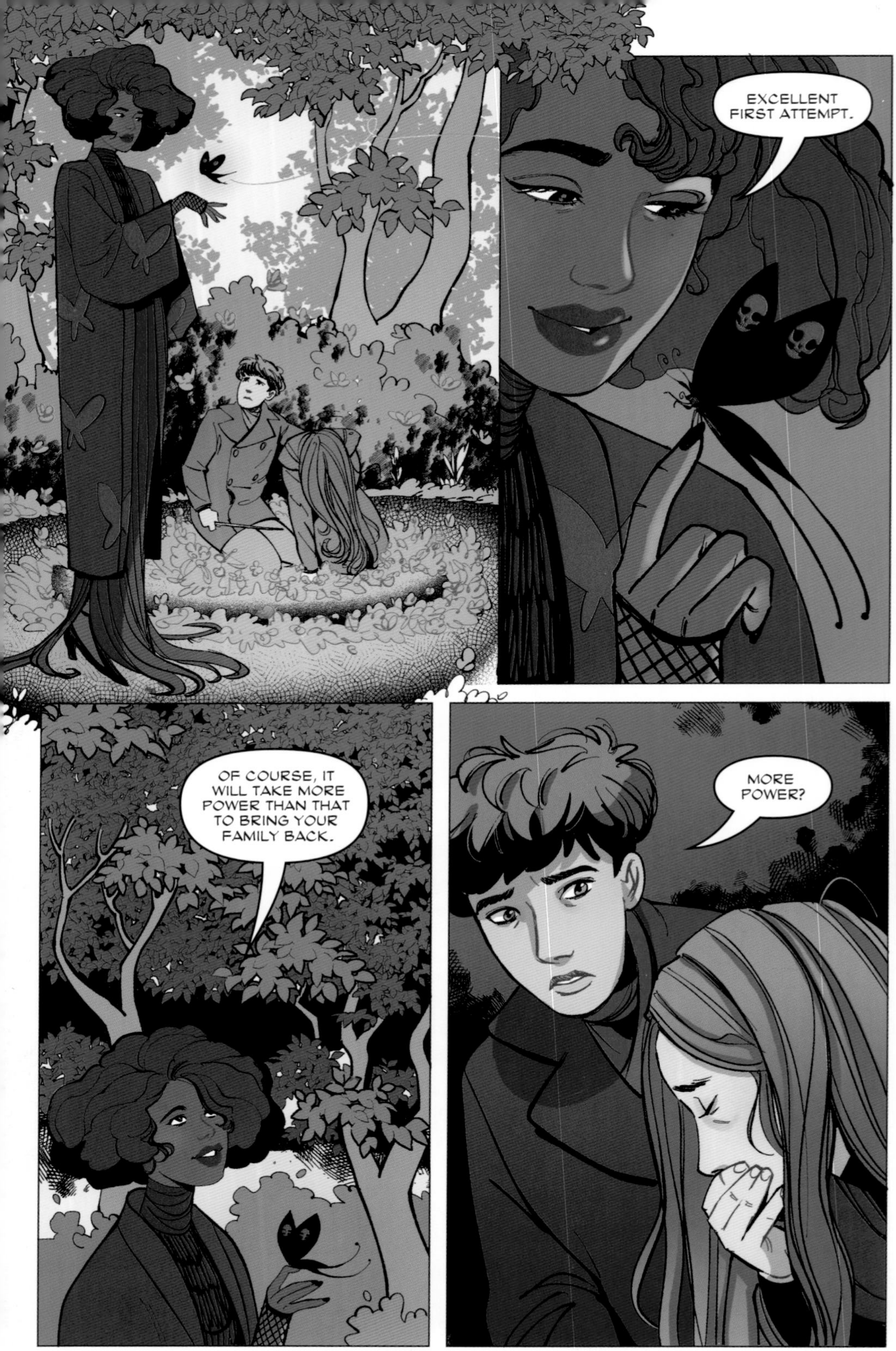
EXCELLENT FIRST ATTEMPT.
OF COURSE, IT WILL TAKE MORE POWER THAN THAT TO BRING YOUR FAMILY BACK.
MORE POWER?

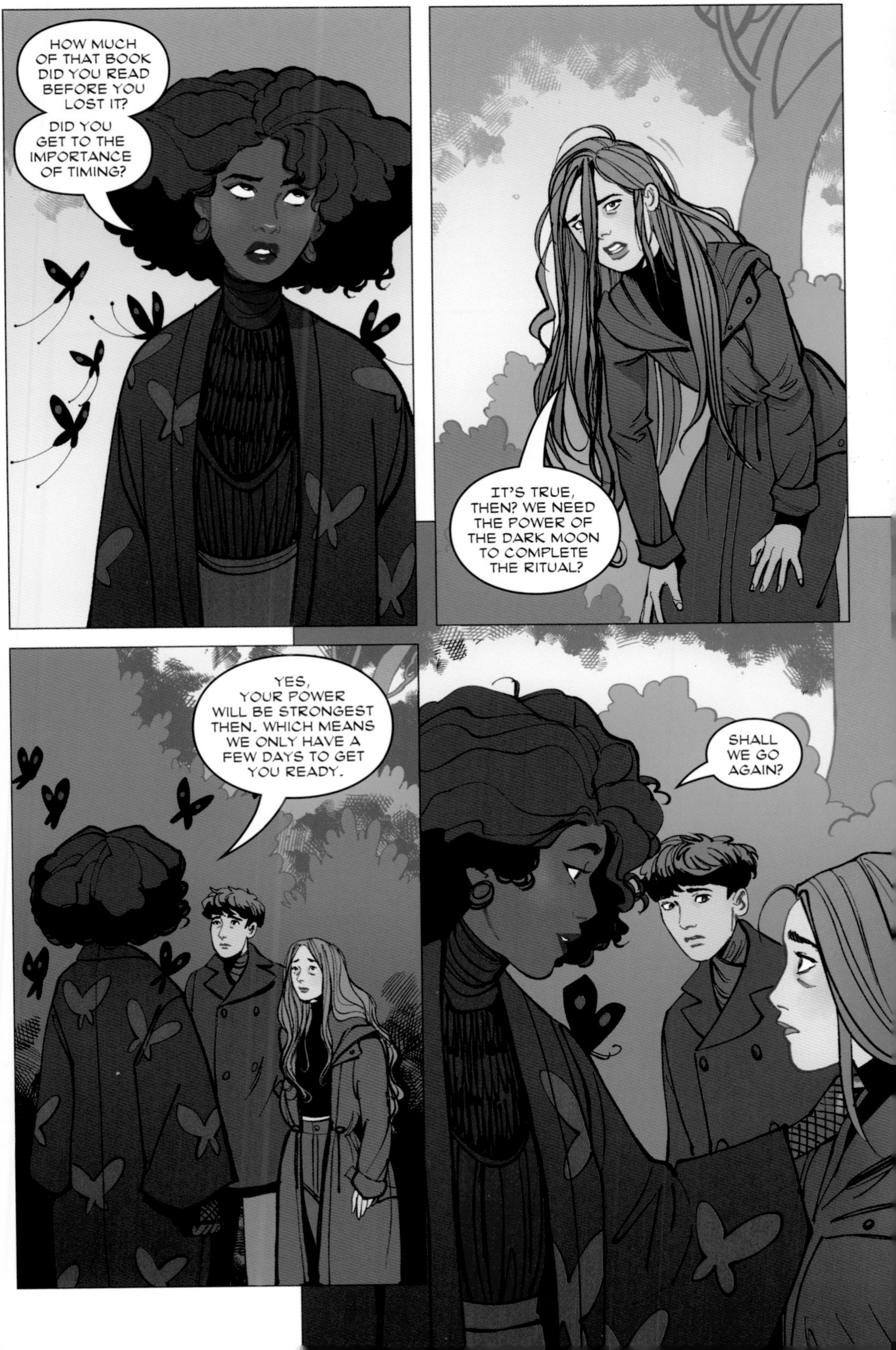
HOW MUCH OF THAT BOOK DID YOU READ BEFORE YOU LOST IT?
DID YOU GET TO THE IMPORTANCE OF TIMING?
IT'S TRUE, THEN? WE NEED THE POWER OF THE DARK MOON TO COMPLETE THE RITUAL?
YES, YOUR POWER WILL BE STRONGEST THEN. WHICH MEANS WE ONLY HAVE A FEW DAYS TO GET YOU READY.
SHALL WE GO AGAIN?

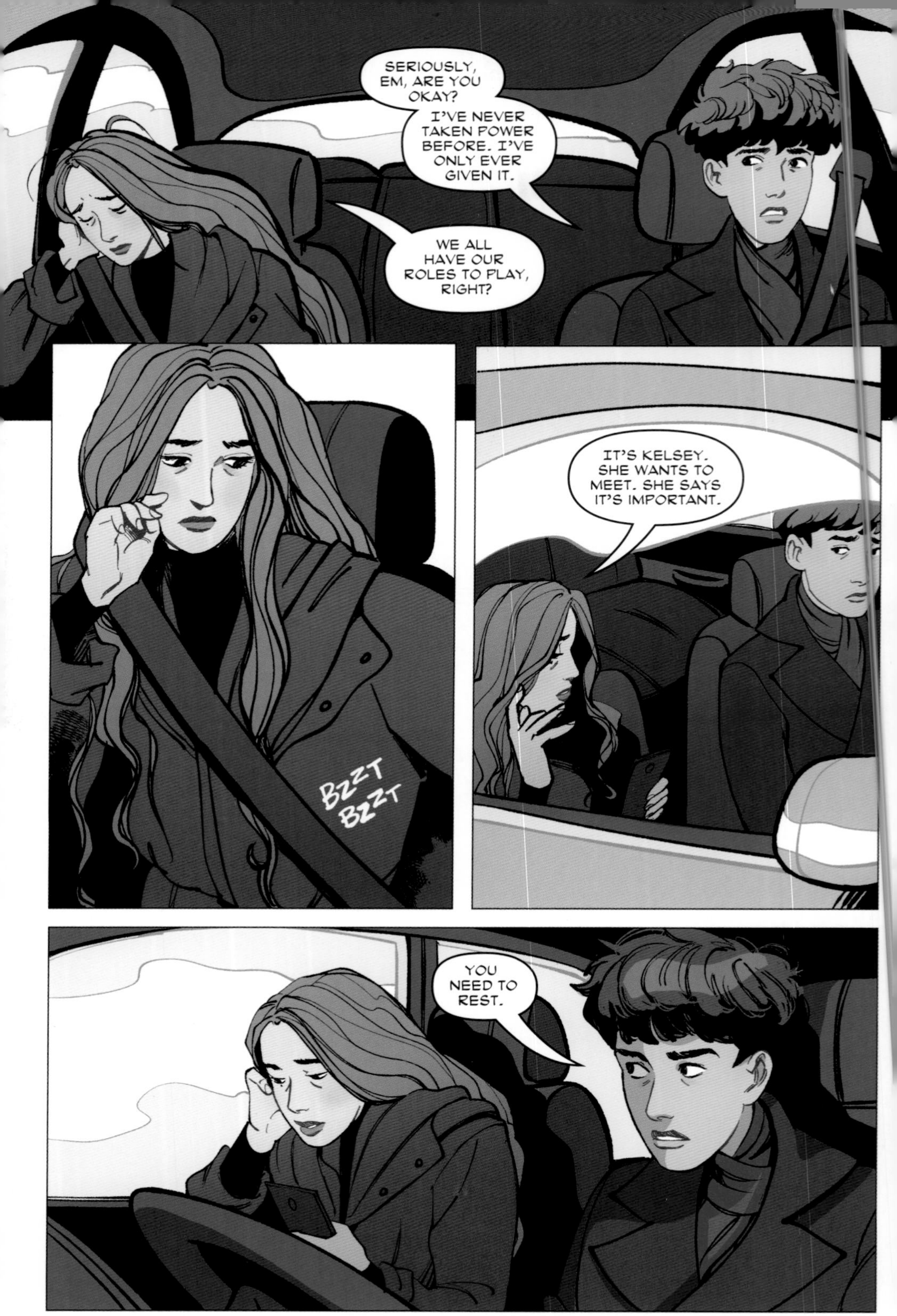
SERIOUSLY, EM, ARE YOU OKAY?
I'VE NEVER TAKEN POWER BEFORE. I'VE ONLY EVER GIVEN IT.
WE ALL HAVE OUR ROLES TO PLAY, RIGHT?
BZZT BZZT
IT'S KELSEY. SHE WANTS TO MEET. SHE SAYS IT'S IMPORTANT.
YOU NEED TO REST.

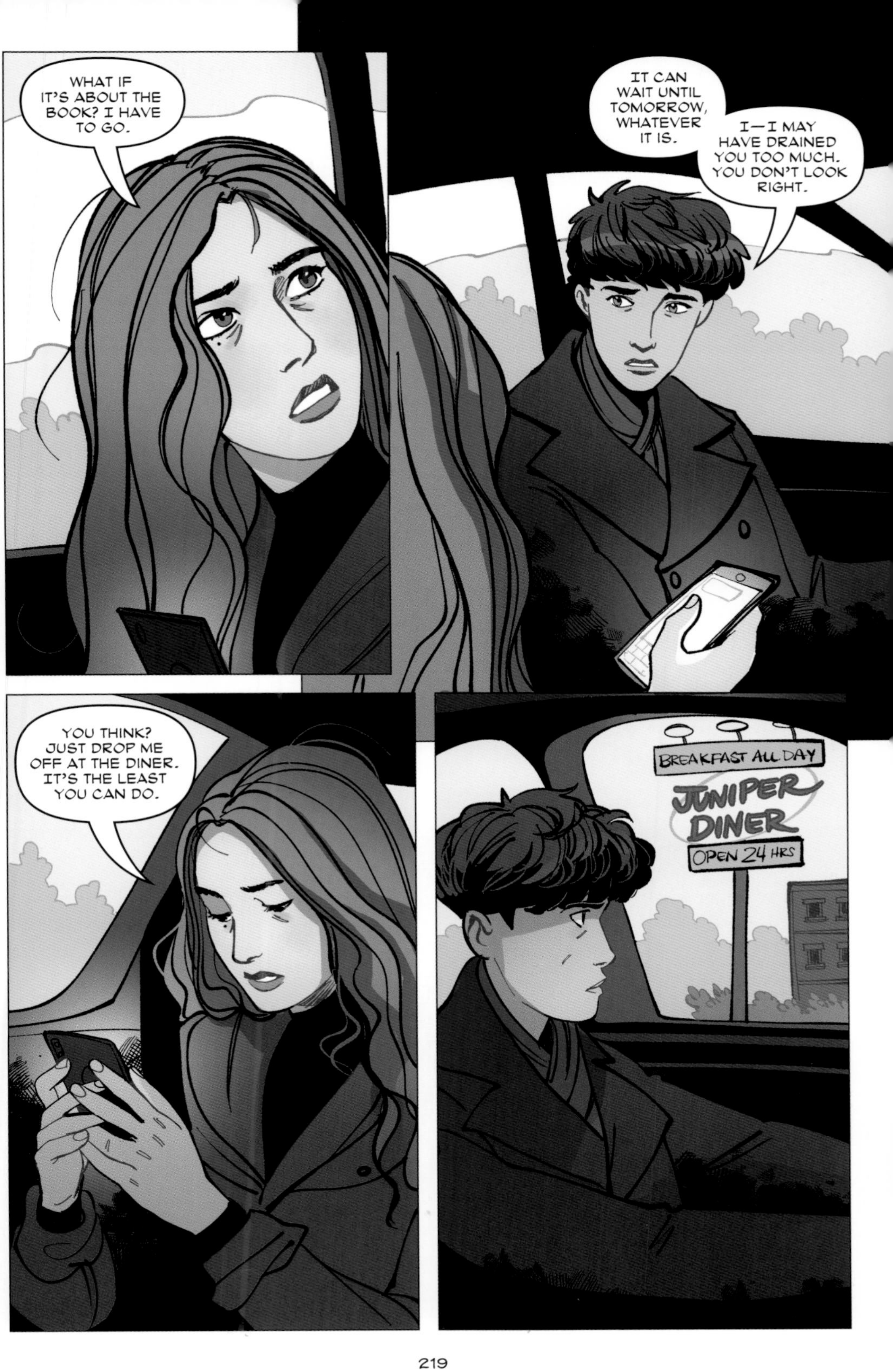
WHAT IF IT'S ABOUT THE BOOK? I HAVE TO GO.
IT CAN WAIT UNTIL TOMORROW, WHATEVER IT IS.
I—I MAY HAVE DRAINED YOU TOO MUCH. YOU DON'T LOOK RIGHT.
YOU THINK? JUST DROP ME OFF AT THE DINER. IT'S THE LEAST YOU CAN DO.
BREAKFAST ALL DAY
JUNIPER DINER
OPEN 24 HRS

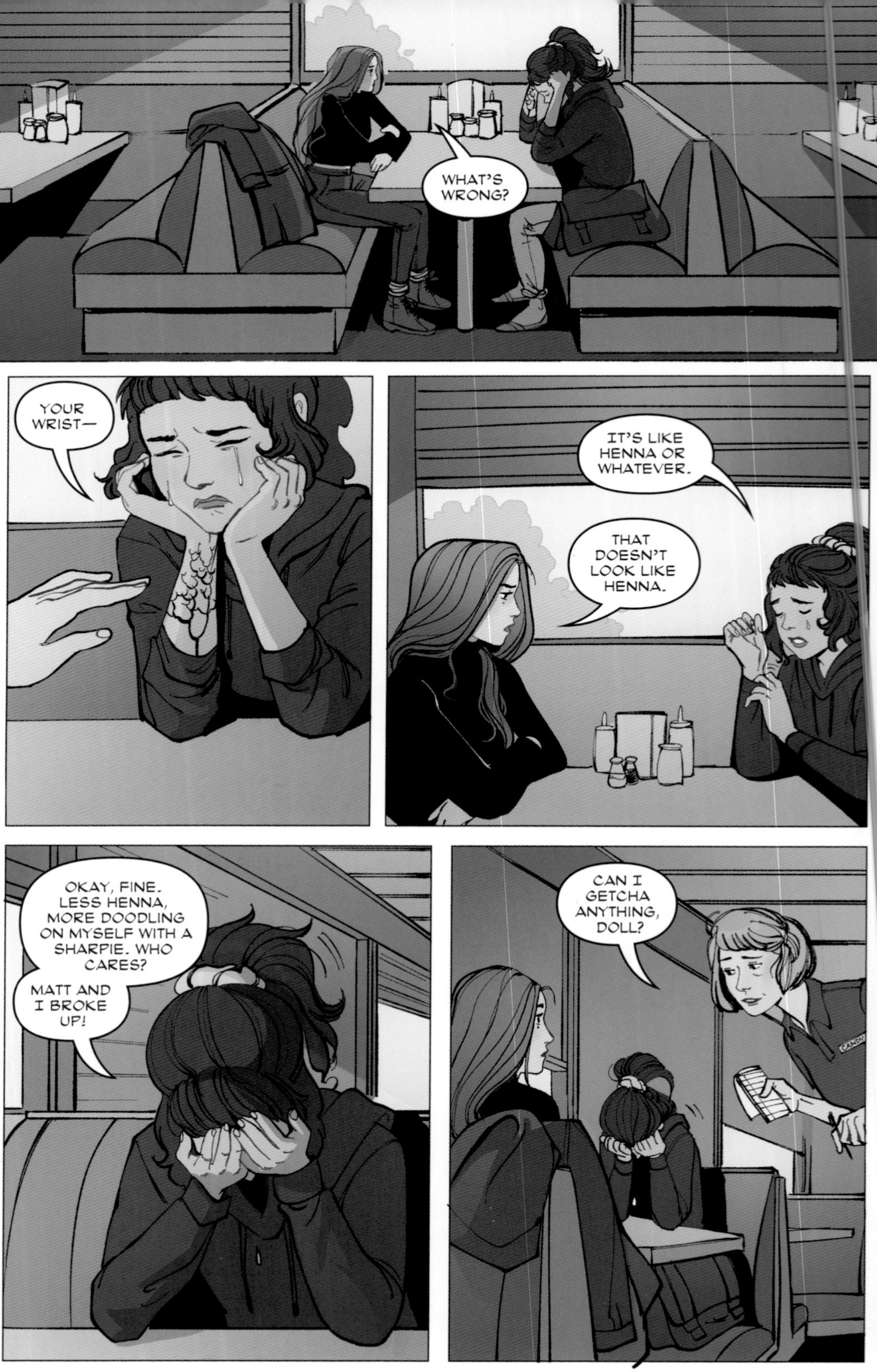
WHAT'S WRONG?
YOUR WRIST—
IT'S LIKE HENNA OR WHATEVER.
THAT DOESN'T LOOK LIKE HENNA.
OKAY, FINE. LESS HENNA, MORE DOODLING ON MYSELF WITH A SHARPIE. WHO CARES?
MATT AND I BROKE UP!
CAN I GETCHA ANYTHING, DOLL?

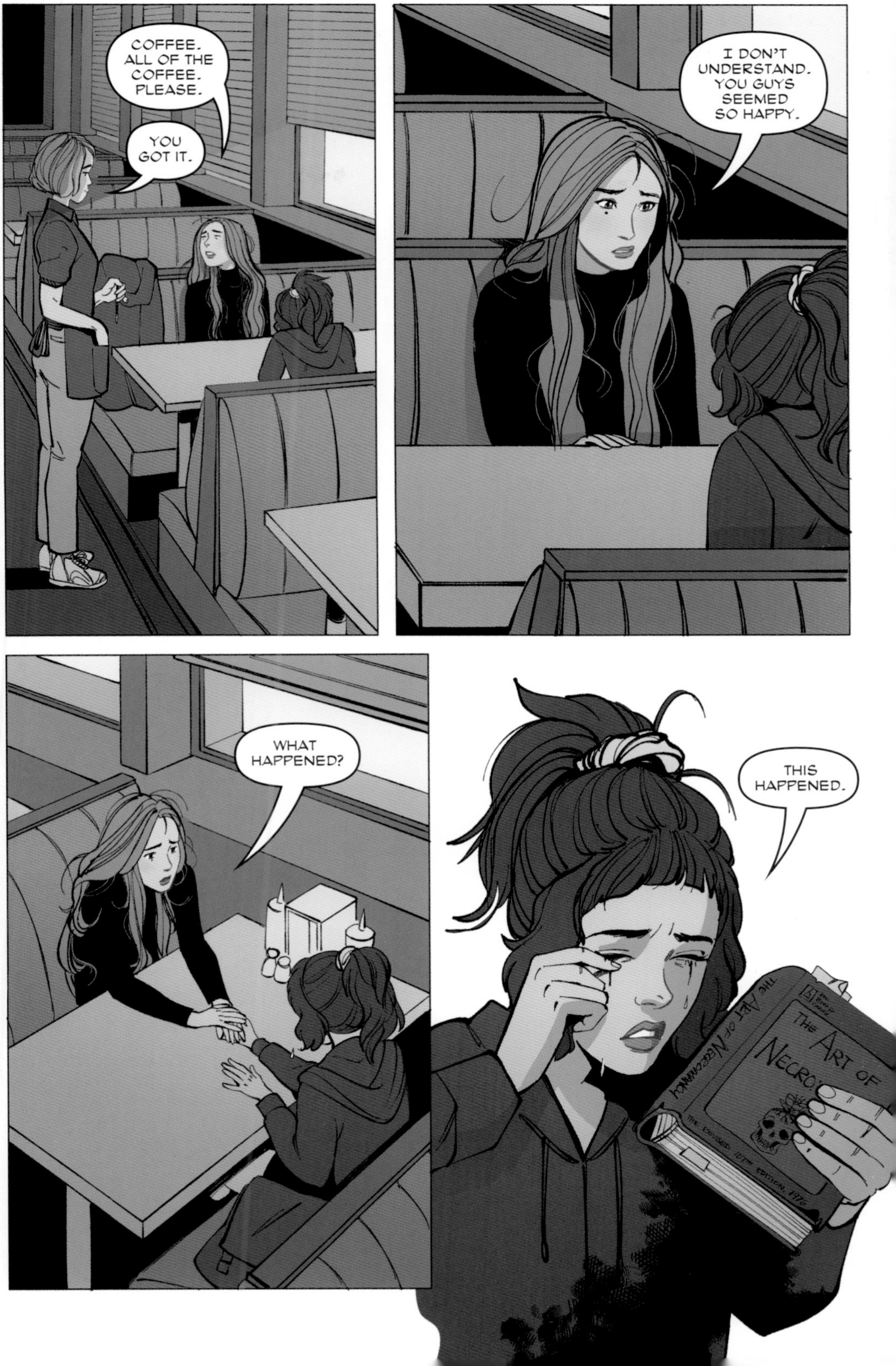
COFFEE. ALL OF THE COFFEE. PLEASE.
YOU GOT IT.
I DON'T UNDERSTAND. YOU GUYS SEEMED SO HAPPY.
WHAT HAPPENED?
THIS HAPPENED.

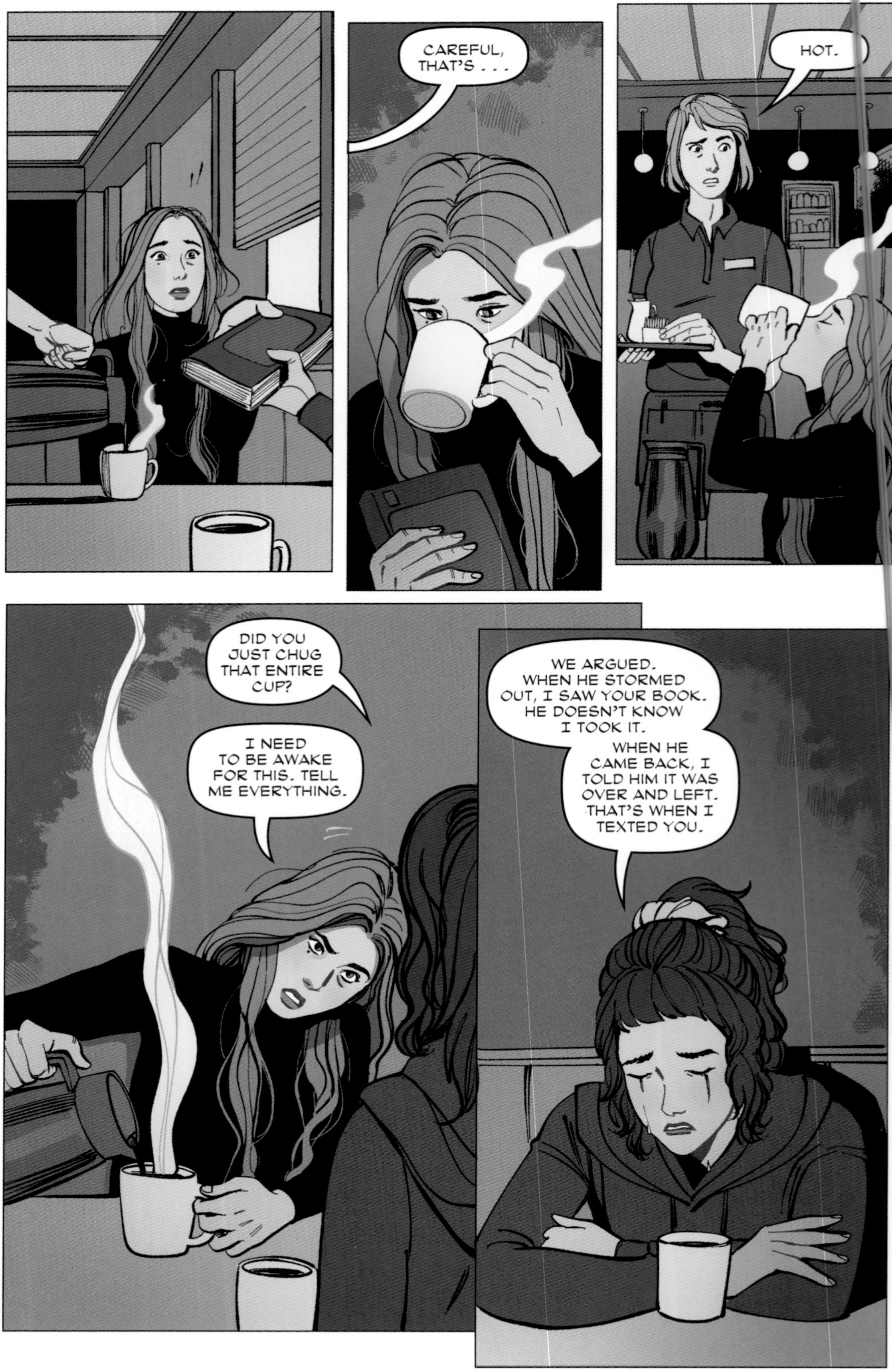
CAREFUL, THAT'S . . .
HOT.
DID YOU JUST CHUG THAT ENTIRE CUP?
I NEED TO BE AWAKE FOR THIS. TELL ME EVERYTHING.
WE ARGUED. WHEN HE STORMED OUT, I SAW YOUR BOOK. HE DOESN'T KNOW I TOOK IT.
WHEN HE CAME BACK, I TOLD HIM IT WAS OVER AND LEFT. THAT'S WHEN I TEXTED YOU.

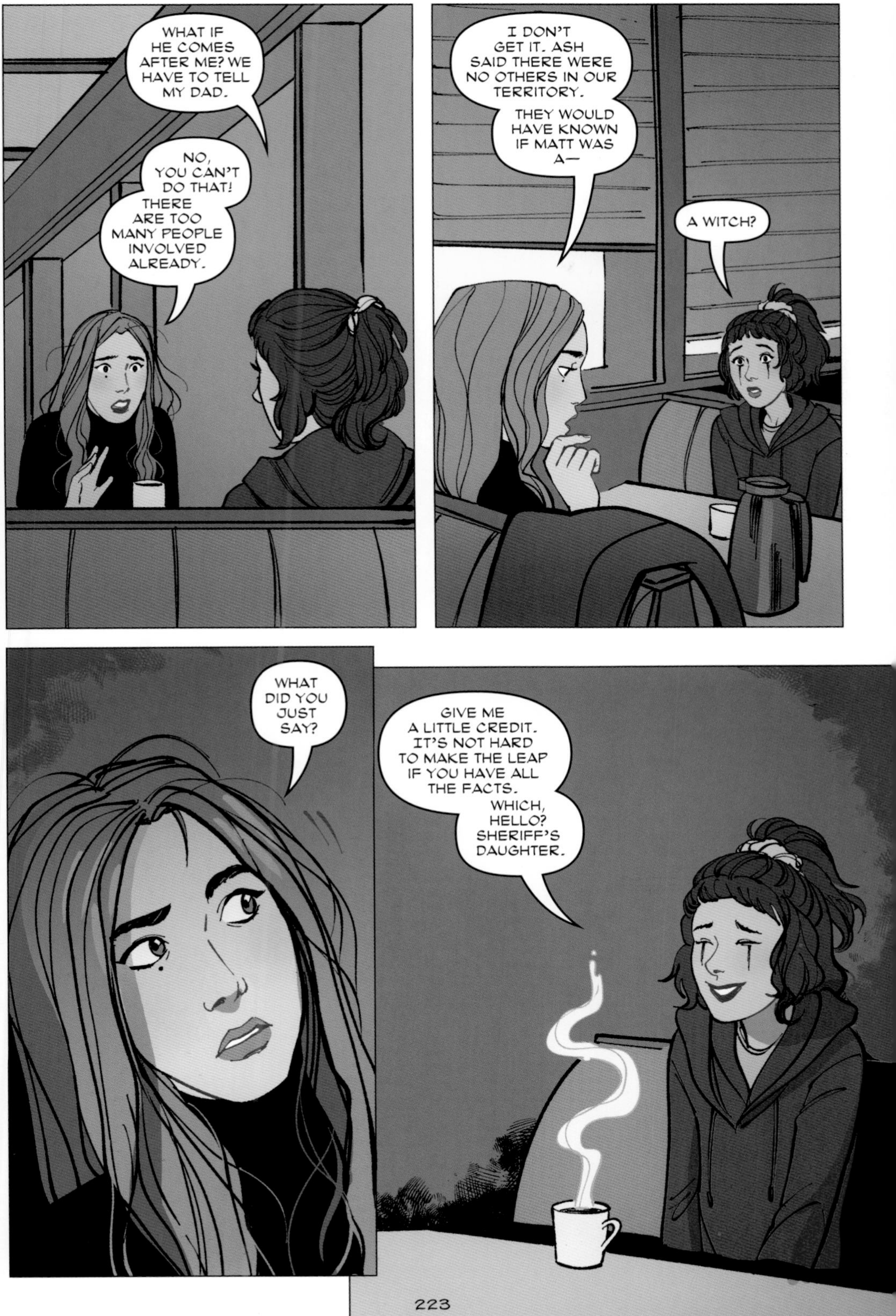
WHAT IF HE COMES AFTER ME? WE HAVE TO TELL MY DAD.
NO, YOU CAN'T DO THAT! THERE ARE TOO MANY PEOPLE INVOLVED ALREADY.
I DON'T GET IT. ASH SAID THERE WERE NO OTHERS IN OUR TERRITORY.
THEY WOULD HAVE KNOWN IF MATT WAS A—
A WITCH?
WHAT DID YOU JUST SAY?
GIVE ME A LITTLE CREDIT. IT'S NOT HARD TO MAKE THE LEAP IF YOU HAVE ALL THE FACTS.
WHICH, HELLO? SHERIFF'S DAUGHTER.

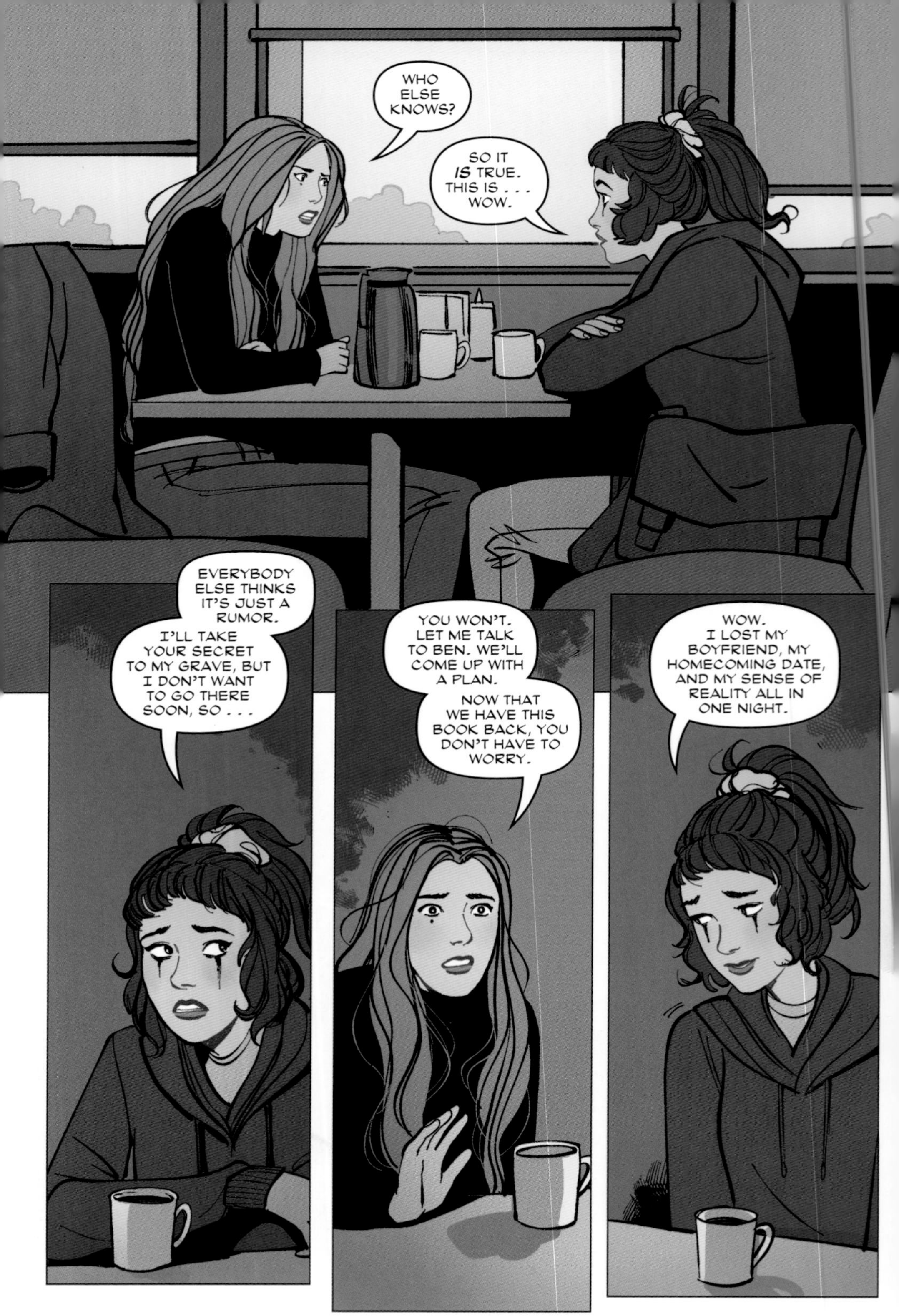
WHO ELSE KNOWS?
SO IT IS TRUE. THIS IS . . . WOW.
EVERYBODY ELSE THINKS IT'S JUST A RUMOR.
I'LL TAKE YOUR SECRET TO MY GRAVE, BUT I DON'T WANT TO GO THERE SOON, SO . . .
YOU WON'T. LET ME TALK TO BEN. WE'LL COME UP WITH A PLAN.
NOW THAT WE HAVE THIS BOOK BACK, YOU DON'T HAVE TO WORRY.
WOW. I LOST MY BOYFRIEND, MY HOMECOMING DATE, AND MY SENSE OF REALITY ALL IN ONE NIGHT.

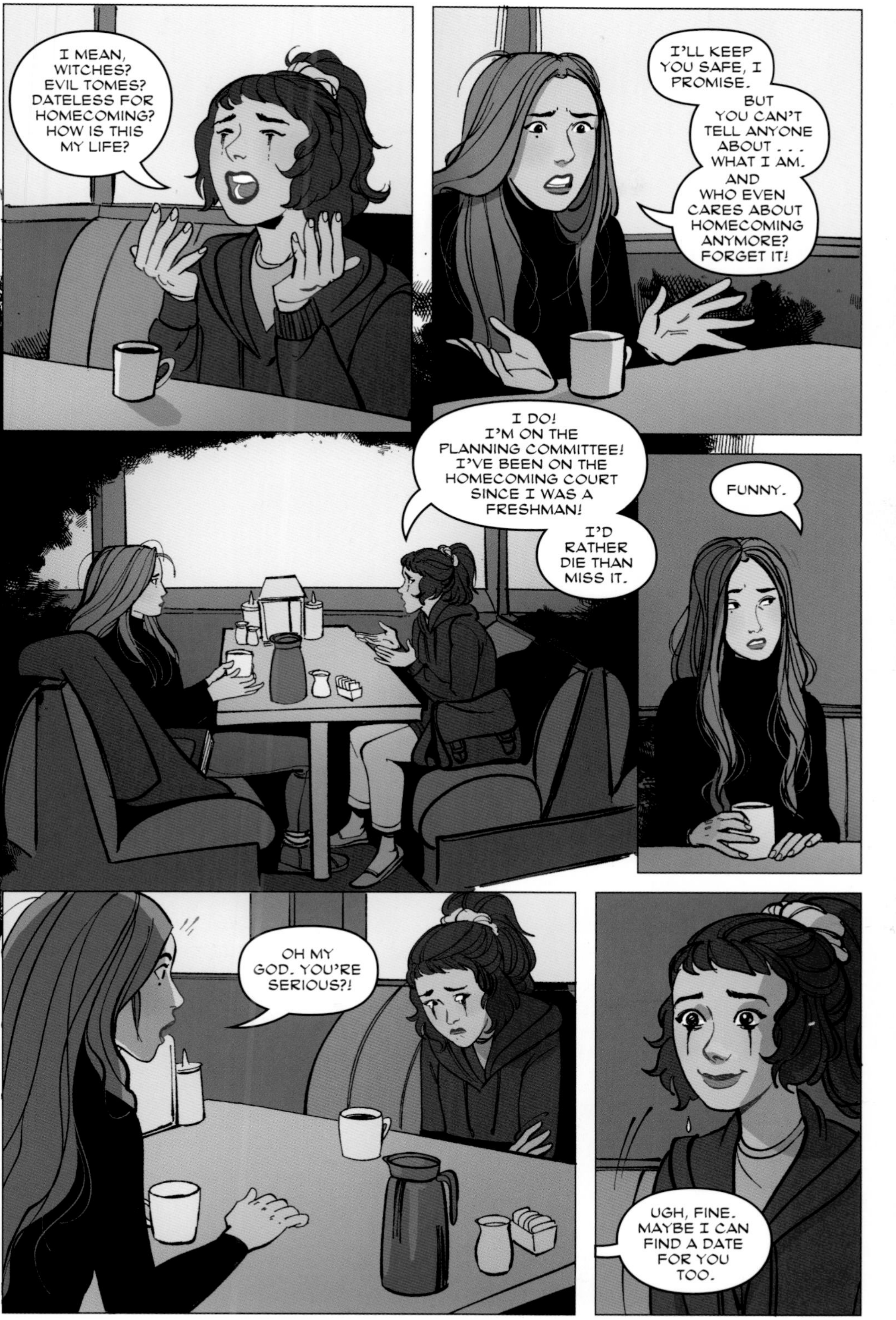

I MEAN, WITCHES? EVIL TOMES? DATELESS FOR HOMECOMING? HOW IS THIS MY LIFE?
I'LL KEEP YOU SAFE, I PROMISE.
BUT YOU CAN'T TELL ANYONE ABOUT . . . WHAT I AM.
AND WHO EVEN CARES ABOUT HOMECOMING ANYMORE? FORGET IT!
I DO! I'M ON THE PLANNING COMMITTEE! I'VE BEEN ON THE HOMECOMING COURT SINCE I WAS A FRESHMAN!
I'D RATHER DIE THAN MISS IT.
FUNNY.
OH MY GOD. YOU'RE SERIOUS?!
UGH, FINE. MAYBE I CAN FIND A DATE FOR YOU TOO.

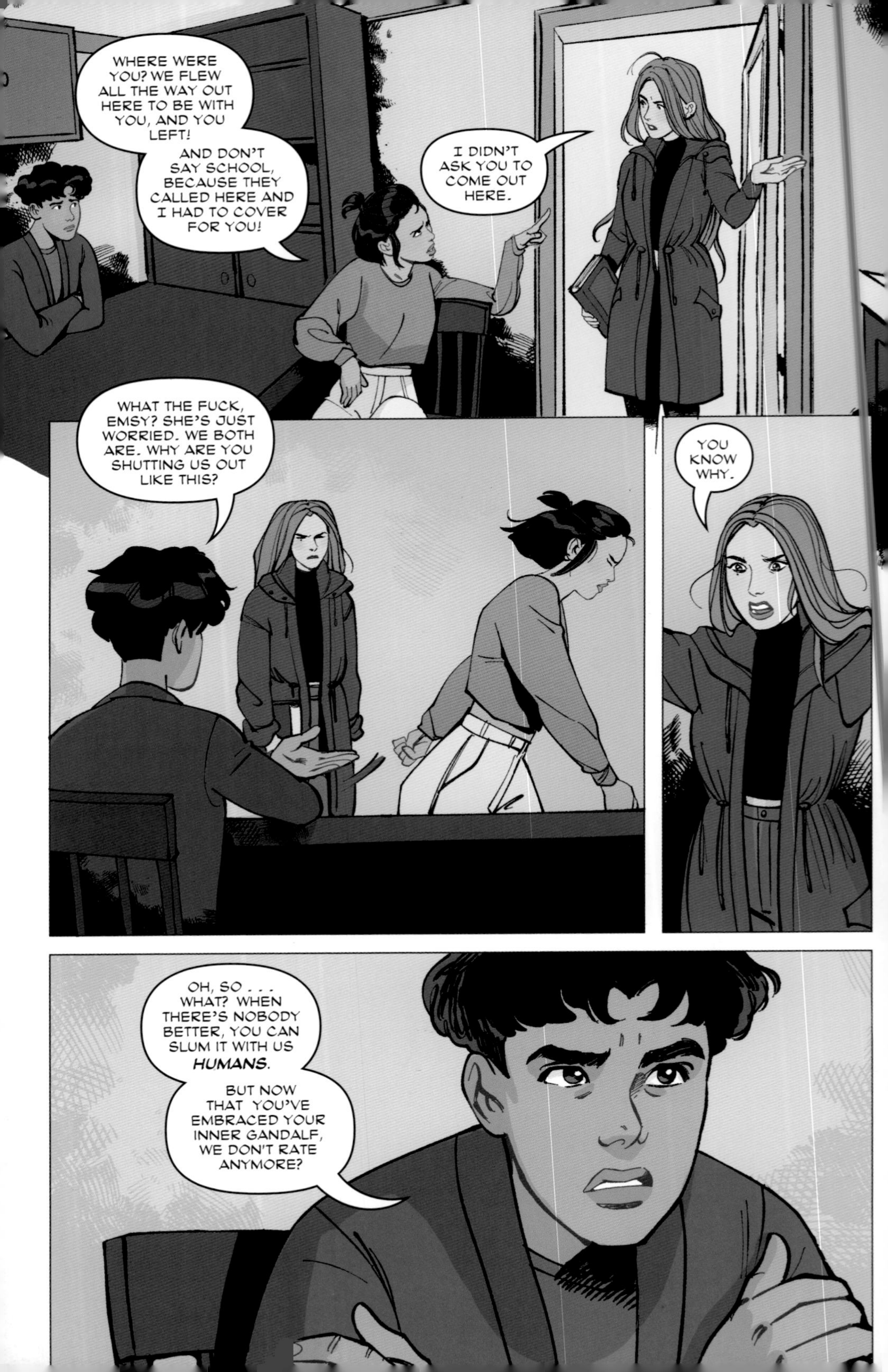
WHERE WERE YOU? WE FLEW ALL THE WAY OUT HERE TO BE WITH YOU, AND YOU LEFT!
AND DON'T SAY SCHOOL, BECAUSE THEY CALLED HERE AND I HAD TO COVER FOR YOU!
I DIDN'T ASK YOU TO COME OUT HERE.
WHAT THE FUCK, EMSY? SHE'S JUST WORRIED. WE BOTH ARE. WHY ARE YOU SHUTTING US OUT LIKE THIS?
YOU KNOW WHY.
OH, SO . . . WHAT? WHEN THERE'S NOBODY BETTER, YOU CAN SLUM IT WITH US *HUMANS*.
BUT NOW THAT YOU'VE EMBRACED YOUR INNER GANDALF, WE DON'T RATE ANYMORE?

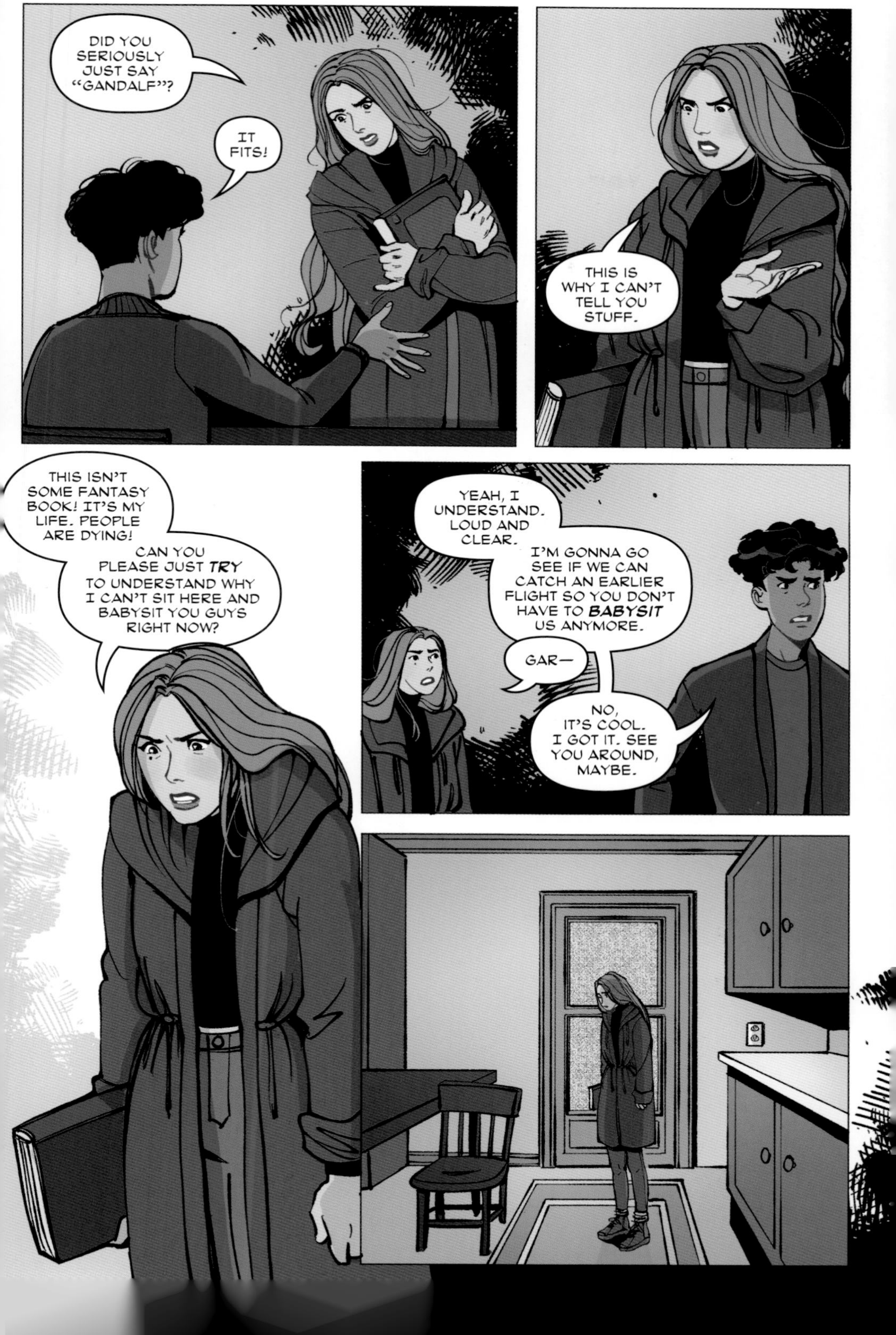
DID YOU SERIOUSLY JUST SAY "GANDALF"?
IT FITS!
THIS IS WHY I CAN'T TELL YOU STUFF.
THIS ISN'T SOME FANTASY BOOK! IT'S MY LIFE. PEOPLE ARE DYING!
CAN YOU PLEASE JUST *TRY* TO UNDERSTAND WHY I CAN'T SIT HERE AND BABYSIT YOU GUYS RIGHT NOW?
YEAH, I UNDERSTAND. LOUD AND CLEAR.
I'M GONNA GO SEE IF WE CAN CATCH AN EARLIER FLIGHT SO YOU DON'T HAVE TO ***BABYSIT*** US ANYMORE.
GAR—
NO, IT'S COOL. I GOT IT. SEE YOU AROUND, MAYBE.

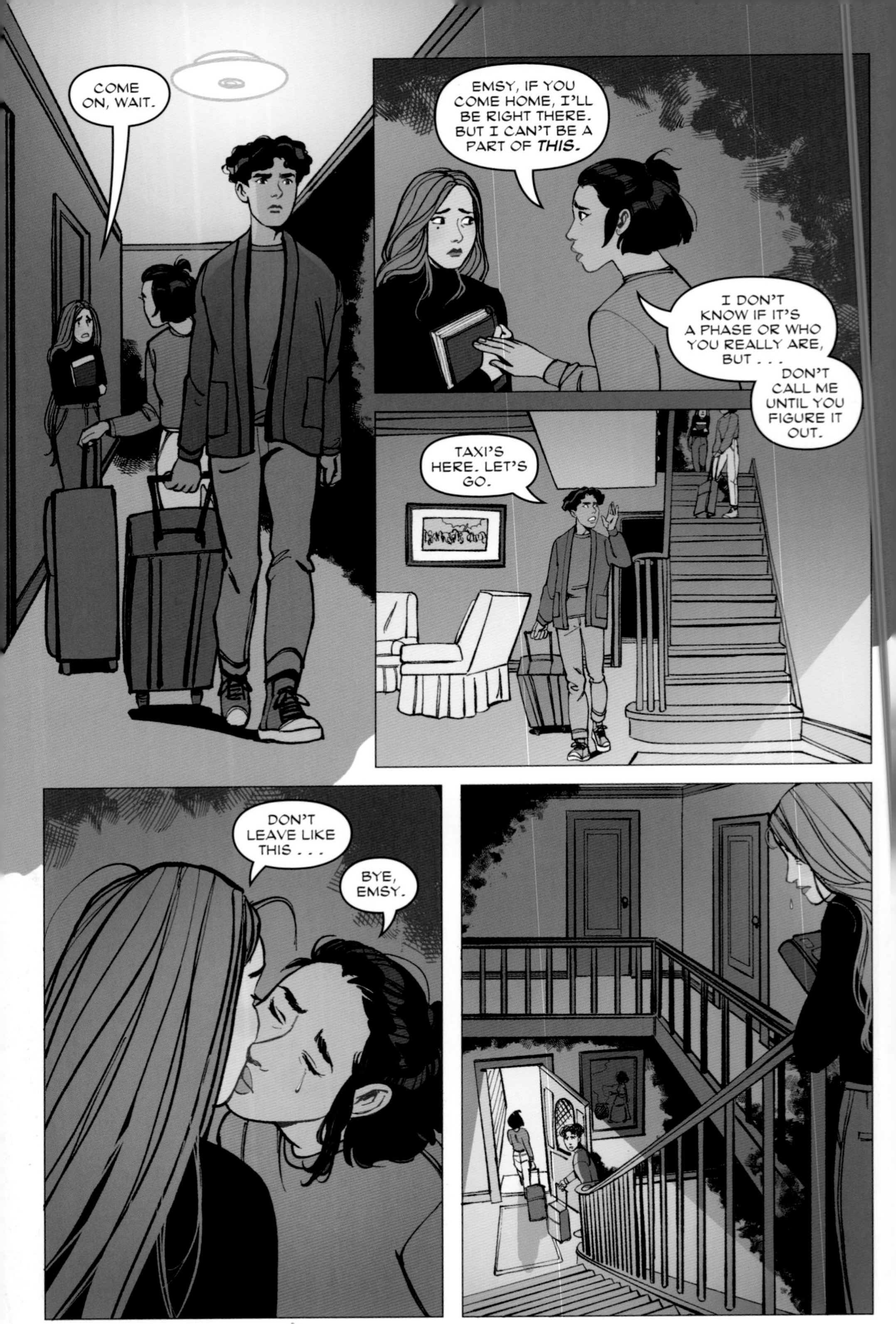
COME ON, WAIT.
EMSY, IF YOU COME HOME, I'LL BE RIGHT THERE. BUT I CAN'T BE A PART OF *THIS.*
I DON'T KNOW IF IT'S A PHASE OR WHO YOU REALLY ARE, BUT . . .
DON'T CALL ME UNTIL YOU FIGURE IT OUT.
TAXI'S HERE. LET'S GO.
DON'T LEAVE LIKE THIS . . .
BYE, EMSY.

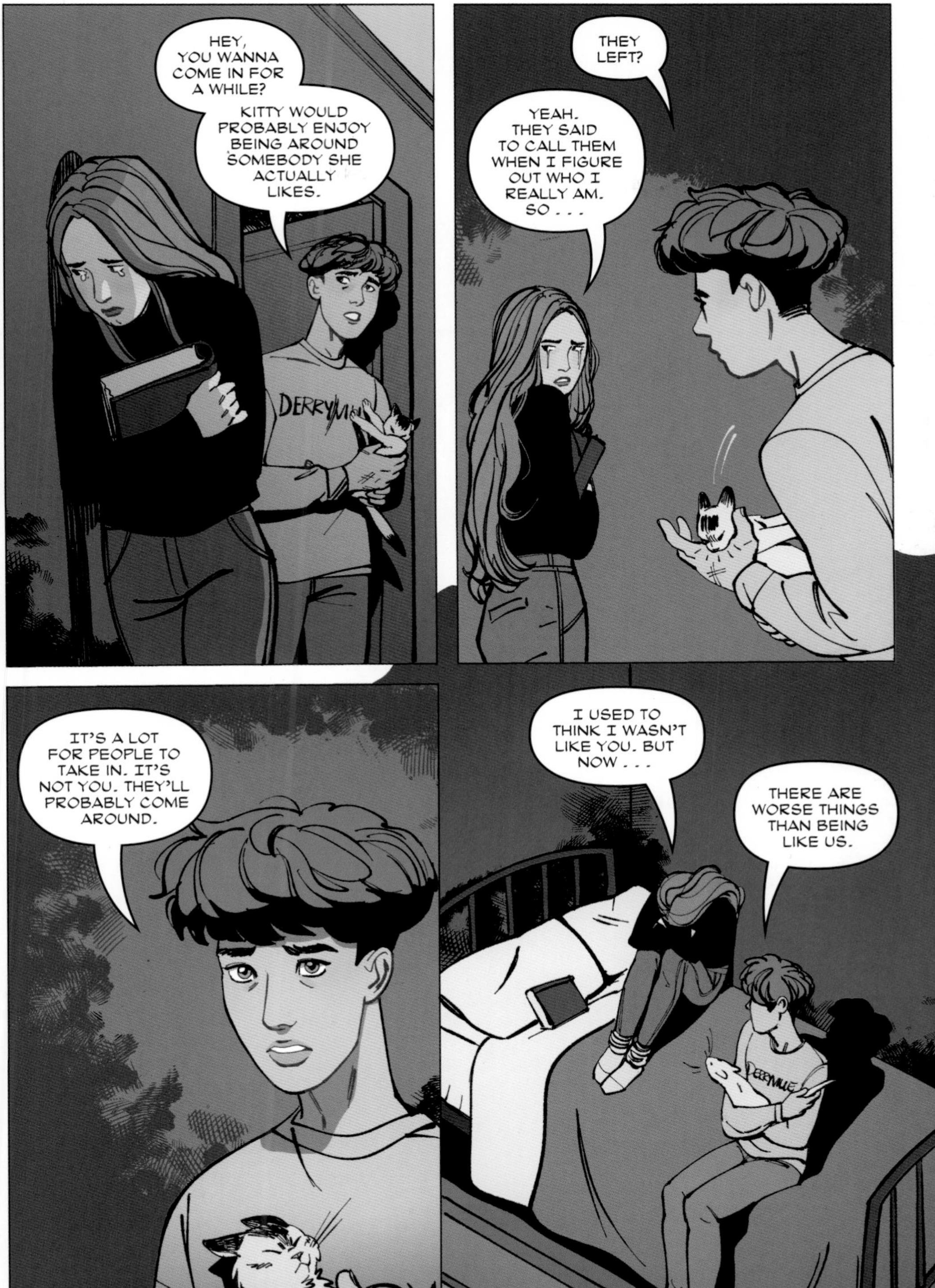
HEY, YOU WANNA COME IN FOR A WHILE?
KITTY WOULD PROBABLY ENJOY BEING AROUND SOMEBODY SHE ACTUALLY LIKES.
DERRYVILLE
THEY LEFT?
YEAH. THEY SAID TO CALL THEM WHEN I FIGURE OUT WHO I REALLY AM. SO . . .
IT'S A LOT FOR PEOPLE TO TAKE IN. IT'S NOT YOU. THEY'LL PROBABLY COME AROUND.
I USED TO THINK I WASN'T LIKE YOU. BUT NOW . . .
THERE ARE WORSE THINGS THAN BEING LIKE US.
DERRYVILLE

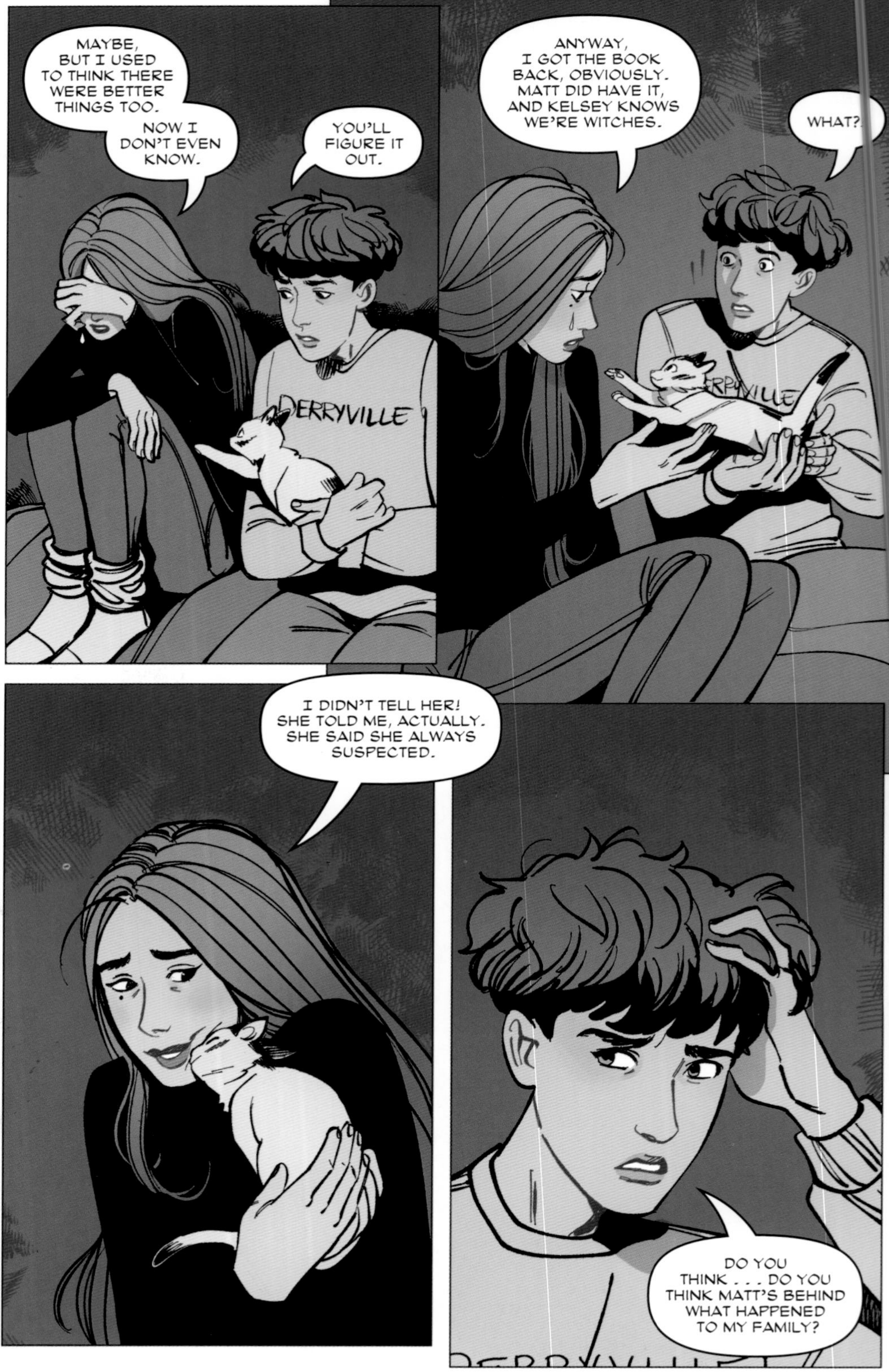
MAYBE, BUT I USED TO THINK THERE WERE BETTER THINGS TOO.
NOW I DON'T EVEN KNOW.
YOU'LL FIGURE IT OUT.
DERRYVILLE
ANYWAY, I GOT THE BOOK BACK, OBVIOUSLY. MATT DID HAVE IT, AND KELSEY KNOWS WE'RE WITCHES.
WHAT?
I DIDN'T TELL HER! SHE TOLD ME, ACTUALLY. SHE SAID SHE ALWAYS SUSPECTED.
DO YOU THINK . . . DO YOU THINK MATT'S BEHIND WHAT HAPPENED TO MY FAMILY?

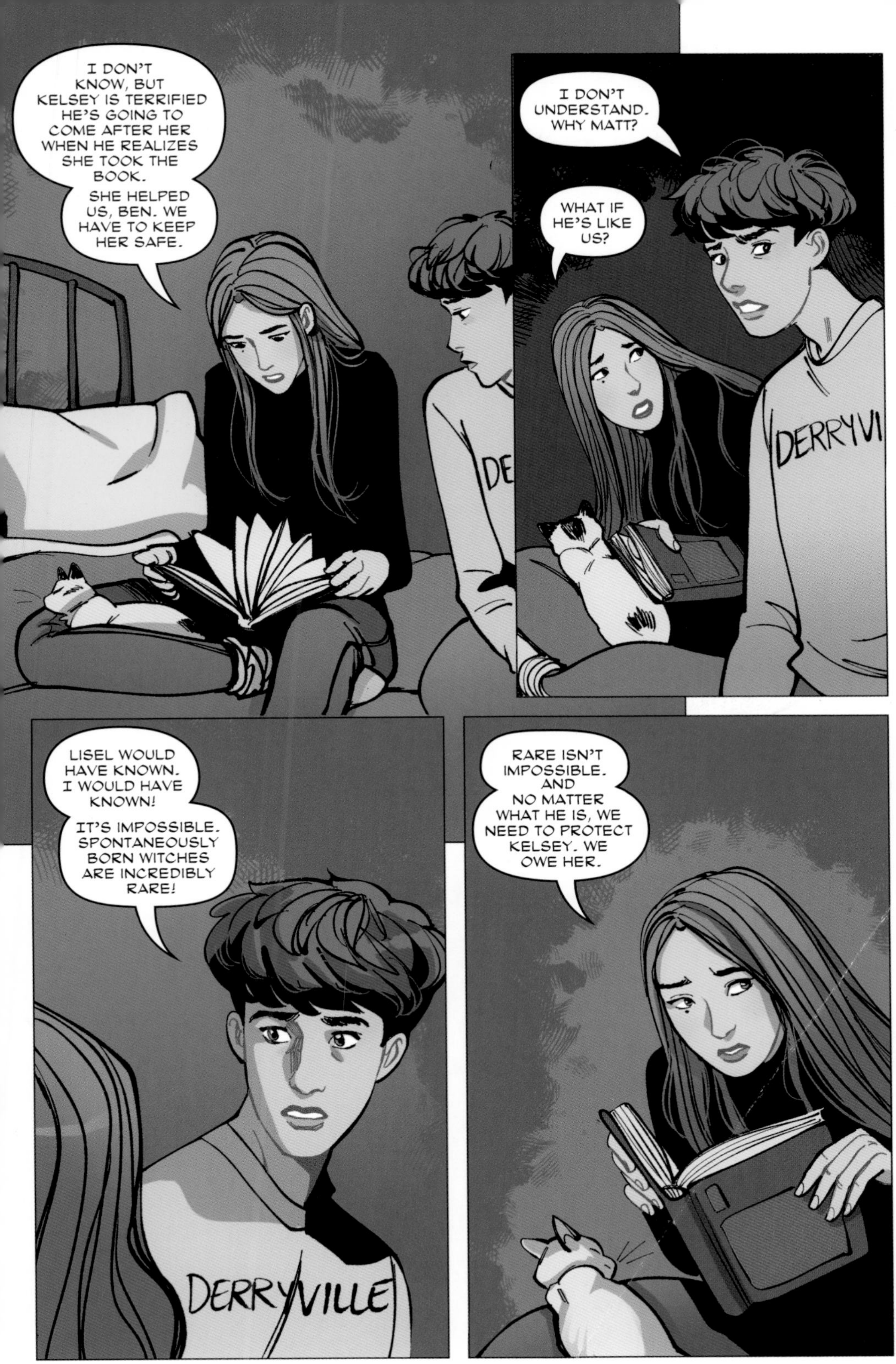
I DON'T KNOW, BUT KELSEY IS TERRIFIED HE'S GOING TO COME AFTER HER WHEN HE REALIZES SHE TOOK THE BOOK.
SHE HELPED US, BEN. WE HAVE TO KEEP HER SAFE.
I DON'T UNDERSTAND. WHY MATT?
WHAT IF HE'S LIKE US?
DERRYVI
LISEL WOULD HAVE KNOWN. I WOULD HAVE KNOWN!
IT'S IMPOSSIBLE. SPONTANEOUSLY BORN WITCHES ARE INCREDIBLY RARE!
DERRYVILLE
RARE ISN'T IMPOSSIBLE. AND NO MATTER WHAT HE IS, WE NEED TO PROTECT KELSEY. WE OWE HER.

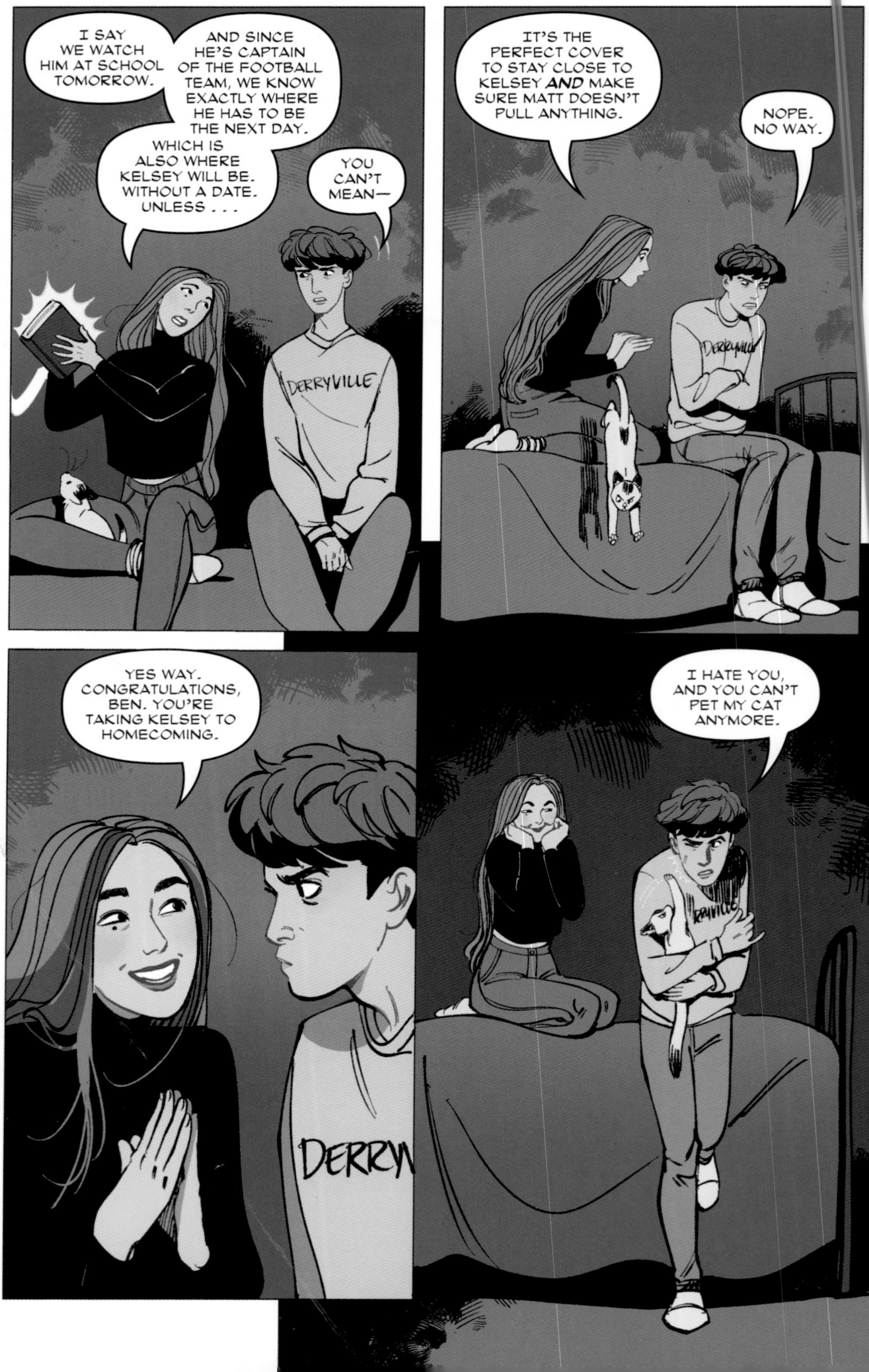

I SAY WE WATCH HIM AT SCHOOL TOMORROW.
AND SINCE HE'S CAPTAIN OF THE FOOTBALL TEAM, WE KNOW EXACTLY WHERE HE HAS TO BE THE NEXT DAY.
WHICH IS ALSO WHERE KELSEY WILL BE. WITHOUT A DATE. UNLESS . . .
YOU CAN'T MEAN—
DERRYVILLE
IT'S THE PERFECT COVER TO STAY CLOSE TO KELSEY **AND** MAKE SURE MATT DOESN'T PULL ANYTHING.
NOPE. NO WAY.
DERRYVILLE
YES WAY. CONGRATULATIONS, BEN. YOU'RE TAKING KELSEY TO HOMECOMING.
DERRYV
I HATE YOU, AND YOU CAN'T PET MY CAT ANYMORE.

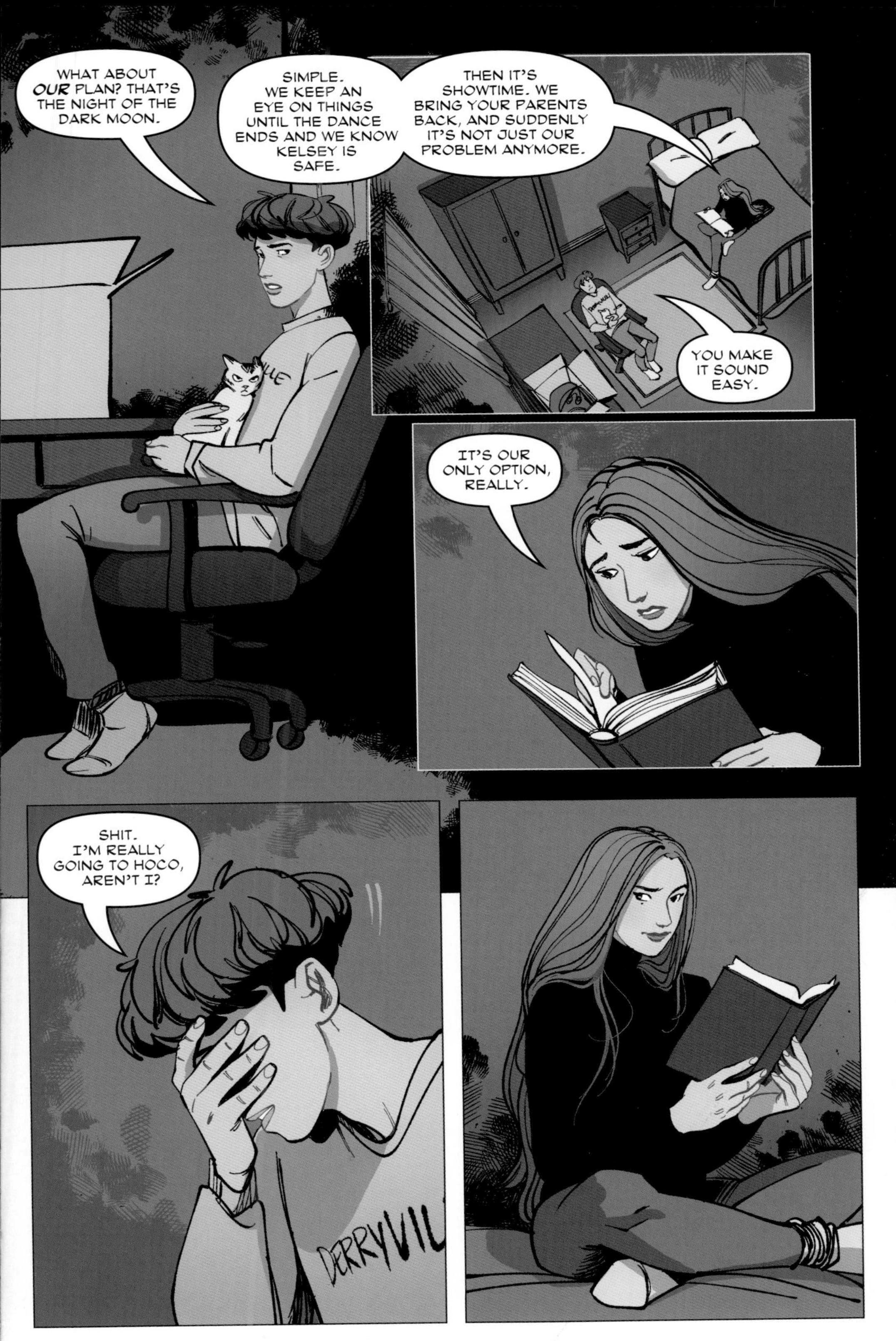
WHAT ABOUT OUR PLAN? THAT'S THE NIGHT OF THE DARK MOON.
SIMPLE. WE KEEP AN EYE ON THINGS UNTIL THE DANCE ENDS AND WE KNOW KELSEY IS SAFE.
THEN IT'S SHOWTIME. WE BRING YOUR PARENTS BACK, AND SUDDENLY IT'S NOT JUST OUR PROBLEM ANYMORE.
YOU MAKE IT SOUND EASY.
IT'S OUR ONLY OPTION, REALLY.
SHIT. I'M REALLY GOING TO HOCO, AREN'T I?
DERRYVIL

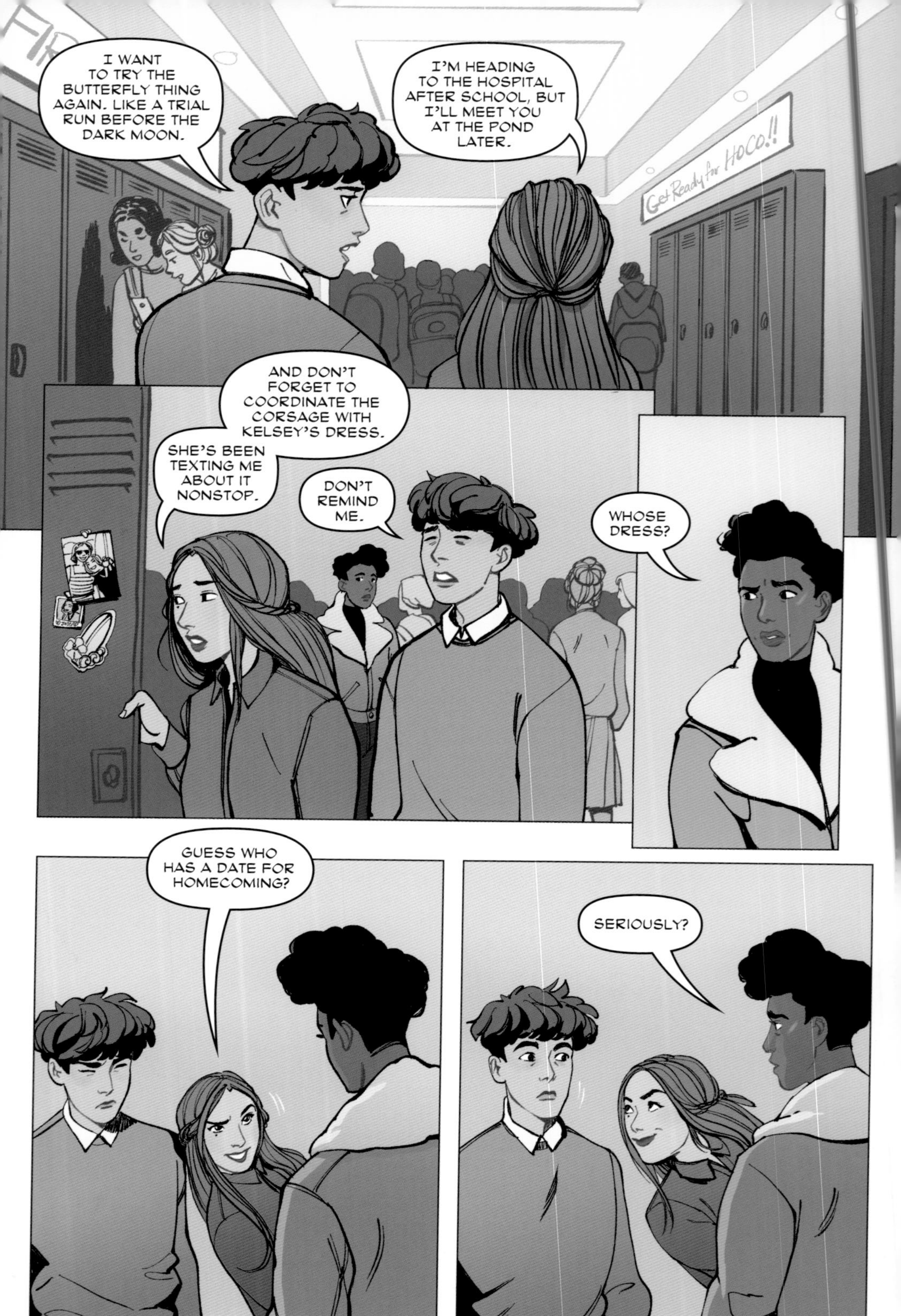
I WANT TO TRY THE BUTTERFLY THING AGAIN. LIKE A TRIAL RUN BEFORE THE DARK MOON.
I'M HEADING TO THE HOSPITAL AFTER SCHOOL, BUT I'LL MEET YOU AT THE POND LATER.
Get Ready for HoCo!!
AND DON'T FORGET TO COORDINATE THE CORSAGE WITH KELSEY'S DRESS.
SHE'S BEEN TEXTING ME ABOUT IT NONSTOP.
DON'T REMIND ME.
WHOSE DRESS?
GUESS WHO HAS A DATE FOR HOMECOMING?
SERIOUSLY?

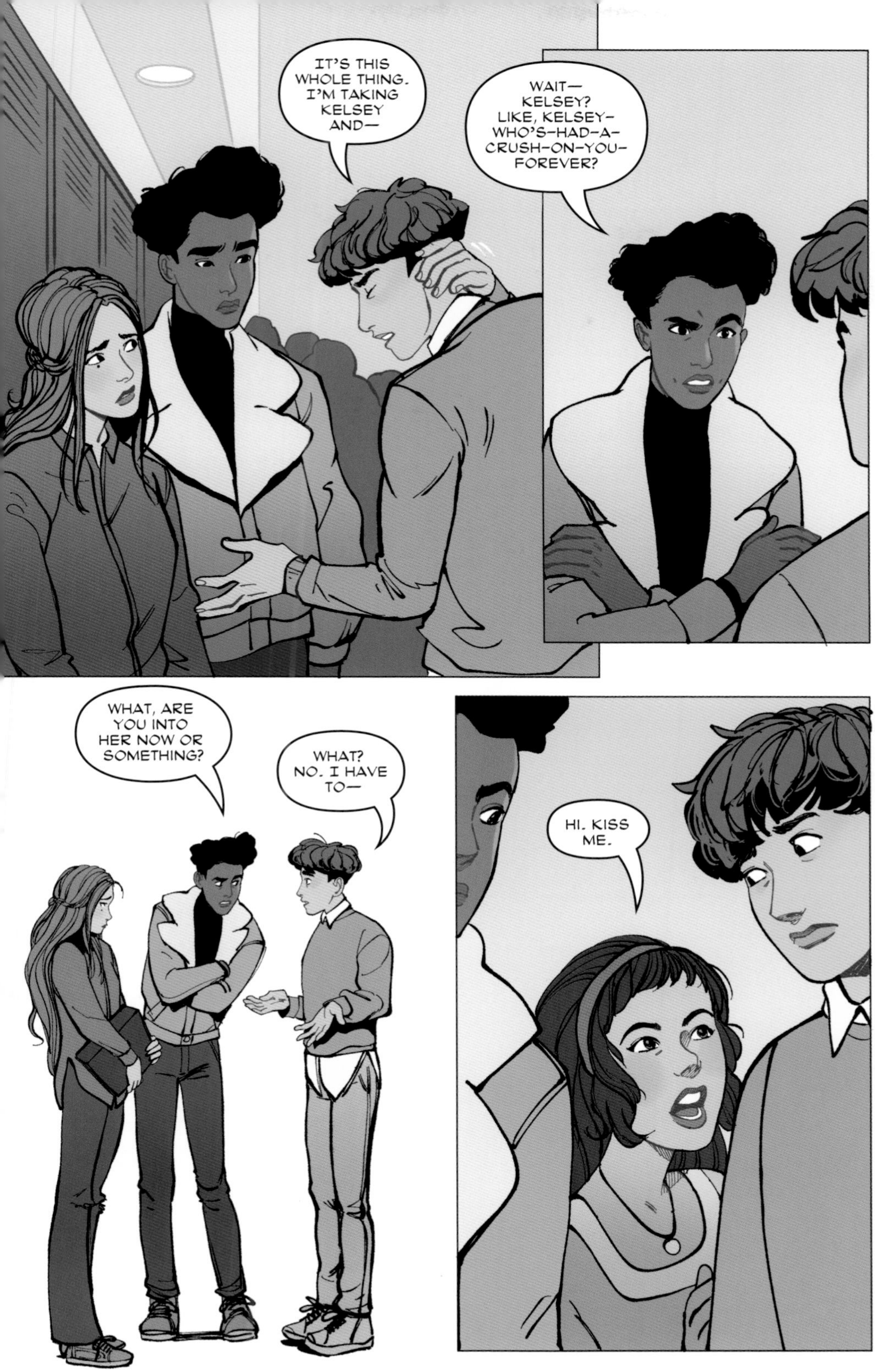
IT'S THIS WHOLE THING. I'M TAKING KELSEY AND—
WAIT— KELSEY? LIKE, KELSEY-WHO'S-HAD-A-CRUSH-ON-YOU-FOREVER?
WHAT, ARE YOU INTO HER NOW OR SOMETHING?
WHAT? NO. I HAVE TO—
HI. KISS ME.

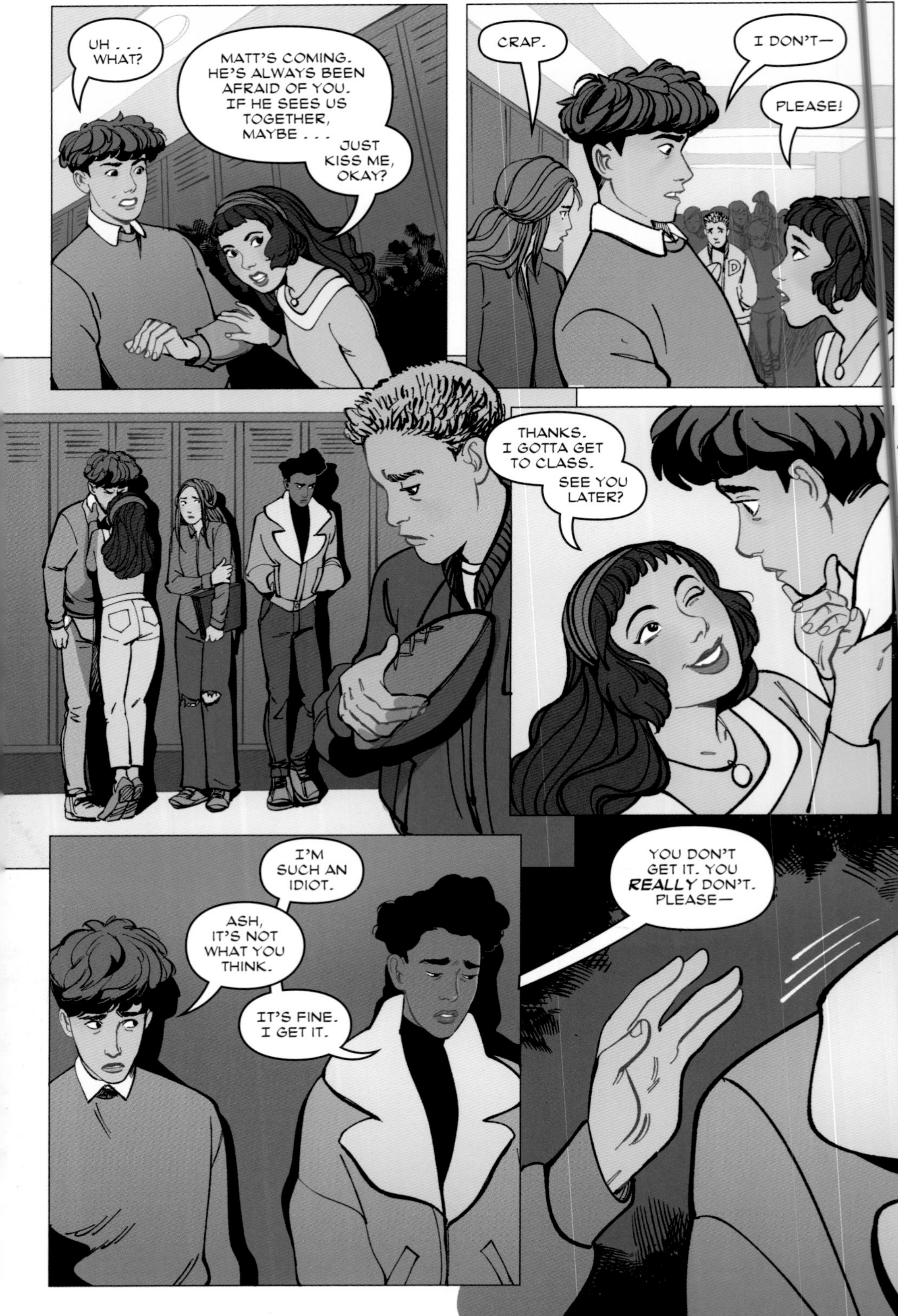
UH . . . WHAT?
MATT'S COMING. HE'S ALWAYS BEEN AFRAID OF YOU. IF HE SEES US TOGETHER, MAYBE . . .
JUST KISS ME, OKAY?
CRAP.
I DON'T—
PLEASE!
THANKS. I GOTTA GET TO CLASS.
SEE YOU LATER?
I'M SUCH AN IDIOT.
ASH, IT'S NOT WHAT YOU THINK.
IT'S FINE. I GET IT.
YOU DON'T GET IT. YOU *REALLY* DON'T. PLEASE—

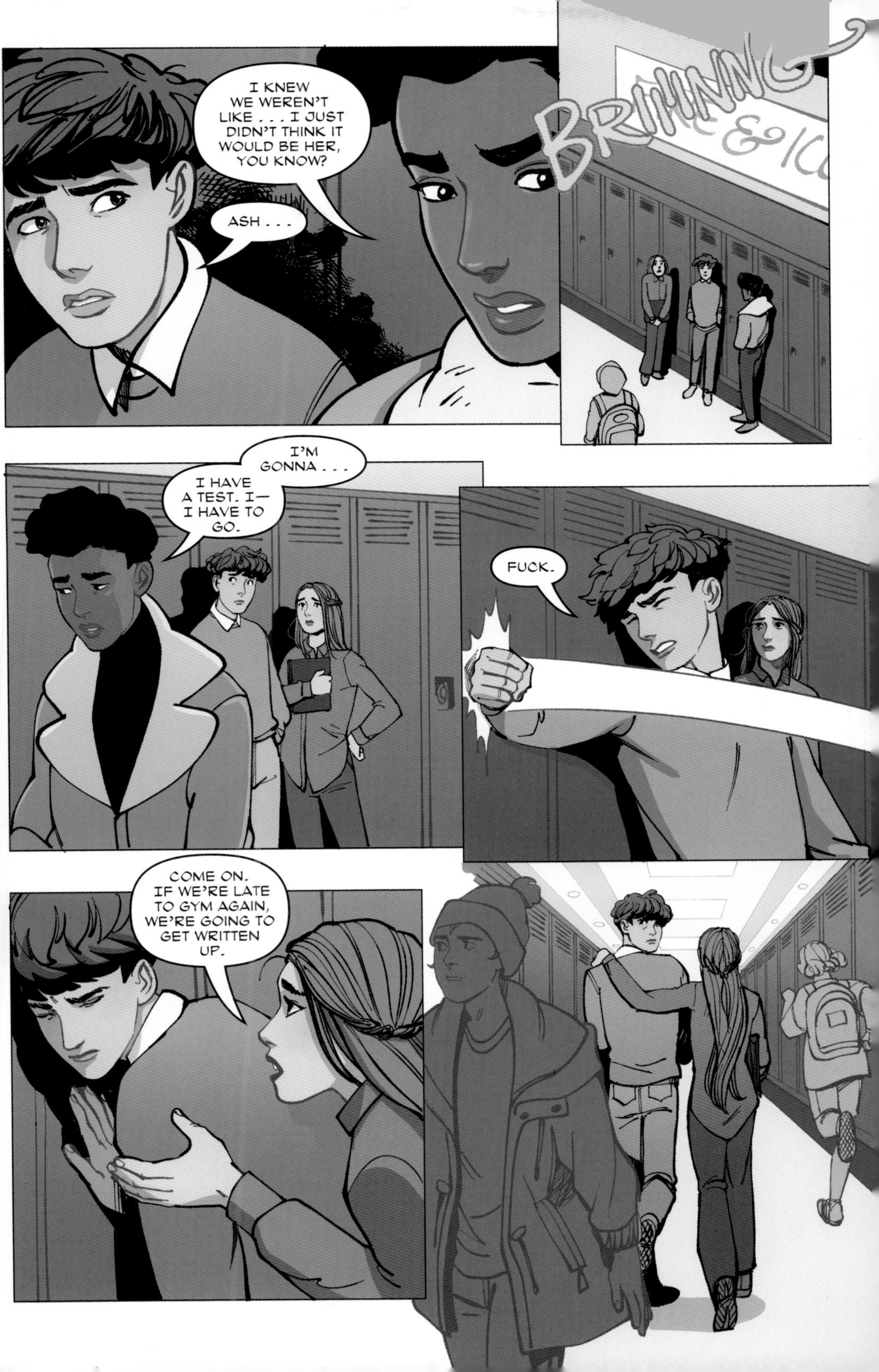
I KNEW WE WEREN'T LIKE . . . I JUST DIDN'T THINK IT WOULD BE HER, YOU KNOW?
ASH . . .
BRIIINNG
I HAVE A TEST. I— I HAVE TO GO.
I'M GONNA . . .
FUCK.
COME ON. IF WE'RE LATE TO GYM AGAIN, WE'RE GOING TO GET WRITTEN UP.

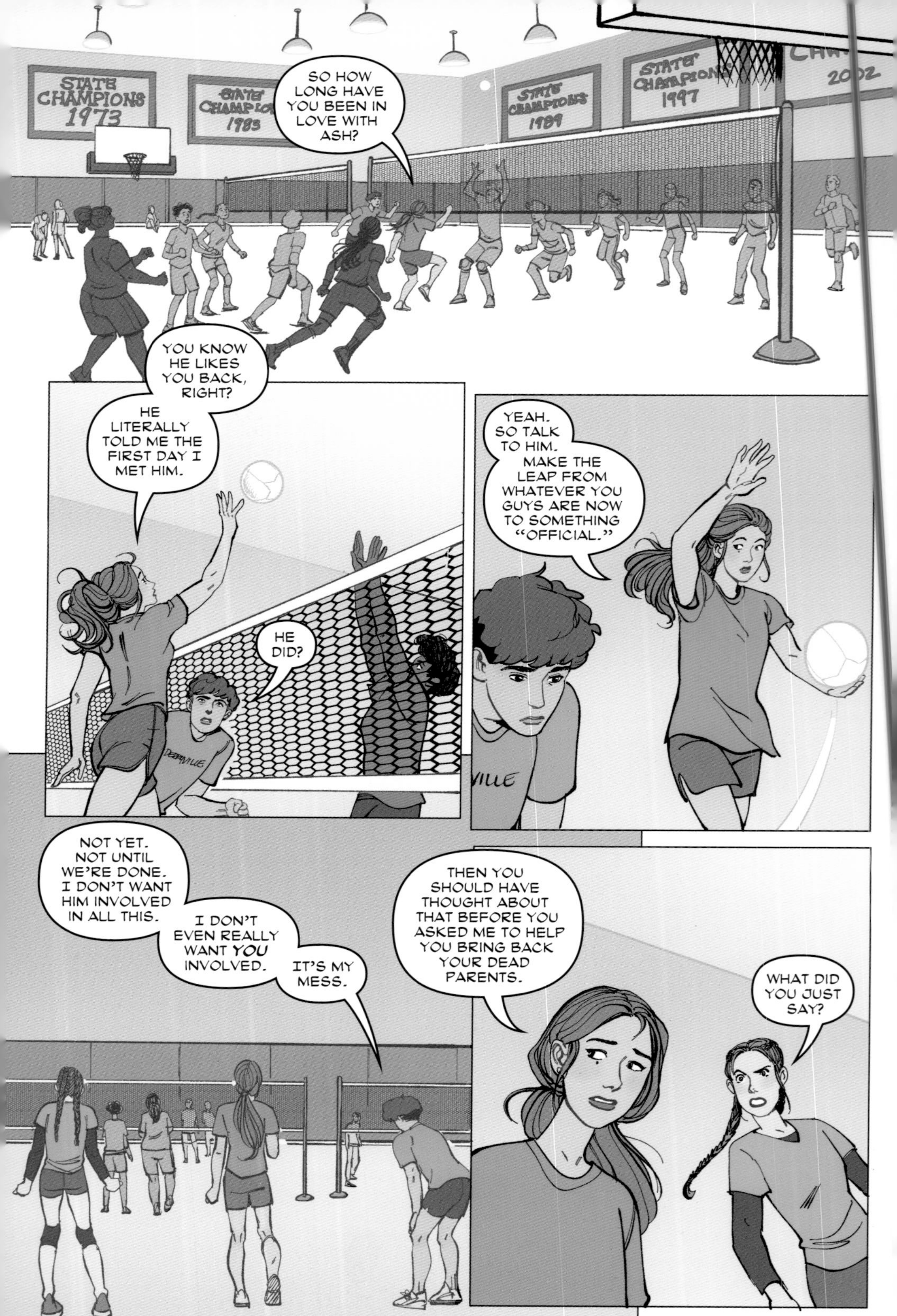
STATE CHAMPIONS 1973
STATE CHAMPIONS 1983
SO HOW LONG HAVE YOU BEEN IN LOVE WITH ASH?
STATE CHAMPIONS 1989
STATE CHAMPIONS 1997
2002
YOU KNOW HE LIKES YOU BACK, RIGHT?
HE LITERALLY TOLD ME THE FIRST DAY I MET HIM.
HE DID?
DEERVILLE
YEAH. SO TALK TO HIM.
MAKE THE LEAP FROM WHATEVER YOU GUYS ARE NOW TO SOMETHING "OFFICIAL."
VILLE
NOT YET. NOT UNTIL WE'RE DONE. I DON'T WANT HIM INVOLVED IN ALL THIS.
I DON'T EVEN REALLY WANT *YOU* INVOLVED.
IT'S MY MESS.
THEN YOU SHOULD HAVE THOUGHT ABOUT THAT BEFORE YOU ASKED ME TO HELP YOU BRING BACK YOUR DEAD PARENTS.
WHAT DID YOU JUST SAY?

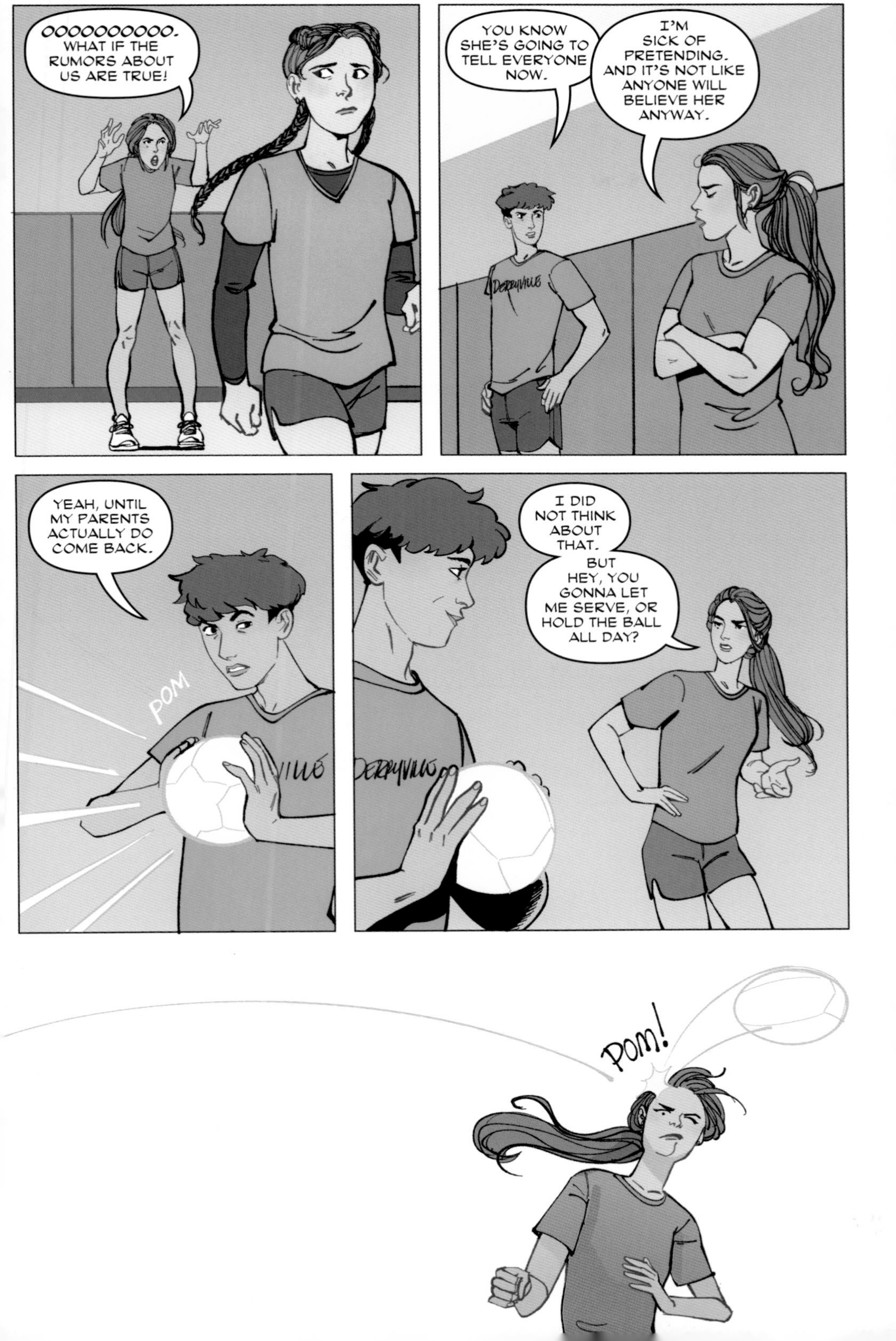
OOOOOOOOOO-
WHAT IF THE RUMORS ABOUT US ARE TRUE!
YOU KNOW SHE'S GOING TO TELL EVERYONE NOW.
I'M SICK OF PRETENDING. AND IT'S NOT LIKE ANYONE WILL BELIEVE HER ANYWAY.
DERRYVILLE
YEAH, UNTIL MY PARENTS ACTUALLY DO COME BACK.
POM
I DID NOT THINK ABOUT THAT.
BUT HEY, YOU GONNA LET ME SERVE, OR HOLD THE BALL ALL DAY?
POM!

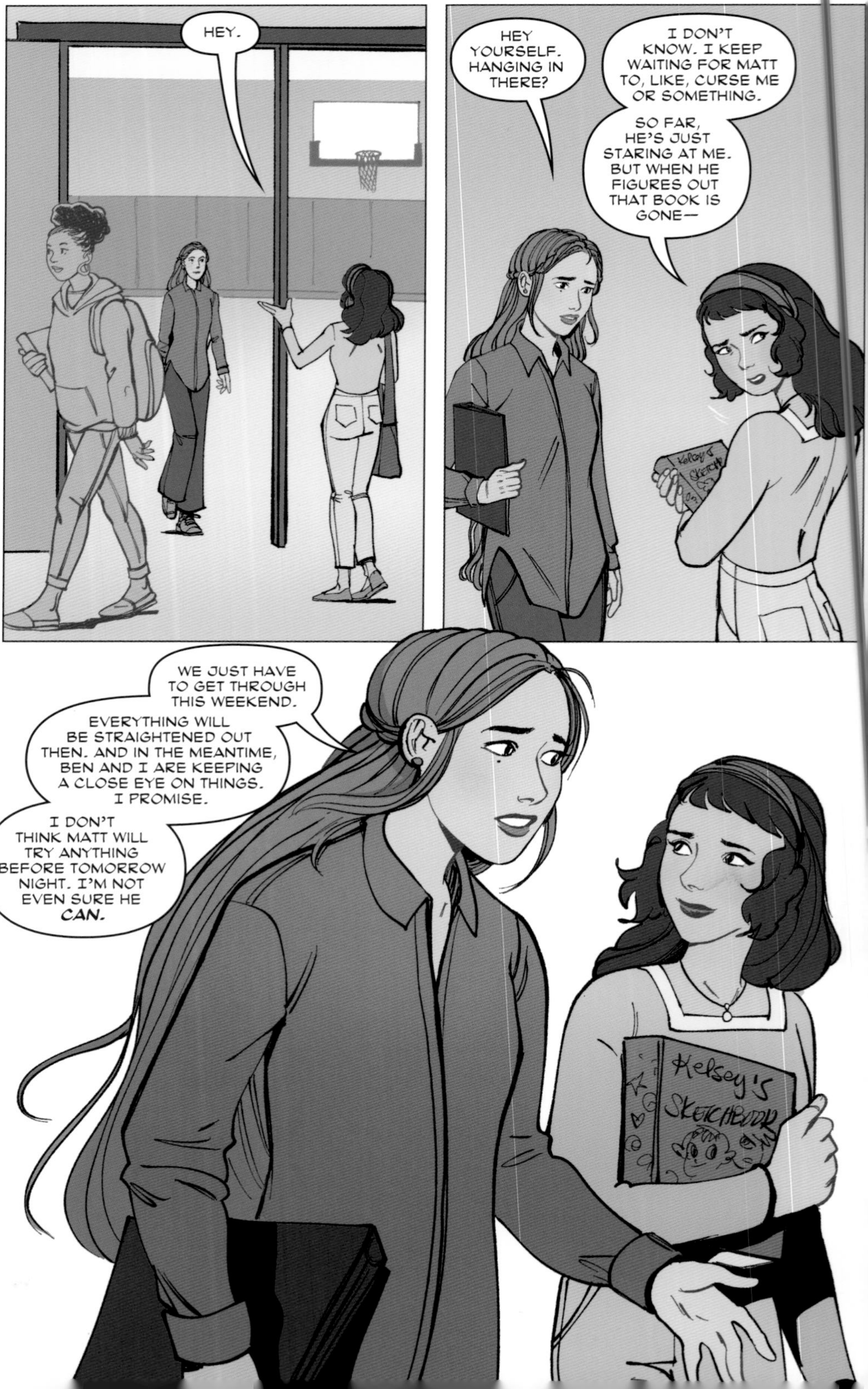
HEY.
HEY YOURSELF. HANGING IN THERE?
I DON'T KNOW. I KEEP WAITING FOR MATT TO, LIKE, CURSE ME OR SOMETHING.
SO FAR, HE'S JUST STARING AT ME. BUT WHEN HE FIGURES OUT THAT BOOK IS GONE—
WE JUST HAVE TO GET THROUGH THIS WEEKEND.
EVERYTHING WILL BE STRAIGHTENED OUT THEN. AND IN THE MEANTIME, BEN AND I ARE KEEPING A CLOSE EYE ON THINGS. I PROMISE.
I DON'T THINK MATT WILL TRY ANYTHING BEFORE TOMORROW NIGHT. I'M NOT EVEN SURE HE CAN.
Kelsey's SKETCHBOOK

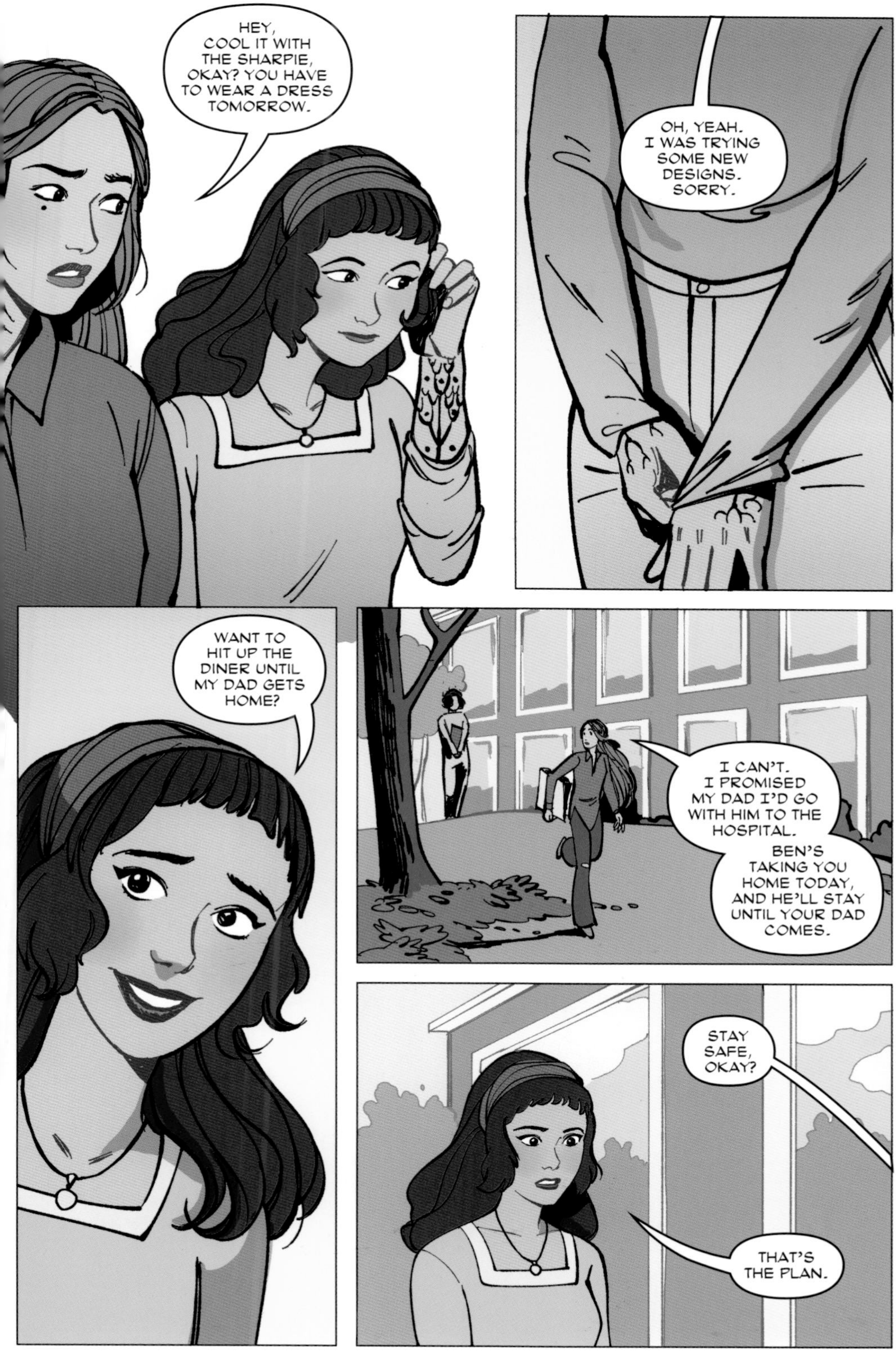
HEY, COOL IT WITH THE SHARPIE, OKAY? YOU HAVE TO WEAR A DRESS TOMORROW.
OH, YEAH. I WAS TRYING SOME NEW DESIGNS. SORRY.
WANT TO HIT UP THE DINER UNTIL MY DAD GETS HOME?
I CAN'T. I PROMISED MY DAD I'D GO WITH HIM TO THE HOSPITAL.
BEN'S TAKING YOU HOME TODAY, AND HE'LL STAY UNTIL YOUR DAD COMES.
STAY SAFE, OKAY?
THAT'S THE PLAN.

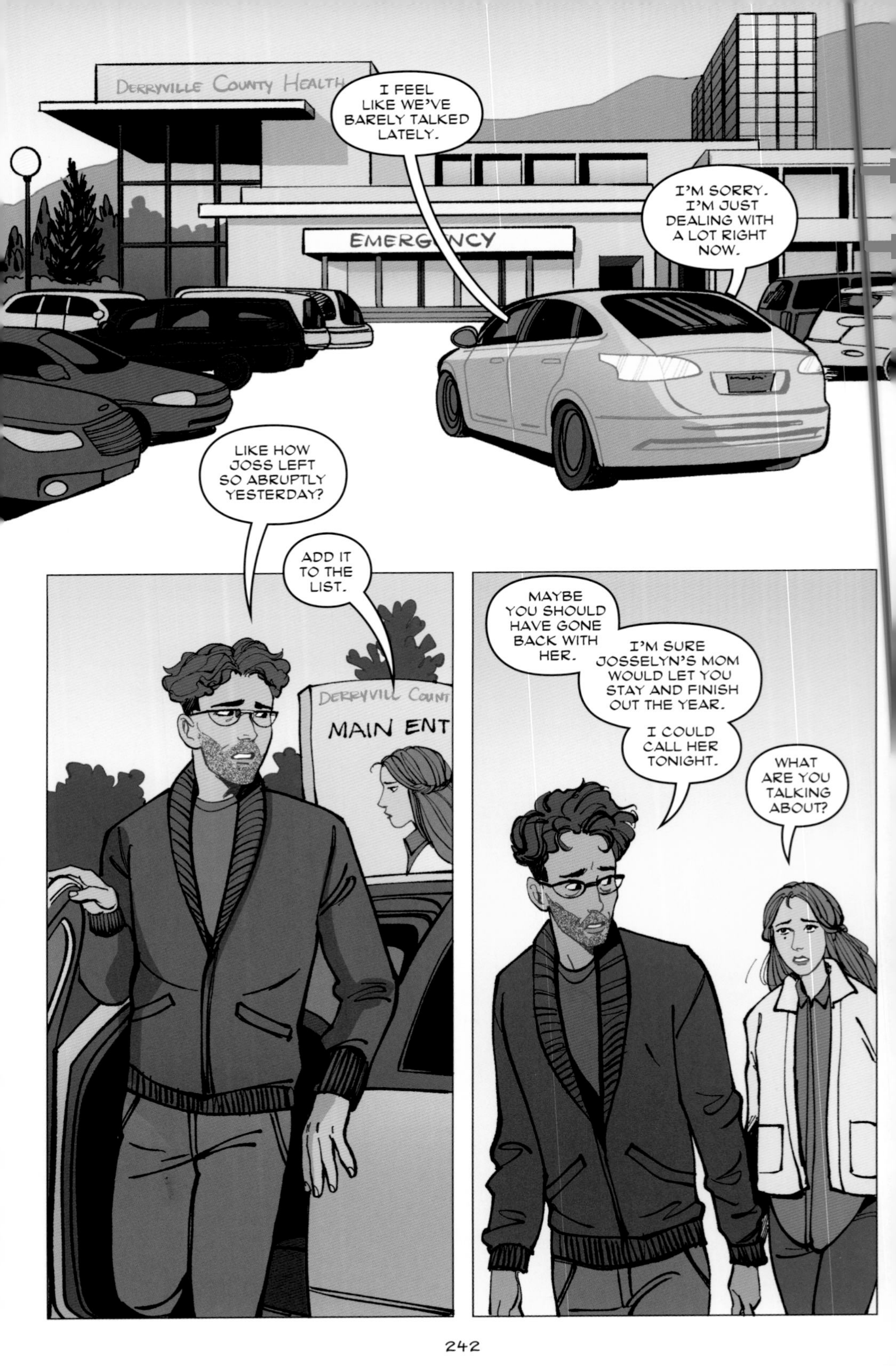
DERRYVILLE COUNTY HEALTH
I FEEL LIKE WE'VE BARELY TALKED LATELY.
I'M SORRY. I'M JUST DEALING WITH A LOT RIGHT NOW.
LIKE HOW JOSS LEFT SO ABRUPTLY YESTERDAY?
ADD IT TO THE LIST.
MAIN ENT
MAYBE YOU SHOULD HAVE GONE BACK WITH HER.
I'M SURE JOSSELYN'S MOM WOULD LET YOU STAY AND FINISH OUT THE YEAR.
I COULD CALL HER TONIGHT.
WHAT ARE YOU TALKING ABOUT?

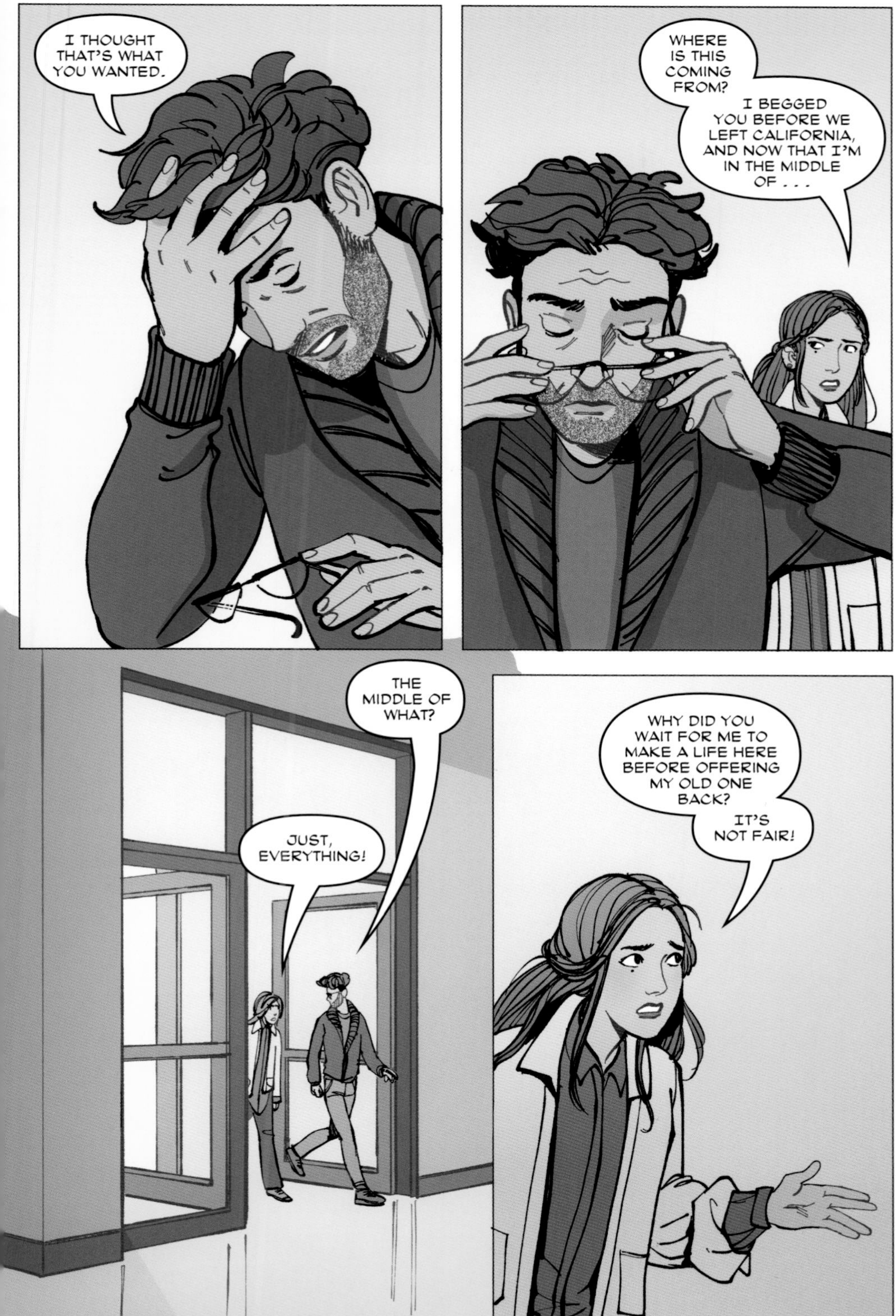
I THOUGHT THAT'S WHAT YOU WANTED.
WHERE IS THIS COMING FROM?
I BEGGED YOU BEFORE WE LEFT CALIFORNIA, AND NOW THAT I'M IN THE MIDDLE OF . . .
THE MIDDLE OF WHAT?
JUST, EVERYTHING!
WHY DID YOU WAIT FOR ME TO MAKE A LIFE HERE BEFORE OFFERING MY OLD ONE BACK?
IT'S NOT FAIR!

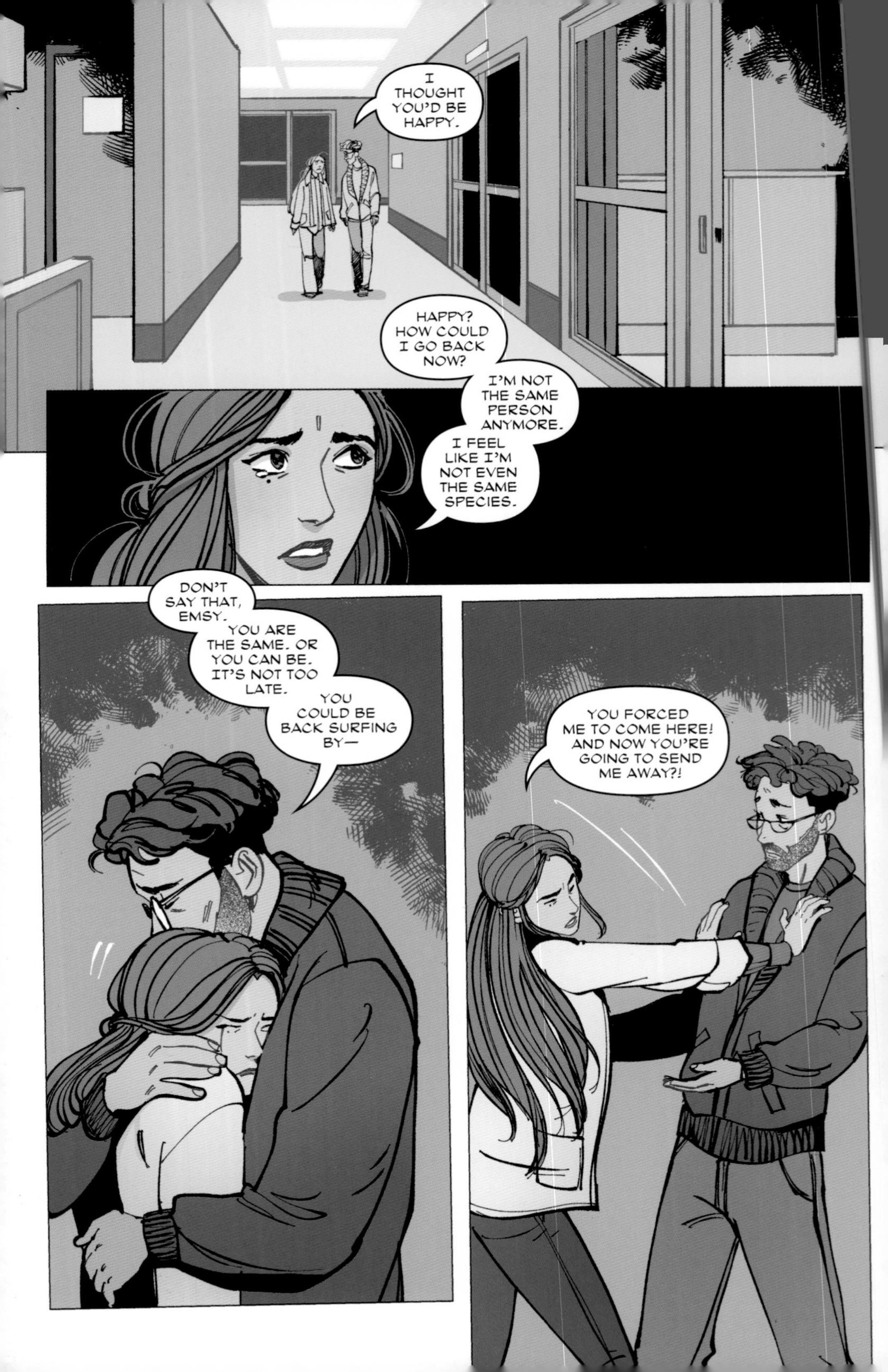
I THOUGHT YOU'D BE HAPPY.
HAPPY? HOW COULD I GO BACK NOW?
I'M NOT THE SAME PERSON ANYMORE.
I FEEL LIKE I'M NOT EVEN THE SAME SPECIES.
DON'T SAY THAT, EMSY.
YOU ARE THE SAME. OR YOU CAN BE. IT'S NOT TOO LATE.
YOU COULD BE BACK SURFING BY—
YOU FORCED ME TO COME HERE! AND NOW YOU'RE GOING TO SEND ME AWAY?!

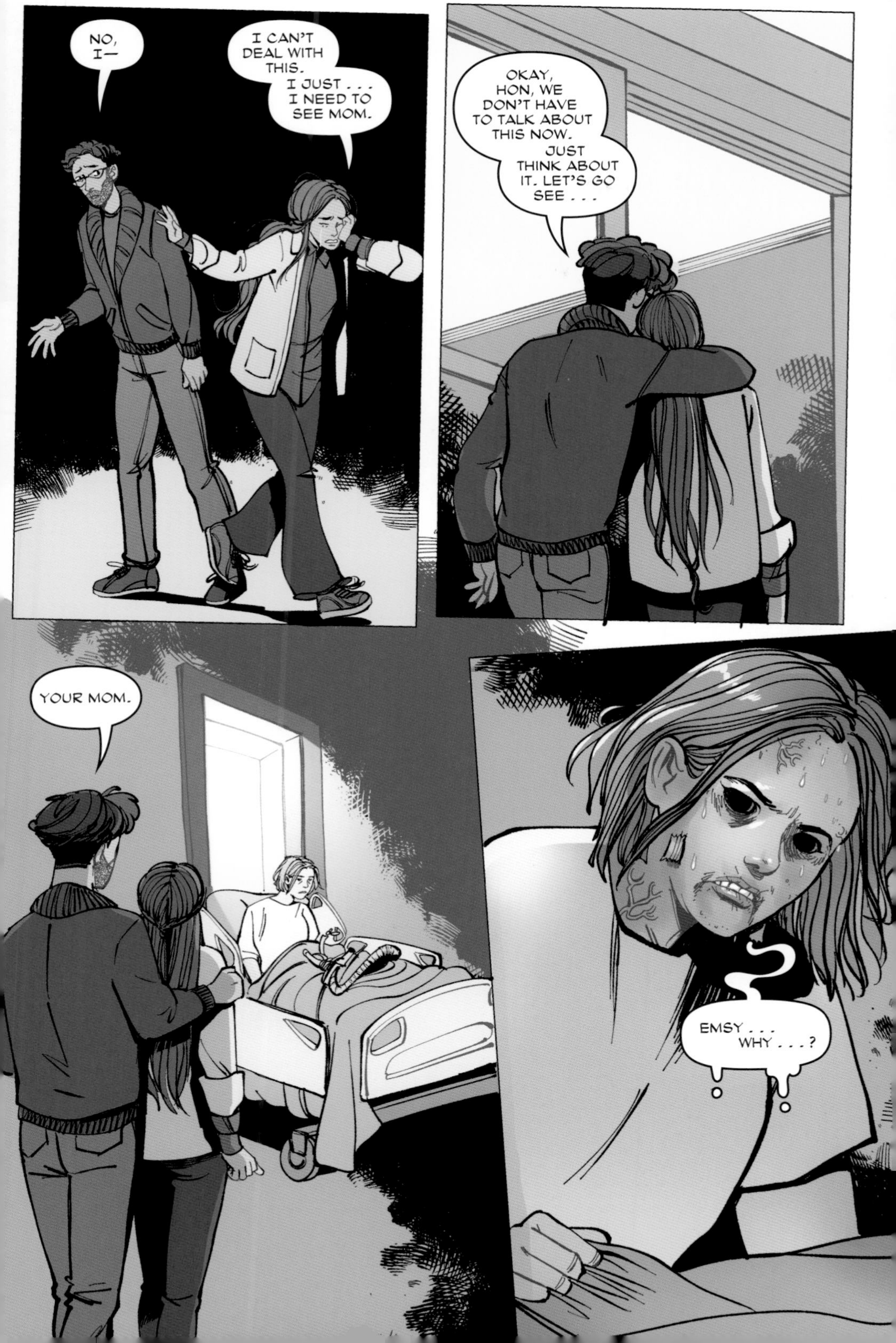
NO, I—
I CAN'T DEAL WITH THIS. I JUST . . . I NEED TO SEE MOM.
OKAY, HON, WE DON'T HAVE TO TALK ABOUT THIS NOW. JUST THINK ABOUT IT. LET'S GO SEE . . .
YOUR MOM.
EMSY . . . WHY . . . ?

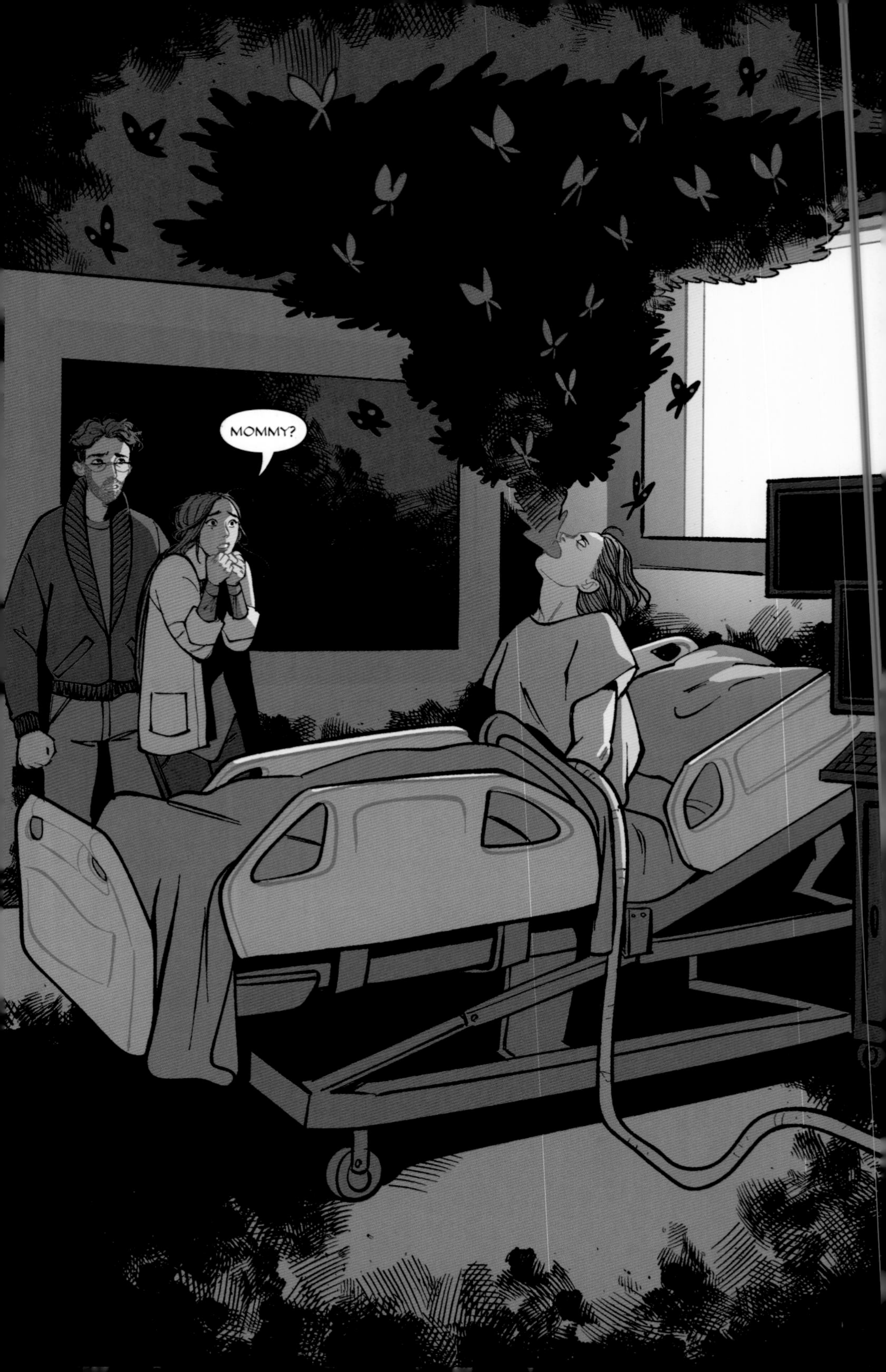
MOMMY?

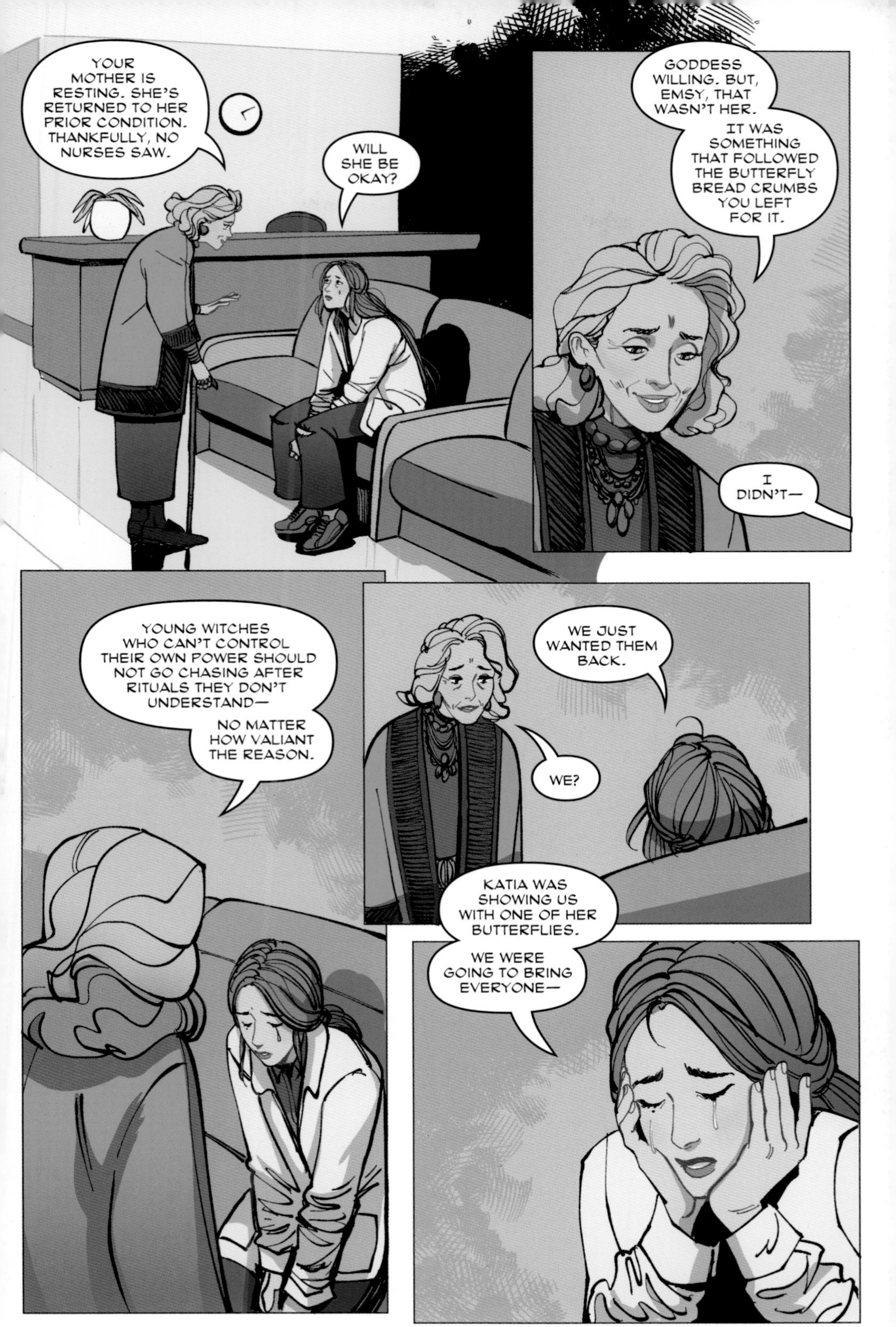
YOUR MOTHER IS RESTING. SHE'S RETURNED TO HER PRIOR CONDITION. THANKFULLY, NO NURSES SAW.
WILL SHE BE OKAY?
GODDESS WILLING. BUT, EMSY, THAT WASN'T HER.
IT WAS SOMETHING THAT FOLLOWED THE BUTTERFLY BREAD CRUMBS YOU LEFT FOR IT.
I DIDN'T—
YOUNG WITCHES WHO CAN'T CONTROL THEIR OWN POWER SHOULD NOT GO CHASING AFTER RITUALS THEY DON'T UNDERSTAND—
NO MATTER HOW VALIANT THE REASON.
WE JUST WANTED THEM BACK.
WE?
KATIA WAS SHOWING US WITH ONE OF HER BUTTERFLIES.
WE WERE GOING TO BRING EVERYONE—

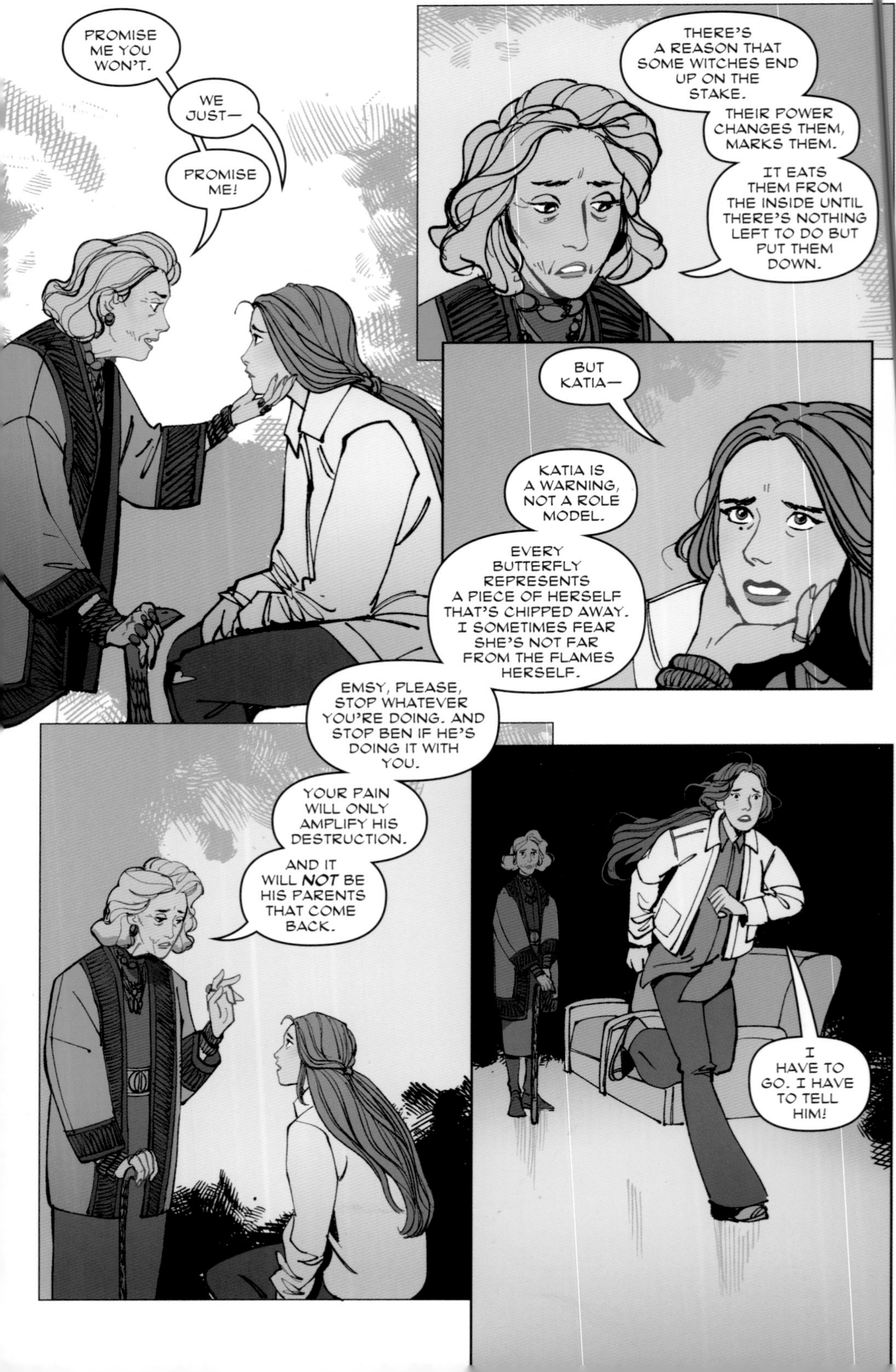
PROMISE ME YOU WON'T.
WE JUST—
PROMISE ME!
THERE'S A REASON THAT SOME WITCHES END UP ON THE STAKE.
THEIR POWER CHANGES THEM, MARKS THEM.
IT EATS THEM FROM THE INSIDE UNTIL THERE'S NOTHING LEFT TO DO BUT PUT THEM DOWN.
BUT KATIA—
KATIA IS A WARNING, NOT A ROLE MODEL.
EVERY BUTTERFLY REPRESENTS A PIECE OF HERSELF THAT'S CHIPPED AWAY. I SOMETIMES FEAR SHE'S NOT FAR FROM THE FLAMES HERSELF.
EMSY, PLEASE, STOP WHATEVER YOU'RE DOING. AND STOP BEN IF HE'S DOING IT WITH YOU.
YOUR PAIN WILL ONLY AMPLIFY HIS DESTRUCTION.
AND IT WILL NOT BE HIS PARENTS THAT COME BACK.
I HAVE TO GO. I HAVE TO TELL HIM!

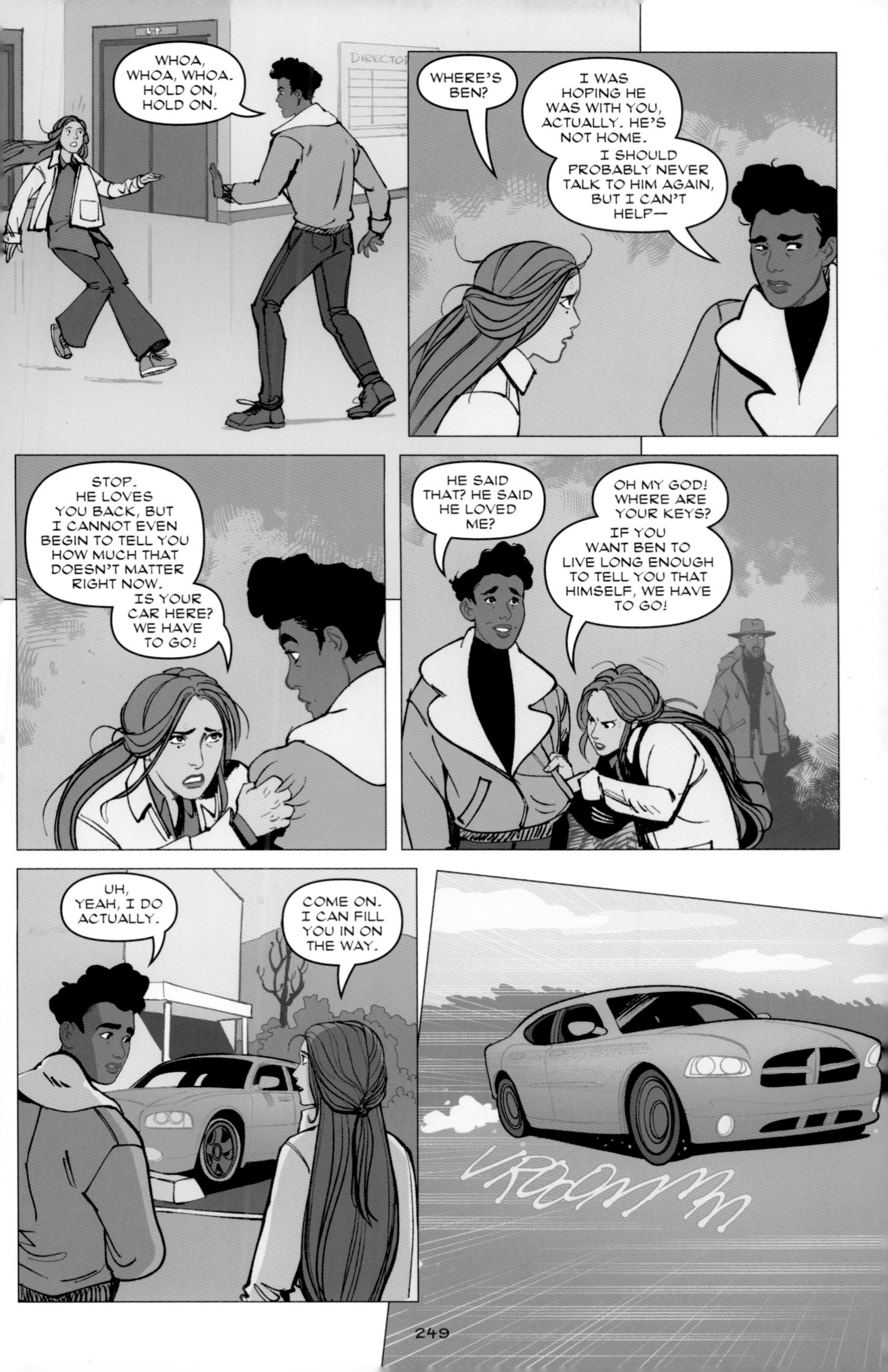

WHOA, WHOA, WHOA. HOLD ON, HOLD ON.
DIRECTOR
WHERE'S BEN?
I WAS HOPING HE WAS WITH YOU, ACTUALLY. HE'S NOT HOME.
I SHOULD PROBABLY NEVER TALK TO HIM AGAIN, BUT I CAN'T HELP—
STOP. HE LOVES YOU BACK, BUT I CANNOT EVEN BEGIN TO TELL YOU HOW MUCH THAT DOESN'T MATTER RIGHT NOW.
IS YOUR CAR HERE? WE HAVE TO GO!
HE SAID THAT? HE SAID HE LOVED ME?
OH MY GOD! WHERE ARE YOUR KEYS?
IF YOU WANT BEN TO LIVE LONG ENOUGH TO TELL YOU THAT HIMSELF, WE HAVE TO GO!
UH, YEAH, I DO ACTUALLY.
COME ON. I CAN FILL YOU IN ON THE WAY.
VROOMMM

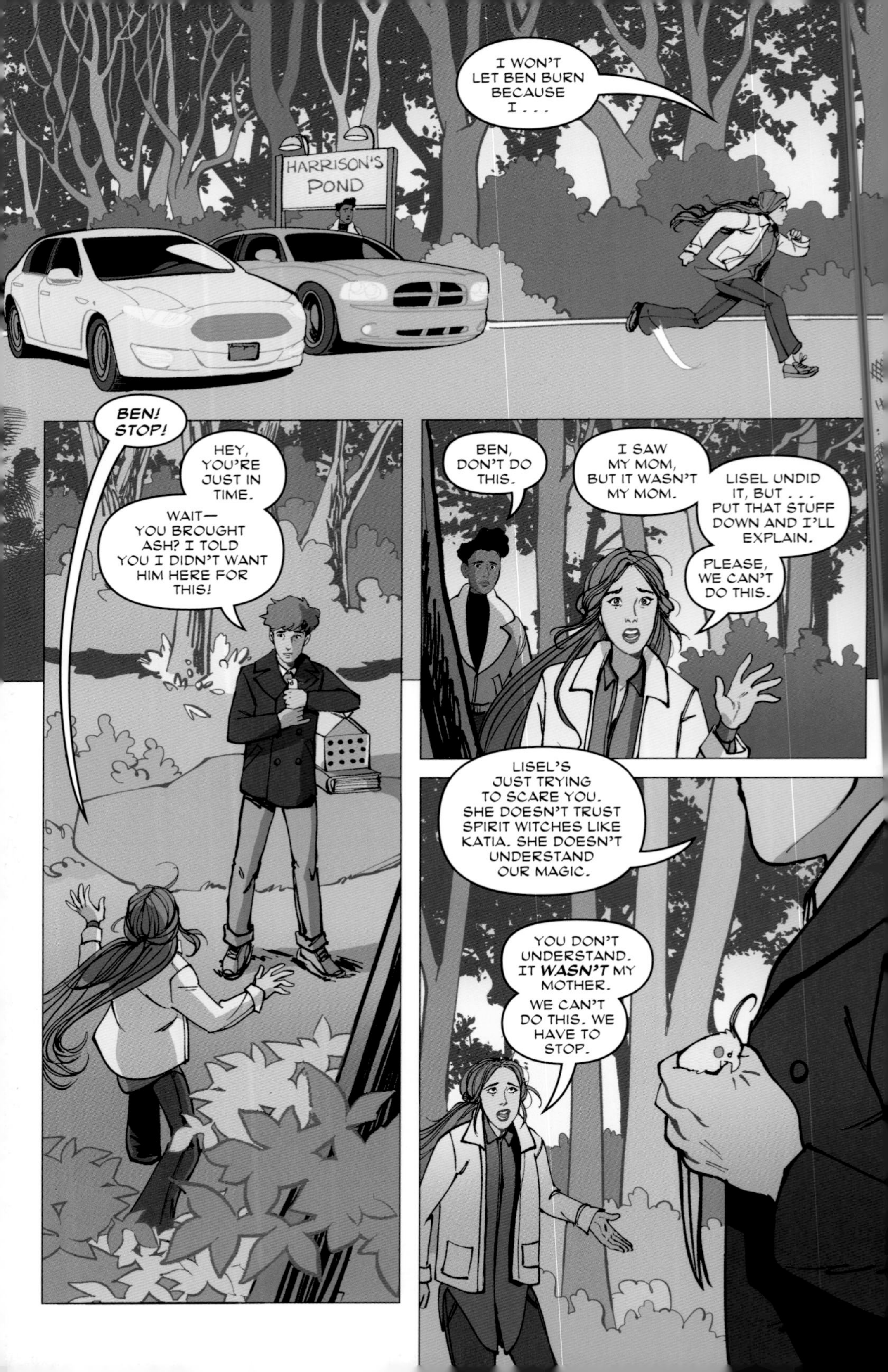
I WON'T LET BEN BURN BECAUSE I . . .
HARRISON'S POND
BEN! STOP!
HEY, YOU'RE JUST IN TIME.
WAIT— YOU BROUGHT ASH? I TOLD YOU I DIDN'T WANT HIM HERE FOR THIS!
BEN, DON'T DO THIS.
I SAW MY MOM, BUT IT WASN'T MY MOM.
LISEL UNDID IT, BUT . . . PUT THAT STUFF DOWN AND I'LL EXPLAIN.
PLEASE, WE CAN'T DO THIS.
LISEL'S JUST TRYING TO SCARE YOU. SHE DOESN'T TRUST SPIRIT WITCHES LIKE KATIA. SHE DOESN'T UNDERSTAND OUR MAGIC.
YOU DON'T UNDERSTAND. IT WASN'T MY MOTHER.
WE CAN'T DO THIS. WE HAVE TO STOP.

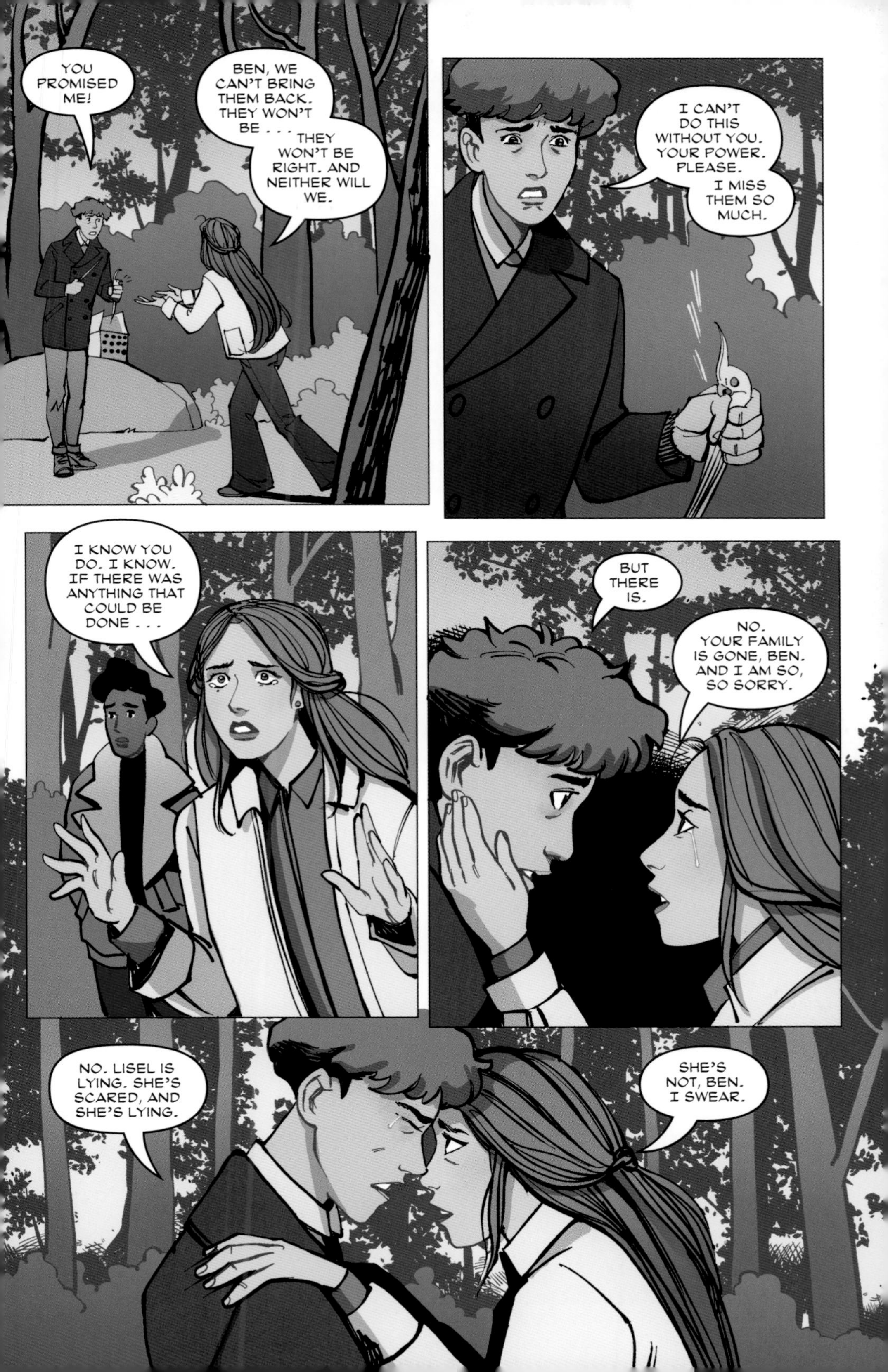
YOU PROMISED ME!
BEN, WE CAN'T BRING THEM BACK. THEY WON'T BE . . .
THEY WON'T BE RIGHT. AND NEITHER WILL WE.
I CAN'T DO THIS WITHOUT YOU. YOUR POWER. PLEASE.
I MISS THEM SO MUCH.
I KNOW YOU DO. I KNOW. IF THERE WAS ANYTHING THAT COULD BE DONE . . .
BUT THERE IS.
NO. YOUR FAMILY IS GONE, BEN. AND I AM SO, SO SORRY.
NO. LISEL IS LYING. SHE'S SCARED, AND SHE'S LYING.
SHE'S NOT, BEN. I SWEAR.

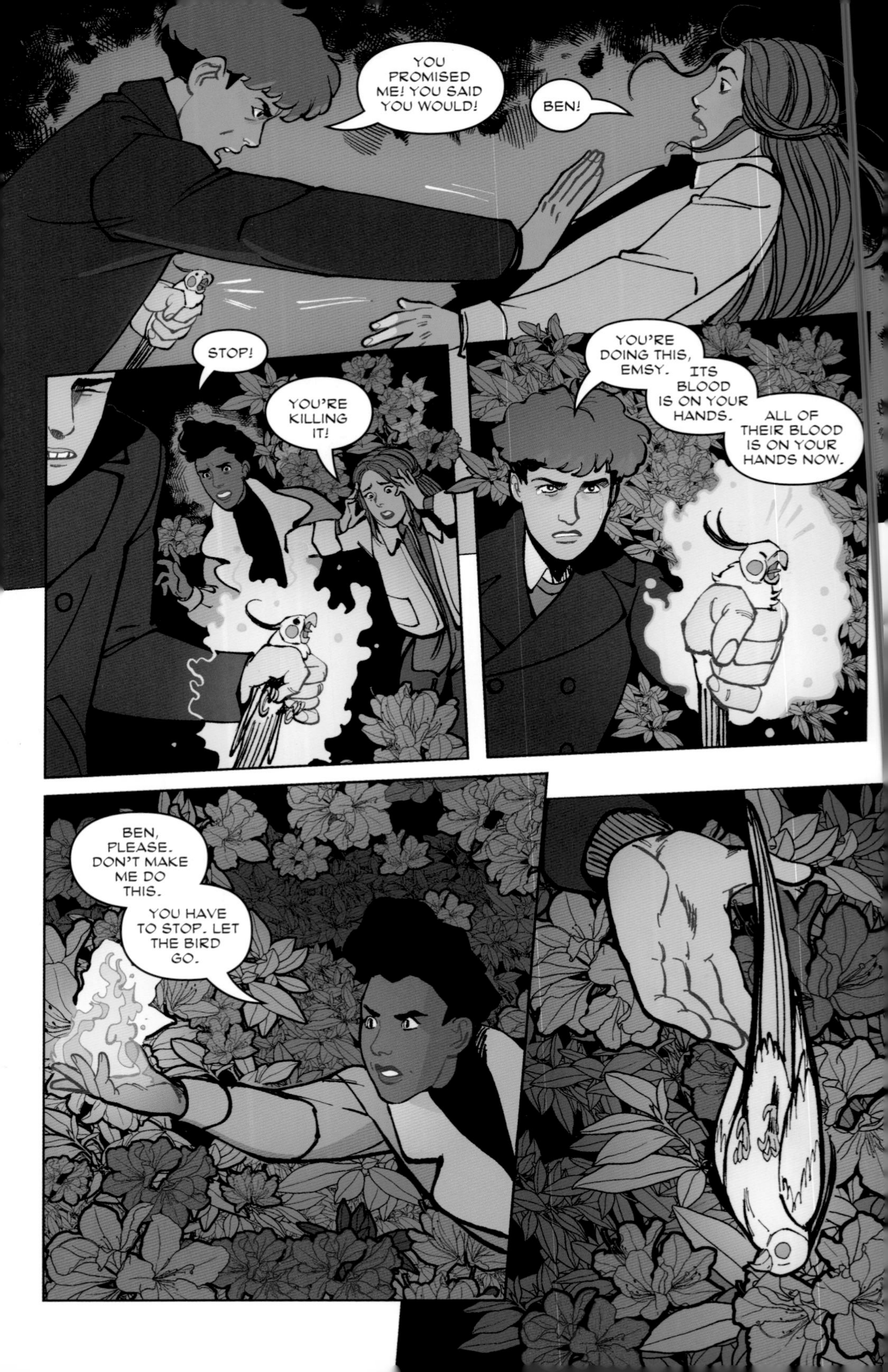
YOU PROMISED ME! YOU SAID YOU WOULD!
BEN!
STOP!
YOU'RE KILLING IT!
YOU'RE DOING THIS, EMSY.
ITS BLOOD IS ON YOUR HANDS.
ALL OF THEIR BLOOD IS ON YOUR HANDS NOW.
BEN, PLEASE. DON'T MAKE ME DO THIS.
YOU HAVE TO STOP. LET THE BIRD GO.

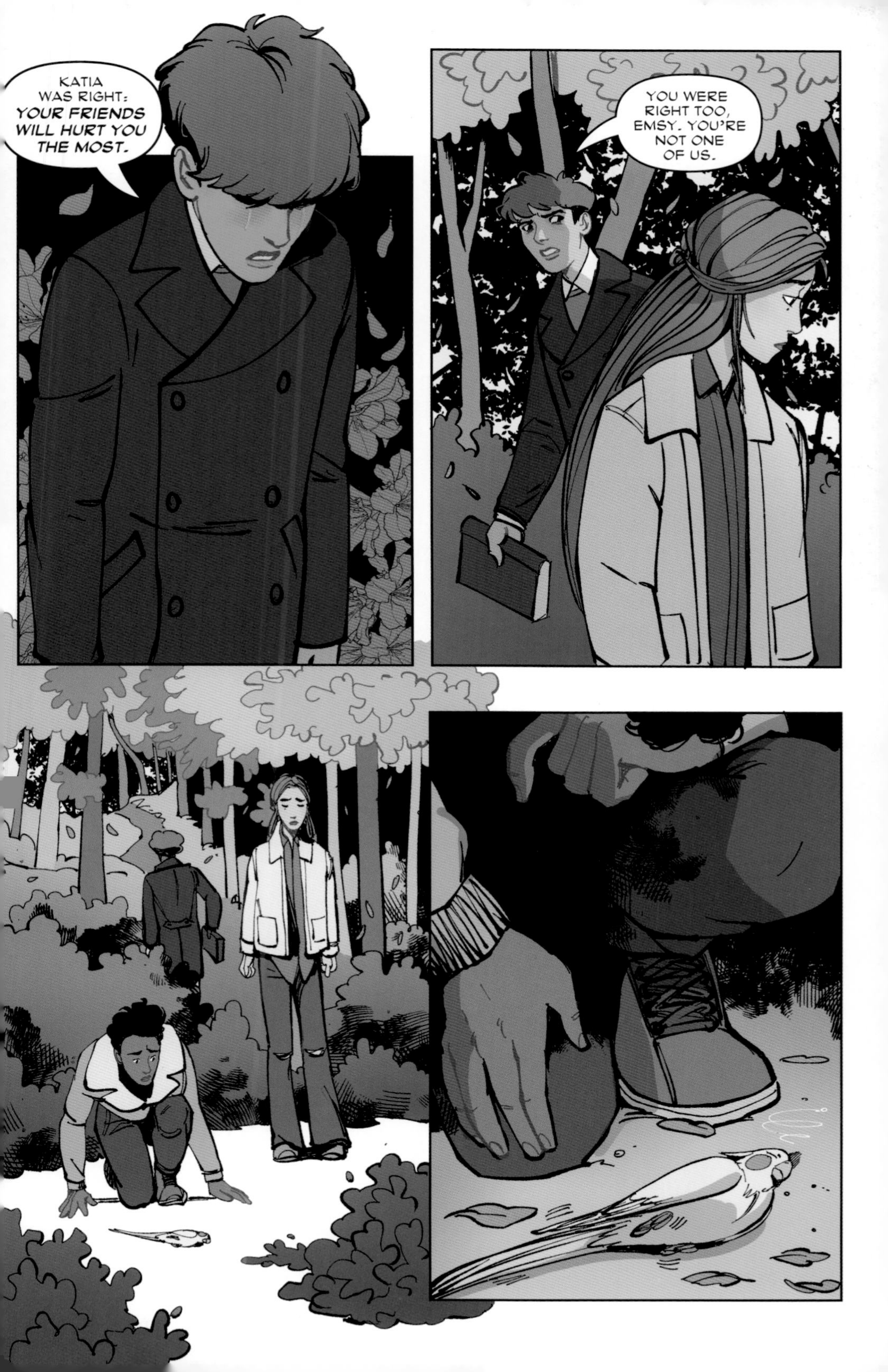
KATIA WAS RIGHT: *YOUR FRIENDS WILL HURT YOU THE MOST.*
YOU WERE RIGHT TOO, EMSY. YOU'RE NOT ONE OF US.

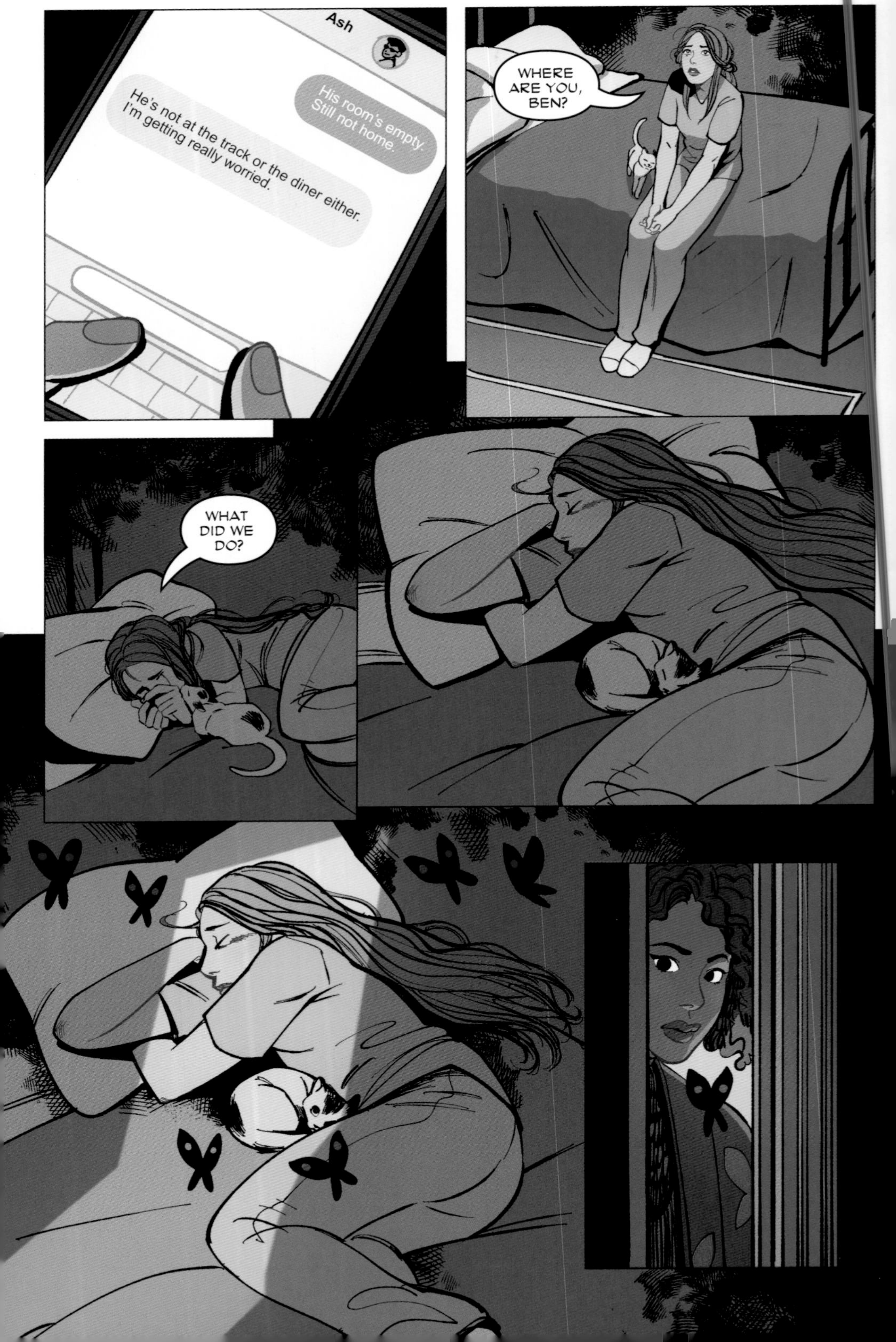

Ash
His room's empty. Still not home.
He's not at the track or the diner either. I'm getting really worried.
WHERE ARE YOU, BEN?
WHAT DID WE DO?

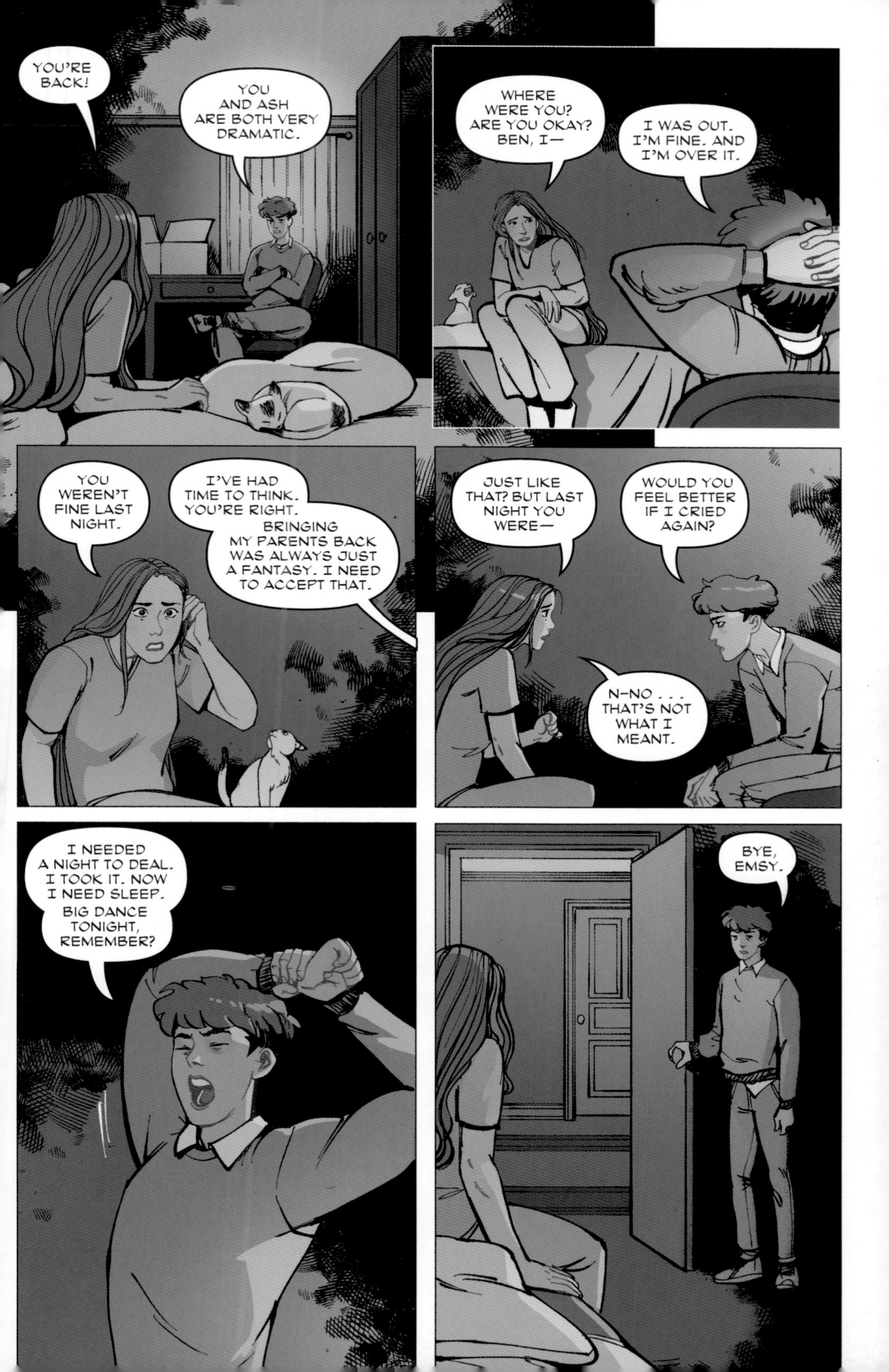
YOU'RE BACK!
YOU AND ASH ARE BOTH VERY DRAMATIC.
WHERE WERE YOU? ARE YOU OKAY? BEN, I—
I WAS OUT. I'M FINE. AND I'M OVER IT.
YOU WEREN'T FINE LAST NIGHT.
I'VE HAD TIME TO THINK. YOU'RE RIGHT.
BRINGING MY PARENTS BACK WAS ALWAYS JUST A FANTASY. I NEED TO ACCEPT THAT.
JUST LIKE THAT? BUT LAST NIGHT YOU WERE—
WOULD YOU FEEL BETTER IF I CRIED AGAIN?
N–NO . . . THAT'S NOT WHAT I MEANT.
I NEEDED A NIGHT TO DEAL. I TOOK IT. NOW I NEED SLEEP.
BIG DANCE TONIGHT, REMEMBER?
BYE, EMSY.

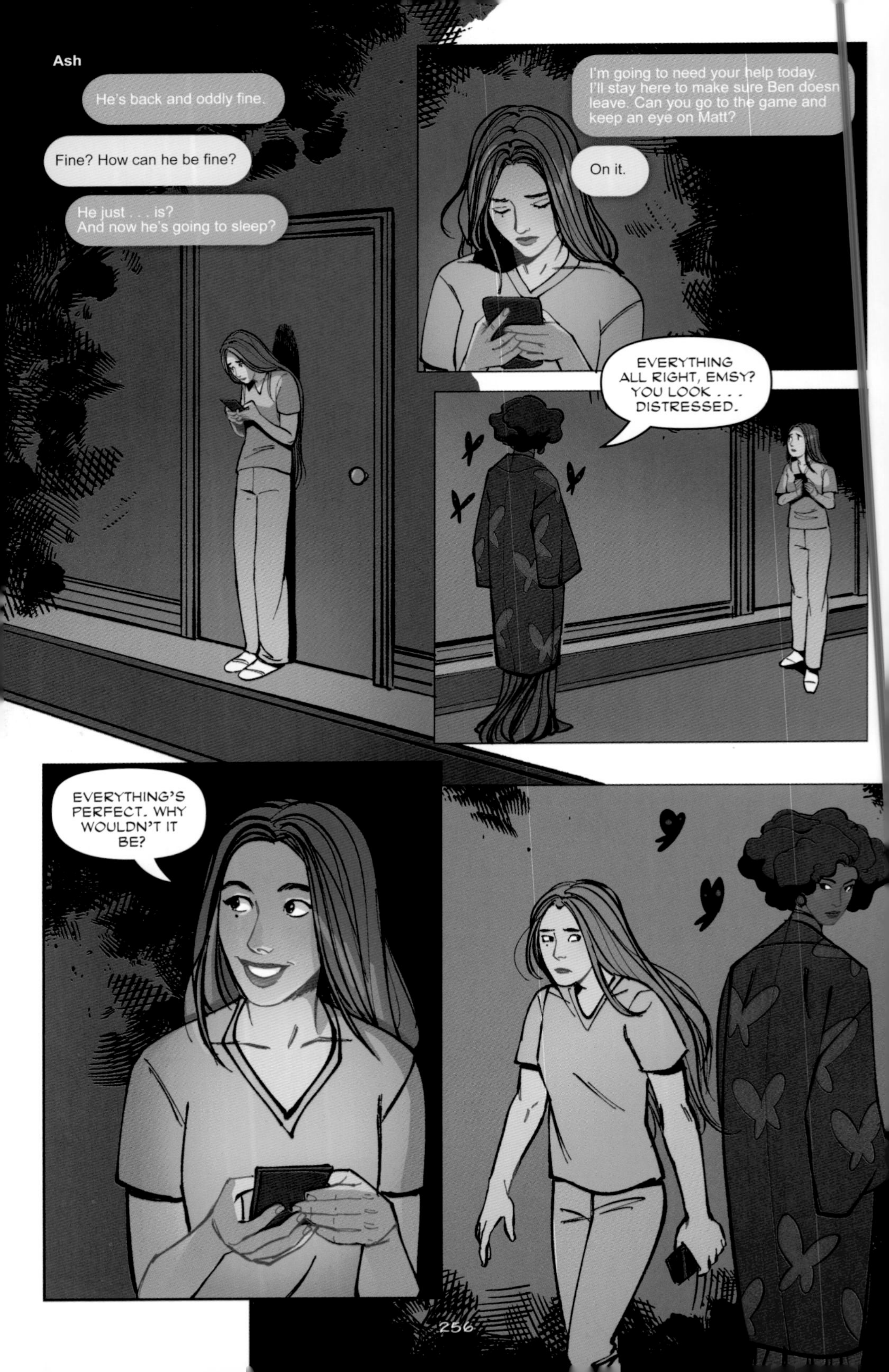
Ash
He's back and oddly fine.
Fine? How can he be fine?
He just . . . is?
And now he's going to sleep?
I'm going to need your help today. I'll stay here to make sure Ben doesn leave. Can you go to the game and keep an eye on Matt?
On it.
EVERYTHING ALL RIGHT, EMSY? YOU LOOK . . . DISTRESSED.
EVERYTHING'S PERFECT. WHY WOULDN'T IT BE?

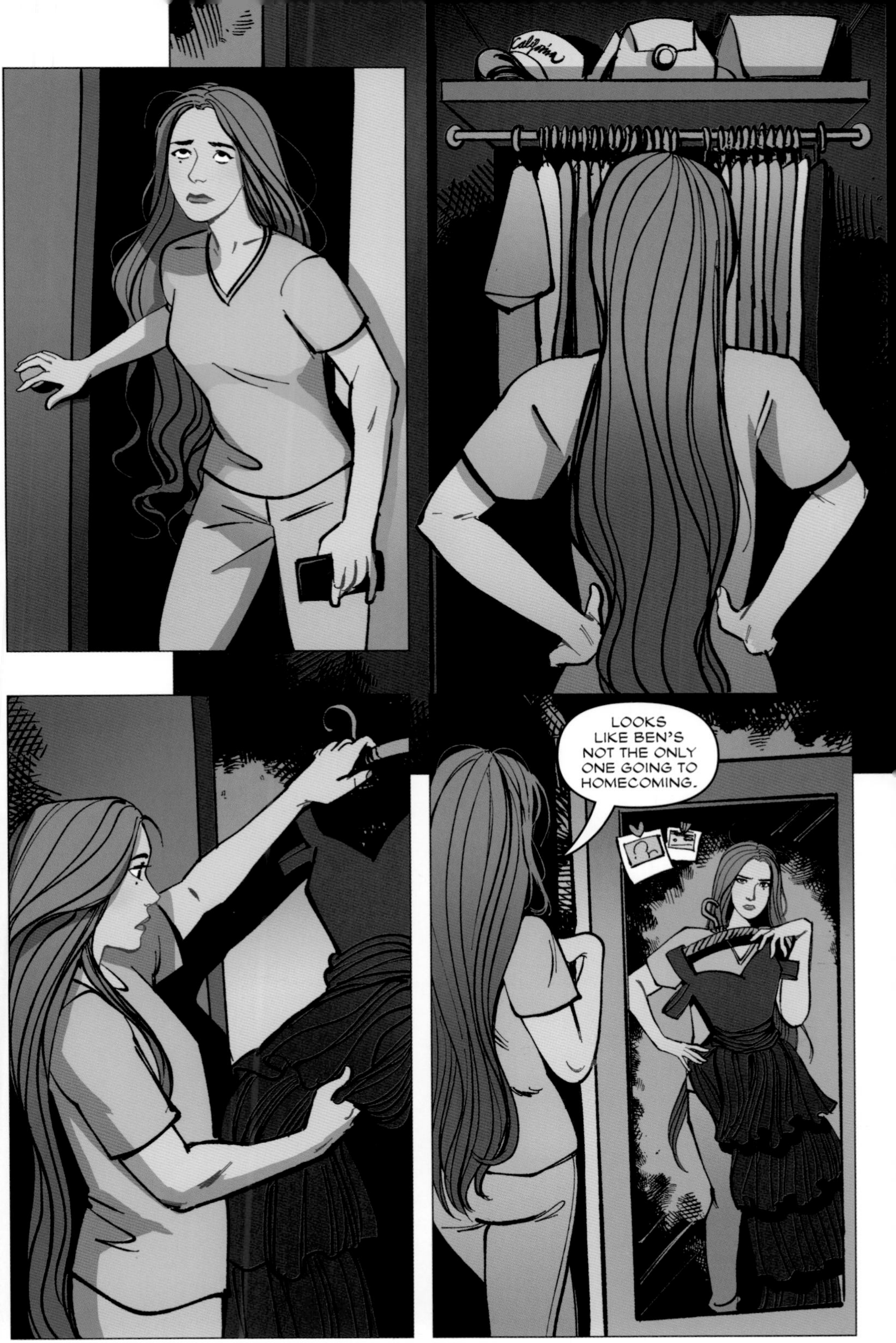
California
LOOKS LIKE BEN'S NOT THE ONLY ONE GOING TO HOMECOMING.

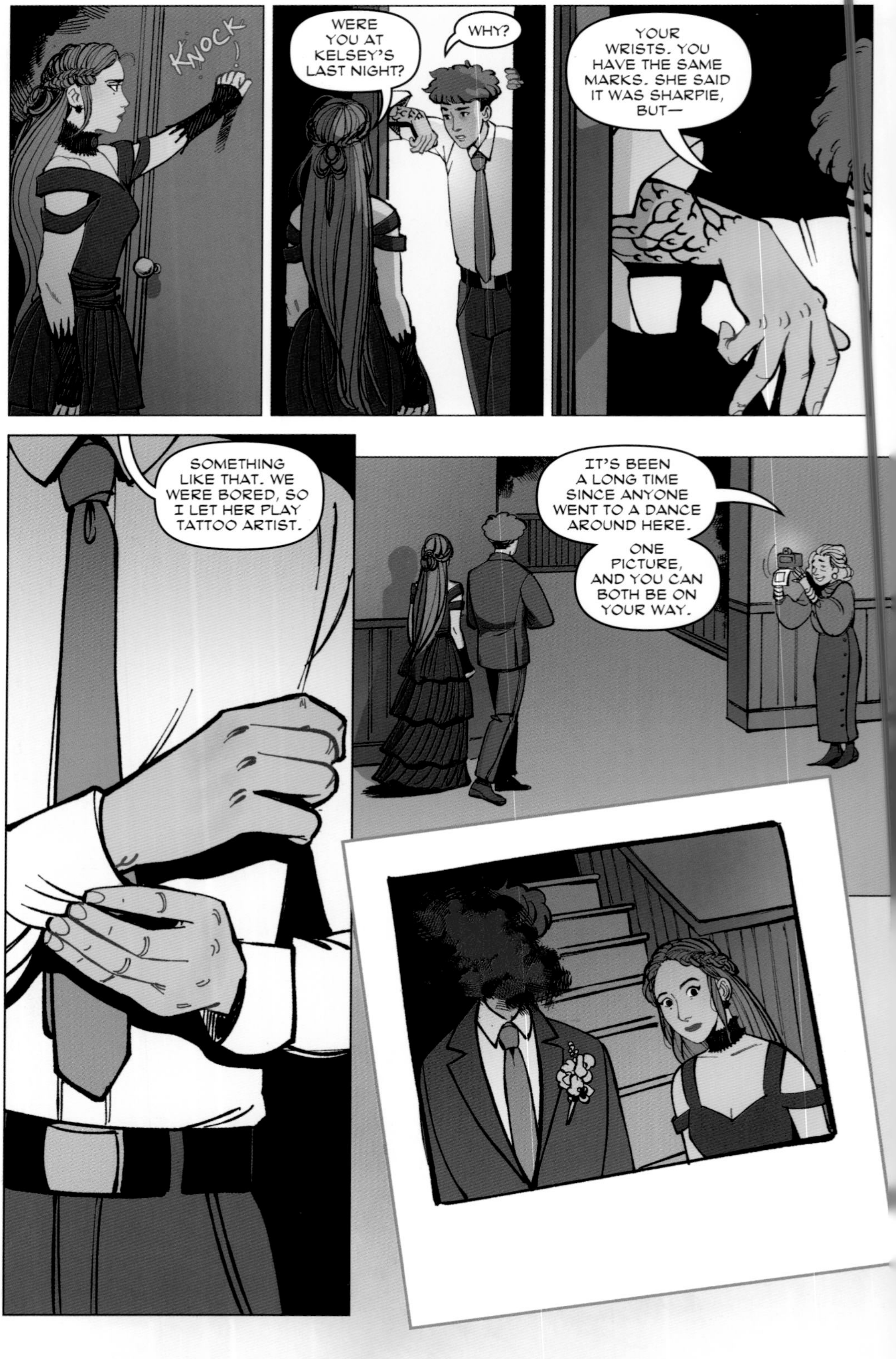
KNOCK
WERE YOU AT KELSEY'S LAST NIGHT?
WHY?
YOUR WRISTS. YOU HAVE THE SAME MARKS. SHE SAID IT WAS SHARPIE, BUT—
SOMETHING LIKE THAT. WE WERE BORED, SO I LET HER PLAY TATTOO ARTIST.
IT'S BEEN A LONG TIME SINCE ANYONE WENT TO A DANCE AROUND HERE.
ONE PICTURE, AND YOU CAN BOTH BE ON YOUR WAY.

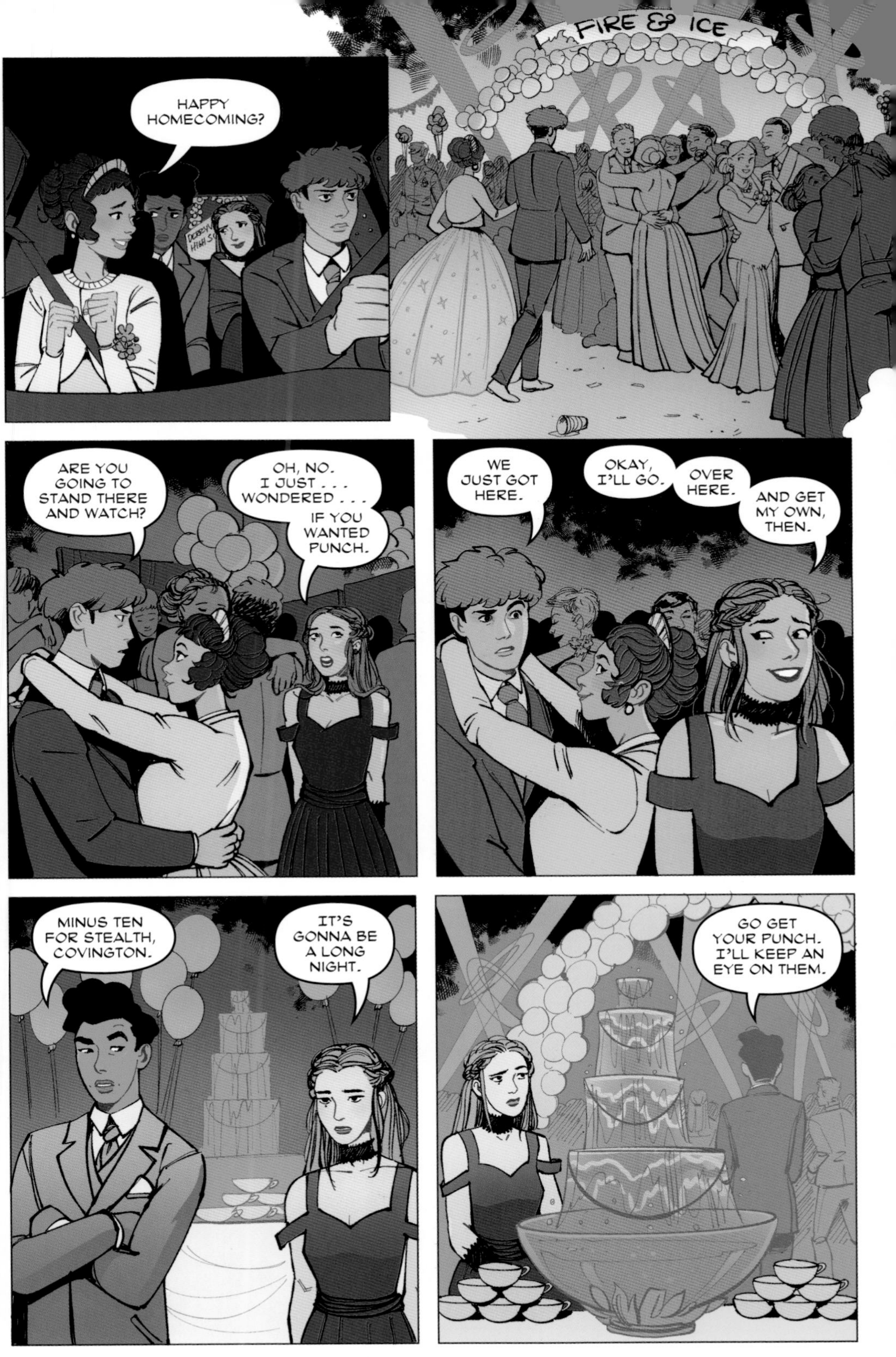
HAPPY HOMECOMING?
DERBYVILLE HIGH SC
FIRE & ICE
ARE YOU GOING TO STAND THERE AND WATCH?
OH, NO. I JUST . . . WONDERED . . .
IF YOU WANTED PUNCH.
WE JUST GOT HERE.
OKAY, I'LL GO.
OVER HERE.
AND GET MY OWN, THEN.
MINUS TEN FOR STEALTH, COVINGTON.
IT'S GONNA BE A LONG NIGHT.
GO GET YOUR PUNCH. I'LL KEEP AN EYE ON THEM.

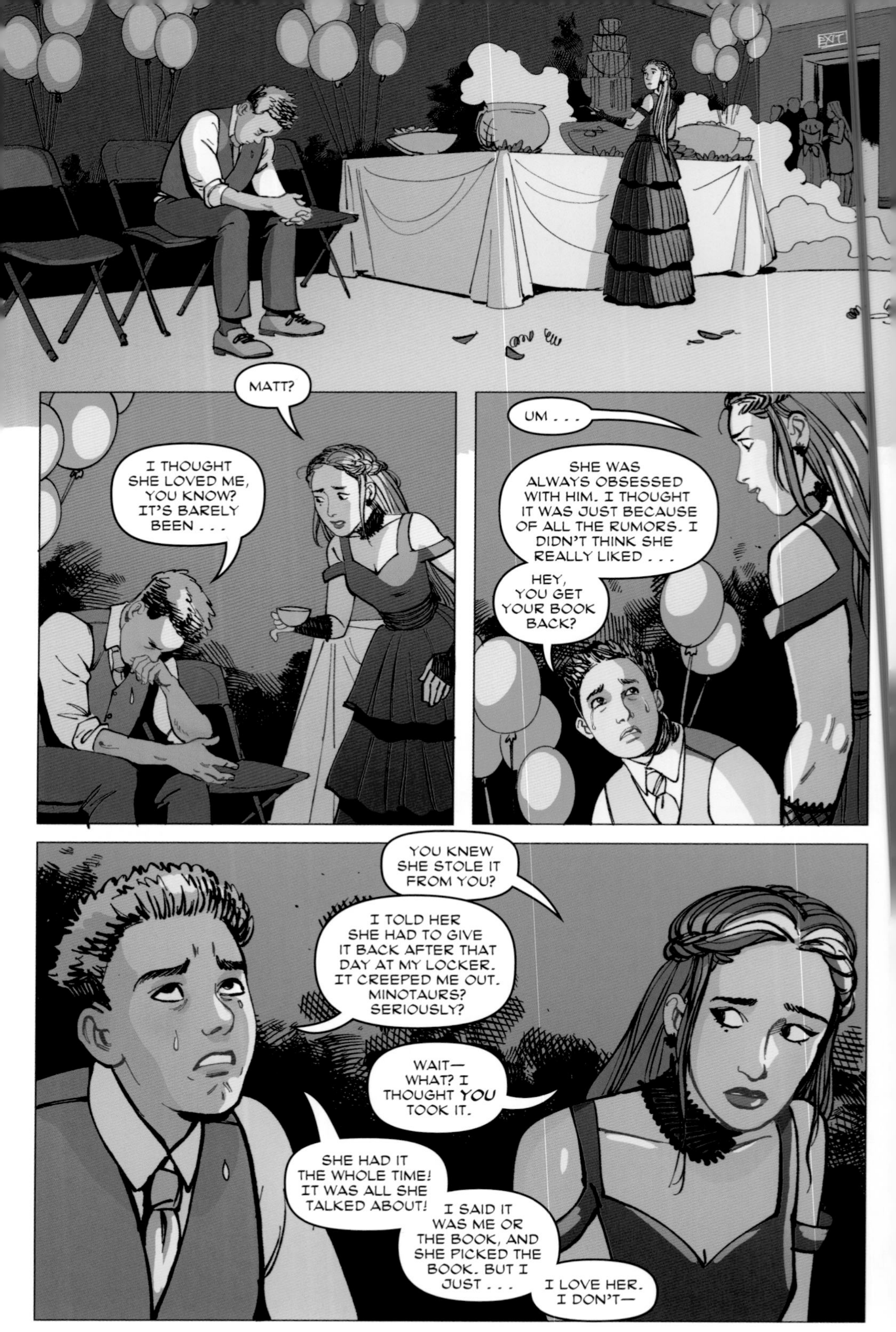
MATT?
I THOUGHT SHE LOVED ME, YOU KNOW? IT'S BARELY BEEN . . .
UM . . .
SHE WAS ALWAYS OBSESSED WITH HIM. I THOUGHT IT WAS JUST BECAUSE OF ALL THE RUMORS. I DIDN'T THINK SHE REALLY LIKED . . .
HEY, YOU GET YOUR BOOK BACK?
YOU KNEW SHE STOLE IT FROM YOU?
I TOLD HER SHE HAD TO GIVE IT BACK AFTER THAT DAY AT MY LOCKER. IT CREEPED ME OUT. MINOTAURS? SERIOUSLY?
WAIT— WHAT? I THOUGHT *YOU* TOOK IT.
SHE HAD IT THE WHOLE TIME! IT WAS ALL SHE TALKED ABOUT!
I SAID IT WAS ME OR THE BOOK, AND SHE PICKED THE BOOK. BUT I JUST . . .
I LOVE HER. I DON'T—

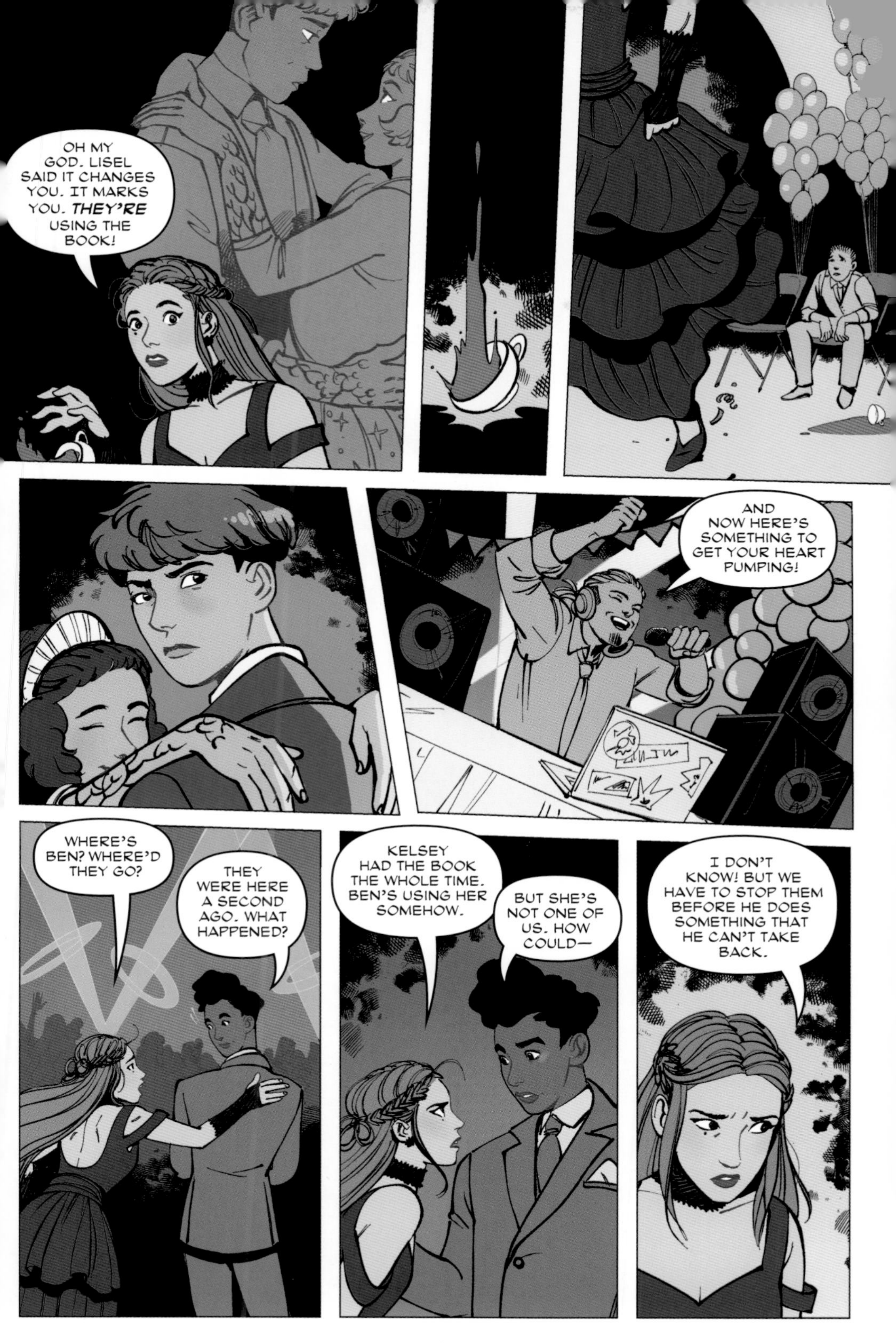
OH MY GOD. LISEL SAID IT CHANGES YOU. IT MARKS YOU. *THEY'RE* USING THE BOOK!
AND NOW HERE'S SOMETHING TO GET YOUR HEART PUMPING!
WHERE'S BEN? WHERE'D THEY GO?
THEY WERE HERE A SECOND AGO. WHAT HAPPENED?
KELSEY HAD THE BOOK THE WHOLE TIME. BEN'S USING HER SOMEHOW.
BUT SHE'S NOT ONE OF US. HOW COULD—
I DON'T KNOW! BUT WE HAVE TO STOP THEM BEFORE HE DOES SOMETHING THAT HE CAN'T TAKE BACK.

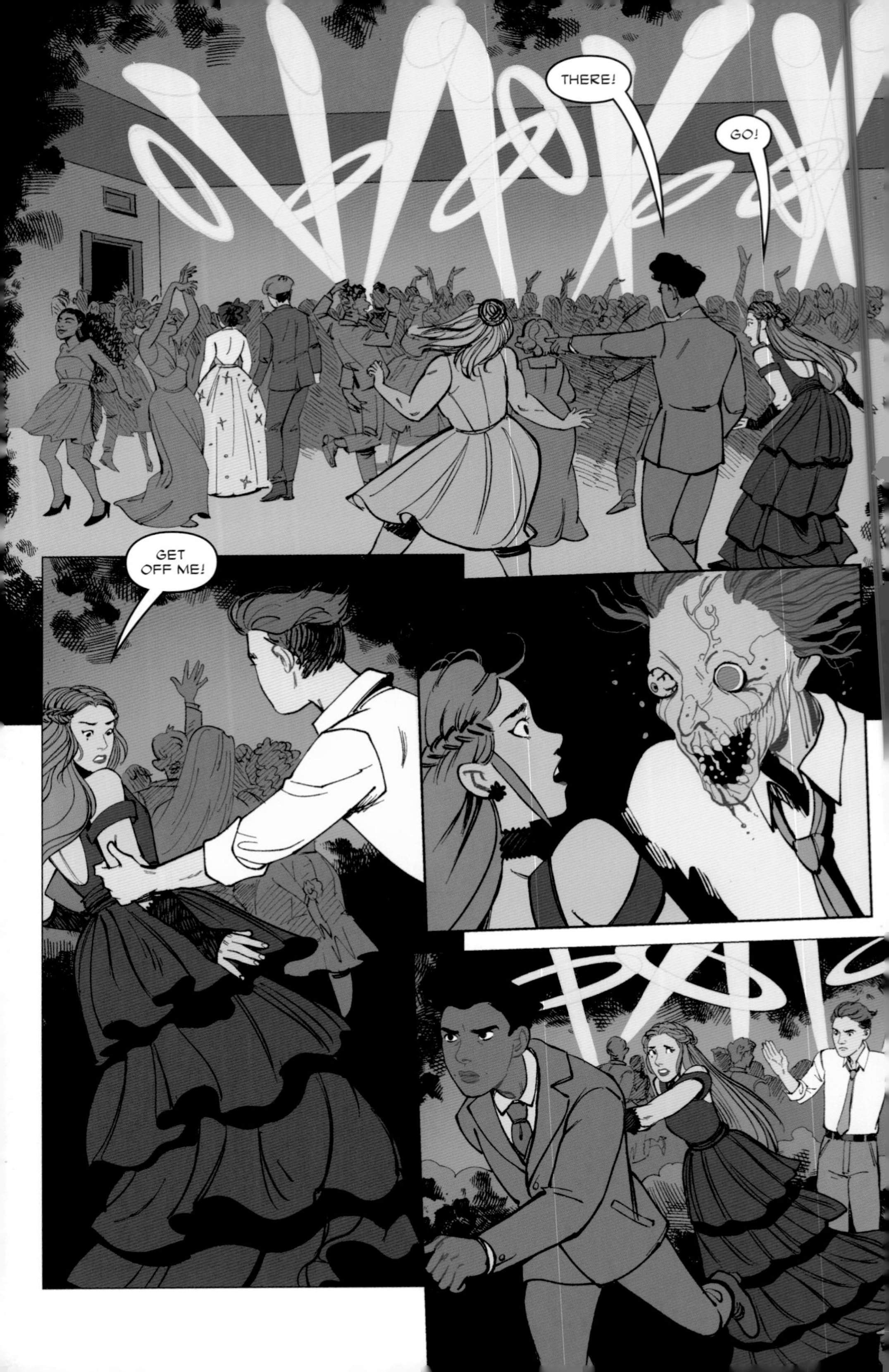
THERE!
GO!
GET OFF ME!

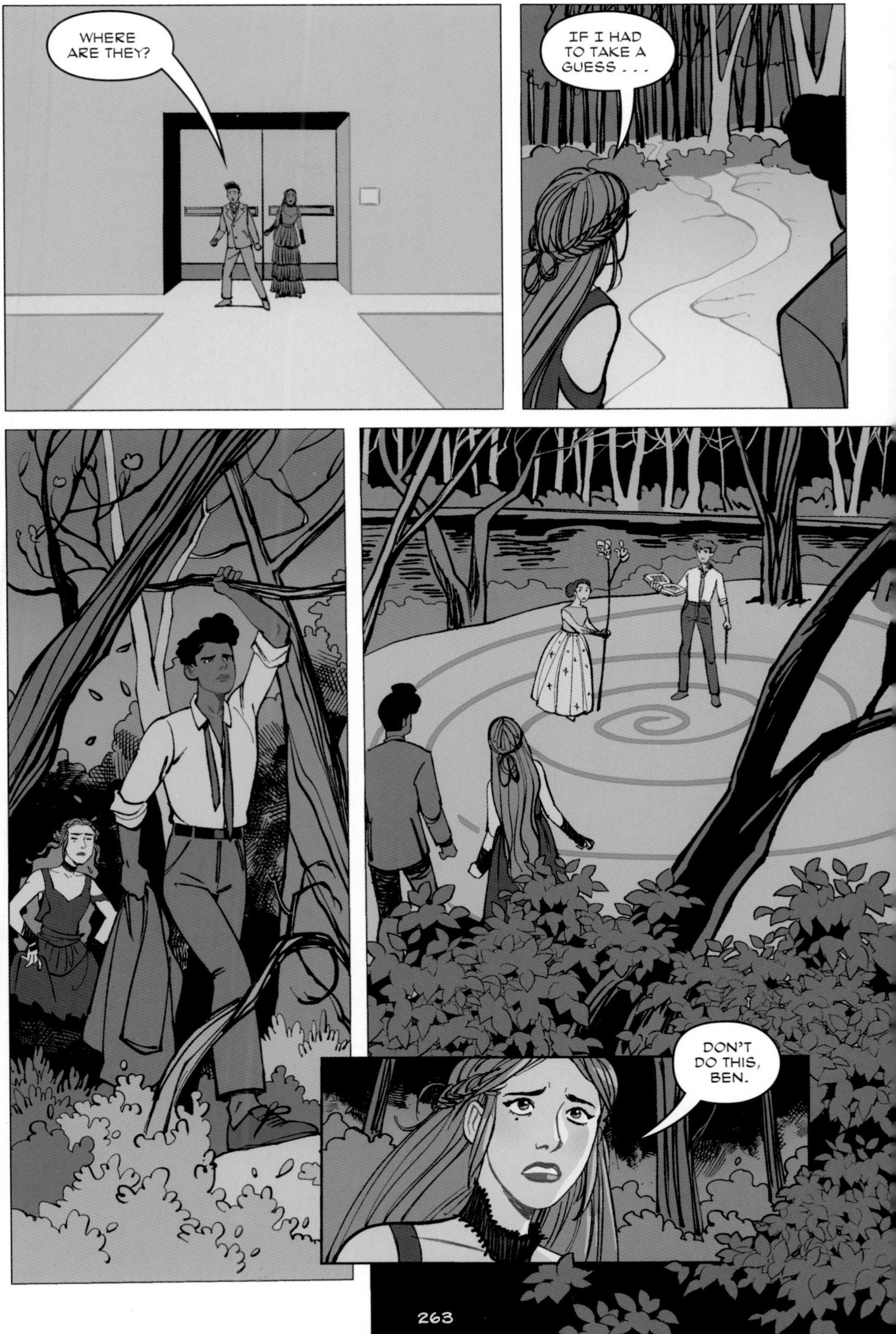
WHERE ARE THEY?
IF I HAD TO TAKE A GUESS . . .
DON'T DO THIS, BEN.

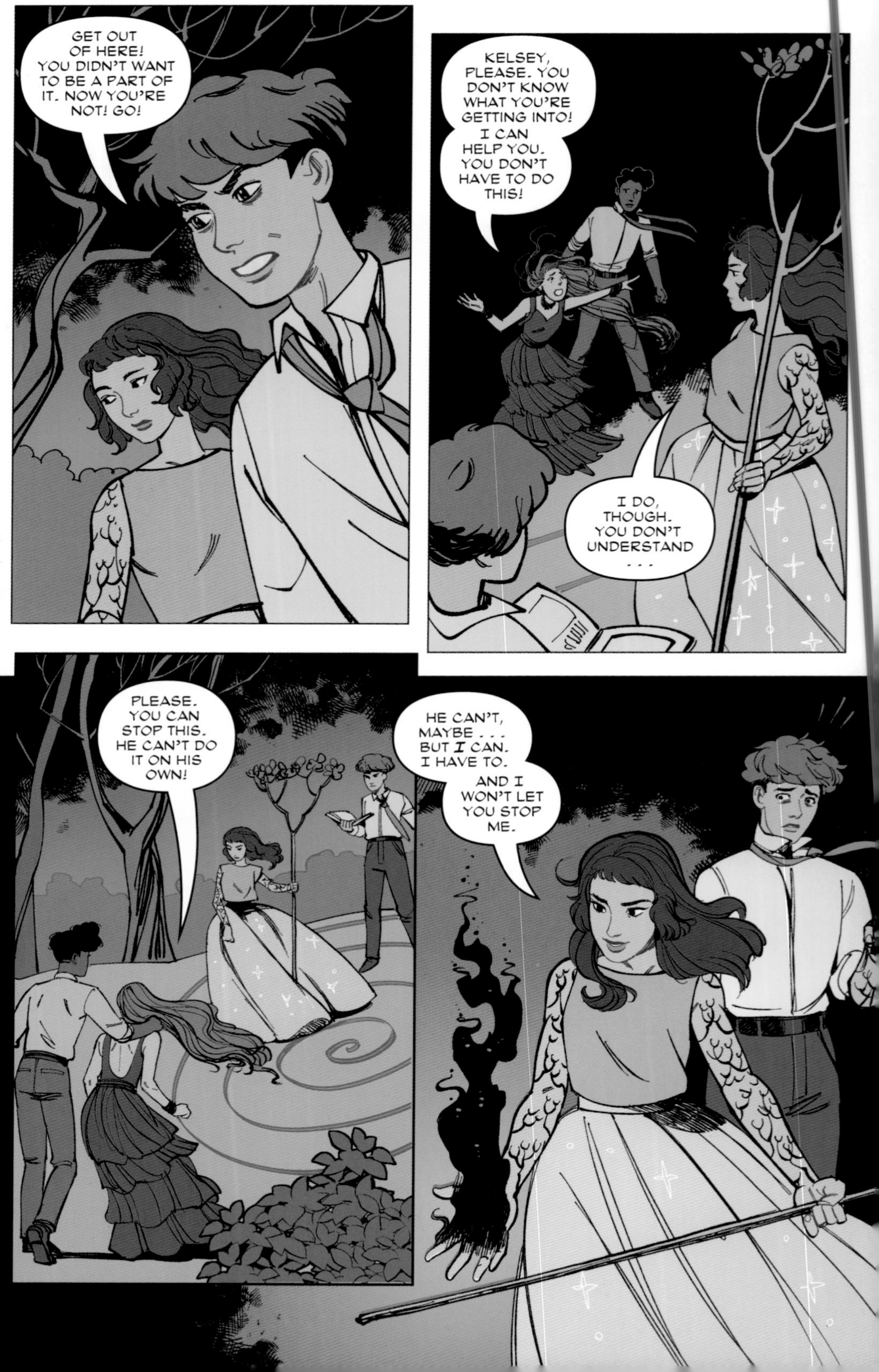
GET OUT OF HERE! YOU DIDN'T WANT TO BE A PART OF IT. NOW YOU'RE NOT! GO!
KELSEY, PLEASE. YOU DON'T KNOW WHAT YOU'RE GETTING INTO!
I CAN HELP YOU. YOU DON'T HAVE TO DO THIS!
I DO, THOUGH. YOU DON'T UNDERSTAND . . .
PLEASE. YOU CAN STOP THIS. HE CAN'T DO IT ON HIS OWN!
HE CAN'T, MAYBE . . . BUT *I* CAN. I HAVE TO.
AND I WON'T LET YOU STOP ME.

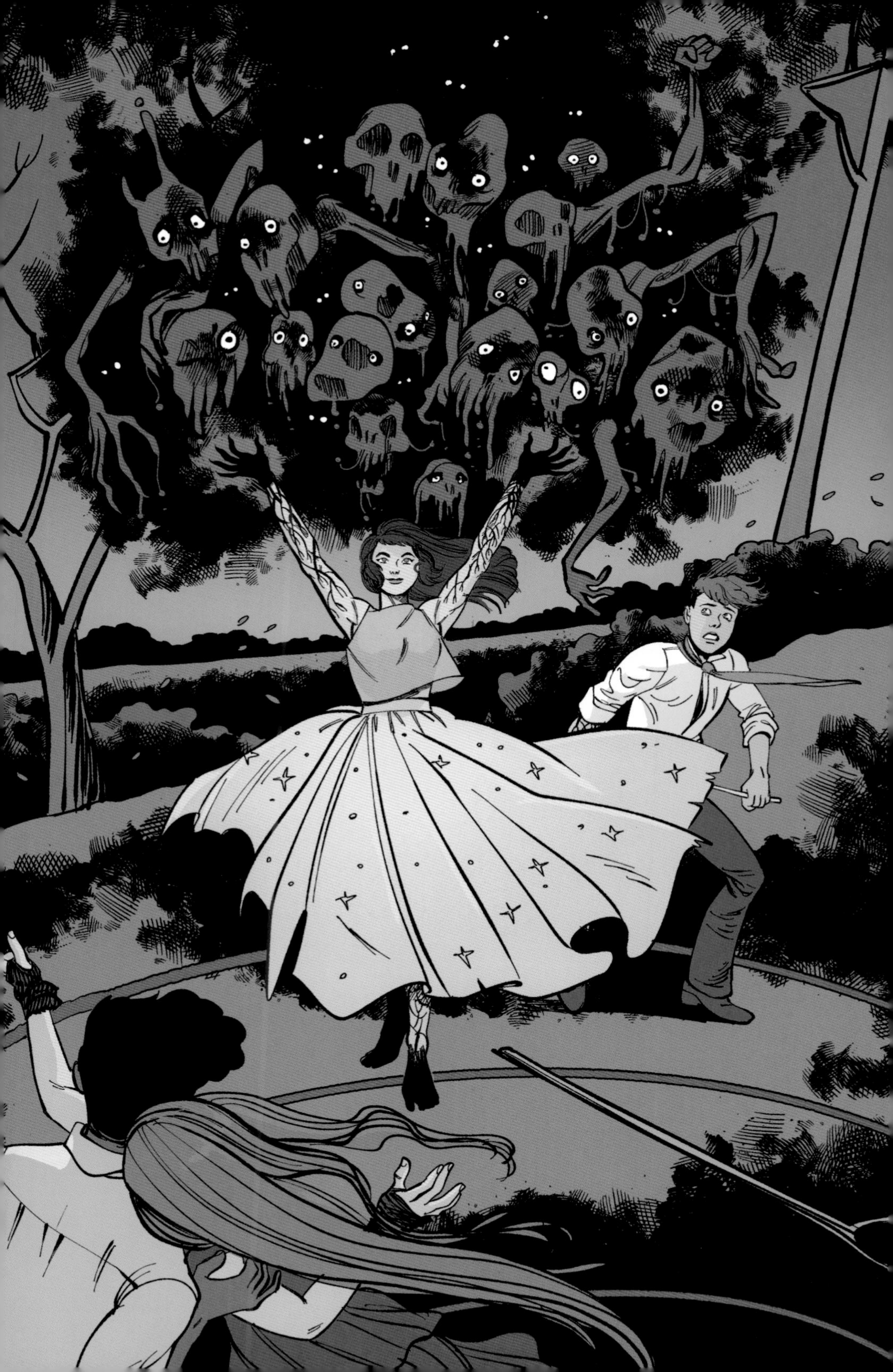

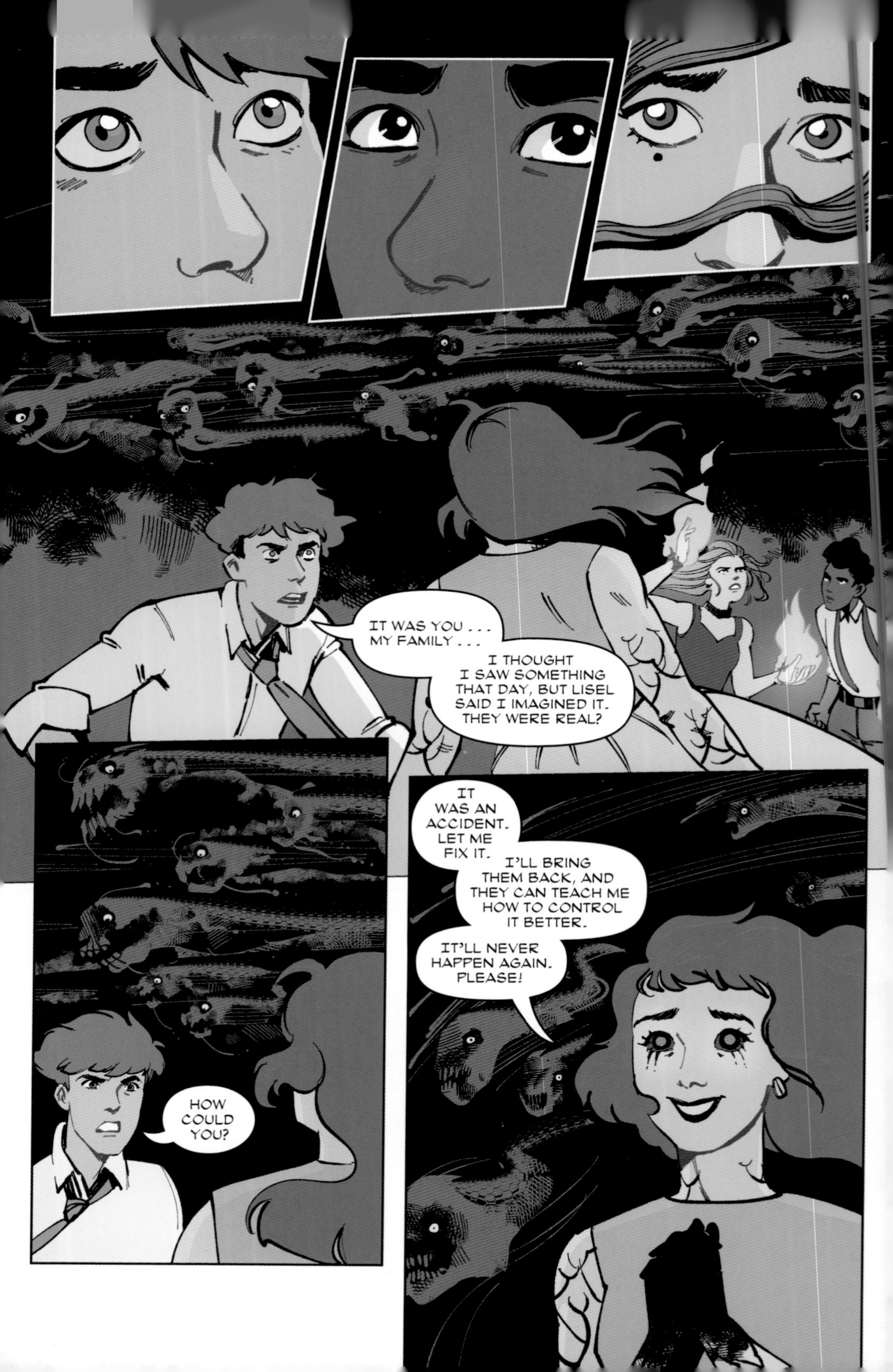
IT WAS YOU . . . MY FAMILY . . .
I THOUGHT I SAW SOMETHING THAT DAY, BUT LISEL SAID I IMAGINED IT. THEY WERE REAL?
HOW COULD YOU?
IT WAS AN ACCIDENT. LET ME FIX IT.
I'LL BRING THEM BACK, AND THEY CAN TEACH ME HOW TO CONTROL IT BETTER.
IT'LL NEVER HAPPEN AGAIN. PLEASE!

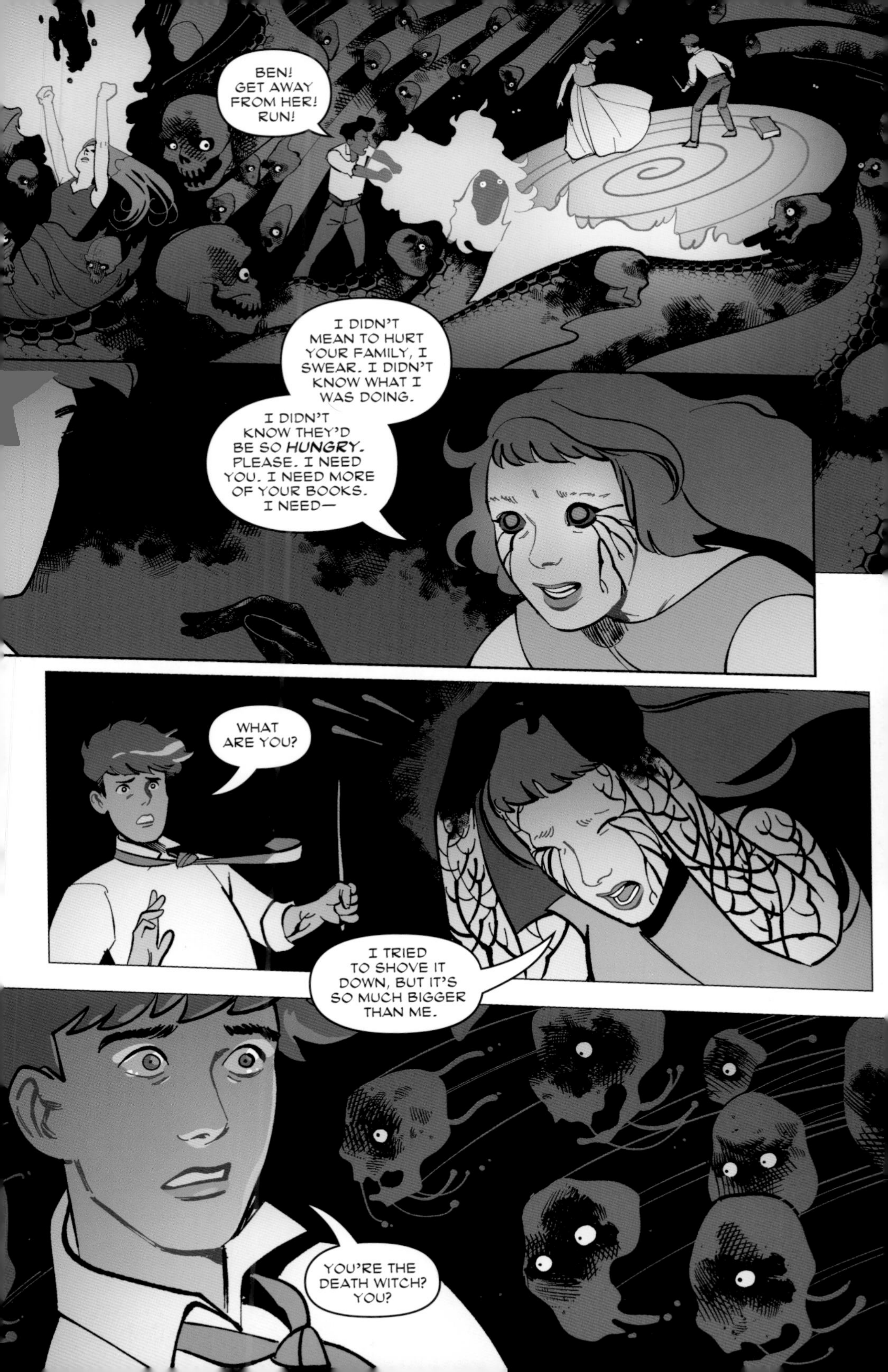

BEN! GET AWAY FROM HER! RUN!
I DIDN'T MEAN TO HURT YOUR FAMILY, I SWEAR. I DIDN'T KNOW WHAT I WAS DOING.
I DIDN'T KNOW THEY'D BE SO *HUNGRY.* PLEASE. I NEED YOU. I NEED MORE OF YOUR BOOKS. I NEED—
WHAT ARE YOU?
I TRIED TO SHOVE IT DOWN, BUT IT'S SO MUCH BIGGER THAN ME.
YOU'RE THE DEATH WITCH? YOU?

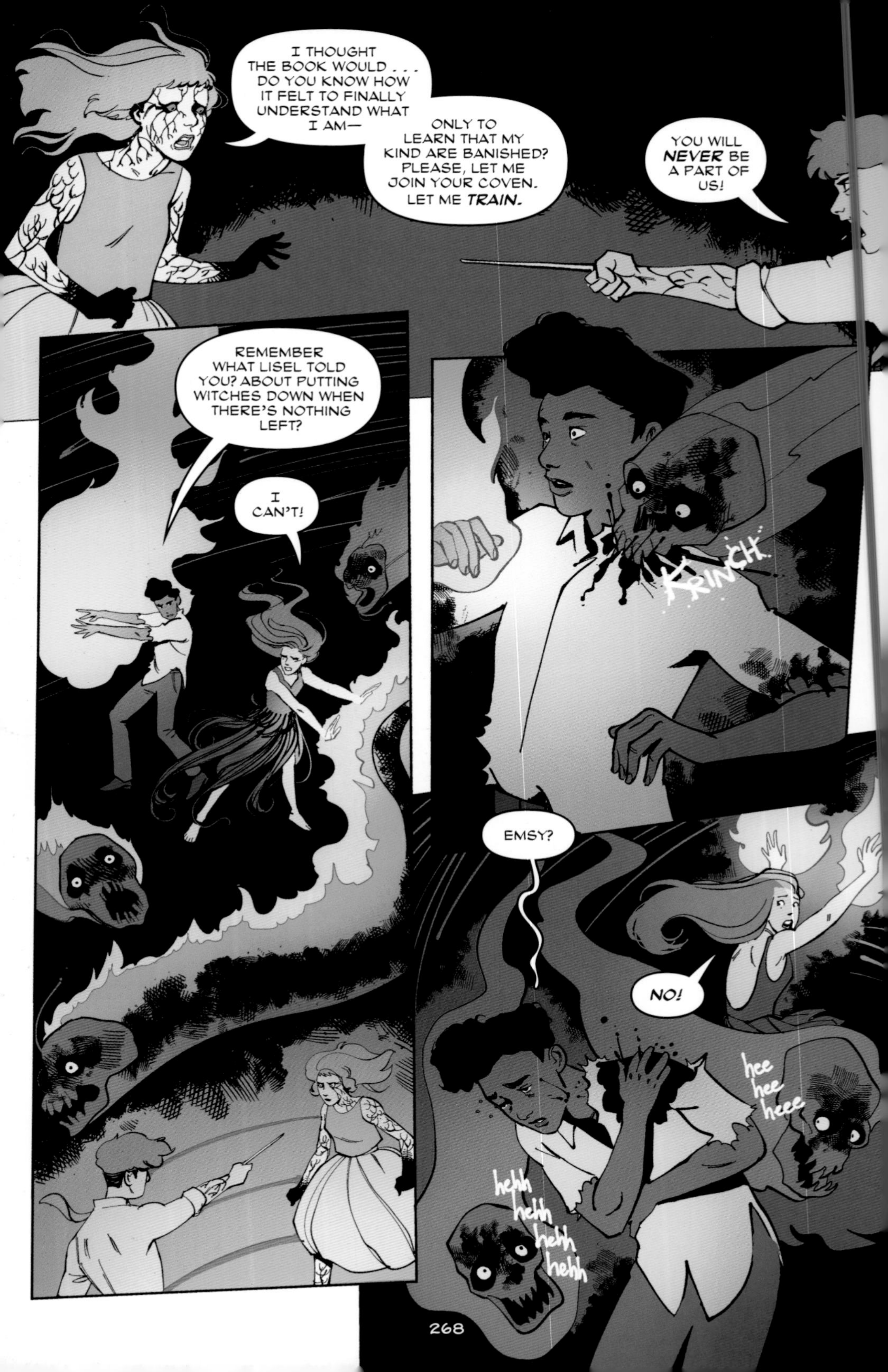
I THOUGHT THE BOOK WOULD . . . DO YOU KNOW HOW IT FELT TO FINALLY UNDERSTAND WHAT I AM—
ONLY TO LEARN THAT MY KIND ARE BANISHED? PLEASE, LET ME JOIN YOUR COVEN. LET ME TRAIN.
YOU WILL NEVER BE A PART OF US!
REMEMBER WHAT LISEL TOLD YOU? ABOUT PUTTING WITCHES DOWN WHEN THERE'S NOTHING LEFT?
I CAN'T!
KRINCH
EMSY?
NO!
hee hee heee
hehh hehh hehh hehh

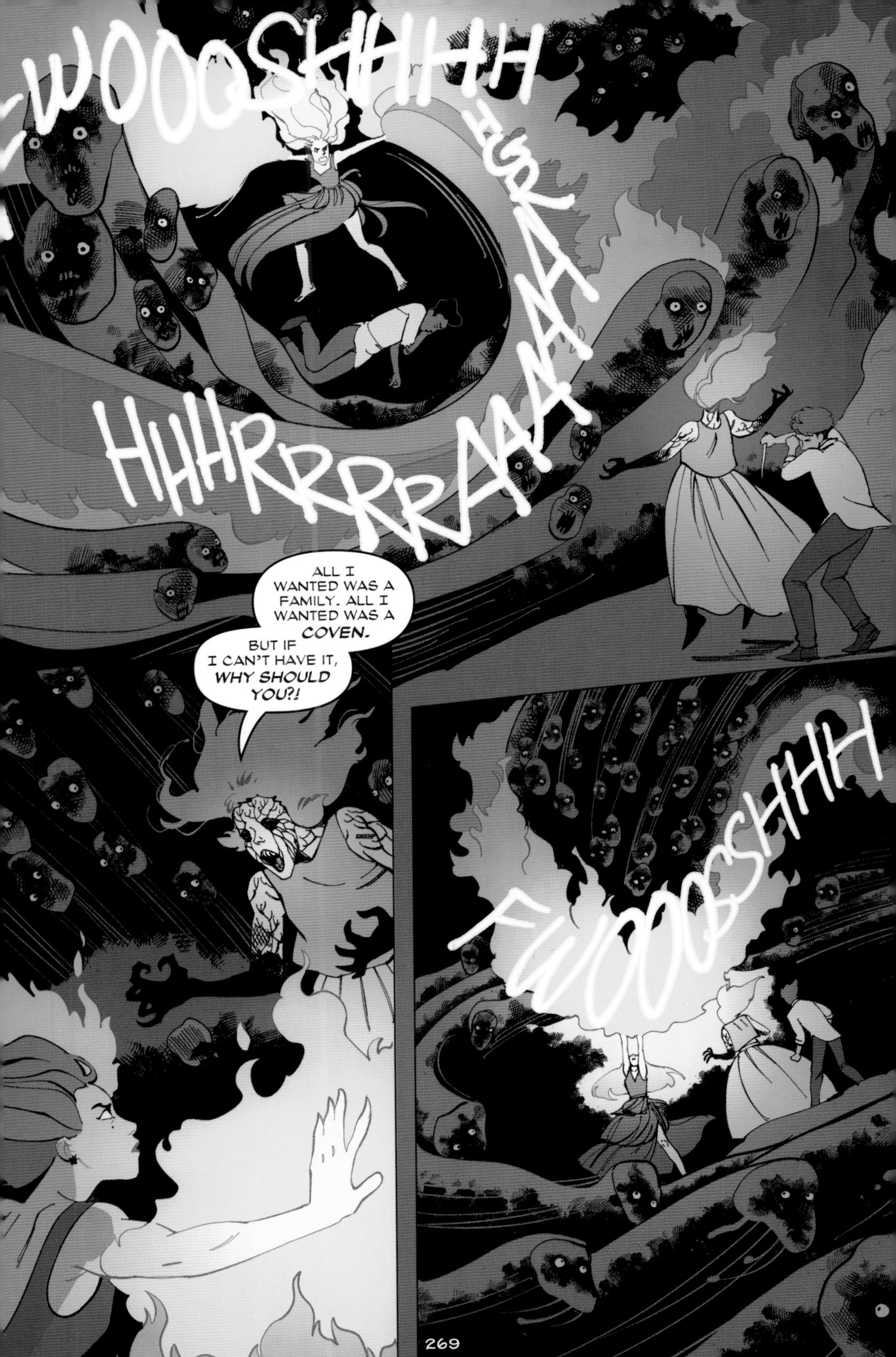
WOOOSHHHH
ALL I WANTED WAS A FAMILY. ALL I WANTED WAS A *COVEN.*
BUT IF I CAN'T HAVE IT, ***WHY SHOULD YOU?!***
FWOOOSHHH

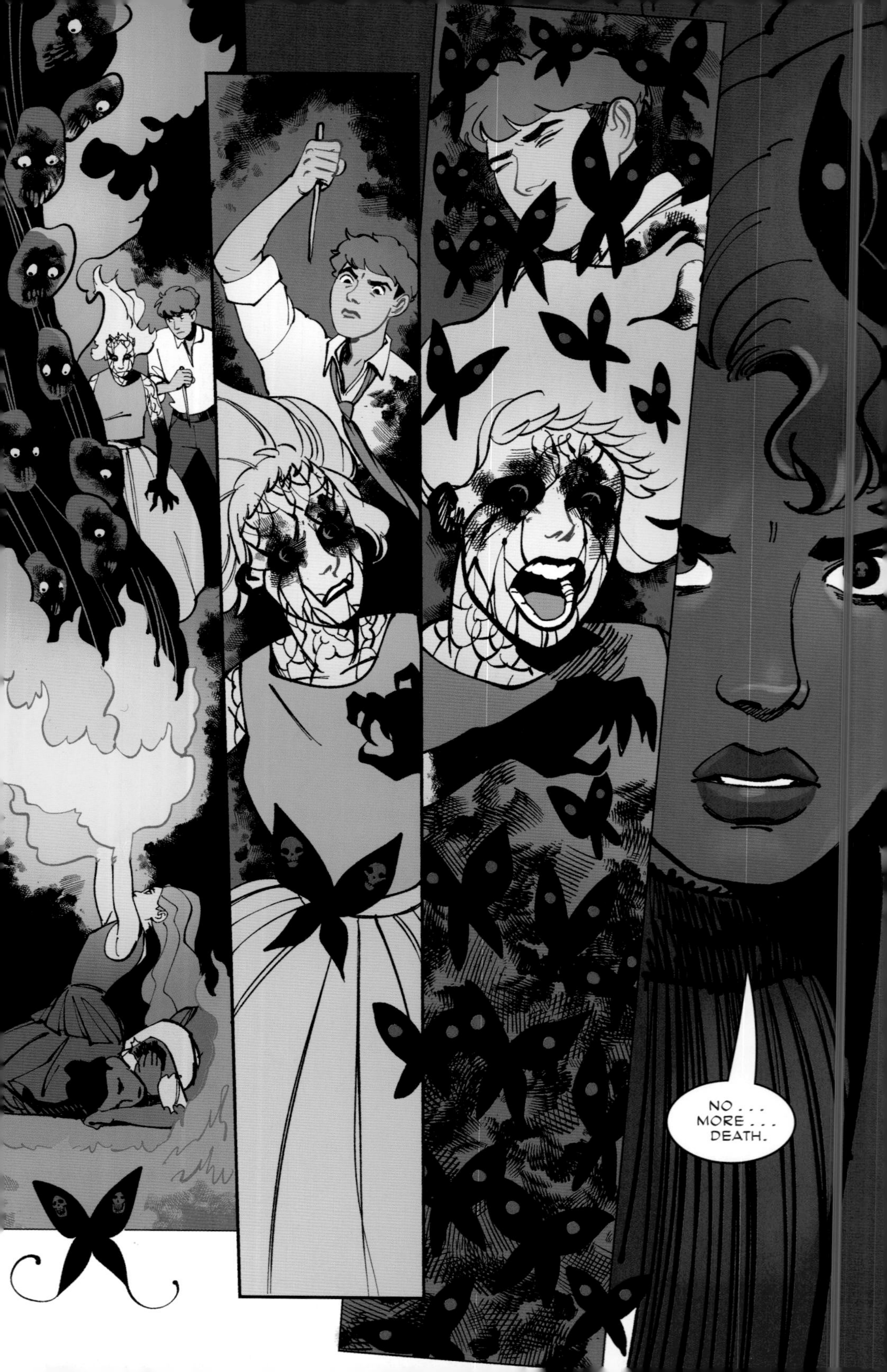
NO . . . MORE . . . DEATH.

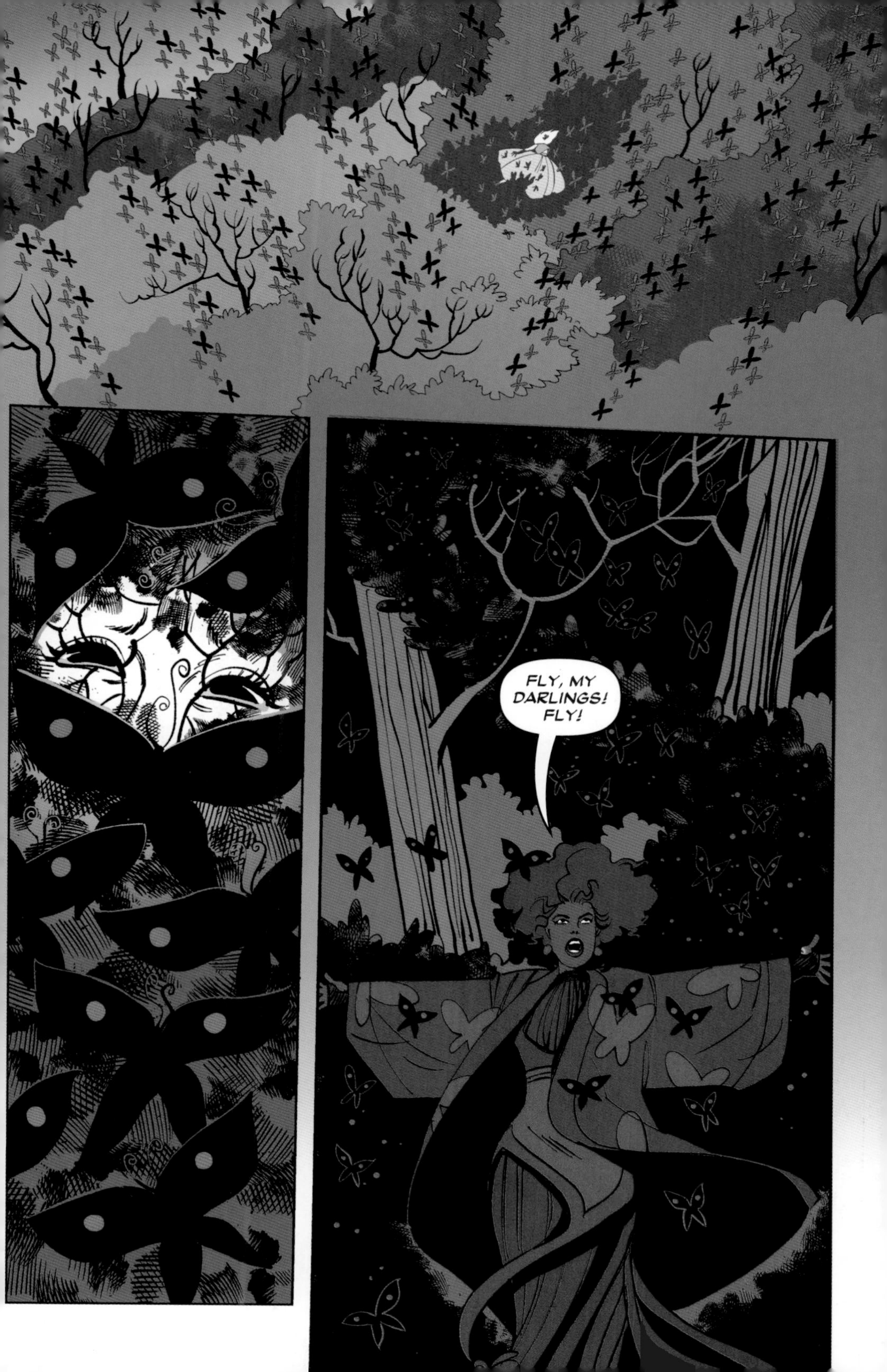
FLY, MY DARLINGS! FLY!

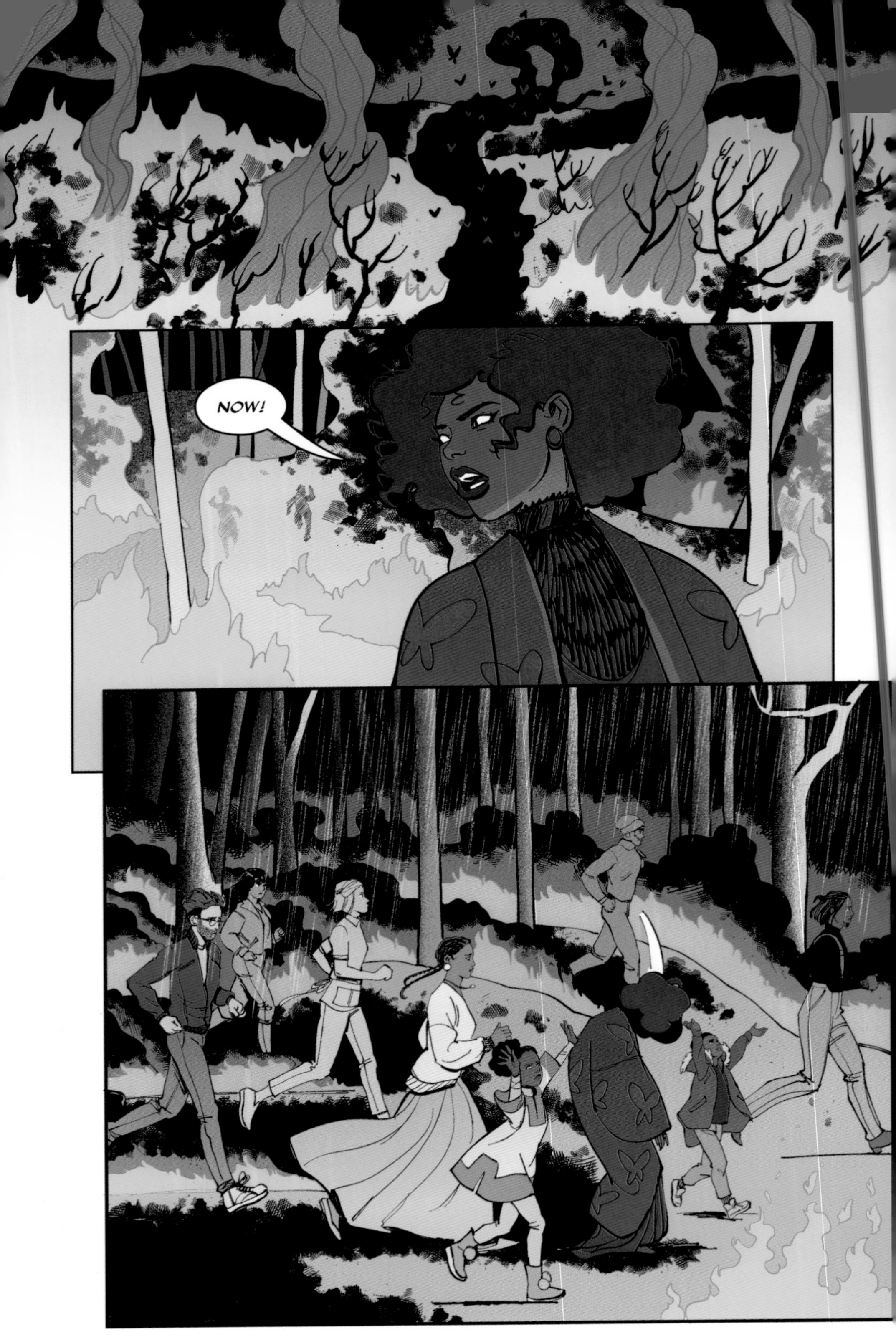
NOW!

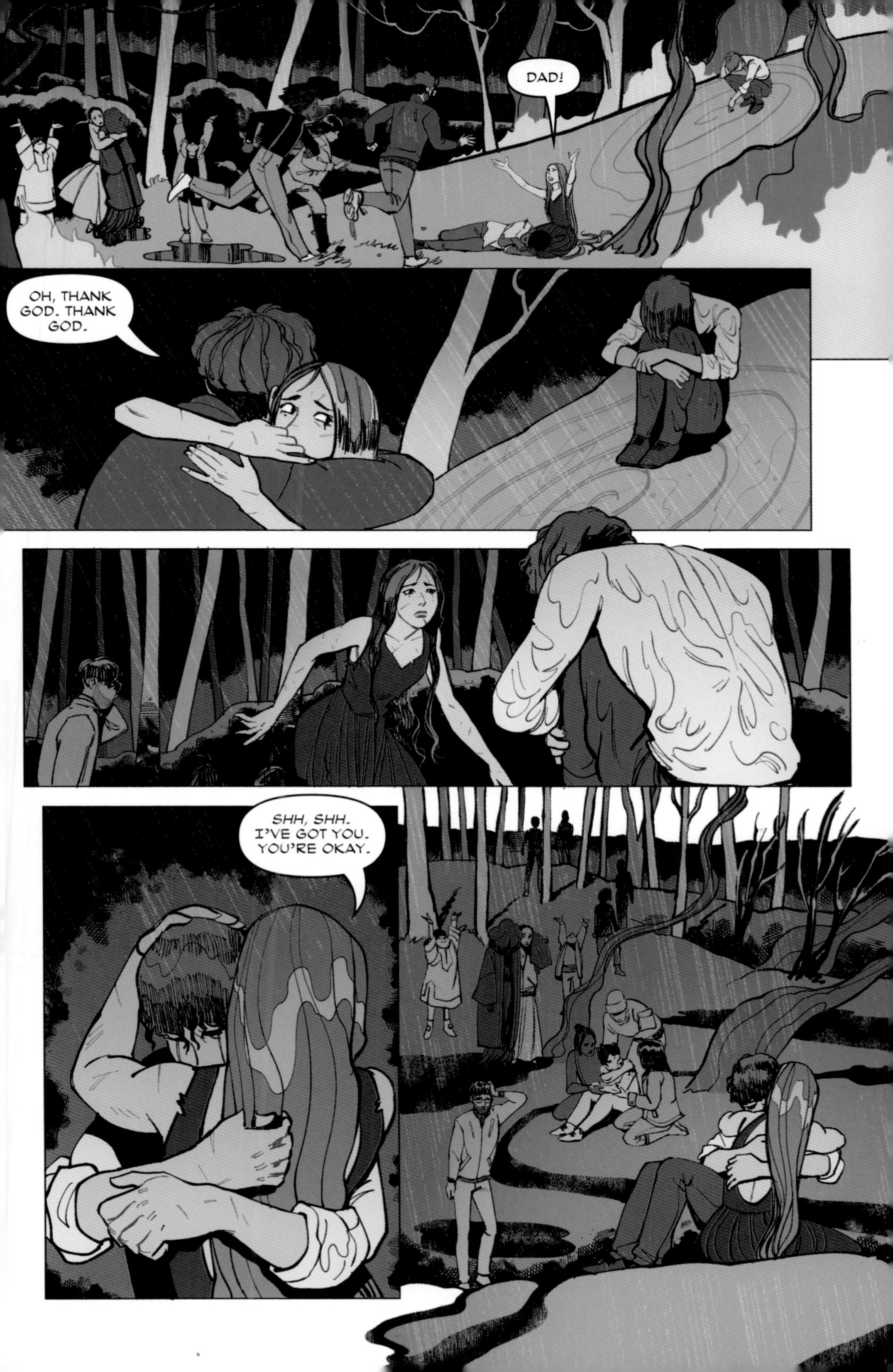
DAD!
OH, THANK GOD. THANK GOD.
SHH, SHH. I'VE GOT YOU. YOU'RE OKAY.

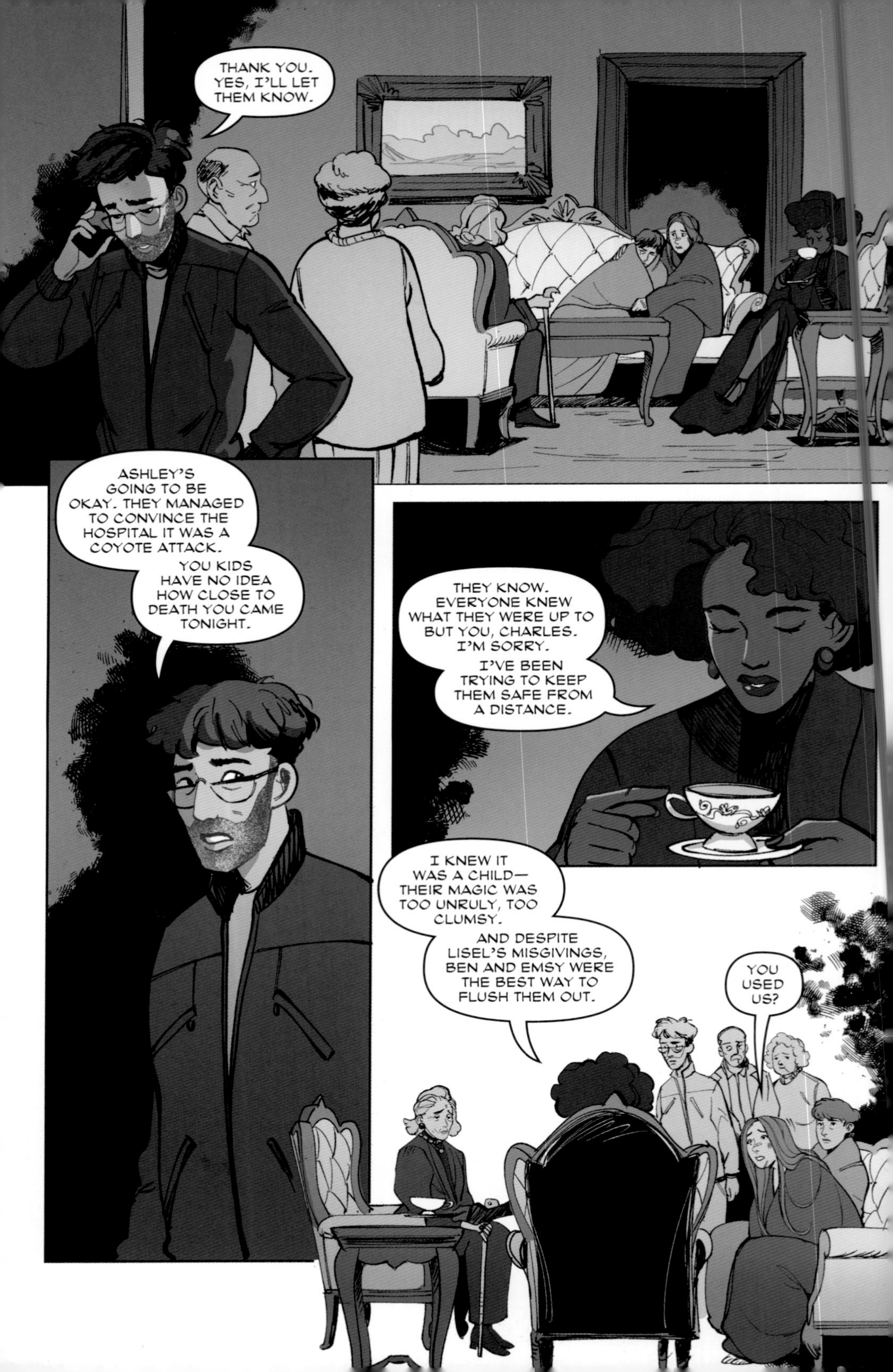
THANK YOU. YES, I'LL LET THEM KNOW.
ASHLEY'S GOING TO BE OKAY. THEY MANAGED TO CONVINCE THE HOSPITAL IT WAS A COYOTE ATTACK.
YOU KIDS HAVE NO IDEA HOW CLOSE TO DEATH YOU CAME TONIGHT.
THEY KNOW. EVERYONE KNEW WHAT THEY WERE UP TO BUT YOU, CHARLES. I'M SORRY.
I'VE BEEN TRYING TO KEEP THEM SAFE FROM A DISTANCE.
I KNEW IT WAS A CHILD— THEIR MAGIC WAS TOO UNRULY, TOO CLUMSY.
AND DESPITE LISEL'S MISGIVINGS, BEN AND EMSY WERE THE BEST WAY TO FLUSH THEM OUT.
YOU USED US?

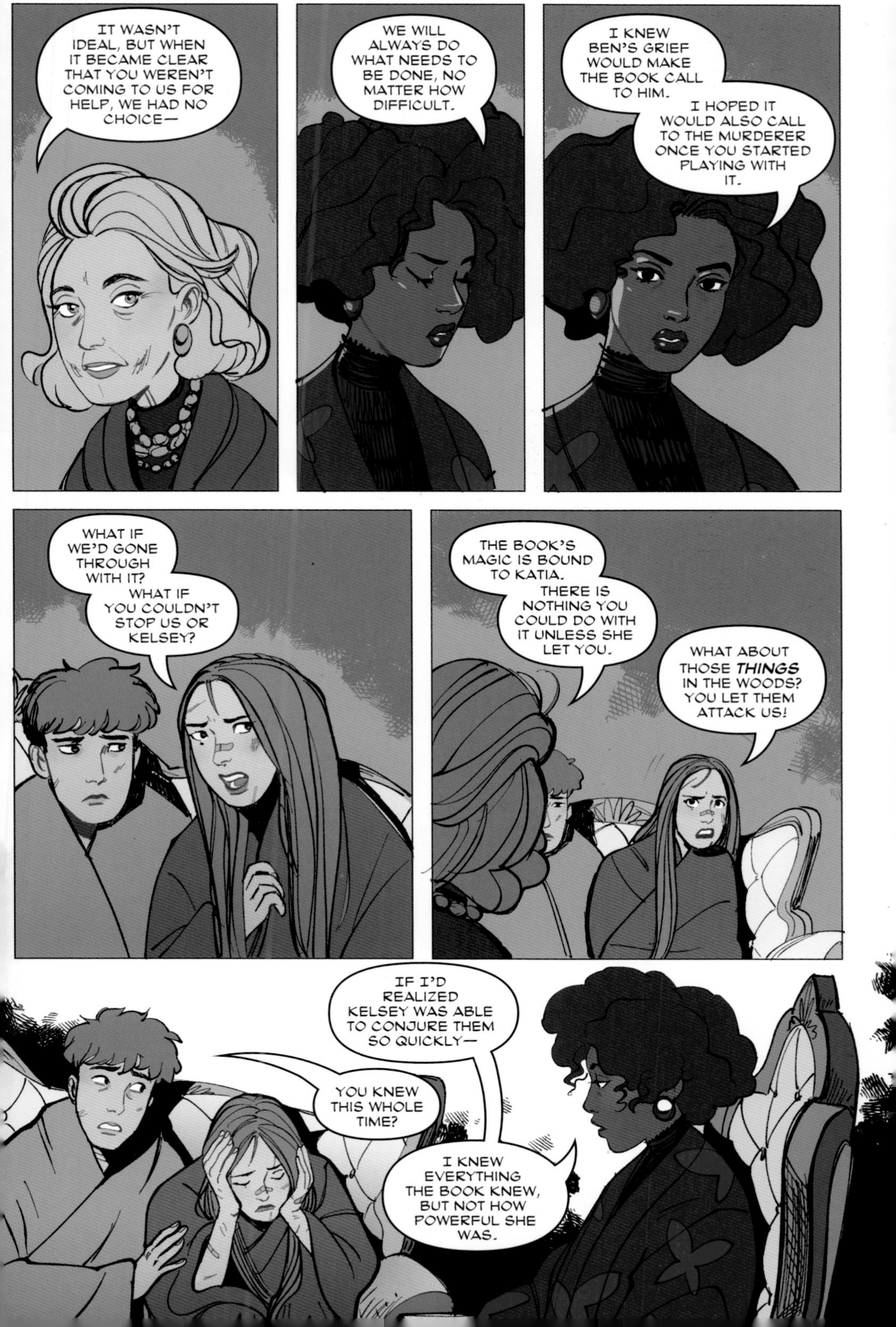
IT WASN'T IDEAL, BUT WHEN IT BECAME CLEAR THAT YOU WEREN'T COMING TO US FOR HELP, WE HAD NO CHOICE—
WE WILL ALWAYS DO WHAT NEEDS TO BE DONE, NO MATTER HOW DIFFICULT.
I KNEW BEN'S GRIEF WOULD MAKE THE BOOK CALL TO HIM.
I HOPED IT WOULD ALSO CALL TO THE MURDERER ONCE YOU STARTED PLAYING WITH IT.
WHAT IF WE'D GONE THROUGH WITH IT?
WHAT IF YOU COULDN'T STOP US OR KELSEY?
THE BOOK'S MAGIC IS BOUND TO KATIA.
THERE IS NOTHING YOU COULD DO WITH IT UNLESS SHE LET YOU.
WHAT ABOUT THOSE ***THINGS*** IN THE WOODS? YOU LET THEM ATTACK US!
IF I'D REALIZED KELSEY WAS ABLE TO CONJURE THEM SO QUICKLY—
YOU KNEW THIS WHOLE TIME?
I KNEW EVERYTHING THE BOOK KNEW, BUT NOT HOW POWERFUL SHE WAS.

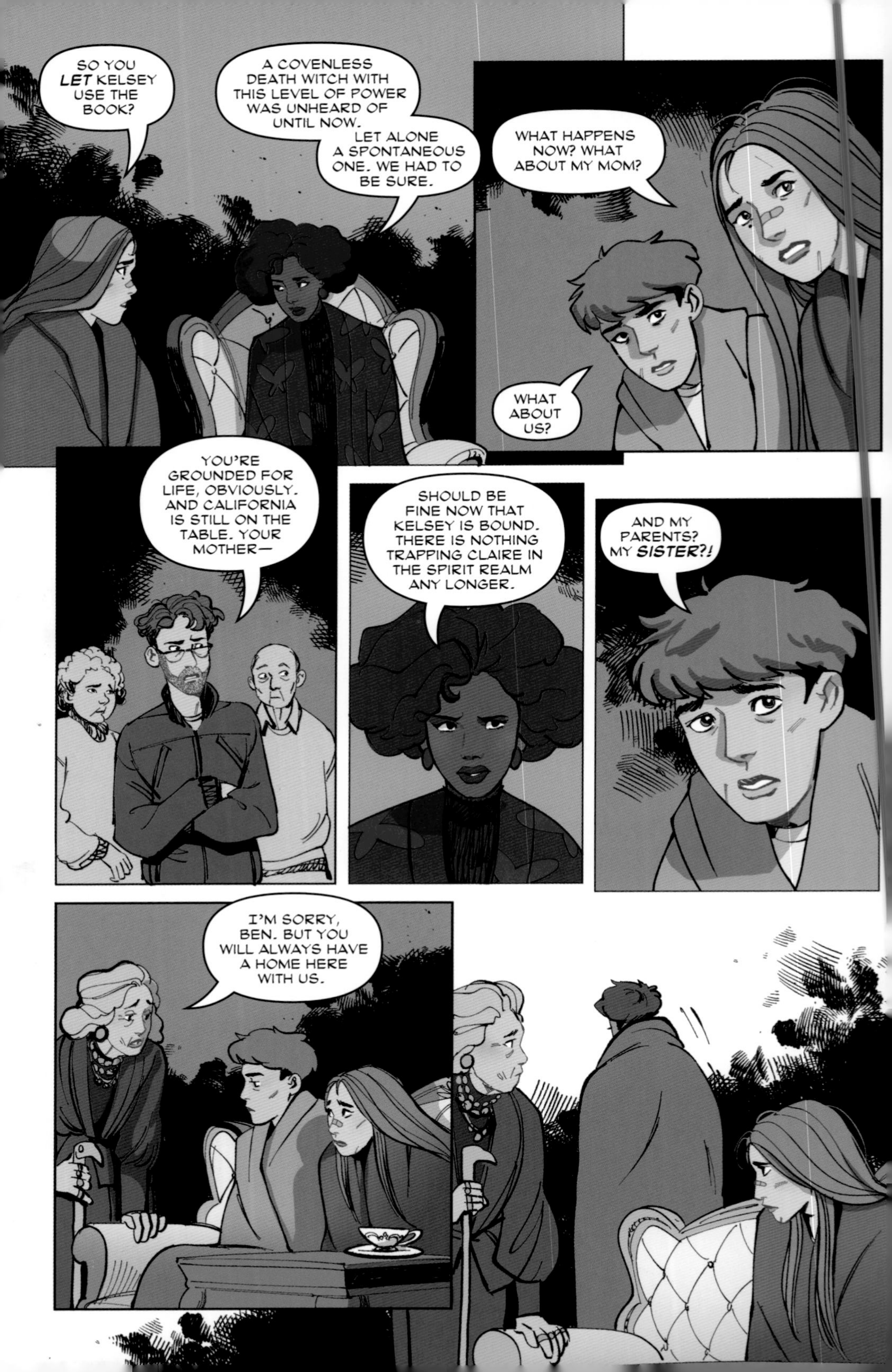
SO YOU *LET* KELSEY USE THE BOOK?
A COVENLESS DEATH WITCH WITH THIS LEVEL OF POWER WAS UNHEARD OF UNTIL NOW.
LET ALONE A SPONTANEOUS ONE. WE HAD TO BE SURE.
WHAT HAPPENS NOW? WHAT ABOUT MY MOM?
WHAT ABOUT US?
YOU'RE GROUNDED FOR LIFE, OBVIOUSLY. AND CALIFORNIA IS STILL ON THE TABLE. YOUR MOTHER—
SHOULD BE FINE NOW THAT KELSEY IS BOUND. THERE IS NOTHING TRAPPING CLAIRE IN THE SPIRIT REALM ANY LONGER.
AND MY PARENTS? MY *SISTER?!*
I'M SORRY, BEN. BUT YOU WILL ALWAYS HAVE A HOME HERE WITH US.

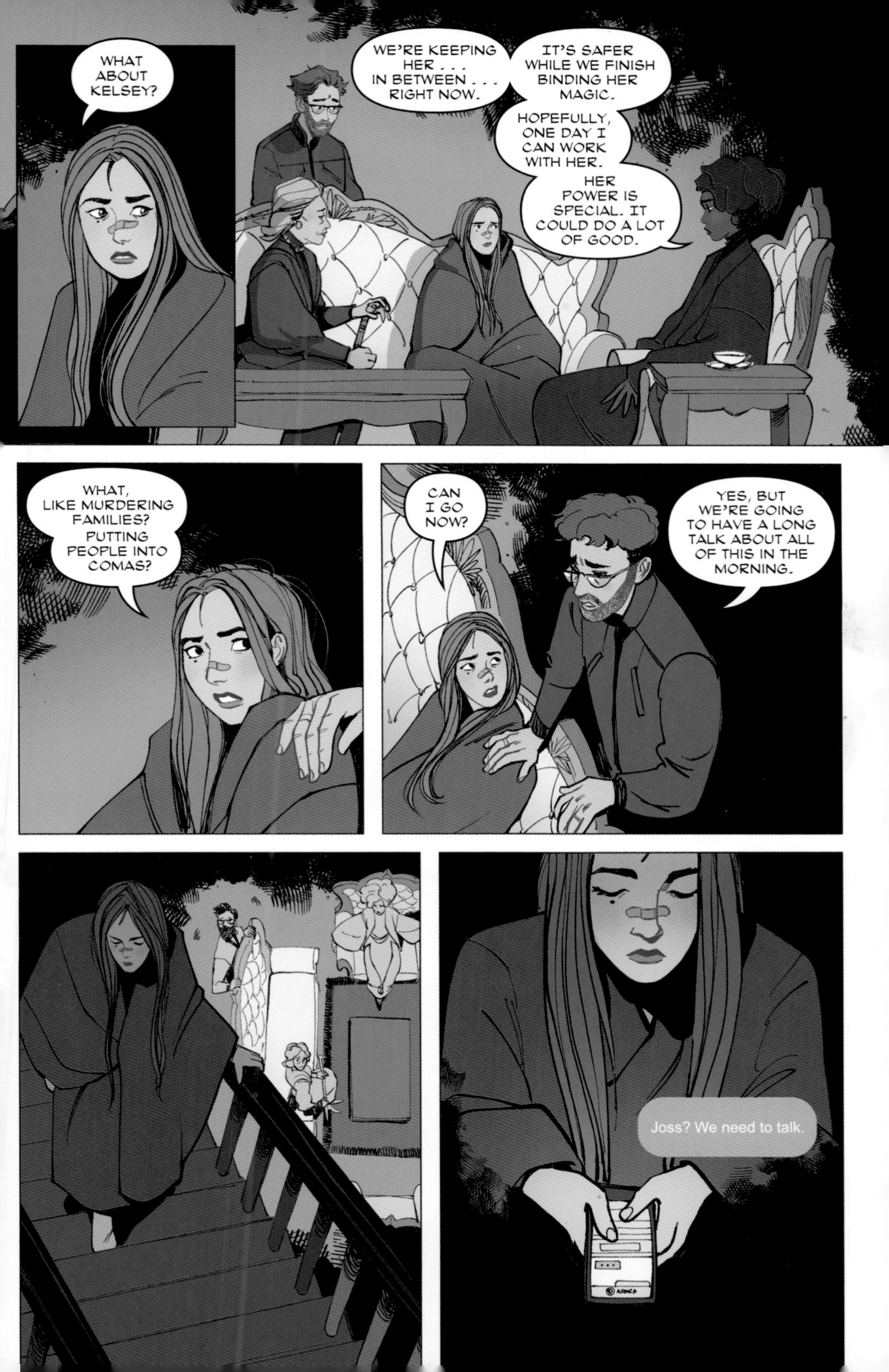
WHAT ABOUT KELSEY?
WE'RE KEEPING HER . . . IN BETWEEN . . . RIGHT NOW.
IT'S SAFER WHILE WE FINISH BINDING HER MAGIC.
HOPEFULLY, ONE DAY I CAN WORK WITH HER.
HER POWER IS SPECIAL. IT COULD DO A LOT OF GOOD.
WHAT, LIKE MURDERING FAMILIES? PUTTING PEOPLE INTO COMAS?
CAN I GO NOW?
YES, BUT WE'RE GOING TO HAVE A LONG TALK ABOUT ALL OF THIS IN THE MORNING.
Joss? We need to talk.

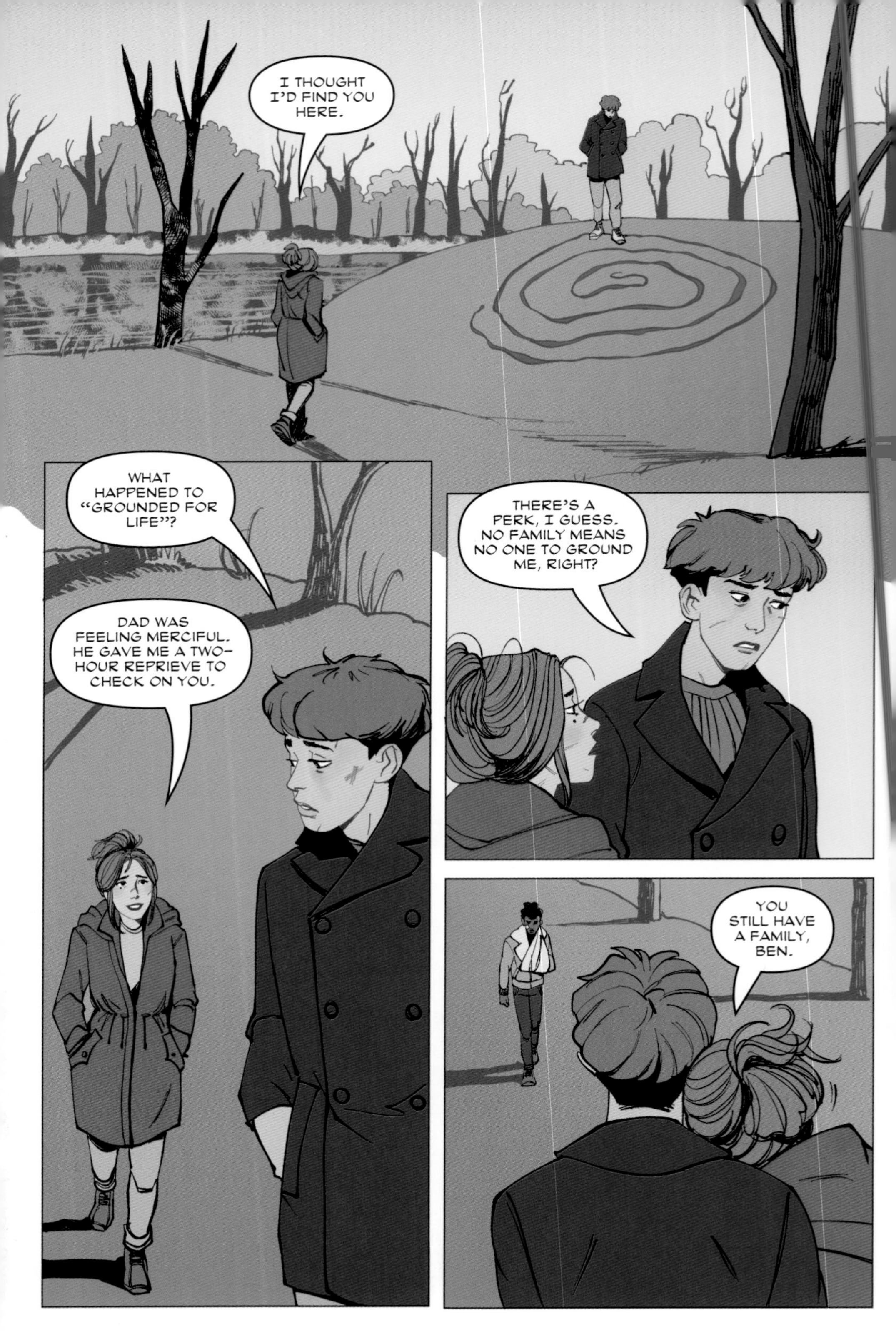
I THOUGHT I'D FIND YOU HERE.
WHAT HAPPENED TO "GROUNDED FOR LIFE"?
DAD WAS FEELING MERCIFUL. HE GAVE ME A TWO-HOUR REPRIEVE TO CHECK ON YOU.
THERE'S A PERK, I GUESS. NO FAMILY MEANS NO ONE TO GROUND ME, RIGHT?
YOU STILL HAVE A FAMILY, BEN.

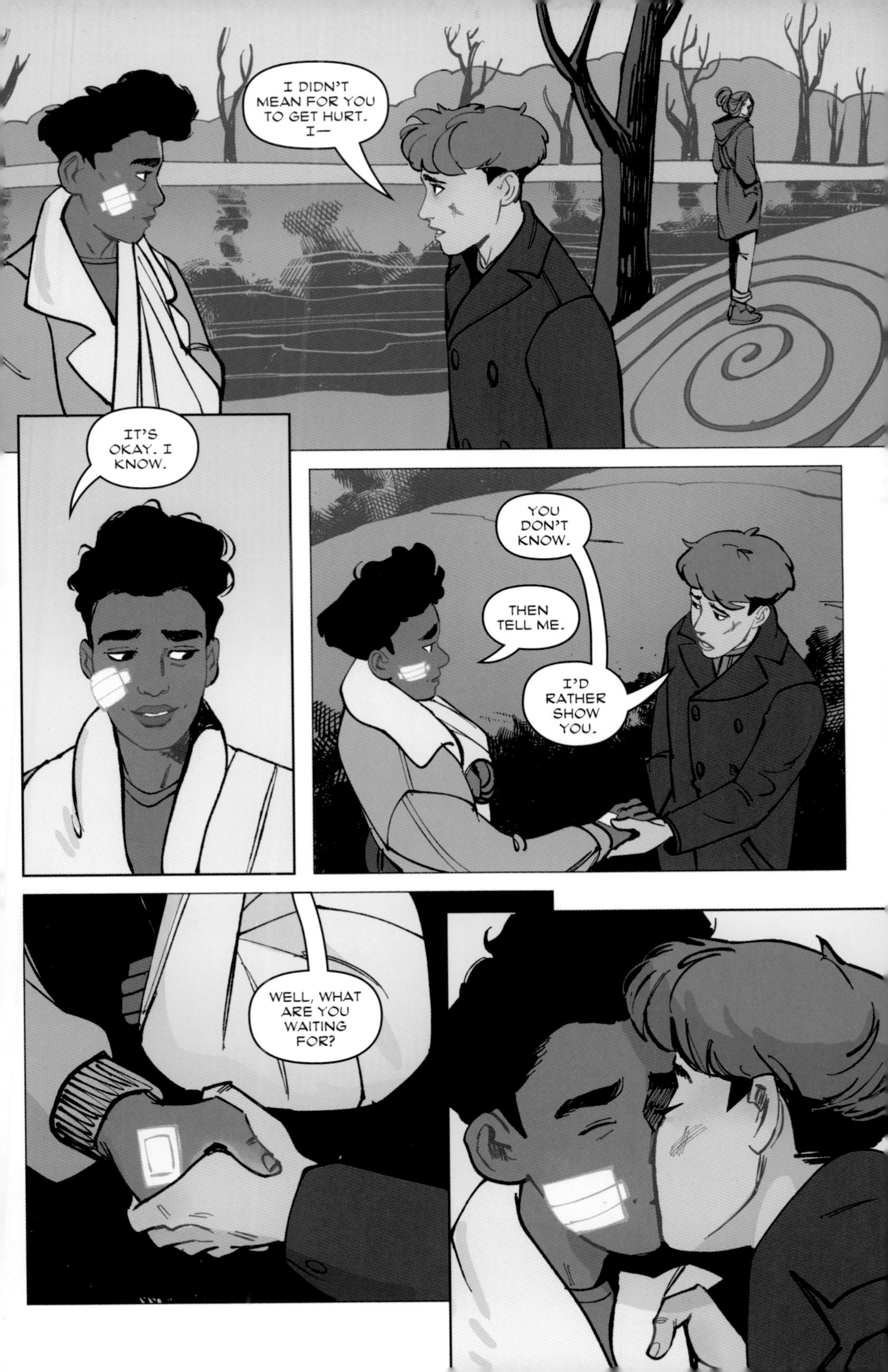
I DIDN'T MEAN FOR YOU TO GET HURT. I—
IT'S OKAY. I KNOW.
YOU DON'T KNOW.
THEN TELL ME.
I'D RATHER SHOW YOU.
WELL, WHAT ARE YOU WAITING FOR?

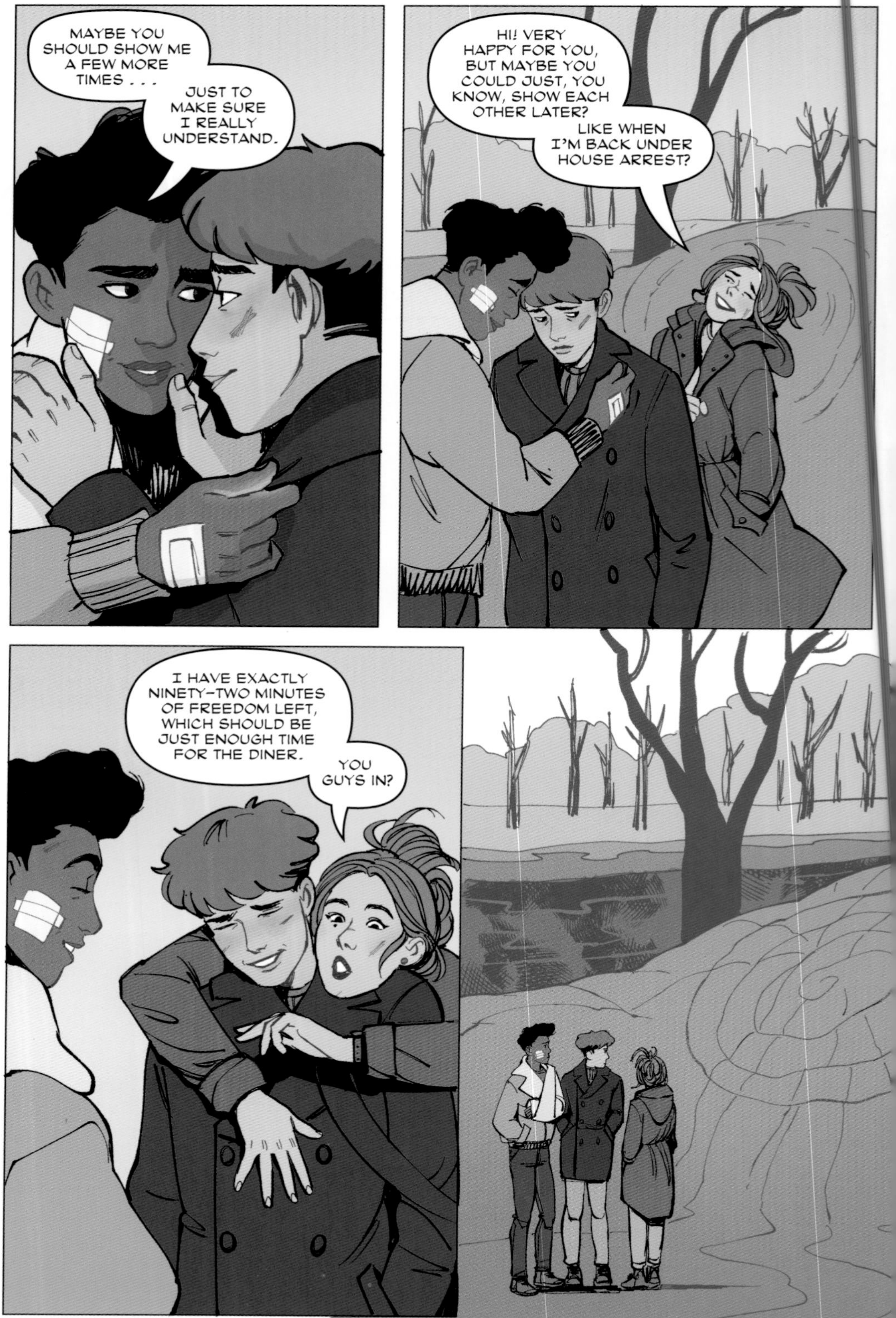
MAYBE YOU SHOULD SHOW ME A FEW MORE TIMES . . .
JUST TO MAKE SURE I REALLY UNDERSTAND.
HI! VERY HAPPY FOR YOU, BUT MAYBE YOU COULD JUST, YOU KNOW, SHOW EACH OTHER LATER?
LIKE WHEN I'M BACK UNDER HOUSE ARREST?
I HAVE EXACTLY NINETY-TWO MINUTES OF FREEDOM LEFT, WHICH SHOULD BE JUST ENOUGH TIME FOR THE DINER.
YOU GUYS IN?

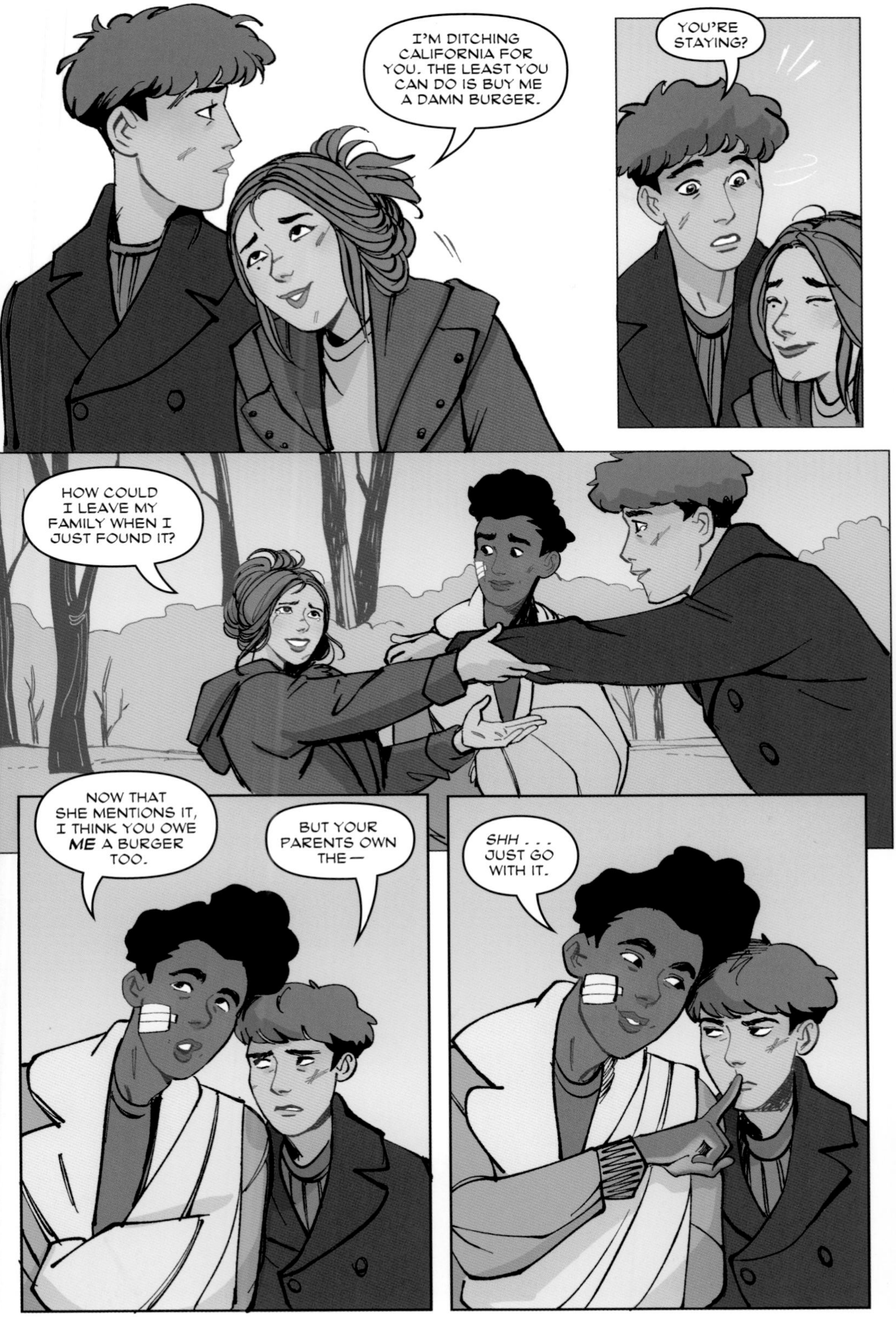
I'M DITCHING CALIFORNIA FOR YOU. THE LEAST YOU CAN DO IS BUY ME A DAMN BURGER.
YOU'RE STAYING?
HOW COULD I LEAVE MY FAMILY WHEN I JUST FOUND IT?
NOW THAT SHE MENTIONS IT, I THINK YOU OWE *ME* A BURGER TOO.
BUT YOUR PARENTS OWN THE—
SHH . . . JUST GO WITH IT.

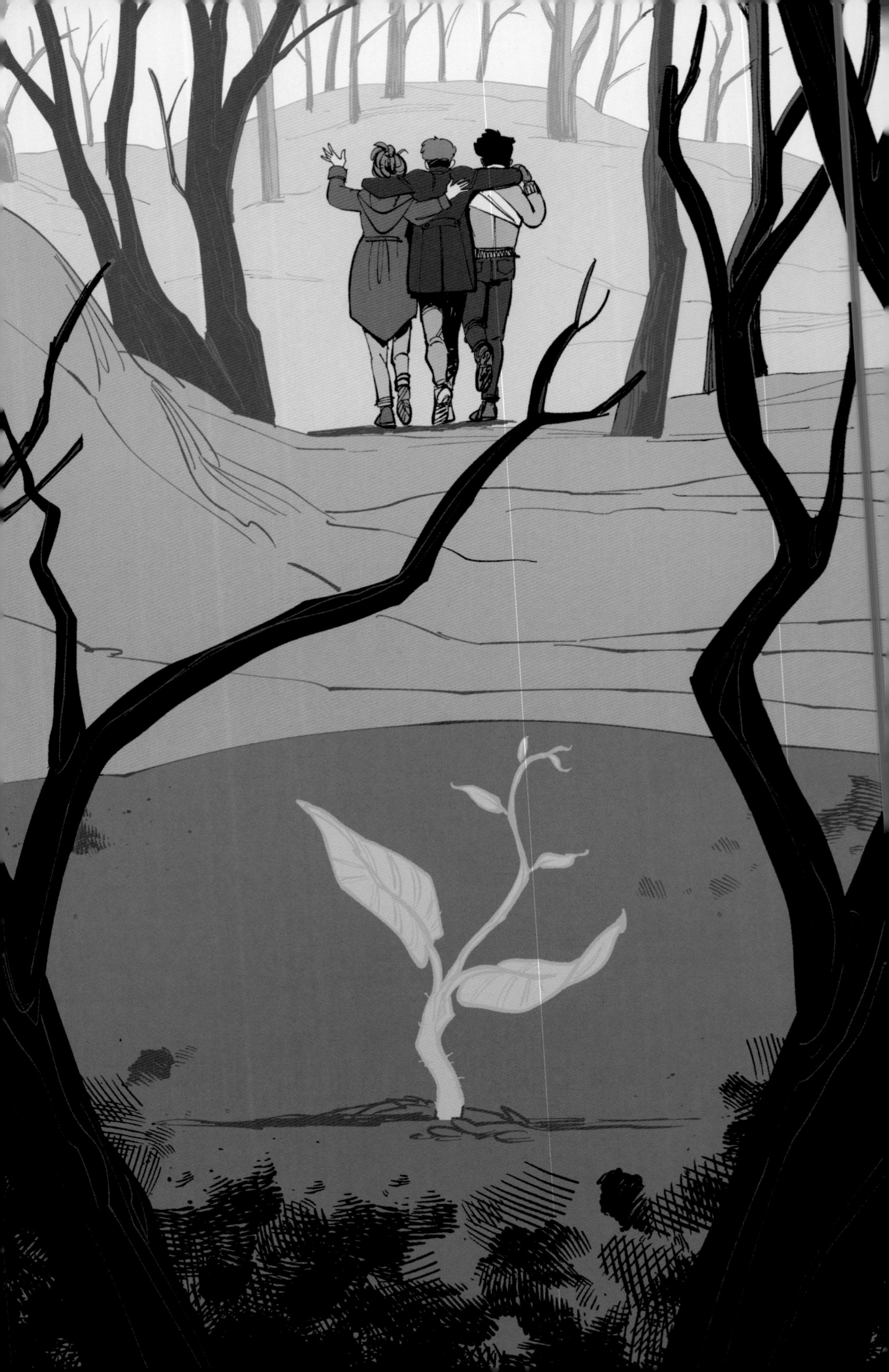

AUTHOR ACKNOWLEDGMENTS:

First and foremost, thanks to Kit Seaton, who is the best creative partner I could ever wish for. Thank you to Stephanie Pitts, Jen Klonsky, Matt Phipps, and the entire Penguin Teen and Putnam family, who have worked tirelessly to help bring this book to life despite a global pandemic, a crumbling supply chain, and everything else life threw at us. I am forever grateful. Thanks to Sara Crowe for adopting this book and fighting for it as if she had been here from the start. Thanks to Dennis and to Joe, Brody, Olivia, Bonks, Phinny, and LuLu for being endless sources of love and inspiration. To my family, and to Shannon, Jeff, Rory, Isabel, and Karen for keeping me humble, happy, motivated, and everything in between.

To my readers, and to the bloggers, booktokers, bookstagrammers, and bookstore workers: Thank you for your support. None of this would be possible without you.

ILLUSTRATOR ACKNOWLEDGMENTS:

I'd like to thank the amazing team I worked with on this book: Jenn Dugan, our author, for her enthusiasm and passion for this project; Cecilia Yung and Eileen Savage, whose art direction and technical prowess helped me manage many a speed bump; and our editor, Stephanie Pitts, for her encouragement and thoughtful feedback. I'd also like to shout out my friend Leila del Duca and my family for being the best support system I could ask for while working on this book.

JENNIFER DUGAN is a writer, a geek, and a romantic who writes the kinds of stories she wishes she'd had growing up. She's the author of the young adult novels *Melt With You*, *Some Girls Do*, *Verona Comics*, and *Hot Dog Girl*, which was called "a great, fizzy rom-com" by *Entertainment Weekly* and "one of the best reads of the year, hands down" by *Paste* magazine. She lives in upstate New York with her family, their dog, a strange kitten who enjoys wearing sweaters, and an evil cat who is no doubt planning to take over the world.

You can visit Jennifer at

JLDugan.com

Or follow her on Twitter and Instagram

@JL__Dugan

KIT SEATON has illustrated the graphic novel adaptations of Leigh Bardugo's *Wonder Woman: Warbringer* and Alexandra Bracken's *Brightly Woven*. She is the co-creator of the comics *Norroway* and *Afar*. She lives with her family, which includes a gang of three cats and two poodles, in a grove of live oaks in Savannah, Georgia, a haunted city known for hot sticky summers, the maddening hum of cicadas, and the unpredictable crunch of a palmetto bug underfoot. Kit loves all things spooky, so she feels right at home.

You can visit Kit at

kitseaton.com

Or follow her on Instagram

@kitandcatcomics

To the tiniest frog in the tiniest pond —J.D.

To all students of the arts, practical or esoteric —K.S.

G. P. Putnam's Sons
An imprint of Penguin Random House LLC, New York

First published in the United States of America by G. P. Putnam's Sons,
an imprint of Penguin Random House LLC, 2022

Text copyright © 2022 by Jennifer Dugan
Illustrations copyright © 2022 by Kit Seaton

G. P. Putnam's Sons is a registered trademark of Penguin Random House LLC.
Penguin Books & colophon are registered trademarks of Penguin Books Limited.

Visit us online at penguinrandomhouse.com

Library of Congress Cataloging-in-Publication Data is available.

Manufactured in China

ISBN 9780593112168 (hardcover)
1 3 5 7 9 10 8 6 4 2

ISBN 9780593112182 (paperback)
1 3 5 7 9 10 8 6 4 2

TOPL

Design by Eileen Savage and Cindy De la Cruz | Text set in Atland BB and Serenity